FYODOR
DOSTOYEVSKY

GREAT CLASSIC LIBRARY

FYODOR DOSTOYEVSKY

CRIME AND PUNISHMENT

THE GAMBLER

NOTES FROM THE UNDERGROUND

LONGMEADOW
PRESS

Crime and Punishment was first published in Russian in 1866. This translation was first published in 1914
The Gambler was first published in Russian in 1867. This translation was first published in 1913
Notes from the Underground was first published in Russian in 1864. This translation was first published in 1913 under the title *Letters from the Underworld*

Crime and Punishment translated by Constance Garnett.
The Gambler and *Notes fron the Underground* translated by C.J. Hogarth.

This collected volume published in 1994 by Longmeadow Press,
201 High Ridge Road, Stamford, CT 06904. All rights reserved.
No part of this book may be reproduced or utilized in any form or by any means, electronic or mechanical, including photocopying, recording or by any information storage and retrieval system, without permission in writing from the Publisher.
Longmeadow Press and the colophon are registered trademarks.

Cover design by Les Needham
Interior design by Gwyn Lewis
ISBN: 0-681-00777-X
Printed in Great Britain
First Longmeadow Press Edition
0 9 8 7 6 5 4 3 2 1

Contents

CRIME AND PUNISHMENT

Translated from the Russian by Constance Garnett

⇛ TRANSLATOR'S PREFACE ⇚

A FEW WORDS ABOUT DOSTOEVSKY himself may help the English reader to understand his work.

Dostoevsky was the son of a doctor. His parents were very hard-working and deeply religious people, but so poor that they lived with their five children in only two rooms. The father and mother spent their evenings in reading aloud to their children, generally from books of a serious character.

Though always sickly and delicate Dostoevsky came out third in the final examination of the Petersburg school of Engineering. There he had aldely begun his first work, "Poor Folk".

This story was published by the poet Nekrassov in his review and was received with acclamations. The shy, unknown youth found himself instantly something of a celebrity. A brilliant and successful career seemed to open before him, but those hopes were soon dashed. In 1849 he was arrested.

Though neither by temperament nor conviction a revolutionist, Dosto-evsky was one of a little group of young men who met together to read Fourier and Proudhon. He was accused of 'taking part in conversations against the censorship, of reading a letter from Byelinsky to Gogol, and of knowing of the intention to set up a printing press'. Under Nicholas I, (that 'stern and just man, as Maurice Baring calls him) this was enough, and he was condemned to death. After eight months' imprisonment he was with twenty-one others taken out to the Semyonovsky Square to be shot. Writing to his brother Mihail, Dostoevsky says: 'They snapped words over our heads, and they made us put on the white shirts worn by persons condemned to death. Thereupon we were bound in threes to stakes, to suffer execution. Being the third in the row, I concluded I had only a few minutes of life before me. I thought of you and your dear ones and I contrived to kiss Plestcheiev and Dourov, who were next to me, and to bid them farewell. Suddenly the troops beat a tattoo, we were unbound, brought back upon the scaffold, and informed that his Majesty has spared us our lives.' The sentence was commuted to hard labour.

One of the prisoners, Grigoryev, went mad as soon as he was untied and never regained his sanity.

The intense suffering of this experience left a lasting stamp on Dostoevsky's mind. Though his religious temper led him in the end to accept every suffering with resignation and to regard it as a blessing in his own case, he constantly recurs to the subject in his writings. He describes the awful agony of the condemned man and insists on the cruelty of inflicting such torture. Then followed four years of penal servitude, spent in the company of common criminals in Siberia, where he began the 'Dead House', and some years of service in a disciplinary battalion.

He had shown signs of some obscure nervous disease before his arrest and this now developed into violent attacks of epilepsy, from which he suffered for the rest of his life. The fits occurred three or four times a year and were more frequent in periods of great strain. In 1859 he was allowed to return to Russia. He started a journal — 'Vremya', which was forbidden by the Censorship through a misunderstanding. In 1864 he lost his first wife and his brother Mihail. He was in terrible poverty, yet he took upon himself the payment of his brother's debts. He started another journal – 'The Epoch', which within a few months was also prohibited. He was weighed down by debt, his brother's family was dependent on him, he was forced to write at heart-breaking speed, and is said never to have corrected his work. The later years of his life were much softened by the tenderness and devotion of his second wife.

In June 1880 he made his famous speech at the unveiling of the monument to Pushkin in Moscow and he was received with extraordinary demonstrations of love and honour.

A few months later Dostoevsky died. He was followed to the grave by a vast multitude of mourners, who 'gave the hapless man the funeral of a king'. He is still probably the most widely read writer in Russia.

In the words of a Russian critic, who seeks to explain the feeling inspired by Dostoevsky: 'He was one of ourselves, a man of our blood and our bone, but one who has suffered and has seen so much more deeply than we have his insight impresses us as wisdom . . . that wisdom of the heart which we seek that we may learn from it how to live. All his other gifts came to him from nature, this he won for himself and through it he became great.'

PART ONE

❦ ONE ❧

ON AN EXCEPTIONALLY HOT EVENING early in July a young man came out of the garret in which he lodged in S. Place and walked slowly, as though in hesitation, towards K. bridge.

He had successfully avoided meeting his landlady on the staircase. His garret was under the roof of a high, five-storied house, and was more like a cupboard than a room. The landlady, who provided him with garret, dinners, and attendance, lived on the floor below, and every time he went out he was obliged to pass her kitchen, the door of which invariably stood open. And each time he passed, the young man had a sick, frightened feeling, which made him scowl and feel ashamed. He was hopelessly in debt to his landlady, and was afraid of meeting her.

This was not because he was cowardly and abject, quite the contrary; but for some time past he had been in an overstrained, irritable condition, verging on hypochondria. He had become so completely absorbed in himself, and isolated from his fellows that he dreaded meeting, not only his landlady, but any one at all. He was crushed by poverty, but the anxieties of his position had of late ceased to weigh upon him. He had given up attending to matters of practical importance; he had lost all desire to do so. Nothing that any landlady could do had a real terror for him. But to be stopped on the stairs, to be forced to listen to her trivial, irrelevant gossip, to pestering demands for payment, threats and complaints, and to rack his brains for excuses, to prevaricate, to lie – no, rather than that, he would creep down the stairs like a cat and slip out unseen.

This evening, however, on coming out into the street, he became acutely aware of his fears.

'I want to attempt a thing *like that* and am frightened by these trifles,' he thought, with an odd smile. 'Hm . . . yes, all is in a man's hands and he lets it all slip from cowardice, that's an axiom. It would be interesting to know what it is men are most afraid of. Taking a new step, uttering a new word is what they fear most. . . . But I am talking too much. It's because I chatter that I do nothing. Or perhaps it is that I chatter because I do nothing. I've learned to chatter this last month, lying for days together in

5

my den thinking . . . of Jack the Giant-killer. Why am I going there now? Am I capable of *that*? Is *that* serious? It is not serious at all. It's simply a fantasy to amuse myself; a plaything! Yes, maybe it is a plaything.'

The heat in the street was terrible: and the airlessness, the bustle and the plaster, scaffolding, bricks, and dust all about him, and that special Petersburg stench, so familiar to all who are unable to get out of town in summer – all worked painfully upon the young man's already over-wrought nerves. The insufferable stench from the pot-houses, which are particularly numerous in that part of the town, and the drunken men whom he met continually, although it was a working day, completed the revolting misery of the picture. An expression of the profoundest disgust gleamed for a moment in the young man's refined face. He was, by the way, exceptionally handsome, above the average in height, slim, well-built, with beautiful dark eyes and dark brown hair. Soon he sank into deep thought, or more accurately speaking into a complete blankness of mind; he walked along not observing what was about him and not caring to observe it. From time to time, he would mutter something, from the habit of talking to himself, to which he had just confessed. At these moments he would become conscious that his ideas were sometimes in a tangle and that he was very weak; for two days he had scarcely tasted food.

He was so badly dressed that even a man accustomed to shabbiness would have been ashamed to be seen in the street in such rags. In that quarter of the town, however, scarcely any short-coming in dress would have created surprise. Owing to the proximity of the Hay Market, the number of establishments of bad character, the preponderance of the trading and working class population crowded in these streets and alleys in the heart of Petersburg, types so various were to be seen in the streets that no figure, however queer, would have caused surprise. But there was such accumulated bitterness and contempt in the young man's heart that, in spite of all the fastidiousness of youth, he minded his rags least of all in the street. It was a different matter when he met with acquaintances or with former fellow students, whom, indeed, he disliked meeting at any time. And yet when a drunken man who, for some unknown reason, was being taken somewhere in a huge waggon dragged by a heavy dray horse, suddenly shouted at him as he drove past: 'Hey there, German hatter!' bawling at the top of his voice and pointing at him – the young man stopped suddenly and clutched tremulously at his hat. It was a tall round hat from Zimmerman's, but completely worn out, rusty with age, all torn and bespattered, brimless and bent on one side in a most unseemly fashion. Not shame, however, but quite another feeling akin to terror had overtaken him.

'I knew it,' he muttered in confusion, 'I thought so! That's the worst of all! Why, a stupid thing like this, the most trivial detail might spoil the whole plan. Yes, my hat is too noticeable. . . . It looks absurd and that makes it noticeable. . . . With my rags I ought to wear a cap, any sort of old pancake, but not this grotesque thing. Nobody wears such a hat, it would be noticed a mile off, it would be remembered. . . . What matters is that people would remember it, and that would give them a clue. For this business one should be as little conspicuous as possible. . . . Trifles, trifles are what matter! Why, it's just such trifles that always ruin everything. . . .'

He had not far to go; he knew indeed how many steps it was from the gate of his lodging house: exactly seven hundred and thirty. He had counted them once when he had been lost in dreams. At the time he had put no faith in those dreams and was only tantalizing himself by their hideous but daring recklessness. Now, a month later, he had begun to look upon them differently, and, in spite of the monologues in which he jeered at his own impotence and indecision, he had involuntarily come to regard this 'hideous' dream as an exploit to be attempted, although he still did not realize this himself. He was positively going now for a 'rehearsal' of his project, and at every step his excitement grew more and more violent.

With a sinking heart and a nervous tremor, he went up to a huge house which on one side looked on to the canal, and on the other into the street. This house was let out in tiny tenements and was inhabited by working people of all kinds – tailors, locksmiths, cooks, Germans of sorts, girls picking up a living as best they could, petty clerks, etc. There was a continual coming and going through the two gates and in the two court-yards of the house. Three or four door-keepers were employed on the building. The young man was very glad to meet none of them, and at once slipped unnoticed through the door on the right, and up the stair-case. It was a back staircase, dark and narrow, but he was familiar with it already, and knew his way, and he liked all these surroundings: in such darkness even the most inquisitive eyes were not to be dreaded.

'If I am so scared now, what would it be if it somehow came to pass that I were really going to do it?' he could not help asking himself as he reached the fourth storey. There his progress was barred by some porters who were engaged in moving furniture out of a flat. He knew that the flat had been occupied by a German clerk in the civil service, and his family. This German was moving out then, and so the fourth floor on this staircase would be untenanted except by the old woman. 'That's a good thing anyway,' he thought to himself, as he rang the bell to the old woman's flat. The bell gave a faint tinkle as though it were made of tin and not of copper. The little flats in such houses always have bells that ring like that. He had forgotten the note of that bell, and now its peculiar tinkle seemed to remind him of something and to bring it clearly before him. . . . He started, his nerves were terribly overstrained by now. In a little while, the door was opened a tiny crack: the old woman eyed her visitor with evident distrust through the crack, and nothing could be seen but her little eyes, glittering in the darkness. But, seeing a number of people on the landing, she grew bolder, and opened the door wide. The young man stepped into the dark entry, which was partitioned off from the tiny kitchen. The old woman stood facing him in silence and looking inquiringly at him. She was a diminutive, withered-up old woman of sixty, with sharp malignant eyes and a sharp little nose. Her colourless, somewhat grizzled hair was thickly smeared with oil, and she wore no kerchief over it. Round her thin long neck, which looked like a hen's leg, was knotted some sort of flannel rag, and, in spite of the heat, there hung flapping on her shoulders, a mangy fur cape, yellow with age. The old woman coughed and groaned at every instant. The young man must have looked at her with a rather peculiar expression, for a gleam of mistrust came into her eyes again.

'Raskolnikov, a student, I came here a month ago,' the young man made haste to mutter, with a half-bow, remembering that he ought to be more polite.

'I remember, my good sir, I remember quite well your coming here,' the old woman said distinctly, still keeping her inquiring eyes on his face.

'And here . . . I am again on the same errand,' Raskolnikov continued, a little disconcerted and surprised at the old woman's mistrust. 'Perhaps she is always like that though, only I did not notice it the other time,' he thought with an uneasy feeling.

The old woman paused, as though hesitating; then stepped on one side, and pointing to the door of the room, she said, letting her visitor pass in front of her:

'Step in, my good sir.'

The little room into which the young man walked, with yellow paper on the walls, geraniums and muslin curtains in the windows, was brightly lighted up at that moment by the setting sun.

'So the sun will shine like this *then* too!' flashed as it were by chance through Raskolnikov's mind, and with a rapid glance he scanned everything in the room, trying as far as possible to notice and remember its arrangement. But there was nothing special in the room. The furniture, all very old and of yellow wood, consisted of a sofa with a huge bent wooden back, an oval table in front of the sofa, a dressing-table with a looking-glass fixed on it between the windows, chairs along the walls and two or three halfpenny prints in yellow frames, representing German damsels with birds in their hands – that was all. In the corner a light was burning before a small ikon. Everything was very clean; the floor and the furniture were brightly polished; everything shone.

'Lizaveta's work,' thought the young man. There was not a speck of dust to be seen in the whole flat.

'It's in the houses of spiteful old widows that one finds such cleanliness,' Raskolnikov thought again, and he stole a curious glance at the cotton curtain over the door leading into another tiny room, in which stood the old woman's bed and chest of drawers and into which he had never looked before. These two rooms made up the whole flat.

'What do you want?' the old woman said severely, coming into the room and, as before, standing in front of him so as to look him straight in the face.

'I've brought something to pawn here,' and he drew out of his pocket an old-fashioned flat silver watch, on the back of which was engraved a globe; the chain was of steel.

'But the time is up for your last pledge. The month was up the day before yesterday.'

'I will bring you the interest for another month; wait a little.'

'But that's for me to do as I please, my good sir, to wait or to sell your pledge at once.'

'How much will you give me for the watch, Alyona Ivanovna?'

'You come with such trifles, my good sir, it's scarcely worth anything. I gave you two roubles last time for your ring and one could buy it quite new at a jeweller's for a rouble and a half.'

'Give me four roubles for it, I shall redeem it, it was my father's. I shall be getting some money soon.'

'A rouble and a half, and interest in advance, if you like!'

'A rouble and a half' cried the young man.

'Please yourself' – and the old woman handed him back the watch. The young man took it, and was so angry that he was on the point of going away; but checked himself at once, remembering that there was nowhere else he could go, and that he had had another object also in coming.

'Hand it over,' he said roughly.

The old woman fumbled in her pocket for her keys, and disappeared behind the curtain into the other room. The young man, left standing alone in the middle of the room, listened inquisitively, thinking. He could hear her unlocking the chest of drawers.

'It must be the top drawer,' he reflected. 'So she carries the keys in a pocket on the right. All in one bunch on a steel ring. . . . And there's one key there, three times as big as all the others, with deep notches; that can't be the key of the chest of drawers . . . then there must be some other chest or strong box . . . that's worth knowing. Strong-boxes always have keys like that . . . but how degrading it all is.'

The old woman came back.

'Here, sir: as we say ten copecks the rouble a month, so I must take fifteen copecks from a rouble and a half for the month in advance. But for the two roubles I lent you before, you owe me now twenty copecks on the same reckoning in advance. That makes thirty-five copecks altogether. So I must give you a rouble and fifteen copecks for the watch. Here it is.'

'What! only a rouble and fifteen copecks now!'

'Just so.'

The young man did not dispute it and took the money. He looked at the old woman, and was in no hurry to get away, as though there was still something he wanted to say or to do, but he did not himself quite know what.

'I may be bringing you something else in a day or two, Alyona Ivanovna – a valuable thing – silver – a cigarette-box, as soon as I get it back from a friend . . .' he broke off in confusion.

'Well, we will talk about it then, sir.'

'Good-bye – are you always at home alone, your sister is not here with you?' He asked her as casually as possible as he went out into the passage.

'What business is she of yours, my good sir?'

'Oh, nothing particular, I simply asked. You are too quick. . . . Good-day, Alyona Ivanovna.'

Raskolnikov went out in complete confusion. This confusion became more and more intense. As he went down the stairs, he even stopped short, two or three times, as though suddenly struck by some thought. When he was in the street he cried out, 'Oh, God, how loathsome it all is! and can I, can I possibly. . . . No, it's nonsense, it's rubbish!' he added resolutely. 'And how could such an atrocious thing come into my head? What filthy things my heart is capable of. Yes, filthy above all, disgusting, loathsome, loathsome! – and for a whole month I've been. . . .' But no words, no exclamations, could express his agitation. The feeling of intense repulsion, which had begun to oppress and torture his heart while he was on his way to the old woman, had by now reached such a pitch and had taken such a definite form that he did not know what to do with himself to escape from his wretchedness. He walked along the pavement like a drunken man, regardless of the passers-by, and jostling against them, and only came to his senses when he was in the next street. Looking round, he noticed that he was standing close to a tavern which was

10

entered by steps leading from the pavement to the basement. At that instant two drunken men came out of the door, and abusing and supporting one another, they mounted the steps. Without stopping to think, Raskolnikov went down the steps at once. Till that moment he had never been into a tavern, but now he felt giddy and was tormented by a burning thirst. He longed for a drink of cold beer, and attributed his sudden weakness to the want of food. He sat down at a sticky little table in a dark and dirty corner; ordered some beer, and eagerly drank off the first glassful. At once he felt easier; and his thoughts became clear.

'All that's nonsense,' he said hopefully, 'and there is nothing in it all to worry about! It's simply physical derangement. Just a glass of beer, a piece of dry bread – and in one moment the brain is stronger, the mind is clearer and the will is firm! Phew, how utterly petty it all is!'

But in spite of this scornful reflection, he was by now looking cheerful as though he were suddenly set free from a terrible burden: and he gazed round in a friendly way at the people in the room. But even at that moment he had a dim foreboding that this happier frame of mind was also not normal.

There were few people at the time in the tavern. Besides the two drunken men he had met on the steps, a group consisting of about five men and a girl with a concertina had gone out at the same time. Their departure left the room quiet and rather empty. The persons still in the tavern were a man who appeared to be an artisan, drunk, but not extremely so, sitting before a pot of beer, and his companion, a huge, stout man with a grey beard, in a short full-skirted coat. He was very drunk: and had dropped asleep on the bench; every now and then, he began, as though in his sleep, cracking his fingers, with his arms wide apart and the upper part of his body bounding about on the bench, while he hummed some meaningless refrain, trying to recall some such lines as these:

> *'His wife a year he fondly loved*
> *His wife a – a year he – fondly loved.'*

Or suddenly waking up again:

> *'Walking along the crowded row*
> *He met the one he used to know.'*

But no one shared his enjoyment: his silent companion looked with positive hostility and mistrust at all these manifestations. There was another man in the room who looked somewhat like a retired government clerk.

He was sitting apart, now and then sipping from his pot and looking round at the company. He, too, appeared to be in some agitation.

⇒ TWO ⇐

RASKOLNIKOV WAS NOT USED TO crowds, and, as we said before, he avoided society of every sort, more especially of late. But now all at once he felt a desire to be with other people. Something new seemed to be taking place within him, and with it he felt a sort of thirst for company. He was so weary after a whole month of concentrated wretchedness and gloomy excitement that he longed to rest, if only for a moment, in some other world, whatever it might be; and, in spite of the filthiness of the surroundings, he was glad now to stay in the tavern.

The master of the establishment was in another room, but he frequently came down some steps into the main room, his jaunty, tarred boots with red turn-over tops coming into view each time before the rest of his person. He wore a full coat and a horribly greasy black satin waistcoat, with no cravat, and his whole face seemed smeared with oil like an iron lock. At the counter stood a boy of about fourteen, and there was another boy somewhat younger who handed whatever was wanted. On the counter lay some sliced cucumber, some pieces of dried black bread, and some fish, chopped up small, all smelling very bad. It was insufferably close, and so heavy with the fumes of spirits that five minutes in such an atmosphere might well make a man drunk.

There are chance meetings with strangers that interest us from the first moment, before a word is spoken. Such was the impression made on Raskolnikov by the person sitting a little distance from him, who looked like a retired clerk. The young man often recalled this impression afterwards, and even ascribed it to presentiment. He looked repeatedly at the clerk, partly no doubt because the latter was staring persistently at him, obviously anxious to enter into conversation. At the other persons in the room, including the tavern-keeper, the clerk looked as though he were used to their company, and weary of it, showing a shade of condescending contempt for them as persons of station and culture inferior to his own, with whom it would be useless for him to converse. He was a man over fifty, bald and grizzled, of medium height, and stoutly built. His face, bloated from continual drinking, was of a yellow, even greenish, tinge, with swollen eyelids, out of which keen, reddish eyes gleamed like little chinks. But there was something very strange in him; there was a light in his eyes as though of intense feeling – perhaps there were even thought and intelligence, but at the same time there was a gleam of something like madness. He was wearing an old and hopelessly ragged black dress coat, with all its buttons missing except one, and that one he had buttoned, evidently clinging to this last trace of respectability. A crumpled shirt front, covered with spots and stains, protruded from his canvas waistcoat. Like a clerk, he wore no beard, nor moustache, but had been so long unshaven that his chin looked like a stiff greyish brush. And there was something respectable and like an official about his manner too. But he was restless; he ruffled up his hair and from time to time let his head drop into his hands dejectedly resting his ragged elbows on the stained and sticky table. At last he looked straight at Raskolnikov, and said loudly and resolutely:

'May I venture, honoured sir, to engage you in polite conversation? Forasmuch as, though your exterior would not command respect, my experience admonishes me that you are a man of education and not accustomed to drinking. I have always respected education when in conjunction with genuine sentiments, and I am besides a titular counsellor in rank. Marmeladov – such is my name; titular counsellor. I make bold to inquire – have you been in the service?'

'No, I am studying,' answered the young man, somewhat surprised at the grandiloquent style of the speaker and also at being so directly addressed. In spite of the momentary desire he had just been feeling for company of any sort, on being actually spoken to he felt immediately his habitual irritable and uneasy aversion for any stranger who approached or attempted to approach him.

'A student then, or formerly a student,' cried the clerk. 'Just what I thought! I'm a man of experience, immense experience, sir,' and he tapped his forehead with his fingers in self-approval. 'You've been a student or have attended some learned institution! . . . But allow me . . .' He got up, staggered, took up his jug and his glass, and sat down beside the young man, facing him a little sideways. He was drunk, but spoke fluently and boldly, only occasionally losing the thread of his sentences and drawling his words. He pounced upon Raskolnikov as greedily as though he too had not spoken to a soul for a month.

'Honoured sir,' he began almost with solemnity, 'poverty is not a vice, that's a true saying. Yet I know too that drunkenness is not a virtue, and that that's even truer. But beggary, honoured sir, beggary is a vice. In poverty you may still retain your innate nobility of soul, but in begggary – never – no one. For beggary a man is not chased out of human society with a stick, he is swept out with a broom, so as to make it as humiliating as possible; and quite right too, forasmuch as in beggary I am ready to be the first to humiliate myself. Hence the pot-house! Honoured sir, a month ago Mr. Lebeziatnikov gave my wife a beating, and my wife is a very different matter from me! Do you understand? Allow me to ask you another question out of simple curiosity: have you ever spent a night on a hay barge, on the Neva?'

'No, I have not happened to,' answered Raskolnikov. 'What do you mean?'

'Well, I've just come from one and it's the fifth night I've slept so. . . .' He filled his glass, emptied it and paused. Bits of hay were in fact clinging to his clothes and sticking to his hair. It seemed quite probable that he had not undressed or washed for the last five days. His hands, particularly, were filthy. They were fat and red, with black nails.

His conversation seemed to excite a general though languid interest. The boys at the counter fell to sniggering. The inn-keeper came down from the upper room, apparently on purpose to listen to the 'funny fellow' and sat down at a little distance, yawning lazily, but with dignity. Evidently Marmeladov was a familiar figure here, and he had most likely acquired his weakness for high-flown speeches from the habit of frequently entering into conversation with strangers of all sorts in the tavern. This habit develops into a necessity in some drunkards, and especially in those who are looked after sharply and kept in order at home. Hence in the company of other drinkers they try to justify themselves and even if possible obtain consideration.

'Funny fellow!' pronounced the inn-keeper. 'And why don't you work, why aren't you at your duty, if you are in the service?'

'Why am I not at my duty, honoured sir?' Marmaladov went on, addressing himself exclusively to Raskolnikov, as though it had been he who put that question to him. 'Why am I not at my duty? Does not my heart ache to think what a useless worm I am? A month ago when Mr. Lebeziatnikov beat my wife with his own hands, and I lay drunk, didn't I suffer? Excuse me, young man, has it ever happened to you . . . hm . . . well, to petition hopelessly for a loan?'

'Yes, it has. But what do you mean by "hopelessly"?'

'Hopelessly in the fullest sense, when you know beforehand that you will get nothing by it. You know, for instance, beforehand with positive certainty that this man, this most reputable and exemplary citizen will on no consideration give you money; and indeed I ask you why should he? For he knows of course that I shan't pay it back. From compassion? But Mr. Lebeziatnikov who keeps up with modern ideas explained the other day that compassion is forbidden nowadays by science itself, and that

that's what is done now in England, where there is political economy. Why, I ask you, should he give it to me? And yet though I know before-hand that he won't, I set off to him and . . .'

'Why do you go?' put in Raskolnikov.

'Well, when one has no one, nowhere else one can go! For every man must have somewhere to go. Since there are times when one absolutely must go somewhere! When my own daughter first went out with a yellow ticket, then I had to go . . . (for my daughter has a yellow passport,') he added in parenthesis, looking with a certain uneasiness at the young man. 'No matter, sir, no matter!' he went on hurriedly and with apparent composure when both the boys at the counter guffawed and even the inn-keeper smiled— 'No matter, I am not confounded by the wagging of their heads; for every one knows everything about it already, and all that is secret is made open. And I accept it all not with contempt, but with humility. So be it! So be it! "Behold the man!" Excuse me, young man, can you. . . . No, to put it more strongly and more distinctly; not *can* you but *dare* you, looking upon me, assert that I am not a pig?'

The young man did not answer a word.

'Well,' the orator began again stolidly and with even increased dignity, after waiting for the laughter in the room to subside. 'Well, so be it, I am a pig, but she is a lady! I have the semblance of a beast, but Katerina Ivanovna, my spouse, is a person of education and an officer's daughter. Granted, granted, I am a scoundrel, but she is a woman of a noble heart, full of sentiments, refined by education. And yet . . . oh, if only she felt for me! Honoured sir, honoured sir, you know every man ought to have at least one place where people feel for him!! But Katerina Ivanovna, though she is magnanimous, she is unjust. . . . And yet, although I realize that when she pulls my hair she only does it out of pity – for I repeat without being ashamed, she pulls my hair, young man,' he declared, with redoubled dignity, hearing the sniggering again – 'but, my God, if she would but once. . . . But no, no! It's all in vain and it's no use talking! No use talking! For more than once, my wish did come true and more than once she has felt for me but . . . such is my fate and I am a beast by nature!'

'Rather!' assented the inn-keeper, yawning. Marmeladov struck his fist resolutely on the table.

'Such is my fate! Do you know, sir, do you know, I have sold her very stockings for drink? Not her shoes – that would be more or less in the order of things, but her stockings, her stockings I have sold for drink! Her mohair shawl I sold for drink, a present to her long ago, her own prop-erty, not mine; and we live in a cold room and she caught cold this winter and has begun coughing and spitting blood too. We have three little children and Katrina Ivanovna is at work from morning till night; she is scrubbing and cleaning and washing the children, for she's been used to cleanliness from a child. But her chest is weak and she has a tendency to consumption and I feel it! Do you suppose I don't feel it? And the more I drink the more I feel it. That's why I drink too. I try to find sympathy and feeling in drink. . . . I drink so that I may suffer twice as much!' And as though in despair he laid his head down on the table.

'Young man,' he went on, raising his head again, 'in your face I seem to read some trouble of mind. When you came in I read it, and that was why I addressed you at once. For in unfolding to you the story of my life, I do not wish to make myself a laughing-stock before these idle listeners, who indeed know all about it already, but I am looking for a man of feeling and education. Know then that my wife was educated in a high-class school for the daughters of noblemen, and on leaving, she danced the shawl dance before the governor and other personages for which she was presented with a gold medal and a certificate of merit. The medal . . . well, the medal of course was sold – long ago, hm . . . but the certificate of merit is in her trunk still and not long ago she showed it to our landlady. And although she is most continually on bad terms with the landlady, yet she wanted to tell someone or other of her past honours and of the happy days that are gone. I don't condemn her for it, I don't blame her, for the one thing left her is recollection of the past, and all the rest is dust and ashes. Yes, yes, she is a lady of spirit, proud and determined. She scrubs the floors herself and has nothing but black bread to eat, but won't allow herself to be treated with disrespect. That's why she would not overlook Mr. Lebeziatnikov's rudeness to her, and so when he gave her a beating for it, she took to her bed more from the hurt to her feelings than from the blows. She was a widow when I married her, with three children, one smaller than the other. She married her first husband, an infantry officer, for love, and ran away with him from her father's house. She was exceedingly fond of her husband; but he gave way to cards, got into trouble and with that he died. He used to beat her at the end: and although she paid him back, of which I have authentic documentary evidence, to this day she speaks of him with tears and she throws him up at me; and I am glad, I am glad that, though only in imagination, she should think of herself as having once been happy. . . . And she was left at his death with three children in a wild and remote district where I happened to be at the time; and she was left in such hopeless poverty that, although I have seen many ups and downs of all sorts, I don't feel equal to describing it even. Her relations had all thrown her off. And she was proud, too, excessively proud. . . . And then, honoured sir, and then, I, being at the time a widower, with a daughter of fourteen left me by my first wife, offered her my hand, for I could not bear the sight of such suffering. You can judge the extremity of her calamities, that she, a woman of education and culture and distinguished family, should have consented to be my wife. But she did! Weeping and sobbing and wringing her hands, she married me! For she had nowhere to turn! Do you understand, sir, do you understand what it means when you have absolutely nowhere to turn? No, that you don't understand yet. . . . And for a whole year, I performed my duties conscientiously and faithfully, and did not touch this' (he tapped the jug with his finger), 'for I have feelings. But even so, I could not please her; and then I lost my place too, and that through no fault of mine but through changes in the office; and then I did touch it! . . . It will be a year and a half ago soon since we found ourselves at last after many wanderings and numerous calamities in this magnificent capital, adorned with innumerable monuments. Here too I obtained a situation. . . . I obtained it and I lost it again. Do you understand? This time it was through my own fault I lost it: for my weakness had come out. . . . We have now part of a room at Amalia Fyodorovna Lippevechsel's; and what we live upon and what we pay our rent with, I could not say. There are a lot of people living there beside ourselves. Dirt and disorder a perfect Bedlam . . . hm . . . yes. . . . And meanwhile my daughter by my first wife has grown up; and what my daughter has had to put up with from her step-mother whilst she was growing up, I won't speak of. For, though Katerina Ivanovna is full of generous feelings, she is a spirited lady, irritable and short-tempered. . . . Yes. But it's no use going over that! Sonia, as you may well fancy, has had no education. I did make an effort four years ago to give her a course of geography and universal history, but as I was not very well up in those subjects myself and we had no suitable books, and what books we had . . . hm, anyway we have not even those now, so all our instruction came to an end. We stopped at Cyrus of Persia. Since she has attained years of maturity, she has read other books of romantic tendency and of late she has read with great interest a book she got through Mr. Lebeziatnikov, Lewes' Physiology – do you know it? – and even recounted extracts from it to us: and that's the whole of her education. And now may I venture to address you, honoured sir, on my own account with a private question? Do you suppose that a respectable poor girl can earn much by honest work? Not fifteen farthings a day can she earn, if she is respectable and has no special talent and that without putting her work down for an instant! And what's more, Ivan Ivanitch Klopstock the civil counsellor – have you heard of him? – has not to this day paid her for the half-dozen linen shirts she made him and drove her roughly away, stamping and reviling her, on the pretext that the shirt collars were not made like the

pattern and were put in askew. And there are the little ones hungry. . . .
And Katerina Ivanovna walking up and down and wringing her hands,
her cheeks flushed red, as they always are in that disease: "Here you live
with us," says she, "you eat and drink and are kept warm and you do
nothing to help." And much she gets to eat and drink when there is not
a crust for the little ones for three days! I was lying at the time . . . well,
what of it! I was lying drunk and I heard my Sonia speaking (she is a
gentle creature with a soft little voice . . . fair hair and such a pale, thin
little face). She said: "Katerina Ivanovna, am I really to do a thing like
that?" And Darya Frantsovna, a woman of evil character and very well
known to the police, and two or three times tried to get at her through
the landlady. "And why not?" said Katerina Ivanovna with a jeer, "you
are something mighty precious to be so careful of" But don't blame her,
don't blame her, honoured sir, don't blame her! She was not herself when
she spoke, but driven to distraction by her illness and the crying of the
hungry children; and it was said more to wound her than anything
else. . . . For that's Katerina Ivanovna's character, and when children cry,
even from hunger, she falls to beating them at once. At six o'clock I saw
Sonia get up, put on her kerchief and her cape, and go out of the room
and about nine o'clock she came back. She walked straight up to Katerina
Ivanovna and she laid thirty roubles on the table before her in silence.
She did not utter a word, she did not even look at her, she simply picked
up our own big green *drap de dames* shawl (we have a shawl, made of
drap de dames), put it over her head and face and lay down on the bed
with her face to the wall; and her little shoulders and her body kept
shuddering. . . . And I went on lying there, just as before. . . . And then I
saw, young man, I saw Katerina Ivanovna, in the same silence go up to
Sonia's little bed; she was on her knees all the evening kissing Sonia's
feet, and would not get up, and then they both fell asleep in each other's
arms . . . together, together . . . yes . . . and I . . . lay drunk.'

Marmeladov stopped short, as though his voice had failed him. Then
he hurriedly filled his glass, drank, and cleared his throat.

'Since then, sir,' he went on after a brief pause – 'Since then, owing
to an unfortunate occurrence and through information given by evil-
intentioned persons – in all which Darya Frantsovna took a leading part
on the pretext that she had been treated with want of respect – since then
my daughter Sofya Semyonovna has been forced to take a yellow ticket,
and owing to that she is unable to go on living with us. For our landlady,
Amalia Fyodorovna, would not hear of it (though she had backed up
Darya Frantsovna before) and Mr. Lebeziatnikov too . . . hm. . . . All the
trouble between him and Katerina Ivanovna was on Sonia's account. At
first he was for making up to Sonia himself and then all of a sudden he

stood on his dignity: "how," said he, "can a highly educated man like me live in the same rooms with a girl like that?" And Katerina Ivanovna would not let it pass, she stood up for her . . . and so that's how it happened. And Sonia comes to us now, mostly after dark; she comforts Katerina Ivanovna and gives her all she can. . . . She has a room at the Kapernaumovs' the tailors, she lodges with them; Kapernaumov is a lame man with a cleft palate and all of his numerous family have cleft palates too. And his wife, too, has a cleft palate. They all live in one room, but Sonia has her own, partitioned off. . . . Hm . . . yes . . . very poor people and all with cleft palates . . . yes. Then I got up in the morning, put on my rags, lifted up my hands to heaven and set off to his excellency Ivan Afanasyvitch. His excellency Ivan Afanasyvitch, do you know him? No? Well, then, it's a man of God you don't know. He is wax . . . wax before the face of the Lord; even as wax melteth! . . . His eyes were dim when he heard my story. "Marmeladov, once already you have deceived my expectations . . . I'll take you once more on my own responsibility" – that's what he said, "remember," he said, "and now you can go." I kissed the dust at his feet – in thought only, for in reality he would not have allowed me to do it, being a statesman and a man of modern political and enlightened ideas. I returned home, and when I announced that I'd been taken back into the service and should receive a salary, heavens, what a to-do there was . . . !'

Marmeladov stopped again in violent excitement. At that moment a whole party of revellers already drunk came in from the street, and the sounds of a hired concertina and the cracked piping voice of a child of seven singing "The Hamlet" were heard in the entry. The room was filled with noise. The tavern-keeper and the boys were busy with the newcomers. Marmeladov paying no attention to the new arrivals continued his story. He appeared by now to be extremely weak, but as he became more and more drunk, he became more and more talkative. The recollection of his recent success in getting the situation seemed to revive him, and was positively reflected in a sort of radiance on his face. Raskolnikov listened attentively.

'That was five weeks ago, sir. Yes. . . . As soon as Katerina Ivanovna and Sonia heard of it, mercy on us, it was as though I stepped into the kingdom of Heaven. It used to be: you can lie like a beast, nothing but abuse. Now they were walking on tiptoe, hushing the children. "Semyon Zaharovitch is tired with his work at the office, he is resting, shh!" They made me coffee before I went to work and boiled cream for me! They began to get real cream for me, do you hear that? And how they managed to get together the money for a decent outfit – eleven roubles, fifty copecks – I can't guess. Boots, cotton shirt-fronts – most magnificent, a uniform, they got up all in splendid style, for eleven roubles and a half. The first morning I came back from the office I found Katerina Ivanovna had cooked two courses for dinner – soup and salt meat with horseradish – which we had never dreamed of till then. She has not any dresses . . . none at all, but she got herself up as though she were going on a visit; and not that she'd anything to do it with, she smartened herself up with nothing at all, she'd done her hair nicely, put on a clean collar of some sort, cuffs, and there she was, quite a different person, she was younger and better-looking, Sonia, my little darling, had only helped with money "for the time," she said, "it won't do for me to come and see you too often. After dark maybe when no one can see." Do you hear, do you hear? I lay down for a nap after dinner and what do you think? though Katerina Ivanovna had quarrelled to the last degree with our landlady Amalia Fyodorovna only a week before, she could not resist then asking her in to coffee. For two hours they were sitting, whispering together. "Semyon Zaharovitch is in the service again, now, and receiving a salary," says she, "and he went himself to his excellency and his excellency himself came out to him, made all the others wait and led Semyon Zaharovitch by the hand before everybody into his study." Do you hear, do you hear? "To be sure," says he, "Semyon Zaharovitch, remembering your past services," says he, "and in spite of your propensity to that foolish weakness, since you promise now and since moreover we've got on badly without you," (do you hear, do you hear?) "and so," says he, "I rely now on your word as a gentleman." And all that, let me tell you, she has simply made up for herself, and not simply out of wantonness, for the sake of bragging; no, she believes it all herself, she amuses herself with her own fancies, upon my word she does! And I don't blame her for it, no, I don't blame her! . . . Six days ago when I brought her my first earnings in full – twenty-three roubles forty copecks altogether – she called me her poppet: "poppet," said she "my little poppet". And when we were by ourselves, you understand? You would not think me a beauty, you would not think much of me as a husband, would you? . . . Well, she pinched my cheek, "my little poppet", said she.'

Marmeladov broke off, tried to smile, but suddenly his chin began to twitch. He controlled himself, however. The tavern, the degraded appearance of the man, the five nights in the hay barge, and the pot of spirits, and yet this poignant love for his wife and children bewildered his listener. Raskolnikov listened intently but with a sick sensation. He felt vexed that he had come here.

'Honoured sir, honoured sir,' cried Marmeladov, recovering himself – 'Oh, sir, perhaps all this seems a laughing matter to you, as it does to others, and perhaps I am only worrying you with the stupidity of all the trivial details of my home life, but it is not a laughing matter to me. For I can feel it all. . . . And the whole of that heavenly day of my life and the whole of that evening I passed in fleeting dreams of how I would arrange it all, and how I would dress all the children, and how I should give her rest, and how I should rescue my own daughter from dishonour and restore her to the bosom of her family. . . . And a great deal more. . . . Quite excusable, sir. Well, then sir' (Marmeladov suddenly gave a sort of start, raised his head and gazed intently at his listener), 'well, on the very next day after all those dreams, that is to say, exactly five days ago, in the evening, by a cunning trick, like a thief in the night, I stole from Katerina Ivanovna the key of her box, took out what was left of my earnings, how much it was I have forgotten, and now look at me, all of you! It's the fifth day since I left home, and they are looking for me there and it's the end of my employment, and my uniform is lying in a tavern on the Egyptian bridge. I exchanged it for the garments I have on . . . and it's the end of everything!'

Marmeladov struck his forehead with his fist, clenched his teeth, closed his eyes and leaned heavily with his elbow on the table. But a minute later his face suddenly changed and with a certain assumed slyness and affectation of bravado, he glanced at Raskolnikov, laughed and said:

'This morning I went to see Sonia, I went to ask her for a pick-me up! He-he-he!'

'You don't say she gave it to you?' cried one of the new-comers; he shouted the words and went off into a guffaw.

'This very quart was bought with her money,' Marmeladov declared, addressing himself exclusively to Raskolnikov. 'Thirty copecks she gave me with her own hands, her last, all she had, as I saw. . . . She said nothing, she only looked at me without a word. . . . Not on earth, but up yonder . . . they grieve over men, they weep, but they don't blame them, they don't blame them! But it hurts more, it hurts more when they don't blame! Thirty copecks, yes! And maybe she needs them now, eh? What do you think, my dear sir? For now she's got to keep up her appearance. It costs money, that smartness, that special smartness, you know? Do you understand? And there's pomatum too, you see, she must have things; petticoats, starched ones, shoes too, real jaunty ones to show off her foot when she has to step over a puddle. Do you understand, sir, do you understand, what all that smartness means? And here I, her own father, here I took thirty copecks of that money for a drink! And I am drinking it! And I have already drunk it! Come, who will have pity on a man like me, eh? Are you sorry for me, sir, or not? Tell me, sir, are you sorry or not? He-he-he!'

He would have filled his glass, but there was no drink left. The pot was empty.

'What are you to be pitied for?' shouted the tavern-keeper, who was again near them.

Shouts of laughter and even oaths followed. The laughter and the oaths came from those who were listening and also from those who had heard nothing, but were simply looking at the figure of the discharged government clerk.

'To be pitied! Why am I to be pitied?' Marmeladov suddenly declaimed, standing up with his arm outstretched, as though he had been only waiting for that question.

'Why am I to be pitied, you say? Yes! There's nothing to pity me for! I ought to be crucified, crucified on a cross, not pitied! Crucify me, oh judge, crucify me but pity me! And then I will go of myself to be crucified, for it's not merry-making I seek but tears and tribulation! . . . Do you suppose, you that sell, that this pint of yours has been sweet to me? It was tribulation I sought at the bottom of it, tears and tribulation, and have found it, and I have tasted it; but He will pity as Who has had pity on all men, Who has understood all men and all things, He is the One, He too is the judge. He will come in that day and He will ask: "Where is the daughter who gave herself for her cross, consumptive step-mother and for the little children of another? Where is the daughter who had pity upon the filthy drunkard, her earthly father, undismayed by his beastliness?" And He will say, "Come to Me! I have already forgiven thee once. . . . I have forgiven thee once. . . . Thy sins which are many are forgiven thee, for thou hast loved much. . . ." And He will forgive my Sonia, He will forgive, I know it . . . I felt it in my heart when I was with her just now! And He will judge and will forgive all, the good and the evil, the wise and the meek. . . . And when He has done with all of them, then He will summon us. "You too come forth," He will say. "Come forth, ye drunkards, come forth, ye weak ones, come forth, ye children of shame!" And we shall all come forth, without shame and shall stand before him. And He will say unto us: "Ye are swine, made in the Image of the Beast and with his mark; but come ye also!" And the wise ones and those of understanding will say: "Oh Lord, why dost Thou receive these men?" And He will say: "This is why I receive them, oh ye wise, this is why I receive them, oh ye of understanding, that not one of them believed himself to be worthy of this." And He will hold out His hands to us and we shall fall down before Him . . . and we shall weep . . . and we shall understand all things! Then we shall understand all! . . . and all will understand, Katerina Ivanovna even . . . she will understand . . . Lord, Thy kingdom come!' And he sank down on the bench exhausted, and helpless, looking at no one, apparently oblivious of his surroundings and plunged in deep thought. His words had created a certain impression; there was a moment of silence; but soon laughter and oaths were heard again.

'That's his notion!'

'Talked himself silly!'

'A fine clerk he is!'

And so on, and so on.

'Let us go, sir,' said Marmeladov all at once, raising his head and addressing Raskolnikov – 'come along with me . . . Kozel's house, looking into the yard. I'm gong to Katerina Ivanovna – time I did.'

Raskolnikov had for some time been wanting to go and he had meant to help him. Marmeladov was much unsteadier on his legs than in his speech and leaned heavily on the young man. They had two or three hundred paces to go. The drunken man was more and more overcome by dismay and confusion as they drew nearer the house.

'It's not Katerina Ivanovna I am afraid of now,' he muttered in agitation – 'and that she will begin pulling my hair. What does my hair matter! Bother my hair! That's what I say! Indeed it will be better if she does begin pulling it, that's not what I am afraid of . . . it's her eyes I am afraid of . . . yes, her eyes . . . the red on her cheeks, too, frightens me . . . and her breathing too. . . . Have you noticed how people in that disease breathe . . . when they are excited? I am frightened of the children's crying, too. . . . For if Sonia has not taken them food . . . I don't know what's happened! I don't know! But blows I am not afraid of. . . . Know, sir, that such blows are not a pain to me, but even an enjoyment. In fact I can't get on without it. . . . It's better so. Let her strike me, it relieves her heart . . . it's better so. . . . There is the house. The house of Kozel, the cabinet-maker . . . a German, well-to-do. Lead the way!'

They went in from the yard and up to the fourth storey. The staircase got darker and darker as they went up. It was nearly eleven o'clock, and although in summer in Petersburg there is no real night, yet it was quite dark at the top of the stairs.

A grimy little door at the very top of the stairs stood ajar. A very poor-looking room about ten paces long was lighted up by a candle-end; the whole of it was visible from the entrance. It was all in disorder, littered up with rags of all sorts, especially children's garments. Across the farthest corner was stretched a ragged sheet. Behind it probably was the bed. There was nothing in the room except two chairs and a sofa covered with American leather, full of holes, before which stood an old deal kitchen-table, unpainted and uncovered. At the edge of the table stood a smouldering tallow-candle in an iron candlestick. It appeared that the family had a room to themselves, not part of a room, but their room was practically a passage. The door leading to the other rooms, or rather cupboards, into which Amalia Lippevechsel's flat was divided stood half open, and there was shouting, uproar and laughter within. People seemed to be playing cards and drinking tea there. Words of the most unceremonious kind flew out from time to time.

Raskolnikov recognized Katerina Ivanovna at once. She was a rather tall, slim and graceful woman, terribly emaciated, with magnificent dark brown hair and with a hectic flush in her cheeks. She was pacing up and down in her little room, pressing her hands against her chest; her lips were parched and her breathing came in nervous broken gasps. Her eyes glittered as in fever and looked about with a harsh immovable stare. And that consumptive and excited face with the last flickering light of the candle-end playing upon it made a sickening impression. She seemed to Raskolnikov about thirty years old and was certainly a strange wife for Marmeladov.... She had not heard them and did not notice them coming in. She seemed to be lost in thought, hearing and seeing nothing. The room was close, but she had not opened the window; a stench rose from the staircase, but the door on to the stairs was not closed. From the inner rooms clouds of tobacco smoke floated in, she kept coughing, but did not close the door. The youngest child, a girl of six, was asleep, sitting curled up on the floor with her head on the sofa. A boy a year older stood crying and shaking in the corner, probably he had just had a beating. Beside him stood a girl of nine years old, tall and thin, wearing a thin and ragged chemise with an ancient cashmere pelisse flung over her bare shoulders, long outgrown and barely reaching her knees. Her arm, as thin as a stick, was round her brother's neck. She was trying to comfort him, whispering something to him, and doing all she could to keep him from whimpering again. At the same time her large dark eyes, which looked larger still from the thinness of her frightened face, were watching her mother with alarm. Marmeladov did not enter the door, but dropped on his knees in the very doorway, pushing Raskolnikov in front of him. The woman seeing a stranger stopped indifferently facing him, coming to herself for a moment and apparently wondering what he had come for. But evidently she decided that he was going into the next room, as he had to pass through hers to get there. Taking no further notice of him, she walked towards the outer door to close it and uttered a sudden scream on seeing her husband on his knees in the doorway.

'Ah!' she cried out in a frenzy, 'he has come back! The criminal! the monster!... And where is the money? What's in your pocket, show me! And your clothes are all different! Where are your clothes? Where is the money? Speak!'

And she fell to searching him. Marmeladov submissively and obediently held up both arms to facilitate the search. Not a farthing was there.

'Where is the money?' she cried – 'Mercy on us, can he have drunk it all? There were twelve silver roubles left in the chest!' and in a fury she seized him by the hair and dragged him into the room. Marmeladov seconded her efforts by meekly crawling along on his knees.

'And this is a consolation to me! This does not hurt me, but is a positive con-so-la-tion, ho-nou-red, sir,' he called out, shaken to and fro by his hair and even once striking the ground with his forehead. The child asleep on the floor woke up, and began to cry. The boy in the corner losing all control began trembling and screaming and rushed to his sister in violent terror, almost in a fit. The eldest girl was shaking like a leaf.

'He's drunk it! he's drunk it all,' the poor woman screamed in despair – 'and his clothes are gone! And they are hungry, hungry!' – and wringing her hands she pointed to the children. 'Oh, accursed life! And you, are you not ashamed' – she pounced all at once upon Raskolnikov – 'from the tavern! Have you been drinking with him? You have been drinking with him, too! Go away!'

The young man was hastening away without uttering a word. The inner door was thrown wide open and inquisitive faces were peering in at it. Coarse laughing faces with pipes and cigarettes and heads wearing caps thrust themselves in at the doorway. Further in could be seen figures in dressing-gowns flung open, in costumes of unseemly scantiness, some of them with cards in their hands. They were particularly diverted, when Marmeladov, dragged about by his hair, shouted that it was a consolation to him. They even began to come into the room; at last a sinister shrill outcry was heard: this came from Amalia Lippevechsel herself pushing her way amongst them and trying to restore order after her own fashion and for the hundredth time to frighten the poor woman by ordering her with coarse abuse to clear out of the room next day. As he went out, Raskolnikov had time to put his hand into his pocket, to snatch up the coppers he had received in exchange for his rouble in the tavern and to lay them unnoticed on the window. Afterwards, on the stairs, he changed his mind and would have gone back.

'What a stupid thing I've done,' he thought to himself, 'they have Sonia and I want it myself.' But reflecting that it would be impossible to take it back now and that in any case he would not have taken it, he dismissed it with a wave of his hand and went back to his lodging. 'Sonia wants pomatum, too,' he said as he walked along the street, and he laughed malignantly – 'such smartness costs money.... Hm! And maybe Sonia herself will be bankrupt to-day, for there is always a risk, hunting big-game ... digging for gold ... then they would all be without a crust to-morrow except for my money. Hurrah for Sonia! What a mine they've dug there! And they're making the most of it! Yes, they are making the most of it! They've wept over it and grown used to it. Man grows used to everything, the scoundrel!'

He sank into thought.

'And what if I am wrong?' he cried suddenly after a moment's thought. 'What if man is not really a scoundrel, man in general , I mean, the whole race of mankind – then all the rest is prejudice, simply artificial terrors and there are no barriers and it's all as it should be.'

➤ THREE ◄

HE WAKED UP LATE NEXT DAY AFTER a broken sleep. But his sleep had not refreshed him; he waked up bilious, irritable, ill-tempered, and looked with hatred at his room. It was a tiny cupboard of a room about six paces in length. It had a poverty-striken appearance with its dusty yellow paper peeling off the walls, and it was so low-pitched that a man of more than average height was ill at ease in it and felt every moment that he would knock his head against the ceiling. The furniture was in keeping with the room: there were three old chairs, rather rickety; a painted table in the corner on which lay a few manuscripts and books; the dust that lay thick upon them showed that they had been long untouched. A big, clumsy sofa occupied almost the whole of one wall and half the floor space of the room; it was once covered with chintz, but was now in rags and served Raskolnikov as a bed. Often he went to sleep on it, as he was, without undressing, without sheets, wrapped in his old student's overcoat, with his head on one little pillow, under which he heaped up all the linen he had, clean and dirty, by way of a bolster. A little table stood in front of the sofa.

It would have been difficult to sink to a lower ebb of disorder, but to Raskolnikov in his present state of mind this was positively agreeable. He had got completely away from everyone, like a tortoise in its shell, and even the sight of a servant girl who had to wait upon him and looked sometimes into his room made him writhe with nervous irritation. He was in the condition that overtakes some monomaniacs entirely concentrated upon one thing. His landlady had for the last fortnight given up sending him in meals, and he had not yet thought of expostulating with her, though he went without his dinner. Nastasya, the cook and only servant, was rather pleased at the lodger's mood and had entirely given up sweeping and doing his room, only once a week or so she would stray into his room with a broom. She waked him up that day.

'Get up, why are you asleep?' she called to him. 'It's past nine, I have brought you some tea; will you have a cup? I should think you're fairly starving?'

Raskolnikov opened his eyes, started and recognized Nastasya.

'From the landlady, eh?' he asked, slowly and with a sickly face sitting up on the sofa.

'From the landlady, indeed!'

She set before him her own cracked teapot full of weak and stale tea and laid two yellow lumps of sugar by the side of it.

'Here, Nastasya, take it, please,' he said, fumbling in his pocket (for he had slept in his clothes) and taking out a handful of coppers – 'run and buy me a loaf. And get me a little sausage, the cheapest, at the pork-butcher's.'

'The loaf I'll fetch you this very minute, but wouldn't you rather have some cabbage soup instead of sausage? It's capital soup, yesterday's. I saved it for you yesterday, but you came in late. It's fine soup.'

When the soup had been brought, and he had begun upon it, Nastasya sat down beside him on the sofa and began chatting. She was a country peasant-woman, and a very talkative one.

'Praskovya Pavlovna means to complain to the police about you,' she said.

He scowled.

'To the police? What does she want?'

'You don't pay her money and you won't turn out of the room. That's what she wants, to be sure.'

'The devil, that's the last straw,' he muttered, grinding his teeth, 'no, that would not suit me . . . just now. She is a fool,' he added aloud. 'I'll go and talk to her to-day.'

'Fool she is and no mistake, just as I am. But why, if you are so clever, do you lie here like a sack and have nothing to show for it? One time you used to go out, you say, to teach children. But why is it you do nothing now?'

'I am doing . . .' Raskolnikov began sullenly and reluctantly.

'What are you doing?'

'Work . . .'

'What sort of work?'

'I am thinking,' he answered seriously after a pause.

Nastasya was overcome with a fit of laughter. She was given to laughter and when anything amused her she laughed inaudibly, quivering and shaking all over till she felt ill.

'And have you made much money by your thinking?' she managed to articulate at last.

'One can't go out to give lessons without boots. And I'm sick of it.'

'Don't quarrel with your bread and butter.'

'They pay so little for lessons. What's the use of a few coppers?' he answered, reluctantly, as though replying to his own thought.

'And you want to get a fortune all at once?'

He looked at her strangely.

'Yes, I want a fortune,' he answered firmly, after a brief pause.

'Don't be in such a hurry, you quite frighten me! Shall I get you the loaf or not?'

'As you please.'

'Ah, I forgot! A letter came for you yesterday when you were out.'

'A letter? for me! from whom?'

'I can't say. I gave three copecks of my own to the postman for it. Will you pay me back?'

'Then bring it to me, for God's sake, bring it,' cried Raskolnikov greatly excited – 'good God!'

A minuter later the letter was brought him. That was it: from his mother, from the province of R – . He turned pale when he took it. It was a long while since he had received a letter, but another feeling also suddenly stabbed his heart.

'Nastasya, leave me alone, for goodness' sake; here are your three copecks, but for goodness' sake make haste and go!'

The letter was quivering in his hand; he did not want to open it in her presence; he wanted to be left *alone* with this letter. When Nastasya had gone out, he lifted it quickly to his lips and kissed it; then he gazed intently at the address, the small, sloping handwriting, so dear and familiar, of the mother who had once taught him to read and write. He delayed; he seemed almost afraid of something. At last he opened it: it was a thick heavy letter, weighing over two ounces, two large sheets of notepaper were covered with very small handwriting.

'My dear Rodya,' wrote his mother – 'it's two months since I last had a talk with you by letter which has distressed me and even kept me awake at night, thinking. But I am sure you will not blame me for my inevitable silence. You know how I love you; you are all we have to look to, Dounia and I, you are our all, our one hope, our one stay. What a grief it was to me when I heard that you had given up the university some months ago, for want of means to keep yourself and that you had lost your lessons and your other work! How could I help you out of my hundred and twenty roubles a year pension? The fifteen roubles I sent you four months ago I borrowed, as you know, on security of my pension, from Vassily Ivanovitch Vahrushin a merchant of this town. He is a kind-hearted man and was a friend of your father's too. But having given him the right to receive the pension, I had to wait till the debt was paid off and that is only just done, so that I've been unable to send you anything all this time. But now, thank God, I believe I shall be able to send you something more and in fact we may congratulate ourselves on our good fortune now, of which I hasten to inform you. In the first place, would you have guessed, dear Rodya, that your sister has been living with me for the last six weeks and we shall not be separated in the future. Thank God, her sufferings are over, but I will tell you everything in order, so that you may know just how everything has happened and all that we have hitherto concealed from you. When you wrote to me two months ago that you had heard that Dounia had a great deal to put up with in the Svidrigaïlovs' house, when you wrote that and asked me to tell you all about it – what could I write in answer to you? If I had written the whole truth to you, I dare say you would have thrown up everything and have come to us, even if you had to walk all the way, for I know your character and your feelings, and you would not let your sister be insulted. I was in despair myself, but what could I do? And, besides, I did not know the whole truth myself then. What made it all so difficult was that Dounia received a hundred roubles in advance when she took the place as governess in their family, on condition of part of her salary being deducted every month, and so it was impossible to throw up the situation without repaying the debt. This sum (now I can explain it all to you, my precious Rodya) she took chiefly in order to send you sixty roubles, which you needed so terribly then and which you received from us last year. We deceived you then, writing that this money came from Dounia's savings, but that was not so, and now I tell you all about it, because, thank God, things have suddenly changed for the better, and that you may know how Dounia loves you and what a heart she has. At first indeed Mr. Svidrigaïlov treated her very rudely and used to make disrespectful and jeering remarks at table. . . . But I don't want to go into all those painful details, so as not to worry you for nothing when it is now all over. In short, in spite of the kind and generous behaviour of Marfa Petrovna, Mr. Svidrigaïlov's wife, and all the rest of the household, Dounia had a very hard time, especially when Mr. Svidrigaïlov, relapsing into his old regimental habits, was under the influence of Bacchus. And how do you think it was all explained later on? Would you believe that the crazy fellow had conceived a passion for Dounia from the beginning, but had concealed it under a show of rudeness and contempt. Possibly he was ashamed and horrified himself at his own flighty hopes, considering his years and his being the father of a family; and that made him angry with Dounia. And possibly, too, he hoped by his rude and sneering behaviour to hide the truth from others. But at last he lost all control and had the face to make Dounia an open and shameful proposal, promising her all sorts of inducements and offering, besides, to throw up everything and take her to another estate of his, or even abroad. You can imagine all she went through! To leave her situation at once was impossible not only on account of the money debt, but also to spare the feelings of Marfa Petrovna, whose suspicions would have been aroused: and then Dounia would have been the cause of a rupture in the family. And it would have meant a terrible scandal for Dounia too; that would have been inevitable. There were various other reasons owning to which Dounia could not hope to escape from that awful house for another six weeks. You know Dounia, of course; you know how clever she is and what a strong will she has. Dounia can endure a great deal and even in the most difficult cases she has the fortitude to maintain her firmness. She did not even write to me about everything for fear of upsetting me, although we were constantly in communication. It all ended very unexpectedly. Marfa Petrovna accidentally overheard her husband imploring Dounia in the garden, and, putting a wrong interpretation on the position, threw the blame upon her, believing her to be the cause of it all. An awful scene took place between them on the spot in the garden; Marfa Petrovna went so far as to strike Dounia, refused to hear anything and was shouting at her for a whole hour and then gave orders that Dounia should be packed off at once to me in a plain peasant's cart, into which they flung all her things, her linen and her clothes, all pell-mell, without folding it up and packing it. And a heavy shower of rain came on, too, and Dounia, insulted and put to shame, had to drive with a peasant in an open cart all the seventeen versts into town. Only think now what answer could I have sent to the letter I received from you two months ago and what could I have written? I was in despair; I dared not write to you the truth because you would have been very unhappy, mortified and indignant, and yet what could you do? You could only perhaps ruin yourself, and, besides, Dounia would not allow it; and fill up my letter with trifles when my heart was so full of sorrow, I could not. For a whole month the town was full of gossip about this scandal and it came to such a pass that Dounia and I dared not even go to church on account of the contemptuous looks, whispers, and even remarks made aloud about us. All our acquaintances avoided us, nobody even bowed to us in the street, and I learnt that some shopmen and clerks were intending to insult us in a shameful way, smearing the gates of our house with pitch, so that the landlord began to tell us we must leave. All this was set going by Marfa Petrovna, who managed to slander Dounia and throw dirt at her in every family. She knows everyone in the neighbourhood, and that month she was continually coming into the town, and as she is rather talkative and fond of gossiping about her family affairs and particularly of complaining to all and each of her husband – which is not at all right – so in a short time she had spread her story not only in the town, but over the whole surrounding district. It made me ill, but Dounia bore it better than I did, and if only you could have seen how she endured it all and tried to comfort me and cheer me up! She is an angel! But by God's mercy, our sufferings were cut short: Mr. Svidrigaïlov returned to his senses and repented and, probably feeling sorry for Dounia, he laid before Marfa Petrovna a complete and unmistakable proof of Dounia's innocence, in the form of a letter Dounia had been forced to write and give to him, before Marfa Petrovna came upon them in the garden. This letter, which remained in Mr. Svidrigaïlov's hands after her departure, she had written to refuse personal explanations and secret interviews, for which he was entreating her. In that letter she reproached him with great heat and indignation for the baseness of his behaviour in regard to Marfa Petrovna, reminding him that he was the father and head of a family and telling him how infamous it was of him to torment and make unhappy a defenceless girl, unhappy enough already. Indeed, dear Rodya, the letter was so nobly and touchingly written that I sobbed when I read it and to this day I cannot read it without tears. Moreover, the evidence of the servants, too, cleared Dounia's reputation; they had seen and known a great deal more than Mr. Svidrigaïlov had himself supposed – as indeed is always the case with servants. Marfa Petrovna was completely taken aback, and "again crushed" as she said herself to us, but she was completely convinced of Dounia's innocence. The very next day, being Sunday, she went straight to the Cathedral, knelt down and prayed with tears to Our Lady to give her strength to bear this new trial and to do her duty. Then she came straight from the Cathedral to us, told us the whole story, wept bitterly and, fully penitent, she embraced Dounia and besought her to forgive her. The same morning, without any delay, she went round to all the houses in the town and everywhere, shedding tears, she asserted in the most flattering terms Dounia's innocence and the nobility of her feelings and her behaviour. What was more, she showed and read to everyone the letter in Dounia's handwriting to Mr. Svidrigaïlov and even allowed them to take copies of it – which I must say I think was superfluous. In this way she was busy for several days in driving about the whole town, because some people had taken offence through precedence having been given to others. And therefore they had to take turns, so that in every house she was expected before she arrived, and everyone knew that on such and such a day Marfa Petrovna would be reading the letter in such and such a place and people assembled for every reading of it, even many who had heard it several times already both in their own houses and in other people's. In my opinion a great deal, a very great deal of all this was unnecessary; but that's Marfa Petrovna's character. Anyway she succeeded in completely re-establishing Dounia's reputation and the whole ignominy of this affair rested as an indelible disgrace upon her husband, as the only person to blame, so that I really began to feel sorry for him; it was really treating the crazy fellow too harshly. Dounia was at once asked to give lessons in several families, but she refused. All of a sudden everyone began to treat her with marked respect and all this did much to bring about the event by which, you may say, our whole fortunes are now transformed. You must know, dear Rodya, that Dounia has a suitor and that she has already consented to marry him. I hasten to tell you all about the matter, and though it has been arranged without asking your counsel, I think you will not be aggrieved with me or with your sister on that account, for you will see that we could not wait and put off our decision till we heard from you. And you could not have judged all the facts without being on the spot. This was how it happened. He is already of the rank of a counsellor, Pyotr Petrovitch Luzhin, and is distantly related to Marfa Petrovna, who has been very active in bringing the match about. It began with his expressing through her his desire to make our acquaintance. He was properly received, drank coffee with us and the very next day he sent us a letter in which he very courteously made an offer and begged for a speedy and decided answer. He is a very busy man and is in a great hurry to get to Petersburg, so that every moment is precious to him. At first, of course, we were greatly surprised, as it had all happened so quickly and unexpectedly. We thought and talked it over the whole day. He is a well-to-do man, to be depended upon, he has two posts in the government and has already made his fortune. It is true that he is forty-five years old, but he is of a fairly prepossessing appearance, and might still be thought attractive by women, and he is altogether a very respectable and presentable man, only he seems a little morose and somewhat conceited. But possibly that may only be the impression he makes at first sight. And beware, dear Rodya, when he comes to Petersburg, as he shortly will do, beware of judging him too hastily and severely, as your way is, if there is anything you do not like in him at first sight. I give you this warning, although I feel sure that he will make a favourable impression upon you. Moreover, in order to understand any man one must be deliberate and careful to avoid forming prejudices and mistaken ideas, which are very difficult to correct and get over afterwards. And Pyotr Petrovitch, judging by many indications, is a thoroughly estimable man. At his first visit, indeed, he told us that he was a practical man, but still he shares, as he expressed it, many of the convictions "of our most rising generation" and he is an opponent of all prejudices. He said a good deal more, for he seems a little conceited and likes to be listened to, but this is scarcely a vice. I, of course, understood very little of it, but Dounia explained to me that, though he is not a man of great education, he is clever and seems to be good-natured. You know your sister's character, Rodya. She is a resolute, sensible, patient and generous girl, but she has a passionate heart, as I know very well. Of course, there is no great love either on his side or on hers, but Dounia is a clever girl and has the heart of an angel, and will make it her duty to make her husband happy who on his side will make her happiness his care. Of that we have no good reason to doubt, though it must be admitted the matter has been arranged in great haste. Besides he is a man of great prudence and he will see, to be sure, of himself, that his own happiness will be the more secure, the happier Dounia is with him. And as for some defects of character, for some habits and even certain differences of opinion – which indeed are inevitable even in the happiest marriages – Dounia has said that, as regards all that, she relies on herself, that there is nothing to be uneasy about, and that she is ready to put up with a great deal, if only their future relationship can be an honourable and straightforward one. He struck me, for instance, at first, as rather abrupt, but that may well come from his being an outspoken man, and that is no doubt how it is. For instance, at his second visit, after he had received Dounia's consent, in the course of conversation he declared that before making Dounia's acquaintance he had made up his mind to marry a girl of good reputation, without dowry and, above all, one who had experienced poverty, because, as he explained, a man ought not to be indebted to his wife, but that it is better for a wife to look upon her husband as her benefactor. I must add that he expressed it more nicely and politely than I have done, for I have forgotten his actual phrases and only remember the meaning. And, besides, it was obviously not said of design, but slipped out in the heat of conversation, so that he tried afterwards to correct himself and smooth it over, but all the same it did strike me as somewhat rude, and I said so afterwards to Dounia. But Dounia was vexed, and answered that "words are not deeds", and that, of course, is perfectly true. Dounia did not sleep all night before she made up her mind, and, thinking that I was asleep, she got out of bed and was walking up and down the room all night; at last she knelt down before the ikon and prayed long and fervently and in the morning she told me that she had decided.

I have mentioned already that Pyotr Petrovitch is just setting off for Petersburg, where he has a great deal of business, and he wants to open a legal bureau. He has been occupied for many years in conducting civil and commercial litigation, and only the other day he won an important case. He has to be in Petersburg because he has an important case before the Senate. So, Rodya dear, he may be of the greatest use to you, in every way indeed, and Dounia and I have agreed that from this very day you could definitely enter upon your career and might consider that your future is marked out and assured for you. Oh, if only this comes to pass! This would be such a benefit that we could only look upon it as a providential blessing. Dounia is dreaming of nothing else. We have even ventured already to drop a few words on the subject to Pyotr Petrovitch. He was cautious in his answer, and said that, of course, as he could not get on without a secretary, if would be better to be paying a salary to a relation than to a stranger, if only the former were fitted for the duties (as though there could be doubt of your being fitted!), but then he expressed doubts whether your studies at the university would leave you time for work at his office. The matter dropped for the time, but Dounia is thinking of nothing else now. She has been in a sort of fever for the last few days, and has already made a regular plan for your becoming in the end an associate and even a partner in Pyotr Petrovitch's legal business, which might well be, seeing that you are a student of law. I am in complete agreement with her, Rodya, and share all her plans and hopes, and think there is every probability of realizing them. And in spite of Pyotr Petrovitch's evasiveness, very natural at present (since he does not know you), Dounia is firmly persuaded that she will gain everything by her good influence over her future husband; this she is reckoning upon. Of course we are careful not to talk of any of these remote plans to Pyotr Petrovitch, especially of your becoming his partner. He is a practical man and might take this very coldly, it might all seem to him simply a daydream. Nor has either Dounia or I breathed a word to him of the great hopes we have of his helping us to pay for your university studies; we have not spoken of it, in the first place, because it will come to pass of itself, later on, and he will no doubt without wasting words offer to do it of himself (as though he could refuse Dounia that) the more readily since you may by your own efforts become his right hand in the office, and receive this assistance not as a charity, but as a salary earned by your own work. Dounia wants to arrange it all like this and I quite agree with her. And we have not spoken of our plans for another reason, that is, because I particularly wanted you to feel on an equal footing when you first meet him. When Dounia spoke to him with enthusiasm about you, he answered that one could never judge a man without seeing him close, for oneself, and that he looked forward to forming his own opinion when he makes your acquaintance. Do you know, my precious Rodya, I think that perhaps for some reasons (nothing to do with Pyotr Petrovitch though, simply for my own personal, perhaps old-womanish, fancies) I should do better to go on living by myself, apart, than with them, after the wedding. I am convinced that he will be generous and delicate enough to invite me and to urge me to remain with my daughter for the future, and if he has said nothing about it hitherto, it is simply because it has been taken for granted; but I shall refuse. I have noticed more than once in my life that husbands don't quite get on with their mothers-in-law, and I don't want to be the least in anyone's way, and for my own sake, too, would rather be quite independent, so long as I have a crust of bread of my own, and such children as you and Dounia. If possible, I would settle somewhere near you, for the most joyful piece of news, dear Rodya, I have kept for the end of my letter: know then, my dear boy, that we may perhaps be all together in a very short time and may embrace one another again after a separation of almost three years! It is settled *for certain* that Dounia and I are to set off for Petersburg, exactly when I don't know, but very, very soon, possibly in a week. It all depends on Pyotr Petrovitch who will let us know when he has had time to look round him in Petersburg. To suit his own arrangements he is anxious to have the ceremony as soon as possible, even before the fast of Our Lady, if it could be managed, or if that is too soon to be ready, immediately after. Oh, with what happiness I shall press you to my heart! Dounia is all excitement at the joyful thought of seeing you, she said one day in joke that she would be ready to marry Pyotr Petrovitch for that alone. She is an angel! She is not writing anything to you now, and has only told me to write that she has so much, so much to tell you that she is not going to take up her pen now, for a few lines would tell you nothing, and it would only mean upsetting herself; she bids me send you her love and innumerable kisses. But although we shall be meeting so soon, perhaps I shall send you as much money as I can in a day or two. Now that everyone has heard that Dounia is to marry Pyotr Petrovitch, my credit has suddenly improved and I knew that Afanasy Ivanovitch will trust me now even to seventy-five roubles on the security of my pension, so that perhaps I shall be able to send you twenty-five or even thirty roubles. I would send you more, but I am uneasy about our travelling expenses; for though Pyotr Petrovitch has been so kind as to undertake part of the expenses of the journey, that is to say, he has taken upon himself the conveyance of our bags and big trunk (which will be conveyed through some acquaintances of his), we must reckon upon some expense on our arrival in Petersburg, where we can't be left without a halfpenny, at least for the first few days. But we have calculated it all, Dounia and I, to the last penny, and we see that the journey will not cost very much. It is only ninety versts from us to the railway and we have come to an agreement with a driver we know, so as to be in readiness; and from there Dounia and I can travel quite comfortably third class. So that I may very likely be able to send you not twenty-five but thirty roubles. But enough; I have covered two sheets already and there is no space left for more; our whole history, but so many events have happened! And now, my precious Rodya, I embrace you and send you a mother's blessing till we meet. Love Dounia your sister, Rodya; love her as she loves you and understand that she loves you beyond everything, more than herself. She is an angel and you, Rodya, you are everything to me – our one hope, our one consolation. If only you are happy, we shall be happy. Do you still say your prayers, Rodya, and believe in the mercy of our Creator and our Redeemer? I am afraid in my heart that you may have been visited by the new spirit of infidelity that is abroad to-day; If it is so, I pray for you. Remember, dear boy, how in your childhood, when your father was living, you used to lisp your prayers at my knee, and how happy we all were in those days. Goody-bye, till we meet then – I embrace you warmly, warmly, with many kisses.

> 'Yours till death,
>
> 'PULCHERIA RASKOLNIKOV.'

Almost from the first, while he read the letter, Raskolnikov's face was wet with tears; but when he finished it, his face was pale and distorted and a bitter, wrathful and malignant smile was on his lips. He laid his head down on his threadbare dirty pillow and pondered, pondered a long time. His heart was beating violently, and his brain was in a turmoil. At last he felt cramped and stifled in the little yellow room that was like a cupboard or a box. His eyes and his mind craved for space. He took up his hat and went out, this time without dread of meeting anyone; he had forgotten his dread. He turned in the direction of the Vassilyevsky Ostrov, walking along Vassilyevsky Prospect, as though hastening on some business, but he walked, as his habit was, without noticing his way, muttering and even speaking aloud to himself, to the astonishment of the passers-by. Many of them took him to be drunk.

✦ FOUR ✦

HIS MOTHER'S LETTER HAD BEEN a torture to him, but as regards the chief fact in it, he had felt not one moment's hesitation, even whilst he was reading the letter. The essential question was settled, and irrevocably settled, in his mind: 'Never such a marriage while I am alive and Mr. Luzhin be damned!' 'The thing is perfectly clear,' he muttered to himself, with a malignant smile anticipating the triumph of his decision. 'No, mother, no, Dounia, you won't deceive me! and then they apologize for not asking my advice and for taking the decision without me! I dare say! They imagine it is arranged now and can't be broken off; but we will see whether it can or not! A magnificent excuse: "Pyotr Petrovitch is such a busy man that even his wedding has to be in post-haste, almost by express." No, Dounia, I see it all and I know what you want to say to me; and I know too what you were thinking about, when you walked up and down all night, and what your prayers were like before the Holy Mother of Kazan who stands in mother's bedroom. Bitter is the ascent of Golgotha. . . . Hm . . . so it is finally settled; you have determined to marry a sensible business man, Avdotya Romanovna, one who has a fortune (has *already* made his fortune, that is so much more solid and impressive), a man who holds two government posts and who shares the ideas of our most rising generation, as mother writes, and who *seems* to be kind, as Dounia herself observes. That *seems* beats everything! And that very Dounia for that very "*seems*" is marrying him! Splendid! splendid!

'. . . But I should like to know why mother has written to me about "our most rising generation"? Simply as a descriptive touch, or with the idea of prepossessing me in favour of Mr. Luzhin? Oh, the cunning of them! I should like to know one thing more: how far they were open with one another that day and night and all this time since? Was it all put into *words*, or did both understand that they had the same thing at heart and in their minds, so that there was no need to speak of it aloud, and better not to speak of it? Most likely it was partly like that, from mother's letter it's evident: he struck her as rude *a little*, and mother in her simplicity took her observations to Dounia. And she was sure to be vexed and "answered her angrily". I should think so! Who would not be angered when it was quite clear without any naïve questions and when it was understood that it was useless to discuss it? And why does she write to me, "love Dounia, Rodya, and she loves you more than herself"? Has she a secret conscience-prick at sacrificing her daughter to her son? "You are our one comfort, you are everything to us." Oh, mother!'

His bitterness grew more and more intense, and if he had happened to meet Mr. Luzhin at the moment, he might have murdered him.

'Hm . . . yes, that's true,' he continued, pursuing the whirling idea that chased each other in his brain, 'it is true that "it needs time and care to get to know a man", but there is no mistake about Mr. Luzhin. The chief thing is he is "a man of business and *seems* kind", that was something, wasn't it, to send the bags and big box for them! A kind man, no doubt, after that! But his *bride* and her mother are to drive in a peasant's cart covered with sacking (I know, I have been driven in it). No matter! It is only ninety versts and then they can "travel very comfortably, third class", for a thousand versts! Quite right, too. One must cut one's coat according to one's cloth, but what about you, Mr. Luzhin? She is your bride. . . . And you must be aware that her mother has to raise money on her pension for the journey. To be sure it's a matter of business, a partnership for mutual benefit, with equal shares and expense: – food and drink provided, but pay for your tobacco. The business man has got the better of them, too. The luggage will cost less than their fares and very likely go for nothing. How is it that they don't both see all that, or is it that they don't want to see? And they are pleased, pleased! And to think that this is only the first blossoming, and that the real fruits are to come! But what really matters is not the stinginess, is not the meanness, but the *tone* of the whole thing. For that will be the tone after marriage, it's a foretaste of it. And mother too, why should she be so lavish? What will she have by the time she gets to Petersburg? Three silver roubles or two "paper ones" as *she* says . . . that old woman . . . hm. What does she expect to live upon in Petersburg afterwards? She has her reasons already for guessing that she *could not* live with Dounia after the marriage, even for the first few months. The good man has no doubt let slip something on that subject also, though mother would deny it: "I shall refuse," says she. On whom is she reckoning then? Is she counting on what is left of her hundred and twenty roubles of pension when Afanasy Ivanovitch's debt is paid? She knits woollen shawls and embroiders cuffs, ruining her old eyes. And all her shawls don't add more than twenty roubles a year to her hundred and twenty, I know that. So she is building all her hopes all the time on Mr. Luzhin's generosity; "he will offer it of himself, he will press it on me". You may wait a long time for that! That's how it always is with these Schilleresque noble hearts; till the last moment every goose is a swan with them, till the last moment, they hope for the best and will see nothing wrong, and although they have an inkling of the other side of the picture, yet they won't face the truth till they are forced to; the very thought of it makes them shiver; they thrust the truth away with both hands, until the men they deck out in false colours puts a fool's cap on them with his own hands. I should like to know whether Mr. Luzhin has any orders of merit; I bet he has the Anna in his buttonhole and that he puts it on when he goes to dine with contractors or merchants. He will be sure to have it for his wedding, too! Enough of him, confound him!

'Well . . . mother I don't wonder at, it's like her, God bless her, but how could Dounia? Dounia darling, as though I did not know you! You were nearly twenty when I saw you last: I understood you then. Mother writes that "Dounia can put up with a great deal". I know that very well. I knew that two years and a half ago, and for the last two and a half years I have been thinking about it, thinking of just that, that "Dounia can put up with a great deal". If she could put up with Mr. Svidrigaïlov and all the rest of it, she certainly can put up with a great deal. And now mother and she have taken it into their heads that she can put up with Mr. Luzhin, who propounds the theory of the superiority of wives raised from destitution and owing everything to their husbands' bounty – who propounds it, too, almost at the first interview. Granted that he "let it slip", though he is a sensible man (yet maybe it was not a slip at all, but he meant to make himself clear as soon as possible), but Dounia, Dounia? She understands the man, of course, but she will have to live with the man. Why! she'd live on black bread and water, she would not sell her soul, she would not barter her moral freedom for comfort; she would not barter it for all Schleswig-Holstein, much less Mr. Luzhin's money. No, Dounia was not that sort when I knew her and . . . she is still the same, of course! Yes, there's no denying, the Svidrigaïlovs are a bitter pill! It's a bitter thing to spend one's life a governess in the provinces for two hundred roubles, but I know she would rather be a nigger on a plantation or a Lett with a German master than degrade her soul, and her moral dignity, by binding herself for ever to a man whom she does not respect and with whom she has nothing in common – for her own advantage. And if Mr. Luzhin had been of unalloyed gold, or one huge diamond, she would never have consented to become his legal concubine. Why is she consenting then? What's the point of it? What's the answer? It's clear enough: for herself, for her comfort, to save her life she would not sell herself, but for someone else she is doing it! For one she loves, for one she adores, she will sell herself! That's what it all amounts to; for her brother, for her mother, she will sell herself! She will sell everything! In such cases, "we overcome our moral feeling if necessary", freedom, peace, conscience even, all, all are brought into the market. Let my life go, if only my dear ones may be happy! More than that, we become casuists, we learn to be Jesuitical and for a time maybe we can soothe ourselves, we can persuade ourselves that it is one's duty for a good object. That's just like us, it's as clear as daylight. It's clear that Rodion Romanovitch Raskolnikov is the central figure in the business, and no one else. Oh yes, she can ensure his happiness, keep him in the university, make him a partner in the office, make his whole future secure; perhaps he may even be a rich man later on, prosperous, respected, and may even end his life a famous man! But my mother? It's all Rodya, precious Rodya, her firstborn! For such a son who would not sacrifice such a daughter! Oh, loving, over-partial hearts! Why, for his sake we would not shrink even from Sonia's fate. Sonia, Sonia Marmeladov, the eternal victim so long as the world lasts. Have you taken the measure of your sacrifice, both of you? Is it right? Can you bear it? Is it any use? Is there sense in it? And let me tell you, Dounia, Sonia's life is no worse than life with Mr. Luzhin. "There can be no question of love," mother writes. And what if there can be no respect either, if on the contrary there is aversion, contempt, repulsion, what then? So you will have to "keep up your appearance", too. Is not that so? Do you understand what that smartness means? Do you understand that the Luzhin smartness is just the same thing as Sonia's and may be worse, viler, baser, because in your case, Dounia, it's a bargain for luxuries, after all, but with Sonia it's simply a question of starvation. It has to be paid for, it has to be paid for, Dounia, this smartness. And what if it's more than you can bear afterwards, if you regret it? The bitterness, the misery, the curses, the tears hidden from all the world, for you are not a Marfa Petrovna. And how will your mother feel then? Even now she is uneasy, she is worried, but then, when she sees it all clearly? And I? Yes, indeed, what have you taken me for? I won't have your sacrifice, Dounia, I won't have it, mother! It shall not be, so long as I am alive, shall not, it shall not! I won't accept it!'

He suddenly paused in his reflections and stood still.

'It shall not be? But what are you going to do to prevent it? You'll forbid it? And what right have you? What can you promise them on your side to give you such a right? Your whole life, your whole future, you will devote to them *when you have finished your studies and obtained a post*? Yes, we have heard all that before, and that's all *words*, but now? Now something must be done, now, do you understand that? And what are you doing now? You are living upon them. They borrow on their hundred roubles pension. They borrow from the Svidrigaïlovs. How are you going to save them from the Svidrigaïlovs, from Afanasy Ivanovitch Vahrushin, oh, future millionaire Zeus, who would arrange their lives for them? In another ten years? In another ten years, mother will be blind with knitting shawls, maybe with weeping too. She will be worn to a shadow with fasting; and my sister? Imagine for a moment what may have become of your sister in ten years? What may happen to her during those ten years? Can you fancy?'

So he tortured himself, fretting himself with such questions, and finding a kind of enjoyment in it. And yet all these questions were not new ones suddenly confronting him, they were old familiar aches. It was long since they had first begun to grip and rend his heart. Long, long ago his present anguish had its first beginnings; it had waxed and gathered strength, it had matured and concentrated, until it had taken the form of a fearful, frenzied and fantastic question, which tortured his heart and his mind, clamouring insistently for an answer. Now his mother's letter had burst on him like a thunderclap. It was clear that he must not now suffer passively, worrying himself over unsolved questions, but that he must do something, do it at once, and do it quickly. Anyway he must decide on something, or else. . . .

'Or throw up life altogether!' he cried suddenly, in a frenzy – 'accept one's lot humbly as it is, once for all and stifle everything in oneself, giving up all claim to activity, life and love!'

'Do you understand, sir, do you understand what it means when you have absolutely nowhere to turn?' Marmeladov's question came suddenly into his mind, 'for every man must have somewhere to turn'. . . .

He gave a sudden start: another thought, that he had had yesterday, slipped back into his mind. But he did not start at the thought recurring to him, for he knew, he had *felt beforehand*, that it must come back, he was expecting it; besides it was not only yesterday's thought. The difference was that a month ago, yesterday even, the thought was a mere dream: but now . . . now it appeared not a dream at all, it had taken a new menacing and quite unfamiliar shape, and he suddenly became aware of this himself. . . . He felt a hammering in his head, and there was a darkness before his eyes.

He looked round hurriedly, he was searching for something. He wanted to sit down and was looking for a seat; he was walking along the K – Boulevard. There was a seat about a hundred paces in front of him. He walked towards it as fast as he could; but on the way he met with a little adventure which absorbed all his attention. Looking for the seat, he had noticed a woman walking some twenty paces in front of him, but at first he took no more notice of her than of other objects that crossed his path. It had happened to him many times going home not to notice the road by which he was going, and he was accustomed to walk like that. But there was at first sight something so strange about the woman in front of him, that gradually his attention was riveted upon her, at first reluctantly and, as it were, resentfully, and then more and more intently. He felt a sudden desire to find out what it was that was so strange about the woman. In the first place, she appeared to be a girl quite young, and she was walking in the great heat bareheaded and with no parasol or gloves, waving her arms about in an absurd way. She had on a dress of some light silky material, but put on strangely awry, not properly hooked up, and torn open at the top of the skirt, close to the waist: a great piece was rent and hanging loose. A little kerchief was flung about her bare throat, but lay slanting on one side. The girl was walking unsteadily, too, stumbling and staggering from side to side. She drew Raskolnikov's whole attention at last. He overtook the girl at the seat, but, on reaching it, she dropped down on it, in the corner; she let her head sink on the back of the seat and closed her eyes, apparently in extreme exhaustion. Looking at her closely, he saw at once that she was completely drunk. It was a strange and shocking sight. He could hardly believe that he was not mistaken. He saw before him the face of a quite young, fair-haired girl – sixteen, perhaps not more than fifteen, years old, a pretty little face, but flushed and heavy-looking and, as it were, swollen. The girl seemed hardly to know what she was doing; she crossed one leg over the other, lifting it indecorously, and showed every sign of being unconscious that she was in the street.

Raskolnikov did not sit down, but he felt unwilling to leave her, and stood facing her in perplexity. This boulevard was never much frequented; and now, at two o'clock, in the stifling heat, it was quite deserted. And yet on the further side of the boulevard, about fifteen paces away, a gentleman was standing on the edge of the pavement, he, too, would apparently have liked to approach the girl with some object of his own. He, too, had probably seen her in the distance and had followed her, but found Raskolnikov in his way. He looked angrily at him, though he tried to escape his notice, and stood impatiently biding his time, till the unwelcome man in rags should have moved away. His intentions were unmistakable. The gentleman was a plump, thickly-set man, about thirty, fashionably dressed, with a high colour, red lips and moustaches. Raskolnikov felt furious; he had a sudden longing to insult this fat dandy in some way. He left the girl for a moment and walked towards the gentleman.

'Hey! You Svidrigaïlov! What do you want here?' he shouted, clenching his fists and laughing, spluttering with rage.

'What do you mean?' the gentleman asked sternly, scowling in haughty astonishment.

'Get away, that's what I mean.'

'How dare you, you low fellow!'

He raised his cane. Raskolnikov rushed at him with his fists, without reflecting that the stout gentleman was a match for two men like himself. But at that instant someone seized him from behind, and a police constable stood between them.

'That's enough, gentlemen, no fighting, please, in a public place. What do you want? Who are you?' he asked Raskolnikov sternly, noticing his rags.

Raskolnikov looked at him intently. He had a straightforward, sensible, soldierly face, with grey moustaches and whiskers.

'You are just the man I want,' Raskolnikov cried, catching at his arm. 'I am a student, Raskolnikov. . . . You may as well know that too,' he added, addressing the gentleman, 'come along, I have something to show you.'

And taking the policeman by the hand he drew him towards the seat.

'Look here, hopelessly drunk, and she has just come down the boulevard. There is no telling who and what she is, she does not look like a professional. It's more likely she has been given drink and deceived somewhere . . . for the first time . . . you understand? and they've put her out into the street like that. Look at the way her dress is torn, and the way it has been put on: she has been dressed by somebody, she has not dressed herself, and dressed by unpractised hands, by a man's hands; that's evident. And now look there: I don't know that dandy with whom I was going to fight, I see him for the first time, but he, too, has seen her on the road, just now, drunk, not knowing what she is doing and now he is very eager to get hold of her, to get her away somewhere while she is in this state . . . that's certain, believe me, I am not wrong. I saw him myself watching her and following her, but I prevented him, and he is just waiting for me to go away. Now he has walked away a little, and is standing still, pretending to make a cigarette. . . . Think how can we keep her out of his hands, and how are we to get her home?'

The policeman saw it all in a flash. The stout gentleman was easy to understand, he turned to consider the girl. The policeman bent over to examine her more closely, and his face worked with genuine compassion.

'Ah, what a pity!' he said, shaking his head – 'why, she is quite a child! She has been deceived, you can see that at once. Listen, lady,' he began addressing her, 'where do you live?' The girl opened her weary and sleepy-looking eyes, gazed blankly at the speaker and waved her hand.

'Here,' said Raskolnikov, feeling in his pocket and finding twenty copecks, 'here, call a cab and tell him to drive her to her address. The only thing is to find out her address!'

'Missy, missy!' the policeman began again, taking the money. 'I'll fetch you a cab and take you home myself. Where shall I take you, eh? Where do you live?'

'Go away! They won't let me alone,' the girl muttered, and once more waved her hand.

'Ach, ach, how shocking! It's shameful, missy, it's a shame!' He shook his head again, shocked, sympathetic and indignant.

'It's a difficult job,' the policeman said to Raskolnikov, and as he did so, he looked him up and down in a rapid glance. He, too, must have seemed a strange figure to him: dressed in rags and handing him money!

'Did you meet her far from here?' he asked him.

'I tell you she was walking in front of me, staggering, just here, in the boulevard. She only just reached the seat and sank down on it.'

'Ah, the shameful things that are done in the world nowadays, God have mercy on us! An innocent creature like that, drunk already! She has been deceived, that's a sure thing. See how her dress has been torn too. . . . Ah, the vice one sees nowadays! And as likely as not she belongs to gentlefolk too, poor ones maybe. . . . There are many like that nowadays. She looks refined, too, as though she were a lady,' and he bent over her once more.

Perhaps he had daughters growing up like that, 'looking like ladies and refined', with pretensions to gentility and smartness. . . .

'The chief thing is,' Raskolnikov persisted, 'to keep her out of this scoundrel's hands! Why should he outrage her? It's as clear as day what he is after; ah, the brute, he is not moving off!'

Raskolnikov spoke aloud and pointed to him. The gentleman heard him, and seemed about to fly into a rage again, but thought better of it, and confined himself to a contemptuous look. He then walked slowly another ten paces away and again halted.

'Keep her out of his hands we can,' said the constable thoughtfully, 'if only she'd tell us where to take her, but as it is. . . . Missy, hey, missy!' he bent over her once more.

She opened her eyes fully all of a sudden, looked at him intently, as though realizing something, got up from the seat and walked away in the direction from which she had come. 'Oh, shameful wretches, they won't let me alone!' she said, waving her hand again. She walked quickly, though staggering as before. The dandy followed her, but along another avenue, keeping his eye on her.

'Don't be anxious, I won't let him have her,' the policeman said resolutely, and he set off after them.

'Ah, the vice one sees nowadays!' he repeated aloud, sighing.

At that moment something seemed to sting Raskolnikov; in an instant a complete revulsion of feeling came over him.

'Hey, here!' he shouted after the policeman.

The latter turned round.

'Let them be! What is it to do with you? Let her go! Let him amuse himself.' He pointed at the dandy, 'What is it to do with you?'

The policeman was bewildered, and stared at him open-eyed. Raskolnikov laughed.

'Well!' ejaculated the policeman, with a gesture of contempt, and he walked after the dandy and the girl, probably taking Raskolnikov for a madman or something even worse.

'He has carried off my twenty copecks,' Raskolnikov murmured angrily when he was left alone. 'Well, let him take as much from the other fellow to allow him to have the girl and so let it end. And why did I want to interfere? Is it for me to help? Have I any right to help? Let them devour each other alive – what is it to me? How did I dare to give him twenty copecks? Were they mine?'

In spite of those strange words he felt very wretched. He sat down on the deserted seat. His thoughts strayed aimlessly. . . . He found it hard to fix his mind on anything at that moment. He longed to forget himself altogether, to forget everything, and then to wake up and begin life anew. . . .

'Poor girl!' he said, looking at the empty corner where she had sat – 'She will come to herself and weep, and then her mother will find out. . . . She will give her a beating, a horrible, shameful beating and then, maybe, turn her out of doors. . . . And even if she does not, the Darya Frantsovnas will get wind of it, and the girl will soon be slipping out on the sly here and there. Then there will be the hospital directly (that's always the luck of those girls with respectable mothers, who go wrong on the sly) and then . . . again the hospital . . . drink . . . the taverns . . . and more hospital, in two or three years – a wreck, and her life over at eighteen or nineteen. . . . Have not I seen cases like that? And how have they been brought to it? Why, they've all come to it like that. Ugh! But what does it matter? That's as it should be, they tell us. A certain percentage, they tell us, must every year go . . . that way . . . to the devil, I suppose, so that the rest may remain chaste, and not be interfered with. A percentage! What splendid words they have; they are so scientific, so consolatory. . . . Once you've said "perentage" there's nothing more to worry about. If we had any other word . . . maybe we might feel more uneasy. . . . But what if Dounia were one of the percentage? Of another one if not that one?

'But where am I going?' he thought suddenly. 'Strange. I came out for something. As soon as I had read the letter I came out. . . . I was going to Vassilyevsky Ostrov, to Razumihin. That's what it was . . . now I remember. What for, though? And what put the idea of going to Razumihin into my head just now? That's curious.'

He wondered at himself. Razumihin was one of his old comrades at the university. It was remarkable that Raskolnikov had hardly any friends at the university; he kept aloof from everyone, went to see no one, and did not welcome anyone who came to see him, and indeed everyone soon gave him up. He took no part in the students' gatherings, amusements or conversations. He worked with great intensity without sparing himself, and he was respected for this, but no one liked him. He was very poor, and there was a sort of haughty pride and reserve about him, as though he were keeping something to himself. He seemed to some of his comrades to look down upon them all as children, as though he were superior in development, knowledge and convictions, as though their beliefs and interests were beneath him.

With Razumihin he had got on, or, at least, he was more unreserved and communicative with him. Indeed it was impossible to be on any other terms with Razumihin. He was an exceptionally good-humoured and candid youth, good-natured to the point of simplicity, though both depth and dignity lay concealed under that simplicity. The better of his comrades understood this, and all were fond of him. He was extremely intelligent, though he was certainly rather a simpleton at times. He was of striking appearance – tall, thin, black-haired and always badly shaved. He was sometimes uproarious and was reputed to be of great physical strength. One night, when out in a festive company, he had with one blow laid a gigantic policeman on his back. There was no limit to his drinking powers, but he could abstain from drink altogether; he sometimes went too far in his pranks; but he could do without pranks altogether. Another thing striking about Razumihin, no failure distressed him, and it seemed as though no unfavourable circumstances could crush him. He could lodge anywhere, and bear the extremes of cold and hunger. He was very poor, and kept himself entirely on what he could earn by work of one sort or another. He knew of no end of resources by which to earn money. He spent one whole winter without lighting his stove, and used to declare that he liked it better, because one slept more soundly in the cold. For the present he, too, had been obliged to give up the university, but it was only for a time, and he was working with all his might to save enough to return to his studies again. Raskolnikov had not been to see him for the last four months, and Razumihin did not even know his address. About two months before, they had met in the street, but Raskolnikov had turned away and even crossed to the other side that he might not be observed. And though Razumihin noticed him, he passed him by, as he did not want to annoy him.

✤ FIVE ✦

'OF COURSE, I'VE BEEN MEANING lately to go to Razumihin's to ask for work, to ask him to get me lessons or something...' Raskolnikov thought, 'but what help can he be to me now? Suppose he gets me lessons, suppose he shares his last farthing with me, if he has any farthings, so that I could get some boots and make myself tidy enough to give lessons... hm... Well and what then? What shall I do with the few coppers I earn? That's not what I want now. It's really absurd for me to go to Razumihin....'

The question why he was now going to Razumihin agitated him even more than he was himself aware; he kept uneasily seeking for some sinister significance in this apparently ordinary action.

'Could I have expected to set it all straight and to find a way out by means of Razumihin alone?' he asked himself in perplexity.

He pondered and rubbed his forehead, and, strange to say, after long musing, suddenly, as it were spontaneously and by chance, a fantastic thought came into his head.

'Hm... to Razumihin's,' he said all at once, calmly, as though he had reached a final determination. 'I shall go to Razumihin's, of course, but... not now, I shall go to him... on the next day after It, when It will be over and everything will begin afresh....'

And suddenly he realized what he was thinking.

'After It,' he shouted, jumping up from the seat, 'but is It really going to happen? Is it possible it really will happen?' He left the seat, and went off almost at a run; he meant to turn back, homewards, but the thought of going home suddenly filled him with intense loathing; in that hole, in that awful little cupboard of his, all *this* had for a month past been growing up in him; and he walked on at random.

His nervous shudder had passed into a fever that made him feel shivering; in spite of the heat he felt cold. With a kind of effort he began almost unconsciously, from some inner craving, to stare at all the objects before him, as though looking for something to distract his attention; but he did not succeed, and kept dropping every moment into brooding. When with a start he lifted his head again and looked round, he forgot at once what he had just been thinking about and even where he was going. In this

47

way he walked right across Vassilyevsky Ostrov, came out on to the Lesser Neva, crossed the bridge and turned towards the islands. The greenness and freshness were at first restful to his weary eyes after the dust of the town and the huge houses that hemmed him in and weighed upon him. Here there were no taverns, no stifling closeness, no stench. But soon these new pleasant sensations passed into morbid irritability. Sometimes he stood still before a brightly painted summer villa standing among green foliage, he gazed through the fence, he saw in the distance smartly dressed women on the verandahs and balconies, and children running in the gardens. The flowers especially caught his attention; he gazed at them longer than at anything. He was met, too, by luxurious carriages and by men and women on horseback; he watched them with curious eyes and forgot about them before they had vanished from his sight. Once he stood still and counted his money; he found he had thirty copecks. 'Twenty to the policeman, three to Nastasya for the letter, so I must have given forty-seven or fifty to the Marmeladovs yesterday,' he thought, reckoning it up for some unknown reason, but he soon forgot with what object he had taken the money out of his pocket. He recalled it on passing an eating-house or tavern, and felt that he was hungry. . . . Going into the tavern he drank a glass of vodka and ate a pie of some sort. He finished eating it as he walked away. It was a long while since he had taken vodka and it had an effect upon him at once, though he only drank a wineglassful. His legs felt suddenly heavy and a great drowsiness came upon him. He turned homewards, but reaching Petrovsky Ostrov he stopped completely exhausted, turned off the road into the bushes, sank down upon the grass and instantly fell asleep.

In a morbid condition of the brain, dreams often have a singular actuality, vividness and extraordinary semblance of reality. At times monstrous images are created, but the setting and the whole picture are so truthlike and filled with details so delicate, so unexpected, but so artistically consistent, that the dreamer, were he an artist like Pushkin or Turgenev even, could never have invented them in the waking state. Such sick dreams always remain long in the memory and make a powerful impression on the overwrought and deranged nervous system.

Raskolnikov had a fearful dream. He dreamt he was back in his childhood in the little town of his birth. He was a child about seven years old, walking into the country with his father on the evening of a holiday. It was a grey and heavy day, the country was exactly as he remembered it; indeed he recalled it far more vividly in his dream than he had done in memory. The little town stood on a level flat as bare as the hand, not even a willow near it; only in the far distance, a copse lay, a dark blur on the very edge of the horizon. A few paces beyond the last market garden stood a tavern, a big tavern, which had always aroused in him a feeling of aversion, even of fear, when he walked by it with his father. There was always a crowd there, always shouting, laughter and abuse, hideous hoarse singing and often fighting. Drunken and horrible-looking figures were hanging about the tavern. He used to cling close to his father, trembling all over when he met them. Near the tavern the road became a dusty track, the dust of which was always black. It was a winding road, and about a hundred paces further on, it turned to the right to the graveyard. In the middle of the graveyard stood a stone church with a green cupola where he used to go to mass two or three times a year with his father and mother, when a service was held in memory of his grandmother, who had long been dead, and whom he had never seen. On these occasions they used to take on a white dish tied up in a table napkin a special sort of rice pudding with raisins stuck in it in the shape of a cross. He loved that church, the old-fashioned, unadorned ikons and the old priest with the shaking head. Near his grandmother's grave, which was marked by a stone, was the little grave of his younger brother who had died at six months old. He did not remember him at all, but he had been told about his little brother, and whenever he visited the graveyard he used religiously and reverently to cross himself and to bow down and kiss the little grave. And now he dreamt that he was walking with his father past the tavern on the way to the graveyard; he was holding his father's hand and looking with dread at the tavern. A peculiar circumstance attracted his attention: there seemed to be some kind of festivity going on, there were crowds of gaily dressed townspeople, peasant women, their husbands, and riff-raff of all sorts, all singing and all more or less drunk. Near the entrance of the tavern stood a cart, but a strange cart. It was one of those big carts usually drawn by heavy cart-horses and laden with casks of wine or other heavy goods. He always liked looking at those great cart-horses, with their long manes, thick legs, and slow even pace, drawing along a perfect mountain with no appearance of effort, as though it were easier going with a load than without it. But now, strange to say, in the shafts of such a cart he saw a thin little sorrel beast, one of those peasants' nags which he had often seen straining their utmost under a heavy load of wood or hay, especially when the wheels were stuck in the mud or in a rut. And the peasants would beat them so cruelly, sometimes even about the nose and eyes, and he felt so sorry, so sorry for them that he almost cried, and his mother always used to take him away from the window. All of a sudden there was a great uproar of shouting, singing and the balalaïka, and from the tavern a number of big and very drunken peasants came out, wearing red and blue shirts and coats thrown over their shoulders.

'Get in, get in!' shouted one of them, a young thick-necked peasant with a fleshy face red as a carrot. 'I'll take you all, get in!'

But at once there was an outbreak of laughter and exclamations in the crowd.

'Take us all with a beast like that!'

'Why, Mikolka, are you crazy to put a nag like that in such a cart?'

'And this mare is twenty if she is a day, mates!'

'Get in, I'll take you all,' Mikolka shouted again, leaping first into the cart, seizing the reins and standing straight up in front. 'The bay has gone with Matvey,' he shouted from the cart – 'and this brute, mates, is just breaking my heart, I feel as if I could kill her. She's just eating her head off. Get in, I tell you! I'll make her gallop! She'll gallop!' and he picked up the whip, preparing himself with relish to flog the little mare.

'Get in! Come along!' The crowd laughed. 'D'you hear? she'll gallop!'

'Gallop indeed! She has not had a gallop in her for the last ten years!'

'She'll jog along!'

'Don't you mind her, mates, bring a whip each of you, get ready!'

'All right! Give it to her!'

They all clambered into Mikolka's cart, laughing and making jokes. Six men got in and there was still room for more. They hauled in a fat, rosy-cheeked woman. She was dressed in red cotton, in a pointed, beaded headdress and thick leather shoes; she was cracking nuts and laughing. The crowd round them was laughing too and indeed, how could they help laughing? That wretched nag was to drag all the cartload of them at a gallop! Two young fellows in the cart were just getting whips ready to help Mikolka. With the cry of 'now,' the mare tugged with all her might, but far from galloping, could scarcely move forward; she struggled with her legs, gasping and shrinking from the blows of the three whips which were showered upon her like hail. The laughter in the cart and in the crowd was redoubled, but Mikolka flew into a rage and furiously thrashed the mare, as though he supposed she really could gallop.

'Let me get in, too, mates,' shouted a young man in the crowd whose appetite was aroused.

'Get in, all get in,' cried Mikolka, 'she will draw you all. I'll beat her to death!' And he thrashed and thrashed at the mare, beside himself with fury.

'Father, father,' he cried, 'father, what are they doing? Father, they are beating the poor horse!'

'Come along, come along!' said his father. 'They are drunken and foolish, they are in fun; come away, don't look!' and he tried to draw him away, but he tore himself away from his hand, and, beside himself with horror, ran to the horse. The poor beast was in a bad way. She was gasping, standing still, then tugging again and almost falling.

'Beat her to death,' said Mikolka, 'it's come to that. I'll do for her!'

'What are you about, are you a Christian, you devil?' shouted an old man in the crowd.

'Did anyone ever see the like? A wretched nag like that pulling such a cartload,' said another.

'You'll kill her,' shouted the third.

'Don't meddle! It's my property, I'll do what I choose. Get in, more of you! Get in, all of you! I will have her go at a gallop! . . .'

All at once laughter broke into a roar and covered everything: the mare, roused by the shower of blows, began feebly kicking. Even the old man could not help smiling. To think of a wretched little beast like that trying to kick!

Two lads in the crowd snatched up whips and ran to the mare to beat her about the ribs. One ran each side.

'Hit her in the face, in the eyes, in the eyes,' cried Mikolka.

'Give us a song, mates,' shouted someone in the cart, and everyone in the cart joined in a riotous song, jingling a tambourine and whistling. The woman went on cracking nuts and laughing.

. . . He ran beside the mare, ran in front of her, saw her being whipped across the eyes, right in the eyes! He was crying, he felt choking, his tears were streaming. One of the men gave him a cut with the whip across the face, he did not feel it. Wringing his hands and screaming, he rushed up to the grey-headed old man with the grey beard, who was shaking his head in disapproval. One woman seized him by the hand and would have taken him away, but he tore himself from her and ran back to the mare. She was almost at the last gasp, but began kicking once more.

'I'll teach you to kick,' Mikolka shouted ferociously. He threw down the whip, bent forward and picked up from the bottom of the cart a long, thick shaft, he took hold of one end with both hands and with an effort brandished it over the mare.

'He'll crush her,' was shouted round him, 'He'll kill her!'

'It's my property' shouted Mikolka and brought the shaft down with a swinging blow. There was a sound of a heavy thud.

'Thrash her, thrash her! Why have you stopped?' shouted voices in the crowd.

And Mikolka swung the shaft a second time and it fell a second time on the spine of the luckless mare. She sank back on her haunches, but lurched forward and tugged forward with all her force, tugged first on one side and then on the other, trying to move the cart. But the six whips were attacking her in all directions, and the shaft was raised again and fell upon her a third time, then a fourth, with heavy measured blows. Mikolka was in a fury that he could not kill her at one blow.

'She's a tough one,' was shouted in the crowd.

'She'll fall in a minute, mates, there will soon be an end of her,' said an admiring spectator in the crowd.

'Fetch an axe to her! Finish her off,' shouted a third.

'I'll show you! Stand off,' Mikolka screamed frantically; he threw down the shaft, stooped down in the cart and picked up an iron crowbar. 'Look out,' he shouted, and with all his might he dealt a stunning blow at the poor mare. The blow fell; the mare staggered, sank back, tried to pull, but the bar fell again with a swinging blow on her back and she fell on the ground like a log.

'Finish her off,' shouted Mikolka and he leapt, beside himself, out of the cart. Several young men, also flushed from drink, seized anything they could come across – whips, sticks, poles – and ran to the dying mare. Mikolka stood on one side and began dealing random blows with the crowbar. The mare stretched out her head, draw a long breath and died.

'You butchered her,' some shouted in the crowd.

'Why wouldn't she gallop then?'

'My property!' shouted Mikolka, with bloodshot eyes, brandishing the bar in his hands. He stood as though regretting that he had nothing more to beat.

'No mistake about it, you are not a Christian,' many voices were shouting in the crowd.

But the poor boy, beside himself, made his way, screaming, through the crowd to the sorrel nag, put his arms round her bleeding dead head and kissed it, kissed the eyes and kissed the lips. . . . Then he jumped up and flew in a frenzy with his little fists out at Mikolka. At that instant his father, who had been running after him, snatched him up and carried him out of the crowd.

'Come along, come! Let us go home,' he said to him.

'Father! Why did they . . . kill . . . the poor horse?' he sobbed, but his voice broke and the words came in shrieks from his panting chest.

'They are drunk. . . . They are brutal . . . it's not your business!' said his father. He put his arms round his father but he felt choked, choked. He tried to draw a breath, to cry out – and woke up.

He waked up, gasping for breath, his hair soaked with perspiration, and stood up in terror.

'Thank God, that was only a dream,' he said, sitting down under a tree and drawing deep breaths. 'But what is it? Is it some fever coming on? Such a hideous dream!'

He felt utterly broken: darkness and confusion were in his soul. He rested his elbows on his knees and leaned his head on his hands.

'Good God!' he cried, 'can it be, can it be, that I shall really take an axe, that I shall strike her on the head, split her skull open . . . that I shall tread in the sticky warm blood, break the lock, steal and tremble; hide, all spattered in the blood . . . with the axe . . . Good God, can it be?'

He was shaking like a leaf as he said this.

'But why am I going on like this?' he continued, sitting up again, as it were in profound amazement. 'I knew that I could never bring myself to it, so what have I been torturing myself for till now? Yesterday, yesterday, when I went to make that . . . *experiment*, yesterday I realized completely that I could never bear to do it. . . . Why am I going over it again, then? Why am I still hesitating? As I came down the stairs yesterday, I said myself that it was base, loathsome, vile, vile . . . the very thought of it made me feel sick and filled me with horror.

'No, I couldn't do it, I couldn't do it! Granted, granted that there is no flaw in all that reasoning, that all that I have concluded this last month is clear as day, true as arithmetic. . . . My God! Anyway I couldn't bring myself to it! I couldn't do it, I couldn't do it! Why, why then am I still . . .?'

He rose to his feet, looked round in wonder as though surprised at finding himself in this place, and went towards the bridge. He was pale, his eyes glowed, he was exhausted in every limb, but he seemed suddenly to breathe more easily. He felt he had cast off that fearful burden that had so long been weighing upon him, and all at once there was a sense of relief and peace in his soul. 'Lord,' he prayed, 'show me my path – I renounce that accursed . . . dream of mine.'

Crossing the bridge, he gazed quietly and calmly at the Neva, at the glowing red sun setting in the glowing sky. In spite of his weakness he was not conscious of fatigue. It was as though an abscess that had been forming for a month past in his heart had suddenly broken. Freedom, freedom! He was free from that spell, that sorcery, that obsession!

Later on, when he recalled that time and all that happened to him during those days, minute by minute, point by point, he was superstitiously impressed by one circumstance, which, though in itself not very exceptional, always seemed to him afterwards the predestined turning-point of his fate. He could never understand and explain to himself why, when he was tired and worn out, when it would have been more convenient for him to go home by the shortest and most direct way, he had returned by the Hay Market where he had no need to go. It was obviously and quite unnecessarily out of his way, though not much so. It is true that it happened to him dozens of times to return home without noticing what streets he passed through. But why, he was always asking himself, why had such an important, such a decisive and at the same time such an absolutely chance meeting happened in the Hay Market (where he had moreover no reason to go) at the very hour, the very minute of his life when he was just in the very mood and in the very circumstances in which that meeting was able to exert the gravest and most decisive influence on his whole destiny? As though it had been lying in wait for him on purpose!

It was about nine o'clock when he crossed the Hay Market. At the tables and the barrows, at the booths and the shops, all the market people were closing their establishments or clearing away and packing up their wares and, like their customers, were going home. Rag pickers and costermongers of all kinds were crowding round the taverns in the dirty and stinking courtyards of the Hay Market. Raskolnikov particularly liked this place and the neighbouring alleys, when he wandered aimlessly in the streets. Here his rags did not attract contemptuous attention, and one could walk about in any attire without scandalizing people. At the corner of an alley a huckster and his wife had two tables set out with tapes, thread, cotton handkerchiefs, etc. They, too, had got up to go home, but were lingering in conversation with a friend, who had just come up to them. This friend was Lizaveta Ivanovna, or, as everyone called her, Lizaveta, the younger sister of the old pawnbroker, Alyona Ivanovna, whom Raskolnikov had visited the previous day to pawn his watch and make his *experiment*. . . . He already knew all about Lizaveta and she knew him a little too. She was a single woman of about thirty-five, tall, clumsy, timid, submissive and almost idiotic. She was a complete slave and went in fear and trembling of her sister, who made her work day and night, and even beat her. She was standing with a bundle before the huckster and his wife, listening earnestly and doubtfully. They were talking of something with special warmth. The moment Raskolnikov caught sight of her, he was overcome by a strange sensation as it were of intense astonishment, though there was nothing astonishing about this meeting.

'You could make up your mind for yourself, Lizaveta Ivanovna,' the huckster was saying aloud. 'Come around tomorrow about seven. They will be here too.'

'To-morrow?' said Lizaveta slowly and thoughtfully, as though unable to make up her mind.

'Upon my word, what a fright you are in of Alyona Ivanovna,' gabbled the huckster's wife, a lively woman. 'I look at you, you are like some little babe. And she is not your own sister either – nothing but a stepsister and what a hand she keeps over you!'

'But this time don't say a word to Alyona Ivanovna,' her husband interrupted; 'that's my advice, but come round to us without asking. It will be worth your while. Later on your sister herself may have a notion.'

'Am I to come?'

'About seven o'clock to-morrow. And they will be here. You will be able to decide for yourself.'

'And we'll have a cup of tea,' added his wife.

'All right, I'll come,' said Lizaveta, still pondering, and she began slowly moving away.

Raskolnikov had just passed and heard no more. He passed softly, unnoticed, trying not to miss a word. His first amazement was followed by a thrill of horror, like a shiver running down his spine. He had learnt, he had suddenly quite unexpectedly learnt, that the next day at seven o'clock Lizaveta, the old woman's sister and only companion, would be away from home and that therefore at seven o'clock precisely the old woman *would be left alone*.

He was only a few steps from his lodging. He went in like a man condemned to death. He thought of nothing and was incapable of thinking; but he felt suddenly in his whole being that he had no more freedom of thought, no will, and that everything was suddenly and irrevocably decided.

Certainly, if he had to wait whole years for a suitable opportunity, he could not reckon on a more certain step towards the success of the plan than that which had just presented itself. In any case, it would have been difficult to find out beforehand and with certainty, with greater exactness and less risk, and without dangerous inquiries and investigations, that next day at a certain time an old woman, on whose life an attempt was contemplated, would be at home and entirely alone.

⇜ SIX ⇝

LATER ON, RASKOLNIKOV HAPPENED to find out why the huckster and his wife had invited Lizaveta. It was a very ordinary matter and there was nothing exceptional about it. A family who had come to the town and been reduced to poverty were selling their household goods and clothes, all women's things. As the things would have fetched little in the market, they were looking for a dealer. This was Lizaveta's business. She understood such jobs and was frequently employed, as she was very honest and always fixed a fair price and stuck to it. She spoke as a rule little and, as we have said already, she was very submissive and timid.

But Raskolnikov had become superstitious of late. The traces of superstition remained in him long after, and were almost ineradicable. And in all this he was always afterwards disposed to see something strange and mysterious, as it were the presence of some peculiar influences and coincidences. In the previous winter a student he knew called Pokorev, who had left for Harkov, had chanced in conversation to give him an address of Alyona Ivanovna, the old pawnbroker, in case he might want to pawn anything. For a long while he did not go to her, for he had lessons and managed to get along somehow. Six weeks ago he had remembered the address; he had two articles that could be pawned: his father's old silver watch and a little gold ring with three red stones, a present from his sister at parting. He decided to take the ring. When he found the old woman he had felt an insurmountable repulsion for her at the first glance, though he knew nothing special about her. He got two roubles from her and went into a miserable little tavern on his way home. He asked for tea, sat down and sank into deep thought. A strange idea was pecking at his brain like a chicken in the egg, and very, very much absorbed him.

Almost beside him at the next table there was sitting a student, whom he did not know and had never seen, and with him a young officer. They had played a game of billiards and began drinking tea. All at once he heard the student mention to the officer the pawnbroker Alyona Ivanovna and give him her address. This of itself seemed strange to Raskolnikov; he had just come from her and here at once heard her name. Of course it was chance, but he could not shake off a very extraordinary impression, and here someone seemed to be speaking expressly for him; the student began telling his friend various details about Alyona Ivanovna.

'She is first-rate,' he said. 'You can always get money from her. She is as rich as a Jew, she can give you five thousand roubles at a time and she is not above taking a pledge for a rouble. Lots of our fellows have had dealings with her. But she is an awful old harpy. . . .'

And he began describing how spiteful and uncertain she was, how if you were only a day late with your interest the pledge was lost; how she gave a quarter of the value of an article and took five and even seven per cent, a month on it and so on. The student chattered on, saying that she had a sister Lizaveta, whom the wretched little creature was continually beating, and kept in complete bondage like a small child, though Lizaveta was at least six feet high.

'There's a phenomenon for you,' cried the student and he laughed.

They began talking about Lizaveta. The student spoke about her with a peculiar relish and was continually laughing and the officer listened with great interest and asked him to send Lizaveta to do some mending for him. Raskolnikov did not miss a word and learned everything about her. Lizaveta was younger than the old woman and was her half-sister, being the child of a different mother. She was thirty-five. She worked day and night for her sister, and besides doing the cooking and the washing, she did sewing and worked as a charwoman and gave her sister all she earned. She did not dare to accept an order or job of any kind without her sister's permission. The old woman had already made her will, and Lizaveta knew of it, and by this will she would not get a farthing; nothing but the movables, chairs and so on; all the money was left to a monastery in the province of N—, that prayers might be said for her in perpetuity. Lizaveta was of lower rank than her sister, unmarried and awfully uncouth in appearance, remarkably tall with long feet that looked as if they were bent outwards. She always wore battered goatskin shoes, and was clean in her person. What the student expressed most surprise and amusement about was the fact that Lizaveta was continually with child.

'But you say she is hideous?' observed the officer.

'Yes, she is so dark-skinned and looks like a soldier dressed up, but you know she is not at all hideous. She has such a good-natured face and eyes. Strikingly so. And the proof of it is that lots of people are attracted by her. She is such a soft, gentle creature, ready to put up with anything, always willing, willing to do anything. And her smile is really very sweet.'

'You seem to find her attractive yourself,' laughed the officer.

'From her queerness. No, I'll tell you what. I could kill that damned old woman and make off with her money, I assure you, without the faintest conscience-prick,' the student added with warmth. The officer laughed again while Raskolnikov shuddered. How strange it was!

'Listen, I want to ask you a serious question,' the student said hotly. 'I was joking of course, but look here; on one side we have a stupid, senseless, worthless, spiteful, ailing, horrid old woman, not simply useless but doing actual mischief, who has not an idea what she is living for herself, and who will die in a day or two in any case. You understand? You understand?'

'Yes, yes, I understand,' answered the officer, watching his excited companion attentively.

'Well, listen then. On the other side, fresh young lives thrown away for want of help and by thousands, on every side! A hundred thousand good deeds could be done and helped, on that old woman's money which will be buried in a monastery! Hundreds, thousands perhaps, might be set on the right path; dozens of families saved from destitution, from ruin, from vice, from the Lock hospitals – and all with her money. Kill her, take her money and with the help of it devote oneself to the service of humanity and the good of all. What do you think, would not one tiny crime be wiped out by thousands of good deeds? For one life thousands would be saved from corruption and decay. One death, and a hundred lives in exchange – it's simple arithmetic! Besides, what value has the life of that sickly, stupid, ill-natured old woman in the balance of existence? No more than the life of a louse, of a black-beetle, less in fact because the old woman is doing harm. She is wearing out the lives of others; the other day she bit Lizaveta's finger out of spite; it almost had to be amputated.'

'Of course she does not deserve to live,' remarked the officer, 'but there it is, it's nature.'

'Oh well, brother, but we have to correct and direct nature, and, but for that, we should drown in an ocean of prejudice. But for that, there would never have been a single great man. They talk of duty, conscience – I don't want to say anything against duty and conscience; – but the point is, what do we mean by them? Stay, I have another question to ask you. Listen!'

'No, you stay, I'll ask you a question. Listen!'

'Well!'

'You are talking and speechifying away, but tell me, would you kill the old woman *yourself*?'

'Of course not! I was only arguing the justice of it. . . . It's nothing to do with me. . . .'

'But I think, if you would not do it yourself, there's no justice about it. . . . Let us have another game.'

Raskolnikov was violently agitated. Of course, it was all ordinary youthful talk and thought, such as he had often heard before in different forms and on different themes. But why had he happened to hear such a discussion and such ideas at the very moment when his own brain was just conceiving . . . *the very same ideas*? And why, just at the moment when he had brought away the embryo of his idea from the old woman, had he dropped at once upon a conversation about her? This coincidence always seemed strange to him. This trivial talk in a tavern had an immense influence on him in his later action; as though there had really been in it something preordained, some guiding hint. . . .

On returning from the Hay Market he flung himself on the sofa and sat for a whole hour without stirring. Meanwhile it got dark; he had no candle and, indeed, it did not occur to him to light up. He could never recollect whether he had been thinking about anything at that time. At last he was conscious of his former fever and shivering, and he realized with relief that he could lie down on the sofa. Soon heavy, leaden sleep came over him, as it were crushing him.

He slept an extraordinarily long time and without dreaming. Nastasya, coming into his room at ten o'clock the next morning, had difficulty in rousing him. She brought him in tea and bread. The tea was again the second brew and again in her own teapot.

'My goodness, how he sleeps!' she cried indignantly. 'And he is always asleep.'

He got up with an effort. His head ached, he stood up, took a turn in his garret and sank back on the sofa again.

'Going to sleep again,' cried Nastasya. 'Are you ill, eh?'

He made no reply.

'Do you want some tea?'

'Afterwards,' he said with an effort, closing his eyes again and turning to the wall.

Nastasya stood over him.

'Perhaps he really is ill,' she said, turned and went out. She came in again at two o'clock with soup. He was lying as before. The tea stood untouched. Nastasya felt positively offended and began wrathfully rousing him.

'Why are you lying like a log?' she shouted, looking at him with repulsion.

He got up, and sat down again, but said nothing and stared at the floor.

'Are you ill or not?' asked Nastasya and again received no answer. 'You'd better go out and get a breath of air,' she said after a pause. 'Will you eat it or not?'

'Afterwards,' he said weakly. 'You can go.'

And he motioned her out.

She remained a little longer, looked at him with compassion and went out.

A few minutes afterwards, he raised his eyes and looked for a long while at the tea and the soup. Then he took the bread, took up a spoon and began to eat.

He ate a little, three or four spoonfuls, without appetite, as it were mechanically. His head ached less. After his meal he stretched himself on the sofa again, but now he could not sleep; he lay without stirring, with his face in the pillow. He was haunted by day-dreams and such strange day-dreams; in one, that kept recurring, he fancied that he was in Africa, in Egypt, in some sort of oasis. The caravan was resting, the camels were peacefully lying down; the palms stood all round in a complete circle; all the party were at dinner. But he was drinking water from a spring which flowed gurgling close by. And it was so cool, it was wonderful, wonderful, blue, cold water running among the parti-coloured stones and over the clean sand which glistened here and there like gold. . . . Suddenly he heard a clock strike. He started, roused himself, raised his head, looked out of the window, and seeing how late it was, suddenly jumped up wide awake as though someone had pulled him off the sofa. He crept on tiptoe to the door, stealthily opened it and began listening on the staircase. His heart beat terribly. But all was quiet on the stairs as if everyone were asleep. . . . It seemed to him strange and monstrous that he could have slept in such forgetfulness from the previous day and had done nothing, had prepared nothing yet. . . . And meanwhile perhaps it has struck six. And his drowsiness and stupefaction were followed by an extraordinary, feverish, as it were distracted haste. But the preparations to be made were few. He concentrated all his energies on thinking of everything and forgetting nothing; and his heart kept beating and thumping so that he could hardly breathe. First he had to make a noose and sew it into his overcoat – a work of a moment. He rummaged under his pillow and picked out amongst the linen stuffed away under it a worn-out, old unwashed shirt. From its rags he tore a long strip, a couple of inches wide and about sixteen inches long. He folded this strip in two, took off his wide, strong summer overcoat of some stout cotton material (his only outer garment) and began sewing the two ends of the rag on the inside, under the left armhole. His hands shook as he sewed, but he did it successfully so that nothing showed outside when he put the coat on again. The needle and thread he had got ready long before and they lay on his table in a piece of paper. As for the noose, it was a very ingenious device of his own; the noose was intended for the axe. It was impossible for him to carry the axe through the street in his hands. And if hidden under his coat he would still have had to support it with his hand, which would have been noticeable. Now he had only to put the head of the axe in the noose, and it would hang quietly under his arm on the inside. Putting his hand in his coat pocket, he could hold the end of the handle all the way, so that it did not swing; and as the coat was very full, a regular sack in fact, it could not be seen from outside that he was holding something with the hand that was in the pocket. This noose, too, he had designed a fortnight before.

When he had finished with this, he thrust his hand into a little opening between his sofa and the floor, fumbled in the left corner and drew out the *pledge*, which he had got ready long before and hidden there. This pledge was, however, only a smoothly planed piece of wood the size and thickness of a silver cigarette-case. He picked up this piece of wood in one of his wanderings in a court-yard where there was some sort of workshop. Afterwards he had added to the wood a thin smooth piece of iron, which he had also picked up at the same time in the street. Putting the iron which was a little the smaller on the piece of wood, he fastened them very firmly, crossing and recrossing the thread around them; then wrapped them carefully and daintily in clean, white paper and tied up the parcel so that it would be very difficult to untie it. This was in order to divert the attention of the old woman for a time, while she was trying to undo the knot, and so to gain a moment. The iron strip was added to give weight, so that the woman might not guess the first minute that the 'thing' was made of wood. All this had been stored by him beforehand under the sofa. He had only just got the pledge out when he heard someone suddenly shout in the yard.

'It struck six long ago.'

'Long ago! My God!'

He rushed to the door, listened, caught up his hat and began to descend his thirteen steps cautiously, noiselessly, like a cat. He had still the most important thing to do – to steal the axe from the kitchen. That the deed must be done with an axe he had decided long ago. He had also a pocket pruning-knife, but he could not rely on the knife and still less on his own strength, and so resolved finally on the axe. We may note, in passing, one peculiarity in regard to all the final resolutions taken by him in the matter; they had one strange characteristic; the more final they were, the more hideous and the more absurd they at once became in his eyes. In spite of all his agonising inward struggle, he never for a single instant all that time could believe in the carrying out of his plans.

And, indeed, if it had ever happened that everything to the least point could have been considered and finally settled, and no uncertainty of any kind had remained, he would, it seems have renounced it all as something absurd, monstrous and impossible. But a whole mass of unsettled points and uncertainties remained. As for getting the axe, that trifling business cost him no anxiety, for nothing could be easier. Nastasya was continually out of the house, especially in the evenings; she would run in to the neighbours or to a shop, and always left the door ajar. It was the one thing the landlady was always scolding her about. And so, when the time came, he would only have to go quietly into the kitchen and to take the axe, and an hour later (when everything was over) go in and put it back again. But these were doubtful points. Supposing he returned an hour later to put it back, and Nastasya had come back and was on the spot. He would of course have to go by and wait till she went out again. But supposing she were in the meantime to miss the axe, look for it, make an outcry – that would mean suspicion or at least grounds for suspicion.

But those were all trifles which he had not even begun to consider, and indeed he had no time. He was thinking of the chief point, and put off trifling details, until he *could believe in it all*. But that seemed utterly unattainable. So it seemed to himself at least. He could not imagine, for instance, that he would sometimes leave off thinking, get up and simply go there.... Even his late experiment (*i.e.* his visit with the object of a final survey of the place) was simply an attempt at an experiment, far from being the real thing, as though one should say, 'Come, let us go and try it – why dream about it)' – and at once he had broken down and run away cursing, in a frenzy with himself. Meanwhile it would seem, as regards the moral question, that his analysis was complete; his casuistry had become keen as a razor, and he could not find rational objections in himself. But in the last resort he simply ceased to believe in himself, and doggedly, slavishly sought arguments in all directions, fumbling for them, as though someone were forcing and drawing him to it.

At first – long before indeed – he had been much occupied with one question; why almost all crimes are so badly concealed and so easily detected, and why almost all criminals leave such obvious traces? He had come gradually to many different and curious conclusions, and in his opinion the chief reason lay not so much in the material impossibility of concealing the crime as in the criminal himself. Almost every criminal is subject to a failure of will and reasoning power by a childish and phenomenal heedlessness, at the very instant when prudence and caution are most essential. It was his conviction that this eclipse of reason and failure of will-power attacked a man like a disease developed gradually and reached its highest point just before the perpetration of the crime, continued with equal violence at the moment of the crime and for longer or shorter time after, according to the individual case, and then passed off like any other disease. The question whether the disease gives rise to the crime, or whether the crime from its own peculiar nature is always accompanied by something of the nature of disease, he did not yet feel able to decide.

When he reached these conclusions, he decided that in his own case there could not be such a morbid reaction, that his reason and will would remain unimpaired at the time of carrying out his design, for the single reason that his design was 'not a crime....' We will omit all the process by means of which he arrived at this last conclusion; we have run too far ahead already.... We may add only that the practical, purely material difficulties of the affair occupied a secondary position in his mind. 'One has but to keep all one's will-power and reason to deal with them, and they will all be overcome at the time when once one has familiarized oneself with the minutest details of the business....' But this preparation had never been begun. His final decisions were what he came to trust least, and when the hour struck, it all came to pass quite differently, as it were accidentally and unexpectedly.

One trifling circumstance upset his calculations before he even left the staircase. When he reached the landlady's kitchen, the door of which was open as usual, he glanced cautiously in to see whether, in Nastasya's absence, the landlady herself was there, or if not, whether the door to her own room was closed, so that she might not peep out when he went in for the axe. But what was his amazement when he suddenly saw that Nastasya was not only at home in the kitchen, but was occupied there, taking linen out of a basket and hanging it on a line. Seeing him, she left off hanging the clothes, turned to him and stared at him all the time he was passing. He turned away his eyes, and walked past as though he noticed nothing. But it was the end of everything; he had not the axe! He was overwhelmed.

'What made me think,' he reflected, as he went under the gateway. 'What made me think that she would be sure not to be home at that moment? Why, why, why did I assume this so certainly?'

He was crushed and even humiliated. He could have laughed at himself in his anger. . . . A dull animal rage boiled within him.

He stood hesitating in the gateway. To go into the street, to go a walk for appearance' sake was revolting; to go back to his room, even more revolting. 'And what a chance I have lost for ever!' he muttered, standing aimlessly in the gateway, just opposite the porter's little dark room, which was also open. Suddenly he started. From the porter's room, two paces away from him, something shining under the bench to the right caught his eyes. . . . He looked about him – nobody. He approached the room on tiptoe, went down two steps into it and in a faint voice called the porter. 'Yes, not at home! Somewhere near though, in the yard, for the door is wide open.' He dashed to the axe (it was an axe) and pulled it out from under the bench, where it lay between two chunks of wood; at once, before going out, he made it fast in the noose, he thrust both hands into his pockets and went out of the room; no one had noticed him! 'When reason fails, the devil helps!' he thought with a strange grin. This chance raised his spirits extraordinarily.

He walked along quietly and sedately, without hurry, to avoid awakening suspicion. He scarcely looked at the passers-by, tried to escape looking at their faces at all, and to be as little noticeable as possible. Suddenly he thought of his hat. 'Good heavens! I had the money the day before yesterday and did not get a cap to wear instead!' A curse rose from the bottom of his soul.

Glancing out of the corner of his eye into a shop, he saw by a clock on the wall that it was ten minutes past seven. He had to make haste and at the same time to go some way round, so as to approach the house from the other side. . . .

When he had happened to imagine all this beforehand, he had sometimes thought that he would be very much afraid. But he was not very much afraid now, was not afraid at all, indeed. His mind was even occupied by irrelevant matters, but by nothing for long. As he passed the Yusupov garden, he was deeply absorbed in considering the building of great fountains, and of their refreshing effect on the atmosphere in all the squares. By degrees he passed to the conviction that if the summer garden were extended to the field of Mars, and perhaps joined to the garden of the Mihailovsky Palace, it would be a splendid thing and a great benefit to the town. Then he was interested by the question why in all great towns men are not simply driven by necessity, but in some peculiar way inclined to live in those parts of the town where there are no gardens nor fountains; where there are most dirt and smell and all sorts of nastiness. Then his own walks through the Hay Market came back to his mind, and for a moment he waked up to reality. 'What nonsense!' he thought, 'better think of nothing at all!'

'So probably men led to execution clutch mentally at every object that meets them on the way,' flashed through his mind, but simply flashed, like lightning; he made haste to dismiss this thought. . . . And by now he was near; here was the house, here was the gate. Suddenly a clock somewhere struck once. 'What! can it be half-past seven? Impossible, it must be fast!'

Luckily for him, everything went well again at the gates. At that very moment, as though expressly for his benefit, a huge waggon of hay had just driven in at the gate, completely screening him as he passed under the gateway, and the waggon had scarcely had time to drive through into the yard before he had slipped in a flash to the right. On the other side of the waggon he could hear shouting and quarrelling; but no one noticed him and no one met him. Many windows looking into that huge quadrangular yard were open at that moment, but he did not raise his head – he had not the strength to. The staircase leading to the old woman's room was close by, just on the right of the gateway. He was already on the stairs. . . .

Drawing a breath, pressing his hand against his throbbing heart, and once more feeling for the axe and setting it straight, he began softly and cautiously ascending the stairs, listening every minute. But the stairs, too, were quite deserted; all the doors were shut; he met no one. One flat indeed on the first floor was wide open and painters were at work on it, but they did not glance at him. He stood still, thought a minute and went on. 'Of course it would be better if they had not been here, but . . . it's two storeys above them.'

And here was the fourth storey, here was the door, here was the flat opposite, the empty one. The flat underneath the old woman's was apparently empty also; the visiting card nailed on the door had been torn off – they had gone away! . . . He was out of breath. For one instant the thought floated through his mind, 'Shall I go back?' But he made no answer and began listening at the old woman's door, a dead silence. Then he listened again on the staircase, listened long and intently . . . then looked about him for the last time, pulled himself together, drew himself up, and once more tried the axe in the noose. 'Am I very pale?' he wondered. 'Am I not evidently agitated? She is mistrustful. . . . Had I better wait a little longer . . . till my heart leaves off thumping?'

But his heart did not leave off. On the contrary, as though to spite him, it throbbed more and more violently. He could stand it no longer, he slowly put out his hand to the bell and rang. Half a minute later he rang again, more loudly.

No answer. To go on ringing was useless and out of place. The old woman was, of course, at home, but she was suspicious and alone. He had some knowledge of her habits . . . and once more he put his ear to the door. Either his senses were peculiarly keen (which it is difficult to suppose), or the sound was really very distinct. Anyway, he suddenly heard something like the cautious touch of a hand on the lock and the rustle of a skirt at the very door. Someone was standing stealthily close to the lock and, just as he was doing on the outside, was secretly listening within, and seemed to have her ear to the door. . . . He moved a little on purpose and muttered something aloud that he might not have the appearance of hiding, then rang a third time, but quietly, soberly and without impatience. Recalling it afterwards, that moment stood out in his mind vividly, distinctly, for ever; he could not make out how he had had such cunning, for his mind was as it were clouded at moments and he was almost unconscious of his body. . . . An instant later he heard the latch unfastened.

✦ SEVEN ✦

THE DOOR WAS AS BEFORE OPENED a tiny crack, and again two sharp and suspicious eyes stared at him out of the darkness. Then Raskolnikov lost his head and nearly made a great mistake.

Fearing the old woman would be frightened by their being alone, and not hoping that the sight of him would disarm her suspicions, he took hold of the door and drew it towards him to prevent the old woman from attempting to shut it again. Seeing this she did not pull the door back, but she did not let go the handle so that he almost dragged her out with it on to the stairs. Seeing that she was standing in the doorway not allowing him to pass, he advanced straight upon her. She stepped back in alarm, tried to say something, but seemed unable to speak and stared with open eyes at him.

'Good evening, Alyona Ivanovna,' he began, trying to speak easily, but his voice would not obey him, it broke and shook. 'I have come . . . I have brought something . . . but we'd better come in . . . to the light . . .'

And leaving her, he passed straight into the room uninvited. The old woman ran after him; her tongue was unloosed.

'Good heavens! What is it? Who is it? What do you want?'

'Why Alyona Ivanovna, you know me . . . Raskolnikov . . . here, I brought you the pledge I promised the other day. . . .' And he held out the pledge.

The old woman glanced for a moment at the pledge, but at once stared in the eyes of her uninvited visitor. She looked intently, maliciously and mistrustfully. A minute passed; he even fancied something like a sneer in her eyes, as though she had already guessed everything. He felt that he was losing his head, that he was almost frightened, so frightened that if she were to look like that and not say a word for another half-minute, he thought he would have run away from her.

'Why do you look at me as though you did not know me?' he said suddenly, also with malice. 'Take it if you like, if not I'll go elsewhere, I am in a hurry.'

He had not even thought of saying this, but it was suddenly said of itself. The old woman recovered herself, and her visitor's resolute tone evidently restored her confidence.

'But why, my good sir, all of a minute . . . What is it?' she asked, looking at the pledge.

'The silver cigarette-case; I spoke of it last time, you know.' She held out her hand.

'But how pale you are, to be sure . . . and your hands are trembling too? Have you been bathing, or what?'

'Fever,' he answered abruptly. 'You can't help getting pale . . . if you've nothing to eat,' he added, with difficulty articulating the words.

His strength was failing him again. But his answer sounded like the truth; the old woman took the pledge.

'What is it?' she asked once more, scanning Raskolnikov intently and weighing the pledge in her hand.

'A thing . . . cigarette case. . . . Silver. . . . Look at it.'

'It does not seem somehow like silver. . . . How he has wrapped it up!'

Trying to untie the string and turning to the window, to the light (all her windows were shut, in spite of the stifling heat), she left him altogether for some seconds and stood with her back to him. He unbuttoned his coat and freed the axe from the noose, but did not yet take it out altogether, simply holding it in his right hand under the coat. His hands were fearfully weak, he felt them every moment growing more numb and more wooden. He was afraid he would let the axe slip and fall. . . . A sudden giddiness came over him.

'But what has he tied it up like this for?' the old woman cried with vexation and moved towards him.

He had not a minute more to lose. He pulled the axe quite out, swung it with both arms, scarcely conscious of himself, and almost without effort, almost mechanically, brought the blunt side down on her head. He seemed not to use his own strength in this. But as soon as he had once brought the axe down, his strength returned to him.

The old woman was as always bareheaded. Her thin, light hair, streaked with grey, thickly smeared with grease, was plaited in a rat's tail and fastened by a broken horn comb which stood out on the nape of her neck. As she was so short, the blow fell on the very top of her skull. She cried out, but very faintly, and suddenly sank all of a heap on the floor, raising her hands to her head. In one hand she still held 'the pledge'. Then he dealt her another and another blow with the blunt side and on the same spot. The blood gushed as from an overturned glass, the body fell back. He stepped back, let it fall, and at once bent over her face; she was dead. Her eyes seemed to be starting out of their sockets, the brow and the whole face were drawn and contorted convulsively.

He laid the axe on the ground near the dead body and felt at once in her pocket (trying to avoid the streaming blood) – the same right-hand pocket from which she had taken the key on his last visit. He was in full possession of his faculties, free from confusion or giddiness, but his hands were still trembling. He remembered afterwards that he had been particularly collected and careful, trying all the time not to get smeared with blood. . . . He pulled out the keys at once, they were all, as before, in one bunch on a steel ring. He ran at once into the bedroom with them. It was a very small room with a whole shrine of holy images. Against the other wall stood a big bed, very clean and covered with a silk patchwork wadded quilt. Against a third wall was a chest of drawers. Strange to say, so soon as he began to fit the keys into the chest, so soon as he heard their jingling, a convulsive shudder passed over him. He suddenly felt tempted again to give it all up and go away. But that was only for an instant; it was too late to go back. He positively smiled at himself, when suddenly another terrifying idea occurred to his mind. He suddenly fancied that the old woman might still be alive and might recover her senses. Leaving the keys in the chest, he ran back to the body, snatched up the axe and lifted it once more over the old woman, but did not bring it down. There was no doubt that she was dead. Bending down and examining her again more closely, he saw clearly that the skull was broken and even battered in on one side. He was about to feel it with his finger, but drew back his hand and indeed it was evident without that. Meanwhile there was a perfect pool of blood. All at once he noticed a string on her neck; he tugged at it, but the string was strong and did not snap and, besides, it was soaked with blood. He tried to pull it out from the front of her dress, but something held it and prevented its coming. In his impatience he raised the axe to cut the string from above on the body, but did not dare, and with difficulty, smearing his hand and the axe in the blood, after two minutes' hurried effort, he cut the string and took it off without touching the body with the axe; he was not mistaken – it was a purse. On the string were two crosses, one of Cyprus wood and one of copper, and an image in silver-filigree, and with them a small greasy chamois leather purse with a steel rim and ring. The purse was stuffed very full; Raskolnikov thrust it in his pocket without looking at it, flung the crosses on the old woman's body and rushed back into the bedroom, this time taking the axe with him.

He was in terrible haste, he snatched the keys, and began trying them again. But he was unsuccessful. They would not fit in the locks. It was not so much that his hands were shaking, but that he kept making mistakes; though he saw for instance that a key was not the right one and would not fit, still he tried to put it in. Suddenly he remembered and realized that the big key with the deep notches, which was hanging there with the small keys, could not possibly belong to the chest of drawers (on his last visit this had struck him) but to some strong box, and that everything perhaps was hidden in that box. He left the chest of drawers, and at once felt under the bedstead, knowing that old women usually kept boxes under their beds. And so it was; there was a good-sized box under the bed, at least a yard in length, with an arched lid covered with red leather and studded with steel nails. The notched key fitted at once and unlocked it. At the top, under a white sheet, was a coat of red brocade lined with hareskin; under it was a silk dress, then a shawl and it seemed as though there was nothing below but clothes. The first thing he did was to wipe his blood-stained hands on the red brocade. 'It's red, and on red blood will be less noticeable,' the thought passed through his mind; then he suddenly came to himself, 'Good God, am I going out of my senses?' he thought with terror.

But no sooner did he touch the clothes than a gold watch slipped from under the fur coat. He made haste to turn them all over. There turned out to be various articles made of gold among the clothes – probably all pledges, unredeemed or waiting to be redeemed – bracelets, chains, earrings, pins and such things. Some were in cases, others simply wrapped in newspaper, carefully and exactly folded, and tied round with tape. Without any delay, he began filling up the pockets of his trousers and overcoat without examining or undoing the parcels and cases; but he had not time to take many. . . .

He suddenly heard steps in the room where the old woman lay. He stopped short and was still as death. But all was quiet, so it must have been his fancy. All at once he heard distinctly a faint cry, as though someone had uttered a low broken moan. Then again dead silence for a minute or two. He sat squatting on his heels by the box and waited holding his breath. Suddenly he jumped up, seized the axe and ran out of the bedroom.

In the middle of the room stood Lizaveta with a big bundle in her arms. She was gazing in stupefaction at her murdered sister, white as a sheet and seeming not to have the strength to cry out. Seeing him run out of the bedroom, she began faintly quivering all over, like a leaf, a shudder ran down her face; she lifted her hand, opened her mouth, but still did not scream. She began slowly backing away from him into the corner, staring intently, persistently at him, but still uttered no sound, as though she could not get breath to scream. He rushed at her with the axe; her mouth twitched piteously, as one sees babies' mouths, when they begin to be frightened, stare intently at what frightens them and are on the point of screaming. And this hapless Lizaveta was so simple and had been so thoroughly crushed and scared that she did not even raise a hand to guard her face, though that was the most necessary and natural action at the moment, for the axe was raised over her face. She only put up her empty left hand, but not to her face, slowly holding it out before her as though motioning him away. The axe fell with the sharp edge just on the skull and split at one blow all the top of the head. She fell heavily at once. Raskolnikov completely lost his head, snatching up her bundle, dropped it again and ran into the entry.

Fear gained more and more mastery over him, especially after this second, quite unexpected murder. He longed to run away from the place as fast as possible. And if at that moment he had been capable of seeing and reasoning more correctly, if he had been able to realise all the difficulties of his position, the hopelessness, the hideousness and the absurdity of it, if he could have understood how many obstacles and, perhaps, crimes he had still to overcome or to commit to get out of that place and to make his way home, it is very possible that he would have flung up everything, and would have gone to give himself up, and not from fear, but from simple horror and loathing of what he had done. The feeling of loathing especially surged up within him and grew stronger every minute. He would not now have gone to the box or even into the room for anything in the world.

But a sort of blankness, even dreaminess, had begun by degrees to take possession of him; at moments he forgot himself, or rather forgot what was of importance and caught at trifles. Glancing, however, into the kitchen and seeing a bucket half full of water on a bench, he bethought him of washing his hands and the axe. His hands were sticky with blood. He dropped the axe with the blade in the water, snatched a piece of soap that lay in a broken saucer on the window, and began washing his hands in the bucket. When they were clean, he took out the axe, washed the blade and spent a long time, about three minutes, washing the wood where there were spots of blood, rubbing them with soap. Then he wiped it all with some linen that was hanging to dry on a line in the kitchen and then he was a long while attentively examining the axe at the window. There was no trace left on it, only the wood was still damp. He carefully hung the axe in the noose under his coat. Then as far as was possible, in the dim light in the kitchen, he looked over his overcoat, his trousers and his boots. At the first glance there seemed to be nothing but stains on the boots. He wetted the rag and rubbed the boots. But he knew he was not looking thoroughly, that there might be something quite noticeable that he was overlooking. He stood in the middle of the room, lost in thought. Dark agonizing ideas rose in his mind – the idea that he was mad and that at that moment he was incapable of reasoning, of protecting himself, that he ought perhaps to be doing something utterly different from what he was now doing. 'Good God!' he muttered, 'I must fly, fly,' and he rushed into the entry. But here a shock of terror awaited him such as he had never known before.

He stood and gazed and could not believe his eyes: the door, the outer door from the stairs, at which he had not long before waited and rung, was standing unfastened and at least six inches open. No lock, no bolt, all the time, all that time! The old woman had not shut it after him perhaps as a precaution. But, good God! Why, he had failed Lizaveta afterwards! And how could he, how could he have failed to reflect that she must have come in somehow! She could not have come through the wall!

He dashed to the door and fastened the latch.

'But no, the wrong thing again! I must get away, get away. . . .'

He unfastened the latch, opened the door and began listening on the staircase.

He listened a long time. Somewhere far away, it might be in the gateway, two voices were loudly and shrilly shouting, quarrelling and scolding. 'What are they about?' He waited patiently. At last all was still, as though suddenly cut off; they had separated. He was meaning to go out, but suddenly, on the floor below, a door was noisily opened and someone began going downstairs humming a tune. 'How is it they all make such a noise?' flashed through his mind. Once more he closed the door and waited. At last all was still, not a soul stirring. He was just taking a step towards the stairs when he heard fresh footsteps.

The steps sounded very far off, at the very bottom of the stairs, but he remembered quite clearly and distinctly that from the first sound he began for some reason to suspect that this was someone coming *there*, to the fourth floor, to the old woman. Why? Were the sounds somehow peculiar, significant? The steps were heavy, even and unhurried. Now *he* had passed the first floor, now he was mounting higher, it was growing more and more distinct! He could hear his heavy breathing. And now the third storey had been reached. Coming here! And it seemed to him all at once that he was turned to stone, that it was like a dream in which one is being pursued, nearly caught and will be killed, and is rooted to the spot and cannot even move one's arms.

At last when the unknown was mounting to the fourth floor, he suddenly started, and succeeded in slipping neatly and quickly back into the flat and closing the door behind him. Then he took the hook and softly, noiselessly, fixed it in the catch. Instinct helped him. When he had done this, he crouched, holding his breath, by the door. The unknown visitor was by now also at the door. They were now standing opposite one another, as he had just before been standing with the old woman, when the door divided them and he was listening.

The visitor panted several times. 'He must be a big, fat man,' thought

Raskolnikov, squeezing the axe in his hand. It seemed like a dream indeed. The visitor took hold of the bell and rang it loudly.

As soon as the tin bell tinkled, Raskolnikov seemed to be aware of something moving in the room. For some seconds he listened quite seriously. The unknown rang again, waited and suddenly tugged violently and impatiently at the handle of the door. Raskolnikov gazed in horror at the hook shaking in its fastening, and in blank terror expected every minute that the fastening would be pulled out. It certainly did seem possible, so violently was he shaking it. He was tempted to hold the fastening, but *he* might be aware of it. A giddiness came over him again. 'I shall fall down!' flashed through his mind, but the unknown began to speak and he recovered himself at once.

'What's up? Are they asleep, or murdered? D-damn them!' he bawled in a thick voice. 'Hey, Alyona Ivanovna, old witch! Lizaveta Ivanovna, hey, my beauty! open the door! Oh, damn them! Are they asleep or what?'

And again, enraged, he tugged with all his might a dozen times at the bell. He must certainly be a man of authority and an intimate acquaintance.

At this moment light hurried steps were heard not far off, on the stairs. Someone else was approaching. Raskolnikov had not heard them at first.

'You don't say there's no one at home,' the new-comer cried in a cheerful, ringing voice, addressing the first visitor who still went on pulling the bell. 'Good evening, Koch.'

'From his voice he must be quite young,' thought Raskolnikov.

'Who the devil can tell? I've almost broken the lock,' answered Koch. 'But how do you come to know me?'

'Why! The day before yesterday I beat you three times running at billiards at Gambrinus'.'

'Oh!'

'So they are not at home? That's queer. It's awfully stupid though. Where could the old woman have gone? I've come on business.'

'Yes; and I have business with her, too.'

'Well, what can we do? Go back, I suppose. Aie – aie! And I was hoping to get some money!' cried the young man.

'We must give it up, of course, but what did she fix this time for? The old witch fixed the time for me to come herself. It's out of my way. And where the devil she can have got to, I can't make out. She sits here from year's end to year's end, the old hag; her legs are bad and yet here all of a sudden she is out for a walk!'

'Hadn't we better ask the porter?'

'What?'

'Where she's gone and when she'll be back.'

'Hm.... Damn it all!... We might ask.... But you know she never does go anywhere.'

And he once more tugged at the door-handle.

'Damn it all. There's nothing to be done, we must go!'

'Stay!' cried the young man suddenly. 'Do you see how the door shakes if you pull it?'

'Well?'

'That shows it's not locked, but fastened with the hook! Do you hear how the hook clanks?'

'Well?'

'Why, don't you see? That proves that one of them is at home. If they were all out, they would have locked the door from outside with the key and not with the hook from inside. There, do you hear how the hook is clanking? To fasten the hook on the inside they must be at home, don't you see? So there they are sitting inside and don't open the door!'

'Well! And so they must be!' cried Koch, astonished. 'What are they about in there?' And he began furiously shaking the door.

'Stay!' cried the young man again. 'Don't pull at it! There must be something wrong.... Here, you've been ringing and pulling at the door and still they don't open! So either they've both fainted or ...'

'What?'

'I tell you what. Let's go and fetch the porter, let him wake them up.'

'All right.'

Both were going down.

'Stay. You stop here while I run down for the porter.'

'What for?'

'Well, you'd better.'

'All right.'

'I'm studying the law, you see! It's evident, e-vi-dent there's something wrong here!' the young man cried hotly, and he ran downstairs.

Koch remained. Once more he softly touched the bell which gave one tinkle, then gently, as though reflecting and looking about him, began touching the door-handle, pulling it and letting it go to make sure once more that it was only fastened by the hook. Then puffing and panting he bent down and began looking at the keyhole: but the key was in the lock on the inside and so nothing could be seen.

Raskolnikov stood keeping tight hold of the axe. He was in a sort of delirium. He was even making ready to fight when they should come in. While they were knocking and talking together, the idea several times occurred to him to end it all at once and shout to them through the door. Now and then he was tempted to swear at them, to jeer at them, while they could not open the door! 'Only make haste!' was the thought that flashed through his mind.

'But what the devil is he about? . . .' Time was passing, one minute, and another – no one came. Koch began to be restless.

'What the devil!' he cried suddenly and in impatience deserting his sentry duty, he, too, went down, hurrying and thumping with his heavy boots on the stairs. The steps died away.

'Good heavens! What am I to do?'

Raskolnikov unfastened the hook, opened the door – there was no sound. Abruptly, without any thought at all, he went out, closing the door as thoroughly as he could, and went downstairs.

He had gone down three flights when he suddenly heard a loud noise below – where could he go? There was nowhere to hide. He was just going back to the flat.

'Hey there! Catch the brute!'

Somebody dashed out of a flat below, shouting, and rather fell than ran down the stairs, bawling at the top of his voice:

'Mitka! Mitka! Mitka! Mitka! Mitka! Blast him!'

The shout ended in a shriek; the last sounds came from the yard; all was still. But at the same instant several men talking loudly and fast began noisily mounting the stairs. There were three or four of them. He distinguished the ringing voice of the young man. 'They!'

Filled with despair he went straight to meet them, feeling 'come what must!' If they stopped him – all was lost; if they let him pass – all was lost too; they would remember him. They were approaching; they were only a flight from him – and suddenly deliverance! A few steps from him, on the right, there was an empty flat with the door wide open, the flat on the second floor, where the painters had been at work, and which, as though for his benefit, they had just left. It was they, no doubt, who had just run down, shouting. The floor had only just been painted, in the middle of the room stood a pail and a broken pot with paint and brushes. In one instant he had whisked in at the open door and hidden behind the wall and only in the nick of time; they had already reached the landing. Then they turned and went on up to the fourth floor, talking loudly. He waited, went out on tiptoe and ran down the stairs.

No one was on the stairs, nor in the gateway. He passed quickly through the gateway and turned to the left in the street.

He knew, he knew perfectly well that at that moment they were at the flat, that they were greatly astonished at finding it unlocked, as the door had just been fastened, that by now they were looking at the bodies, that before another minute had passed they would guess and completely realize that the murderer had just been there, and had succeeded in hiding somewhere, slipping by them and escaping. They would guess most likely that he had been in the empty flat, while they were going upstairs. And meanwhile he dared not quicken his pace much, though the next turning was still nearly a hundred yards away. 'Should he slip through some gateway and wait somewhere in an unknown street? No, hopeless! Should he fling away the axe? Should he take a cab? Hopeless, hopeless!'

At last he reached the turning. He turned down it more dead than alive. Here he was half-way to safety, and he understood it; it was less risky because there was a great crowd of people, and he was lost in it like a grain of sand. But all he had suffered had so weakened him that he could scarcely move. Perspiration ran down him in drops, his neck was all wet. 'My word, he has been going it!' someone shouted at him when he came out on the canal bank.

He was only dimly conscious of himself now, and the farther he went the worse it was. He remembered, however, that on coming out on to the canal bank he was alarmed at finding few people there and so being more conspicuous, and he had thought of going back. Though he was almost falling from fatigue, he went a long way round so as to get home from quite a different direction.

He was not fully conscious when he passed through the gateway of his house; he was already on the staircase before he recollected the axe. And yet he had a very grave problem before him, to put it back and to escape observation as far as possible in doing so. He was of course incapable of reflecting that it might perhaps be far better not to restore the axe at all, but to drop it later on in somebody's yard. But it all happened fortunately, the door of the porter's room was closed but not locked, so that it seemed most likely that the porter was at home. But he had so completely lost all power of reflection that he walked straight to the door and opened it. If the porter had asked him, 'What do you want?' he would perhaps have simply handed him the axe. But again the porter was not at home, and he succeeded in putting the axe back under the bench and even covering it with the chunk of wood as before. He met no one, not a soul, afterwards on the way to his room; the landlady's door was shut. When he was in his room, he flung himself on the sofa just as he was – he did not sleep, but sank into blank forgetfulness. If anyone had come into his room then, he would have jumped up at once and screamed. Scraps and shreds of thoughts were simply swarming in his brain, but he could not catch at one, he could not rest on one, in spite of all his efforts. . . .

PART TWO

✤ ONE ✤

So HE LAY A VERY LONG WHILE. Now and then he seemed to wake up, and at such moments he noticed that it was far into the night, but it did not occur to him to get up. At last he noticed that it was beginning to get light. He was lying on his back, still dazed from his recent oblivion. Fearful, despairing cries rose shrilly from the street, sounds which he heard every night, indeed, under his window after two o'clock. They woke him up now.

'Ah! the drunken men are coming out of the taverns,' he thought, 'it's past two o'clock,' and at once he leaped up, as though someone had pulled him from the sofa.

'What! Past two o'clock!'

He sat down on the sofa – and instantly recollected everything! All at once, in a flash, he recollected everything.

For the first moment he thought he was going mad. A dreadful chill came over him; but the chill was from the fever that had begun long before in his sleep. Now he was suddenly taken with violent shivering, so that his teeth chattered and all his limbs were shaking. He opened the door and began listening – everything in the house was asleep. With amazement he gazed at himself and everything in the night around him, wondering how he could have come in the night before without fastening the door, and have flung himself on the sofa without undressing, without even taking his hat off. It had fallen off and was lying on the floor near his pillow.

'If anyone had come in, what would he have thought? That I'm drunk but . . .'

He rushed to the window. There was light enough, and he began hurriedly looking himself all over from head to foot, all his clothes; were there no traces? But there was no doing it like that; shivering with cold, he began taking off everything and looking over again. He turned everything over to the last threads and rags, and mistrusting himself, went through his search three times.

But there seemed to be nothing, no trace, except in one place, where some thick drops of congealed blood were clinging to the frayed edge of his trousers. He picked up a big clasp-knife and cut off the frayed threads. There seemed to be nothing more.

Suddenly he remembered that the purse and the things he had taken out of the old woman's box were still in his pockets! He had not thought till then of taking them out and hiding them! He had not even thought of them while he was examining his clothes! What next? Instantly he rushed to take them out and fling them on the table. When he had pulled out everything, and turned the pocket inside out to be sure there was nothing left, he carried the whole heap to the corner. The paper had come off the bottom of the wall and hung there in tatters. He began stuffing all the things into the hole under the paper: 'They're in! All out of sight, and the purse too!' he thought gleefully, getting up and and gazing blankly at the hole which bulged out more than ever. Suddenly he shuddered all over with horror' 'My God!' he whispered in despair; 'what's the matter with me? Is that hidden? Is that the way to hide things?'

He had not reckoned on having trinkets to hide. He had only thought of money, and so had not prepared a hiding-place.

'But now, now what am I glad of?' he thought. 'Is that hiding things? My reason's deserting me – simply!'

He sat down on the sofa in exhaustion and was at once shaken by another unbearable fit of shivering. Mechanically he drew from a chair beside him his old student's winter coat, which was still warm though almost in rags, covered himself up with it and once more sank into drowsiness and delirium. He lost consciousness.

Not more than five minutes had passed when he jumped up a second time, and at once pounced in a frenzy on his clothes again.

'How could I go to sleep again with nothing done? Yes, yes; I have not taken the loop off the armhole! I forgot it, forgot a thing like that! Such a piece of evidence!'

He pulled off the noose, hurriedly cut it to pieces and threw the bits among his linen under the pillow.

'Pieces of torn linen couldn't rouse suspicion, whatever happened; I think not, I think not, anyway!' he repeated, standing in the middle of the room, and with painful concentration he fell to gazing about him again, at the floor and everywhere, trying to make sure he had not forgotten anything. The conviction that all his faculties, even memory, and the simplest power of reflection were failing him began to be an insufferable torture.

'Surely it isn't beginning already! Surely it isn't my punishment coming upon me? It is!'

The frayed rags he had cut off his trousers were actually lying on the floor in the middle of the room, where anyone coming in would see them!

'What is the matter with me?' he cried again, like one distraught.

Then a strange idea entered his head; that, perhaps, all his clothes were covered with blood, that, perhaps, there were a great many stains, but that he did not see them, did not notice them because his perceptions were failing, were going to pieces . . . his reason was clouded . . . Suddenly he remembered that there had been blood on the purse too. 'Ah! Then there must be blood on the pocket too, for I put the wet purse in my pocket!'

In a flash he had turned the pocket inside out and, yes! – there were traces, stains on the lining of the pocket!

'So my reason has not quite deserted me, so I still have some sense and memory, since I guessed it of myself,' he thought triumphantly, with a deep sigh of relief; 'it's simply the weakness of fever, a moment's delirium,' and he tore the whole lining out of the left pocket of his trousers. At that instant the sunlight fell on his left boot; on the sock which poked out from the boot, he fancied there were traces! He flung off his boots; 'traces indeed! The tip of the sock was soaked with blood;' he must have unwarily stepped into that pool . . . 'But what am I to do with this now? Where am I to put the sock and rags and pocket?'

He gathered them all up in his hands and stood in the middle of the room.

'In the stove? But they would ransack the stove first of all. Burn them? But what can I burn them with? There are no matches even. No, better go out and throw it all away somewhere. Yes, better throw it away,' he repeated, sitting down on the sofa again, 'and at once, this minute, without lingering . . .'

But his head sank on the pillow instead. Again the unbearable icy shivering came over him; again he drew his coat over him.

And for a long while, for some hours, he was haunted by the impulse to 'go off somewhere at once, this moment, and fling it all away, so that it may be out of sight and done with, at once, at once!' Several times he tried to rise from the sofa, but could not.

He was thoroughly waked up at the last by a violent knocking at his door.

'Open, do, are you dead or alive? He keeps sleeping here!' shouted Nastasya, banging with her fist on the door. 'For whole days together he's snoring here like a dog! A dog he is too. Open, I tell you. It's past ten.'

'Maybe he's not at home,' said a man's voice.

'Ha! that's the porter's voice . . . What does he want?'

He jumped up and sat on the sofa. The beating of his heart was a positive pain.

'Then who can have latched the door?' retorted Natasya. 'He's taken to bolting himself in! As if he were worth stealing! Open, you stupid, wake up!'

'What do they want? Why the porter? All's discovered. Resist or open? Come what may! . . .'

He half rose, stooped forward and unlatched the door.

His room was so small that he could undo the latch without leaving the bed. Yes; the porter and Natasya were standing there.

Natasya stared at him in a strange way. He glanced with a defiant and desperate air at the porter, who without a word held out a grey folded paper sealed with bottle-wax.

'A notice from the office,' he announced, as he gave him the paper.

'From what office?'

'A summons to the police office, of course. You know which office.'

'To the police? . . . What for? . . .'

'How can I tell? You're sent for, so you go.'

The man looked at him attentively, looked round the room and turned to go away.

'He's downright ill!' observed Natasya, not taking her eyes off him. The porter turned his head for a moment. 'He's been in a fever since yesterday,' she added.

Raskolnikov made no response and held the paper in his hands, without opening it. 'Don't you get up then,' Natasya went on compassionately, seeing that he was letting his feet down from the sofa. 'You're ill, and so you don't go; there's no such hurry. What have you got there?'

He looked; in his right hand he held the shreds he had cut from his trousers, the sock, and the rags of the pocket. So he had been asleep with them in his hand. Afterwards reflecting upon it, he remembered that, half waking up in his fever, he had grasped all this tightly in his hand and so fallen asleep again.

'Look at the rags he's collected and sleeps with them, as though he has got hold of a treasure . . .'

And Natasya went off into her hysterical giggle.

Instantly, he thrust them all under his greatcoat and fixed his eyes intently upon her. Far as he was from being capable of rational reflection at that moment, he felt that no one would behave like that with a person who was going to be arrested. 'But . . . the police?'

'You'd better have some tea! Yes? I'll bring it, there's some left.'

'No . . . I'm going; I'll go at once,' he muttered, getting on to his feet.

'Why, you'll never get downstairs!'

'Yes, I'll go.'

'As you please.'

She followed the porter out.

At once he rushed to the light to examine the sock and the rags.

'There are stains, but not very noticeable; all covered with dirt, and rubbed and already discoloured. No one who had no suspicion could distinguish anything. Natasya from a distance could not have noticed, thank God!' Then with a tremor he broke the seal of the notice and began reading; he was a long while reading, before he understood. It was an ordinary summons from the district police-station to appear that day at half-past nine at the office of the district superintendent.

'But when has such a thing happened? I never have anything to do with the police! And why just to-day?' he thought in agonizing bewilderment. 'Good God, only get it over soon!'

He was flinging himself on his knees to pray, but broke into laughter – not at the idea of prayer, but at himself.

He began, hurriedly dressing, 'If I'm lost, I am lost, I don't care! Shall I put the sock on?' he suddenly wondered, 'it will get dustier still and the traces will be gone.'

But no sooner had he put it on than he pulled it off again in loathing and horror. He pulled it off, but reflecting that he had no other socks, he picked it up and put it on again – and again he laughed.

'That's all conventional, that's all relative, merely a way of looking at it,' he thought in a flash, but only on the top surface of his mind, while he was shuddering all over, 'there, I've got it on! I have finished by getting it on!'

But his laughter was quickly followed by despair.

'No, it's too much for me . . .' he thought. His legs shook. 'From fear,' he muttered. His head swam and ached with fever. 'It's a trick! They want to decoy me there and confound me over everything,' he mused, as he went out on to the stairs – 'the worst of it is I'm almost light-headed . . . I may blurt out something stupid . . .'

On the stairs he remembered that he was leaving all the things just as they were in the hole in the wall, 'and very likely, it's on purpose to search when I'm out,' he thought, and stopped short. But he was possessed by such despair, such cynicism of misery, if one may so call it, that with a wave of his hand he went on. 'Only to get it over!'

In the street the heat was insufferable again; not a drop of rain had fallen all those days. Again dust, bricks and mortar, again the stench from the shops and pot-houses, again the drunken men, the Finnish pedlars and half-broken-down cabs. The sun shone straight into his eyes, so that it hurt him to look out of them, and he felt his head going round – as a man in a fever is apt to feel when he comes out into the street on a bright sunny day.

83

When he reached the turning into *the* street, in an agony of trepidation he looked down it . . . at *the* house . . . and at once averted his eyes.

'If they question me, perhaps I'll simply tell,' he thought, as he drew near the police-station.

The police-station was about a quarter of a mile off. It had lately been moved to new rooms on the fourth floor of a new house. He had been once for a moment in the old office, but long ago. Turning in at the gateway, he saw on the right a flight of stairs which a peasant was mounting with a book in his hand. 'A house-porter, no doubt; so then, the office is here,' and he began ascending the stairs on the chance. He did not want to ask questions of anyone.

'I'll go in, fall on my knees, and confess everything . . .' he thought, as he reached the fourth floor.

The staircase was steep, narrow and all sloppy with dirty water. The kitchens of the flats opened on to the stairs and stood open almost the whole day. So there was a fearful smell and heat. The staircase was crowded with porters going up and down with their books under their arms, policemen, and persons of all sorts and both sexes. The door at the office, too, stood wide open. Peasants stood waiting within. There, too, the heat was stifling and there was a sickening smell of fresh paint and stale oil from the newly decorated room.

After waiting a little, he decided to move forward into the next room. All the rooms were small and low-pitched. A fearful impatience drew him on and on. No one paid attention to him. In the second room some clerks sat writing, dressed hardly better than he was, and rather a queer-looking set. He went up to one of them.

'What is it?'

He showed them the notice he had received.

'You are a student?' the man asked, glancing at the notice.

'Yes, formerly a student.'

The clerk looked at him, but without the slightest interest. He was a particularly unkempt person with the look of a fixed idea in his eye.

'There would be no getting anything out of him, because he has no interest in anything,' thought Raskolnikov.

'Go in there to the head clerk.' said the clerk, pointing towards the furthest room.

He went into that room – the fourth in order; it was a small room and packed full of people, rather better dressed than in the outer rooms. Among them were two ladies. One, poorly dressed in mourning, sat at the table opposite the chief clerk, writing something at his dictation. The other, a very stout, buxom woman with a purplish-red, blotchy face, excessively smartly dressed with a brooch on her bosom as big as a saucer, was standing on one side, apparently waiting for something. Raskolnikov thrust his notice upon the head clerk. The latter glanced at it, said: 'Wait a minute,' and went on attending to the lady in mourning.

He breathed more freely. 'It can't be that!'

By degrees he began to regain confidence, he kept urging himself to have courage and be calm.

'Some foolishness, some trifling carelessness, and I may betray myself Hm! . . . it's a pity there's no air here,' he added, 'it's stifling . . . It makes one's head dizzier than, than ever . . . and one's mind too . . .'

He was conscious of a terrible inner turmoil. He was afraid of losing his self-control; he tried to catch at something and fix his mind on it, something quite irrelevant, but he could not succeed in this at all. Yet the head clerk greatly interested him, he kept hoping to see through him and guess something from his face.

He was a very young man, about two-and-twenty, with a dark mobile face that looked older than his years. He was fashionably dressed and foppish, with his hair parted in the middle, well combed and pomaded, and wore a number of rings on his well-scrubbed fingers and a gold chain on his waistcoat. He said a couple of words in French to a foreigner who was in the room, and said them fairly correctly.

'Luise Ivanovna, you can sit down,' he said casually to the gaily-dressed, purple-faced lady, who was still standing as though not venturing to sit down, though there was a chair beside her.

'Ich danke,' said the latter, and softly, with a rustle of silk she sank into the chair. Her light-blue dress trimmed with white lace floated about the table like an air-balloon and filled almost half the room. She smelt of scent. But she was obviously embarrassed at filling half the room and smelling so strongly of scent; and though her smile was impudent as well as cringing, it betrayed evident uneasiness.

The lady in mourning had done at last, and got up. All at once, with some noise, an officer walked in very jauntily, with a peculiar swing of his shoulders at each step. He tossed his cockaded cap on the table and sat down in an easy-chair. The smart lady positively skipped from her seat on seeing him, and fell to curtsying in a sort of ecstasy; but the officer took not the smallest notice of her, and she did not venture to sit down again in his presence. He was the assistant superintendent. He had a reddish moustache that stood out horizontally on each side of his face, and extremely small features, expressive of nothing much except a certain insolence. He looked askance and rather indignantly at Raskolnikov; he was so very badly dressed, and in spite of his humiliating position, his bearing was by no means in keeping with his clothes. Raskolnikov had unwarily fixed a very long and direct look on him, so that he felt positively affronted.

'What do you want?' he shouted, apparently astonished that such a ragged fellow was not annihilated by the majesty of his glance.

'I was summoned . . . by a notice . . .' Raskolnikov faltered.

'For the recovery of money due, from *the student*,' the head clerk interfered hurriedly, tearing himself from his papers. 'Here!' and he flung Raskolnikov a document and pointed out the place. 'Read that!'

'Money? What money?' thought Raskolnikov, 'but . . . then . . . it's certainly not *that*.'

And he trembled with joy. He felt sudden intense indescribable relief. A load was lifted from his back.

'And pray, what time were you directed to appear, sir?' shouted the assistant superintendent, seeming for some unknown reason more and more aggrieved. 'You are told to come at nine, and now it's twelve!'

'The notice was only brought me a quarter of an hour ago,' Raskolnikov answered loudly over his shoulder. To his own surprise he, too, grew suddenly angry and found a certain pleasure in it. 'And it's enough that I have come here ill with fever.'

'Kindly refrain from shouting!'

'I'm not shouting, I'm speaking very quietly, it's you who are shouting at me. I'm a student, and allow no one to shout at me.'

The assistant superintendant was so furious that for the first minute he could only splutter inarticulately. He leaped up from his seat.

'Be silent! You are in a government office. Don't be impudent, sir!'

'You're in a government office, too,' cried Raskolnikov, 'and you're smoking a cigarette as well as shouting, so you are showing disrespect to all of us.'

He felt an indescribable satisfaction at having said this.

The head clerk looked at him with a smile. The angry assistant superintendent was obviously disconcerted.

'That's not your business!' he shouted at last with unnatural loudness. 'Kindly make the declaration demanded of you. Show him, Alexandr Grigorievitch. There is a complaint against you! You don't pay your debts! You're a fine bird!'

But Raskolnikov was not listening now; he had eagerly clutched at the paper, in haste to find an explanation. He read it once, and a second time, and still did not understand.

'What is this?' he asked the head clerk.

'It is for the recovery of money on an I O U, a writ. You must either pay it, with all expenses, costs and so on, or give a written declaration when you can pay it, and at the same time an undertaking not to leave the capital without payment, and not to sell or conceal your property. The creditor is at liberty to sell your property, and proceed against you according to the law.'

'But I . . . am not in debt to anyone!'

'That's not our business. Here, an I O U for a hundred and fifteen roubles, legally attested, and due for payment, has been brought us for recovery, given by you to the widow of the assessor Zarnitsyn, nine months ago, and paid over by the widow Zarnitsyn to one Mr. Tchebarov. We therefore summon you, hereupon.'

'But she is my landlady!'

'And what if she is your landlady?'

The head clerk looked at him with a condescending smile of compassion, and at the same time with a certain triumph, as at a novice under fire for the first time – as though he would say: 'Well, how do you feel now?' But what did he care now for an I O U, for a writ of recovery? Was that worth worrying about now, was it worth attention even? He stood, he read, he listened, he answered, he even asked questions himself, but all mechanically. The triumphant sense of security, of deliverance from overwhelming danger, that was what filled his whole soul that moment without thought for the future, without analysis, without suppositions or surmises, without doubts and without questioning. It was an instant of full, direct, purely instinctive joy. But at that very moment something like a thunderstorm took place in the office. The assistant superintendent, still shaken by Raskolnikov's disrespect, still fuming and obviously anxious to keep up his wounded dignity, pounced on the unfortunate smart lady, who had been gazing at him ever since he came in with an exceedingly silly smile.

'You shameful hussy!' he shouted suddenly at the top of his voice. (The lady in mourning had left the office.) 'What was going on at your house last night? Eh? A disgrace again, you're a scandal to the whole street. Fighting and drinking again. Do you want the house of correction? Why, I have warned you ten times over that I would not let you off the eleventh! And here you are again, again you . . . you . . .!'

The paper fell out of Raskolnikov's hands, and he looked wildly at the smart lady who was so unceremoniously treated. But he soon saw what it meant, and at once began to find positive amusement in the scandal. He listened with pleasure, so that he longed to laugh and laugh . . . all his nerves were on edge.

'Ilya Petrovitch!' the head clerk was beginning anxiously, but stopped short, for he knew from experience that the enraged assistant could not be stopped except by force.

As for the smart lady, at first she positively trembled before the storm.

But, strange to say, the more numerous and violent the terms of abuse became, the more amiable she looked, and the more seductive the smiles she lavished on the terrible assistant. She moved uneasily, and curtsied incessantly, waiting impatiently for a chance of putting in her word: and at last she found it.

'There was no sort of noise or fighting in my house, Mr. Captain,' she pattered all at once, like peas dropping, speaking Russian confidently, though with a strong German accent, 'and no sort of scandal, and his honour came drunk, and it's the whole truth I am telling, Mr. Captain, and I am not to blame . . . Mine is an honourable house, Mr. Captain, and honourable behaviour, Mr. Captain, and I always, always dislike any scandal myself. But he came quite tipsy, and asked for three bottles again, and then he lifted up one leg, and began playing the pianoforte with one foot, and that is not at all right in an honourable house, and he *ganz* broke the piano, and it was very bad manners indeed and I said so. And he took up a bottle and began hitting everyone with it. And then I called the porter, and Karl came, and he took Karl and hit him in the eye; and he hit Henriette in the eye, too, and gave me five slaps on the cheek. And it was so ungentlemanly in an honourable house, Mr. Captain, and I screamed. And he opened the window over the canal, and stood in the window, squealing like a little pig; it was a disgrace. The idea of squealing like a little pig at the window into the street! Fie upon him! And Karl pulled him away from the window by his coat, and it is true, Mr Captain, he tore *sein rock*. And then he shouted that *man muss* pay him fifteen roubles damages. And I did pay him, Mr. Captain, five roubles for *sein rock*. And he is an ungentlemanly visitor and caused all the scandal. "I will show you up," he said, "for I can write to all the papers about you." '

'Then he was an author?'

'Yes, Mr. Captain, and what an ungentlemanly visitor in an honourable house . . .'

'Now then! Enough! I have told you already . . .'

'Ilya Petrovitch!' the head clerk repeated significantly.

The assistant glanced rapidly at him; the head clerk slightly shook his head.

'. . . So I tell you this, most respectable Luise Ivanovna, and I tell it you for the last time,' the assistant went on. 'If there is a scandal in your honourable house once again, I will put you yourself in the lock-up, as it is called in polite society. Do you hear? So a literary man, an author, took five roubles for his coat-tail in an "honourable house"? A nice set, these authors!'

And he cast a contemptuous glance at Raskolnikov. 'There was a scandal the other day in a restaurant, too. An author had eaten his dinner and would not pay; "I'll write a satire on you," says he. And there was another of them on a steamer last week used the most disgraceful language to the respectable family of a civil councillor, his wife and daughter. And there was one of them turned out of a confectioner's shop the other day. They are like that, authors, literary men, students, town-criers . . . Pfoo! You get along! I shall look in upon you myself one day. Then you had better be careful! Do you hear?'

With hurried deference, Luise Ivanovna fell to curtsying in all directions, and so curtsied herself to the door. But at the door, she stumbled backwards against a good-looking officer with a fresh, open face and splendid thick fair whiskers. This was the superintendent of the district himself, Nikodim Fomitch. Luise Ivanovna made haste to curtsy almost to the ground, and with mincing little steps, she fluttered out of the office.

'Again thunder and lightning – a hurricane!' said Nikodim Fomitch to Ilya Petrovitch in a civil and friendly tone. 'You are aroused again, you are fuming again! I heard it on the stairs!'

'Well, what then!' Ilya Petrovitch drawled, with gentlemanly nonchalance; and he walked with some papers to another table, with a jaunty swing of his shoulders at each step. 'Here, if you will kindly look: an author, or a student, has been one at least, does not pay his debts, has given an I O U, won't clear out of his room, and complaints are constantly being lodged against him, and here he has been pleased to make a protest against my smoking in his presence! He behaves like a cad himself, and just look at him, please. Here's the gentleman, and very attractive he is!'

'Poverty is not a vice, my friend, but we know you go off like powder, you can't bear a slight. I daresay you took offence at something and went too far yourself,' continued Nikodim Fomitch, turning affably to Raskolnikov. 'But you were wrong there; he is a capital fellow, I assure you, but explosive, explosive! He gets hot, fires up, boils over, and no stopping him! And then it's all over! And at the bottom he's a heart of gold! His nickname in the regiment was the Explosive Lieutenant . . .'

'And what a regiment it was, too,' cried Ilya Petrovitch much gratified at this agreeable banter, though still sulky.

Raskolnikov had a sudden desire to say something exceptionally pleasant to them all. 'Excuse me, Captain,' he began easily, suddenly addressing Nikodim Fomitch, 'will you enter into my position? . . . I am ready to ask pardon, if I have been ill-mannered. I am a poor student, sick and shattered (shattered was the word he used) by poverty. I am not studying, because I cannot keep myself now, but I shall get money . . . I have a mother and sister in the province of X. They will send it to me, and I will pay. My landlady is a good-hearted woman, but she is so exasperated at my having lost my lessons and not paying her for the last four months, that she does not even send up my dinner . . . and I don't understand this I O U at all. She is asking me to pay her on this I O U. How am I to pay her? Judge for yourselves! . . .'

'But that is not our business, you know,' the head clerk was observing.

'Yes, yes. I perfectly agree with you. But allow me to explain . . .' Raskolnikov put in again, still addressing Nikodim Fomitch, but trying his best to address Ilya Petrovitch also, though the latter persistently appeared to be rummaging among his papers and to be contemptuously oblivious of him. 'Allow me to explain that I have been living with her for nearly three years at first . . . at first . . . for why should I not confess it, at the very beginning I promised to marry her daughter, it was a verbal promise, freely given . . . she was a girl . . . indeed, I liked her, though I was not in love with her . . . a youthful affair in fact . . . that is, I mean to say, that my landlady gave me credit freely in those days, and I led a life of . . . I was very heedless . . .'

'Nobody asks you for these personal details, sir, we've no time to waste.' Ilya Petrovitch interposed roughly and with a note of triumph; but Raskolnikov stopped him hotly, though he suddenly found it exceedingly difficult to speak.

'But excuse me, excuse me. It is for me to explain . . . how it all happened . . . In my turn . . . though I agree with you . . . it is unnecessary. But a year ago, the girl died of typhus. I remained lodging there as before, and when my landlady moved into her present quarters, she said to me . . . and in a friendly way . . . that she had complete trust in me, but still, would I not give her an I O U for one hundred and fifteen roubles, all the debt I owed her. She said if only I gave her that, she would trust me again, as much as I liked, and that she would never, never – those were her own words – make use of that I O U till I could pay of myself . . . and now, when I have lost my lessons and having nothing to eat, she takes action against me. What am I to say to that?'

'All these affecting details are no business of ours,' Ilya Petrovitch interrupted rudely. 'You must give a written undertaking, but as for your love affairs and all these tragic events, we have nothing to do with that.'

'Come now . . . you are harsh,' muttered Nikodim Fomitch, sitting down at the table and also beginning to write. He looked a little ashamed.

'Write!' said the head clerk to Raskolnikov.

'Write what?' the latter asked, gruffly.

'I will dictate to you.'

Raskolnikov fancied that the head clerk treated him more casually and contemptuously after his speech, but strange to say he suddenly felt completely indifferent to anyone's opinion, and this revulsion took place in a flash, in one instant. If he had cared to think a little, he would have been amazed indeed that he could have talked to them like that a minute before, forcing his feelings upon them. And where had those feelings come from? Now if the whole room had been filled, not with police officers but with those nearest and dearest to him, he would not have found one human word for them, so empty was his heart. A gloomy sensation of agonising, everlasting solitude and remoteness, took conscious form in his soul. It was not the meanness of the latter's triumph over him that had caused this sudden revulsion in his heart. Oh, what had he to do now with his own baseness, with all these petty vanities, officers, German women, debts, police-offices? If he had been sentenced to be burnt at that moment, he would not have stirred, would hardly have heard the sentence to the end. Something was happening to him entirely new, sudden and unknown. It was not that he understood, but he felt clearly with all the intensity of sensation that he could never more appeal to these people in the police-office with sentimental effusions like his recent outburst, or with anything whatever; and that if they had been his own brothers and sisters and not police-officers, it would have been utterly out of the question to appeal to them in any circumstance of life. He had never experienced such a strange and awful sensation. And what was most agonising – it was more a sensation than a conception or idea, a direct sensation, the most agonising of all the sensations he had known in his life.

The head clerk began dictating to him the usual form of declaration, that he could not pay, that he undertook to do so at a future date, that he would not leave the town, nor sell his property, and so on.

'But you can't write, you can hardly hold the pen,' observed the head clerk, looking with curiosity at Raskolnikov. 'Are you ill?'

'Yes, I am giddy. Go on!'

'That's all. Sign it.'

The head clerk took the paper, and turned to attend to others.

Raskolnikov gave back the pen; but instead of getting up and going away, he put his elbows on the table and pressed his head in his hands. He felt as if a nail were being driven into his skull. A strange idea suddenly occurred to him, to get up at once, to go up to Nikodim Fomitch, and tell him everything that had happened yesterday, and then to go with him to his lodgings and to show him the things in the hole in the corner. The impulse was so strong that he got up from his seat to carry it out. 'Hadn't I better think a minute?' flashed through his mind. 'No, better cast off the burden without thinking.' But all at once he stood still, rooted to the spot. Nikodim Fomitch was talking eagerly with Ilya Petrovitch, and the words reached him:

'It's impossible, they'll both be released. To begin with, the whole story contradicts itself. Why should they have called the porter, if it had been their doing? To inform against themselves? Or as a blind? No, that would be too cunning! Besides, Pestryakov, the student, was seen at the gate by both the porters and a woman as he went in. He was walking with three friends, who left him only at the gate, and he asked the porters to direct him, in the presence of the friends. Now, would he have asked his way if he had been going with such an object? As for Koch, he spent half an hour at the silversmith's below, before he went up to the old woman and he left him at exactly a quarter to eight. Now just consider . . .'

'But excuse me, how do you explain this contradiction? They state themselves that they knocked and the door was locked; yet three minutes later when they went up with the porter, it turned out the door was unfastened.'

'That's just it; the murderer must have been there and bolted himself in' and they'd have caught him for a certainty if Koch had not been an ass and gone to look for the porter too. *He* must have seized the interval to get downstairs and slip by them somehow. Kock keeps crossing himself and saying: "If I had been there, he would have jumped out and killed me with his axe." He is going to have a thanksgiving service – ha, ha!'

'And no one saw the murderer?'

'They might well not see him; the house is a regular Noah's Ark,' said the head clerk, who was listening.

'It's clear, quite clear,' Nikodim Fomitch repeated warmly.

'No, it is anything but clear,' Ilya Petrovitc maintained.

Raskolnikov picked up his hat and walked towards the door, but he did not reach it . . .

When he recovered consciousness, he found himself sitting in a chair, supported by someone on the right side, while someone else was standing on the left, holding a yellowish glass filled with yellow water, and Nikodim Fomitch standing before him, looking intently at him. He got up from the chair.

'What's this? Are you ill?' Nikodim Fomitch asked, rather sharply.

'He could hardly hold his pen when he was signing,' said the head clerk, settling back in his place, and taking up his work again.

'Have you been ill long?' cried Ilya Petrovitch from his place, where he, too, was looking through papers. He had, of course, come to look at the sick man when he fainted, but retired at once when he recovered.

'Since yesterday,' muttered Raskolnikov in reply.

'Did you go out yesterday?'

'Yes.'

'Though you were ill?'

'Yes.'

'At what time?'

'About seven.'

'And where did you go, may I ask?'

'Along the street.'

'Short and clear.'

Raskolnikov, white as a handkerchief, had answered sharply, jerkily, without dropping his black feverish eyes before Ilya Petrovitch's stare.

'He can scarcely stand upright. And you . . .' Nikodim Fomitch was beginning.

'No matter,' Ilya Petrovitch pronounced rather peculiarly.

Nikodim Fomitch would have made some further protest, but glancing at the head clerk who was looking very hard at him, he did not speak. There was a sudden silence. It was strange.

'Very well, then,' concluded Ilya Petrovitch,' we will not detain you.'

Raskolnikov went out. He caught the sound of eager conversation on his departure, and above the rest rose the questioning voice of Nikodim Fomitch. In the street, his faintness passed off completely.

'A search – there will be a search at once,' he repeated to himself, hurrying home. 'The brutes! they suspect.'

His former terror mastered him completely again.

⇒ TWO ⇐

'AND WHAT IF THERE HAS BEEN a search already? What if I find them in my room?'

But here was his room. Nothing and no one in it. No one had peeped in. Even Nastasya had not touched it. But heavens! how could he have left all those things in the hole?

He rushed to the corner, slipped his hand under the paper, pulled the things out and filled his pockets with them. There were eight articles in all; two little boxes with ear-rings or something of the sort, he hardly looked to see; then four small leather cases. There was a chain, too, merely wrapped in newspaper and something else in newspaper, that looked like a decoration. . . . He put them all in the different pockets of his overcoat, and the remaining pocket of his trousers, trying to conceal them as much as possible. He took the purse, too. Then he went out of his room, leaving the door open. He walked quickly and resolutely, and though he felt shattered, he had his senses about him. He was afraid of pursuit, he was afraid that in another half-hour, another quarter of an hour perhaps, instructions would be issued for his pursuit, and so at all costs he must hide all traces before then. He must clear everything up while he still had some strength, some reasoning power left him . . . Where was he to go?

That had long been settled: 'Fling them into the canal, and all traces hidden in the water, the thing would be at an end.' So he had decided in the night of his delirium when several times he had had the impulse to get up and go away, to make haste, and get rid of it all. But to get rid of it, turned out to be a very difficult task. He wandered along the bank of the Ekaterininsky Canal for half an hour or more and looked several times at the steps running down to the water, but he could not think of carrying out his plan; either rafts stood at the steps' edge, and women were washing clothes on them, or boats were moored there, and people were swarming everywhere. Moreover he could be seen and noticed from the banks on all sides; it would look suspicious for a man to go down on purpose, stop, and throw something into the water. And what if the boxes were to float instead of sinking? And of course they would. Even as it was, everyone he met seemed to stare and look round, as if they had nothing to do but to watch him. 'Why is it, or can it be my fancy?' he thought.

At last the thought struck him that it might be better to go to the Neva. There were not so many people there, he would be less observed, and it would be more convenient in every way, above all it was further off. He wondered how he could have been wandering for a good half-hour, worried and anxious in this dangerous past without thinking of it before. And that half-hour he had lost over an irrational plan, simply because he had thought of it in delirium! He had become extremely absent and forgetful and he was aware of it. He certainly must make haste.

He walked towards the Neva along V– Prospect, but on the way another idea struck him. 'Why to the Neva? Would it not be better to go somewhere far off, to the Islands again, and there hide the things in some solitary place, in a wood or under a bush, and mark the spot perhaps? And though he felt incapable of clear judgment, the idea seemed to him a sound one. But he was not destined to go there. For coming out of V– Prospect towards the square, he saw on the left a passage leading between two blank walls to a courtyard. On the right hand, the blank unwhite-washed wall of a four-storied house stretched far into the court; on the left, a wooden hoarding ran parallel with it for twenty paces into the court, and then turned sharply to the left. Here was a deserted fenced-off place where rubbish of different sorts was lying. At the end of the court, the corner of a low, smutty, stone shed, apparently part of some workshop, peeped from behind the hoarding. It was probably a carriage-builder's or carpenter's shed; the whole place from the entrance was black with coal-dust. Here would be the place to throw it, he thought. Not seeing anyone in the hard, he slipped in, and at once saw near the gate a sink, such as is often put in yards where there are many workmen or cab-drivers; and on the hoarding above had been scribbled in chalk the time-honoured witticism, 'Standing here strictly forbidden'. That was all the better, for there would be nothing suspicious about his going in. 'Here I could throw it all in a heap and get away!'

Looking round once more, with his hand already in his pocket, he noticed against the outer wall, between the entrance and the sink, a big unhewn stone, weighing perhaps sixty pounds. The other side of the wall was a street. He could hear passers-by, always numerous in that part, but he could not be seen from the entrance, unless someone came in from the street, which might well happen indeed, so there was need of haste.

He bent down over the stone, seized the top of it firmly in both hands, and using all his strength turned it over. Under the stone was a small hollow in the ground, and he immediately emptied his pocket into it. The purse lay at the top, and yet the hollow was not filled up. Then he seized the stone again and with one twist turned it back, so that it was in the same position again, though it stood a very little higher. But he scraped the earth about it and pressed it at the edges with his foot. Nothing could be noticed.

Then he went out, and turned into the square. Again an intense, almost unbearable joy overwhelmed him for an instant, as it had in the police office. 'I have buried my tracks! and who, who can think of looking under that stone? It has been lying there most likely ever since the house was built, and will lie as many years more. And if it were found, who would think of me? It is all over! No clue!' And he laughed. Yes, he remembered that he began laughing a thin, nervous noiseless laugh, and went on laughing all the time he was crossing the square. But when he reached the K – Boulevard where two days before he had come upon that girl, his laughter suddenly ceased. Other ideas crept into his mind. He felt all at once that it would be loathsome to pass that seat on which, after the girl was gone, he had sat and pondered, and that it would be hateful, too, to meet that whiskered policeman to whom he had given the twenty copecks: 'Damn him!'

He walked, looking about him angrily and distractedly. All his ideas now seemed to be circling round some single point, and he felt that there really was such a point, and that now, now, he was left facing that point – and for the first time, indeed, during the last two months.

'Damn it all!' he thought suddenly, in a fit of ungovernable fury. 'If it has begun, then it has begun. Hang the new life! Good Lord, how stupid it is! . . . And what lies I told to-day! How despicably I fawned upon that wretched Ilya Petrovitch! But that is all folly! What do I care for them all, and my fawning upon them! It is not that at all! It is not that at all!'

Suddenly he stopped; a new utterly unexpected and exceedingly simple question perplexed and bitterly confounded him.

'If it all has really been done deliberately and not idiotically, if I really had a certain and definite object, how is it I did not even glance into the purse and don't know what I had there, for which I have undergone these agonies, and have deliberately undertaken this base, filthy, degrading business? And here I wanted to once throw into the water the purse together with all the things which I had not seen either . . . how's that?'

Yes, that was so, that was all so. Yet he had known it all before, and it was not a new question for him, even when it was decided in the night without hesitation and consideration, as though so it must be, as though it could not possibly be otherwise . . . Yes, he had known it all, and understood it all; it surely had all been settled even yesterday at the moment when he was bending over the box and pulling the jewel-cases out of it . . . Yes, so it was.

'It is because I am very ill,' he decided grimly at last, 'I have been worrying and fretting myself, and I don't know what I am doing . . . Yesterday and the day before yesterday and all this time I have been worrying myself . . . I shall get well and I shall not worry . . . But what if I don't get well at all? Good God, how sick I am of it all!'

He walked on without resting. He had a terrible longing for some distraction, but he did not know what to do, what to attempt. A new overwhelming sensation was gaining more and more mastery over him every moment; this was an immeasurable, almost physical, repulsion for everything surrounding him, an obstinate, malignant feeling of hatred. All who met him were loathsome to him – he loathed their faces, their movements, their gestures. If anyone had addressed him, he felt that he might have spat at him or bitten him . . .

He stopped suddenly, on coming out on the bank of the Little Neva, near the bridge to Vassilyevsky Ostrov. 'Why, he lives here, in that house,' he thought, 'why, I have not come to Razumihin of my own accord! Here it's the same thing over again . . . Very interesting to know, though; have I come on purpose or have I simply walked here by chance? Never mind, I said the day before yesterday that I would go and see him the day *after*; well, and so I will! Besides I really cannot go further now.'

He went up to Razumihin's room on the fifth floor.

The latter was at home in his garret, busily writing at the moment, and he opened the door himself. It was four months since they had seen each other. Razumihin was sitting in a ragged dressing-gown, with slippers on his bare feet, unkempt, unshaved and unwashed. His face showed surprise.

'Is it you?' he cried. He looked his comrade up and down; then after a brief pause, he whistled. 'As hard up as all that! Why, brother you've cut me out!' he added, looking at Raskolnikov's rags. 'Come sit down, you are tired, I'll be bound.'

And when he had sunk down on the American leather sofa, which was in even worse condition than his own, Razumihin saw at once that his visitor was ill.

'Why, you are seriously ill, do you know that?' He began feeling his pulse. Raskolnikov pulled away his hand.

'Never mind,' he said, 'I have come for this: I have no lessons . . . I wanted . . . but I don't really want lessons . . .'

'But I say! You are delirious, you know!' Razumihin observed, watching him carefully.

'No, I'm not.'

Raskolnikov got up from the sofa. As he had mounted the stairs to Razumihin's, he had not realized that he would be meeting his friend face to face. Now, in a flash, he knew that what he was least of all disposed for at that moment was to be face to face with anyone in the wide world. His spleen rose within him. He almost choked with rage at himself as soon as he crossed Razumihin's threshold.

'Good-bye,' he said abruptly, and walked to the door.

'Stop, stop! You queer fish.'

'I don't want to,' said the other, again pulling away his hand.

'Then why the devil have you come? Are you mad, or what? Why, this is . . . almost insulting! I won't let you go like that.'

'Well, then, I came to you because I know no one but you who could help . . . to begin . . . because you are kinder than anyone – cleverer, I mean, and can judge . . . and now I see that I want nothing. Do you hear? Nothing at all . . . no one's services . . . no one's sympathy. I am by myself . . . alone. Come, that's enough. Leave me alone.'

'Stay a minute, you sweep! You are a perfect madman. As you like, for all I care. I have no lessons, do you see, and I don't care about that, but there's a bookseller, Heruvimov – and he takes the place of a lesson. I would not exchange him for five lessons. He's doing publishing of a kind, and issuing natural science manuals and what a circulation they have! The very titles are worth the money! You always maintained that I was a fool, but by Jove, my boy, there are greater fools than I am! Now he is setting up for being advanced, not that he has an inkling of anything, but, of course, I encourage him. Here are two signatures of the German text – in my opinion, the crudest charlatanism; it discusses the question, "Is woman a human being?" And, of course, triumphantly proves that she is. Heruvimov is going to bring out this work as a contribution to the woman question; I am translating it; he will expand these two and a half signatures into six, we shall make up a gorgeous title half a page long and bring it out at half a rouble. It will do! He pays me six roubles the signature, it works out to about fifteen roubles for the job, and I've had six already in advance. When we have finished this, we are going to begin a translation about whales, and then some of the dullest scandals out of the second part of *Les Confessions* we have marked for translation; somebody has told Heruvimov that Rousseau was a kind of Radishchev. You may be sure I don't contradict him, hang him! Well, would you like to do the second signature of *"Is woman a human being?"* If you would, take the German and pens and paper – all those provided, and take three roubles; for as I have had six roubles in advance on the whole thing, three roubles comes to you for your share. And when you have finished the signature there will be another three roubles for you. And please don't think I am doing you a service; quite the contrary, as soon as you came in, I saw how you could help me; to begin with, I am weak in spelling, and secondly, I am sometimes utterly adrift in German, so that I make it up as I go along for the most part. The only comfort is, that it's bound to be a change for the better. Though who can tell, maybe it's sometimes for the worse. Will you take it?'

Raskolnikov took the German sheets in silence, took the three roubles and without a word went out. Razumihin gazed after him in astonishment. But when Raskolnikov was in the next street, he turned back, mounted the stairs to Razumihin's again and laying on the table the German article and the three roubles, went out again, still without uttering a word.

'Are you raving, or what?' Razumihin shouted, roused to fury at last. 'What farce is this? You'll drive me crazy too . . . what did you come to see me for, damn you?'

'I don't want . . . translation,' muttered Raskolnikov from the stairs.

'Then what the devil do you want?' shouted Razumihin from above. Raskolnikov continued descending the staircase in silence.

'Hey, there!' Where are you living?'

No answer.

'Well, confound you then!'

But Raskolnikov was already stepping into the street. On the Nikolaevsky Bridge he was roused to full consciousness again by an unpleasant incident. A coachman, after shouting at him two or three times, gave him a violent lash on the back with his whip, for having almost fallen under his horses' hoofs. The lash so infuriated him that he dashed away to the railing (for some unknown reason he had been walking in the very middle of the bridge in the traffic). He angrily clenched and ground his teeth. He heard laughter, of course.

'Serve him right!'

'A pickpocket, I dare say.'

'Pretending to be drunk, for sure, and getting under the wheels on purpose; and you have to answer for him.'

'It's a regular profession, that's what it is.'

But while he stood at the railing, still looking angry and bewildered after the retreating carriage, and rubbing his back, he suddenly felt someone thrust money into his hand. He looked. It was an elderly woman in a kerchief and goatskin shoes, with a girl, probably her daughter wearing a hat, and carrying a green parasol.

'Take it, my good man, in Christ's name.'

He took it and they passed on. It was a piece of twenty copecks. From his dress and appearance they might well have taken him for a beggar asking alms in the streets, and the gift of the twenty copecks he doubtless owed to the blow, which made them feel sorry for him.

He closed his hand on the twenty copecks, walked on for ten paces, and turned facing the Neva, looking towards the palace. The sky was without a cloud and the water was almost bright blue, which is so rare in the Neva. The cupola of the cathedral, which is seen at its best from the bridge about twenty paces from the chapel, glittered in the sunlight, and in the pure air every ornament on it could be clearly distinguished. The pain from the lash went off, and Raskolnikov forgot about it; one uneasy and not quite definite idea occupied him now completely. He stood still, and gazed long and intently into the distance; this spot was especially familiar to him. When he was attending the university he had hundreds of times – generally on his way home – stood still on this spot, gazed at this truly magnificent spectacle and almost always marvelled at a vague and mysterious emotion it roused in him. It left him strangely cold; this gorgeous picture was for him blank and lifeless. He wondered every time at his sombre and enigmatic impression and, mistrusting himself, put off finding the explanation of it. He vividly recalled those old doubts and perplexities, and it seemed to him that it was no mere chance that he recalled them now. It struck him as strange and grotesque that he should have stopped at the same spot as before, as though he actually imagined he could think the same thoughts, be interested in the same theories and pictures that had interested him . . . so short a time ago. He felt it almost amusing, and yet it wrung his heart. Deep down, hidden far away out of sight all that seemed to him now – all his old past, his old thoughts, his old problems and theories, his old impressions and that picture and himself and all, all . . . He felt as though he were flying upwards, and everything were vanishing from his sight. Making an unconscious movement with his hand, he suddenly became aware of the piece of money in his fist. He opened his hand, stared at the coin, and with a sweep of his arm flung it into the water; then he turned and went home. It seemed to him, he had cut himself off from everyone and from everything at that moment.

Evening was coming on when he reached home, so that he must have been walking about six hours. How and where he came back he did not remember. Undressing, and quivering like an over-driven horse, he lay down on the sofa, drew his greatcoat over him, and at once sank into oblivion . . .

It was dusk when he was waked up by a fearful scream. Good God, what a scream! Such unnatural sounds, such howling, wailing, grinding, tears, blows and curses he had never heard.

He could never have imagined such brutality, such frenzy. In terror he sat up in bed, almost swooning with agony. But the fighting, the wailing and cursing grew louder and louder. And then to his intense amazement he caught the voice of his landlady. She was howling, shrieking and wailing, rapidly, hurriedly, incoherently, so that he could not make out what she was talking about; she was beseeching, no doubt, not to be beaten, for she was being mercilessly beaten on the stairs. The voice of her assailant was so horrible from spite and rage that it was almost a croak; but he, too, was saying something, and just as quickly and indistinctly, hurrying and spluttering. All at once Raskolnikov trembled; he recognized the voice – it was the voice of Ilya Petrovitch. Ilya Petrovitch here and beating the landlady! He is kicking her, banging her head against the steps – that's clear, that can be told from the sounds, from the cries and the thuds. How is it, is the world topsy-turvy? He could hear people running in crowds from all the storeys and all the staircases; he heard voices, exclamations, knocking, doors banging. 'But why, why, and how could it be?' he repeated, thinking seriously that he had gone mad. But no, he heard too distinctly! And they would come to him then next, 'for no doubt . . . it's all about that . . . about yesterday . . . Good God!' He would have fastened his door with the latch, but he could not lift his hand . . . besides, it would be useless. Terror gripped his heart like ice, tortured him and numbed him . . . But at last all this uproar, after continuing about ten minutes, began gradually to subside. The landlady was moaning and groaning; Ilya Petrovitch was still uttering threats and curses. . . . But at last he, too, seemed to be silent, and now he could not be heard. 'Can he have gone away? Good Lord!' Yes, and now the land-lady is going too, still weeping and moaning . . . and then her door slammed . . . Now the crowd was going from the stairs to their rooms, exclaiming, disputing, calling to one another, raising their voices to a shout, dropping them to a whisper. There must have been numbers of them – almost all the inmates of the block. 'But? good God, how could it be? And why, why had he come here?'

Raskolnikov sank worn out on the sofa, but could not close his eyes. He lay for half an hour in such anguish, such an intolerable sensation of infinite terror as he had never experienced before. Suddenly a bright light flashed into his room. Nastasya came in with a candle and a plate of soup. Looking at him carefully and ascertaining that he was not asleep, she set the candle on the table and began to lay out what she had brought – bread, salt, a plate, a spoon.

'You've eaten nothing since yesterday, I warrant. You've been trudging about all day, and you're shaking with fever.'

'Nastasya . . . what were they beating the landlady for?'

She looked intently at him.

'Who beat the landlady?'

'Just now . . . half an hour ago, Ilya Petrovitch, the assistant super-intendant, on the stairs . . . Why was he ill-treating her like that, and . . . why was he here?'

Nastasya scrutinized him, silent and frowning, and her scrutiny lasted a long time. He felt uneasy, even frightened at her searching eyes.

'Nastasya, why don't you speak?' he said timidly at last in a weak voice.

'It's the blood,' she answered at last softly, as though speaking to herself.

'Blood? What blood?' he muttered, growing white and turning towards the wall.

Nastasya still looked at him without speaking.

'Nobody has been beating the landlady,' she declared at last in a firm, resolute voice.

He gazed at her, hardly able to breathe.

'I heard it myself . . . I was not asleep . . . I was sitting up,' he said still more timidly. 'I listened a long while. The assistant superintendent came . . . Everyone ran out on to the stairs from all the flats.'

'No one has been here. That's the blood crying in your ears. When there's no outlet for it and it gets clotted, you begin fancying things . . . Will you eat something?'

He made no answer. Nastasya still stood over him, watching him.

'Give me something to drink . . . Nastasya.'

She went downstairs and returned with a white earthenware jug of water. He remembered only swallowing one sip of the cold water and spilling some on his neck. Then followed forgetfulness.

➤ THREE ✦

HE WAS NOT COMPLETELY UNCONSCIOUS, however, all the time he was ill; he was in a feverish state, sometimes delirious, sometime half conscious. He remembered a great deal afterwards. Sometimes it seemed as though there were a number of people round him; they wanted to take him away somewhere, there was a great deal of squabbling and discussing about him. Then he would be alone in the room; they had all gone away afraid of him, and only now and then opened the door a crack to look at him; they threatened him, plotted something together, laughed, and mocked at him. He remembered Nastasya often at his bedside; he distinguished another person, too, whom he seemed to know very well, though he could not remember who he was, and this fretted him, even made him cry. Sometimes he fancied he had been lying there a month; at other times it all seemed part of the same day. But of *that* – of *that* he had no recollection, and yet every minute he felt that he had forgotten something he ought to remember. He worried and tormented himself trying to remember, moaned, flew into a rage, or sank into awful, intolerable terror. Then he struggled to get up, would have run away, but someone always prevented him by force, and he sank back into impotence and forgetfulness. At last he returned to complete consciousness.

It happened at ten o'clock in the morning. On fine days the sun shone into the room at that hour, throwing a streak of light on the right wall and the corner near the door. Nastasya was standing beside him with another person, a complete stranger, who was looking at him very inquisitively. He was a young man with a beard, wearing a full, short-waisted coat, and looked like a messenger. The landlady was peeping at the half-opened door. Raskolnikov sat up.

'Who is this, Nastasya?' he asked, pointing to the young man.

'I say, he's himself again!' she said.

'He is himself,' echoed the man.

Concluding that he had returned to his senses, the landlady closed the door and disappeared. She was always shy and dreaded conversations or discussions. She was a woman of forty, not at all bad-looking, fat and buxom, with black eyes and eyebrows, good-natured from fatness and laziness, and absurdly bashful.

'Who . . . are you?' he went on, addressing the man. But at that moment the door was flung open, and, stooping a little, as he was so tall, Razumihin came in.

'What a cabin it is!' he cried. 'I am always knocking my head. You call this a lodging! So you are conscious, brother? I've just heard the news from Pashenka.'

'He has just come to,' said Nastasya.

'Just come to,' echoed the man again, with a smile.

'And who are you?' Razumihin asked, suddenly addressing him. 'My name is Vrazumihin, at your service; not Razumihin, as I am always called, but Vrazumihin, a student and gentleman; and he is my friend. And who are you?'

'I am the messenger from our office, from the merchant Shelopaev, and I've come on business.'

'Please sit down.' Razumihin seated himself on the other side of the table. 'It's a good thing you've come to, brother,' he went on to Raskolnikov. 'For the last four days you have scarcely eaten or drunk anything. We had to give you tea in spoonfuls. I brought Zossimov to see you twice. You remember Zossimov? He examined you carefully and said at once it was nothing serious – something seemed to have gone to your head. Some nervous nonsense, the result of bad feeling, he says you have not had enough beer and radish, but it's nothing much, it will pass and you will be all right. Zossimov is a first-rate fellow! He is making quite a name. Come, I won't keep you,' he said, addressing the man again. 'Will you explain what you want? You must know, Rodya, this is the second time they have sent from the office; but it was another man last time, and I talked to him. Who was it came before?'

'That was the day before yesterday, I venture to say, if you please, sir. That was Alexey Semyonovitch; he is in our office, too.'

'He was more intelligent than you, don't you think so?'

'Yes, indeed, sir, he is of more weight than I am.'

'Quite so; go on.'

'At your mamma's request, through Afanasy Ivanovitch Vahrushin, of whom I presume you have heard more than once, a remittance is sent to you from our office,' the man began, addressing Raskolnikov. 'If you are in an intelligible condition, I've thirty-five roubles to remit to you, as Semyon Semyonovitch has received from Afanasy Ivanovitch at your mamma's request instructions to that effect, as on previous occasions. Do you know him, sir?'

'Yes, I remember . . . Vahrushin,' Raskolnikov said dreamily.

'You hear, he knows Vahrushin,' cried Razumihin. 'He is in "an intelligible condition"! And I see you are an intelligent man too. Well, it's always pleasant to hear words of wisdom.'

'That's the gentleman, Vahrushin, Afanasy Ivanovitch. And at the request of your mamma, who has sent you a remittance once before in the same manner through him, he did not refuse this time also, and sent instructions to Semyon Semyonovitch some days since to hand you thirty-five roubles in the hope of better to come.'

'That "hoping for better to come" is the best thing you've said, though "your mamma" is not bad either. Come then, what do you say? Is he fully conscious, eh?'

'That's all right. If only he can sign this little paper.'

'He can scrawl his name. Have you got the book?'

'Yes, here's the book.'

'Give it to me. Here, Rodya, sit up. I'll hold you. Take the pen and scribble "Raskolnikov" for him. For just now, brother, money is sweeter to us than treacle.'

'I don't want it,' said Raskolnikov, pushing away the pen.

'Not want it?'

'I won't sign it.'

'How the devil can you do without signing it?'

'I don't want . . . the money.'

'Don't want the money! Come, brother, that's nonsense, I bear witness. Don't trouble, please, it's only that he is on his travels again. But that's pretty common with him at all times though . . . You are a man of judgment and we will take him in hand, that is, more simply, take his hand and he will sign it. Here.'

'But I can come another time.'

'No, no. Why should we trouble you? You are a man of judgment . . . Now, Rodya, don't keep your visitor, you see he is waiting,' and he made ready to hold Raskolnikov's hand in earnest.

'Stop, I'll do it alone,' said the latter, taking the pen and signing his name.

The messenger took out the money and went away.

'Bravo! And now, brother, are you hungry?'

'Yes,' answered Raskolnikov.

'Is there any soup?'

'Some of yesterday's,' answered Nastasya, who was still standing there.

'With potatoes and rice in it?'

'Yes.'

'I know it by heart. Bring soup and give us some tea.'

'Very well.'

Raskolnikov looked at all this with profound astonishment and a dull, unreasoning terror. He made up his mind to keep quiet and see what would happen. 'I believe I am not wandering. I believe it's reality,' he thought.

In a couple of minutes Nastasya returned with the soup, and announced that the tea would be ready directly. With the soup she brought two spoons, two plates, salt, pepper, mustard for the beef, and so on. The table was set as it had not been for a long time. The cloth was clean.

'It would not be amiss, Nastasya, if Praskovya Pavlovna were to send us up a couple of bottles of beer. We could empty them.'

'Well, you are a cool hand,' muttered Nastasya, and she departed to carry out his orders.

Raskolnikov still gazed wildly with strained attention. Meanwhile Razumihin sat down on the sofa beside him, as clumsily as a bear put his left arm round Raskolnikov's head, although he was able to sit up, and with his right hand gave him a spoonful of soup, blowing on it that it might not burn him. But the soup was only just warm. Raskolnikov swallowed one spoonful greedily, then a second, then a third. But after giving him a few more spoonfuls of soup, Razumihin suddenly stopped, and said that he must ask Zossimov whether he ought to have more.

Nastasya came in with two bottles of beer.

'And will you have tea?'

'Yes.'

'Cut along, Nastasya, and bring some tea, for tea we may venture on without the faculty. But here is the beer!' He moved back to his chair, pulled the soup and meat in front of him, and began eating as though he had not touched food for three days.

'I must tell you, Rodya, I dine like this here every day now,' he mumbled with his mouth full of beef, 'and it's all Pashenka, your dear little landlady, who sees to that; she loves to do anything for me. I don't ask for it, but, of course, I don't object. And here's Nastasya with the tea. She is a quick girl. Nastasya, my dear, won't you have some beer?'

'Get along with your nonsense!'

'A cup of tea, then?'

'A cup of tea, maybe.'

'Pour it out. Stay, I'll pour it out myself. Sit down.'

He poured out two cups, left his dinner, and sat on the sofa again. As before, he put his left arm round the sick man's head, raised him up and gave him tea in spoonfuls, again blowing each spoonful steadily and earnestly, as though this process was the principal and most effective means towards his friend's recovery. Raskolnikov said nothing and made no resistance, though he felt quite strong enough to sit up on the sofa without support and could not merely have held a cup or spoon, but even perhaps could have walked about. But from some queer, almost animal, cunning he conceived the idea of hiding his strength and lying low for a time, pretending if necessary not to be yet in full possession of his faculties, and meanwhile listening to find out what was going on. Yet he could not overcome his sense of repugnance. After sipping a dozen spoonfuls of tea, he suddenly released his head, pushed the spoon away capriciously, and sank back on the pillow. There were actually real pillows under his head now, down pillows in clean cases, he observed that, too, and took note of it.

'Pashenka must give us some raspberry jam to-day to make him some raspberry tea,' said Razumihin, going back to his chair and attacking his soup and beer again.

'And where is she to get raspberries for you?' asked Nastasya, balancing a saucer on her five outspread fingers and sipping tea through a lump of sugar.

'She'll get it at the shop, my dear. You see, Rodya, all sorts of things have been happening while you have been laid up. When you decamped in that rascally way without leaving your address, I felt so angry that I resolved to find you out and punish you. I set to work that very day. How I ran about making inquiries for you! This lodging of yours I had forgotten, though I never remembered it, indeed, because I did not know it; and as for your old lodgings, I could only remember it was at the Five Corners, Harlamov's house. I kept trying to find that Harlamov's house, and afterwards it turned out that it was not Harlamov's, but Buch's. How one muddles up sounds sometimes! So I lost my temper, and I went on the chance to the address bureau next day, and only fancy, in two minutes they looked you up! Your name is down there.'

'My name!'

'I should think so; and yet a General Kobelev they could not find while I was there. Well, it's a long story. But as soon as I did land on this place, I soon got to know all your affairs – all, all, brother, I knew everything; Nastasya here will tell you. I made the acquaintance of Nikodim Fomitch and Ilya Petrovitch and the house-porter and Mr. Zametov, Alexandr Griforievitch, the head clerk in the police office, and, last but not least, of Pashenka; Nastasya here knows . . .'

'He's got round her,' Nastasya murmured, smiling slyly.

'Why don't you put the sugar in your tea, Nastasya Nikiforovna?'

'You are a one!' Nastasya cried suddenly, going off into a giggle. 'I am not Nikiforovna, but Petrovna,' she added suddenly, recovering from her mirth.

'I'll make a note of it. Well, brother, to make a long story short, I was going in for a regular explosion here to uproot all malignant influences in the locality, but Pashenka won the day. I had not expected, brother, to find her so . . . prepossessing. Eh, what do you think?'

Raskolnikov did not speak, but he still kept his eyes fixed upon him, full of alarm.

'And all that could be wished, indeed, in every respect,' Razumihin went on, not at all embarrassed by his silence.

'Ah, the sly dog!' Nastasya shrieked again. This conversation afforded her unspeakable delight.

'It's a pity, brother, that you did not set to work in the right way at first. You ought to have approached her differently. She is, so to speak, a most unaccountable character. But we will talk about her character later . . . How could you let things come to such a pass that she gave up sending you your dinner? And that I O U? You must have been mad to sign an I O U. And that promise of marriage when her daughter, Natalya Yegorovna, was alive? . . . I know all about it! But I see that's a delicate matter and I am an ass; forgive me. But, talking of foolishness, do you know Praskovya Pavlovna is not nearly so foolish as you would think at first sight?'

'No,' mumbled Raskolnikov, looking away, but feeling that it was better to keep up the conversation.

'She isn't, is she?' cried Razumihin, delighted to get an answer out of him. 'But she is not very clever either, eh? She is essentially, essentially an unaccountable character! I am sometimes quite at a loss, I assure you . . . She must be forty; she says she is thirty-six, and of course she has every right to say so. But I swear I judge her intellectually, simply from the metaphysical point of view; there is a sort of symbolism sprung up between us, a sort of algebra or what not! I don't understand it! Well, that's all nonsense. Only, seeing that you are not a student now and have lost your lessons and your clothes, and that through the young lady's death she has no need to treat you as a relation, she suddenly took fright; and as you hid in your den and dropped all your old relations with her, she planned to get rid of you. And she's been cherishing that design a long time, but was sorry to lose the I O U, for you assured her yourself that your mother would pay.'

'It was base of me to say that . . . My mother herself is almost a beggar . . . and I told a lie to keep my lodging . . . and be fed,' Raskolnikov said loudly and distinctly.

'Yes, you did very sensibly. But the worst of it is that at that point Mr. Tchebarov turns up, a business man. Pashenka would never have thought of doing anything on her own account, she is too retiring; but the business man is by no means retiring, and first thing he puts the question, "Is there any hope of realizing the I O U?" Answer; there is, because he has a mother who would save her Rodya with her hundred and twenty-five roubles pension, if she has to starve herself; and a sister, too, who would go into bondage for his sake. That's what he was building upon . . . Why do you start? I know all the ins and outs of your affairs now, my dear boy – it's not for nothing that you were so open with Pashenka when you were her prospective son-in-law, and I say all this as a friend . . . But I tell you what it is: an honest and sensitive man is open; and a business man "listens and goes on eating" you up. Well, then she gave the I O U by way of payment to this Tchebarov, and without hesitation he made a formal demand for payment. When I heard all of this I insisted on stopping the whole affair, engaging that you would pay. I went security for you, brother. Do you understand? We called Tchebarov, flung him ten roubles and got the I O U back from him, and here I have the honour of presenting it to you. She trusts your word now. Here, take it, you see I have torn it.'

Razumihin put the note on the table. Raskolnikov looked at him and turned to the wall without uttering a word. Even Razumihin felt a twinge.

'I see, brother,' he said a moment later, 'that I have been playing the fool again. I thought I should amuse you with my chatter, and I believe I have only made you cross.'

'Was it you I did not recognize when I was delirious?' Raskolnikov asked, after a moment's pause without turning his head.

'Yes, and you flew into a rage about it, especially when I brought Zametov one day.'

'Zametov? The head clerk? What for?' Raskolnikov turned round quickly and fixed his eyes on Razumihin.

'What's the matter with you? . . . What are you upset about? He wanted to make your acquaintance because I talked to him a lot about you . . . How could I have found out so much except from him? He is a capital fellow, brother, first rate . . . in his own way, of course. Now we are friends – see each other almost every day. I have moved into this part, you know. I have only just moved. I've been with him to Luise Ivanovna once or twice . . . Do you remember Luise, Luise Ivanovna?'

'Did I say anything in delirium?'

'I should think so! You were beside yourself.'

'What did I rave about?'

'What next? What did you rave about? What people do rave about . . .

Well, brother, now I must not lose time. To work.' He got up from the table and took up his cap.

'What did I rave about?'

'How he keeps on! Are you afraid of having let out some secret? Don't worry yourself; you said nothing about a countess. But you said a lot about a bulldog, and about earrings and chains, and about Krestovsky Island, and some porter, and Nikodim Fomitch and Ilya Petrovitch, the assistant superintendent. And another thing that was of special interest to you was your own sock. You whined, "Give me my sock" Zametov hunted all about your room for your socks, and with his own scented, ring-bedecked fingers he gave you the rag. And only then were you comforted, and for the next twenty-four hours you held the wretched thing in your hand; we could not get it from you. It is most likely somewhere under your quilt at this moment. And then you asked so piteously for fringe for your trousers. We tried to find out what sort of fringe, but we could not make it out. Now to business! Here are thirty-five roubles; I take ten of them, and shall give you an account of them in an hour or two. I will let Zossimov know at the same time, though he ought to have been here long ago, for it is nearly twelve. And you, Nastasya, look in pretty often while I am away, to see whether he wants a drink or anything else. And I will tell Pashenka what is wanted myself. Good-bye!'

'He calls her Pashenka! Ah, he's a deep one!' said Nastasya as he went out; then she opened the door and stood listening, but could not resist running downstairs after him. She was very eager to hear what he would say to the landlady. She was evidently quite fascinated by Razumihin.

No sooner had she left the room than the sick man flung off the bed-clothes and leapt out of bed like a madman. With burning, twitching impatience he had waited for them to be gone so that he might set to work. But to what work? Now, as though to spite him, it eluded him.

'Good God, only tell me one thing: do they know of it yet or not? What if they know it and are only pretending, mocking me while I am laid up, and then they will come in and tell me that it's been discovered long ago and that they have only . . . What am I to do now? That's what I've forgotten, as though on purpose; forgotten it all at once, I remembered a minute ago.'

He stood in the middle of the room and gazed in miserable bewilderment about him; he walked to the door, opened it, listened; but that was not what he wanted. Suddenly, as though recalling something, he rushed to the corner where there was a hole under the paper, began examining it, put his hand into the hole, fumbled – but that was not it. He went to the stove, opened it and began rummaging in the ashes; the frayed edges of his trousers and the rags cut off his pocket were lying there just as he had thrown them. No one had looked, then! Then he remembered the sock about which Razumihin had just been telling him. Yes, there it lay on the sofa under the quilt, but it was so covered with dust and grime that Zametov could not have seen anything on it.

'Bah, Zametov! The police office! And why am I sent for to the police office? Where's the notice? Bah! I am mixing it up: that was then. I looked at my sock then, too, but now . . . now I have been ill. But what did Zametov come for? Why did Razumihin bring him?' he muttered, helplessly sitting on the sofa again. 'What does it mean? Am I still in delirium, or is it real? I believe it is real . . . Ah, I remember; I must escape! Make haste to escape. Yes, I must, I must escape! Yes . . . but where? And where are my clothes? I've no boots. They've taken them away! They've hidden them! I understand! Ah, here is my coat – they passed that over! And here is money on the table, thank God! And here's the I O U . . . I'll take the money and go and take another lodging. They won't find me! . . . Yes, but the address bureau? They'll find me, Razumihin will find me. Better escape altogether . . . far away . . . to America, and let them do their worst! And take the I O U . . . it would be of use there . . . What else shall I take? They think I am ill! They don't know that I can walk, ha-ha-ha! I could see by their eyes that they know all about it! If only I could get downstairs! And what if they have set a watch there – policemen! What's this, tea? Ah, and here is a beer left, half a bottle, cold!'

He snatched up the bottle, which still contained a glassful of beer, and gulped it down with relish, as though quenching a flame in his breast. But in another minute the beer had gone to his head, and a faint and even pleasant shiver ran down his spine. He lay down and pulled the quilt over him. His sick and incoherent thoughts grew more and more disconnected, and soon a light, pleasant drowsiness came upon him. With a sense of comfort he nestled his head into the pillow, wrapped more closely about him the soft, wadded quilt which had replaced the old, ragged greatcoat, sighed softly and sank into a deep, sound, refreshing sleep.

He woke up, hearing someone come in. He opened his eyes and saw Razumihin standing in the doorway, uncertain whether to come in or not. Raskolnikov sat up quickly on the sofa and gazed at him, as though trying to recall something.

'Ah, you are not asleep! Here I am! Nastasya, bring in the parcel!' Razumihin shouted down the stairs. 'You shall have the account directly.'

'What time is it?' asked Raskolnikov, looking round uneasily.

'Yes, you had a fine sleep, brother, it's almost evening, it will be six o'clock directly. You have slept more than six hours.'

'Good heavens! Have I?'

'And why not? It will do you good. What's the hurry? A tryst, is it? We've all time before us. I've been waiting for the last three hours for you; I've been up twice and found you asleep. I've called on Zossimov twice: not at home, only fancy! But no matter, he will turn up. And I've been out on my own business, too. You know I've been moving to-day, moving with my uncle. I have an uncle living with me now. But that's no matter, to business. Give me the parcel, Nastasya. We will open it directly. And how do you feel now, brother?'

'I am quite well, I am not ill. Razumihin, have you been here long?'

'I tell you I've been waiting for the last three hours.'

'No, before.'

'How do you mean?'

'How long have you been coming here?'

'Why, I told you all about it this morning. Don't you remember?'

Raskolnikov pondered. The morning seemed like a dream to him. He could not remember alone, and looked inquiringly at Razumihin.

'Hm!' said the latter, 'he has forgotten. I fancied then that you were not quite yourself. Now you are better for your sleep. . . . You really look much better. First-rate! Well, to business. Look here, my dear boy.'

He began untying the bundle, which evidently interested him.

'Believe me, brother, this is something specially near my heart. For we must make a man of you. Let's begin from the top. Do you see this cap?' he said, taking out of the bundle a fairly good though cheap and ordinary cap. 'Let me try it on.'

'Presently, afterwards,' said Raskolnikov, waving it off pettishly.

'Come, Rodya my boy, don't oppose it, afterward will be too late; and I shan't sleep all night, for I bought it by guess, without measure. Just right!' he cried triumphantly, fitting it on, 'just your size! A proper head-covering is the first thing in dress and a recommendation in its own way. Tolstyakov, a friend of mine, is always obliged to take off his pudding basin when he goes into any public place where other people wear their hats or caps. People think he does it from slavish politeness, but it's simply because he is ashamed of his bird's nest; he is such a boastful fellow! Look, Nastasya, here are two specimens of headgear: this Palmerston' – he took from the corner Raskolnikov's old, battered hat, which for some unknown reason he called a Palmerston – 'or this jewel! Guess the price, Rodya, what do you suppose I paid for it, Nastasya?' he said, turning to her, seeing that Raskolnikov did not speak.

'Twenty copecks, no more, I dare say,' answered Nastasya.

'Twenty copecks, silly!' he cried, offended. 'Why, nowadays you would cost more than that – eighty copecks! And that only because it has been worn. And it's bought on condition that when it's worn out, they will give you another next year. Yes, on my word! Well, now let us pass to the United States of America, as they called them at school. I assure you I am proud of these breeches,' and he exhibited to Raskolnikov a pair of light, summer trousers of grey woollen material. 'No holes, no spots, and quite respectable, although a little worn; and a waistcoat to match, quite in the fashion. And its being worn really is an improvement, it's softer, smoother. . . . You see, Rodya, to my thinking, the great thing for getting on in the world is always to keep to the seasons; if you don't insist on having asparagus in January, you keep your money in your purse; and it's the same with this purchase. It's summer now, so I've been buying summer things – warmer materials will be wanted for autumn, so you will have to throw these away in any case . . . especially as they will be done for by then from their own lack of coherence if not your higher standard of luxury. Come, price them! What do you say? Two roubles twenty-five copecks! And remember the condition: if you wear these out, you will have another suit for nothing! They only do business on that system at Fedyaev's; if you've bought a thing once, you are satisfied for life, for you will never go there again of your own free will. Now for the boots. What do you say? You see that they are a bit worn, but they'll last a couple of months, for it's foreign work and foreign leather; the secretary of the English Embassy sold them last week – he had only worn them six days, but he was very short of cash. Price – a rouble and a half. A bargain?'

'But perhaps they won't fit,' observed Nastasya.

'Not fit? Just look!' and he pulled out of his pocket Raskolnikov's old, broken boot, stiffly coated with dry mud. 'I did not go empty-handed – they took the size from this monster. We all did our best. And as to your linen, your landlady has seen to that. Here, to begin with are three shirts, hempen but with a fashionable front. . . . Well now then, eighty copecks the cap, two roubles twenty-five copecks the suit – together three roubles five copecks – a rouble and a half for the boots – for you see, they are very good – and that makes four roubles fifty-five copecks; five roubles for the underclothes – they were bought in the lot – which makes exactly nine roubles fifty-five copecks. Forty-five copecks change in coppers. Will you take it? And so, Rodya, you are set up with a complete new rig-out, for your overcoat will serve, and even has a style of its own. That comes from getting one's clothes from Sharmer's! As for your socks and other things, I leave them to you; we've twenty-five roubles left. And as for Pashenka and paying for your lodging, don't you worry. I tell you she'll trust you for anything. And now, brother, let me change your linen, for I daresay you will throw off your illness with your shirt.'

'Let me be! I don't want to!' Raskolnikov waved him off. He had listened with disgust to Razumihin's efforts to be playful about his purchases.

'Come, brother, don't tell me I've been trudging around for nothing,' Razumihin insisted. 'Natasya, don't be bashful, but help me – that's it,' and in spite of Raskolnikov's resistance he changed his linen. The latter sank back on the pillows and for a minute or two said nothing.

'It will be long before I get rid of them,' he thought. 'What money was all that bought with?' he asked at last, gazing at the wall.

'Money? Why, your own, what the messenger brought from Vahrushin, your mother sent it. Have you forgotten that, too?'

'I remember now,' said Raskolnikov after a long, sullen silence. Razumihin looked at him, frowning and uneasy.

The door opened and a tall, stout man whose appearance seemed familiar to Raskolnikov came in.

'Zossimov! At last!' cried Razumihin, delighted.

❧ FOUR ❧

ZOSSIMOV WAS A TALL, FAT MAN with a puffy, colourless, cleanshaven face and straight flaxen hair. He wore spectacles, and a big gold ring on his fat finger. He was twenty-seven. He had on a light grey fashionable loose coat, light summer trousers, and everything about him loose, fashionable and spick and span; his linen was irreproachable, his watch-chain was massive. In manner he was slow and, as it were, nonchalant, and at the same time studiously free and easy; he made efforts to conceal his self-importance, but it was apparent at every instant. All his acquaintances found him tedious, but said he was clever at his work.

'I've been to you twice to-day, brother. You see, he's come to himself,' cried Razumihin.

'I see, I see; and how do we feel now, eh?' said Zossimov to Raskolnikov, watching him carefully and, sitting down at the foot of the sofa, he settled himself as comfortably as he could.

'He is still depressed,' Razumihin went on. 'We've just changed his linen and he almost cried.'

'That's very natural; you might have put it off if he did not wish it. . . . His pulse is first-rate. Is your head still aching, eh?'

'I am well, I am perfectly well!' Raskolnikov declared positively and irritably. He raised himself on the sofa and looked at them with glittering eyes, but sank back on to the pillow at once and turned to the wall. Zossimov watched him intently.

'Very good. . . . Going on all right,' he said lazily. 'Has he eaten anything?'

They told him, and asked what he might have.

'He may have anything . . . soup, tea . . . mushrooms and cucumbers, of course, you must not give him; he'd better not have meat either, and . . . but no need to tell you that!' Razumihin and he looked at each other. 'No more medicine or anything. I'll look at him again to-morrow. Perhaps, to-day even . . . but never mind . . .'

'To-morrow evening I shall take him for a walk,' said Razumihin. 'We are going to the Yusupov garden and then to the Palais de Cristal.'

'I would not disturb him to-morrow at all, but I don't know . . . a little, maybe . . . but we'll see.'

'Ach, what a nuisance! I've got a house-warming party to-night; it's only a step from here. Couldn't he come? He could lie on the sofa. You are coming?' Razumihin said to Zossimov. 'Don't forget, you promised.'

'All right, only rather later. What are you going to do?'

'Oh, nothing – tea, vodka, herrings. There will be a pie . . . just our friends.'

'And who?'

'All neighbours here, almost all new friends, except my old uncle, and he is new too – he only arrived in Petersburg yesterday to see to some business of his. We meet once in five years.'

'What is he?'

'He's been stagnating all his life as a district postmaster; gets a little pension. He is sixty-five – not worth talking about . . . But I am fond of him. Porfiry Petrovitch, the head of the Investigation Department here . . . But you know him.'

'Is he a relation of yours, too?'

'A very distant one. But why are you scowling? Because you quarrelled once, won't you come then?'

'I don't care a damn for him!'

'So much the better. Well, there will be some students, a teacher, a government clerk, a musician, an officer and Zametov.'

'Do tell me, please, what you or he' – Zossimov nodded at Raskolnikov – 'can have in common with this Zametov?'

'Oh, you particular gentleman! Principles! You are worked by principles, as it were by springs: you won't venture to turn round on your own account. If a man is a nice fellow, that's the only principle I go upon. Zametov is a delightful person.'

'Though he does take bribes.'

'Well, he does! and what of it? I don't care if he does take bribes,' Razumihin cried with unnatural irritability. 'I don't praise him for taking bribes. I only say he is a nice man in his own way! But if one looks at men in all ways – are there many good ones left? Why, I am sure I shouldn't be worth a baked onion myself . . . perhaps with you thrown in.'

'That's too little; I'd give two for you.'

'And I wouldn't give more than one for you. No more of your jokes! Zametov is no more than a boy, I can pull his hair and one must draw him and not repel him. You'll never improve a man by repelling him, especially a boy. One has to be twice as careful with a boy. Oh, you progressive dullards! You don't understand. You harm yourselves running another man down. . . . But if you want to know, we really have something in common.'

'I should like to know what.'

'Why, it's all about a house-painter. . . . We are getting him out of a mess! Though indeed there's nothing to fear now. The matter is absolutely self-evident. We only put on steam.'

'A painter?'

'Why, haven't I told you about it? I only told you the beginning then about the murder of the old pawnbroker-woman. Well, the painter is mixed up in it . . .'

'Oh, I heard about that murder before and was rather interested in it . . . partly . . . for one reason . . . I read about it in the papers, too. . . .'

'Lizaveta was murdered, too,' Nastasya blurted out, suddenly addressing Raskolnikov. She remained in the room all the time, standing by the door listening.

'Lizaveta,' murmured Raskolnikov hardly audible.

'Lizaveta, who sold old clothes. Didn't you know her? She used to come here. She mended a shirt for you, too.'

Raskolnikov turned to the wall where in the dirty, yellow paper he picked out one clumsy, white flower with brown lines on it and began examining how many petals there were in it, how many scallops in the petals and how many lines on them. He felt his arms and legs as lifeless as though they had been cut off. He did not attempt to move, but stared obstinately at the flower.

'But what about the painter?' Zossimov interrupted Nastasya's chatter with marked displeasure. She sighed and was silent.

'Why, he was accused of the murder,' Razumihin went on hotly.

'Was there evidence against him then?'

'Evidence, indeed! Evidence that was no evidence, and that's what we had to prove. It was just as they pitched on those fellows, Koch and Pestryakov, at first. Foo! how stupidly it's all done, it makes one sick, though it's not one's business! Pestryakov may be coming to-night. . . . By the way, Rodya, you've heard about the business already; it happened before you were ill, the day before you fainted at the police office while they were talking about it.'

Zossimov looked curiously at Raskolnikov. He did not stir.

'But I say, Razumihin. I wonder at you. What a busybody you are!' Zossimov observed.

'Maybe I am, but we will get him off anyway,' shouted Razumihin, bringing his fist down on the table. 'What's the most offensive is not their lying – one can always forgive lying – lying is a delightful thing, for it leads to truth – what is offensive is that they lie and worship their own lying. . . . I respect Porfiry, but . . . What threw them out at first? The door was locked, and when they came back with the porter it was open. So it followed that Koch and Pestryakov were the murderers – that was their logic!'

'But don't excite yourself; they simply detained them, they could not help that. . . . And, by the way, I've met that man Koch. He used to buy unredeemed pledges from the old woman? Eh?'

'Yes, he is a swindler. He buys up bad debts, too. He makes a profession of it. But enough of him! Do you know what makes me angry? It's their sickening, rotten, petrified routine. . . . And this case might be the means of introducing a new method. One can show from the psychological data alone how to get on the track of the real man. "We have facts," they say. But facts are not everything – at least half the business lies in how you interpret them!'

'Can you interpret them, then?'

'Anyway, one can't hold one's tongue when one has a feeling, a tangible feeling, that one might be a help if only . . . Eh? Do you know the details of the case?'

'I am waiting to hear about the painter.'

'Oh yes! Well, here's the story. Early on the third day after the murder, when they were still dandling Koch and Pestryakov – though they accounted for every step they took and it was as plain as a pikestaff – an unexpected fact turned up. A peasant called Dushkin, who keeps a dram-shop facing the house, brought to the police office a jeweller's case containing some gold ear-rings, and told a long rigmarole. "The day before yesterday, just after eight o'clock" – mark the day and the hour! – "a journeyman house-painter, Nikolay, who had been in to see me already that day, brought me this box of gold ear-rings and stones, and asked me to give him two roubles for them. When I asked him where he got them, he said that he picked them up in the street. I did not ask him anything more." I am telling you Dushkin's story. "I gave him a note" – a rouble, that is – "for I thought if he did not pawn it with me he would with another. It would all come to the same thing – he'd spend it on drink, so the thing had better be with me. The further you hide it the quicker you will find it, and if anything turns up, if I hear any rumours, I'll take it to the police." Of course, that's all taradiddle; he lies like a horse, for I know this Dushkin, he is a pawnbroker and a receiver of stolen goods, and he did not cheat Nikolay out of a thirty-rouble trinket in order to give it to the police. He was simply afraid. But no matter, to return to Dushkin's story. "I've known this peasant, Nikolay Dementyev, from a child; he comes from the same province and district of Zaraïsk, we are both Ryazan men. And though Nikolay is not a drunkard, he drinks, and I knew he had a job in that house, painting, working with Dmitri, who comes from the same village, too. As soon as he got the rouble, he changed it, had a couple of glasses, took his change and went out. But I did not see Dmitri with him then. And the next day I heard that someone had murdered Alyona Ivanovna and her sister, Lizaveta Ivanovna, with an axe. I knew then, and I felt suspicious about the ear-rings at once, for I knew the murdered woman lent money on pledges. I went to the house, and began to make careful inquiries without saying a word to anyone. First of all I asked, 'Is Nikolay here?' Dmitri told me that Nikolay had gone off on the spree; he had come home at daybreak drunk, stayed in the house about ten minutes, and went out again. Dmitri didn't see him again and is finishing the job alone. And their job is on the same staircase as the murder, on the second floor. When I heard all that I did not say a word to anyone" – that's Dushkin's tale – "but I found out what I could about the murder, and went home feeling as suspicious as ever. And at eight o'clock this morning" – that was the third day, you understand – "I saw Nikolay coming in, not sober, though not to say very drunk – he could understand what was said to him. He sat down on the bench and did not speak. There was only one stranger in the bar and a man I knew asleep on a bench and our two boys. 'Have you seen Dmitri?' said I. 'No, I haven't,' said he. 'And you've not been here either?' 'Not since the day before yesterday,' said he. 'And where did you sleep last night?' 'In Peski, with the Kolomensky men.' 'And where did you get those ear-rings?' I asked. 'I found them in the street,' and the way he said it was a bit queer; he did not look at me. 'Did you hear what happened that very evening, at the very hour, on that same staircase?' said I. 'No,' said he, 'I had not heard,' and all the while he was listening, his eyes were starting out of his head and he turned as white as chalk. I told him all about it and he took his hat and began getting up. I wanted to keep him. 'Wait a bit, Nikolay,' said I, 'won't you have a drink?' And I signed to the boy to hold the door, and I came out from behind the bar; but he darted out and down the street to the turning at a run. I have not seen him since. Then my doubts were at an end – it was his doing, as clear as could be. . . ." '

'I should think so,' said Zossimov.

'Wait! Hear the end. Of course they sought high and low for Nikolay; they detained Dushkin and searched his house; Dmitri, too, was arrested; the Kolomensky men also were turned inside out. And the day before yesterday they arrested Nikolay in a tavern at the end of the town. He had gone there, taken the silver cross off his neck and asked for a dram for it. They gave it to him. A few minutes afterwards the woman went to the cowshed, and through a crack in the wall she saw in the stable adjoining he had made a noose of his sash from the beam, stood on a block of wood, and was trying to put his neck in the noose. The woman screeched her hardest; people ran in. "So that's what you are up to!" "Take me," he says, "to such-and-such a police office; I'll confess everything." Well, they took him to that police station – that is here – with a suitable escort. So they asked him this and that, how old he is, "twenty-two," and so on. At the question, "When you were working with Dmitri, didn't you see anyone on the staircase at such-and-such a time?" – answer: "To be sure folks may have gone up and down, but I did not notice them." "And didn't you hear anything, any noise, and so on?" "We heard nothing special." "And did you hear, Nikolay, that on the same day Widow So-and-so and her sister were murdered and robbed?" "I never knew a thing about it. The first I heard of it was from Afanasy Pavlovitch the day before yesterday." "And where did you find the ear-rings?" "I found them on the pavement." "Why didn't you go to work with Dmitri the other day?" "Because I was drinking." "And where were you drinking?" "Oh in such-and-such a place." "And why did you run away from Dushkin's?" "Because I was awfully frightened." "What were you frightened of?" "That I should be accused." "How could you be frightened if you felt free from guilt?" Now, Zossimov, you may not believe me, that question was put literally in those words. I know it for a fact, it was repeated to me exactly! What do you say to that?'

'Well, anyway, there's the evidence.'

'I am not talking of the evidence now, I am talking about that question, of their own idea of themselves. Well, so they squeezed and squeezed him and he confessed: "I did not find it in the street but in the flat where I was painting with Dmitri." "And how was that?" "Why, Dmitri and I were painting there all day, and we were just getting ready to go, and Dmitri took a brush and painted my face, and he ran off and I after him. I ran after him, shouting my hardest, and at the bottom of the stairs I ran right against the porter and some gentlemen – and how many gentlemen were there I don't remember. And the porter swore at me, and the other porter swore, too, and the porter's wife came out, and swore at us, too; and a gentleman came into the entry with a lady, and he swore at us, too, for Dmitri and I lay right across the way. I got hold of Dmitri's hair and knocked him down and began beating him. And Dmitri, too, caught me by the hair and began beating me. But we did it all not for temper but in a friendly way, for sport. And then Dmitri escaped and ran into the street, and I ran after him; but I did not catch him, and went back to the flat alone; I had to clear up my things. I began putting them together, expecting Dmitri to come, and there in the passage, in the corner by the door, I stepped on the box. I saw it lying there wrapped up in paper. I took off the paper, saw some little hooks, undid them, and in the box were the ear-rings. . . .'"

'Behind the door? Lying behind the door? Behind the door?' Raskolnikov cried suddenly, staring with a blank look of terror at Razumihin, and he slowly sat up on the sofa, leaning on his hand.

'Yes . . . why? What's the matter? What's wrong?' Razumihin, too, got up from his set.

'Nothing,' Raskolnikov answered faintly, turning to the wall. All were silent for a while.

'He must have waked from a dream,' Razumihin said at last, looking inquiringly at Zossimov. The latter slightly shook his head.

'Well, go on,' said Zossimov. 'What next?'

'What next? As soon as he saw the ear-rings, forgetting Dmitri and everything, he took up his cap and ran to Dushkin and, as we know, got a rouble from him. He told a lie saying he found them in the street, and went off drinking. He keeps repeating his old story about the murder: "I know nothing of it, never heard of it till the day before yesterday." "And why didn't you come to the police till now?" "I was frightened." "And why did you try to hang yourself?" "From anxiety." "What anxiety?" "That I should be accused of it." Well, that's the whole story. And now what do you suppose they deduced from that?'

'Why, there's no supposing. There's a clue, such as it is, a fact. You wouldn't have your painter set free?'

'Now they've simply taken him for the murderer. They haven't a shadow of doubt.'

'That's nonsense. You are excited. But what about the ear-rings? You must admit that if, on the very same day and hour ear-rings from the old woman's box have come into Nikolay's hands, they must have come there somewhere. That's a good deal in such a case.'

'How did they get there? How did they get there?' cried Razumihin.

'How can you, a doctor, whose duty it is to study man and who has more opportunity than anyone else for studying human nature – how can you fail to see the character of the man in the whole story? Don't you see at once that the answers he has give in the examination are the holy truth? They came into his hands precisely as he has told us – he stepped on the box and picked it up.'

'The holy truth! But didn't he own himself that he told a lie at first?'

'Listen to me, listen attentively. The porter and Koch and Pestryakov and the other porter and the wife of the first porter and the woman who was sitting in the porter's lodge and the man Kryukov, who had just got out of a cab at that minute and went in at the entry with a lady on his arm, that is eight or ten witnesses, agree that Nikolay had Dmitri on the ground, was lying on him beating him, while Dmitri hung on to his hair, beating him, too. They lay right across the way, blocking the thoroughfare. They were sworn at on all sides while they "like children" (the very words of the witnesses) were falling over one another, squealing, fighting and laughing with the funniest faces, and, chasing one another like children, they ran into the street. Now take careful note. The bodies upstairs were warm, you understand, warm when they found them! If they, or Nikolay alone, had murdered them and broken open the boxes, or simply taken part in the robbery, allow me to ask you one question: do their state of mind, their squeals and giggles and scuffling at the gate fit in with axes, bloodshed, fiendish cunning, robbery? They'd just killed them, not five or ten minutes before, for the bodies were still warm, and at once, leaving the flat open, knowing that people would go there at once, flinging away their booty, they rolled about like children, laughing and attracting general attention. And there are a dozen witnesses to swear to that!'

'Of course it is strange! It's impossible, indeed, but . . .'

'No, brother, no *buts*. And if the ear-rings being found in Nikolay's hands at the very day and hour of the murder constitutes an important piece of circumstantial evidence against him – although the explanation given by him accounts for it, and therefore it does not tell seriously against him – one must take into consideration the facts which prove him innocent, especially as they are facts that *cannot be denied*. And do you suppose, from the character of our legal system, that they will accept, or that they are in a position to accept, this fact – resting simply on a psychological impossibility – as irrefutable and conclusively breaking down the circumstantial evidence for the prosecution? No, they won't accept it, they certainly won't, because they found the jewel-case and the man tried to hang himself, "which he could not have done if he hadn't felt guilty". That's the point, that's what excites me, you must understand!'

'Oh, I see you are excited! Wait a bit. I forgot to ask you; what proof is there that the box came from the old woman?'

'That's been proved,' said Razumihin with apparent reluctance, frowning. 'Koch recognised the jewel-case and gave the name of the owner, who proved conclusively that it was his.'

'That's bad. Now another point. Did anyone see Nikolay at the time that Koch and Pestryakov were going upstairs at first, and is there no evidence about that?'

'Nobody did see him,' Razumihin answered with vexation. 'That's the worst of it. Even Koch and Pestryakov did not notice them on their way upstairs, though, indeed, their evidence could not have been worth much. They said they saw the flat was open, and that there must be work going on in it, but they took no special notice and could not remember whether there actually were men at work in it.'

'Hm! . . . So the only evidence for the defence is that they were beating one another and laughing. That constitutes a strong presumption, but . . . How do you explain the facts yourself?'

'How do I explain them? What is there to explain? It's clear. At any rate, the direction in which explanation is to be sought is clear, and the jewel-case points to it. The real murderer dropped those ear-rings. The murderer was upstairs, locked in, when Koch and Pestryakov knocked at the door. Koch, like an ass, did not stay at the door; so the murderer popped out and ran down, too; for he had no other way of escape. He hid from Koch, Pestryakov and the porter in the flat when Nikolay and Dmitri had just run out of it. He stopped there while the porter and others were going upstairs, waited till they were out of hearing, and then went calmly downstairs at the very minute when Dmitri and Nikolay ran out into the street and there was no one in the entry; possibly he was seen, but not noticed. There are lots of people going in and out. He must have dropped the ear-rings out of his pocket when he stood behind the door, and did not notice he dropped them, because he had other things to think of. The jewel-case is a conclusive proof that he did stand there . . . That's how I explain it.'

'Too clever! No, my boy, you're too clever. That beats everything!'

'But, why, why?'

'Why, because everything fits too well . . . it's too melodramatic.'

'A-ach!' Razumihin was exclaiming, but at the moment the door opened and a personage came in who was a stranger to all present.

⇥ FIVE ⇤

THIS WAS A GENTLEMAN NO LONGER young, of a stiff and portly appearance, and a cautious and sour countenance. He began by stopping short in the doorway, staring about him with offensive and undisguised astonishment, as though asking himself what sort of place he had come to. Mistrustfully and with an affectation of being alarmed and almost affronted, he scanned Raskolnikov's low and narrow 'cabin'. With the same amazement he stared at Raskolnikov, who lay undressed, dishevelled, unwashed, on his miserable dirty sofa, looking fixedly at him. Then with the same deliberation he scrutinised the uncouth, unkempt figure and unshaven face of Razumihin, who looked him boldly and inquiringly in the face without rising from his seat. A constrained silence lasted for a couple of minutes and then, as might be expected, some scene-shifting took place. Reflecting, probably from certain fairly unmistakable signs, that he would get nothing in this 'cabin' by attempting to overawe them, the gentleman softened somewhat, and civilly, though with some severity, emphasizing every syllable of his question, addressed Zossimov:

'Rodion Romanovitch Raskolnikov, a student, or formerly a student?'

Zossimov made a slight movement, and would have answered, had not Razumihin anticipated him.

'Here he is lying on the sofa. What do you want?'

This familiar 'what do you want?' seemed to cut the ground from the feet of the pompous gentleman. He was turning to Razumihin, but checked himself in time and turned to Zossimov again.

'This is Raskolnikov,' mumbled Zossimov, nodding towards him. Then he gave a prolonged yawn, opening his mouth as widely as possible. Then he lazily put his hand into his waistcoat-pocket, pulled out a huge gold watch in a round hunter's case, opened it, looked at it and as slowly and lazily proceeded to put it back.

Raskolnikov himself lay without speaking, on his back, gazing persistently, though without understanding, at the stranger. Now that his face was turned away from the strange flower on the paper, it was extremely pale and wore a look of anguish, as though he had just undergone an agonising operation or just been taken from the rack. But the new-comer gradually began to arouse his attention, then his wonder, then suspicion and even alarm. When Zossimov said 'This is Raskolnikov' he jumped up quickly, sat on the sofa and with an almost defiant, but weak and breaking, voice articulated:

'Yes, I am Raskolnikov! What do you want?'

The visitor scrutinised him and pronounced impressively:

'Pyotr Petrovitch Luzhin. I believe I have reason to hope that my name is not wholly unknown to you?'

But Raskolnikov, who had expected something quite different, gazed blankly and dreamily at him, making no reply, as though he heard the name of Pyotr Petrovitch for the first time.

'Is it possible that you can up to the present have received no information?' asked Pyotr Petrovitch somewhat disconcerted.

In reply Raskolnikov sank languidly back on the pillow, put his hands behind his head and gazed at the ceiling. A look of dismay came into Luzhin's face. Zossimov and Razumihin stared at him more inquisitively than ever, and at last he showed unmistakable signs of embarrassment.

'I had presumed and calculated,' he faltered, 'that a letter posted more than ten days, if not a fortnight ago . . .'

'I say, why are you standing in the doorway?' Razumihin interrupted suddenly. 'If you've something to say, sit down. Nastasya and you are so crowded. Nastasya, make room. Here's a chair, thread your way in!'

He moved his chair back from the table, made a little space between the table and his knees, and waited in a rather cramped position for the visitor to 'thread his way in'. The minute was so chosen that it was impossible to refuse, and the visitor squeezed his way through, hurrying and stumbling. Reaching the chair, he sat down, looking suspiciously at Razumihin.

'No need to be nervous,' the latter blurted out. 'Rodya has been ill for the last five days and delirious for three, but now he is recovering and has got an appetite. This is his doctor, who has just had a look at him. I am a comrade of Rodya's, like him, formerly a student, and now I am nursing him; so don't you take any notice of us, but go on with your business.'

'Thank you. But shall I not disturb the invalid by my presence and conversation?' Pyotr Petrovitch asked of Zossimov.

'N-no,' mumbled Zossimov; 'you may amuse him.' He yawned again.

'He has been conscious a long time, since this morning,' went on Razumihin, whose familiarity seemed so much like unaffected, good-nature that Pyotr Petrovitch began to be more cheerful, partly, perhaps, because this shabby and impudent person had introduced himself as a student.

'Your mamma,' began Luzhin.

'Hm!' Razumihin cleared his throat loudly. Luzhin looked at him inquiringly.

'That's all right, go on.'

Luzhin shrugged his shoulders.

'Your mamma had commenced a letter to you while I was sojourning in her neighbourhood. On my arrival here I purposely allowed a few days to elapse before coming to see you, in order that I might be fully assured that you were in full possession of the tidings; but now, to my astonishment . . .'

'I know, I know!' Raskolnikov cried suddenly with impatient vexation. 'So you are the *fiancé*? I know, and that's enough.'

There was no doubt about Pyotr Petrovitch's being offended this time, but he said nothing. He made a violent effort to understand what it all meant. There was a moment's silence.

Meanwhile, Raskolnikov, who had turned a little towards him when he answered, began suddenly staring at him again with marked curiosity, as though he had not had a good look at him yet, or as though something new had struck him; he rose from his pillow on purpose to stare at him. There certainly was something peculiar in Pyotr Petrovitch's whole appearance, something which seemed to justify the title of 'fiancé' so unceremoniously applied to him. In the first place, it was evident, far too much so indeed, that Pyotr Petrovitch had made eager use of his few days in the capital to get himself up and rig himself out in expectation of his betrothed – a perfectly innocent and permissible proceeding, indeed. Even his own, perhaps too complacent, consciousness of the agreeable improvement in his appearance might have been forgiven in such circumstances, seeing that Pyotr Petrovitch had taken up the rôle of fiancé. All his clothes were fresh from the tailor's and were all right, except for being too new and too distinctly appropriate. Even the stylish new round hat had the same significance. Pyotr Petrovitch treated it too respectfully and held it too carefully in his hands. The exquisite pair of lavender gloves, real Louvain, told the same tale, if only from the fact of his not wearing them, but carrying them in his hand for show. Light and youthful colours predominated in Pyotr Petrovitch's attire. He wore a charming summer jacket of a fawn shade, light thin trousers, a waistcoat of the same, new and fine linen, a cravat of the lightest cambric with pink stripes on it, and the best of it was, this all suited Pyotr Petrovitch. His very fresh and even handsome face looked younger than his forty-five years at all times. His dark, mutton-chop whiskers made an agreeable setting on both sides, growing thickly upon his shining, clean-shaven chin. Even his hair, touched here and there with grey, though it had been combed and curled at a hairdresser's, did not give him a stupid appearance, as curled hair usually does, by inevitably suggesting a German on his wedding day. If there really was something unpleasing and repulsive in his rather good-looking and imposing countenance, it was due to quite other causes. After scanning Mr. Luzhin unceremoniously, Raskolnikov smiled malignantly, sank back on the pillow and stared at the ceiling as before.

But Mr. Luzhin hardened his heart and seemed to determine to take no notice of their oddities.

'I feel the greatest regret at finding you in this situation,' he began, again breaking the silence with an effort. 'If I had been aware of your illness I should have come earlier. But you know what business is. I have, too, a very important legal affair in the Senate, not to mention other preoccupations which you may well conjecture. I am expecting your mamma and sister any minute.'

Raskolnikov made a movement and seemed about to speak; his face showed some excitement. Pyotr Petrovitch paused, waited, but as nothing followed, he went on:

'. . . Any minute. I have found a lodging for them on their arrival.'

'Where?' asked Raskolnikov weakly.

'Very near here, in Bakaleyev's house.'

'That's in Voskresensky,' put in Razumihin. 'There are two storeys of rooms, let by a merchant called Yushin; I've been there.'

'Yes, rooms . . .'

'A disgusting place – filthy, stinking and, what's more, of doubtful character. Things have happened there, and there are all sorts of queer people living there. And I went there about a scandalous business. It's cheap, though . . .'

'I could not, of course, find out so much about it, for I am a stranger in Petersburg myself,' Pyotr Petrovitch replied huffily. 'However, the two rooms are exceedingly clean, and as it is for so short a time . . . I have already taken a permanent, that is, our future flat,' he said, addressing Raskolnikov, 'and I am having it done up. And meanwhile I am myself cramped for room in a lodging with my friend Andrey Semyonovitch Lebeziatnikov, in the flat of Madame Lippeveschsel; it was he who told me of Bakaleyev's house, too . . .'

'Lebeziatnikov?' said Raskolnikov slowly, as if recalling something.

'Yes, Andrey Semyonovitch Lebeziatnikov, a clerk in the Ministry. Do you know him?'

'Yes . . . no,' Raskolnikov answered.

'Excuse me, I fancied so from your inquiry. I was once his guardian. . . . A very nice young man and advanced. I like to meet young people: one learns new things from them.' Luzhin looked round hopefully at them all.

'How do you mean?' asked Razumihin.

'In the most serious and essential matters,' Pyotr Petrovitch replied, as though delighted at the question. 'You see, it's ten years since I visited Petersburg. All the novelties, reforms, ideas have reached us in the provinces, but to see it all more clearly one must be in Petersburg. And it's my notion that you observe and learn most by watching the younger generation. And I confess I am delighted . . .'

'At what?'

'Your question is a wide one. I may be mistaken, but I fancy I find clearer views, more, so to say, criticism, more practicality . . .'

'That's true,' Zossimov let drop.

'Nonsense! There's no practicality.' Razumihin flew at him. 'Practicality is a difficult thing to find; it does not drop down from heaven. And for the last two hundred years we have been divorced from all practical life. Ideas, if you like, are fermenting,' he said to Pyotr Petrovitch, 'and desire for good exists, though it's in a childish form, and honesty you may find, although there are crowds of brigands. Anyway, there's no practicality. Practicality goes well shod.'

'I don't agree with you,' Pyotr Petrovitch replied, with evident enjoyment. 'Of course, people do get carried away and make mistakes, but one must have indulgence; those mistakes are merely evidence of enthusiasm for the cause and of abnormal external environment. If little has been done, the time has been but short; of means I will not speak. It's my personal view, if you care to know, that something has been accomplished already. New valuable ideas, new valuable works are circulating in the place of our old dreamy and romantic authors. Literature is taking a maturer form, many injurious prejudices have been rooted up and turned into ridicule. . . . In a word, we have cut ourselves off irrevocably from the past, and that, to my thinking, is a great thing . . .'

'He's learnt it by heart to show off' Raskolnikov pronounced suddenly.

'What?' asked Pyotr Petrovitch, not catching his words; but he received no reply.

'That's all true,' Zossimov hastened to interpose.

'Isn't it so?' Pyotr Petrovitch went on, glancing affably at Zossimov. 'You must admit,' he went on, addressing Razumihin with a shade of triumph and superciliousness – he almost added 'young man' – 'that there is an advance, or, as they say now, progress in the name of science and economic truth . . .'

'A commonplace.'

'No, not a commonplace! Hitherto, for instance, if I were told, "love they neighbour", what came of it?' Pyotr Petrovitch went on, perhaps with excessive haste. 'It came to my tearing my coat in half to share with my neighbour and we both were left half naked. As a Russian proverb has it, "Catch several hares and you won't catch one". Science now tells us, love yourself before all men, for everything in the world rests on self-interest. You love yourself and manage your own affairs properly and your coat remains whole. Economic truth adds that the better private affairs are organized in society – the more whole coats, so to say – the firmer are its foundations and the better is the common welfare organized too. Therefore, in acquiring wealth solely and exclusively for myself, I am acquiring, so to speak, for all, and helping to bring to pass my neighbour's getting a little more than a torn coat; and that not from private, personal liberality, but as a consequence of the general advance. The idea is simple, but unhappily it has been a long time reaching us, being hindered by idealism and sentimentality. And yet it would seem to want very little wit to perceive it . . .'

'Excuse me, I've very little wit myself,' Razumihin cut in sharply, 'and so let us drop it. I began this discussion with an object, but I've grown so sick during the last three years of this chattering to amuse oneself, of this incessant flow of commonplaces, always the same, that, by Jove, I blush even when other people talk like that. You are in a hurry, no doubt, to exhibit your acquirements; and I don't blame you, that's quite pardonable. I only wanted to find out what sort of man you are, for so many unscrupulous people have got hold of the progressive cause of late and have so distorted in their own interests everything they touched, that the whole cause has been dragged in the mire. That's enough!'

'Excuse me, sir,' said Luzhin, affronted, and speaking with excessive dignity. 'Do you mean to suggest so unceremoniously that I too . . .'

'Oh, my dear sir . . . how could I? . . . Come, that's enough,' Razumihin concluded, and he turned abruptly to Zossimov to continue their previous conversation.

Pyotr Petrovitch had the good sense to accept the disavowal. He made up his mind to take leave in another minute or two.

'I trust our acquaintance,' he said, addressing Raskolnikov, 'may, upon your recovery and in view of the circumstances of which you are aware, become closer . . . Above all, I hope for your return to health . . .'

Raskolnikov did not even turn his head. Pyotr Petrovitch began getting up from his chair.

'One of her customers must have killed her,' Zossimov declared positively.

'Not a doubt of it,' replied Razumihin. 'Porfiry doesn't give his opinion, but is examining all who have pledges with her there.'

'Examining them?' Raskolnikov asked aloud.

'Yes. What then?'

'Nothing.'

'How does he get hold of them?' asked Zossimov.

'Koch has given the names of some of them, other names are on the wrappers of the pledges and some have come forward of themselves.'

'It must have been a cunning and practised ruffian! The boldness of it! The coolness!'

'That's just what it wasn't!' interposed Razumihin. 'That's what throws you all off the scent. But I maintain that he is not cunning, not practised, and probably this was his first crime! The supposition that it was a calculated crime and a cunning criminal doesn't work. Suppose him to have been inexperienced, and it's clear that it was only a chance that saved him – and chance may do anything. Why, he did not foresee obstacles, perhaps! And how did he set to work? He took jewels worth ten or twenty roubles, stuffing his pockets with them, ransacked the old woman's trunks, her rags – and they found fifteen hundred roubles, besides notes, in a box in the top drawer of the chest! He did not know how to rob; he could only murder. It was his first crime, I assure you, his first crime; he lost his head. And he got off more by luck than good counsel!'

'You are talking of the murder of the old pawnbroker. I believe?' Pyotr Petrovitch put in, addressing Zossimov. He was standing, hat and gloves in hand, but before departing he felt disposed to throw off a few more intellectual phrases. He was evidently anxious to make a favourable impression and his vanity overcame his prudence.

'Yes. You've heard of it?'

'Oh, yes, being in the neighbourhood.'

'Do you know the details?'

'I can't say that; but another circumstance interests me in the case – the whole question, so to say. Not to speak of the fact that crime has been greatly on the increase among the lower classes during the last five years, not to speak of the cases of robbery and arson everywhere, what strikes me as the strangest thing is that in the higher classes, too, crime is increasing proportionately. In one place one hears of a student's robbing the mail on the high road; in another place people of good social position forge false banknotes; in Moscow of late a whole gang has been captured who used to forge lottery tickets, and one of the ringleaders was a lecturer in universal history; then our secretary abroad was murdered from some obscure motive of gain . . . And if this old woman, the pawnbroker, has been murdered by someone of a higher class in society – for peasants don't pawn gold trinkets – how are we to explain this demoralisation of the civilised part of our society?'

'There are many economic changes,' put in Zossimov.

'How are we to explain it?' Razumihin caught him up. 'It might be explained by our inveterate impracticality.'

'How do you mean?'

'What answer had your lecturer in Moscow to make to the question why he was forging notes? "Everybody is getting rich one way or another, so I want to make haste to get rich too." I don't remember the exact words, but the upshot was that he wants money for nothing, without waiting or working! We've grown used to having everything ready-made, to walking on crutches, to having our food chewed for us. Then the great hour struck,* and every man showed himself in his true colours.'

'But morality? And so to speak, principles . . .'

'But why do you worry about it?' Raskolnikov interposed suddenly. 'It's in accordance with your theory!'

'In accordance with my theory?'

'Why, carry out logically the theory you were advocating just now, and it follows that people may be killed . . .'

'Upon my word!' cried Luzhin.

'No, that's not so,' put in Zossimov.

Raskolnikov lay with a white face and twitching upper lip, breathing painfully.

'There's a measure in all things,' Luzhin went on superciliously. 'Economic ideas are not an incitement to murder, and one has but to suppose . . .'

'And is it true,' Raskolnikov interposed once more suddenly, again in a voice quivering with fury and delight in insulting him, 'is it true that you told your *fiancée* . . . within an hour of her acceptance, that what pleased you most . . . was that she was a beggar . . . because it was better to raise a wife from poverty, so that you may have complete control over her, and reproach her with your being her benefactor?'

'Upon my word!' Luzhin cried wrathfully and irritably, crimson with confusion, 'to distort my words in this way! Excuse me, allow me to assure you that the report which has reached you, or rather, let me say, has been conveyed to you, has no foundation in truth, and I . . . suspect who . . . in a word . . . this arrow . . . in a word, your mamma . . . She seemed to me in other things, with all her excellent qualities, of a somewhat high-flown and romantic way of thinking. . . . But I was a thousand miles from supposing that she would misunderstand and misrepresent things in so fanciful a way. . . . And indeed . . . indeed . . .'

* The emancipation of the serfs in 1861 is meant. – TRANSLATOR'S NOTES.

'I tell you what,' cried Raskolnikov, raising himself on his pillow and fixing his piercing, glittering eyes upon him, 'I tell you what.'

'What?' Luzhin stood still, waiting with a defiant and offended face. Silence lasted for some seconds.

'Why, if ever again . . . you dare to mention a single word . . . about my mother . . . I shall send you flying downstairs!'

'What's the matter with you?' cried Razumihin.

'So that's how it is?' Luzhin turned pale and bit his lip. 'Let me tell you, sir,' he began deliberately, doing his utmost to restrain himself but breathing hard, 'at the first moment I saw you were ill-disposed to me, but I remained here on purpose to find out more. I could forgive a great deal in a sick man and a connection, but you . . . never after this . . .'

'I am not ill,' cried Raskolnikov.

'So much the worse . . .'

'Go to hell!'

But Luzhin was already leaving without finishing his speech, squeezing between the table and the chair; Razumihin got up this time to let him pass. Without glancing at anyone, and not even nodding to Zossimov, who had for some time been making signs to him to let the sick man alone, he went out, lifting his hat to the level of his shoulder to avoid crushing it as he stooped to go out of the door. And even the curve of his spine was expressive of the horrible insult he had received.

'How could you – how could you!' Razumihin said, shaking his head in perplexity.

'Let me alone – let me alone, all of you!' Raskolnikov cried in a frenzy. 'Will you ever leave off tormenting me? I am not afraid of you! I am not afraid of anyone, anyone now! Get away from me! I want to be alone, alone, alone!'

'Come along,' said Zossimov, nodding to Razumihin.

'But we can't leave him like this!'

'Come along,' Zossimov repeated insistently, and he went out. Razumihin thought a minute and ran to overtake him.

'It might be worse not to obey him,' said Zossimov on the stairs. 'He mustn't be irritated.

'What's the matter with him?'

'If only he could get some favourable shock, that's what would do it! At first he was better . . . You know he has got something on his mind! Some fixed idea weighing on him. . . . I am very much afraid so; he must have!'

'Perhaps it's that gentleman, Pyotr Petrovitch. From his conversation I gather he is going to marry his sister, and that he had received a letter about it just before his illness . . .'

'Yes, confound the man! he may have upset the case altogether. But have you noticed, he takes no interest in anything, he does not respond to anything except one point on which he seems excited – that's the murder?'

'Yes, yes,' Razumihin agreed, 'I noticed that, too. He is interested, frightened. It gave him a shock on the day he was ill in the police office; he fainted.'

'Tell me more about that this evening and I'll tell you something afterwards. He interests me very much! In half an hour I'll go and see him again. . . . There'll be no inflammation though.'

'Thanks! And I'll wait with Pashenka meantime and will keep watch on him through Nastasya. . . .'

Raskolnikov, left alone, looked with impatience and misery at Nastasya, but she still lingered.

'Won't you have some tea now?' she asked.

'Later! I am sleepy! Leave me.'

He turned abruptly to the wall; Nastasya went out.

✦ SIX ✦

BUT AS SOON AS SHE WENT OUT, he got up, latched the door, undid the parcel which Razumihin had brought in that evening and had tied up again, and began dressing. Strange to say, he seemed immediately to have become perfectly calm; not a trace of his recent delirium nor of the panic fear that had haunted him of late. It was the first moment of a strange sudden calm. His movements were precise and definite; a firm purpose was evident in them. 'To-day, to-day,' he muttered to himself. He understood that he was still weak, but his intense spiritual concentration gave him strength and self-confidence. He hoped, moreover, that he would not fall down in the street. When he had dressed in entirely new clothes, he looked at the money lying on the table, and after a moment's thought put it in his pocket. It was twenty-five roubles. He took also all the copper change from the ten roubles spent by Razumihin on the clothes. Then he softly unlatched the door, went out, slipped downstairs and glanced in at the open kitchen door. Nastasya was standing with her back to him, blowing up the landlady's samovar. She heard nothing. Who would have dreamed of his going out, indeed? A minute later he was in the street.

It was nearly eight o'clock, the sun was setting. It was a stifling as before, but he eagerly drank in the stinking, dusty town air. His head felt rather dizzy; a sort of savage energy gleamed suddenly in his feverish eyes and his wasted, pale and yellow face. He did not know and did not think where he was going, he had one thought only: 'that all *this* must be ended to-day, once for all, immediately; that he would not return home without it, because he *would not go on living like that.*' How, with what to make an end? He had not an idea about it, he did not even want to think of it. He drove away thought; thought tortured him. All he knew, all he felt was that everything must be changed 'one way or another', he repeated with desperate and immovable self-confidence and determination.

From old habit he took his usual walk in the direction of the Hay Market. A dark-haired young man with a barrel-organ was standing in the road in front of a little general shop and was grinding out a very sentimental song. He was accompanying a girl of fifteen, who stood on the pavement in front of him. She was dressed in a crinoline, a mantle and a straw hat with a flame-coloured feather in it, all very old and shabby. In a strong and rather agreeable voice, cracked and coarsened by street singing, she sang in hope of getting a copper from the shop. Raskolnikov joined two or three listeners, took out a five-copeck piece and put it in the girl's hand. She broke off abruptly on a sentimental high note, shouted sharply to the organ-grinder 'Come on,' and both moved on to the next shop.

'Do you like street music?' said Raskolnikov, addressing a middle-aged man standing idly by him. The man looked at him, startled and wondering.

'I love to hear singing to a street organ,' said Raskolnikov, and his manner seemed strangely out of keeping with the subject – 'I like it on cold, dark, damp autumn evenings – they must be damp – when all the passers-by have pale green, sickly faces, or better still when wet snow is falling straight down, when there's no wind – you know what I mean? – and the street lamps shine through it . . .'

'I don't know. . . . Excuse me . . .' muttered the stranger, frightened by the question and Raskolnikov's strange manner, and he crossed over to the other side of the street.

Raskolnikov walked straight on and came out at the corner of the Hay Market, where the huckster and his wife had talked with Lizaveta; but they were not there now. Recognizing the place, he stopped, looked round and addressed a young fellow in a red shirt who stood gaping before a corn-chandler's shop.

'Isn't there a man who keeps a booth with his wife at this corner?'

'All sorts of people keep booths here,' answered the young man, glancing superciliously at Raskolnikov.

'What's his name?'

'What he was christened.'

'Aren't you a Zaraïsky man, too? Which province?'

The young man looked at Raskolnikov again.

'It's not a province, your excellency, but a district. Graciously forgive me, your excellency!'

'Is that a tavern at the top there?'

'Yes, it's an eating-house and there's a billiard-room and you'll find princesses there too. . . . La-la!'

Raskolnikov crossed the square. In that corner there was a dense crowd of peasants. He pushed his way into the thickest part of it, looking at the faces. He felt an unaccountable inclination to enter into conversation with people. But the peasants took no notice of him; they were all shouting in groups together. He stood and thought a little and took a turning to the right in the direction of V.

He had often crossed that little street which turns at an angle, leading from the market-place to Sadovy Street. Of late he had often felt drawn to wander about this district, when he felt depressed, that he might feel more so.

Now he walked along, thinking of nothing. At that point there is a great block of buildings, entirely let out in dram shops and eating-houses; women were continually running in and out, bare-headed and in their indoor clothes. Here and there they gathered in groups, on the pavement, especially about the entrances to various festive establishments in the lower storeys. From one of these a loud din, sounds of singing, the tinkling of a guitar and shouts of merriment, floated into the street. A crowd of women were thronging round the door; some were sitting on the steps, others on the pavement, others were standing talking. A drunken soldier, smoking a cigarette, was walking near them in the road, swearing; he seemed to be trying to find his way somewhere, but had forgotten where. One beggar was quarrelling with another, and a man dead drunk was lying right across the road. Raskolnikov joined the throng of women, who were talking in husky voices. They were bare-headed and wore cotton dresses and goatskin shoes. There were women of forty and some not more than seventeen; almost all had blackened eyes.

He felt strangely attracted by the singing and all the noise and uproar in the saloon below. . . . Someone could be heard within dancing frantically, marking time with his heels to the sounds of the guitar and of a thin falsetto voice singing a jaunty air. He listened intently, gloomily and dreamily, bending down at the entrance and peeping inquisitively in from the pavement.

> *'Oh, my handsome soldier,*
> *Don't beat me for nothing.'*

trilled the thin voice of the singer. Raskolnikov felt a great desire to make out what he was singing, as though everything depended on that.

'Shall I go in?' he thought. 'They are laughing. From drink. Shall I get drunk?'

'Won't you come in?' one of the women asked him. Her voice was still musical and less thick than the others, she was young and not repulsive – the only one of the group.

'Why, she's pretty,' he said, drawing himself up and looking at her.

She smiled, much pleased at the compliment.

'You're very nice-looking yourself,' she said.

'Isn't he thin though!' observed another woman in a deep bass. 'Have you just come out of hospital?'

'They're all generals' daughters, it seems, but they have all snub noses,' interposed a tipsy peasant with a sly smile on his face, wearing a loose coat. 'See how jolly they are.'

'Go along with you!'

'I'll go, sweetie!'

And he darted down into the saloon below. Raskolnikov moved on.

'I say, sir,' the girl shouted after him.

'What is it?'

She hesitated.

'I'll always be pleased to spend an hour with you, kind gentleman, but now I feel shy. Give me six copecks for a drink, there's a nice young man!'

Raskolnikov gave her what came first – fifteen copecks.

'Ah, what a good-natured gentleman!'

'What's your name?'

'Ask for Duclida.'

'Well, that's too much,' one of the women observed, shaking her head at Duclida. 'I don't know how you can ask like that. I believe I should drop with shame. . . .'

Raskolnikov looked curiously at the speaker. She was a pock-marked wench of thirty, covered with bruises, with her upper lip swollen. She made her criticism quietly and earnestly. 'Where is it?' thought Raskolnikov. 'Where is it I've read that someone condemned to death says or thinks, an hour before his death, that if he had to live on some high rock, on such a narrow ledge that he'd only room to stand, and the ocean, everlasting darkness, everlasting solitude, everlasting tempest around him, if he had to remain standing on a square yard of space all his life, a thousand years, eternity, it were better to live so than to die at once! Only to live, to live and live! Life, whatever it may be! . . . How true it is! Good God, how true! Man is a vile creature! . . . And vile is he who calls him vile for that,' he added a moment later.

He went into another street. 'Bah, the Palais de Cristal! Razumihin was just talking of the Palais de Cristal. But what on earth was it I wanted? Yes, the newspapers. . . . Zossimov said he'd read it in the papers. Have you the papers?' he asked, going into a very spacious and positively clean restaurant, consisting of several rooms, which were, however, rather empty. Two or three people were drinking tea, and in a room further away were sitting four men drinking champagne. Raskolnikov fancied that Zametov was one of them, but he could not be sure at that distance. 'What if it is?' he thought.

'Will you have vodka?' asked the waiter.

'Give me some tea and bring me the papers, the old ones for the last five days, and I'll give you something.'

'Yes, sir, here's to-day's. No vodka?'

The old newspapers and the tea were brought. Raskolnikov sat down and began to look through them.

'Oh, damn . . . these are the items of intelligence. An accident on a staircase, spontaneous combustion of a shopkeeper from alcohol, a fire in Peski . . . a fire in the Petersburg quarter . . . another fire in the Petersburg quarter . . . and another fire in the Petersburg quarter . . . Ah, here it is!' He found at last what he was seeking and began to read it. The lines danced before his eyes, but he read it all and began eagerly seeking later additions in the following numbers. His hands shook with nervous impatience as he turned the sheets. Suddenly someone sat down beside him at his table. He looked up, it was the head clerk Zametov, looking just the same, with the rings on his fingers and the watch-chain, with the curly, black hair, parted and pomaded, with the smart waistcoat, rather shabby coat and doubtful linen. He was in a good humour, at least he was smiling very gaily and good-humouredly. His dark face was rather flushed from the champagne he had drunk.

'What, you here?' he began in surprise, speaking as though he'd known him all his life. 'Why, Razumihin told me only yesterday you were unconscious. How strange! And do you know I've been to see you?'

Raskolnikov knew he would come up to him. He laid aside the papers and turned to Zametov. There was a smile on his lips, and a new shade of irritable impatience was apparent in that smile.

'I know you have,' he answered. 'I've heard it. You looked for my sock. . . . And you know Razumihin has lost his heart to you? He says you've been with him to Luise Ivanovna's – you know, the woman you tried to befriend, for whom you winked to the Explosive Lieutenant and he would not understand. Do you remember? How could he fail to understand – it was quite clear, wasn't it?'

'What a hot head he is!'

'The explosive one?'

'No, your friend Razumihin.'

'You must have a jolly life, Mr. Zametov; entrance free to the most agreeable places. Who's been pouring champagne into you just now?'

'We've just been . . . having a drink together. . . . You talk about pouring it into me!'

'By way of a fee! You profit by everything!' Raskolnikov laughed, 'it's all right, my dear boy,' he added, slapping Zametov on the shoulder. 'I am not speaking from temper, but in a friendly way, for sport, as that workman of yours said when he was scuffling with Dmitri, in the case of the old woman. . . .'

'How do you know about it?'

'Perhaps I know more about it than you do.'

'How strange you are. . . . I am sure you are still very unwell. You oughtn't to have come out.'

'Oh, do I seem strange to you?'

'Yes. What are you doing, reading the papers?'

'Yes.'

'There's a lot about the fires.'

'No, I am not reading about the fires.' Here he looked mysteriously at Zametov; his lips were twisted again in a mocking smile. 'No, I am not reading about the fires,' he went on, winking at Zametov. 'But confess now, my dear fellow, you're awfully anxious to know what I am reading about?'

'I am not in the least. Mayn't I ask a question? Why do you keep on . . .'

'Listen, you are a man of culture and education?'

'I was in the sixth class at the gymnasium,' said Zametov with some dignity.

'Sixth class! Ah, my cock-sparrow! With your parting and your rings – you are a gentleman of fortune. Foo! what a charming boy!' Here Raskolnikov broke into a nervous laugh right in Zametov's face. The latter drew back, more amazed than offended.

'Foo! how strange you are!' Zametov repeated, very seriously. 'I can't help thinking you are still delirious.'

'I am delirious? You are fibbing, my cock-sparrow! So I am strange? You find me curious, do you?'

'Yes, curious.'

'Shall I tell you what I was reading about, what I was looking for? See what a lot of papers I've made them bring me. Suspicious, eh?'

'Well, what is it?'

'You prick up your ears?'

'How do you mean – "prick up my ears"?'

'I'll explain that afterwards, but now, my boy, I declare to you . . . no, better, "I confess" . . . No, that's not right either; "I make a deposition and you take it", I depose that I was reading, that I was looking and searching. . . .' he screwed up his eyes and paused. 'I was searching – and came here on purpose to do it – for news of the murder of the old pawnbroker woman,' he articulated at last, almost in a whisper, bringing his face exceedingly close to the face of Zametov. Zametov looked at him steadily, without moving or drawing his face away. What struck Zametov afterwards as the strangest part of it all was that silence followed for exactly a minute, and that they gazed at one another all the while.

'What if you have been reading about it?' he cried at last, perplexed and impatient. 'That's no business of mine! What of it?'

'The same old woman,' Raskolnikov went on in the same whisper, not heeding Zametov's explanation, 'about whom you were talking in the police-office, you remember, when I fainted. Well, do you understand now?'

'What do you mean? Understand . . . what?' Zametov brought out, almost alarmed.

Raskolnikov's set and earnest face was suddenly transformed, and he suddenly went off into the same nervous laugh as before, as though utterly unable to restrain himself. And in one flash he recalled with extra-ordinary vividness of sensation a moment in the recent past, that moment when he stood with the axe behind the door, while the latch trembled and the men outside swore and shook it, and he had a sudden desire to shout at them, to swear at them, to put out his tongue at them, to mock them, to laugh, and laugh, and laugh!

'You are either mad, or . . .' began Zametov, and he broke off, as though stunned by the idea that had suddenly flashed into his mind.

'Or? Or what? What? Come, tell me!'

'Nothing,' said Zametov, angrily, 'it's all nonsense!'

Both were silent. After his sudden fit of laughter Raskolnikov became suddenly thoughtful and melancholy. He put his elbow on the table and leaned his head on his hand. He seemed to have completely forgotten Zametov. The silence lasted for some time.

'Why don't you drink your tea? It's getting cold,' said Zametov.

'What! Tea? Oh, yes. . . .' Raskolnikov sipped the tea, put a morsel of bread in his mouth and, suddenly looking at Zametov, seemed to remember everything and pulled himself together. At the same moment his face resumed its original mocking expression. He went on drinking tea.

'There have been a great many of these crimes lately,' said Zametov. 'Only the other day I read in the *Moscow News* that a whole gang of false coiners had been caught in Moscow. It was a regular society. They used to forge tickets!'

'Oh, but it was a long time ago! I read about it a month ago,' Raskolnikov answered calmly. 'So you consider them criminals?' he added, smiling.

'Of course they are criminals.'

'They? They are children, simpletons, not criminals! Why, half a hundred people meeting for such an object – what an idea! Three would be too many, and then they want to have more faith in one other than in themselves! One has only to blab in his cups and it all collapses. Simpletons! They engaged untrustworthy people to change the notes – what a thing to trust to a casual stranger! Well, let us suppose that these simpletons succeed and each makes a million, and what follows for the rest of their lives? Each dependent on the others for the rest of his life! Better hang oneself at once! And they did not know how to change the notes either; the man who changed the notes took five thousand roubles, and his hands trembled. He counted the first four thousand, but did not count the fifth thousand – he was in such a hurry to get the money into his pocket and run away. Of course he roused suspicion. And the whole thing came to a crash through one fool! Is it possible?'

'That his hands trembled?' observed Zametov, 'yes, that's quite possible. That, I feel quite sure, is possible. Sometimes one can't stand things.'

'Can't stand that?'

'Why, could you stand it then? No, I couldn't. For the sake of a hundred roubles to face such a terrific experience? To go with false notes into a bank where it's their business to spot that sort of thing! No, I should not have the face to do it. Would you?'

Raskolnikov had an intense desire again 'to put his tongue out'. Shivers kept running down his spine.

'I should do it quite differently,' Raskolnikov began. 'This is how I would change the notes: I'd count the first thousand three or four times backwards and forwards, looking at every note and then I'd set to the second thousand; I'd count that half-way through and then hold some fifty-rouble notes to the light, then turn it, then hold it to the light again – to see whether it was a good one. "I am afraid," I would say, "a relation of mine lost twenty-five roubles the other day through a false note," and then I'd tell them the whole story. And after I began counting the third,

"No, excuse me," I would say, "I fancy I made a mistake in the seventh hundred in that second thousand, I am not sure." And so I would give up on the third thousand and go back to the second and so on to the end. And when I had finished, I'd pick out one from the fifth and one from the second thousand and take them again to the light and ask again, "Change them, please," and put the clerk into such a stew that he would not know how to get rid of me. When I'd finished and had gone out, I'd come back, "No, excuse me," and ask for some explanation. That's how I'd do it.'

'Foo! what terrible things you say!' said Zametov, laughing. 'But all that is only talk. I dare say when it came to deeds you'd make a slip. I believe that even a practised, desperate man cannot always reckon on himself, much less you and I. To take an example near home – that old woman murdered in our district. The murderer seems to have been a desperate fellow, he risked everything in open daylight, was saved by a miracle – but his hands shook, too. He did not succeed in robbing the place, he couldn't stand it. That was clear from the . . .'

Raskolnikov seemed offended.

'Clear? Why don't you catch him then?' he cried, maliciously gibing at Zametov.

'Well, they will catch him.'

'Who? You? Do you suppose you could catch him? You've a tough job! A great point for you is whether a man is spending money or not. If he had no money and suddenly begins spending, he must be the man. So that any child can mislead you.'

'The fact is they always do that, though,' answered Zametov. 'A man will commit a clear murder at the risk of his life and then at once he goes drinking in a tavern. They are caught spending money, they are not all as cunning as you are. You wouldn't go to a tavern, of course?'

Raskolnikov frowned and looked steadily at Zametov.

'You seem to enjoy the subject and would like to know how I should behave in that case, too?' he asked with displeasure.

'I should like to,' Zametov answered firmly and seriously. Somewhat too much earnestness began to appear in his words and looks.

'Very much?'

'Very much!'

'All right then. This is how I should behave.' Raskolnikov began, again bringing his face close to Zametov's, again staring at him and speaking in a whisper, so that the latter positively shuddered. 'This is what I should have done. I should have taken the money and jewels, I should have walked out of there and have gone straight to some deserted place with fences round it and scarcely anyone to be seen, some kitchen garden or place of that sort. I should have looked out beforehand some stone weighing a hundredweight or more which had been lying in the corner from the time the house was built. I would lift that stone – there would sure to be a hollow under it, and I would put the jewels and money in that hole. Then I'd roll the stone back so that it would look as before, would press it down with my foot and walk away. And for a year or two, three maybe, I would not touch it. And, well, they could search! There'd be no trace.'

'You are a madman,' said Zametov, and for some reason he too spoke in a whisper, and moved away from Raskolnikov, whose eyes were glittering. He had turned fearfully pale and his upper lip was twitching and quivering. He bent down as close as possible to Zametov, and his lips began to move without uttering a word. This lasted for half a minute; he knew what he was doing, but could not restrain himself. The terrible word trembled on his lips, like the latch on that door; in another moment it will break out, in another moment he will let it go, he will speak out.

'And what if it was I who murdered the old woman and Lizaveta?' he said suddenly and – realized what he had done.

Zametov looked wildly at him and turned white as the tablecloth. His face wore a contorted smile.

'But is it possible?' he brought out faintly. Raskolnikov looked wrathfully at him.

'Own up that you believed it, yes, you did?'

'Not a bit of it, I believe it less than ever now,' Zametov cried hastily.

'I've caught my cock-sparrow! So you did believe it before, if now you believe it less than ever?'

'Not at all,' cried Zametov, obviously embarrassed. 'Have you been frightening me so as to lead up to this?'

'You don't believe it then? What were you talking about behind my back when I went out of the police-office? And why did the explosive lieutenant question me after I fainted? Hey, there,' he shouted to the waiter, getting up and taking his cap 'how much?'

'Thirty copecks,' the latter replied, running up.

'And here is twenty copecks for the vodka. See what a lot of money!' he held out his shaking hand to Zametov with notes in it. 'Red notes and blue, twenty-five roubles. Where did I get them? And where did my new clothes come from? You know I had not a copeck. You've cross-examined my landlady, I'll be bound. . . . Well, that's enough! *Assez causé!* Till we meet again!'

He went out, trembling all over from a sort of wild hysterical sensation, in which there was an element of insufferable rapture. Yet he was gloomy and terribly tired. His face was twisted as after a fit. His fatigue increased rapidly. Any shock, any irritating sensation stimulated and revived his energies at once, but his strength failed as quickly when the stimulus was removed.

Zametov, left alone, sat for a long time in the same place, plunged in thought. Raskolnikov had unwittingly worked a revolution in his brain on a certain point and had made up his mind for him conclusively.

'Ilya Petrovitch is a blockhead,' he decided.

Raskolnikov had hardly opened the door of the restaurant when he stumbled against Razumihin on the steps. They did not see each other till they almost knocked against each other. For a moment they stood looking each other up and down, Razumihin was greatly astounded, then anger, real anger gleamed fiercely in his eyes.

'So here you are!' he shouted at the top of his voice – 'you ran away from your bed! And here I've been looking for you under the sofa! We went up to the garret. I almost beat Nastasya on your account. And here he is after all. Rodya! What is the meaning of it? Tell me the whole truth! Confess! Do you hear?'

'It means that I'm sick to death of you all and I want to be alone,' Raskolnikov answered calmly.

'Alone? When you are not able to walk, when your face is as white as a sheet and you are gasping for breath! Idiot! . . . What have you been doing in the Palais de Cristal? Own up at once!'

'Let me go!' said Raskolnikov, and tried to pass him. This was too much for Razumihin; he gripped him firmly by the shoulder.

'Let you go? You dare tell me to let you go? Do you know what I'll do with you directly? I'll pick you up, tie you up in a bundle, carry you home under my arm and lock you up!'

'Listen, Razumihin,' Raskolnikov began quietly, apparently calm – 'can't you see that I don't want your benevolence? A strange desire you have to shower benefits on a man who . . . curses them, who feels them a burden in fact! Why did you seek me out at the beginning of my illness? Maybe I was very glad to die. Didn't I tell you plainly enough to-day that you were torturing me, that I was . . . sick of you! You seem to want to torture people! I assure you that all that is seriously hindering my recovery, because it's continually irritating me. You saw Zossimov went away just now to avoid irritating me. You leave me alone, too, for goodness' sake! What right have you, indeed, to keep me by force? Don't you see that I am in possession of all my faculties now? How, how can I persuade you not to persecute me with your kindness? I may be ungrateful, I may be mean, only let me be, for God's sake, let me be! Let me be, let me be!'

He began calmly, gloating beforehand over the venomous phrases he was about to utter, but finished, panting for breath, in a frenzy, as he had been with Luzhin.

Razumihin stood a moment, thought and let his hand drop.

'Well, go to hell then,' he said gently and thoughtfully. 'Stay,' he roared, as Raskolnikov was about to move. 'Listen to me. Let me tell you that you are all a set of babbling, posing idiots! If you've any little trouble you brood over it like a hen over an egg. And you are plagiarists even in that! There isn't a sign of independent life in you! You are made of spermaceti ointment and you've lymph in your veins instead of blood. I don't believe in any one of you! In any circumstances the first thing for all of you is to be unlike a human being! Stop!' he cried with redoubled fury, noticing that Raskolnikov was again making a movement – 'hear me out! You know I'm having a house-warming this evening, I dare say they've arrived by now, but I left my uncle there – I just ran in – to receive the guests. And if you weren't a fool, a common fool, a perfect fool, if you were an original instead of a translation ... you see, Rodya, I recognize you're a clever fellow, but you're a fool! – and if you weren't a fool you'd come round to me this evening instead of wearing out your boots in the street! Since you have gone out, there's no help for it! I'd give you a snug easy-chair, my landlady has one ... a cup of tea, company.... Or you could lie on the sofa – anyway, you would be with us.... Zossimov will be there too. Will you come?'

'No.'

'R-rubbish!' Razumihin shouted, out of patience. 'How do you know? You can't answer for yourself You don't know anything about it.... Thousands of times I've fought tooth and nail with people and run back to them afterwards.... One feels ashamed and goes back to a man! So remember, Potchinkov's house on the third storey....'

'Why, Mr. Razumihin, I do believe you'd let anybody beat you from sheer benevolence.'

'Beat? Whom? Me? I'd twist his nose off at the mere idea! Potchinkov's house, 47, Babushkin's flat....'

'I shall not come, Razumihin.' Raskolnikov turned and walked away.

'I bet you will,' Razumihin shouted after him. 'I refuse to know you if you don't! Stay, hey, is Zametov in there?'

'Yes.'

'Did you see him?'

'Yes.'

'Talked to him?'

'Yes.'

'What about? Confound you, don't tell me then. Potchinkov's house, 47, Babushkin's flat, remember!'

Raskolnikov walked on and turned the corner into Sadovy Street.

Razumihin looked after him thoughtfully. Then with a wave of his hand he went into the house but stopped short on the stairs.

'Confound it,' he went on almost aloud. 'He talked sensibly but yet . . . I am a fool! As if madmen didn't talk sensibly! And this was just what Zossimov seemed afraid of.' He struck his finger on his forehead. 'What if . . . how could I let him go off alone? He may drown himself. . . . Ach, what a blunder! I can't.' And he ran back to overtake Raskolnikov, but there was no trace of him. With a curse he returned with rapid steps to the Palais de Cristal to question Zametov.

Raskolnikov walked straight to X—Bridge, stood in the middle, and leaning both elbows on the rail stared into the distance. On parting with Razumihin, he felt so much weaker that he could scarcely reach this place. He longed to sit or lie down somewhere in the street. Bending over the water, he gazed mechanically at the last pink flush of the sunset, at the row of houses growing dark in the gathering twilight, at one distant attic window on the left bank, flashing as though on fire in the last rays of the setting sun, at the darkening water of the canal, and the water seemed to catch his attention. At last red circles flashed before his eyes, the houses seemed moving, the passers-by, the canal banks, the carriages, all danced before his eyes. Suddenly he started, saved again perhaps from swooning by an uncanny and hideous sight. He became aware of someone standing on the right side of him; he looked and saw a tall woman with a kerchief on her head, with a long, yellow, wasted face and red sunken eyes. She was looking straight at him, but obviously she saw nothing and recognized no one. Suddenly she leaned her right hand on the parapet, lifted her right leg over the railing, then her left and threw herself into the canal. The filthy water parted and swallowed up its victim for a moment, but an instant later the drowning woman floated to the surface, moving slowly with the current, her head and legs in the water, her skirt inflated like a balloon over her back.

'A woman drowning! A woman drowning!' shouted dozens of voices; people ran up, both banks were thronged with spectators, on the bridge people crowded about Raskolnikov, pressing up behind him.

'Mercy on us! it's our Afrosinya!' a woman cried tearfully close by. 'Mercy! save her! kind people, pull her out!'

'A boat, a boat!' was shouted in the crowd. But there was no need of a boat; a policeman ran down the steps to the canal, threw off his greatcoat and his boots and rushed into the water. It was easy to reach her: she floated within a couple of yards from the steps, he caught hold of her clothes with his right hand and with his left seized a pole which a comrade held out to him; the drowning woman was pulled out at once. They laid her on the granite pavement of the embankment. She soon recovered consciousness, raised her head, sat up and began sneezing and coughing, stupidly wiping her wet dress with her hands. She said nothing.

'She's drunk herself out of her senses,' the same woman's voice wailed at her side. 'Out of her senses. The other day she tried to hang herself, we cut her down. I ran out to the shop just now, left my little girl to look after her – and here she's in trouble again! A neighbour, gentleman, a neighbour, we live close by, the second house from the end, see yonder. . . .'

The crowd broke up, the police still remained round the woman, someone mentioned the police station. . . . Raskolnikov looked on with a strange sensation of indifference and apathy. He felt disgusted. 'No, that's loathsome . . . water . . . it's not good enough,' he muttered to himself. 'Nothing will come of it,' he added, 'no use to wait. What about the police office . . .? And why isn't Zametov at the police office? The police office is open till ten o'clock. . . .' He turned his back to the railing and looked about him.

'Very well then!' he said resolutely; he moved from the bridge and walked in the direction of the police office. His heart felt hollow and empty. He did not want to think. Even his depression had passed, there was not a trace now of the energy with which he had set out 'to make an end of it all'. Complete apathy had succeeded to it.

'Well, it's a way out of it,' he thought, walking slowly and listlessly along the canal bank. 'Anyway, I'll make an end, for I want to. . . . But is it a way out? What does it matter? There'll be the square yard of space – ha! But what an end! Is it really the end? Shall I tell them or not? Ah . . . damn! How tired I am! If I could find somewhere to sit or lie down soon! What I am most ashamed of is its being so stupid. But I don't care about that either! What idiotic ideas come into one's head.'

To reach the police office he had to go straight forward and take the second turning to the left. It was only a few paces away. But at the first turning he stopped and, after a minute's thought, turned into a side street and went two streets out of his way, possibly without any object, or possibly to delay a minute and gain time. He walked, looking at the ground; suddenly someone seemed to whisper in his ear; he lifted his head and saw that he was standing at the very gate of *the* house. He had not passed it, he had not been near it since *that* evening. An overwhelming, unaccountable prompting drew him on. He went into the house, passed through the gateway, then into the first entrance on the right, and began mounting the familiar staircase to the fourth storey. The narrow, steep staircase was very dark. He stopped at each landing and looked round him with curiosity; on the first landing the framework of the window had been taken out. 'That wasn't so then,' he thought. Here was the flat on the second storey where Nikolay and Dmitri had been working. 'It's shut up and the door newly painted. So it's to let.' Then the third storey and the fourth. 'Here!' He was perplexed to find the door of the flat wide open. There were men there, he could hear voices; he had not expected that. After brief hesitation he mounted the last stairs and went into the flat. It, too, was being done up; there were workmen in it. This seemed to amaze him; he somehow fancied that he would find everything as he left it, even perhaps the corpses in the same places on the floor. And now, bare walls, no furniture; it seemed strange. He walked to the window and sat down on the window-sill. There were two workmen, both young fellows, but one much younger than the other. They were papering the walls with a new white paper covered with lilac flowers, instead of the old, dirty, yellow one. Raskolnikov for some reason felt horribly annoyed by this. He looked at the new paper with dislike, as though he felt sorry to have it all so changed. The workmen had obviously stayed beyond their time and now they were hurriedly rolling up their paper and getting ready to go home. They took no notice of Raskolnikov's coming in; they were talking. Raskolnikov folded his arms and listened.

'She comes to me in the morning,' said the elder to the younger, 'very early, all dressed up. "Why are you preening and prinking?" says I. "I am ready to do anything to please you, Tit Vassilitch!" That's a way of going on! And she dressed up a regular fashion book!'

'And what is a fashion book?' the younger one asked. He obviously regarded the other as an authority.

'A fashion book is a lot of pictures, coloured, and they come to the tailors here every Saturday, by post from abroad, to show folks how to dress, the male sex as well as the female. They're pictures. The gentlemen are generally wearing fur coats and as for the ladies' fluffles, they're beyond anything you can fancy.'

'There's nothing you can't find in Petersburg,' the younger cried enthusiastically, 'except father and mother, there's everything!'

'Except them, there's everything to be found, my boy,' the elder declared sententiously.

Raskolnikov got up and walked into the other room where the strong box, the bed, and the chest of drawers had been; the room seemed to him very tiny without furniture in it. The paper was the same; the paper in the corner showed where the case of ikons had stood. He looked at it and went to the window. The elder workman looked at him askance.

'What do you want?' he asked suddenly.

Instead of answering Raskolnikov went into the passage and pulled the bell. The same bell, the same cracked note. He rang it a second and a third time; he listened and remembered. The hideous and agonizingly fearful sensation he had felt then began to come back more and more vividly. He shuddered at every ring and it gave him more and more satisfaction.

'Well, what do you want? Who are you?' the workman shouted, going out to him. Raskolnikov went inside again.

'I want to take a flat,' he said. 'I am looking round.'

'It's not the time to look at rooms at night; and you ought to come up with the porter.'

'The floors have been washed, will they be painted?' Raskolnikov went on. 'Is there no blood?'

'What blood?'

'Why, the old woman and her sister were murdered here. There was a perfect pool there.'

'But who are you?' the workman cried, uneasy.

'Who am I?'

'Yes.'

'You want to know? Come to the police station. I'll tell you.'

The workmen looked at him in amazement.

'It's time for us to go, we are late. Come along, Alyoshka. We must lock up,' said the elder workman.

'Very well, come along,' said Raskolnikov indifferently, and going out first, he went slowly downstairs. 'Hey, porter,' he cried in the gateway.

At the entrance several people were standing, staring at the passers-by; the two porters, a peasant woman, a man in a long coat and a few others. Raskolnikov went straight up to them.

'What do you want?' asked one of the porters.

'Have you been to the police office?'

'I've just been there. What do you want?'

'Is it open?'

'Of course.'

'Is the assistant there?'

'He was there for a time. What do you want?'

Raskolnikov made no reply, but stood beside them lost in thought.

'He's been to look at the flat,' said the elder workman, coming forward.

'Which flat?'

'Where we are at work. "Why have you washed away the blood?" says he. "There has been a murder here," says he, and "I've come to take it." And he began ringing at the bell, all but broke it. "Come to the police station," says he, "I'll tell you everything there." He wouldn't leave us.'

The porter looked at Raskolnikov, frowning and perplexed.

'Who are you?' he shouted as impressively as he could.

'I am Rodion Romanovitch Raskolnikov, formerly a student, I live in Shil's house, not far from here, flat Number 14, ask the porter, he knows me.' Raskolnikov said all this in a lazy, dreamy voice, not turning round, but looking intently into the darkening street.

'Why have you been to the flat?'

'To look at it.'

'What is there to look at?'

'Take him straight to the police station,' the man in the long coat jerked in abruptly.

Raskolnikov looked intently at him over his shoulder and said in the same slow, lazy tones:

'Come along.'

'Yes, take him,' the man went on more confidently. 'Why was he going into *that*, what's in his mind, eh?'

'He's not drunk, but God knows what's the matter with him,' muttered the workman.

'But what do you want?' the porter shouted again, beginning to get angry in earnest – 'Why are you hanging about?'

'You funk the police station then?' said Raskolnikov jeeringly.

'How funk it? Why are you hanging about?'

'He's a rogue!' shouted the peasant woman.

'Why waste time talking to him?' cried the other porter, a huge peasant in a full open coat and with keys on his belt. 'Get along! He is a rogue and no mistake. Get along!'

And seizing Raskolnikov by the shoulder he flung him into the street. He lurched forward, but recovered his footing, looked at the spectators in silence and walked away.

'Strange man!' observed the workman.

'There are strange folks about nowadays,' said the woman.

'You should have taken him to the police station all the same,' said the man in the long coat.

'Better have nothing to do with him,' decided the big porter. 'A regular rogue! Just what he wants, you may be sure, but once take him up, you won't get rid of him. . . . We know the sort!'

'Shall I go there or not?' thought Raskolnikov, standing in the middle of the thoroughfare at the cross-roads, and he looked about him, as though expecting from someone a decisive word. But no sound came, all was dead and silent like the stones on which he walked, dead to him, to him alone. . . . All at once at the end of the street, two hundred yards away, in the gathering dusk he saw a crowd and heard talk and shouts. In the middle of the crowd stood a carriage. . . . A light gleamed in the middle of the street. 'What is it?' Raskolnikov turned to the right and went up to the crowd. He seemed to clutch at everything and smiled coldly when he recognized it, for he had fully made up his mind to go to the police station and knew that it would all soon be over.

➤ SEVEN ◄

AN ELEGANT CARRIAGE STOOD IN the middle of the road with a pair of spirited grey horses; there was no one in it, and the coachman had got off his box and stood by; the horses were being held by the bridle. . . . A mass of people had gathered round, the police standing in front. One of them held a lighted lantern which he was turning on something lying close to the wheels. Everyone was talking, shouting, exclaiming; the coachman seemed at a loss and kept repeating:

'What a misfortune! Good Lord, what a misfortune!'

Raskolnikov pushed his way in as far as he could, and succeeded at last in seeing the object of the commotion and interest. On the ground a man who had been run over lay apparently unconscious, and covered with blood; he was very badly dressed, but not like a workman. Blood was flowing from his head and face; his face was crushed, mutilated and disfigured. He was evidently badly injured.

'Merciful heaven!' wailed the coachman, 'what more could I do? If I'd been driving fast or had not shouted to him, but I was going quietly, not in a hurry. Everyone could see I was going along just like everybody else. A drunken man can't walk straight, we all know. . . . I saw him crossing the street, staggering and almost falling. I shouted again and a second and a third time, then I held the horses in, but he fell straight under their feet! Either he did it on purpose or he was very tipsy. . . . The horses are young and ready to take fright . . . they started, he screamed . . . that made them worse. That's how it happened!'

'That's just how it was,' a voice in the crowd confirmed.

'He shouted, that's true, he shouted three times,' another voice declared.

'Three times it was, we all heard it,' shouted a third.

But the coachman was not very much distressed and frightened. It was evident that the carriage belonged to a rich and important person who was awaiting it somewhere; the police, of course, were in no little anxiety to avoid upsetting his arrangements. All they had to do was to take the injured man to the police station and the hospital. No one knew his name.

Meanwhile Raskolnikov had squeezed in and stooped closer over him. The lantern suddenly lighted up the unfortunate man's face. He recognized him.

'I know him! I know him!' he shouted, pushing to the front. 'It's a government clerk retired from the service, Marmeladov. He lives close by in Kozel's house. . . . Make haste for a doctor! I will pay, see?' He pulled money out of his pocket and showed it to the policeman. He was in violent agitation.

The police were glad that they had found out who the man was. Raskolnikov gave his own name and address, and, as earnestly as if it had been his father, he besought the police to carry the unconscious Marmeladov to his lodging at once.

'Just here, three houses away,' he said eagerly, 'the house belongs to Kozel, a rich German. He was going home, no doubt drunk. I know him, he is a drunkard. He has a family there, a wife, children, he has one daughter. . . . It will take time to take him to the hospital, and there is sure to be a doctor in the house. I'll pay, I'll pay! At least he will be looked after at home . . . they will help him at once. But he'll die before you get him to the hospital.' He managed to slip something unseen into the policeman's hand. But the thing was straightforward and legitimate, and in any case help was closer here. They raised the injured man; people volunteered to help.

Kozel's house was thirty yards away. Raskolnikov walked behind, carefully holding Marmeladov's head and showing the way.

'This way, this way! We must take him upstairs head foremost. Turn round! I'll pay, I'll make it worth your while,' he muttered.

Katerina Ivanovna had just begun, as she always did at every free moment, walking to and fro in her little room from window to stove and back again, with her arms folded across her chest, talking to herself and coughing. Of late she had begun to talk more than ever to her eldest girl, Polenka, a child of ten, who, though there was much she did not understand, understood very well that her mother needed her, and so always watched her with her big clever eyes and strove her utmost to appear to understand. This time Polenka was undressing her little brother, who had been unwell all day and was going to bed. The boy was waiting for her to take off his shirt, which had to be washed at night. He was sitting straight and motionless on a chair, with a silent, serious face, with his legs stretched out straight before him – heels together and toes turned out.

He was listening to what his mother was saying to his sister, sitting perfectly still with pouting lips and wide-open eyes, just as all good little boys have to sit when they are undressed to go to bed. A little girl, still younger, dressed literally in rags, stood at the screen, waiting for her turn. The door on to the stairs was open to relive them a little from the clouds of tobacco smoke which floated in from the other rooms and brought on long terrible fits of coughing in the poor, consumptive woman. Katerina Ivanovna seemed to have grown even thinner during that week and the hectic flush on her face was brighter than ever.

'You wouldn't believe, you can't imagine, Polenka,' she said, walking about the room, 'what a happy luxurious life we had in my papa's house and how this drunkard has brought me, and will bring you all, to ruin! Papa was a civil colonel and only a step from being a governor; so that everyone who came to see him said: "We look upon you, Ivan Mihailov-itch, as our governor!" When I . . . when . . .' she coughed violently, 'oh, cursed life,' she cried, clearing her throat and pressing her hand to her breast, 'when I . . . when at the last ball . . . at the marshal's . . . Princess Bezzemelny saw me – who gave me the blessing when your father and I were married, Polenka – she asked at once: "Isn't that the pretty girl who danced the shawl dance at the breaking-up?" (You must mend that tear, you must take your needle and darn it as I showed you, or tomorrow – cough, cough, cough – he will make the hole bigger,' she articulated with effort.) Prince Schegolskoy, a kammer-junker, had just come from Petersburg then . . . he danced the mazurka with me and wanted to make me an offer next day; but I thanked him in flattering expressions and told him that my heart had long been another's. That other was your father, Polya; papa was fearfully angry. . . . Is the water ready? Give me the shirt, and the stockings! Lida,' said she to the youngest one, 'you must manage without your chemise tonight . . . and lay your stockings out with it . . . I'll wash them together. . . . How is it that drunken vagabond doesn't come in? He has worn his shirt till it looks like a dish-clout, he has torn it to rags! I'd do it all together, so as not to have to work two nights running! Oh, dear! (Cough, cough, cough, cough!) Again! What's this?' she cried, noticing a crowd in the passage and the men, who were pushing into her room, carrying a burden. 'What is it? What are they bringing? Mercy on us!'

'Where are we to put him?' asked the policeman, looking round when Marmeladov, unconscious and covered with blood, had been carried in.

'On the sofa! Put him straight on the sofa, with his head this way,' Raskolnikov showed him.

'Run over in the road! Drunk!' someone shouted in the passage.

Katerina Ivanovna stood, turning white and gasping for breath. The children were terrified. Little Lida screamed, rushed to Polenka and clutched at her, trembling all over.

Having laid Marmeladov down, Raskolnikov flew to Katerina Ivanovna.

'For God's sake be calm, don't be frightened!' he said, speaking quickly, 'he was crossing the road and was run over by a carriage, don't be frightened, he will come to, I told them to bring him here ... I've been here already, you remember? He will come to; I'll pay!'

'He's done it this time!' Katerina Ivanovna cried despairingly and she rushed to her husband.

Raskolnikov noticed at once that she was not one of those women who swoon easily. She instantly placed under the luckless man's head a pillow, which no one had thought of and began undressing and examining him. She kept her head, forgetting herself, biting her trembling lips and stifling the screams which were ready to break from her.

Raskolnikov meanwhile induced someone to run for a doctor. There was a doctor, it appeared, next door but one.

'I've sent for a doctor,' he kept assuring Katerina Ivanovna, 'don't be uneasy, I'll pay. Haven't you water? . . . and give me a napkin or a towel, anything, as quick as you can. . . . He is injured, but not killed, believe me. . . . We shall see what the doctor says!'

Katerina Ivanovna ran to the window; there, on a broken chair in the corner, a large earthenware basin full of water had been stood, in readiness for washing her children's and husband's linen that night. This washing was done by Katerina Ivanovna at night at least twice a week, if not oftener. For the family had come to such a pass that they were practically without change of linen, and Katerina Ivanovna could not endure uncleanliness and, rather than see dirt in the house, she preferred to wear herself out at night, working beyond her strength when the rest were asleep, so as to get the wet linen hung on a line and dry by the morning. She took up the basin of water at Raskolnikov's request, but almost fell down with her burden. But the latter had already succeeded in finding a towel, wetted it and began washing the blood off Marmeladov's face.

Katerina Ivanovna stood by, breathing painfully and pressing her hands to her breast. She was in need of attention herself. Raskolnikov began to realize that he might have made a mistake in having the injured man brought here. The policeman, too, stood in hesitation.

'Polenka,' cried Katerina Ivanovna, 'run to Sonia, make haste. If you don't find her at home, leave word that her father has been run over and that she is to come here at once . . . when she comes in. Run, Polenka! there, put on the shawl.'

'Run your fastest!' cried the little boy on the chair suddenly, after which he relapsed into the same dumb rigidity, with round eyes, his heels thrust forward and his toes spread out.

Meanwhile the room had become so full of people that you couldn't have dropped a pin. The policeman left, all except one, who remained for a time, trying to drive out the people who came in from the stairs. Almost all Madame Lippevechsel's lodgers had streamed in from the inner rooms of the flat; at first they were squeezed together in the doorway, but afterwards they overflowed into the room. Katerina Ivanovna flew into a fury.

'You might let him die in peace, at least,' she shouted at the crowd, 'is it a spectacle for you to gape at? With cigarettes! (Cough, cough, cough!) You might as well keep your hats on.... And there is one in his hat!... Get away! You should respect the dead, at least!'

Her cough choked her – but her reproaches were not without result. They evidently stood in some awe of Katerina Ivanovna. The lodgers, one after another, squeezed back into the doorway with that strange inner feeling of satisfaction which may be observed in the presence of a sudden accident, even in those nearest and dearest to the victim, from which no living man is exempt, even in spite of the sincerest sympathy and compassion.

Voices outside were heard, however, speaking of the hospital and saying that they'd do no business to make a disturbance here.

'No business to die!' cried Katerina Ivanovna, and she was rushing to the door to vent her wrath upon them, but in the doorway came face to face with Madame Lippevechsel who had only just heard of the accident and ran in to restore order. She was a particularly quarrelsome and irresponsible German.

'Ah, my God!' she cried, clasping her hands, 'your husband drunken horses have trampled! To the hospital with him! I am the landlady!'

'Amalia Ludwigovna, I beg you to recollect what you are saying,' Katerina Ivanovna began haughtily (she always took a haughty tone with the landlady that she might 'remember her place' and even now could not deny herself this satisfaction). 'Amalia Ludwigovna ...'

'I have you once before told that you that you to call me Amalia Ludwigovna may not dare; I am Amalia Ivanovna.'

'You are not Amalia Ivanovna, but Amalia Ludwigovna, and as I am not one of your despicable flatterers like Mr. Lebeziatnikov, who's laughing behind the door at this moment (a laugh and a cry of "they are at it again" was in fact audible at the door), so I shall always call you Amalia Ludwigovna, though I fail to understand why you dislike that name. You can see for yourself what has happened to Semyon Zaharovitch; he is dying. I beg you to close that door at once and to admit no one. Let him at least die in peace! Or I warn you the Governor-General, himself, shall be informed of your conduct to-morrow. The prince knew me as a girl; he remembers Semyon Zaharovitch well and has often been a benefactor to him. Everyone knows that Semyon Zaharovitch had many friends and protectors, whom he abandoned himself from an honourable pride, knowing his unhappy weakness, but now (she pointed to Raskolnikov) a generous young man has come to our assistance, who has wealth and connections and whom Semyon Zaharovitch has known from a child. You may rest assured, Amalia Ludwigovna . . .'

All this was uttered with extreme rapidity, getting quicker and quicker, but a cough suddenly cut short Katerina Ivanovna's eloquence. At that instant the dying man recovered consciousness and uttered a groan; she ran to him. The injured man opened his eyes and without recognition or understanding gazed at Raskolnikov who was bending over him. He drew deep, slow, painful breaths; blood oozed at the corners of his mouth and drops of perspiration came out on his forehead. Not recognizing Raskolnikov, he began looking round uneasily. Katerina Ivanovna looked at him with a sad but stern face, and tears trickled from her eyes.

'My God! His whole chest is crushed! How he is bleeding!' she said in despair. 'We must take off his clothes. Turn a little, Semyon Zaharovitch, if you can,' she cried to him.

Marmeladov recognized her.

'A priest,' he articulated huskily.

Katerina Ivanovna walked to the window, laid her head against the window frame and exclaimed in despair:

'Oh, cursed life!'

'A priest,' the dying man said again after a moment's silence.

'They've gone for him,' Katerina Ivanovna shouted to him; he obeyed her shout and was silent. With sad and timid eyes he looked for her; she returned and stood by his pillow. He seemed a little easier, but not for long.

Soon his eyes rested on little Lida, his favourite, who was shaking in the corner, as though she were in a fit, and staring at him with her wondering childish eyes.

'A – ah,' he signed towards her uneasily. He wanted to say something.

'What now?' cried Katerina Ivanovna.

'Barefoot, barefoot!' he muttered, indicating with frenzied eyes the child's bare feet.

'Be silent,' Katerina Ivanovna cried irritably, 'you know why she is barefooted.'

'Thank God, the doctor,' exclaimed Raskolnikov, relieved.

The doctor came in, a precise little old man, a German, looking about him mistrustfully; he went up to the sick man, took his pulse, carefully felt his head and with the help of Katerina Ivanovna he unbuttoned the blood-stained shirt, and bared the injured man's chest. It was gashed, crushed and fractured, several ribs on the right side were broken. On the left side, just over the heart, was a large, sinister-looking yellowish-black bruise – a cruel kick from the horse's hoof. The doctor frowned. The policeman told him that he was caught in the wheel and turned round with it for thirty yards on the road.

'It's wonderful that he has recovered consciousness,' the doctor whispered softly to Raskolnikov.

'What do you think of him?' he asked.

'He will die immediately.'

'Is there really no hope?'

'Not the faintest! He is at the last gasp. . . . His head is badly injured, too . . . Hm . . . I could bleed him if you like, but . . . it would be useless. He is bound to die within the next five or ten minutes.'

'Better bleed him then.'

'If you like. . . . But I warn you it will be perfectly useless.'

At that moment other steps were heard; the crowd in the passage parted, and the priest, a little, grey old man, appeared in the doorway bearing the sacrament. A policeman had gone for him at the time of the accident. The doctor changed places with him, exchanging glances with him. Raskolnikov begged the doctor to remain a little while. He shrugged his shoulders and remained.

All stepped back. The confession was soon over. The dying man probably understood little; he could only utter indistinct broken sounds. Katerina Ivanovna took little Lida, lifted the boy from the chair, knelt down in the corner by the stove and made the children kneel in front of her. The little girl was still trembling; but the boy, kneeling on his little bare knees, lifted his hand rhythmically, crossing himself with precision and bowed down, touching the floor with his forehead, which seemed to afford him especial satisfaction. Katerina Ivanovna bit her lips and held back her tears; she prayed, too, now and then pulling straight the boy's shirt, and managed to cover the girl's bare shoulders with a kerchief, which she took from the chest without rising from her knees or ceasing to pray. Meanwhile the door from the inner rooms was opened inquisitively again. In the passage the crowd of spectators from all the flats on the staircase grew denser and denser, but they did not venture beyond the threshold. A single candle-end lighted up the scene.

At that moment Polenka forced her way through the crowd at the door. She came in panting from running so fast, took off her kerchief, looked for her mother, went up to her and said, 'She's coming, I met her in the street'. Her mother made her kneel beside her.

Timidly and noiselessly a young girl made her way through the crowd, and strange was her appearance in that room, in the midst of want, rags, death and despair. She, too, was in rags, her attire was all of the cheapest, but decked out in gutter finery of a special stamp, unmistakably betraying its shameful purpose. Sonia stopped short in the doorway and looked about her bewildered, unconscious of everything. She forgot her fourth-hand, gaudy silk dress, so unseemly here with its ridiculous long train, and her immense crinoline that filled up the whole doorway, and her light-coloured shoes, and the parasol she brought with her, though it was no use at night, and the absurd round straw hat with its flaring flame-coloured feather. Under this rakishly-tilted hat was a pale, frightened little face with lips parted and eyes staring in terror. Sonia was a small thin girl of eighteen with fair hair, rather pretty, with wonderful blue eyes. She looked intently at the bed and the priest; she too was out of breath with running. At last whispers, some words in the crowd probably, reached her. She looked down and took a step forward into the room, still keeping close to the door.

The service was over. Katerina Ivanovna went up to her husband again. The priest stepped back and turned to say a few words of admonition and consolation to Katerina Ivanovna on leaving.

'What am I to do with these?' she interrupted sharply and irritably, pointing to the little ones.

'God is merciful; look to the Most High for succour,' the priest began.

'Ach! He is merciful, but not to us.'

'That's a sin, a sin, madam,' observed the priest, shaking his head.

'And isn't that a sin?' cried Katerina Ivanovna, pointing to the dying man.

'Perhaps those who have involuntarily caused the accident will agree to compensate you, at least for the loss of his earnings.'

'You don't understand!' cried Katerina Ivanovna angrily waving her hand. 'And why should they compensate me? Why, he was drunk and threw himself under the horses! What earnings? He brought us in nothing but misery. He drank everything away, the drunkard! He robbed us to get drink, he wasted our lives and mine for drink! And thank God he's dying! One less to keep!'

'You must forgive in the hour of death, that's a sin, madam, such feelings are a great sin.'

Katerina Ivanovna was busy with the dying man; she was giving him water, wiping the blood and sweat from his head, setting his pillow straight, and had only turned now and then for a moment to address the priest. Now she flew at him almost in a frenzy.

'Ah, father! That's words and only words! Forgive! If he'd not been run over, he'd have come home to-day drunk and his only shirt dirty and in rags and he'd have fallen asleep like a log, and I should have been sousing and rinsing till daybreak, washing his rags and the children's and then drying them by the window and as soon as it was daylight I should have been darning them. That's how I spend my nights! . . . What's the use of talking of forgiveness! I have forgiven as it is!'

A terrible hollow cough interrupted her words. She put her handkerchief to her lips and showed it to the priest, pressing her other hand to her aching chest. The handkerchief was covered with blood. The priest bowed his head and said nothing.

Marmeladov was in the last agony; he did not take his eyes off the face of Katerina Ivanovna, who was bending over him again. He kept trying to say something to her; he began moving his tongue with difficulty and articulating indistinctly, but Katerina Ivanovna, understanding that he wanted to ask her forgiveness, called peremptorily to him:

'Be silent! No need! I know what you want to say!' And the sick man was silent, but at the same instant his wandering eyes strayed to the doorway and he saw Sonia.

Till then he had not noticed her: she was standing in the shadow in a corner.

'Who's that? Who's that?' he said suddenly in a thick gasping voice, in agitation, turning his eyes in horror towards the door where his daughter was standing, and trying to sit up.

'Lie down! Lie do-own!' cried Katerina Ivanovna.

With unnatural strength he had succeeded in propping himself on his elbow. He looked wildly and fixedly for some time on his daughter, as though not recognizing her. He had never seen her before in such attire. Suddenly he recognized her, crushed and ashamed in her humiliation and gaudy finery, meekly awaiting her turn to say good-bye to her dying father. His face showed intense suffering.

'Sonia! Daughter! Forgive!' he cried, and he tried to hold out his hand to her, but, losing his balance, he fell off the sofa, face downwards on the floor. They rushed to pick him up, they put him on the sofa; but he was dying. Sonia with a faint cry ran up, embraced him and remained so without moving. He died in her arms.

'He's got what he wanted,' Katerina Ivanovna cried, seeing her husband's dead body. 'Well, what's to be done now? How am I to bury him? What can I give them to-morrow to eat?'

Raskolnikov went up to Katerina Ivanovna.

'Katerina Ivanovna,' he began, 'last week your husband told me all his life and circumstances. . . . Believe me, he spoke of you with passionate reverence. From that evening, when I learnt how devoted he was to you all and how he loved and respected you especially, Katerina Ivanovna, in spite of his unfortunate weakness, from that evening we became friends. . . . Allow me now . . . to do something . . . to repay my debt to my dead friend. Here are twenty roubles, I think – and if that can be of any assistance to you, then . . . I . . . in short, I will come again, I will be sure to come again . . . I shall, perhaps, come again to-morrow. . . . Goodbye!'

And he went quickly out of the room, squeezing his way through the crowd to the stairs. But in the crowd he suddenly jostled against Nikodim Fomitch, who had heard of the accident and had come to give instructions in person. They had not met since the scene at the police station, but Nikodim Fomitch knew him instantly.

'Ah, is that you?' he asked him.

'He's dead,' answered Raskolnikov. 'The doctor and the priest have been, all as it should have been. Don't worry the poor woman too much, she is in consumption as it is. Try and cheer her up, if possible . . . you are a kind-hearted man, I know . . .' he added with a smile, looking straight in his face.

'But you are spattered with blood,' observed Nikodim Fomitch, noticing in the lamplight some fresh stains on Raskolnikov's waistcoat.

'Yes . . . I'm covered with blood,' Raskolnikov said with a peculiar air; then he smiled, nodded and went downstairs.

He walked down slowly and deliberately, feverish but not conscious of it, entirely absorbed in a new overwhelming sensation of life and strength that surged up suddenly within him. This sensation might be compared to that of a man condemned to death who has suddenly been pardoned. Half-way down the staircase he was overtaken by the priest on his way home; Raskolnikov let him pass, exchanging a silent greeting with him. He was just descending the last steps when he heard rapid footsteps behind him. Someone overtook him; it was Polenka. She was running after him, calling 'Wait! wait!'

He turned round. She was at the bottom of the staircase and stopped short a step above him. A dim light came in from the yard. Raskolnikov could distinguish the child's thin but pretty little face, looking at him with a bright childish smile. She had run after him with a message which she was evidently glad to give.

'Tell me, what is your name? . . . and where do you live?' she said hurriedly in a breathless voice.

He laid both hands on her shoulders and looked at her with a sort of rapture. It was such a joy to him to look at her, he could not have said why.

'Who sent you?'

'Sister Sonia sent me,' answered the girl, smiling still more brightly.

'I knew it was sister Sonia sent you.'

'Mamma sent me, too . . . when sister Sonia was sending me, mamma came up, too, and said, "Run fast, Polenka".'

'Do you love sister Sonia?'

'I love her more than anyone,' Polenka answered with a peculiar earnestness, and her smile became graver.

'And will you love me?'

By way of answer he saw the little girl's face approaching him, her full lips naïvely held out to kiss him. Suddenly her arms as thin as sticks held him tightly, her head rested on his shoulder and the little girl wept softly, pressing her face against him.

'I am sorry for father,' she said a moment later, raising her tear-stained face and brushing away the tears with her hands. 'It's nothing but misfortunes now,' she added suddenly with that peculiarly sedate air which children try hard to assume when they want to speak like grown-up people.

'Did your father love you?'

'He loved Lida most,' she went on very seriously without a smile, exactly like grown-up people, 'he loved her because she is little and because she is ill, too. And he always used to bring her presents. But he taught us to read and me grammar and scripture, too,' she added with dignity. 'And mother never used to say anything, but we knew that she liked it and father knew it, too. And mother wants to teach me French, for it's time my education began.'

'And do you know your prayers?'

'Of course we do! We knew them long ago. I say my prayers to myself as I am a big girl now, but Kolya and Lida say them aloud with mother. First they repeat the "Ave Maria" and then another prayer: "Lord forgive and bless sister Sonia", and then another, "Lord, forgive and bless our second father". For our elder father is dead and this is another one, but we do pray for the other as well.'

'Polenka, my name is Rodion. Pray sometimes for me, too. "And Thy servant Rodion", nothing more.'

'I'll pray for you all the rest of my life,' the little girl declared hotly, and suddenly smiling again she rushed at him and hugged him warmly once more.

Raskolnikov told her his name and address and promised to be sure to come next day. The child went away quite enchanted with him. It was past ten when he came out into the street. In five minutes he was standing on the bridge at the spot where the woman had jumped in.

'Enough,' he pronounced resolutely and triumphantly. 'I've done with fancies, imaginary terrors and phantoms! Life is real! haven't I lived just now? My life has not yet died with that old woman! The Kingdom of Heaven to her – and now enough, madam, leave me in peace! Now for the reign of reason and light . . . and of will, and of strength . . . and now we will see! We will try our strength!' he added defiantly, as though challenging some power of darkness. 'And I was ready to consent to live in a square of space!

'I am very weak at this moment, but . . . I believe my illness is all over. I knew it would be over when I went out. By the way, Potchinkov's house is only a few steps away. I certainly must go to Razumihin even if it were not close by . . . let him win his bet! Let us give him some satisfaction, too – no matter! Strength, strength is what one wants, you can get nothing without it, and strength must be won by strength – that's what they don't know,' he added proudly and self-confidently and he walked with flagging footsteps from the bridge. Pride and self-confidence grew continually stronger in him; he was becoming a different man every moment. What was it had happened to work this revolution in him? He did not know himself; like a man catching at a straw, he suddenly felt that he, too, 'could live, that there was still life for him, that his life had not died with the old woman'. Perhaps he was in too great a hurry with his conclusions, but he did not think of that.

'But I did ask her to remember "Thy servant Rodion" in her prayers,' the idea struck him. 'Well, that was . . . in case of emergency,' he added and laughed himself at his boyish sally. He was in the best of spirits.

He easily found Razumihin; the new lodger was already known at Potchinkov's and the porter at once showed him the way. Half-way upstairs he could hear the noise and animated conversation of a big gathering of people. The door was wide open on the stairs; he could hear exclamations and discussion. Razumihin's room was fairly large; the company consisted of fifteen people. Raskolnikov stopped in the entry, where two of the landlady's servants were busy behind a screen with two samovars, bottles, plates and dishes of pie and savouries, brought up from the landlady's kitchen. Raskolnikov sent in for Razumihin. He ran out delighted. At the first glance it was apparent that he had had a great deal to drink and, though no amount of liquor made Razumihin quite drunk, this time he was perceptibly affected by it.

'Listen,' Raskolnikov hastened to say, 'I've only just come to tell you you've won your bet and that no one really knows what may not happen to him. I can't come in; I am so weak that I shall fall down directly. And so good evening and good-bye! Come and see me to-morrow.'

'Do you know what? I'll see you home. If you say you're weak yourself, you must . . .'

'And your visitors? Who is the curly-headed one who has just peeped out?'

'He? Goodness only knows! Some friend of uncle's, I expect, or perhaps he has come without being invited . . . I'll leave uncle with them, he is an invaluable person, pity I can't introduce you to him now. But confound them all now! They won't notice me, and I need a little fresh air, for you've come just in the nick of time – another two minutes and I should have come to blows! They are talking such a lot of wild stuff . . . you simply can't imagine what men will say! Though why shouldn't you imagine? Don't we talk nonsense ourselves? And let them . . . that's the way to learn not to! . . . Wait a minute, I'll fetch Zossimov.'

Zossimov pounced upon Raskolnikov almost greedily; he showed a special interest in him; soon his face brightened.

'You must go to bed at once,' he pronounced, examining the patient as far as he could, 'and take something for the night. Will you take it? I got it ready some time ago . . . a powder.'

'Two, if you like,' answered Raskolnikov. The powder was taken at once.

'It's a good thing you are taking him home,' observed Zossimov to Razumihin – 'we shall see how he is to-morrow, to-day he's not at all amiss: a considerable change since the afternoon. Live and learn . . .'

'Do you know what Zossimov whispered to me when we were coming out?' Razumihin blurted out, as soon as they were in the street. 'I won't tell you everything, brother, because they are such fools. Zossimov told me to talk freely to you on the way and get you to talk freely to me, and afterwards I am to tell him about it, for he's got a notion in his head that you are . . . mad or close on it. Only fancy! In the first place, you've three times the brains he has; in the second, if you are not mad, you needn't care a hang that he has got such a wild idea; and thirdly, that piece of beef whose speciality is surgery has gone mad on mental diseases, and what's brought him to this conclusion about you was your conversation to-day with Zametov.'

'Zametov told you all about it?'

'Yes, and he did well. Now I understand what it all means and so does Zametov. . . . Well, the fact is, Rodya . . . the point is . . . I am a little drunk now. . . . But that's . . . no matter . . . the point is that this idea . . . you understand? was just being hatched in their brains . . . you understand? That is, no one ventured to say it aloud, because the idea is too absurd and especially since the arrest of that painter, that bubble's burst and gone for ever. But why are they such fools? I gave Zametov a bit of a thrashing at the time – that's between ourselves, brother; please don't let out a hint that you know of it; I've noticed he is a ticklish subject; it was at Luise Ivanovna's. But to-day, to-day it's all cleared up. That Ilya Petrovitch is at the bottom of it! He took advantage of your fainting at the police station, but he is ashamed of it himself now; I know that . . .'

Raskolnikov listened greedily. Razumihin was drunk enough to talk too freely.

'I fainted then because it was so close and the smell of paint,' said Raskolnikov.

'No need to explain that! And it wasn't the paint only: the fever had been coming on for a month; Zossimov testifies to that! But how crushed that boy is now, you wouldn't believe! "I am not worth his little finger," he says. Yours, he means. He has good feelings at times, brother. But the lesson, the lesson you gave him to-day in the Palais de Cristal, that was too good for anything! You frightened him at first, you know, he nearly went into convulsions! You almost convinced him again of the truth of all that hideous nonsense, and then you suddenly – put out your tongue at him: "There now, what do you make of it?" It was perfect! He is crushed, annihilated now! It was masterly, by Jove, it's what they deserve! Ah, that I wasn't there! He was hoping to see you awfully. Porfiry, too, wants to make your acquaintance . . .'

'Ah! . . . he too . . . but why did they put me down as mad?'

'Oh, not mad. I must have said too much, brother. . . . What struck him, you see, was that only that subject seemed to interest you; now it's clear why it did interest you; knowing all the circumstances . . . and how that irritated you and worked in with your illness . . . I am a little drunk, brother, only, confound him, he has some idea of his own . . . I tell you, he's mad on mental diseases. But don't you mind him . . .'

For half a minute both were silent.

'Listen, Razumihin,' began Raskolnikov, 'I want to tell you plainly: I've just been at a death-bed, a clerk who died . . . I gave them all my money . . . and besides I've just been kissed by someone who, if I had killed anyone, would just the same . . . in fact I saw someone else there . . . with a flame-coloured feather . . . but I am talking nonsense; I am very weak, support me . . . we shall be at the stairs directly . . .'

'What's the matter? What's the matter with you?' Razumihin asked anxiously.

'I am a little giddy, but that's not the point, I am so sad, so sad . . . like a woman. Look, what's that? Look, look!'

'What is it?'

'Don't you see? A light in my room, you see? Through the crack . . .'

They were already at the foot of the last flight of stairs, at the level of the landlady's door, and they could, as a fact, see from below that there was a light in Raskolnikov's garret.

'Queer! Nastasya, perhaps,' observed Razumihin.

'She is never in my room at this time and she must be in bed long ago, but . . . I don't care! Good-bye!'

'What do you mean? I am coming with you, we'll come in together!'

'I know we are going in together, but I want to shake hands here and say good-bye to you here. So give me your hand, good-bye!'

'What's the matter with you, Rodya?'

'Nothing . . . come along . . . you shall be witness.'

They began mounting the stairs, and the idea struck Razumihin that perhaps Zossimov might be right after all. 'Ah, I've upset him with my chatter!' he muttered to himself.

When they reached the door they heard voices in the room.

'What is it?' cried Razumihin.

Raskolnikov was the first to open the door; he flung it wide and stood still in the doorway, dumbfoundered.

His mother and sister were sitting on his sofa and had been waiting an hour and a half for him. Why had he never expected, never thought of them, though the news that they had started, were on their way and would arrive immediately, had been repeated to him only that day? They had spent that hour and a half plying Nastasya with questions. She was still standing before them and had told them everything by now. They were beside themselves with alarm when they heard of his 'running away' to-day, ill and, as they understood from her story, delirious! 'Good Heavens, what had become of him?' Both had been weeping, both had been in anguish for that hour and a half.

A cry of joy, of ecstasy, greeted Raskolnikov's entrance. Both rushed to him. But he stood like one dead; a sudden intolerable sensation struck him like a thunderbolt. He did not lift his arms to embrace them, he could not. His mother and sister clasped him in their arms, kissed him, laughed and cried. He took a step, tottered and fell to the ground, fainting.

Anxiety, cries of horror, moans . . . Razumihin who was standing in the doorway flew into the room, seized the sick man in his strong arms and in a moment had him on the sofa.

'it's nothing, nothing!' he cried to the mother and sister – 'It's only a faint, a mere trifle! Only just now the doctor said he was much better, that he is perfectly well! Water! See, he is coming to himself, he is all right again!'

And seizing Dounia by the arm so that he almost dislocated it, he made her bend down to see that 'he is all right again'. The mother and sister looked on him with emotion and gratitude, as their Providence. They had heard already from Nastasya all that had been done for their Rodya during his illness, by this 'very competent young man', as Pulcheria Alexandrovna Raskolnikov called him that evening in conversation with Dounia.

PART THREE

❧ ONE ❧

Raskolnikov GOT UP, AND SAT down on the sofa. He waved his hand weakly to Razumihin to cut short the flow of warm and incoherent consolations he was addressing to his mother and sister, took them both by the hand and for a minute or two gazed from one to the other without speaking. His mother was alarmed by his expression. It revealed an emotion agonizingly poignant, and at the same time something immovable, almost insane. Pulcheria Alexandrovna began to cry.

Pulcheria Alexandrovna was pale; her hand trembled in her brother's.

'Go home ... with him,' he said in a broken voice, pointing to Razumihin, 'good-bye till to-morrow; to-morrow everything. . . . Is it long since you arrived?'

'This evening, Rodya,' answered Pulcheria Alexandrovna, 'the train was awfully late. But, Rodya, nothing would induce me to leave you now! I will spend the night here, near you. . . .'

'Don't torture me!' he said with a gesture of irritation.

'I will stay with him,' cried Razumihin, 'I won't leave him for a moment. Bother all my visitors! Let them rage to their hearts' content! My uncle is presiding there.'

'How, how can I thank you!' Pulcheria Alexandrovna was beginning, once more pressing Razumihin's hands, but Raskolnikov interrupted her again.

'I can't have it! I can't have it!' he repeated irritably, 'don't worry me! Enough, go away. . . . I can't stand it!'

'Come, mamma, come out of the room at least for a minute,' Dounia whispered in dismay; 'we are distressing him, that's evident.'

'Mayn't I look at him after three years?' wept Pulcheria Alexandrovna.

'Stay,' he stopped them again, 'you keep interrupting me, and my ideas get muddled ... Have you seen Luzhin?'

'No Rodya, but he knows already of our arrival. We have heard, Rodya, that Pyotr Petrovitch was so kind as to visit you today,' Pulcheria Alexandrovna added somewhat timidly.

'Yes ... he was so kind ... Dounia, I promised Luzhin I'd throw him downstairs and told him to go to hell. . . .'

'Rodya, what are you saying? Surely, you don't mean to tell us . . .' Pulcheria Alexandrovna began in alarm, but she stopped, looking at Dounia.

Avdotya Romanovna was looking attentively at her brother, waiting for what would come next. Both of them had heard of the quarrel from Nastasya, so far as she had succeeded in understanding and reporting it, and were in painful perplexity and suspense.

'Dounia,' Raskolnikov continued with an effort, 'I don't want that marriage, so at the first opportunity tomorrow you must refuse Luzhin, so that we may never hear his name again.'

'Good heavens!' cried Pulcheria Alexandrovna.

'Brother, think what you are saying!' Avdotya Romanovna began impetuously, but immediately checked herself. 'You are not fit to talk now, perhaps; you are tired,' she added gently.

'You think I am delirious? No. . . . You are marrying Luzhin for *my* sake. But I won't accept the sacrifice. And so write a letter before tomorrow, to refuse him. . . . Let me read it in the morning and that will be the end of it!'

'That I can't do!' the girl cried, offended, 'what right have you . . .'

'Dounia, you are hasty, too, be quiet, to-morrow. . . . Don't you see' . . . the mother interposed in dismay. 'Better come away!'

'He is raving,' Razumihin cried tipsily, 'or how would he dare! To-morrow all this nonsense will be over. . . . To-day he certainly did drive him away. That was so. And Luzhin got angry, too. . . . He made speeches here, wanted to show off his learning and went out crest-fallen. . . .'

'Then it's true?' cried Pulcheria Alexandrovna.

'Good-bye till to-morrow, brother,' said Dounia compassionately – 'let us go, mother. . . . Good-bye, Rodya.'

'Do you hear, sister,' he repeated after them, making a last effort, 'I am not delirious; this marriage is – an infamy. Let me act like a scoundrel, but you mustn't . . . one is enough . . . and though I am a scoundrel, I wouldn't own such a sister. It's me or Luzhin! Go now. . . .'

'But you're out of your mind! Despot!' roared Razumihin; but Raskolnikov did not and perhaps could not answer. He lay down on the sofa, and turned to the wall, utterly exhausted. Avdotya Romanovna looked with interest at Razumihin; her black eyes flashed; Razumihin positively started at her glance.

Pulcheria Alexandrovna stood overwhelmed.

'Nothing would induce me to go,' she whispered in despair to Razumihin. 'I will stay somewhere here . . . escort Dounia home.'

'You'll spoil everything,' Razumihin answered in the same whisper, losing patience – 'come out on to the stairs, anyway. Nastasya, show a light! I assure you,' he went on in a half-whisper on the stairs – 'that he was almost beating the doctor and me this afternoon! Do you understand? The doctor himself! Even he gave way and left him, so as not to irritate him. I remained downstairs on guard, but he dressed at once and slipped off. And he will slip off again if you irritate him, at this time of night, and will do himself some mischief. . . .'

'What are you saying?'

'And Avdotya Romanovna can't possibly be left in those lodgings without you. Just think where you are staying! That blackguard Pyotr Petrovitch couldn't find you better lodgings. . . . But you know I've had a little to drink, and that's what makes me . . . swear; don't mind it. . . .'

'But I'll go to the landlady here,' Pulcheria Alexandrovna insisted, 'I'll beseech her to find some corner for Dounia and me for the night. I can't leave him like that, I cannot!'

This conversation took place on the landing just before the landlady's door. Nastasya lighted them from a step below. Razumihin was in extraordinary excitement. Half an hour earlier, while he was bringing Raskolnikov home, he had indeed talked too freely, but he was aware of it himself, and his head was clear in spite of the vast quantities he had imbibed. Now he was in a state bordering on ecstasy, and all that he had drunk seemed to fly to his head with redoubled effect. He stood with the two ladies, seizing both by their hands, persuading them, and giving them reasons with astonishing plainness of speech, and at almost every word he uttered, probably to emphasize his arguments, he squeezed their hands painfully as in a vice. He stared at Avdotya Romanovna without the least regard for good manners. They sometimes pulled their hands out of his huge bony paws, but far from noticing what was the matter he drew them all the closer to him. If they'd told him to jump head foremost from the staircase, he would have done it without thought or hesitation in their service. Though Pulcheria Alexandrovna felt that the young man was really too eccentric and pinched her hand too much, in her anxiety over her Rodya she looked on his presence as providential, and was unwilling to notice all his peculiarities. But though Avdotya Romanovna shared her anxiety, and was not of timorous disposition, she could see the glowing light in his eyes without wonder and almost alarm. It was only the unbounded confidence inspired by Nastasya's account of her brother's queer friend, which prevented her from trying to run away from him, and to persuade her mother to do the same. She realized, too, that even running away was perhaps impossible now. Ten minutes later, however, she was considerably reassured; it was characteristic of Razumihin that he showed his true nature at once, whatever mood be might be in, so that people quickly saw the sort of man they had to deal with.

'You can't go to the landlady, that's perfect nonsense!' he cried. 'If you stay, though you are his mother, you'll drive him into a frenzy, and then goodness knows what will happen! Listen, I'll tell you what I'll do: Nastasya will stay with him now, and I'll conduct you both home, you can't be in the streets alone; Petersburg is an awful place in that way. . . . But no matter! Then I'll run straight back here and a quarter of an hour later, on my word of honour, I'll bring you news how he is, whether he is asleep, and all that. Then, listen! Then I'll run home in a twinkling – I've a lot of friends there, all drunk – I'll fetch Zossimov – that's the doctor who is looking after him, he is there, too, but he is not drunk; he is not drunk, he is never drunk! I'll drag him to Rodya, and then to you, so that you'll get two reports in the hour – from the doctor, you understand, from the doctor himself, that's a very different thing from my account of him! If there's anything wrong, I swear I'll bring you here myself, but, if it's all right, you go to bed. And I'll spend the night here, in the passage, he won't hear me, and I'll tell Zossimov to sleep at the landlady's, to be at hand. Which is better for him: you or the doctor? So come home then! But the landlady is out of the question; it's all right for me, but it's out of the question for you: she wouldn't take you, for she's . . . for she's a fool. . . . She'd be jealous on my account of Avdotya Romanovna and of you, too, if you want to know . . . of Avdotya Romanovna certainly. She is an absolutely, absolutely unaccountable character! But I am a fool, too! . . . No matter! Come along! Do you trust me? Come, do you trust me or not?'

'Let us go mother,' said Avdotya Romanovna, 'he will certainly do what he has promised. He has saved Rodya already, and if the doctor really will consent to spend the night here, what could be better?'

'You see, you . . . you . . . understand me, because you are an angel!' Razumihin cried in an ecstasy, 'let us go! Nastasya! Fly upstairs and sit with him with a light; I'll come in a quarter of an hour.'

Though Pulcheria Alexandrovna was not perfectly convinced, she made no further resistance. Razumihin gave an arm to each and drew them down the stairs. He still made her uneasy, as though he was competent and good-natured, was he capable of carrying out his promise? He seemed in such a condition. . . .

'Ah, I see you think I am in such a condition!' Razumihin broke in upon her thoughts, guessing them, as he strolled along the pavement with huge steps, so that the two ladies could hardly keep up with him, a fact he did not observe, however. 'Nonsense! That is . . . I am drunk like a fool, but that's not it; I am not drunk from wine. It's seeing you has turned my head.... But don't mind me! Don't take any notice: I am talking nonsense, I am not worthy of you.... I am utterly unworthy of you! The minute I've taken you home, I'll pour a couple of pailfuls of water over my head in the gutter here, and then I shall be all right.... If only you knew how I love you both! Don't laugh, and don't be angry! You may be angry with anyone, but not with me! I am his friend, and therefore I am your friend, too. I want to be.... I had a presentiment... last year there was a moment... though it wasn't a presentiment really, for you seem to have fallen from heaven. And I expect I shan't sleep all night.... Zossimov was afraid a little time ago that he would go mad... that's why he mustn't be irritated.'

'What do you say?' cried the mother.

'Did the doctor really say that?' asked Avdotya Romanovna, alarmed.

'Yes, but it's not so, not a bit of it. He gave him some medicine, a powder, I saw it, and then your coming here.... Ah! It would have been better if you had come tomorrow. It's a good thing we went away. And in an hour Zossimov himself will report to you about everything. He is not drunk! And I shan't be drunk.... And what made me get so tight? Because they got me into an argument, damn them! I've sworn never to argue! They talk such trash! I almost came to blows! I've left my uncle to preside. Would you believe, they insist on complete absence of individualism and that's just what they relish! Not to be themselves, to be as unlike themselves as they can. That's what they regard as the highest point of progress. If only their nonsense were their own, but as it is...'

'Listen!' Pulcheria Alexandrovna interrupted timidly, but it only added fuel to the flames.

'What do you think?' shouted Razumihin, louder than ever, 'you think I am attacking them for talking nonsense? Not a bit! I like them to talk nonsense. That's man's one privilege over all creation. Through error you come to the truth! I am a man because I err! You never reach any truth without making fourteen mistakes and very likely a hundred and fourteen. And a fine thing, too, in its way; but we can't even make mistakes on our own account! Talk nonsense, but talk your own nonsense, and I'll kiss you for it. To go wrong in one's own way is better than to go right in someone else's. In the first case you are a man, in the second you're no better than a bird. Truth won't escape you, but life can be cramped. There have been examples. And what are we doing now? In science, development, thought, invention, ideals, aims, liberalism, judgment, experience and everything, everything, everything, we are still in the preparatory class at school. We prefer to live on other people's ideas, it's what we are used to! Am I right, am I right?' cried Razumihin, pressing and shaking the two ladies' hands.

'Oh mercy, I do not know,' cried poor Pulcheria Alexandrovna.

'Yes, yes . . . though I don't agree with you in everything,' added Avdotya Romanovna earnestly and at once uttered a cry, for he squeezed her hand so painfully.

'Yes you say yes . . . well, after that you . . . you . . .' he cried in a transport, 'you are a fount of goodness, purity, sense . . . and perfection. Give me your hand . . . you give me yours too! I want to kiss your hands here at once, on my knees . . .' and he fell on his knees on the pavement, fortunately at that time deserted.

'Leave off, I entreat you, what are you doing?' Pulcheria Alexandrovna cried, greatly distressed.

'Get up, get up!' said Dounia laughing, though she, too, was upset.

'Not for anything till you let me kiss you hands! That's it! Enough! I get up and we'll go on! I am a luckless fool, I am unworthy of you and drunk . . . and I am ashamed . . . I am not worthy to love you, but to do homage to you is the duty of every man who is not a perfect beast! And I've done homage. . . . Here are your lodgings, and for that alone Rodya was right in driving your Pyotr Petrovitch away. . . . How dare he! how dare he put you in such lodgings! It's a scandal! Do you know the sort of people they take in here? And you his betrothed! You are his betrothed? Yes? Well, then, I tell you, your *fiancé* is a scoundrel.'

'Excuse me, Mr. Razumihin, you are forgetting . . .' Pulcheria Alexandrovna was beginning.

'Yes, yes, you are right, I did forget myself, I am ashamed of it.' Razumihin made haste to apologise. 'But . . . but you can't be angry with me for speaking so! For I speak sincerely and not because . . . hm, hm! That would be disgraceful; in fact not because I'm in . . . hm! Well anyway, I won't say why, I daren't. . . . But we all saw to-day when he came in that that man is not of our sort. Not because he had his hair curled at the barber's, not because he was in such a hurry to show his wit, but because he is a spy, a speculator, because he is a skinflint and a buffoon. That's evident. Do you think him clever? No, he is a fool, a fool. And is he a match for you? Good heavens! Do you see, ladies?' he stopped suddenly on the way upstairs to their rooms, 'though all my friends there are drunk, yet they are all honest, and though we do talk a lot of trash, and I do, too, yet we shall talk our way to the truth at last, for we are on the right path, while Pyotr Petrovitch . . . is not on the right path. Though I've been calling them all sorts of names just now, I do respect them all . . . though I don't respect Zametov, I like him, for he is a puppy, and that bullock Zossimov, because he is an honest man and knows his work. But enough, it's all said and forgiven. Is it forgiven? Well, then, let's go on. I know this corridor, I've been here, there was a scandal at Number 3. . . .

Where are you here? Which number? eight? Well, lock yourselves in for the night, then. Don't let anybody in. In a quarter of an hour I'll come back with news, and half an hour later I'll bring Zossimov, you'll see! Goodbye, I'll run.'

'Good heavens, Dounia, what is going to happen?' said Pulcheria Alexandrovna, addressing her daughter with anxiety and dismay.

'Don't worry yourself, mother,' said Dounia, taking off her hat and cape. 'God has sent this gentleman to our aid, though he has come from a drinking party. We can depend on him, I assure you. And all that he has done for Rodya . . .'

'Ah, Dounia, goodness knows whether he will come! How could I bring myself to leave Rodya? . . . And how different, how different I had fancied our meeting! How sullen he was, as though not pleased to see us. . . .'

Tears came to her eyes.

'No, it's not that, mother. You didn't see, you were crying all the time. He is quite unhinged by serious illness – that's the reason.'

'Ah, that illness! What will happen, what will happen? And how he talked to you, Dounia!' said the mother, looking timidly at her daughter, trying to read her thoughts and, already half consoled by Dounia's standing up for her brother, which meant that she had already forgiven him. 'I am sure he will think better of it tomorrow,' she added, probing her further.

'And I am sure that he will say the same tomorrow . . . about that,' Avdotya Romanovna said finally. And, of course, there was no going beyond that, for this was a point which Pulcheria Alexandrovna was afraid to discuss. Dounia went up and kissed her mother. The latter warmly embraced her without speaking. Then she sat down to wait anxiously for Razumihin's return, timidly watching her daughter who walked up and down the room with her arms folded, lost in thought. This walking up and down when she was thinking was a habit of Avdotya Romanovna's and the mother was always afraid to break in on her daughter's mood at such moments.

Razumihin, of course, was ridiculous in his sudden drunken infatuation for Avdotya Romanovna. Yet apart from his eccentric condition, many people would have thought it justified, if they had seen Avdotya Romanovna, especially at that moment when she was walking to and fro with folded arms, pensive and melancholy. Avdotya Romanovna was remarkably good-looking; she was tall, strikingly well-proportioned, strong and self-reliant – the latter quality was apparent in every gesture, though it did not in the least detract from the grace and softness of her movements. In face she resembled her brother, but she might be described as really beautiful. Her hair was dark brown, a little lighter than her brother's; there was a proud light in her almost black eyes and yet at times a look of extraordinary kindness. She was pale, but it was a healthy pallor; her face was radiant with freshness and vigour. Her mouth was rather small; the full red lower lip projected a little as did her chin; it was the only irregularity in her beautiful face, but it gave it a peculiarly individual and almost haughty expression. Her face was always more serious and thoughtful than gay; but how well smiles, how well youthful, light-hearted, irresponsible laughter suited her face! It was natural enough that a warm, open, simple-hearted, honest giant like Razumihin, who had never seen anyone like her and was not quite sober at the time, should lose his head immediately. Besides, as chance would have it, he saw Dounia for the first time transfigured by her love for her brother and her joy at meeting him. Afterwards he saw her lower lip quiver with indignation at her brother's insolent, cruel and ungrateful words – and his fate was sealed.

He had spoken the truth, moreover, when he blurted out in his drunken talk on the stairs that Praskovya Pavlovna, Raskolnikov's eccentric land-lady, would be jealous of Pulcheria Alexandrovna as well as of Avdotya Romanovna on his account. Although Pulcheria Alexandrovna was forty-three, her face still retained traces of her former beauty; she looked much younger than her age, indeed, which is almost always the case with women who retain serenity of spirit, sensitiveness and pure sincere warmth of heart to old age. We may add in parenthesis that to preserve all this is the only means of retaining beauty to old age. Her hair had begun to grow grey and thin, there had long been little crow's-foot wrink-les round her eyes, her cheeks were hollow and sunken from anxiety and grief, and yet it was a handsome face. She was Dounia over again, twenty years older, but without the projecting underlip. Pulcheria Alexandrovna was emotional, but not sentimental, timid and yielding, but only to a certain point. She could give way and accept a great deal even of what was contrary to her convictions, but there was a certain barrier fixed by honesty, principle and the deepest convictions which nothing would induce her to cross.

Exactly twenty minutes after Razumihin's departure, there came two subdued but hurried knocks at the door: he had come back.

'I won't come in, I haven't time,' he hastened to say when the door was opened. 'He sleeps like a top, soundly, quietly, and God grant he may sleep ten hours. Nastasya's with him; I told her not to leave till I came. Now I am fetching Zossimov, he will report to you and then you'd better turn in; I can see you are too tired to do anything. . . .'

And he ran off down the corridor.

'What a very competent and . . . devoted young man!' cried Pulcheria Alexandrovna exceedingly delighted.

'He seems a splendid person!' Avdotya Romanovna replied with some warmth, resuming her walk up and down the room.

It was nearly an hour later when they heard footsteps in the corridor and another knock at the door. Both women waited this time completely relying on Razumihin's promise; he actually had succeeded in bringing Zossimov. Zossimov had agreed at once to desert the drinking party to go to Raskolnikov's, but he came reluctantly and with the greatest suspicion to see the ladies, mistrusting Razumihin in his exhilarated condition. But his vanity was at once reassured and flattered; he saw that they were really expecting him as an oracle. He stayed just ten minutes and succeeded in completely convincing and comforting Pulcheria Alexandrovna. He spoke with marked sympathy, but with the reserve and extreme seriousness of a young doctor at an important consultation. He did not utter a word on any other subject and did not display the slightest desire to enter into more personal relations with the two ladies. Remarking at his first entrance the dazzling beauty of Avdotya Romanovna, he endeavoured not to notice her at all during his visit and addressed himself solely to Pulcheria Alexandrovna. All this gave him extraordinary inward satisfaction. He declared that he thought the invalid at this moment going on very satisfactorily. According to his observations the patient's illness was due partly to his unfortunate material surroundings during the last few months, but it had partly also a moral origin, 'was, so to speak, the product of several material and moral influences, anxieties, apprehensions, troubles, certain ideas . . . and so on'. Noticing stealthily that Avdotya Romanovna was following his words with close attention, Zossimov allowed himself to enlarge on this theme. On Pulcheria Alexandrovna's anxiously and timidly inquiring as to 'some suspicion of insanity', he replied with a composed and candid smile that his words had been exaggerated; that certainly the patient had some fixed idea, something approaching a monomania – he, Zossimov, was now particularly studying this interesting branch of medicine – but that it must be recollected that until today the patient had been in delirium and . . . and that no doubt the presence of his family would have a favourable effect on his recovery and distract his mind, 'if only all fresh shocks can be avoided', he added significantly. Then he got up, took his leave with an impressive and affable bow, while blessings, warm gratitude, and entreaties were showered upon him, and Avdotya Romanovna spontaneously offered her hand to him. He went out exceedingly pleased with his visit and still more so with himself.

'We'll talk to-morrow; go to bed at once!' Razumihin said in conclusion, following Zossimov out. 'I'll be with you tomorrow morning as early as possible with my report.'

'That's a fetching little girl, Avdotya Romanovna,' remarked Zossimov, almost licking his lips as they both came out into the street.

'Fetching? You said fetching?' roared Razumihin, and he flew at Zossimov and seized him by the throat. 'If you ever dare . . . Do you understand? Do you understand?' he shouted, shaking him by the collar and squeezing him against the wall. 'Do you hear?'

'Let me go, you drunken devil,' said Zossimov, struggling, and when he had let him go, he stared at him and went off into a sudden guffaw. Razumihin stood facing him in a gloomy and earnest reflection.

'Of course, I am an ass,' he observed, sombre as a storm cloud, 'but still . . . you are another.'

'No, brother, not at all such another. I am not dreaming of any folly.'

They walked along in silence and only when they were close to Raskolnikov's lodgings, Razumihin broke the silence in considerable anxiety.

'Listen,' he said, 'you're a first-rate fellow, but among your other failings, you're a loose fish, that I know, and a dirty one, too. You are a feeble, nervous wretch, and a mass of whims, you're getting fat and lazy and can't deny yourself anything – and I call that dirty because it leads one straight into the dirt. You've let yourself go so slack that I don't know how it is you are still a good, even a devoted doctor. You – a doctor – sleep on a feather bed and get up at night to your patients! In another three or four years you won't get up for your patients. . . . But hang it all, that's not the point! . . . You are going to spend tonight in the landlady's flat here. (Hard work I've had to persuade her!) And I'll be in the kitchen. So here's a chance for you to get to know her better. . . . It's not as you think! There's not a trace of anything of the sort, brother . . .!'

'But I don't think!'

'Here you have modesty, brother, silence, bashfulness, a savage virtue . . . and yet she's sighing and melting like wax, simply melting! Save me from her, by all that's unholy! She's most prepossessing. . . . I'll repay you, I'll do anything. . . .'

Zossimov laughed more violently than ever.

'Well, you are smitten! But what am I to do with her?'

'It won't be much trouble, I assure you. Talk any rot you like to her, as long as you sit by her and talk. You're a doctor, too; try curing her of something. I swear you won't regret it. She has a piano, and you know, I strum a little. I have a song there, a genuine Russian one: "I shed hot tears". She likes the genuine article – and well, it all began with that song; Now you're a regular performer, a *maître*, a Rubinstein. . . . I assure you, you won't regret it!'

'But have you made her some promise? Something signed? A promise of marriage, perhaps?'

'Nothing, nothing, absolutely nothing of the kind! Besides she is not that sort at all. . . . Tchebarov tried that. . . .'

'Well then, drop her!'

'But I can't drop her like that!'

'Why can't you?'

'Well, I can't, that's all about it! There's an element of attraction here, brother.'

'Then why have you fascinated her?'

'I haven't fascinated her; perhaps I was fascinated myself in my folly. But she won't care a straw whether it's you or I, so long as somebody sits beside her, sighing. . . . I can't explain the position, brother . . . look here, you are good at mathematics, and working at it now . . . begin teaching her the integral calculus; upon my soul, I'm not joking, I'm in earnest, it'll be just the same to her. She will gaze at you and sigh for a whole year together. I talked to her once for two days at a time about the Prussian House of Lords (for one must talk of something) – she just sighed and perspired! And you mustn't talk of love – she's bashful to hysterics – but just let her see you can't tear yourself away – that's enough. It's fearfully comfortable; you're quite at home, you can read, sit, lie about, write. You may even venture on a kiss, if you're careful.'

'But what do I want with her?'

'Ach, I can't make you understand! You see, you are made for each other! I have often been reminded of you! . . . You'll come to it in the end! So does it matter whether it's sooner or later? There's the feather-bed element here, brother, – ach! and not only that! There's an attraction here – here you have the end of the world, an anchorage, a quiet haven, the navel of the earth, the three fishes that are the foundation of the world, the essence of pancakes, of savoury fish-pies, of the evening samovar, of soft sighs and warm shawls, and hot stoves to sleep on – as snug as though you were dead, and yet you're alive – the advantages of both at once! Well, hang it, brother, what stuff I'm talking, it's bedtime! Listen. I sometimes wake up at night; so I'll go in and look at him. But there's no need, it's all right. Don't worry yourself, yet if you like, you might just look in once, too. But if you notice anything – delirium or fever – wake me at once. But there can't be. . . .'

✦ TWO ✦

RAZUMIHIN WAKED UP NEXT morning at eight o'clock, troubled and serious. He found himself confronted with many new and unlooked-for perplexities. He had never expected that he would ever wake up feeling like that. He remembered every detail of the previous day and he knew that a perfectly novel experience had befallen him, that he had received an impression unlike anything he had known before. At the same time he recognized clearly that the dream which had fired his imagination was hopelessly unattainable – so unattainable that he felt positively ashamed of it, and he hastened to pass to other more practical cares and difficulties bequeathed him by that 'thrice accursed yesterday'.

The most awful recollection of the previous day was the way he had shown himself 'base and mean', not only because he had been drunk, but because he had taken advantage of the young girl's position to abuse her *fiancé* in his stupid jealousy, knowing nothing of their mutual relations and obligations and next to nothing of the man himself. And what right had he to criticize him in that hasty and unguarded manner? Who had asked his opinion? Was it thinkable that such a creature as Avdotya Romanovna would be marrying an unworthy man for money? So there must be something in him. The lodgings? But after all how could he know the character of the lodgings? He was furnishing a flat . . . Foo! how despicable it all was! And what justification was it that he was drunk? Such a stupid excuse was even more degrading! In wine is truth, and the truth had all come out, 'that is, all the uncleanness of his coarse and envious heart'! And would such a dream ever be permissible to him, Razumihin? What was he beside such a girl – he, the drunken noisy braggart of last night? Was it possible to imagine so absurd and cynical a juxtaposition? Razumihin blushed desperately at the very idea and suddenly the recollection forced itself vividly upon him of how he had said last night on the stairs that the landlady would be jealous of Avdotya Romanovna . . . that was simply intolerable. He brought his fist down heavily on the kitchen stove, hurt his hand and sent one of the bricks flying.

'Of course,' he muttered to himself a minute later with a feeling of self-abasement, 'of course, all these infamies can never be wiped out or smoothed over . . . and so it's useless even to think of it, and I must go to them in silence and . . . do my duty . . . in silence, too . . . and not ask forgiveness, and say nothing . . . for all is lost now!'

And yet as he dressed he examined his attire more carefully than usual. He hadn't another suit – if he had had, perhaps he wouldn't have put it on. 'I would have made a point of not putting it on.' But in any case he could not remain a cynic and a dirty sloven; he had no right to offend the feelings of others, especially when they are in need of his assistance and asking him to see them. He brushed his clothes carefully. His linen was always decent; in that respect he was especially clean.

He washed that morning scrupulously – he got some soap from Nastasya – he washed his hair, his neck and especially his hands. When it came to the question whether to shave his stubbly chin or not (Praskovya Pavlovna had capital razors that had been left by her late husband), the question was angrily answered in the negative. 'Let it stay as it is! What if they think I have shaved on purpose to . . .? They certainly would think so! Not on any account!'

'And . . . the worst of it was he was so coarse, so dirty, he had the manners of a pothouse; and . . . and even admitting that he knew he had some of the essentials of a gentleman . . . what was there in that to be proud of? Everyone ought to be a gentleman and more than that . . . and all the same (he remembered) he, too, had done little things . . . not exactly dishonest, and yet . . . And what thoughts he sometimes had; hm . . . and to set all that beside Avdotya Romanovna! Confound it! So be it! Well, he'd make a point then of being dirty, greasy, pothouse in his manners and he wouldn't care! He'd be worse!'

He was engaged in such monologues when Zossimov, who had spent the night in Praskovya Pavlovna's parlour, came in.

He was going home and was in a hurry to look at the invalid first. Razumihin informed him that Raskolnikov was sleeping like a dormouse. Zossimov gave orders that they shouldn't wake him and promised to see him again about eleven.

'If he is still at home,' he added. 'Damn it all! If one can't control one's patients, how is one to cure them? Do you know whether *he* will go to them, or whether *they* are coming here?'

'They are coming, I think,' said Razumihin, understanding the object of the question, 'and they will discuss their family affairs, no doubt. I'll be off. You, as the doctor, have more right to be here than I.'

'But I am not a father confessor; I shall come and go away; I've plenty to do besides looking after them.'

'One thing worries me,' interposed Razumihin, frowning. 'On the way home I talked a lot of drunken nonsense to him . . . all sorts of things . . . and amongst them that you were afraid that he . . . might become insane.'

'You told the ladies so, too.'

'I know it was stupid! You may beat me if you like! Did you think so seriously?'

'That's nonsense, I tell you, how could I think it seriously? You, yourself, described him as a monomaniac when you fetched me to him . . . and we added fuel to the fire yesterday, you did, that is, with your story about the painter; it was a nice conversation when he was, perhaps, mad on that very point! If only I'd known what happened then at the police station and that some wretch . . . had insulted him with his suspicion! Hm . . . I would not have allowed that conversation yesterday. These monomaniacs will make a mountain out of a mole-hill . . . and see their fancies as solid realities . . . As far as I remember, it was Zametov's story that cleared up half the mystery, to my mind. Why, I know one case in which a hypochondriac, a man of forty, cut the throat of a little boy of eight, because he couldn't endure the jokes he made every day at table! And in this case his rags, the insolent police officer, the fever and this suspicion! All that working upon a man half frantic with hypochondria, and with his morbid exceptional vanity! That may well have been the starting-point of illness. Well, bother it all! . . . And, by the way, that Zametov certainly is a nice fellow, but hm . . . he shouldn't have told all that last night. He is an awful chatterbox!'

'But whom did he tell it to? You and me?'

'And Porfiry.'

'What does that matter?'

'And by the way, have you any influence on them, his mother and sister? Tell them to be more careful with him today . . .'

'They'll get on all right!' Razumihin answered reluctantly.

'Why is he so set against this Luzhin? A man with money and she doesn't seem to dislike him . . . and they haven't a farthing, I suppose? eh?'

'But what business is it of yours?' Razumihin cried with annoyance. 'How can I tell whether they've a farthing? Ask them yourself and perhaps you'll find out . . .'

'Foo! what an ass you are sometimes! Last night's wine has not gone off yet . . . Good-bye; thank your Praskovya Pavlovna from me for my night's lodging. She locked herself in, made no reply to my *bonjour* through the door; she was up at seven o'clock, the samovar was taken into her from the kitchen. I was not vouchsafed a personal interview. . . .'

At nine o'clock precisely Razuhimin reached the lodgings at Bakaleyev's house. Both ladies were waiting for him with nervous impatience. They had risen at seven o'clock or earlier. He entered looking as black as night, bowed awkwardly and was at once furious with himself for it. He had reckoned without his host: Pulcheria Alexandrovna fairly rushed at him, seized him by both hands and was almost kissing them. He glanced timidly at Avdotya Romanovna, but her proud countenance wore at that moment an expression of such gratitude and friendliness, such complete and unlooked-for respect (in place of the sneering looks and ill-disguised contempt he had expected), that it threw him into greater confusion than if he had been met with abuse. Fortunately there was a subject of conversation, and he made haste to snatch at it.

Hearing that everything was going well and that Rodya had not yet waked, Pulcheria Alexandrovna declared that she was glad to hear it, because 'she had something which it was very necessary to talk over beforehand'. Then followed an inquiry about breakfast and an invitation to have it with them; they had waited to have it with him. Avdotya Romanovna rang the bell; it was answered by a ragged dirty waiter, and they asked him to bring tea which was served at last, but in such a dirty and disorderly way that the ladies were ashamed. Razumihin vigorously attacked the lodgings, but, remembering Luzhin, stopped in embarrassment and was greatly relieved by Pulcheria Alexandrovna's questions, which showered in a continual stream upon him.

He talked for three-quarters of an hour, being constantly interrupted by their questions, and succeeded in describing to them all the most important facts he knew of the last year of Raskolnikov's life, concluding with a circumstantial account of his illness. He omitted, however, many things, which were better omitted, including the scene at the police station with all its consequences. They listened eagerly to his story, and, when he thought he had finished and satisfied his listeners, he found that they considered he had hardly begun.

'Tell me, tell me! What do you think . . .? Excuse me, I still don't know your name!' Pulcheria Alexandrovna put in hastily.

'Dmitri Prokofitch.'

'I should like very, very much to know, Dmitri Prokofitch . . . how he looks . . . on things in general now, that is, how can I explain, what are his likes and dislikes? Is he always so irritable? Tell me, if you can, what are his hopes and, so to say, his dreams? Under what influences is he now? In a word, I should like . . .'

'Ah, mother, how can he answer all that at once?' observed Dounia.

'Good heavens, I had not expected to find him in the least like this, Dmitri Prokofitch!'

'Naturally,' answered Razumihin. 'I have no mother, but my uncle comes every year and almost every time he can scarcely recognize me, even in appearance, though he is a clever man; and your three years' separation means a great deal. What am I to tell you? I have known

Rodion for a year and a half; he is morose, gloomy, proud and haughty, and of late – and perhaps for a long time before – he has been suspicious and fanciful. He has a noble nature and a kind heart. He does not like showing his feelings and would rather do a cruel thing than open his heart freely. Sometimes, though he is not at all morbid, but simply cold and inhumanly callous; it's as though he were alternating between two characters. Sometimes he is fearfully reserved! He says he is so busy that everything is a hindrance, and yet he lies in bed doing nothing. He doesn't jeer at things, not because he hasn't the wit, but as though he hadn't time to waste on such trifles. He never listens to what is said to him. He is never interested in what interests other people at any given moment. He thinks very highly of himself and perhaps he is right. Well, what more? I think your arrival will have a most beneficial influence upon him.'

'God grant it may,' cried Pulcheria Alexandrovna, distressed by Razumihin's account of her Rodya.

And Razumihin ventured to look more boldly at Avdotya Romanovna at last. He glanced at her often while he was talking, but only for a moment and looked away again at once. Avdotya Romanovna sat at the table, listening attentively, then got up again and began walking to and fro with her arms folded and her lips compressed, occasionally putting in a question, without stopping her walk. She had the same habit of not listening to what was said. She was wearing a dress of thin dark stuff and she had a white transparent scarf round her neck. Razumihin soon detected signs of extreme poverty in their belongings. Had Avdotya Romanovna been dressed like a queen, he felt he would not be afraid of her, but perhaps just because she was poorly dressed and that he noticed all the misery of her surroundings, his heart was filled with dread and he began to be afraid of every word he uttered, every gesture he made, which was very trying for a man who already felt diffident.

'You've told us a great deal that is interesting about my brother's character . . . and have told it impartially. I am glad. I thought that you were too uncritically devoted to him,' observed Avdotya Romanovna with a smile. 'I think you are right that he needs a woman's care,' she added thoughtfully.

'I didn't say so; but I dare say you are right, only . . .'

'What?'

'He loves no one and perhaps he never will,' Razumihin declared decisively.

'You mean he is not capable of love?'

'Do you know, Avdotya Romanovna, you are awfully like your brother, in everything, indeed!' he blurted out suddenly to his own surprise, but remembering at once what he had just before said of her brother, he turned as red as a crab and was overcome with confusion. Avdotya Romanovna couldn't help laughing when she looked at him.

'You may both be mistaken about Rodya,' Pulcheria Alexandrovna remarked, slightly piqued. 'I am not talking of our present difficulty, Dounia. What Pytor Petrovitch writes in this letter and what you and I have supposed may be mistaken, but you can't imagine, Dmitri Prokofitch, how moody and, so to say, capricious he is. I never could depend on what he would do when he was only fifteen. And I am sure that he might do something now that nobody else would think of doing. . . . Well, for instance, do you know how a year and a half ago he astounded me and gave me a shock that nearly killed me, when he had the idea of marrying that girl – what was her name – his landlady's daughter?'

'Did you hear about that affair?' asked Avdotya Romanovna.

'Do you suppose – ' Pulcheria Alexandrovna continued warmly. 'Do you suppose that my tears, my entreaties, my illness, my possible death from grief, our poverty would have made him pause? No, he would calmly have disregarded all obstacles. And yet it isn't that he doesn't love us!'

'He has never spoken a word of that affair to me,' Razumihin answered cautiously. 'But I did hear something from Praskovya Pavlovna herself, though she is by no means a gossip. And what I heard certainly was rather strange.'

'And what did you hear?' both the ladies asked at once.

'Well, nothing very special. I only learned that the marriage which only failed to take place through the girl's death, was not at all to Praskovya Pavlovna's liking. They say, too, the girl was not at all pretty, in fact I am told positively ugly . . . and such an invalid . . . and queer. But she seems to have had some good qualities. She must have had some good qualities or it's quite inexplicable. . . . She had no money either and he wouldn't have considered her money. . . . But it's always difficult to judge in such matters.'

'I am sure she was a good girl,' Avdotya Romanovna observed briefly.

'God forgive me, I simply rejoiced at her death. Though I don't know which of them would have caused most misery to the other – he to her or she to him,' Pulcheria Alexandrovna concluded. Then she began tentatively questioning him about the scene on the previous day with Luzhin, hesitating and continually glancing at Dounia, obviously to the latter's annoyance. This incident more than all the rest evidently caused her uneasiness, even consternation. Razumihin described it in detail again, but this time he added his own conclusions: he openly blamed

Raskolnikov for intentionally insulting Pyotr Petrovitch, not seeking to excuse him on the score of his illness.

'He had planned it before his illness,' he added.

'I think so, too,' Pulcheria Alexandrovna agreed with a dejected air. But she was very much surprised at hearing Razumihin express himself so carefully and even with a certain respect about Pyotr Petrovitch. Avdotya Romanovna, too, was struck by it.

'So this is your opinion of Pyotr Petrovitch?' Pulcheria Alexandrovna could not resist asking.

'I can have no other opinion of your daughter's future husband,' Razumihin answered firmly and with warmth, 'and I don't say it simply from vulgar politeness, but because ... simply because Avdotya Romanovna has of her own free will deigned to accept this man. If I spoke so rudely of him last night, it was because I was disgustingly drunk and ... mad besides; yes, mad, crazy, I lost my head completely ... and this morning I am ashamed of it.'

He crimsoned and ceased speaking. Avdotya Romanovna flushed, but did not break the silence. She had not uttered a word from the moment they began to speak of Luzhin.

Without her support Pulcheria Alexandrovna obviously did not know what to do. At last, faltering and continually glancing at her daughter, she confessed that she was exceedingly worried by one circumstance.

'You see, Dmitri Prokofitch,' she began. 'I'll be perfectly open with Dmitri Prokofitch, Dounia?'

'Of course, mother,' said Avdotya Romanovna emphatically.

'This is what it is,' she began in haste, as though the permission to speak of her trouble lifted a weight off her mind. 'Very early this morning we got a note from Pyotr Petrovitch in reply to our letter announcing our arrival. He promised to meet us at the station, you know; instead of that he sent a servant to bring us the address of these lodgings and to show us the way; and he sent a message that he would be here himself this morning. But this morning this note came from him. You'd better read it yourself; there is one point in it which worries me very much ... you will soon see what that is, and ... tell me your candid opinion, Dmitri Prokofitch! You know Rodya's character better than anyone and no one can advise us better then you can. Dounia, I must tell you, made her decision at once, but I still don't feel sure how to act and I ... I've been waiting for your opinion.'

Razumihin opened the note which was dated the previous evening and read as follows:

'DEAR MADAM, Pulcheria Alexandrovna, I have the honour to inform you that owing to unforeseen obstacles I was rendered unable to meet you at the railway station; I sent a very competent person with the same object in view. I likewise shall be deprived of the honour of an interview with you to-morrow morning by business in the Senate that does not admit of delay, and also that I may not intrude on your family circle while you are meeting your son, and Avdotya Romanovna her brother. I shall have the honour of visiting you and paying you my respects at your lodgings not later than to-morrow evening at eight o'clock precisely, and herewith I venture to present my earnest and, I may add, imperative request that Rodion Romanovitch may not be present at our interview – as he offered me a gross and unprecedented affront on the occasion of my visit to him in his illness yesterday, and, moreover, since I desire from you personally an indispensable and circumstantial explanation upon a certain point, in regard to which I wish to learn your own interpretation. I have the honour to inform you, in anticipation, that if, in spite of my request, I meet Rodion Romanovitch, I shall be compelled to withdraw immediately and then you have only yourself to blame. I write on the assumption that Rodion Romanovitch, who appeared so ill at my visit, suddenly recovered two hours later and so, being able to leave the house, may visit you also. I was confirmed in that belief by the testimony of my own eyes in the lodging of a drunken man who was run over and has since died, to whose daughter, a young woman of notorious behaviour, he gave twenty-five roubles on the pretext of the funeral, which gravely surprised me knowing what pains you were at to raise that sum. Herewith expressing my special respect to your estimable daughter, Avdotya Romanovna, I beg you to accept the respectful homage of

> 'Your humble servant,
> 'P. LUZHIN.'

What am I to do now, Dmitri Prokofitch?' began Pulcheria Alexandrovna, almost weeping. 'How can I ask Rodya not to come? Yesterday he insisted so earnestly on our refusing Pyotr Petrovitch and now we are ordered not to receive Rodya! He will come on purpose if he knows, and . . . what will happen then?'

'Act on Avdotya Romanovna's decision,' Razumihin answered calmly at once.

'Oh, dear me! She says . . . goodness knows what she says, she doesn't explain her object! She says that it would be best, at least, not that it would be best, but that it's absolutely necessary that Rodya should make a point of being here at eight o'clock and that they must meet . . . I didn't want even to show him the letter, but to prevent him from coming by some stratagem with your help . . . because he is so irritable . . . Besides I don't understand about that drunkard who died and that daughter, and how he could have given the daughter all the money . . . which . . .'

'Which cost you such sacrifice, mother,' put in Avdotya Romanovna.

'He was not himself yesterday,' Razumihin said thoughtfully, 'if you only know what he was up to in a restaurant yesterday, though there was sense in it too. . . . Hm! He did say something, as we were going home yesterday evening, about a dead man and a girl, but I didn't understand a word. . . . But last night I myself . . .'

'The best thing, mother, will be for us to go to him ourselves and there I assure you we shall see at once what's to be done. Besides, it's getting late – good heavens, it's past ten,' she cried, looking at a splendid gold-enamelled watch which hung round her neck on a thin Venetian chain, and looked entirely out of keeping with the rest of her dress. 'A present from her fiancé,' thought Razumihin.

'We must start, Dounia, we must start,' her mother cried in a flutter. 'He will be thinking we are still angry after yesterday, from our coming so late. Merciful heavens!'

While she said this she was hurriedly putting on her hat and mantle; Dounia, too, put on her things. Her gloves, as Razumihin noticed, were not merely shabby but had holes in them, and yet this evident poverty gave the two ladies an air of special dignity, which is always found in people who know how to wear poor clothes. Razumihin looked reverently at Dounia and felt proud of escorting her. 'The queen who mended her stockings in prison,' he thought, 'must have looked then every inch a queen and even more a queen than at sumptuous banquets and levées.'

'My God!' exclaimed Pulcheria Alexandrovna, 'little did I think that I should ever fear seeing my son, my darling, darling Rodya! I am afraid, Dmitri Prokofitch,' she added, glancing at him timidly.

'Don't be afraid, mother,' said Dounia, kissing her, 'better have faith in him.'

'Oh dear, I have faith in him, but I haven't slept all night,' exclaimed the poor woman.

They came out into the street.

'Do you know, Dounia, when I dozed a little this morning I dreamed of Marfa Petrovna . . . she was all in white . . . she came up to me, took my hand, and shook her head at me, but so sternly as though she were blaming me . . . . Is that a good omen ? Oh, dear me! You don't know, Dmitri Prokofitch, that Marfa Petrovna's dead!'

'No, I didn't know; who is Marfa Petrovna?'

'She died suddenly; and only fancy . . .'

'Afterwards, mamma,' put in Dounia. 'He doesn't know who Marfa Petrovna is.'

'Ah, you don't know? And I was thinking that you knew all about us. Forgive me, Dmitri Prokofitch, I don't know what I am thinking about these last few days. I look upon you really as a providence for us, and so I took it for granted that you knew all about us. I look on you as a relation.... Don't be angry with me for saying so. Dear me, what's the matter with your right hand? Have you knocked it?'

'Yes, I bruised it,' muttered Razumihin overjoyed.

'I sometimes speak too much from the heart, so that Dounia finds fault with me.... But, dear me, what a cupboard he lives in! I wonder whether he is awake? Does this woman, his landlady, consider it a room? Listen, you say he does not like to show his feelings, so perhaps I shall annoy him with my ... weaknesses? Do advise me, Dmitri Prokofitch, how am I to treat him? I feel quite distracted, you know.'

'Don't question him too much about anything if you see him frown; don't ask him too much about his health; he doesn't like that.'

'Ah, Dmitri Prokofitch, how hard it is to be a mother! But here are the stairs.... What an awful staircase!'

'Mother, you are quite pale, don't distress yourself, darling,' said Dounia caressing her, then with flashing eyes she added: 'He ought to be happy at seeing you, and you are tormenting yourself so.'

'Wait, I'll peep in and see whether he has waked up.'

The ladies slowly followed Razumihin, who went on before, and when they reached the landlady's door on the fourth storey, they noticed that her door was a tiny crack open and that two keen black eyes were watching them from the darkness within. When their eyes met, the door was suddenly shut with such a slam that Pulcheria Alexandrovna almost cried out.

✦ THREE ✦

'HE IS WELL, QUITE WELL!' Zossimov cried cheerfully as they entered.

He had come in ten minutes earlier and was sitting in the same place as before, on the sofa. Raskolnikov was sitting in the opposite corner, fully dressed and carefully washed and combed, as he had not been for some time past. The room was immediately crowded, yet Nastasya managed to follow the visitors in and stayed to listen.

Raskolnikov really was almost well, as compared with his condition the day before, but he was still pale, listless, and sombre. He looked like a wounded man or one who has undergone some terrible physical suffering. His brows were knitted, his lips compressed, his eyes feverish. He spoke little and reluctantly, as though performing a duty, and there was a restlessness in his movements.

He only wanted a sling on his arm or a bandage on his finger to complete the impression of a man with a painful abscess or a broken arm. The pale, sombre face lighted up for a moment when his mother and sister entered, but this only gave it a look of more intense suffering, in place of its listless dejection. The light soon died away, but the look of suffering remained, and Zossimov, watching and studying his patient with all the zest of a young doctor beginning to practise, noticed in him no joy at the arrival of his mother and sister, but a sort of bitter, hidden determination to bear another hour or two of inevitable torture. He saw later that almost every word of the following conversation seemed to touch on some sore place and irritate it. But at the same time he marvelled at the power of controlling himself and hiding his feelings in a patient who the previous day had, like a monomaniac, fallen into a frenzy at the slightest word.

'Yes, I see myself now that I am almost well,' said Raskolnikov, giving his mother and sister a kiss of welcome which made Pulcheria Alexandrovna radiant at once. 'And I don't say this *as I did yesterday*, he said, addressing Razumihin, with a friendly pressure of his hand.

'Yes, indeed, I am quite surprised at him to-day,' began Zossimov, much delighted at the ladies' entrance, for he had not succeeded in keeping up a conversation with his patient for ten minutes. 'In another three or four days, if he goes on like this, he will be just as before, that is, as he was a month ago, or two . . . or perhaps even three. This has been coming on for a long while . . . eh? Confess, now, that it has been perhaps your own fault?' he added, with a tentative smile, as though still afraid of irritating him.

'It is very possible,' answered Raskolnikov coldly.

'I should say, too,' continued Zossimov with zest, 'that your complete recovery depends solely on yourself. Now that one can talk to you, I should like to impress upon you that it is essential to avoid the elementary, so to speak, fundamental causes tending to produce your morbid condition: in that case you will be cured, if not, it will go from bad to worse. These fundamental causes I don't know, but they must be known to you. You are an intelligent man, and must have observed yourself, of course. I fancy the first stage of your derangement coincides with your leaving the university. You must not be left without occupation, and so, work and a definite aim set before you might, I fancy, be very beneficial.'

'Yes, yes; you are perfectly right . . . I will make haste and return to the university: and then everything will go smoothly . . .'

Zossimov, who had begun his sage advice partly to make an effect before the ladies, was certainly somewhat mystified, when, glancing at his patient, he observed unmistakable mockery on his face. This lasted an instant, however. Pulcheria Alexandrovna began at once thanking Zossimov, especially for his visit to their lodging the previous night.

'What! he saw you last night?' Raskolnikov asked, as though startled. 'Then you have not slept either after your journey.'

'Ach, Rodya, that was only till two o'clock. Dounia and I never go to bed before two at home.'

'I don't know how to thank him either,' Raskolnikov went on, suddenly frowning and looking down. 'Setting aside the question of payment – forgive me for referring to it (he turned to Zossimov) – I really don't know what I have done to deserve such special attention from you! I simply don't understand it . . . and . . . and . . . it weighs upon me, indeed, because I don't understand it. I tell you so candidly.'

'Don't be irritated.' Zossimov forced himself to laugh. 'Assume that you are my first patient – well – we fellows just beginning to practice love our first patients as if they were our children and some almost fall in love with them. And, of course, I am not rich in patients.'

'I say nothing about him,' added Raskolnikov, pointing to Razumihin, 'though he has had nothing from me either but insult and trouble.'

'What nonsense he is talking! Why, you are in a sentimental mood to-day, are you?' shouted Razumihin.

If he had had more penetration he would have seen that there was no trace of sentimentality in him, but something indeed quite the opposite. But Avdotya Romanovna noticed it. She was intently and uneasily watching her brother.

'As for you, mother, I don't dare to speak,' he went on, as though repeating a lesson learned by heart. 'It is only to-day that I have been able to realize a little how distressed you must have been here yesterday, waiting for me to come back.'

When he had said this, he suddenly held out his hand to his sister, smiling without a word. But in this smile there was a flash of real unfeigned feeling. Dounia caught it at once, and warmly pressed his hand, overjoyed and thankful. It was the first time he had addressed her since their dispute the previous day. The mother's face lighted up with ecstatic happiness at the sight of this conclusive unspoken reconciliation. 'Yes, that is what I love him for,' Razumihin, exaggerating it all, muttered to himself, with a vigorous turn in his chair. 'He has these movements.'

'And how well he does it all,' the mother was thinking to herself. 'What generous impulses he has, and how simply, how delicately he put an end to all the misunderstanding with his sister – simply by holding out his hand at the right minute and looking at her like that . . . And what fine eyes he has, and how fine his whole face is! . . . He is even better-looking than Dounia . . . But, good heavens, what a suit – how terribly he's dressed! . . . Vasya, the messenger boy in Afanasy Ivanitch's shop, is better dressed! I could rush at him and hug him . . . weep over him – but I am afraid . . . Oh, dear, he's so strange! He's talking kindly, but I'm afraid! Why, what am I afraid of? . . .'

'Oh, Rodya, you wouldn't believe,' she began suddenly, in haste to answer his words to her, 'how unhappy Douina and I were yesterday! Now that it's all over and done with and we are quite happy again – I can tell you. Fancy, we ran here almost straight from the train to embrace you and that woman – ah, here she is! Good morning, Nastasya! . . . She told us at once that you were lying in a high fever and had just run away from the doctor in delirium, and they were looking for you in the streets. You can't imagine how we felt! I couldn't help thinking of the tragic end of Lieutenant Potanchikov, a friend of your father's – you can't remember him, Rodya – who ran out in the same way in a high fever and fell into the well in the court-yard and they couldn't pull him out till next day. Of course, we exaggerated things. We were on the point of rushing to find Pyotr Petrovitch to ask him to help . . . Because we were alone, utterly alone,' she said plaintively and stopped short, suddenly recollecting it was still somewhat dangerous to speak of Pyotr Petrovitch, although 'we are quite happy again'.

'Yes, yes . . . Of course it's very annoying . . .' Raskolnikov muttered in reply, but with such a preoccupied and inattentive air that Dounia gazed at him in perplexity.

'What else was it I wanted to say?' He went on trying to recollect. 'Oh, yes; mother, and you too, Dounia, please don't think that I didn't mean to come and see you to-day and was waiting for you to come first.'

'What are you saying, Rodya?' cried Pulcheria Alexandrovna. She, too, was surprised.

'Is he answering us as a duty?' Dounia wondered. 'Is he being reconciled and asking forgiveness as though he were performing a rite or repeating a lesson?'

'I've only just waked up, and wanted to go to you, but was delayed owing to my clothes; I forgot yesterday to ask her . . . Nastasya . . . to wash out the blood . . . I've only just got dressed.'

'Blood! What blood?' Pulcheria Alexandrovna asked in alarm.

'Oh, nothing – don't be uneasy. It was when I was wandering about yesterday, rather delirious, I chanced upon a man who had been run over . . . a clerk . . .'

'Delirious? But you remember everything!' Razumihin interrupted.

'That's true,' Raskolnikov answered with special carefulness. 'I remember everything even to the slightest detail, and yet – why I did that and went there and said that, I can't clearly explain now.'

'A familiar phenomenon,' interposed Zossimov, 'actions are sometimes performed in a masterly and most cunning way, while the direction of the actions is deranged and dependent on various morbid impressions – it's like a dream.'

'Perhaps it's a good thing really that he should think me almost a madman,' thought Raskolnikov.

'Why, people in perfect health act in the same way too,' observed Dounia, looking uneasily at Zossimov.

'There is some truth in your observation,' the latter replied. 'In that sense we are certainly all not infrequently like madmen, but with the slight difference that the deranged are somewhat madder, for we must draw a line. A normal man, it is true, hardly exists. Among dozens – perhaps hundreds of thousands – hardly one is to be met with.'

At the word 'madman', carelessly dropped by Zossimov in his chatter on his favourite subject, everyone frowned.

Raskolnikov sat seeming not to pay attention, plunged in thought with a strange smile on his pale lips. He was still meditating on something.

'Well, what about the man who was run over? I interrupted you!' Razumihin cried hastily.

'What?' Raskolnikov seemed to wake up. 'Oh . . . I got spattered with blood helping to carry him to his lodging. By the way, mamma, I did an unpardonable thing yesterday. I was literally out of my mind. I gave away all the money you sent me . . . to his wife for the funeral. She's a widow now, in consumption, a poor creature . . . three little children starving . . . nothing in the house . . . there's a daughter, too . . . perhaps you'd have given it yourself if you'd seen them. But I had no right to do it, I admit, especially as I knew how you needed the money yourself. To help others one must have the right to do it, or else, *Crevez, chiens, si vous n'êtes pas contents*'. He laughed, 'That's right, isn't it, Dounia?'

'No, it's not,' answered Dounia firmly.

'Bah! you, too, have ideals,' he muttered, looking at her almost with hatred, and smiling sarcastically. 'I ought to have considered that . . . Well, that's praiseworthy, and it's better for you . . . and if you reach a line you won't overstep, you will be unhappy . . . and if you overstep it, maybe you will be still unhappier . . . But all that's nonsense,' he added irritably, vexed at being carried away. 'I only meant to say that I beg your forgiveness, mother,' he concluded, shortly and abruptly.

'That's enough, Rodya, I am sure that everything you do is very good,' said his mother, delighted.

'Don't be too sure,' he answered, twisting his mouth into a smile.

A silence followed. There was a certain constraint in all this conversation, and in the silence, and in the reconciliation, and in the forgiveness, and all were feeling it.

'It is as though they were afraid of me,' Raskolnikov was thinking to himself, looking askance at his mother and sister. Pulcheria Alexandrovna was indeed growing more timid the longer she kept silent.

'Yet in their absence I seemed to love them so much,' flashed through his mind.

'Do you know, Rodya, Marfa Petrovna is dead,' Pulcheria Alexandrovna suddenly blurted out.

'What Marfa Petrovna?'

'Oh, mercy on us – Marfa Petrovna Svidrigaïlov. I wrote you so much about her.'

'A-a-h! Yes, I remember . . . So she's dead! Oh, really?' he roused himself suddenly, as if waking up. 'What did she die of?'

'Only imagine, quite suddenly,' Pulcheria Alexandrovna answered hurriedly, encouraged by his curiosity. 'On the very day I was sending you that letter! Would you believe it, that awful man seems to have been the cause of her death. They say he beat her dreadfully.'

'Why, were they on such bad terms?' he asked, addressing his sister.

'Not at all. Quite the contrary indeed. With her, he was always very patient, considerate even. In fact, all those seven years of their married life he gave way to her, too much so indeed, in many cases. All of a sudden he seems to have lost patience.'

'Then he could not have been so awful if he controlled himself for seven years? You seem to be defending him, Dounia?'

'No, no, he's an awful man! I can imagine nothing more awful!' Dounia answered, almost with a shudder, knitting her brows, and sinking into thought.

'That had happened in the morning,' Pulcheria Alexandrovna went on hurriedly. 'And directly afterwards she ordered the horses to be harnessed to drive to the town immediately after dinner. She always used to drive to the town in such cases. She ate a very good dinner, I am told . . .'

'After the beating?'

'That was always her . . . habit; and immediately after dinner, so as not to be late in starting, she went to the bathhouse . . . You see, she was undergoing some treatment with baths. They have a cold spring there, and she used to bathe in it regularly every day, and no sooner had she got into the water when she suddenly had a stroke!'

'I should think so,' said Zossimov.

'And did he beat her badly?'

'What does that matter?' put in Dounia.

'H'm! But I don't know why you want to tell us such gossip, mother,' said Raskolnikov irritably, as it were in spite of himself.

'Ah, my dear, I don't know what to talk about,' broke from Pulcheria Alexandrovna.

'Why, are you all afraid of me?' he asked, with a constrained smile.

'That's certainly true,' said Dounia, looking directly and sternly at her brother. 'Mother was crossing herself with terror as she came up the stairs.'

His face worked, as though in convulsion.

'Ach, what are you saying, Dounia? Don't be angry, please, Rodya . . . Why did you say that, Dounia?' Pulcheria Alexandrovna began, overwhelmed – 'You see, coming here, I was dreaming all the way, in the train, how we should meet, how we should talk over everything together . . . And I was so happy, I did not notice the journey! But what am I saying? I am happy now . . . You should not, Dounia . . . I am happy now – simply in seeing you, Rodya . . .'

'Hush, mother,' he muttered in confusion, not looking at her, but pressing her hand. 'We shall have time to speak freely of everything!'

As he said this, he was suddenly overwhelmed with confusion and turned pale. Again that awful sensation he had known of late passed with deadly chill over his soul. Again it became suddenly plain and perceptible to him that he had just told a fearful lie – that he would never now be able to speak freely of everything – that he would never again be able to *speak* of anything to anyone. The anguish of this thought was such that for a moment he almost forgot himself. He got up from his seat, and not looking at anyone walked towards the door.

'What are you about?' cried Razumihin, clutching him by the arm.

He sat down again, and began looking about him, in silence. They were all looking at him in perplexity.

'But what are you all so dull for?' he shouted, suddenly and quite unexpectedly. 'Do say something! What's the use of sitting like this? Come, do speak. Let us talk . . . We meet together and sit in silence . . . Come, anything!'

'Thank God; I was afraid the same thing as yesterday was beginning again,' said Pulcheria Alexandrovna, crossing herself.

'What is the matter, Rodya?' asked Avdotya Romanovna, distrustfully.

'Oh, nothing! I remembered something,' he answered, and suddenly laughed.

'Well, if you remembered something; that's all right! . . . I was beginning to think . . .' muttered Zossimov, getting up from the sofa. 'It is time
for me to be off. I will look in again perhaps . . . if I can . . .' He made his
bows, and went out.

'What an excellent man!' observed Pulcheria Alexandrovna.

'Yes, excellent, splendid, well-educated, intelligent,' Raskolnikov
began, suddenly speaking with surprising rapidity, and a liveliness he
had not shown till then. 'I can't remember where I met him before my
illness . . . I believe I have met him somewhere – . . . And this is a good
man, too,' he nodded at Razumihin. 'Do you like him, Dounia?' he asked
her; and suddenly, for some unknown reason, laughed.

'Very much,' answered Dounia.

'Foo! – what a pig you are!' Razumihin protested blushing in terrible
confusion, and he got up from his chair. Pulcheria Alexandrovna smiled
faintly, but Raskolnikov laughed aloud.

'Where are you off to?'

'I must go.'

'You need not at all. Stay. Zossimov has gone, so you must. Don't
go. What's the time? Is it twelve o'clock? What a pretty watch you have
got, Dounia. But why are you all silent again? I do all the talking.'

'It was a present from Marfa Petrovna,' answered Dounia.

'And a very expensive one!' added Pulcheria Alexandrovna.

'A-ah! What a big one! Hardly like a lady's.'

'I like that sort,' said Dounia.

'So it is not a present from her fiancé,' thought Razumihin, and was
unreasonably delighted.

'I thought it was Luzhin's present,' observed Raskolnikov.

'No, he has not made Dounia any presents yet.'

'A-ah! And do you remember, mother, I was in love and wanted to get
married?' he said suddenly, looking at his mother, who was disconcerted
by the sudden change of subject and the way he spoke of it.

'Oh, yes, my dear.'

Pulcheria Alexandrovna exchanged glances with Dounia and
Razumihin.

'H'm yes. What shall I tell you? I don't remember much indeed. She
was such a sickly girl,' he went on, growing dreamy and looking down
again. 'Quite an invalid. She was fond of giving alms to the poor, and
was always dreaming of a nunnery, and once she burst into tears when
she began talking to me about it. Yes, yes, I remember. I remember very
well. She was an ugly little thing. I really don't know what drew me to
her then – I think it was because she was always ill. If she had been lame

or hunchback, I believe I should have liked her better still,' he smiled dreamily. 'Yes, it was a sort of spring delirium.'

'No, it was not only spring delirium,' said Dounia, with warm feeling.

He fixed a strained intent look on his sister, but did not hear or did not understand her words. Then, completely lost in thought, he got up, went up to his mother, kissed her, went back to his place and sat down.

'You love her even now?' said Pulcheria Alexandrovna, touched.

'Her? Now? Oh, yes . . . You ask about her? No . . . that's all now, as it were, in another world . . . and so long ago. And indeed everything happening here seems somehow far away.' He looked attentively at him. 'You, now . . . I seem to be looking at you from a thousand miles away . . . but goodness knows why we are talking of that! And what's the use of asking about it?' he added with annoyance, and biting his nails, fell into dreamy silence again.

'What a wretched lodging you have, Rodya! It's like a tomb,' said Pulcheria Alexandrovna, suddenly breaking the oppressive silence. 'I am sure it's quite half through your lodging you have become so melancholy.'

'My lodging,' he answered, listlessly. 'Yes, the lodging had a great deal to do with it . . . I thought that, too . . . If only you knew, though, what a strange thing you said just now, mother,' he said, laughing strangely.

A little more, and their companionship, this mother and this sister, with him after three years' absence, this intimate tone of conversation, in face of the utter impossibility of really speaking about anything, would have been beyond his power of endurance. But there was one urgent matter which must be settled one way or the other that day – so he had decided when he woke. Now he was glad to remember it, as a means of escape.

'Listen, Dounia,' he began, gravely and drily, 'of course I beg your pardon for yesterday, but I consider it my duty to tell you again that I do not withdraw from my chief point. It is me or Luzhin. If I am a scroundrel, you must not be. One is enough. If you marry Luzhin, I cease at once to look on you as a sister.'

'Rodya, Rodya! It is the same as yesterday again,' Pulcheria Alexandrovna cried, mournfully. 'And why do you call yourself a scroundrel? I can't bear it. You said the same yesterday.'

'Brother,' Dounia answered firmly and with the same dryness. 'In all this there is a mistake on your part. I thought it over at night, and found out the mistake. It is all because you seem to fancy I am sacrificing myself to someone and for someone. That is not the case at all. I am simply marrying for my own sake, because things are hard for me. Though, of course, I shall be glad if I succeed in being useful to my family. But that is not the chief motive for my decision . . .'

'She is lying,' he thought to himself, biting his nails vindictively. 'Proud creature! She won't admit she wants to do it out of charity! Too haughty! Oh, base characters! They even love as though they hate ... Oh, how, I ... hate them all!'

'In fact,' continued Dounia, 'I am marrying Pyotr Petrovitch because of two evils I choose the less. I intend to do honestly all he expects of me, so I am not deceiving him ... Why did you smile just now?' She, too, flushed, and there was a gleam of anger in her eyes.

'All?' he asked, with a malignant grin.

'Within certain limits. Both the manner and form of Pyotr Petrovitch's courtship showed me at once what he wanted. He may, of course, think too well of himself, but I hope he esteems me, too ... Why are you laughing again?'

'And why are you blushing again? You are lying, sister. You are intentionally lying, simply from feminine obstinacy, simply to hold your own against me ... You cannot respect Luzhin. I have seen him and talked with him. So you are selling yourself for money, and so in any case you are acting basely, and I am glad at least that you can blush for it.'

'It is not true. I am not lying,' cried Dounia, losing her composure. 'I would not marry him if I were not convinced that he esteems me and thinks highly of me. I would not marry him if I were not firmly convinced that I can respect him. Fortunately, I can have convincing proof of it this very day ... and such a marriage is not a vileness, as you say! And even if you were right, if I really had determined on a vile action, is it not merciless on your part to speak to me like that? Why do you demand of me a heroism that perhaps you have not either? It is despotism; it is tyranny. If I ruin anyone, it is only myself ... I am not committing a murder. Why do you look at me like that? Why are you so pale? Rodya, darling, what's the matter?'

'Good heavens! You have made him faint,' cried Pulcheria Alexandrovna.

'No, no, nonsense! It's nothing. A little giddiness – not fainting. You have fainting on the brain. H'm, yes, what was I saying? Oh, yes. In what way will you get convincing proof to-day that you can respect him, and that he ... esteems you, as you said. I think you said to-day?'

'Mother, show Rodya Pyotr Petrovitch's letter,' said Dounia.

With trembling hands, Pulcheria Alexandrovna gave him the letter. He took it with great interest, but, before opening it, he suddenly looked with a sort of wonder at Dounia.

'It is strange,' he said, slowly, as though struck by a new idea, 'what am I making such a fuss for? What is it all about? Marry whom you like!'

He said this as though to himself, but said it aloud, and looked for some time at his sister, as though puzzled. He opened the letter at last, still with the same look of strange wonder on his face. Then, slowly and attentively, he began reading, and read it through twice. Pulcheria Alexandrovna showed marked anxiety, and all indeed expected something particular.

'What surprises me,' he began, after a short pause, handing the letter to his mother, but not addressing anyone in particular, 'is that he is a business man, a lawyer, and his conversation is pretentious indeed, and yet he writes such an uneducated letter.'

They all started. They had expected something quite different.

'But they all write like that, you know,' Razumihin observed, abruptly.

'Have you read it?'

'Yes.'

'We showed him, Rodya. We ... consulted him just now,' Pulcheria Alexandrovna began, embarrassed.

'That's just the jargon of the courts,' Razumihin put in. 'Legal documents are written like that to this day.'

'Legal? Yes, it's just legal – business language – not so very uneducated, and not quite educated – business language!'

'Pyotr Petrovich makes no secret of the fact that he had a cheap education, he is proud indeed of having made his own way,' Avdotya Romanovna observed, somewhat offended by her brother's tone.

'Well, if he's proud of it, he has reason, I don't deny it. You seem to be offended, sister, at my making only such a frivolous criticism on the letter, and to think thay I speak of such trifling matters on purpose to annoy you. It is quite the contrary, an observation apropos of the style occurred to me that is by no means irrelevant as things stand. There is one expression, "blame yourselves", put in very significantly and plainly, and there is besides a threat that he will go away at once if I am present. That threat to go away is equivalent to a threat to abandon you both if you are disobedient, and to abandon you now after summoning you to Petersburg. Well, what do you think? Can one resent such an expression from Luzhin, as we should if he (he pointed to Razumihin) had written it, or Zossimov, or one of us?'

'N-no,' answered Dounia, with more animation. 'I saw clearly that it was too naïvely expressed, and that perhaps he simply has no skill in writing ... that is a true criticism, brother. I did not expect, indeed ...'

'It is expressed in legal style, and sounds coarser than perhaps he intended. But I must disillusion you a little. There is one expression in the letter, one slander about me, and rather a contemptible one. I gave the money last night to the widow, a woman in consumption, crushed with trouble, and not 'on the pretext of the funeral', but simply to pay for the funeral, and not to the daughter – a young woman, as he writes, of notorious behaviour (whom I saw last night for the first time in my life) – but to the widow. In all this I see a too hasty desire to slander me and to raise dissension between us. It is expressed again in legal jargon, that is to say, with a too obvious display of the aim, and with a very naïve eagerness. He is a man of intelligence, but to act sensibly, intelligence is not enough. It all shows the man and . . . I don't think he has a great esteem for you. I tell you this simply to warn you, because I sincerely wish for your good . . .'

Dounia did not reply. Her resolution had been taken. She was only awaiting the evening.

'Then what is your decision, Rodya?' asked Pulcheria Alexandrovna, who was more uneasy than ever at the sudden, new businesslike tone of his talk.

'What decision?'

'You see Pyotr Petrovitch writes that you are not to be with us this evening, and that he will go away if you come. So will you . . . come?'

'That, of course, is not for me to decide, but for you first, if you are not offended by such a request; and secondly, by Dounia, if she, too, is not offended. I will do what you think best,' he added drily.

'Dounia has already decided, and I fully agree with her,' Pulcheria Alexandrovna hastened to declare.

'I decided to ask you, Rodya, to urge you not to fail to be with us at this interview,' said Dounia. 'Will you come?'

'Yes.'

'I will ask you, too, to be with us at eight o'clock,' she said, addressing Razumihin. 'Mother, I am inviting him, too.'

'Quite right, Dounia. Well, since you have decided,' added Pulcheria Alexandrovna, 'so be it. I shall feel easier myself. I do not like concealment and deception. Better let us have the whole truth . . . Pyotr Petrovitch may be angry or not, now!'

➤ FOUR ◆

AT THAT MOMENT THE DOOR was softly opened, and a young girl walked into the room, looking timidly about her. Everyone turned towards her with surprise and curiosity. At first sight, Raskolnikov did not recognize her. It was Sofya Semyonova Marmeladov. He had seen her yesterday for the first time, but at such a moment, in such surroundings and in such a dress, that his memory retained a very different image of her. Now she was a modestly and poorly-dressed young girl, very young, indeed, almost like a child, with a modest and refined manner, with a candid but somewhat frightened-looking face. She was wearing a very plain indoor dress, and had on a shabby old-fashioned hat, but she still carried a parasol. Unexpectedly finding the room full of people, she was not so much embarrassed as completely overwhelmed with shyness, like a little child. She was even about to retreat. 'Oh ... it's you!' said Raskolnikov, extremely astonished, and he, too, was confused. He at once recollected that his mother and sister knew through Luzhin's letter of 'some young woman of notorious behaviour'. He had only just been protesting against Luzhin's calumny and declaring that he had seen the girl last night for the first time, and suddenly she had walked in. He remembered, too, that he had not protested against the expression 'of notorious behaviour'. All this passed vaguely and fleetingly through his brain, but looking at her more intently, he saw that the humiliated creature was so humiliated that he felt suddenly sorry for her. When she made a movement to retreat in terror, it sent a pang to his heart.

'I did not expect you,' he said hurriedly, with a look that made her stop. 'Please sit down. You come, no doubt, from Katerina Ivanovna. Allow me – not there. Sit here . . .'

At Sonia's entrance, Razumihin, who had been sitting on one of Raskolnikov's three chairs, close to the door, got up to allow her to enter. Raskolnikov had at first shown her the place on the sofa where Zossimov had been sitting, but feeling that the sofa, which served him as a bed, was too *familiar* a place, he hurriedly motioned her to Razumihin's chair.

'You sit here,' he said to Razumihin, putting him on the sofa.

Sonia sat down, almost shaking with terror, and looked timidly at the two ladies. It was evidently almost inconceivable to herself that she could sit down beside them. At the thought of it, she was so frightened that she hurriedly got up again, and in utter confusion addressed Raskolnikov.

'I ... I ... have come for one minute. Forgive me for disturbing you,' she began falteringly. 'I come from Katerina Ivanovna, and she had no one to send. Katerina Ivanovna told me to beg you ... to be at the service ... in the morning ... at the Mitrofanievsky ... and then ... to us ... to her ... to do her the honour ... she told me to beg you ...' Sonia stammered and ceased speaking.

'I will try, certainly, most certainly,' answered Raskolnikov. He, too, stood up, and he, too, faltered and could not finish his sentence. 'Please sit down,' he said, suddenly. 'I want to talk to you. You are perhaps in a hurry, but please, be so kind, spare me two minutes,' and he drew up a chair for her.

Sonia sat down again, and again timidly she took a hurried, frightened look at the two ladies, and dropped her eyes. Raskolnikov's pale face flushed, a shudder passed over him, his eyes glowed.

'Mother,' he said firmly and insistently, 'this is Sofya Semyonovna Marmeladov, the daughter of that unfortunate Mr. Marmeladov who was run over yesterday before my eyes, and of whom I was just telling you.'

Pulcheria Alexandrovna glanced at Sonia, and slightly screwed up her eyes. In spite of her embarrassment before Rodya's urgent and challenging look, she could not deny herself that satisfaction. Dounia gazed gravely and intently into the poor girl' face, and scrutinized her with perplexity. Sonia, hearing herself introduced, tried to raise her eyes again, but was more embarrassed than ever.

'I wanted to ask you,' said Raskolnikov, hastily, 'how things were arranged yesterday. You were not worried by the police, for instance?'

'No, that was all right . . . it was too evident, the cause of death . . . they did not worry us . . . only the lodgers are angry.'

'Why?'

'At the body's remaining so long. You see it is hot now. So that, to-day, they will carry it to the cemetery, into the chapel, until to-morrow. At first Katerina Ivanovna was unwilling, but now she sees herself that it is necessary . . .'

'To-day, then?'

'She begs you to do us the honour to be in the church to-morrow for the service, and then to be present at the funeral lunch.'

'She is giving a funeral lunch?'

'Yes . . . just a little . . . She told me to thank you very much for helping us yesterday. But for you, we should have had nothing for the funeral.'

All at once her lips and chin began trembling, but, with an effort, she controlled herself, looking down again.

During the conversation, Raskolnikov watched her carefully. She had a thin, very thin, pale little face, rather irregular and angular, with a sharp little nose and chin. She could not have been called pretty, but her blue eyes were so clear, and when they lighted up, there was such a kindliness and simplicity in her expression that one could not help being attracted. Her face, and her whole figure indeed, had another peculiar characteristic. In spite of her eighteen years, she looked almost a little girl – almost a child. And in some of her gestures, this childishness seemed almost absurd.

'But has Katerina Ivanovna been able to manage with such small means? Does she even mean to have a funeral lunch?' Raskolnikov asked, persistently keeping up the conversation.

'The coffin will be plain, of course ... and everything will be plain, so it won't cost much. Katerina Ivanovna and I have reckoned it all out, so that there will be enough left ... and Katerina Ivanovna was very anxious it should be so. You know one can't ... it's a comfort to her ... she is like that, you know ...'

'I understand, I understand ... of course ... why do you look at my room like that? My mother has just said it is like a tomb.'

'You gave us everything yesterday,' Sonia said suddenly, in reply, in a loud rapid whisper; and again she looked down in confusion. Her lips and chin were trembling once more. She had been struck at once by Raskolnikov's poor surroundings, and now these words broke out spontaneously. A silence followed. There was a light in Dounia's eyes, and even Pulcheria Alexandrovna looked kindly at Sonia.

'Rodya,' she said, getting up, 'we shall have dinner together, of course. Come, Dounia ... And you, Rodya, had better go for a little walk, and then rest and lie down before you come to see us ... I am afraid we have exhausted you ...'

'Yes, yes, I'll come,' he answered, getting up fussily. 'But I have something to see to.'

'But surely you will have dinner together?' cried Razumihin, looking in surprise at Raskolnikov. 'What do you mean?'

'Yes, yes, I am coming ... of course, of course! And you stay a minute. You do not want him just now, do you, mother? Or perhaps I am taking him from you?'

'Oh, no, no. And will you, Dmitri Prokofitch, do us the favour of dining with us?'

'Please do,' added Dounia.

Razumihin bowed, positively radiant. For one moment, they were all strangely embarrassed.

'Good-bye, Rodya, that is till we meet. I do not like saying good-bye. Good-bye, Nastasya. Ah, I have said good-bye again.'

Pulcheria Alexandrovna meant to greet Sonia, too; but it somehow failed to come off, and she went in a flutter out of the room.

But Avdotya Romanovna seemed to await her turn, and following her mother out, gave Sonia an attentive, courteous bow. Sonia, in confusion, gave a hurried, frightened curtsy. There was a look on poignant discomfort in her face, as though Avdotya Romanovna's courtesy and attention were oppressive and painful to her.

'Dounia, good-bye,' called Raskolnikov, in the passage. 'Give me your hand.'

'Why, I did give it you. Have you forgotten?' said Dounia, turning warmly and awkwardly to him.

'Never mind, give it to me again.' And he squeezed her fingers warmly.

Dounia smiled, flushed, pulled her hand away, and went off quite happy.

'Come, that's capital,' he said to Sonia, going back and looking brightly at her. 'God give peace to the dead, the living have still to live. That is right, isn't it?'

Sonia looked surprised at the sudden brightness of his face. He looked at her for some moments in silence. The whole history of the dead father floated before his memory in those moments . . .

'Heavens, Dounia,' Pulcheria Alexandrovna began, as soon as they were in the street. 'I really feel relieved myself at coming away – more at ease. How little did I think yesterday in the train that I could ever be glad of that.'

'I tell you again mother, he is still very ill. Don't you see it? Perhaps worrying about us upset him. We must be patient, and much, much can be forgiven.'

'Well, you were not very patient!' Pulcheria Alexandrovna caught her up, hotly and jealously. 'Do you know, Dounia, I was looking at you two. You are the very portrait of him, and not so much in face as in soul. You are both melancholy, both morose and hot-tempered, both haughty and both generous, . . . Surely he can't be an egoist, Dounia. Eh? When I think of what is in store for us this evening, my heart sinks!'

'Don't be uneasy, mother. What must be, will be.'

'Dounia, only think what a position we are in! What if Pyotr Petrovitch breaks if off?' poor Pulcheria Alexandrovna blurted out, incautiously.

'He won't be worth much if he does,' answered Dounia, sharply and contemptuously.

'We did well to come away,' Pulcheria Alexandrovna hurriedly broke in. 'He was in a hurry about some business or other. If he gets out and has a breath of air . . . it is fearfully close in his room . . . But where is one to get a breath of air here? The very streets here feel like shut-up rooms. Good heavens! what a town! . . . stay . . . this side . . . they will crush you – carrying something. Why, it is a piano they have got, I declare . . . how they push! . . . I am very much afraid of that young woman, too.'

'What young woman, mother?'

'Why, that Sofya Semyonovna, who was there just now.'

'Why?'

'I have a presentiment, Dounia. Well, you may believe it or not, but as soon as she came in, that very minute, I felt that she was the chief cause of the trouble . . .'

'Nothing of the sort!' cried Dounia, in vexation. 'What nonsense, with your presentiments, mother! He only made her acquaintance the evening before, and he did not know her when she came in.'

'Well, you will see . . . She worries me; but you will see, you will see! I was so frightened. She was gazing at me with those eyes. I could scarcely sit still in my chair when he began introducing her, do you remember? It seems so strange, but Pyotr Petrovitch writes like that about her, and he introduces her to us – to you! So he must think a great deal of her.'

'People will write anything. We were talked about and written about, too. Have you forgotten? I am sure that she is a good girl, and that it is all nonsense.'

'God grant it may be!'

'And Pyotr Petrovitch is a contemptible slanderer,' Dounia snapped out, suddenly.

Pulcheria Alexandrovna was crushed; the conversation was not resumed.

'I will tell you what I want with you,' said Raskolnikov, drawing Razumihin to the window.

'Then I will tell Katerina Ivanovna that you are coming,' Sonia said hurriedly, preparing to depart.

'One minute, Sofya Semyonovna. We have no secrets. You are not in our way. I want to have another word or two with you. Listen!' he turned suddenly to Razumihin again. 'You know that . . . what's his name . . . Porfiry Petrovitch?'

'I should think so! He is a relation. Why?' added the latter, with interest.

'Is not he managing that case . . . you know, about that murder? . . . You were speaking about it yesterday.'

'Yes . . . well?' Razumihin's eyes opened wide.

'He was inquiring for people who had pawned things, and I have some pledges there, too – trifles – a ring my sister gave me as a keepsake when I left home, and my father's silver watch – they are only worth five or six roubles altogether . . . but I value them. So what am I to do now? I do not want to lose the things, especially the watch. I was quaking just now, for fear mother would ask me to look at it, when we spoke of Dounia's watch. It is the only thing of father's left us. She would be ill if it were lost. You know what women are. So tell me what to do. I know I ought to have given notice at the police station, but would it not be better to go straight to Porfiry? Eh? What do you think? The matter might be settled more quickly. You see, mother may ask for it before dinner.'

'Certainly not to the police station. Certainly to Porfiry,' Razumihin shouted in extraordinary excitement. 'Well, how glad I am. Let us go at once. It is a couple of steps. We shall be sure to find him.'

'Very well, let us go.'

'And he will be very, very glad to make your acquaintance. I have often talked to him of you at different times. I was speaking of you yesterday. Let us go. So you knew the old woman? So that's it! It is all turning out splendidly . . . Oh, yes, Sofya Ivanovna . . .'

'Sofya Semyonovna,' corrected Raskolnikov, 'Sofya Semyonovna, this is my friend Razumihin, and he is a good man.'

'If you have to go now,' Sonia was beginning, not looking at Razumihin at all, and still more embarrassed.

'Let us go,' decided Raskolnikov. 'I will come to you to-day, Sofya Semyonovna. Only tell me where you live.'

He was not exactly ill at ease, but seemed hurried, and avoided her eyes. Sonia gave her address, and flushed as she did so. They all went out together.

'Don't lock up?' asked Razumihin, following him on to the stairs.

'Never,' answered Raskolnikov. 'I have been meaning to buy a lock for these two years. People are happy who have no need of locks,' he said, laughing, to Sonia. They stood still in the gateway.

'Do you go to the right, Sofya Semyonovna? How did you find me, by the way?' he added, as though he wanted to say something quite different. He wanted to look at her soft clear eyes, but this was not easy.

'Why, you gave your address to Polenka yesterday.'

'Polenka? Oh, yes; Polenka, that is the little girl. She is your sister? Did I give her the address?'

'Why, had you forgotten?'

'No, I remember.'

'I had heard my father speak of you . . . only I did not know your name, and he did not know it. And now I came . . . and as I had learnt your name, I asked to-day, "Where does Mr. Raskolnikov live?" I did not know you had only a room too . . . Good-bye, I will tell Katrina Ivanovna.'

She was extremely glad to escape at last; she went away looking down, hurrying to get out of sight as soon as possible, to walk the twenty steps to the turning on the right and to be at last alone, and then moving rapidly along, looking at no one, noticing nothing, to think, to remember, to meditate on every word, every detail. Never, never had she felt anything like this. Dimly and unconsciously a whole new world was opening before her. She remembered suddenly that Raskolnikov meant to come to her that day, perhaps that morning, perhaps at once!

'Only not to-day, please, not to-day!' she kept muttering with a sinking heart, as though entreating someone, like a frightened child. 'Mercy! to me . . . to that room . . . he will see . . . oh, dear!'

She was not capable at that instant of noticing an unknown gentleman who was watching her and following at her heels. He had accompanied her from the gateway. At the moment when Razumihin, Raskolnikov, and she stood still at parting on the pavement, this gentleman, who was just passing, started on hearing Sonia's words: 'and I asked where Mr. Raskolnikov lived?' He turned a rapid but attentive look upon all three, then looked back and noted the house. All this was done in an instant as he passed, and trying not to betray his interest, he walked on more slowly as though waiting for something. He was waiting for Sonia; he saw that they were parting, and that Sonia was going home.

'Home? Where? I've seen that face somewhere,' he thought. 'I must find out.'

At the turning he crossed over, looked round, and saw Sonia coming the same way, noticing nothing. She turned the corner. He followed her on the other side. After about fifty paces he crossed over again, overtook her and kept two or three yards behind her.

He was a man about fifty, rather tall and thickly set, with broad high shoulders which made him look as though he stooped a little. He wore good and fashionable clothes, and looked like a gentleman of position. He carried a handsome cane, which he tapped on the pavement at each step; his gloves were spotless. He had a broad, rather pleasant face with high cheekbones and a fresh colour, not often seen in Petersburg. His flaxen hair was still abundant, and only touched here and there with grey, and his thick square beard was even lighter than his hair. His eyes were blue and had a cold and thoughtful look; his lips were crimson. He was a remarkably well-preserved man and looked much younger than his years.

When Sonia came out on the canal bank, they were the only two persons on the pavement. He observed her dreaminess and preoccupation. On reaching the house where she lodged, Sonia turned in at the gate; he followed her, seeming rather surprised. In the courtyard she turned to the right corner. 'Bah!' muttered the unknown gentleman, and mounted the stairs behind her. Only then Sonia noticed him. She reached the third storey, turned down the passage, and rang at No. 9. On the door was inscribed in chalk, 'Kapernaumov, Tailor'. 'Bah!' the stranger repeated again, wondering at the strange coincidence, and he rang next door, at No. 8. The doors were two or three yards apart.

'You lodge at Kapernaumov's,' he said, looking at Sonia and laughing. 'He altered a waistcoat for me yesterday. I am staying close here at Madame Resslich's. How odd!' Sonia looked at him attentively.

'We are neighbours,' he went on gaily. 'I only came to town the day before yesterday. Good-bye for the present.'

Sonia made no reply; the door opened and she slipped in. She felt for some reason ashamed and uneasy.

On the way to Porfiry's, Razumihin, was obviously excited.

'That's capital, brother,' he repeated several times, 'and I am glad! I am glad!'

'What are you glad about?' Raskolnikov thought to himself.

'I didn't know that you pledged things at that old woman's too. And . . . and was it long ago? I mean, was it long since you were there?'

'What a simple-hearted fool he is!'

'When was it?' Raskolnikov stopped still to recollect. 'Two or three days before her death, it must have been. But I am not going to redeem the things now,' he put in with a sort of hurried and conspicuous solicitude about the things. 'I've not more than a silver rouble left . . . after last night's accursed delirium!'

He laid special emphasis on the delirium.

'Yes, yes,' Razumihin hastened to agree – with what was not clear. 'Then that's why you . . . were stuck . . . partly . . . you know in your delirium you were continually mentioning some rings or chains! Yes, yes . . . that's clear, it's all clear now.'

'Hullo! How that idea must have got about among them. Here this man will go to the stake for me, and I find him delighted at having it *cleared up* why I spoke of rings in my delirium! What a hold the idea must have on all of them!'

'Shall we find him?' he asked suddenly.

'Oh, yes,' Razumihin answerd quickly. 'He is a nice fellow, you will see, brother. Rather clumsy, that is to say, he is a man of polished manners, but I mean clumsy in a different sense. He is an intelligent fellow, very much so indeed, but he has his own range of ideas . . . He is incredulous, sceptical, cynical . . . he likes to impose on people, or rather to make fun of them. His is the old, circumstantial method . . . But he understands his work . . . thoroughly . . . Last year he cleared up a case of murder in which the police had hardly a clue. He is very, very anxious to make your acquaintance!'

'On what grounds is he so anxious?'

'Oh, it's not exactly . . . you see, since you've been ill I happen to have mentioned you several times . . . So, when he heard about you . . . about your being a law student and not able to finish your studies, he said, "What a pity!" And so I concluded . . . from everything together, not only that; yesterday Zametov . . . you know, Rodya, I talked some nonsense on the way home to you yesterday, when I was drunk . . . I am afraid, brother, of your exaggerating it, you see.'

'What? That they think I am a madman? Maybe they are right,' he said with a constrained smile.

'Yes, yes . . . That is, pooh, no! . . . But all that I said (and there was something else too) it was all nonsense, drunken nonsense.'

'But why are you apologizing? I am so sick of it all!' Raskolnikov cried with exaggerated irritability. It was partly assumed, however.

'I know, I know, I understand. Believe me, I understand. One's ashamed to speak of it.'

'If you are ashamed, then don't speak of it.'

Both were silent. Razumihin was more than ecstatic and Raskolnikov perceived it with repulsion. He was alarmed, too, by what Razumihin had just said about Porfiry.

'I shall have to pull a long face with him too,' he thought, with a beating heart, and he turned white, 'and do it naturally, too. But the most natural thing would be to do nothing at all. Carefully do nothing at all! No, *carefully* would not be natural again . . . Oh, well, we shall see how it turns out . . . We shall see . . . directly. Is it a good thing to go or not? The butterfly flies to the light. My heart is beating, that's what's bad!'

'In this grey house,' said Razumihin.

'The most important thing, does Porfiry know that I was at the old hag's flat yesterday . . . and asked about the blood? I must find that out instantly, as soon as I go in, find out from his face; otherwise . . . I'll find out, if it's my ruin.'

'I say, brother,' he said suddenly, addressing Razumihin, with a sly smile, 'I have been noticing all day that you seem to be curiously excited. Isn't it so?'

'Excited? Not a bit of it,' said Razumihin, stung to the quick.

'Yes, brother, I assure you it's noticeable. Why, you sat on your chair in a way you never do sit, on the edge somehow, and you seemed to be writhing all the time. You kept jumping up for nothing. One moment you were angry, and the next your face looked like a sweetmeat. You even blushed; especially when you were invited to dinner, you blushed awfully.'

'Nothing of the sort, nonsense! What do you mean?'

'But why are you wriggling out of it, like a schoolboy? By Jove, there, he's blushing again.'

'What a pig you are!'

'But why are you so shamefaced about it? Romeo! Stay, I'll tell of you to-day. Ha-ha-ha! I'll make mother laugh, and someone else, too . . .'

'Listen, listen, listen, this is serious . . . What next, you fiend!'

Razumihin was utterly overwhelmed, turning cold with horror. 'What will you tell them? Come, brother . . . foo! what a pig you are!'

'You are like a summer rose. And if only you knew how it suits you; a Romeo over six foot high! And how you've washed to-day – you cleaned your nails, I declare. Eh? That's something unheard of! Why, I do believe you've got pomatum on your hair! Bend down.'

'Pig!'

Raskolnikov laughed as though he could not restrain himself. So laughing, they entered Porfiry Petrovitch's flat. This is what Raskolnikov wanted: from within they could be heard laughing as the came in, still guffawing in the passage.

'Not a word here or I'll . . . brain you!' Razumihin whispered furiously, seizing Raskolnikov by the shoulder.

❯ FIVE ❮

Raskolnikov was already entering the room. He came in looking as though he had the utmost difficulty not to burst out laughing again. Behind him Razumihin strode in gawky and awkward, shamefaced and red as a peony, with an utterly crestfallen and ferocious expression. His face and whole figure really were ridiculous at that moment and amply justified Raskolnikov's laughter. Raskolnikov, not waiting for an introduction, bowed to Portfiry Petrovitch, who stood in the middle of the room looking inquiringly at them. He held out his hand and shook hands, still apparently making desperate efforts to subdue his mirth and utter a few words to introduce himself. But he had no sooner succeeded in assuming a serious air and muttering something when he suddenly glanced again as though accidentally at Razumihin, and could no longer control himself: his stifled laughter broke out the more irresistibly the more he tried to restrain it. The extraordinary ferocity with which Razumihin received this 'spontaneous' mirth gave the whole scene the appearance of most genuine fun and naturalness. Razumihin strengthened this impression as though on purpose.

'Fool! You fiend,' he roared, waving his arm which at once struck a little round table with an empty tea-glass on it. Everything was sent flying and crashing.

'But why break chairs, gentlemen? You know it's a loss to the Crown,' Porfiry Petrovitch quoted gaily.

Raskolnikov was still laughing, with his hand in Porfiry Petrovitch's, but, anxious not to overdo it, awaited the right moment to put a natural end to it. Razumihin, completely put to confusion by upsetting the table and smashing the glass, gazed gloomily at the fragments, cursed and turned sharply to the window where he stood looking out with his back to the company with a fiercely scowling countenance, seeing nothing Porfiry Petrovitch laughed and was ready to go on laughing, but obviously looked for explanations. Zametov had been sitting in the corner, but he rose at the visitors' entrance and was standing in expectation with a smile on his lips, though he looked with surprise and even it seemed incredulity at the whole scene and at Raskolnikov with a certain embarrassment. Zametov's unexpected presence struck Raskolnikov unpleasantly.

'I've got to think of that,' he thought. 'Excuse me, please,' he began, affecting extreme embarrassment. 'Raskolnikov.'

'Not at all, very pleasant to see you ... and how pleasantly you've come in ... Why, won't he even say good-morning?' Porfiry Petrovitch nodded at Razumihin.

'Upon my honour I don't know why he is in such a rage with me. I only told him as we came along that he was like Romeo ... and proved it. And that was all, I think!'

'Pig!' ejaculated Razumihin, without turning round.

'There must have been very grave grounds for it, if he is so furious at the word,' Porfiry laughed.

'Oh, you sharp lawyer! ... Damn you all!' snapped Razumihin, and suddenly bursting out laughing himself, he went up to Porfiry with a more cheerful face as though nothing had happened. 'That'll do! We are all fools. To come to business, This is my friend Rodion Romanovitch Raskolnikov; in the first place he has heard of you and wants to make your acquaintance, and secondly, he has a little matter of business with you. Bah! Zametov, what brought you here? Have you met before? Have you known each other long?'

'What does this mean?' thought Raskolnikov uneasily.

Zametov seemed taken aback, but not very much so.

'Why, it was at your rooms we met yesterday,' he said easily.

'Then I have been spared the trouble. All last week he was begging me to introduce him to you. Porfiry and you have sniffed each other out without me. Where is your tobacco?'

Porfiry Petrovitch was wearing a dressing-gown, very clean linen, and trodden-down slippers. He was a man of about five-and-thirty, short, stout even to corpulence, and clean-shaven. He wore his hair cut short and had a large round head, paricularly prominent at the back. His soft round, rather snub-nosed face was of a sickly yellowish colour, but had a vigorous and rather ironical expression. It would have been good-natured except for a look in the eyes, which shone with a watery, mawkish light under almost white, blinking eyelashes. The expression of those eyes was strangely out of keeping with his somewhat womanish figure, and gave it something far more serious than could be guessed at first sight.

As soon as Porfiry Petrovitch heard that his visitor had a little matter of business with him, he begged him to sit down on the sofa and sat down himself on the other end, waiting for him to explain his business, with that careful and over-serious attention which is at once oppressive and embarrassing, especially to a stranger, and especially if what you are discussing is in your own opinion of far too little importance for such exceptional solemnity. But in brief and coherent phrases Raskolnikov explained his business clearly and exactly, and was so well satisfied with himself that he even succeeded in taking a good look at Porfiry. Porfiry Petrovitch did not once take his eyes off him. Razumihin, sitting opposite at the same table, listened warmly and impatiently, looking from one to the other every moment with rather excessive interest.

'Fool,' Raskolnikov swore to himself.

'You have to give information to the police,' Porfiry replied, with a most businesslike air, 'that having learnt of this incident, that is of the murder, you beg to inform the lawyer in charge of the case that such and such things belong to you, and that you desire to redeem them . . . or . . . but they will write to you.'

'That's just the point, that at the present moment,' Raskolnikov tried his utmost to feign embarrassment, 'I am not quite in funds . . . and even this trifling sum is beyond me . . . I only wanted, you see, for the present to declare that the things are mine, and that when I have money . . .'

'That's no matter,' answered Porfiry Petrovitch, receiving his explanation of his pecuniary position coldly, 'but you can, if you prefer, write straight to me, to say, that having been informed of the matter, and claiming such and such as your property, you beg . . .'

'On an ordinary sheet of paper?' Raskolnikov interrupted eagerly, again interested in the financial side of the question.

'Oh, the most ordinary,' and suddenly Profiry Petrovitch looked with obvious irony at him, screwing up his eyes and, as it were, winking at him. But perhaps it was Raskolnikov's fancy, for it all lasted but a moment. There was certainly something of the sort, Raskolnikov could have sworn he winked at him, goodness knows why.

'He knows,' flashed through his mind like lightning.

'Forgive my troubling you about such trifles,' he went on, a little disconcerted, 'the things are only worth five roubles, but I prize them particularly for the sake of those from whom they came to me, and I must confess that I was alarmed when I heard . . .'

'That's why you were so much struck when I mentioned to Zossimov that Porfiry was inquiring for everyone who had pledges!' Razumihin put in with obvious intention.

This was really unbearable. Raskolnikov could not help glancing at him with a flash of vindictive anger in his black eyes, but immediately recollected himself.

'You seem to be jeering at me, brother?' he said to him, with a well-feigned irritability. 'I dare say I do seem to you absurdly anxious about such trash; but you mustn't think me selfish or grasping for that, and these two things may be anything but trash in my eyes. I told you just now that the silver watch, though it's not worth a cent, is the only thing left us of my father's. You may laugh at me, but my mother is here,' he turned suddenly to Porfiry, 'and if she knew,' he turned again hurriedly to Razumihin, carefully making his voice tremble, 'that the watch was lost, she would be in despair! You know what women are!'

'Not a bit of it! I didn't mean that at all! Quite the contrary!' shouted Razumihin distressed.

'Was it right? Was it natural? Did I overdo it?' Raskolnikov asked himself in a tremor. 'Why did I say that about women?'

'Oh, your mother is with you?' Porfiry Petrovitch inquired.

'Yes.'

'When did she come?'

'Last night.'

Porfiry paused as though reflecting.

'Your things would not in any case be lost,' he went on calmly and coldly. 'I have been expecting you here for some time.'

And as though that were a matter of no importance, he carefully offered the ash-tray to Razumihin, who was ruthlessly scattering cigarette ash over the carpet. Raskolnikov shuddered, but Porfiry did not seem to be looking at him, and was still concerned with Razumihin's cigarette.

'What? Expecting him? Why, did you know that he had pledges *there*?' cried Razumihin.

Porfiry Petrovitch addressed himself to Raskolnikov.

'Your things, the ring and the watch, were wrapped up together, and on the paper your name was legibly written in pencil, together with the date on which you left them with her . . .'

'How observant you are!' Raskolnikov smiled awkwardly, doing his very utmost to look him straight in the face, but he failed, and suddenly added:

'I say that because I suppose these were a great many pledges . . . so that it must be difficult to remember them all . . . But you remember them all so clearly, and . . . and . . .'

'Stupid! Feeble!' he thought. 'Why did I add that?'

'But we know all who had pledges, and you are the only one who hasn't come forward,' Porfiry answered with hardly perceptible irony.

'I haven't been quite well.'

'I heard that too. I heard, indeed, that you were in great distress about something. You look pale still.'

'I am not pale at all . . . No, I am quite well,' Raskolnikov snapped out rudely and angrily, completely changing his tone. His anger was mounting, he could not repress it. 'And in my anger I shall betray myself,' flashed through his mind again. 'Why are they torturing me?'

'Not quite well!' Razumihin caught him up. 'What next! He was unconscious and delirious till yesterday. Would you believe, Porfiry, as soon as our backs were turned, he dresses, though he could hardly stand, and gave us the slip and went off on the spree somewhere till midnight, delirious all the time! Would you believe it! Extraordinary!'

'Really delirious? You don't say so!; Porfiry shook his head in a womanish way.

'Nonsense! Don't you believe it! But you don't believe it anyway,' Raskolnikov let slip in his anger. But Porfiry Petrovitch did not seem to catch those strange words.

'But how could you have gone out if you hadn't been delirious?' Razumihin got hot suddenly. 'What did you go out for? What was the object of it? And why on the sly? Were you in your senses when you did it? Now that all danger is over I can speak plainly.'

'I was awfully sick of them yesterday.' Raskolnikov addressed Porfiry suddenly with a smile of insolent defiance, 'I ran away from them to take lodgings where they wouldn't find me, and took a lot of money with me. Mr. Zametov there saw it. I say, Mr. Zametov, was I sensible or delirious yesterday? Settle our dispute.'

He could have strangled Zametov at that moment, so hateful were his expression and his silence to him.

'In my opinion you talked sensibly and even artfully, but you were extremely irritable,' Zametov pronounced dryly.

'And Nikodim Fomitch was telling me to-day,' put in Porfiry Petrovitch, 'that he met you very late last night in the lodging of a man who had been run over.'

'And there,' said Razumihin, 'weren't you mad then? You gave your last penny to the widow for the funeral. If you wanted to help, give fifteen or twenty even, but keep three roubles for yourself at least, but he flung away all the twenty-five at once!'

'Maybe I found a treasure somewhere and you know nothing of it? So that's why I was liberal yesterday . . . Mr. Zametov knows I've found a treasure! Excuse us, please, for disturbing you for half an hour with such trivialities,' he said, turning to Porfiry Petrovitch, with trembling lips. 'We are boring you, aren't we?'

'Oh no, quite the contrary, quite the contrary! If only you knew how you interest me! It's interesting to look on and listen . . . and I am really glad you have come forward at last.'

'But you might give us some tea! My throat's dry,' cried Razumihin.

'Capital idea! Perhaps we will all keep you company. Wouldn't you like . . . something more essential before tea?'

'Get along with you!'

Porfiry Petrovitch went out to order tea.

Raskolnikov's thoughts were in a whirl. He was in terrible exasperation.

'The worst of it is they don't disguise it; they don't care to stand on ceremony! And how, if you didn't know me at all, did you come to talk to Nikodim Fomitch about me? So they don't care to hide that they are tracking me like a pack of dogs. They simply spit in my face.' He was shaking with rage. 'Come, strike me openly, don't play with me like a cat with a mouse. It's hardly civil, Porfiry Petrovitch, but perhaps I won't allow it! I shall get up and throw the whole truth in your ugly faces, and you'll see how I despise you.' He could hardly breathe. 'And what if it's only my fancy? What if I am mistaken, and through inexperience I get angry and don't keep up my nasty part? perhaps it's all unintentional. All their phrases are the usual ones, but there is something about them . . . It all might be said, but there is something. Why did he say bluntly, "With her"? Why did Zametov add that I spoke artfully? Why do they speak in that tone? Yes the tone . . . Razumihin is sitting here, why does he see nothing? That innocent blockhead never does see anything! Feverish again! Did Porfiry wink at me just now? Of course it's nonsense! What could he wink for? Are they trying to upset my nerves or are they teasing me? Either it's all fancy or they know! Even Zametov is rude . . . Is Zametov rude? Zametov has changed his mind. I foresaw he would change his mind! He is at home here, while it's my first visit. Porfiry does not consider him a visitor; sits with his back to him. They're as thick as thieves, no doubt, over me! Not a doubt they were talking about me before we came. Do they know about the flat? If only they'd make haste! When I said that I ran away to take a flat he let it pass . . . I put that in cleverly about a flat, it may be of use afterwards . . . Delirious, indeed . . . ha-ha-ha! He knows all about last night! He didn't know of my mother's arrival! The hag had written the date on in pencil! You are wrong, you won't catch me! There are no facts . . . it's all supposition! You produce facts! The flat even isn't a fact but delirium. I know what to say to them . . . Do they know about the flat? I won't go without finding out. What did I come for? But my being angry now, maybe, is a fact! Fool, how irritable I am! Perhaps that's right; to play the invalid . . . He is feeling me. He will try to catch me. Why did I come?'

All this flashed like lightning through his mind.

Porfiry Petrovitch returned quickly. He became suddenly more jovial.

'Your party yesterday, brother, has left my head rather . . . And I am out of sorts altogether,' he began in quite a different tone, laughing to Razumihin.

'Was it interesting? I left you yesterday at the most interesting point. Who got the best of it?'

'Oh, no one, of course. They got on to everlasting questions, floated off into space.'

'Only fancy, Rodya, what we got on to yesterday. Whether there is such a thing as crime. I told you that we talked our heads off.'

'What is there strange? It's an everyday social question,' Raskolnikov answered casually.

'The question wasn't put quite like that,' observed Porfiry.

'Not quite, that's true,' Razumihin agreed at once, getting warm and hurried as usual. 'Listen, Rodion, and tell us your opinion. I want to hear it. I was fighting tooth and nail with them and wanted you to help me. I told them you were coming . . . It began with the socialist doctrine. You know their doctrine; crime is a protest against the abnormality of the social organization and nothing more, and nothing more; no other causes admitted! . . .'

'You were wrong there,' cried Porfiry Petrovitch; he was noticeably animated and kept laughing as he looked at Razumihin, which made him more excited than ever.

'Nothing is admitted,' Razumihin interrupted with heat.

'I am not wrong. I'll show you their pamphlets. Everything with them is "the influence of environment", and nothing else. Their favourite phrase! From which it follows that, if society is normally organized, all crime will cease at once, since there will be nothing to protest against and all men will become righteous in one instant. Human nature is not taken into account, it is excluded, it's not supposed to exist! They don't recognize that humanity, developing by a historical living process, will become at last a normal society, but they believe that a social system that has come out of some mathematical brain is going to organize all humanity at once and make it just and sinless in an instant, quicker than any living process! That's why they instinctively dislike history, "nothing but ugliness and stupidity in it", and they explain it all as stupidity! That's why they so dislike the *living* process of life; they don't want a *living soul*! The living soul demands life, the soul won't obey the rules of mechanics, the soul is an object of suspicion, the soul is retrograde! But what they want though it smells of death and can be made of india-rubber, at least is not alive, has no will, is servile and won't revolt! And it comes in the end to their reducing everything to the building of walls and the planning of rooms and passages in a phalanstery! The phalanstery is ready, indeed, but your human nature is not ready for the phalanstery – it wants life, it hasn't completed its vital process, it's too soon for the graveyard! You can't skip over nature by logic. Logic presupposes three possibilities, but there are millions! Cut away a million, and reduce it all to the question of comfort! That's the easiest solution of the problem! It's seductively clear and you mustn't think about it. That's the great thing, you mustn't think! The whole secret of life in two pages of print!'

'Now he is off, beating the drum! Catch hold of him, do!' laughed Porfiry. 'Can you imagine,' he turned to Raskolnikov, 'six people holding forth like that last night, in one room, with punch as a preliminary! No, brother, you are wrong, environment accounts for a great deal in crime; I can assure you of that.'

'Oh, I know it does, but just tell me: a man of forty violates a child of ten; was it environment drove him to it?'

'Well, strictly speaking, it did,' Porfiry observed with noteworthy gravity; 'a crime of that nature may be very well ascribed to the influence of environment.'

Razumihin was almost in a frenzy. 'Oh, if you like,' he roared, 'I'll prove to you that your white eyelashes may very well be ascribed to the Church of Ivan the Great's being two hundred and fifty feet high, and I will prove it clearly, exactly, progressively, and even with a Liberal tendency! I undertake to! Will you bet on it?'

'Done! Let's hear, please, how he will prove it!'

'He is always humbugging, confound him,' cried Razumihin, jumping up and gesticulating. 'What's the use of talking to you? He does all that on purpose; you don't know him, Rodion! He took their side yesterday, simply to make fools of them. And the things he said yesterday! And they were delighted! He can keep it up for a fortnight together. Last year he persuaded us that he was going into a monastery: he stuck to it for two months. Not long ago he took it into his head to declare he was going to get married, that he had everything ready for the wedding. He ordered

215

new clothes indeed. We all began to congratulate him. There was no bride, nothing, all pure fantasy!'

'Ah, you are wrong! I got the clothes before. It was the new clothes, in fact, that made me think of taking you in.'

'Are you such a good dissembler?' Raskolnikov asked carelessly.

'You wouldn't have supposed it, eh? Wait a bit, I shall take you in, too. Ha-ha-ha! No, I'll tell you the truth. All these questions about crime, environment, children, recall to my mind an article of yours which interested me at the time. "On Crime" . . . or something of the sort, I forget the title, I read it with pleasure two months ago in the *Periodical Review.'*

'My article? In the *Periodical Review*?' Raskolnikov asked in astonishment. 'I certainly did write an article upon a book six months ago when I left the university, but I sent it to the *Weekly Review.'*

'But it came out in the *Periodical.'*

'And the *Weekly Review* ceased to exist, so that's why it wasn't printed at the time.'

'That's true; but when it ceased to exist, the *Weekly Review* was amalgamated with the *Periodical*, and so your article appeared two months ago in the latter. Didn't you know?'

Raskolnikov had not known.

'Why, you might get some money out of them for the article! What a strange person you are! You lead such a solitary life that you know nothing of matters that concern you directly. It's a fact, I assure you.'

'Bravo, Rodya! I knew nothing about it either!' cried Razumihin. 'I'll run to-day to the reading-room and ask for the number. Two months ago? What was the date? It doesn't matter though, I will find it. Think of not telling us!'

'How did you find out that the article was mine! It's only signed with an initial.'

'I only learnt it by chance, the other day. Through the editor; I know him . . . I was very much interested.'

'I analyzed, if I remember, the psychology of a Criminal before and after the crime.'

'Yes, and you maintained that the perpetration of a crime is always accompanied by illness. Very, very original, but . . . it was not that part of your article that interested me so much, but an idea at the end of the article which I regret to say you merely suggested without working it out clearly. There is, if you recollect, a suggestion that there are certain persons who can . . . that is, not precisely are able to, but have perfect right to commit breaches of morality and crimes, and that the law is not for them.'

Raskolnikov smiled at the exaggerated and intentional distortion of his idea.

'What? What do you mean? A right to crime? But not because of the influence of environment?' Razumihin inquired with some alarm even.

'No, not exactly because of it,' answered Porfiry. 'In his article all men are divided into "ordinary" and "extraordinary". Ordinary men have to live in submission, have no right to transgress the law, because, don't you see, they are ordinary. But extraordinary men have a right to commit any crime and to transgress the law in any way, just because they are extraordinary. That was your idea, if I am not mistaken?'

'What do you mean? That can't be right?' Razumihin muttered in bewilderment.

Raskolnikov smiled again. He saw the point at once, and knew where they wanted to drive him. He decided to take up the challenge.

'That wasn't quite my contention,' he began simply and modestly. 'Yet I admit that you have stated it almost correctly; perhaps, if you like, perfectly so.' (It almost gave him pleasure to admit this.) 'The only difference is that I don't contend that extraordinary people are always bound to commit breaches of morals, as you call it. In fact, I doubt whether such an argument could be published. I simply hinted that an "extraordinary" man has the right ... that is not an official right, but an inner right to decide in his own conscience to overstep ... certain obstacles, and only in case it is essential for the practical fulfilment of his idea (sometimes, perhaps, of benefit to the whole of humanity). You say that my article isn't definite; I am ready to make it as clear as I can. Perhaps I am right in thinking you want me to; very well. I maintain that if the discoveries of Kepler and Newton could not have been made known except by sacrificing the lives of one, a dozen, a hundred, or more men, Newton would have had the right, would indeed have been in duty bound ... to *eliminate* the dozen or the hundred men for the sake of making his discoveries known to the whole of humanity. But it does not follow from that that Newton had a right to murder people right and left and to steal every day in the market. Then, I remember, I maintain in my article that all ... well, legislators and leaders of men, such as Lycurgus, Solon, Mahomet, Napoleon, and so on, were all without exception criminals, from the very fact that, making a new law, they transgressed the ancient one, handed down from their ancestors and held sacred by the people, and they did not stop short at bloodshed either, if that bloodshed – often of innocent persons fighting bravely in defence of ancient law – were of use to their cause. It's remarkable, in fact, that the majority, indeed, of these benefactors and leaders of humanity were guilty of terrible carnage. In short, I maintain that all great men or even men a little out of the common, that is to say capable of giving some new word, must from their very nature be criminals – more or less, of course. Otherwise it's hard for them to get out of they common rut; and to remain in the common rut is what they can't submit to, from their very nature again, and to my mind they ought not, indeed, to submit to it. You see that there is nothing particularly new in all that. The same thing has been printed and read a thousand times before. As for my division of people into ordinary and extraordinary, I acknowledge that it's somewhat arbitrary, but I don't insist upon exact numbers. I only believe in my leading idea that men are *in general* divided by a law of nature into two categories, inferior (ordinary), that is, so to say, material that serves only to reproduce its kind, and men who have the gift or the talent to utter *a new word*. There are, of course, innumerable sub-divisions, but the distinguishing features of both categories are fairly well marked. The first category, generally speaking, are men conservative in temperament and law-abiding; they live under control and love to be controlled. To my thinking it is their duty to be controlled, because that's their vocation, and there is nothing humiliating in it for them. The second category all transgress the law; they are destroyers or disposed to destruction according to their capacities. The crimes of these men are of course relative and varied; for the most part they seek in very varied ways the destruction of the present for the sake of the better. But if such a one is forced for the sake of his idea to step over a corpse or wade through blood, he can, I maintain, find within himself, in his conscience, a sanction for wading through blood – that depends on the idea and its dimensions, note that. It's only in that sense I speak of their right to crime in my article (you remember it began with the legal question). There's no need for much anxiety, however; the masses will scarcely ever admit this right, they punish them or hang them (more or less), and in doing so fulfil quite justly their conservative vocation. But the same masses set these criminals on a pedestal in the next generation and worship them (more or less). The first category is always the man of the present, the second the man of the future. The first preserve the world and people it, the second move the world and lead it to its goal. Each class has an equal right to exist. In fact, all have equal rights with me – and *vive la guerre éternelle* – till the New Jerusalem, of course!'

'Then you believe in the New Jerusalem, do you?'

'I do,' Raskolnikov answered firmly; as he said these words and during the whole preceding tirade he kept his eyes on one spot on the carpet.

'And . . . and do you believe in God? Excuse my curiosity.'

'I do,' repeated Raskolnikov, raising his eyes to Porfiry.

'And . . . do you believe in Lazarus' rising from the dead?'

'I . . . I do. Why do you ask all this?'

'You believe it literally?'

'Literally.'

'You don't say so ... I asked from curiosity. Excuse me. But let us go back to the question; they are not always executed. Some, on the contrary ...'

'Triumph in their lifetime? Oh yes, some attain their ends in this life, and then ...'

'They begin executing other people?'

'If it's necessary; indeed, for the most part they do. Your remark is very witty.'

'Thank you. But tell me this: how do you distinguish those extra ordinary people from the ordinary ones? Are there signs at their birth? I feel there ought to be more exactitude, more external definition. Excuse the natural anxiety of a practical law-abiding citizen, but couldn't they adopt a special uniform, for instance, couldn't they wear something, be branded in some way? For you know if confusion arises and a member of one category imagines that he belongs to the other, begins to "eliminate obstacles" as you so happily expressed it, then ...'

'Oh, that very often happens! That remark is wittier than the other.'

'Thank you.'

'No reason to; but take note that the mistake can only arise in the first category, that is among the ordinary people (as I perhaps unfortunately called them). In spite of their predisposition to obedience very many of them, through a playfulness of nature, sometimes vouchsafed even to the cow, like to imagine themselves advanced people, "destroyers", and to push themselves into the "new movement", and this quite sincerely. Meanwhile the really *new* people are very often unobserved by them, or even despised as reactionaries of grovelling tendencies. But I don't think there is any considerable danger here, and you really need not be uneasy, for they never go very far. Of course, they might have a thrashing sometimes for letting their fancy run away with them and to teach them their place, but no more; in fact, even this isn't necessary as they castigate themselves, for they are very conscientious: some perform this service for one another and others chastise themselves with their own hands ... They will impose various public acts of penitence upon themselves with a beautiful and edifying effect; in fact you've nothing to be uneasy about ... It's a law of nature.'

'Well, you have certainly set my mind more at rest on that score; but there's another thing worries me. Tell me, please, are there many people who have the right to kill others, these extraordinary people? I am ready to bow down to them, of course, but you must admit it's alarming if there are a great many of them, eh?'

'Oh, you needn't worry about that either,' Raskolnikov went on in the same tone. 'People with new ideas, people with the faintest capacity for saying something *new*, are extremely few in number, extraordinarily so, in fact. One thing only is clear, that the appearance of all these grades and subdivisions of men must follow with unfailing regularity some law of nature. That law, of course, is unknown at present, but I am convinced that it exists, and one day may become known. The vast mass of mankind is mere material, and only exists in order by some great effort, by some mysterious process, by means of some crossing of races and stocks, to bring into the world at last perhaps one man out of a thousand with a spark of independence. One in ten thousand perhaps – I speak roughly, approximately – is born with some independence, and with still greater independence one in a hundred thousand. The man of genius is one of millions, and the great geniuses, the crown of humanity, appear on earth perhaps one in many thousand millions. In fact I have not peeped into the retort in which all this takes place. But there certainly is and must be a definite law, it cannot be a matter of chance.'

'Why, are you both joking?' Razumihin cried at last. 'There you sit, making fun of one another. Are you serious, Rodya?'

Raskolnikov raised his pale and almost mournful face and made no reply. And the unconcealed, persistent, nervous, and *discourteous* sarcasm of Profiry seemed strange to Razumihin beside that quiet and mournful face.

'Well, brother, if you are really serious . . . You are right, of course, in saying that it's not new, that it's like what we've read and heard a thousand times already; but what is really *original* in all this, and is exclusively your own, to my horror, is that you sanction bloodshed *in the name of conscience*, and, excuse me saying so, with such fanaticism . . . That, I take it, is the point of your article. But that sanction of bloodshed *by conscience* is, to my mind . . . more terrible than the official, legal sanction of bloodshed . . .'

'You are quite right, it is more terrible,' Porfiry agreed.

'Yes, you must have exaggerated! There is some mistake, I shall read it. You can't think that! I shall read it.'

'All that is not in the article, there's only a hint of it,' said Raskolnikov.

'Yes, yes,' Porfiry couldn't sit still. 'Your attitude to crime is pretty clear to me now, but . . . excuse me for my impertience (I am really ashamed to be worrying you like this), you see, you've removed my anxiety as to the two grades getting mixed, but . . . there are various practical possibilities that make me uneasy! What if some man or youth imagines that he is a Lycurgus or Mahomet – a future one, of course – and suppose he begins to remove all obstacles . . . He had some great enterprises before him and needs money for it . . . and tries to get it . . . do you see?'

Zametov gave a sudden guffaw in his corner. Raskolnikov did not even raise his eyes to him.

'I must admit,' he went on calmly, 'that such cases certainly must arise. The vain and foolish are particularly apt to fall into that snare; young people especially.'

'Yes, you see. Well then?'

'What then?' Raskolnikov smiled in reply; 'that's not my fault. So it is and so it always will be. He said just now (he nodded at Razumihin) that I sanction bloodshed. Society is too well protected by prisons, banishment, criminal investigators, penal servitude. There's no need to be uneasy. You have but to catch the thief.'

'And what if we do catch him?'

'Then he gets what he deserves.'

'You are certainly logical. But what of this conscience?'

'Why do you care about that?'

'Simply from humanity.'

'If he has a conscience he will suffer for his mistake. That will be his punishment – as well as the prison.'

'But the real geniuses,' asked Razumihin frowning, 'those who have the right to murder? Oughn't they to suffer at all even for the blood they've shed?'

'Why the word *ought*? It's not a matter of permission or prohibition. He will suffer if he is sorry for his victim. Pain and suffering are always inevitable for a large intelligence and a deep heart. The really great men must, I think, have great sadness on earth,' he added dreamily, not in the tone of the conversation.

He raised his eyes, looked earnestly at them all, smiled, and took his cap. He was too quiet by comparison with his manner at his entrance, and he felt this. Everyone got up.

'Well, you may abuse me, be angry with me if you like,' Porfiry Petrovitch began again, 'but I can't resist. Allow me one little question (I know I am troubling you). There is just one little notion I want to express, simply that I may not forget it.'

'Very good, tell me your little notion,' Raskolnikov stood waiting, pale and grave before him.

'Well, you see . . . I really don't know how to express it properly . . . It's a playful, psychological idea . . . When you were writing your article, surely you couldn't have helped, he-he! fancying yourself . . . just a little, an "extraordinary" man, uttering a *new word* in your sense . . . That's so, isn't it?'

'Quite possibly,' Raskolnikov answered contemptuously.

Razumihin made a movement.

'And, if so, could you bring yourself in case of worldly difficulties and hardship or for some service to humanity – to overstep obstacles? . . . For instance, to rob and murder?'

And again he winked with his left eye, and laughed noiselessly just as before.

'If I did I certainly should not tell you,' Raskolnikov answered with defiant and haughty contempt.

'No, I was only interested on account of your article, from a literary point of view . . .'

'Foo! how obvious and insolent that is!' Raskolnikov thought with repulsion.

'Allow me to observe,' he answered dryly, 'that I don't consider myself a Mahomet or a Napoleon, nor any personage of that kind, and not being one of them I cannot tell you how I should act.'

'Oh, come, don't we all think ourselves Napoleans now in Russia?' Porfiry Petrovitch said with alarming familiarity.

Something peculiar betrayed itself in the very intonation of his voice.

'Perhaps it was one of these future Napoleons who did for Alyona Ivanovna last week?' Zametov blurted out from the corner.

Raskolnikov did not speak, but looked firmly and intently at Porfiry. Razumihin was scowling gloomily. He seemed before this to be noticing something. He looked angrily around. There was a minute of gloomy silence. Raskolnikov turned to go.

'Are you going already?' Porfiry said amiably, holding out his hand with excessive politeness. 'Very, very, glad of your acquaintance. As for your request, have no uneasiness, write just as I told you, or, better still, come to me there yourself in a day or two . . . to-morrow, indeed. I shall be there at eleven o'clock for certain. We'll arrange it all; we'll have a talk. As one of the last to be *there*, you might perhaps be able to tell us something,' he added with a most good-natured expression.

'You want to cross-examine me officially in due form?' Raskolnikov asked sharply.

'Oh, why? That's not necesary for the present. You misunderstand me. I lose no opportunity, you see, and . . . I've talked with all who had pledges . . . I obtained evidence from some of them, and you are the last . . . Yes, by the way,' he cried, seemingly suddenly delighted, 'I just remember, what was I thinking of?' he turned to Razumihin, 'you were talking my ears off about that Nikolay . . . of course, I know, I know very well,' he turned to Raskolnikov, 'that the fellow is innocent, but what is one to do? We had to trouble Dmitri too . . . This is the point, this is all: when you went up the stairs it was past seven, wasn't it?'

'Yes,' answered Raskolnikov, with an unpleasant sensation at the very moment he spoke that he need not have said it.

'Then when you went upstairs between seven and eight, didn't you see in a flat that stood open on a second storey, do you remember? two workmen or at least one of them? They were painting there, didn't you notice them? It's very, very important for them.'

'Painters? No, I didn't see them,' Raskolnikov answered slowly, as though ransacking his memory, while at the same instant he was racking every nerve, almost swooning with anxiety to conjecture as quickly as possible where the trap lay and not to overlook anything. 'No, I didn't see them, and I don't think I noticed a flat like that open . . . But on the fourth storey' (he had mastered the trap now and was triumphant) 'I remember now that someone was moving out of the flat opposite Alyona Ivanovna's . . . I remember . . . I remember it clearly. Some porters were carrying out a sofa and they squeezed me against the wall. But painters . . . no, I don't remember that there were any painters, and I don't think that there was a flat open anywhere, no, there wasn't.'

'What do you mean?' Razumihin shouted suddenly, as though he had reflected and realized. 'Why, it was on the day of the murder the painters were at work, and he was there three days before! What are you asking?'

'Foo! I have muddled it!' Porfiry slapped himself on the forehead. 'Deuce take it! This business is turning my brain!' he addressed Raskolnikov somewhat apologetically. It would be such a great thing for us to find out whether anyone had seen them between seven and eight at the flat, so I fancied you could perhaps have told us something . . . I quite muddled it.'

'Then you should be more careful,' Razumihin observed grimly.

The last words were uttered in the passage. Porfiry Petrovitch saw them to the door with excessive politeness.

They went out into the street gloomy and sullen, and for some steps they did not say a word. Raskolnikov drew a deep breath.

✦ SIX ✦

'I DON'T BELIEVE IT, I CAN'T believe it!' repeated Razumihin, trying in perplexity to refute Raskolnikov's arguments.

They were by now approaching Bakaleyev's lodgings, where Pulcheria Alexandrovna and Dounia had been expecting them a long while. Razumihin kept stopping on the way in the heat of discussion, confused and excited by the very fact that they were for the first time speaking openly about *it*.

'Don't believe it, then!' answered Raskolnikov, with a cold, careless smile. 'You were noticing nothing, as usual, but I was weighing every word.'

'You are suspicious. That is why you weighed their words . . . h'm . . . certainly, I agree, Porfiry's tone was rather strange, and still more that wretch Zametov! . . . You are right, there was something about him – but why? Why?'

'He has changed his mind since last night.'

'Quite the contrary! If they had that brainless idea, they would do their utmost to hide it, and conceal their cards, so as to catch you afterwards . . . But it was all impudent and careless.'

'If they had had facts – I mean, real facts – I mean, real facts – or at least grounds for suspicion, then they would certainly have tried to hide their game, in the hope of getting more (they would have made a search long ago besides). But they have no facts, not one. It is all mirage – all ambiguous. Simply a floating idea. So they try to throw me out by impudence. And perhaps, he was irritated at having no facts, and blurted it out in his vexation – or perhaps he has some plan . . . he seems an intelligent man. Perhaps he wanted to frighten me by pretending to know. They have a psychology of their own, brother. But it is loathsome explaining it all. Stop!'

'And its insulting, insulting! I understand you. But . . . since we have spoken openly now (and it is an excellent thing that we have at last – I am glad) I will own now frankly that I noticed it in them long ago, this idea. Of course the merest hint only – an insinuation – but why an insinuation even? How dare they? What foundation have they? If only you knew how furious I have been. Think only! Simply because a poor student, unhinged by poverty and hypochondria, on the eve of a severe delirious illness (note that), suspicious, vain, proud, who has not seen a soul to speak to for six months, in rags and in boots without soles, has to face some wretched policemen and put up with their insolence; and the unexpected debt thrust under his nose, the I O U presented by Tchebarov, the new paint, thirty degrees Reaumur and a stifling atmosphere, a crowd of people, the talk about the murder of a person where he had been just before, and all that on an empty stomach – he might well have a fainting fit! And that, that is what they found it all on! Damn them! I understand how annoying it is, but in your place, Rodya, I would laugh at them, or better still, spit in their ugly faces, and spit a dozen times in all directions. I'd hit out in all directions, neatly too, and so I'd put an end to it. Damn them! Don't be down-hearted. It's a shame!'

'He really has put it well, though,' Raskolnikov thought.

'Damn them! But the cross-examination again, tomorrow?' he said with bitterness. 'Must I really enter into explanations with them? I feel vexed as it is, that I condescended to speak to Zametov yesterday in the restaurant . . .'

'Damn it! I will go myself to Porfiry, I will squeeze it out of him, as one of the family: he must let me know the ins and outs of it all! And as for Zametov . . .'

'At last he sees through him!' thought Raskolnikov.

'Stay!' cried Razumihin, seizing him by the shoulder again. 'Stay! you were wrong. I have thought it out. You are wrong! How was that a trap? You say that the question about the workmen was a trap. But if you had done *that*, could you have said you had seen them painting the flat . . . and the workmen? On the contrary, you would have seen nothing, even if you had seen it. Who would own it against himself?'

'If I had done *that thing*, I should certainly have said that I had seen the workmen and the flat,' Raskolnikov answered, with reluctance and obvious disgust.

'But why speak against yourself?'

'Because only peasants, or the most inexperienced novices deny everything flatly at examinations. If a man is ever so little developed and experienced, he will certainly try to admit all the external facts that can't be avoided, but will seek other explanations of them, will introduce some special, unexpected turn, that will give them another significance and put them in another light. Porfiry might well reckon that I should be sure to answer so, and say I had seen them to give an air of truth, and then make some explanation.'

'But he would have told you at once that workmen could not have been there two days before, and that therefore you must have been there on the day of the murder at eight o'clock. And so he would have caught you over a detail.'

'Yes, that is what he was reckoning on, that I should not have time to reflect, and should be in a hurry to make the most likely answer, and so would forget that the workmen could not have been there two days before.'

'But how could you forget it?'

'Nothing easier. It is in just such stupid things clever people are most easily caught. The more cunning a man is, the less he suspects that he will be caught in a simple thing. The more cunning a man is, the simpler the trap he must be caught in. Porfiry is not such a fool as you think . . .'

'He is a knave then, if that is so!'

Raskolnikov could not help laughing. But at the very moment, he was struck by the strangeness of his own frankness, and the eagerness with which he had made this explanation, though he had kept up all the preceding conversation with gloomy repulsion, obviously with a motive, from necessity.

'I am getting a relish for certain aspects!' he thought to himself. But almost at the same instant he became suddenly uneasy, as though an unexpected and alarming idea had occurred to him. His uneasiness kept on increasing. They had just reached the entrance to Bakaleyev's.

'Go in alone!' said Raskolnikov suddenly. 'I will be back directly.'

'Where are you going? Why, we are just here.'

'I can't help it . . . I will come in half an hour. Tell them.'

'Say what you like, I will come with you.'

'You, too, want to torture me!' he screamed, with such bitter irritation, such despair in his eyes that Razumihin's hands dropped. He stood for some time on the steps, looking gloomily at Raskolnikov striding rapidly away in the direction of his lodging. At last, gritting his teeth and clenching his fist, he swore he would squeeze Porfiry like a lemon that very day, and went up the stairs to reassure Pulcheria Alexandrovna, who was by now alarmed at their long absence.

When Raskolnikov got home, his hair was soaked with sweat and he was breathing heavily. He went rapidly up the stairs, walked into his unlocked room and at once fastened the latch. Then in senseless terror he rushed to the corner, to that hole under the paper where he had put the things; put his hand in, and for some minutes felt carefully in the hole, in every crack and fold of the paper. Finding nothing, he got up and drew a deep breath. As he was reaching the steps of Bakaleyev's, he suddenly fancied that something, a chain, a stud or even a bit of paper in which they had been wrapped with the old woman's handwriting on it, might somehow have slipped out and been lost in some crack, and then might suddenly turn up as unexpected, conclusive evidence against him.

He stood as though lost in thought, and a strange, humiliated, half-senseless smile strayed on his lips. He took his cap at last and went quietly out of the room. His ideas were all tangled. He went dreamily through the gateway.

'Here he is himself,' shouted a loud voice.

He raised his head.

The porter was standing at the door of his little room and was pointing him out to a short man who looked like an artisan, wearing a long coat and a waistcoat, and looking at a distance remarkably like a woman. He stooped, and his head in a greasy cap hung forward. From his wrinkled flabby face he looked over fifty; his little eyes were lost in fat and they looked out grimly, sternly and discontentedly.

'What is it?' Raskolnikov asked, going up to the porter.

The man stole a look at him from under his brows and he looked at him attentively, deliberately; then he turned slowly and went out of the gate into the street without saying a word.

'What is it?' cried Raskolnikov.

'Why, he there was asking whether a student lived here, mentioned your name and whom you lodged with. I saw you coming and pointed you out and he went away. It's funny.'

The porter too seemed rather puzzled, but not much so, and after wondering for a moment he turned and went back to his room.

Raskolnikov ran after the stranger, and at once caught sight of him walking along the other side of the street with the same even deliberate step with his eyes fixed on the ground, as though in meditation. He soon overtook him, but for some time walked behind him. At last, moving on to a level with him, he looked at his face. The man noticed him at once, looked at him quickly, but dropped his eyes again; and so they walked for a minute side by side without uttering a word.

'You were inquiring for me . . . of the porter?' Raskolnikov said at last, but in a curiously quiet voice.

The man made no answer; he didn't even look at him. Again they were both silent.

'Why do you . . . come and ask for me . . . and say nothing . . . What's the meaning of it?'

Raskolnikov's voice broke and he seemed unable to articulate the words clearly.

The man raised his eyes this time and turned a gloomy sinister look at Raskolnikov.

'Murderer!' he said suddenly in a quiet but clear and distinct voice.

Raskolnikov went on walking beside him. His legs felt suddenly weak, a cold shiver ran down his spine, and his heart seemed to stand still for a moment, then suddenly began throbbing as though it were set free. So they walked for about a hundred paces, side by side in silence.

The man did not look at him.

'What do you mean... what is... Who is the murderer?' muttered Raskolnikov hardly audibly.

'*You* are a murderer,' the man answered still more articulately and emphatically, with a smile of triumphant hatred, and again he looked straight into Raskolnikov's pale face and striken eyes.

They had just reached the cross-roads. The man turned to the left without looking behind him. Raskolnikov remained standing, gazing after him. He saw him turn round fifty paces away and look back at him still standing there. Raskolnikov could not see clearly, but he fancied that he was again smiling the same smile of cold hatred and triumph.

With slow faltering steps, with shaking knees, Raskolnikov made his way back to his little garret, feeling chilled all over. He took off his cap and put it on the table, and for ten minutes he stood without moving. Then he sank exhausted on the sofa and with a weak moan of pain he stretched himself on it. So he lay for half an hour.

He thought of nothing. Some thoughts or fragments of thoughts, some images without order or coherence floated before his mind – faces of people he had seen in his childhood or met somewhere once, whom he would never have recalled, the belfry of the church at V., the billiard table in a restaurant and some officers playing billiards, the smell of cigars in some underground tobacco shop, a tavern room, a back staircase quite dark, all sloppy with dirty water and strewn with egg-shells, and the Sunday bells floating in from somewhere... The images followed one another, whirling like a hurricane. Some of them he liked and tried to clutch at, but they faded and all the while there was an oppression within him, but it was not overwhelming, sometimes it was even pleasant... The slight shivering still persisted, but that too was an almost pleasant sensation.

He heard the hurried footsteps of Razumihin; he closed his eyes and pretended to be asleep. Razumihin opened the door and stood for some time in the doorway as though hesitating, then he stepped softly into the room and went cautiously to the sofa. Raskolnikov heard Nastasya's whisper:

'Don't disturb him! Let him sleep. He can have his dinner later.'

'Quite so,' answered Razumihin. Both withdrew carefully and closed the door. Another half-hour passed. Raskolnikov opened his eyes, turned on his back again, clasping his hands behind his head.

'Who is he? Who is that man who sprang out of the earth? Where was he, what did he see? He had seen it all, that's clear. Where was he then?' And from where did he see? Why has he only now sprung out of the earth? And how could he see? Is it possible? Hm . . .' continued Raskolnikov, turning cold and shivering, 'and the jewel case Nikolay found behind the door – was that possible? A clue? You miss an infinitesimal line and you can build it into a pyramid of evidence! A fly flew by and saw it! Is it possible?' He felt with sudden loathing how weak, how physically weak he had become. 'I ought to have known it,' he thought with a bitter smile. 'And how dared I, knowing myself, knowing how I should be, take up an axe and shed blood! I ought to have known beforehand . . . Ah, but I did know!' he whispered in despair. At times he came to a standstill at some thought.

'No, those men are not made so. The real *Master* to whom all is permitted storms Toulon, makes a massacre in Paris, *forgets* an army in Egypt, *wastes* half a million men in the Moscow expedition and gets off with a jest at Vilna. And altars are set up to him after his death, and so *all* is permitted. No, such people, it seems, are not of flesh but of bronze!'

One sudden irrelevant idea almost made him laugh. Napoleon, the pyramids, Waterloo, and a wretched skinny old woman, a pawnbroker with a red trunk under her bed – it's a nice hash for Porfiry Petrovitch to digest! How can they digest it? It's too inartistic. 'A Napoleon creep under an old woman's bed! Ugh, how loathsome!'

At moments he felt he was raving. He sank into a state of feverish excitement. 'The old woman is of no consequence,' he thought, hotly and incoherently. 'The old woman was a mistake perhaps, but she is not what matters! The old woman was only an illness . . . I was in a hurry to overstep . . . I didn't kill a human being, but a principle! I killed the principle, but I didn't overstep, I stopped on this side . . . I was only capable of killing. And it seems I wasn't even capable of that . . . Principle? Why was that fool Razumihin abusing the socialists? They are industrious, commercial people; "the happiness of all" is their case. No, life is only given to me once and I shall never have it again; I don't want to wait for "the happiness of all". I want to live myself, or else better not live at all. I simply couldn't pass by my mother starving, keeping my rouble in my pocket while I waited for the "happiness of all". I am putting my little brick into the happiness of all and so my heart is at peace. Ha-ha! Why have you let me slip? I only live once, I too want . . . Ach, I am an æsthetic louse and nothing more,' he added suddenly, laughing like a madman. 'Yes, I am certainly a louse,' he went on, clutching at the idea, gloating over it and playing with it with vindictive pleasure. 'In the first place, because I can reason that I am one, and secondly, because for a month past I have been troubling benevolent Providence, calling it to witness that not for my own fleshly lusts did I undertake it, but with a grand and noble object – ha-ha!? Thirdly, because I aimed at carrying it out as justly as possible, weighing, measuring and calculating. Of all the lice I picked out the most useless one and proposed to take from her only as much as I needed for the first step, no more nor less (so the rest would have gone to a monastery, according to her will, ha-ha!). And what shows that I am utterly a louse,' he added, grinding his teeth, 'is that I am perhaps viler and more loathsome than the louse I killed, and *I felt beforehand* that I should tell myself so *after* killing her. Can anything be compared with the horror of that? The vulgarity! The abjectness! I understand the "prophet" with his sabre, on his steed: Allah commands and "trembling" creation must obey! The "prophet" is right, he is right when he sets a battery across the street and blows up the innocent and the guilty without deigning to explain! It's for you to obey, trembling creation, and not *to have desires*, for that's not for you! . . . I shall never, never forgive the old woman!'

His hair was soaked with sweat, his quivering lips were parched, his eyes were fixed on the ceiling.

'Mother, sister – how I loved them! Why do I hate them now? Yes, I hate them, I feel a physical hatred for them, I can't bear them near me . . . I went up to my mother and kissed her, I remember . . . To embrace her and think if she only knew . . . shall I tell her then? That's just what I might do . . . H'm. *She* must be the same as I am,' he added, straining himself to think, as it were struggling with delirium. 'Ah, how I hate the old woman now! I feel I should kill her again if she came to life! Poor Lizaveta! Why did she come in . . . It's strange though, why is it I scarcely ever think of her, as though I hadn't killed her? Lizaveta! Sonia! Poor gentle things, with gentle eyes . . . Dear women! Why don't they weep? Why don't they moan? They give up everything . . . their eyes are soft and gentle . . . Sonia, Sonia! Gentle Sonia!'

He lost consciousness; it seemed strange to him that he didn't remember how he got into the street. It was late evening. The twilight had fallen and the full moon was shining more and more brightly; but there was a peculiar breathlessness in the air. There were crowds of people in the street; workmen and business people were making their way home; other people had come out for a walk; there was a smell of mortar, dust and stagnant water. Raskolnikov walked along, mournful and anxious; he was distinctly aware of having come out with a purpose, of having to do something in a hurry, but what it was he had forgotten. Suddenly he stood still and saw a man standing on the other side of the street, beckoning to him. He crossed over to him, but at once the man turned and walked away with his head hanging, as though he had made no sign to him. 'Stay, did he really beckon?' Raskolnikov wondered, but he tried to overtake him. When he was within ten paces he recognized him and was frightened; it was the same man with stooping shoulders in the long coat. Raskolnikov followed him at a distance; his heart was beating; they went down a turning; the man still did not look round. 'Does he know I am following him?' thought Raskolnikov. The man went into the gateway of a big house. Raskolnikov hastened to the gate and looked in to see whether he would look round and sign to him. In the court-yard the man did turn round and again seemed to beckon him. Raskolnikov at once followed him into the yard, but the man was gone. He must have gone up the first staircase. Raskolnikov rushed after him. He heard slow measured steps two flights above. The staircase seemed strangely familiar. He reached the window on the first floor; the moon shone through the panes with a melancholy and mysterious light; then he reached the second floor. Bah! this is the flat where the painters were at work . . . how was it he did not recognize it at once? The steps of the man above had died away. 'So he must have stopped or hidden somewhere.' He reached the third storey, should he go on? There was a stillness that was dreadful . . . But he went on. The sound of his own footsteps scared and frightened him. How dark it was! The man must be hiding in some corner here. Ah! the flat was standing wide open, he hesitated and went in. It was very dark and empty in the passage, as though everything had been removed; he crept on tiptoe into the parlour which was flooded with moonlight. Everything there was as before, the chairs, the looking-glass, the yellow sofa and the pictures in the frames. A huge, round, copper-red moon looked in at the windows. 'It's the moon that makes it so still, weaving some mystery,' thought Raskolnikov. He stood and waited, waited a long while, and the more silent the moonlight, the more violently his heart beat, till it was painful. And still the same hush. Suddenly he heard a momentary sharp crack like the snapping of a splinter and all was still again. A fly flew up suddenly and struck the window-pane with a plaintive buzz. At that moment he noticed in the corner between the window and the little cupboard something like a cloak hanging on the wall. 'Why is that cloak here?' he thought, 'it wasn't there before . . .' He went up to it quietly and felt that there was someone hiding behind it. He cautiously moved the cloak and saw, sitting on a chair in the corner, the old woman bent double so that he couldn't see her face; but it was she. He stood over her. 'She is afraid,' he thought. He stealthily took the axe from the noose and struck her one blow, then another on the skull. But strange to say she did not stir, as though she were made of wood. He was frightened, bent down nearer and tried to look at her; but she, too, bent her head lower. He bent right down to the ground and peeped up into her face from below, he peeped and turned cold with horror: the old woman was sitting and laughing, shaking with noiseless laughter, doing her utmost that he should not hear it. Suddenly he fancied that the door from the bedroom was opened a little and that there was laughter and whispering within. He was overcome with frenzy and he began hitting the old woman on the head with all his force, but at every blow of the axe the laughter and whispering from the bedroom grew louder and the old woman was simply shaking with mirth. He was rushing away, but the passage was full of people, the doors of the flats stood open and on the landing, on the stairs and everywhere below there were people, rows of heads, all looking, but huddled together in silence and expectation. Something gripped his heart, his legs were rooted to the spot, they would not move . . . He tried to scream and woke up.

He drew a deep breath – but his dream seemed strangely to persist: his door was flung open and a man whom he had never seen stood in the doorway watching him intently.

Raskolnikov had hardly opened his eyes and he instantly closed them again. He lay on his back without stirring.

'Is it still a dream?' he wondered and again raised his eyelids hardly perceptibly; the stranger was standing in the same place, still watching him.

He stepped cautiously into the room, carefully closing the door after him, went up to the table, paused a moment, still keeping his eyes on Raskolnikov, and noiselessly seated himself on the chair by the sofa; he put his hat on the floor beside him and leaned his hands on his cane and his chin on his hands. It was evident that he was prepared to wait indefinitely. As far as Raskolnikov could make out from his stolen glances, he was a man no longer young, stout, with a full, fair, almost whitish beard.

Ten minutes passed. It was still light, but beginning to get dusk. There was complete stillness in the room. Not a sound came from the stairs. Only a big fly buzzed and fluttered against the window-pane. It was unbearable at last. Raskolnikov suddenly got up and sat on the sofa.

'Come, tell me what you want.'

'I knew you were not asleep, but only pretending,' the stranger answered oddly, laughing calmly. 'Arkady Ivanovitch Svidrigaïlov, allow me to introduce myself . . .'

PART FOUR

➤ ONE ❧

'CAN THIS BE STILL A DREAM?' Raskolnikov thought once more.

He looked carefully and suspiciously at the unexpected visitor.

'Svidrigaïlov! What nonsense! It can't be!' he said at last aloud in bewilderment.

His visitor did not seem at all surprised at this exclamation.

'I've come to you for two reasons. In the first place, I wanted to make your personal acquaintance, as I have already heard a great deal about you that is interesting and flattering; secondly, I cherish the hope that you may not refuse to assist me in a matter directly concerning the welfare of your sister, Avdotya Romanovna. For without your support she might not let me come near her now, for she is prejudiced against me, but with your assistance I reckon on . . .'

'You reckon wrongly,' interrupted Raskolnikov.

'They only arrived yesterday, may I ask you?'

Raskolnikov made no reply.

'It was yesterday, I know. I only arrived myself the day before. Well, let me tell you this, Rodion Romanovitch, I don't consider it necessary to justify myself, but kindly tell me what was there particularly criminal on my part in all this business, speaking without prejudice, with common sense?'

Raskolnikov continued to look at him in silence.

'That in my own house I persecuted a defenceless girl and 'insulted her with my infamous proposals' – is that it? (I am anticipating you.) But you've only to assume that I, too, am a man *et nihil humanum* . . . in a word, that I am capable of being attracted and falling in love (which does not depend on our will), then everything can be explained in the most natural manner. The question is, am I a monster, or am I myself a victim? And what if I am a victim? In proposing to the object of my passion to elope with me to America or Switzerland, I may have cherished the deepest respect for her and may have thought that I was promoting our mutual happiness! Reason is the slave of passion, you know; why, probably, I was doing more harm to myself than anyone!'

'But that's not the point,' Raskolnikov interrupted with disgust. 'It's simply that whether you are right or wrong, we dislike you. We don't want to have anything to do with you. We show you the door. Go out!'

Svidrigaïlov broke into a sudden laugh.

'But you're . . . but there's no getting round you,' he said, laughing in the frankest way. 'I hoped to get round you, but you took up the right line at once!'

'But you are trying to get round me still!'

'What of it? What of it?' cried Svidrigaïlov, laughing openly. 'But this is what the French call *bonne guerre*, and the most innocent form of deception! . . . But still you have interrupted me; one way or another, I repeat again: there would never have been any unpleasantness except for what happened in the garden. Marfa Petrovna . . .'

'You have got rid of Marfa Petrovna, too, so they say?' Raskolnikov interrupted rudely.

'Oh, you've heard that, too, then? You'd be sure to, though . . . But as for your question, I really don't know what to say, though my own conscience is quite at rest on that score. Don't suppose that I am in any apprehension about it. All was regular and in order; the medical inquiry diagnosed apoplexy due to bathing immediately after a heavy dinner and a bottle of wine, and indeed it could have proved nothing else. But I'll tell you what I have been thinking to myself of late, on my way here in the train, especially: didn't I contribute to all that . . . calamity, morally, in a way, by irritation or something of the sort. But I came to the conclusion that that, too, was quite out of the question.'

Raskolnikov laughed.

'I wonder you trouble yourself about it!'

'But what are you laughing at? Only consider, I struck her just twice with a switch – there were no marks even . . . don't regard me as a cynic, please; I am perfectly aware how atrocious it was of me and all that; but I know for certain, too, that Marfa Petrovna was very likely pleased at my, so to say, warmth. The story of your sister had been wrung out to the last drop; for the last three days Marfa Petrovna had been forced to sit at home; she had nothing to show herself with in the town. Besides, she had bored them so with that letter (you heard about her reading the letter). And all of a sudden those two switches fell from heaven! Her first act was to order the carriage to be got out . . . Not to speak of the fact that there are cases when women are very, very glad to be insulted in spite of all their show of indignation. There are instances of it with everyone; human beings in general, indeed, greatly love to be insulted, have you noticed that? But it's particularly so with women. One might even say it's their only amusement.'

At one time Raskolnikov thought of getting up and walking out and so finishing the interview. But some curiosity and even a sort of prudence made him linger for a moment.

'You are fond of fighting?' he asked carelessly.

'No, not very,' Svidrigaïlov answered calmly. 'And Marfa Petrovna and I scarcely ever fought. We lived very harmoniously and she was always pleased with me. I only used the whip twice in all our seven years (not counting a third occasion of a very ambiguous character). The first time, two months after our marriage, immediately after we arrived in the country, and the last time was that of which we are speaking. Did you suppose I was such a monster, such a reactionary, such a slave driver? Ha, ha! By the way, do you remember, Rodion Romanovitch, how a few years ago, in those days of beneficent publicity, a nobleman, I've forgotten his name, was put to shame everywhere, in all the papers, for having thrashed a German woman in the railway train? You remember? It was in those days, that very year, I believe, the "disgraceful action of the *Age*" took place (you know, "The Egyptian Nights", that public reading, you remember? The dark eyes, you know! Ah, the golden days of our youth, where are they). Well, as for the gentleman who thrashed the German, I feel no sympathy with him, because after all what need is there for sympathy? But I must say that there are sometimes such provoking "Germans" that I don't believe there is a progressive who could quite answer for himself. No one looked at the subject from that point of view then, but that's the truly humane point of view, I assure you.'

After saying this, Svidrigaïlov broke into a sudden laugh again. Raskolnikov saw clearly that this was a man with a firm purpose in his mind and able to keep it to himself.

'I expect you've not talked to anyone for some days?' he asked.

'Scarcely anyone. I suppose you are wondering at my being such an adaptable man?'

'No, I am only wondering at your being too adaptable a man.'

'Because I am not offended at the rudeness of your questions? Is that it? But why take offence? As you asked, so I answered,' he replied, with a surprising expression of simplicity. 'You know, there's hardly anything I take interest in,' he went on, as it were dreamily, 'especially now, I've nothing to do ... You are quite at liberty to imagine though that I am making up to you with a motive, particularly as I told you I want to see your sister about something. But I'll confess frankly, I am very much bored. The last three days especially, so I am delighted to see you ... Don't be angry, Rodion Romanovitch, but you seem to be somehow awfully strange yourself. Say what you like, there's something wrong with you, and now, too ... not this very minute, I mean, but now, generally . . . Well, well, I won't, I won't, don't scowl! I am not such a bear, you know, as you think.'

Raskolnikov looked gloomily at him.

'You are not a bear, perhaps, at all,' he said. 'I fancy indeed that you are a man of very good breeding, or at least know how on occasion to behave like one.'

'I am not particularly interested in anyone's opinion,' Svidrigaïlov answered, dryly and even with a shade of haughtiness, 'and therefore why not be vulgar at times when vulgarity is such a convenient cloak for our climate . . . and especially if one has a natural propensity that way,' he added, laughing again.

'But I've heard you have many friends here. You are, as they say, "not without connections". What can you want with me, then, unless you've some special object?'

'That's true that I have friends here,' Svidrigaïlov admitted, not replying to the chief point. 'I've met some already. I've been lounging about for the last three days, and I've seen them, or they've seen me. That's a matter of course. I am well dressed and reckoned not a poor man; the emancipation of the serfs hasn't affected me; my property consists chiefly of forests and water meadows. The revenue has not fallen off; but . . . I am not going to see them, I was sick of them long ago. I've been here three days and have called on no one . . . What a town it is! How has it come into existence among us, tell me that? A town of officials and students of all sorts. Yes, there's a great deal I didn't notice when I was here eight years ago, kicking up my heels . . . My only hope now is in anatomy, by Jove, it is!'

'Anatomy?'

'But as for these clubs, Dussauts, parades, or progress, indeed, maybe – well, all that can go on without me,' he went on, again without noticing the question. 'Besides, who wants to be a card-sharper?'

'Why, have you been a card-sharper then?'

'How could I help being? There was a regular set of us, men of the best society, eight years ago; we had a fine time. And all men of breeding, you know, poets, men of property. And indeed as a rule in our Russian society the best manners are found among those who've been thrashed, have you noticed that? I've deteriorated in the country. But I did get into prison for debt, through a low Greek who came from Nezhin. Then Marfa Petrovna turned up; she bargained with him and bought me off for thirty thousand silver pieces (I owed seventy thousand). We were united in lawful wedlock and she bore me off into the country like a treasure. You know she was five years older than I. She was very fond of me. For seven years I never left the country. And, take note, that all my life she held a document over me, the I O U for thirty thousand roubles, so if I were to elect to be restive about anything I should be trapped at once! And she would have done it! Women find nothing incompatible in that.'

'If it hadn't been for that, would you have given her the slip?'

'I don't know what to say. It was scarcely the document restrained me. I didn't want to go anywhere else. Marfa Petrovna herself invited me to go abroad, seeing I was bored, but I've been abroad before, and always felt sick there. For no reason, but the sunrise, the bay of Naples, the sea – you look at them and it makes you sad. What's most revolting is that one is really sad! No, it's better at home. Here at least one blames others for everything and excuses oneself. I should have gone perhaps on an expedition to the North Pole, because *j'ai le vin mauvais* and hate drinking, and there's nothing left but wine. I have tried it. But, I say, I've been told Berg is going up in a great balloon next Sunday from the Yusupov Garden and will take up passengers at a fee. Is it true?'

'Why, would you go up?'

'I . . . No, oh no,' muttered Svidrigaïlov, really seeming to be deep in thought.

'What does he mean? Is he in earnest?' Raskolnikov wondered.

'No, the document didn't restrain me,' Svidrigaïlov went on, meditatively. 'It was my own doing, not leaving the country, and nearly a year ago Marfa Petrovna gave me back the document on my name-day and made me a present of a considerable sum of money, too. She had a fortune, you know. "You see how I trust you, Arkady Ivanovitch' – that was actually her expression. You don't believe she used it? But do you know I managed the estate quite decently, they know me in the neighbourhood. I ordered books, too. Marfa Petrovna at first approved, but afterwards she was afraid of my over-studying.'

'You seem to be missing Marfa Petrovna very much?'

'Missing her? Perhaps. Really, perhaps I am. And, by the way, do you believe in ghosts?'

'What ghosts?'

'Why, ordinary ghosts.'

'Do you believe in them?'

'Perhaps not, *pour vous plaire* . . . I wouldn't say "No" exactly.'

'Do you see them, then?'

Svidrigaïlov looked at him rather oddly.

'Marfa Petrovna is pleased to visit me,' he said, twisting his mouth into a strange smile.

'How do you mean, "she is pleased to visit you"?'

'She has been three times. I saw her first on the very day of the funeral, an hour after she was buried. It was the day before I left to come here. The second time was the day before yesterday, at daybreak, on the journey at the station of Malaya Vishera, and the third time was two hours ago in the room where I am staying. I was alone.'

'Were you awake?'

'Quite awake. I was wide awake every time. She comes, speaks to me for a minute and goes out at the door – always at the door. I can almost hear her.'

'What made me think that something of the sort must be happening to you?' Raskolnikov said suddenly.

At the same moment he was surprised at having said it. He was much excited.

'What! Did you think so?' Svidrigaïlov asked in astonishment. 'Did you really? Didn't I say that there was something in common between us, eh?'

'You never said so!' Raskolnikov cried sharply and with heat.

'Didn't I?'

'No!'

'I thought I did. When I came in and saw you lying with your eyes shut, pretending, I said to myself at once, "Here's the man".'

'What do you mean by "the man"? What are you talking about?' cried Raskolnikov.

'What do I mean? I really don't know ...' Svidrigaïlov muttered ingenuously, as though he, too, were puzzled.

For a minute they were silent. They stared in each other's faces.

'That's all nonsense!' Raskolnikov shouted with vexation. 'What does she say when she comes to you?'

'She? Would you believe it, she talks of the silliest trifles and – man is a strange creature – it makes me angry. The first time she came in (I was tired, you know: the funeral service, the funeral ceremony, the lunch afterwards. At last I was left alone in my study. I lighted a cigar and began to think), she came in at the door. "You've been so busy to-day, Arkady Ivanovitch, you have forgotten to wind the dining-room clock," she said. All those seven years I've wound that clock every week, and if I forgot it she would always remind me. The next day I set off on my way here. I got out at the station at daybreak; I'd been asleep, tired out, with my eyes half open. I was drinking some coffee. I looked up and there was suddenly Marfa Petrovna sitting beside me with a pack of cards in her hand. "Shall I tell your fortune for the journey, Arkady Ivanovitch?" She was a great hand at telling fortunes. I shall never forgive myself for not asking her to. I ran away in a fright, and, besides, the bell rang. I was sitting to-day, feeling very heavy after a miserable dinner from a cook-shop; I was sitting smoking, all of a sudden Marfa Petrovna again. She came in very smart in a new green silk dress with a long train. "Good day, Arkady Ivanovitch! How do you like my dress? Aniska can't make like this." (Aniska was a dressmaker in the country, one of our former serf girls who had been trained in Moscow, a pretty wench.) She stood turning round before me. I looked at the dress, and then I looked carefully, very carefully, at her face. "I wonder you trouble to come to me about such trifles, Marfa Petrovna." "Good gracious, you won't let one disturb you about anything!" To tease her I said, "I want to get married, Marfa Petrovna". "That's just like you, Arkady Ivanovitch; it does you very little credit to come looking for a bride when you've hardly buried your wife. And if you could make a good choice, at least, but I know it won't be for your happiness or hers, you will only be a laughing-stock to all good people." Then she went out and her train seemed to rustle. Isn't it nonsense, eh?'

'But perhaps you are telling lies?' Raskolnikov put in.

'I rarely lie,' answered Svidrigaïlov thoughtfully, apparently not noticing the rudeness of the question.

'And in the past, have you ever seen ghosts before?'

'Y-yes, I have seen them, but only once in my life, six years ago. I had a serf, Filka; just after his burial I called out, forgetting, "Filka, my pipe!" He came in and went to the cupboard where my pipes were. I sat still and thought "he is doing it out of revenge" because we had a violent quarrel just before his death. "How dare you come in with a hole in your elbow?" I said. "Go away, you scamp!" He turned and went out, and never came again. I didn't tell Marfa Petrovna at the time. I wanted to have a service sung for him, but I was ashamed.'

'You should go to a doctor.'

'I know I am not well, without your telling me, though I don't know what's wrong; I believe I am five times as strong as you are. I didn't ask you whether you believe that ghosts are seen, but whether you believe that they exist.'

'No, I won't believe it!' Raskolnikov cried, with positive anger.

'What do people generally say?' muttered Svidrigaïlov, as though speaking to himself, looking aside and bowing his head. 'They say, "You are ill, so what appears to you is only unreal fantasy". But that's not strictly logical. I agree that ghosts only appear to the sick, but that only proves that they are unable to appear except to the sick, not that they don't exist.'

'Nothing of the sort,' Raskolnikov insisted irritably.

'No? You don't think so?' Svidrigaïlov went on, looking at him deliberately. 'But what do you say to this argument? (help me with it); ghosts are, as it were, shreds and fragments of other worlds, the beginning of them. A man in health has, of course, no reason to see them, because he is above all a man of this earth and is bound for the sake of completeness and order to live only in this life. But as soon as one is ill, as soon as the normal earthly order of the organism is broken, one begins to realize the possibility of another world; and the more seriously ill one is, the closer becomes one's contact with that other world, so that as soon as the man dies he steps straight into that world. I thought of that long ago. If you believe in a future life, you could believe in that, too.'

'I don't believe in a future life,' said Raskolnikov.

Svidrigaïlov sat lost in thought.

'And what if there are only spiders there, or something of that sort?' he said suddenly.

'He is a madman,' thought Raskolnikov.

'We always imagine eternity as something beyond our conception, something vast, vast! But why must it be vast? Instead of all that, what if it's one little room, like a bath house in the country, black and grimy and spiders in every corner, and that's all eternity is? I sometimes fancy it like that.'

'Can it be you can imagine nothing juster and more comforting than that?' Raskolnikov cried, with a feeling of anguish.

'Juster? And how can we tell, perhaps that is just, and do you know it's what I would certainly have made it?' answered Svidrigaïlov, with a vague smile.

This horrible answer sent a cold chill through Raskolnikov. Svidrigaïlov raised his head, looked at him, and suddenly began laughing.

'Only think,' he cried, 'half an hour ago we had never seen each other, we regarded each other as enemies; there is a matter unsettled between us; we've thrown it aside, and away we've gone into the abstract! Wasn't I right in saying that we were birds of a feather?'

'Kindly allow me,' Raskolnikov went on irritably, 'to ask you to explain why you have honoured me with your visit ... and ... and I am in a hurry, I have no time to waste. I want to go out.'

'By all means, by all means. Your sister, Avdotya Romanovna, is going to be married to Mr Luzhin, Pyotr Petrovitch?'

'Can you refrain from any question about my sister and from mentioning her name? I can't understand how you dare utter her name in my presence, if you really are Svidrigaïlov.'

'Why, but I've come here to speak about her; how can I avoid mentioning her?'

'Very good, speak, but make haste.'

'I am sure that you must have formed your own opinion of this Mr. Luzhin, who is a connection of mine through my wife, if you have only seen him for half an hour, or heard any facts about him. He is no match for Avdotya Romanovna. I believe Avdotya Romanovna is sacrificing herself generously and imprudently for the sake of . . . for the sake of her family. I fancied from all I had heard of you that you would be very glad if the match could be broken off without the sacrifice of worldy advantages. Now I know you personally, I am convinced of it.'

'All this is very naïve . . . excuse me, I should have said impudent on your part,' said Raskolnikov.

'You mean to say that I am seeking my own ends. Don't be uneasy, Rodion Romanovitch, if I were working for my own advantage I would not have spoken out so directly. I am not quite a fool. I will confess something psychologically curious about that: just now, defending my love for Avdotya Romanovna, I said I was myself the victim. Well, let me tell you that I've no feeling of love now, not the slightest, so that I wonder myself indeed, for I really did feel something . . .'

'Through idleness and depravity,' Raskolnikov put in.

'I certainly am idle and depraved, but your sister has such qualities that even I could not help being impressed by them. But that's all nonsense, as I see myself now.'

'Have you seen that long?'

'I began to be aware of it before, but was only perfectly sure of it the day before yesterday, almost at the moment I arrived in Petersburg. I still fancied in Moscow, though, that I was coming to try to get Avdotya Romanovna's hand and to cut out Mr. Luzhin.'

'Excuse me for interrupting you; kindly be brief, and come to the object of your visit. I am in a hurry, I want to go out . . .'

'With the greatest pleasure. On arriving here and determining on a certain . . . journey, I should like to make some necessary preliminary arrangements. I left my children with an aunt; they are well provided for; and they have no need of me personally. And a nice father I should make, too! I have taken nothing but what Marfa Petrovna gave me a year ago. That's enough for me. Excuse me, I am just coming to the point. Before the journey which may come off, I want to settle Mr. Luzhin, too. It's not that I detest him so much, but it was through him I quarrelled with Marfa Petrovna when I learned that she had dished up this marriage. I want now to see Avdotya Romanovna through your mediation, and if you like in your presence, to explain to her that in the first place she will never gain anything but harm from Mr. Luzhin. Then, begging her pardon for all past unpleasantness, to make her a present of ten thousand roubles and so assist the rupture with Mr. Luzhin, a rupture to which I believe she is herself not disinclined, if she could see the way to it.'

'You are certainly mad,' cried Raskolnikov, not so much angered as astonished. 'How dare you talk like that!'

'I knew you would scream at me; but in the first place, though I am not rich, this ten thousand roubles is perfectly free; I have absolutely no need for it. If Avdotya Romanovna does not accept it, I shall waste it in some more foolish way. That's the first thing. Secondly, my conscience is perfectly easy; I make the offer with no ulterior motive. You may not believe it, but in the end Avdotya Romanovna and you will know. The point is, that I did actually cause your sister, whom I greatly respect, some trouble and unpleasantness, and so, sincerely regretting it, I want – not to compensate, not to repay her for the unpleasantness, but simply to do something to her advantage, to show that I am not, after all, privileged to do nothing but harm. If there were a millionth fraction of self-interest in my offer, I should not have made it so openly; and I should not have offered her ten thousand only, when five weeks ago I offered her more. Besides, I may, perhaps, very soon marry a young lady, and that alone ought to prevent suspicion of any design on Avdotya Romanovna. In conclusion, let me say that in marrying Mr. Luzhin she is taking money just the same, only from another man. Don't be angry, Rodion Romanovitch, think it over coolly and quietly.'

Svidrigaïlov himself was exceedingly cool and quiet as he was saying this.

'I beg you to say no more,' said Raskolnikov. 'In any case this is unpardonable impertinence.'

'Not in the least. Then a man may do nothing but harm to his neighbour in this world, and is prevented from doing the tiniest bit of good by trivial conventional formalities. That's absurd. If I died, for instance, and left that sum to your sister in my will, surely she wouldn't refuse it?'

'Very likely she would.'

'Oh, no, indeed. However, if you refuse it, so be it, though ten thousand roubles is a capital thing to have on occasion. In any case I beg you to repeat what I have said to Avdotya Romanovna.'

'No, I won't.'

'In that case, Rodion Romanovitch, I shall be obliged to try and see her myself and worry her by doing so.'

'And if I do tell her, will you not try to see her?'

'I don't know really what to say. I should like very much to see her once more.'

'Don't hope for it.'

'I'm sorry. But you don't know me. Perhaps we may become better friends.'

'You think we may become friends.'

'And why not?' Svidrigaïlov said, smiling. He stood up and took his hat. 'I didn't quite intend to disturb you and I came here without reckoning on it . . . though I was very much struck by your face this morning.'

'Where did you see me this morning?' Raskolnikov asked uneasily.

'I saw you by chance . . . I keep fancying there is something about you like me . . . But don't be uneasy. I am not intrusive; I used to get on all right with card-sharpers, and I never bored Prince Svirbey, a great personage who is a distant relation of mine, and I could write about Raphael's *Madonna* in Madam Prilukov's album, and I never left Marfa Petrovna's side for seven years, and I used to stay the night at Viazemsky's house in the Hay Market in the old days, and I may go up in a balloon with Berg, perhaps.'

'Oh, all right. Are you starting soon on your travels, may I ask?'

'What travels?'

'Why, on that "journey"; you spoke of it yourself.'

'A journey? Oh, yes. I did speak of a journey. Well, that's a wide subject . . . If only you knew what you are asking,' he added, and gave a sudden, loud, short laugh. 'Perhaps I'll get married instead of the journey. They're making a match for me.'

'Here?'

'Yes.'

'How have you had time for that?'

'But I am very anxious to see Avdotya Romanovna once. I earnestly beg it. Well, good-bye for the present. Oh, yes. I have forgotten something. Tell your sister, Rodion Romanovitch, that Marfa Petrovna remembered her in her will and left her three thousand roubles. That's absolutely certain. Marfa Petrovna arranged it a week before her death, and it was done in my presence. Avdotya Romanovna will be able to receive the money in two or three weeks.'

'Are you telling the truth?'

'Yes, tell her. Well, your servant. I am staying very near you.'

As he went out, Svidrigaïlov ran up against Razumihin in the doorway.

✦ TWO ✦

IT WAS NEARLY EIGHT O'CLOCK. The two young men hurried to Bakaleyev's, to arrive before Luzhin.

'Why, who was that?' asked Razumihin, as soon as they were in the street.

'It was Svidrigaïlov, that landowner in whose house my sister was insulted when she was their governess. Through his persecuting her with his attentions, she was turned out by his wife, Marfa Petrovna. This Marfa Petrovna begged Dounia's forgiveness afterwards, and she's just died suddenly. It was of her we were talking this morning. I don't know why I'm afraid of that man. He came here at once after his wife's funeral. He is very strange, and is determined on doing something . . . We must guard Dounia from him . . . that's what I wanted to tell you, do you hear?'

'Guard her! What can he do to harm Avdotya Romanovna? Thank you, Rodya, for speaking to me like that . . . We will, we will guard her. Where does he live?'

'I don't know.'

'Why didn't you ask? What a pity! I'll find out, though.'

'Did you see him?' asked Raskolnikov after a pause.

'Yes, I noticed him, I noticed him well.'

'You did really see him? You saw him clearly?' Raskolnikov insisted.

'Yes, I remember him perfectly. I should know him in a thousand; I have a good memory for faces.'

They were silent again.

'Hm! . . . that's all right,' muttered Raskolnikov. 'Do you know, I fancied . . . I keep thinking that it may have been an hallucination.'

'What do you mean? I don't understand you.'

'Well, you all say,' Raskolnikov went on, twisting his mouth into a smile, 'that I am mad. I thought just now that perhaps I really am mad, and have only seen a phantom.'

'What do you mean?'

'Why, who can tell? Perhaps I am really mad, and perhaps everything that happened all these days may be only imagination.'

'Ach, Rodya, you have been upset again! . . . But what did he say, what did he come for?'

Raskolnikov did not answer. Razumihin thought a minute.

'Now let me tell you my story,' he began, 'I came to you, you were asleep. Then we had dinner and then I went to Porfiry's, Zametov was still with him. I tried to begin, but it was no use. I couldn't speak in the right way. They don't seem to understand and can't understand, but are not a bit ashamed. I drew Porfiry to the window, and began talking to him, but it was still no use. He looked away and I looked away. At last I shook my fist in his ugly face, and told him as a cousin I'd brain him. He merely looked at me, I cursed and came away. That was all. It was very stupid. To Zametov I didn't say a word. But, you see, I thought I'd made a mess of it, but as I went downstairs a brilliant idea struck me: why should we trouble? Of course if you were in any danger or anything, but why need you care? You needn't care a hang for them. We shall have a laugh at them afterwards, and if I were in your place I'd mystify them more than ever. How ashamed they'll be afterwards! Hang them! We can thrash them afterwards, but let's laugh at them now!'

'To be sure,' answered Raskolnikov. 'But what will you say to-morrow?' he thought to himself. Strange to say, till that moment it had never occurred to him to wonder what Razumihin would think when he knew. As he thought of it, Raskolnikov looked at him. Razumihin's account of his visit to Porfiry had very little interest for him, so much had come and gone since then.

In the corridor they came upon Luzhin; he had arrived punctually at eight, and was looking for the number, so that all three went in together without greeting or looking at one another. The young men walked in first, while Pyotr Petrovitch, for good manners, lingered a little in the passage, taking off his coat. Pulcheria Alexandrovna came forward at once to greet him in the doorway, Dounia was welcoming her brother. Pyotr Petrovitch walked in and quite amiably, though with redoubled dignity, bowed to the ladies. He looked, however, as though he were a little put out and could not yet recover himself. Pulcheria Alexandrovna, who seemed also a little embarrassed, hastened to make them all sit down at the round table where a samovar was boiling. Dounia and Luzhin were facing one another on opposite sides of the table. Razumihin and Raskolnikov were facing Pulcheria Alexandrovna, Razumihin was next to Luzhin and Raskolnikov was beside his sister.

A moment's silence followed. Pyotr Petrovitch deliberately drew out a cambric handkerchief reeking of scent and blew his nose with an air of a benevolent man who felt himself slighted, and was firmly resolved to insist on an explanation. In the passage the idea had occurred to him to keep on his overcoat and walk away, and so give the two ladies a sharp and emphatic lesson and make them feel the gravity of the position. But he could not bring himself to do this. Besides, he could not endure uncertainty, and he wanted an explanation: if his request had been so openly disobeyed, there was something behind it, and in that case it was better to find it out beforehand; it rested with him to punish them and there would always be time for that.

'I trust you had a favourable journey,' he inquired officially of Pulcheria Alexandrovna.

'Oh, very, Pyotr Petrovitch.'

'I am gratified to hear it. And Avdotya Romanovna is not over-fatigued either?'

'I am young and strong, I don't get tired, but it was a great strain for mother,' answered Dounia.

'That's unavoidable! our national railways are of terrible length. "Mother Russia," as they say, is a vast country . . . In spite of all my desire to do so, I was unable to meet you yesterday. But I trust all passed off without inconvenience?'

'Oh, no, Pyotr Petrovitch, it was all terribly disheartening.' Pulcheria Alexandrovna hastened to declare with peculiar intonation, 'and if Dmitri Prokofitch had not been sent us, I really believe by God Himself, we should have been utterly lost. Here he is! Dmitri Prokofitch Razumihin,' she added, introducing him to Luzhin.

'I had the pleasure . . . yesterday,' muttered Pyotr Petrovitch with a hostile glance sidelong at Razumihin; then he scowled and was silent.

Pyotr Petrovitch belonged to that class of persons, on the surface very polite in society, who make a great point of punctiliousness, but who, directly they are crossed in anything, are completely disconcerted, and become more like sacks of flour than elegant and lively men of society. Again all was silent; Raskolnikov was obstinately mute, Avdotya Romanovna was unwilling to open the conversation too soon. Razumihin had nothing to say, so Pulcheria Alexandrovna was anxious again.

'Marfa Petrovna is dead, have you heard?' she began, having recourse to her leading item of conversation.

'To be sure, I heard so. I was immediately informed, and I have come to make you acquainted with the fact that Arkady Ivanovitch Svidrigaïlov set off in haste for Petersburg immediately after his wife's funeral. So at least I have excellent authority for believing.'

'To Petersburg? here?' Dounia asked in alarm and looked at her mother.

'Yes, indeed, and doubtless not without some design, having in view the rapidity of his departure, and all the circumstances preceding it.'

'Good heavens! won't he leave Dounia in peace even here?' cried Pulcheria Alexandrovna.

'I imagine that neither you nor Avdotya Romanovna have any ground for uneasiness, unless, of course, you are yourselves desirious of getting into communication with him. For my part I am on my guard, and am now discovering where he is lodging.'

'Oh, Pyotr Petrovitch, you would not believe what a fright you have given me.' Pulcheria Alexandrovna went on: 'I've only seen him twice, but I thought him terrible, terrible! I am convinced that he was the cause of Marfa Petrovna's death.'

'It's impossible to be certain about that. I have precise information. I do not dispute that he may have contributed to accelerate the course of events by the moral influence, so to say, of the affront; but as to the general conduct and moral characteristics of that personage, I am in agreement with you. I do not know whether he is well off now, and precisely what Marfa Petrovna left him; this will be known to me within a very short period; but no doubt here in Petersburg, if he has any pecuniary resources, he will relapse at once into his old ways. He is the most depraved, and abjectly vicious specimen of that class of men. I have considerable reason to believe that Marfa Petrovna, who was so unfortunate as to fall in love with him and to pay his debts eight years ago, was of service to him also in another way. Solely by her exertions and sacrifices, a criminal charge, involving an element of fantastic and homicidal brutality for which he might well have been sentenced to Siberia, was hushed up. That's the sort of man he is, if you care to know.'

'Good heavens!' cried Pulcheria Alexandrovna. Raskolnikov listened attentively.

'Are you speaking the truth when you say that you have good evidence of this?' Dounia asked sternly and emphatically.

'I only repeat what I was told in secret by Marfa Petrovna. I must observe that from the legal point of view the case was far from clear. There was, and I believe still is, living here a woman called Resslich, a foreigner, who lent small sums of money at interest, and did other commissions, and with this woman Svidrigaïlov had for a long while close and mysterious relations. She had a relation, a niece I believe, living with her, a deaf and dumb girl of fifteen, or perhaps not more than fourteen. Resslich hated this girl, and grudged her every crust; she used to beat her mercilessly. One day the girl was found hanging in the garret. At the inquest the verdict was suicide. After the usual proceedings the matter ended, but, later on, information was given that the child had been . . . cruelly outraged by Svidrigaïlov. It is true, this was not clearly established, the information was given by another German woman of loose character whose word could not be trusted; no statement was actually made to the police, thanks to Marfa Petrovna's money and exertions; it did not get beyond gossip. And yet the story is a very significant one. You heard, no doubt, Avdotya Romanovna, when you were with them the story of the servant Philip who died of ill treatment he received six years ago, before the abolition of serfdom.'

'I heard, on the contrary, that this Philip hanged himself.'

'Quite so, but what drove him, or rather perhaps disposed him, to suicide was the systematic persecution and severity of Mr. Svidrigaïlov.'

'I don't know that,' answered Dounia dryly. 'I only heard a queer story that Philip was a sort of hypochondriac, a sort of domestic philosopher, the servants used to say, "he read himself silly", and that he hanged himself partly on account of Mr. Svidrigaïlov's mockery of him and not his blows. When I was there he behaved well to the servants, and they were actually fond of him, though they certainly did blame him for Philip's death.'

'I perceive, Avdotya Romanovna, that you seem disposed to undertake his defence all of a sudden,' Luzhin observed, twisting his lips into an ambiguous smile, 'there's no doubt that he is an astute man, and insinuating where ladies are concerned, of which Marfa Petrovna, who has died so strangely, is a terrible instance. My only desire has been to be of service to you and your mother with my advice, in view of the renewed efforts which may certainly be anticipated from him. For my part it's my firm conviction that he will end in a debtors' prison again. Marfa Petrovna had not the slightest intention of settling anything substantial on him, having regard for his children's interests, and, if she left him anything, it would only be the merest sufficiency, something insignificant and ephemeral, which would not last a year for a man of his habits.'

'Pyotr Petrovitch, I beg you,' said Dounia, 'say no more of Mr. Svidrigaïlov. It makes me miserable.'

'He has just been to see me,' said Raskolnikov, breaking his silence for the first time.

There were exclamations from all, and they all turned to him. Even Pyotr Petrovitch was roused.

'An hour and half ago, he came in when I was asleep, waked me, and introduced himself,' Raskolnikov continued. 'He was fairly cheerful and at ease, and quite hopes that we shall become friends. He is particularly anxious, by the way, Dounia, for an interview with you, at which he asked me to assist. He has a proposition to make to you, and he told me about it. He told me, too, that a week before her death Marfa Petrovna left you three thousand roubles in her will, Dounia, and that you can receive the money very shortly.'

'Thank God!' cried Pulcheria Alexandrovna, crossing herself. 'Pray for her soul, Dounia!'

'It's a fact!' broke from Luzhin.

'Tell us, what more?' Dounia urged Raskolnikov.

'Then he said that he wasn't rich and all the estate was left to his children who are now with an aunt, then that he was staying somewhere not far from me, but where I don't know, I didn't ask . . .'

'But what, what does he want to propose to Dounia?' cried Pulcheria Alexandrovna in a fright. 'Did he tell you?'

'Yes.'

'What was it?'

'I'll tell you afterwards.'

Raskolnikov ceased speaking and turned his attention to his tea. Pyotr Petrovitch looked at his watch.

'I am compelled to keep a business engagement, and so I shall not be in your way,' he added with an air of some pique and he began getting up.

'Don't go, Pyotr Petrovitch,' said Dounia, 'you intended to spend the evening. Besides, you wrote yourself that you wanted to have an explanation with mother.'

'Precisely so, Avdotya Romanovna,' Pyotr Petrovitch answered impressively, sitting down again, but still holding his hat. 'I certainly desired an explanation with you and your honoured mother upon a very important point indeed. But as your brother cannot speak openly in my presence of some proposals of Mr. Svidrigaïlov, I, too, do not desire and am not able to speak openly . . . in the presence of others . . . of certain matters of the greatest gravity. Moreover, my most weighty and urgent request has been disregarded . . .'

Assuming an aggrieved air, Luzhin relapsed into dignified silence.

'Your request that my brother should not be present at our meeting was disregarded solely at my instance,' said Dounia. 'You wrote that you had been insulted by my brother; I think that this must be explained at once, and you must be reconciled. And if Rodya really has insulted you, then he *should* and *will* apologize.'

Pyotr Petrovitch took a stronger line.

'There are insults, Avdotya Romanovna, which no goodwill can make us forget. There is a line in everything which it is dangerous to overstep; and when it has been overstepped, there is no return.'

'That wasn't what I was speaking of exactly, Pyotr Petrovitch,' Dounia interrupted with some impatience. 'Please understand that our whole future depends now on whether all this is explained and set right as soon as possible. I tell you frankly at the start that I cannot look at it in any other light, and if you have the least regard for me, all this business must be ended to-day, however hard that may be. I repeat that if my brother is to blame he will ask your forgiveness.'

'I am surprised at your putting the question like that,' said Luzhin, getting more and more irritated. 'Esteeming, and so to say, adoring you, I may at the same time, very well indeed, be able to dislike some member of your family. Though I lay claim to the happiness of your hand, I cannot accept duties incompatible with . . .'

'Ah, don't be so ready to take offence, Pyotr Petrovitch,' Dounia interrupted with feeling, 'and be the sensible and generous man I have always considered, and wish to consider, you to be. I've given you a great promise, I am your betrothed. Trust me in this matter and, believe me, I shall be capable of judging impartially. My assuming the part of judge is as much a surprise for my brother as for you. When I insisted on his coming to our interview to-day after your letter, I told him nothing of what I meant to do. Understand that, if you are not reconciled, I must choose between you – it must be either you or he. That is how the question rests on your side and on his. I don't want to be mistaken in my choice, and I must not be. For your sake I must break off with my brother, for my brother's sake I must break off with you. I can find out for certain now whether he is a brother to me, and I want to know it; and of you, whether I am dear to you, whether you esteem me, whether you are the husband for me.'

'Avdotya Romanovna,' Luzhin declared huffily, 'your words are of too much consequence to me; I will say more, they are offensive in view of the position I have the honour to occupy in relation to you. To say nothing of your strange and offensive setting me on a level with an impertinent boy, you admit the possibility of breaking your promise to me. You say "you or he", showing thereby of how little consequence I am in your eyes . . . I cannot let this pass considering the relationship and . . . the obligations existing between us.'

'What!' cried Dounia, flushing. 'I set your interest beside all that has hitherto been most precious in my life, what has made up the *whole* of my life, and here you are offended at my making too *little* account of you.'

Raskolnikov smiled sarcastically, Razumihin fidgeted, but Pyotr Petrovitch did not accept the reproof; on the contrary, at every word he became more persistent and irritable, as though he relished it.

'Love for the future partner of your life, for your husband. ought to outweigh your love for your brother,' he pronounced sententiously, 'and in any case I cannot be put on the same level . . . Although I said so emphatically that I would not speak openly in your brother's presence, nevertheless I intend now to ask your honoured mother for a necessary explanation on a point of great importance closely affecting my dignity. Your son,' he turned to Pulcheria Alexandrovna, 'yesterday, in the presence of Mr. Razsudkin (or . . . I think that's it? excuse me, I have forgotten your surname') (he bowed politely to Razumihin), 'insulted me by misrepresenting the idea I expressed to you in a private conversation, drinking coffee, that is, that marriage with a poor girl who has had experience of trouble is more advantageous from the conjugal point of view than with one who has lived in luxury, since it is more profitable for the moral character. Your son intentionally exaggerated the significance of my words and made them ridiculous, accusing me of malicious intentions, and, as far as I could see, relied upon your correspondence with him. I shall consider myself happy, Pulcheria Alexandrovna, if it is possible for you to convince me of an opposite conclusion, and thereby considerately reassure me. Kindly let me know in what terms precisely you repeated my words in your letter to Rodion Romanovitch.'

'I don't remember,' faltered Pulcheria Alexandrovna. 'I repeated them as I understood them. I don't know how Rodya repeated them to you, perhaps he exaggerated.'

'He could not have exaggerated them, except at your instigation.'

'Pyotr Petrovitch,' Pulcheria Alexandrovna declared with dignity, 'the proof that Dounia and I did not take your words in a very bad sense is the fact that we are here.'

'Good, mother,' said Dounia approvingly.

'Then this is my fault again,' said Luzhin, aggrieved.

'Well, Pyotr Petrovitch, you keep blaming Rodion, but you yourself have just written what was false about him,' Pulcheria Alexandrovna added, gaining courage.

'I don't remember writing anything false.'

'You wrote,' Raskolnikov said sharply, not turning to Luzhin, 'that I gave money yesterday not to the widow of the man who was killed, as was the fact, but to his daughter (whom I had never seen till yesterday). You wrote this to make dissention between me and my family, and for that object added coarse expressions about the conduct of a girl whom you don't know. All that is mean slander.'

'Excuse me, sir,' said Luzhin, quivering with fury. 'I enlarged upon your qualities and conduct in my letter solely in response to your sister's and mother's inquiries, how I found you, and what impression you made on me. As for what you've alluded to in my letter, be so good as to point out one word of falsehood, show, that is, that you didn't throw away your money, and that there are not worthless persons in that family, however unfortunate.'

'To my thinking, you, with all your virtues, are not worth the little finger of that unfortunate girl at whom you throw stones.'

'Would you go so far then as to let her associate with your mother and sister?'

'I have done so already, if you care to know. I made her sit down to-day with mother and Dounia.'

'Rodya!' cried Pulcheria Alexandrovna. Dounia crimsoned, Razumihin knitted his brows, Luzhin smiled with lofty sarcasm.

'You may see for yourself, Avdotya Romanovna,' he said, 'whether it is possible for us to agree. I hope now that this question is at an end, once and for all. I will withdraw, that I may not hinder the pleasures of family intimacy, and the discussion of secrets.' He got up from his chair and took his hat. 'But in withdrawing, I venture to request that for the future I may be spared similar meetings, and, so to say, compromises. I appeal particularly to you, honoured Pulcheria Alexandrovna, on this subject, the more as my letter was addressed to you and to no one else.'

Pulcheria Alexandrovna was a little offended.

'You seem to think we are completely under your authority, Pyotr Petrovitch. Dounia has told you the reason your desire was disregarded, she had the best intentions. And indeed you write as though you were laying commands upon me. Are we to consider every desire of yours as a command? Let me tell you on the contrary that you ought to show particular delicacy and consideration for us now, because we have thrown up everything, and have come here relying on you, and so we are in any case in a sense in your hands.'

'That is not quite true, Pulcheria Alexandrovna, especially at the present moment, when the news has come of Marfa Petrovna's legacy, which seems indeed very apropos, judging from the new tone you take to me,' he said sarcastically.

'Judging from that remark, we may certainly presume that you were reckoning on our helplessness,' Dounia observed irritably.

'But now in any case I cannot reckon on it, and I particularly desire not to hinder your discussion of the secret proposals of Arkady Ivanovitch Svidrigaïlov, which he has entrusted to your brother and which have, I perceive, a great and possibly a very agreeable interest for you.'

'Good heavens!' cried Pulcheria Alexandrovna.

Razumihin could not sit still on his chair.

'Aren't you ashamed now, sister?' asked Raskolnikov.

'I am ashamed, Rodya,' said Dounia. 'Pyotr Petrovitch, go away,' she turned to him, white with anger.

Pyotr Petrovitch had apparently not at all expected such a conclusion. He had too much confidence in himself, in his power and in the helplessness of his victims. He could not believe it even now. He turned pale, and his lips quivered.

'Avdotya Romanovna, if I go out of this door now, after such a dismissal, then, you may reckon on it, I will never come back. Consider what you are doing. My word is not to be shaken.'

'What insolence!' cried Dounia, springing up from her seat. 'I don't want you to come back again.'

'What! So that's how it stands!' cried Luzhin, utterly unable to the last moment to believe in the rupture and so completely thrown out of his reckoning now. 'So that's how it stands! But do you know, Avdotya Romanovna, that I might protest.'

'What right have you to speak to her like that?' Pulcheria Alexandrovna intervened hotly. 'And what can you protest about? What rights have you? Am I to give my Dounia to a man like you? Go away, leave us altogether! We are to blame for having agreed to a wrong action, and I above all . . .'

'But you have bound me, Pulcheria Alexandrovna,' Luzhin stormed in a frenzy, 'by your promise, and now you deny it and . . . besides . . . I have been led on account of that into expenses . . .'

This last complaint was so characteristic of Pyotr Petrovitch that Raskolnikov, pale with anger and with the effort of restraining it, could not help breaking into laughter. But Pulcheria Alexandrovna was furious.

'Expenses? What expenses? Are you speaking of our trunk? But the conductor brought it for nothing for you. Mercy on us, we have bound you! What are you thinking about, Pyotr Petrovitch, it was you bound us, hand and foot, not we!'

'Enough, mother, no more, please,' Avdotya Romanovna implored. 'Pyotr Petrovitch, do be kind and go!'

'I am going, but one last word,' he said, quite unable to control himself. 'Your mamma seems to have entirely forgotten that I made up my mind to take you, so to speak, after the gossip of the town had spread all over the district in regard to your reputation. Disregarding public opinion for your sake and reinstating your reputation, I certainly might very well reckon on a fitting return, and might indeed look for gratitude on your part. And my eyes have only now been opened! I see myself that I may have acted very, very recklessly in disregarding the universal verdict . . .'

'Does the fellow want his head smashed?' cried Razumihin, jumping up.

'You are a mean and spiteful man!' said Dounia.

'Not a word! Not a movement!' cried Raskolnikov, holding Razumihin back; then going close up to Luzhin, 'kindly leave the room!' he said quietly and distinctly, 'and not a word more or . . .'

Pyotr Petrovitch gazed at him for some seconds with a pale face that worked with anger, then he turned, went out, and rarely has any man carried away in his heart such vindictive hatred as he felt against Raskolnikov. Him, and him alone, he blamed for everything. It is noteworthy that as he went downstairs he still imagined that his case was perhaps not utterly lost, and that, so far as the ladies were concerned, all might 'very well indeed' be set right again.

✤ THREE ✤

THE FACT WAS THAT UP TO THE last moment he had never expected such an ending; he had been overbearing to the last degree, never dreaming that two destitute and defenceless women could escape from his control. This conviction was strengthened by his vanity and conceit, a conceit to the point of fatuity. Pyotr Petrovitch, who had made his way up from insignificance, was morbidly given to self-admiration, had the highest opinion of his intelligence and capacities, and sometimes even gloated in solitude over his image in the glass. But what he loved and valued above all was the money he had amassed by his labour, and by all sorts of devices: that money made him the equal of all who had been his superiors.

When he had bitterly reminded Dounia that he had decided to take her in spite of evil report, Pyotr Petrovitch had spoken with perfect sincerity and had, indeed, felt genuinely indignant at such 'black ingratitude'. And yet, when he made Dounia his offer, he was fully aware of the groundlessness of all the gossip. The story had been everywhere contradicted by Marfa Petrovna, and was by then disbelieved by all the townspeople, who were warm in Dounia's defence. And he would not have denied that he knew all that at the time. Yet he still thought highly of his own resolution in lifting Dounia to his level and regarded it as something heroic. In speaking of it to Dounia, he had let out the secret feeling he cherished and admired, and he could not understand that others should fail to admire it too. He had called on Raskolnikov with the feelings of a benefactor who is about to reap the fruits of his good deeds and to hear agreeable flattery. And as he went downstairs now, he considered himself most undeservedly injured and unrecognized.

Dounia was simply essential to him; to do without her was unthinkable. For many years he had had voluptuous dreams of marriage, but he had gone on waiting and amassing money. He brooded with relish, in profound secret, over the image of a girl – virtuous, poor (she must be poor), very young, very pretty, of good birth and education, very timid, one who had suffered much, and was completely humbled before him, one who would all her life look on him as her saviour, worship him, admire him and only him. How many scenes, how many amorous episodes he had imagined on this seductive and playful theme, when his work was over! And, behold, the dream of so many years was all but realized; the beauty and education of Avdotya Romanovna had impressed him; her helpless position had been a great allurement; in her he had found even more than he dreamed of. Here was a girl of pride, character, virtue, of education and breeding superior to his own (he felt that), and this creature would be slavishly grateful all her life for his heroic condescension, and would humble herself in the dust before him, and he would have absolute, unbounded power over her! . . . Not long before, he had, too, after long reflection and hesitation, made an important change in his career and was now entering on a wider circle of business. With this change he cherished dreams of rising into a higher class of society seemed likely to be realized . . . He was, in fact, determined to try his fortune in Petersburg. He knew that women could do a very great deal. The fascination of a charming, virtuous, highly educated woman might make his way easier, might do wonders in attracting people to him, throwing an aureole round him, and now everything was in ruins! This sudden horrible rupture affected him like a clap of thunder; it was like a hideous joke, an absurdity. He had been only a tiny bit masterful, had not even time to speak out, had simply made a joke, been carried away – and it had ended so seriously. And, of course, too, he did love Dounia in his own way; he already possessed her in his dreams – and all at once! No! The next day, the very next day, it must all be set right, smoothed over, settled. Above all he must crush that conceited milksop who was the cause of it all. With a sick feeling he could not help recalling Razumihin too, but he soon reassured himself on that score; as though a fellow like that could be put on a level with him! The man he really dreaded in earnest was Svidrigaïlov . . . He had, in short, a great deal to attend to . . .

'No, I, I am more to blame than anyone!' said Dounia, kissing and embracing her mother. 'I was tempted by his money, but on my honour, brother, I had no idea he was such a base man. If I had seen through him before, nothing would have tempted me! Don't blame me, brother!'

'God has delivered us! God has delivered us!' Pulcheria Alexandrovna muttered, but half consciously, as though scarcely able to realize what had happened.

They were all relieved, and in five minutes they were laughing. Only now and then Dounia turned white and frowned, remembering what had passed. Pulcheria Alexandrovna was surprised to find that she, too, was glad: she had only that morning thought rupture with Luzhin a terrible misfortune. Razumihin was delighted. He did not yet dare to express his joy fully, but he was in a fever of excitement as though a ton weight had fallen off his heart. Now he had the right to devote his life to them, to serve them ... Anything might happen now! But he felt afraid to think of further possibilities and dared not let his imagination range. But Raskolnikov sat still in the same place, almost sullen and indifferent. Though he had been the most insistent on getting rid of Luzhin, he seemed now the least concerned at what had happened. Dounia could not help thinking that he was still angry with her, and Pulcheria Alexandrovna watched him timidly.

'What did Svidrigaïlov say to you?' said Dounia, approaching him.

'Yes, yes!' cried Pulcheria Alexandrovna.

Raskolnikov raised his head.

'He wants to make you a present of ten thousand roubles and he desires to see you once in my presence.'

'See her! On no account!' cried Pulcheria Alexandrovna. 'And how dare he offer her money!'

Then Raskolnikov repeated (rather dryly) his conversation with Svidrigaïlov, omitting his account of the ghostly visitations of Marfa Petrovna, wishing to avoid all unnecessary talk.

'What answer did you give him?' asked Dounia.

'At first I said I would not take any message to you. Then he said that he would do his utmost to obtain an interview with you without my help. He assured me that his passion for you was a passing infatuation, now he has no feeling for you. He doesn't want you to marry Luzhin ... His talk was altogether rather muddled.'

'How do you explain him to yourself, Rodya? How did he strike you?'

'I must confess I don't quite understand him. He offers you ten thousand, and yet says he is not well off. He says he is going away, and in ten minutes he forgets he has said it. Then he says he is going to be married and has already fixed on the girl ... No doubt he has a motive, and probably a bad one. But it's odd that he should be so clumsy about it if he had any designs against you ... Of course, I refused this money on your account, once for all. Altogether, I thought him very strange ... One might almost think he was mad. But I may be mistaken; that may only be the part he assumes. The death of Marfa Petrovna seems to have made a great impression on him.'

'God rest her soul,' exclaimed Pulcheria Alexandrovna. 'I shall always, always pray for her! Where should we be now, Dounia, without this three thousand! It's as though it had fallen from heaven! Why, Rodya, this morning we had only three roubles in our pocket and Dounia and I were just planning to pawn her watch, so as to avoid borrowing from that man until he offered help.'

Dounia seemed strangely impressed by Svidrigaïlov's offer. She still stood meditating.

'He has got some terrible plan,' she said in a half-whisper to herself, almost shuddering.

Raskolnikov noticed this disproportionate terror.

'I fancy I shall have to see him more than once again,' he said to Dounia.

'We will watch him! I will track him out!' cried Razumihin, vigorously. 'I won't lose sight of him. Rodya has given me leave. He said to me himself just now, 'Take care of my sister'. Will you give me leave, too, Avdotya Romanovna?'

Dounia smiled and held out her hand, but the look of anxiety did not leave her face. Pulcheria Alexandrovna gazed at her timidly, but the three thousand roubles had obviously a soothing effect on her.

A quarter of an hour later, they were all engaged in a lively conversation. Even Raskolnikov listened attentively for some time, though he did not talk. Razumihin was the speaker.

'And why, why should you go away?' he flowed on ecstatically. 'And what are you to do in a little town? The great thing is, you are all here together and you need one another – you do need one another, believe me. For a time, anyway . . . Take me into partnership, and I assure you we'll plan a capital enterprise. Listen! I'll explain it all in detail to you, the whole project! It all flashed into my head this morning, before anything had happened . . . I tell you what; I have an uncle, I must introduce him to you (a most accommodating and respectable old man). This uncle has got a capital of a thousand roubles, and he lives on his pension and has no need of that money. For the last two years he has been bothering me to borrow it from him and pay him six per cent interest. I know what that means; he simply wants to help me. Last year I had no need of it, but this year I resolved to borrow it as soon as he arrived. Then you lend me another thousand of your three and we have enough for a start, so we'll go into partnership, and what are we going to do?'

Then Razumihin began to unfold his project, and he explained at length that almost all our publishers and booksellers know nothing at all of what they are selling, and for that reason they are usually bad publishers, and that any decent publications pay as a rule and give a profit, sometimes a considerable one. Razumihin had, indeed, been dreaming of setting up as a publisher. For the last two years he had been working in publishers' offices, and knew three European languages well, though he had told Raskolnikov six days before that he was 'schwach' in German with an object of persuading him to take half his translation and half the payment for it. He had told a lie then, and Raskolnikov knew he was lying.

'Why, why should we let our chance slip when we have one of the chief means of success – money of our own!' cried Razumihin warmly. 'Of course there will be a lot of work, but we will work, you, Avdotya Romanovna, I, Rodion . . . You get a splendid profit on some books nowadays! And the great point of the business is that we shall know just what wants translating, and we shall be translating, publishing, learning all at once. I can be of use because I have experience. For nearly two years I've been scuttling about among the publishers, and now I know every detail of their business. You need not be a saint to make pots, believe me! And why, why should we let our chance slip! Why, I know – and I keep the secret – two or three books which one might get a hundred roubles simply for thinking of translating and publishing. Indeed, and I would not take five hundred for the very idea of one of them. And what do you think? If I were to tell a publisher, I dare say he'd hesitate – they are such blockheads! And as for the business side, printing, paper, selling, you trust to me, I know my way about. We'll begin in a small way and go on to a large. In any case it will get us our living and we shall get back our capital.'

Dounia's eyes shone.

'I like what you are saying, Dmitri Prokofitch!' she said.

'I know nothing about it, of course,' put in Pulcheria Alexandrovna, 'it may be a good idea, but again God knows. It's new and untried. Of course, we must remain here at least for a time.' She looked at Rodya.

'What do you think, brother?' said Dounia.

'I think he's got a very good idea,' he answered. 'Of course, it's too soon to dream of a publishing firm, but we certainly might bring out five or six books and be sure of success. I know of one book myself which would be sure to go well. And as for his being able to manage it, there's no doubt about that either. He knows the business . . . But we can talk it over later . . .'

'Hurrah!' cried Razumihin. 'Now, stay, there's a flat here in this house belonging to the same owner. It's a special flat apart, not communicating with these lodgings. It's furnished, rent moderate, three rooms. Suppose you take them to begin with. I'll pawn your watch to-morrow and bring you the money, and everything can be arranged then. You can all three live together, and Rodya will be with you. But where are you off to, Rodya?'

'What, Rodya, you are going already?' Pulcheria Alexandrovna asked in dismay.

'At such a minute?' cried Razumihin.

Dounia looked at her brother with incredulous wonder. He held his cap in his hand, he was preparing to leave them.

'One would think you were burying me or saying good-bye for ever' he said somewhat oddly. He attempted to smile, but it did not turn out a smile. 'But who knows, perhaps it is the last time we shall see each other . . .' he let slip accidentally. It was what he was thinking, and it somehow was uttered aloud.

'What is the matter with you?' cried his mother.

'Where are you going, Rodya?' asked Dounia, rather strangely.

'Oh, I'm quite obliged to . . .' he answered vaguely, as though hesitating what he would say. But there was a look of sharp determination in his white face.

'I meant to say . . . as I was coming here . . . I meant to tell you, mother, and you, Dounia, that it would be better for us to part for a time. I feel ill, I am not at peace . . . I will come afterwards, I will come of myself . . . when it's possible. I remember you and love you . . . Leave me, leave me alone. I decided this even before . . . I'm absolutely resolved on it. Whatever may come to me, whether I come to ruin or not, I want to be alone. Forget me altogether, it's better. Don't inquire about me. When I can, I'll come of myself or . . . I'll send for you. Perhaps it will all come back, but now if you love me, give me up . . . else I shall begin to hate you, I feel it . . . Good-bye!'

'Good God!' cried Pulcheria Alexandrovna. Both his mother and his sister were terribly alarmed. Razumihin was also.

'Rodya, Rodya, be reconciled with us! Let us be as before!' cried his poor mother.

He turned slowly to the door and slowly went out of the room. Dounia overtook him.

'Brother, what are you doing to mother?' she whispered, her eyes flashing with indignation.

He looked dully at her.

'No matter, I shall come . . . I'm coming,' he muttered in an undertone, as though not fully conscious of what he was saying, and he went out of the room.

'Wicked, heartless egoist!' cried Dounia.

'He is insane, but not heartless. He is mad! Don't you see it? You're heartless after that!' Razumihin whispered in her ear, squeezing her hand tightly. 'I shall be back directly,' he shouted to the horror-stricken mother, and he ran out of the room.

Raskolnikov was waiting for him at the end of the passage. 'I knew you would run after me,' he said. 'Go back to them – be with them . . . be with them to-morrow and always . . . I . . . perhaps I shall come . . . if I can. Good-bye.'

And without holding out his hand he walked away.

'But where are you going? What are you doing? What's the matter with you? How can you go on like this?' Razumihin muttered at his wits' end.

Raskolnikov stopped once more.

'Once for all, never ask me about anything. I have nothing to tell you. Don't come to see me. Maybe I'll come here . . . Leave me, but *don't leave* them. Do you understand me?'

It was dark in the corridor, they were standing near the lamp. For a minute they were looking at one another in silence. Razumihin remembered that minute all his life. Raskolnikov's burning and intent eyes grew more penetrating every moment, piercing into his soul, into his consciousness. Suddenly Razumihin started. Something strange, as it were, passed between them . . . Some idea, some hint, as it were, slipped, something awful, hideous, and suddenly understood on both sides . . . Razumihin turned pale.

'Do you understand now?' said Raskolnikov, his face twitching nervously. 'Go back, go to them,' he said suddenly, and turning quickly, he went out of the house.

I will not attempt to describe how Razumihin went back to the ladies, how he soothed them, how he protested that Rodya needed rest in his illness, protested that Rodya was sure to come, that he would come every day, that he was very, very much upset, that he must not be irritated, that he, Razumihin, would watch over him, would get him a doctor, the best doctor, a consultation . . . In fact from that evening Razumihin took his place with them as a son and a brother.

➤ FOUR ◄

RASKOLNIKOV WENT STRAIGHT to the house on the canal bank where Sonia lived. It was an old green house of three storeys. He found the porter and obtained from him vague directions as to the whereabouts of Kapernaumov, the tailor. Having found in the corner of the courtyard the entrance to the dark and narrow staircase, he mounted to the second floor and came out into a gallery that ran round the whole second storey over the yard. While he was wandering in the darkness, uncertain where to turn for Kapernaumov's door, a door opened three paces from him; he mechanically took hold of it.

'Who is there?' a woman's voice asked uneasily.

'It's I . . . come to see you,' answered Raskolnikov, and he walked into the tiny entry.

On a broken chair stood a candle in a battered copper candlestick.

'It's you! Good heavens!' cried Sonia weakly, and she stood rooted to the spot.

'Which is your room? This way?' and Raskolnikov, trying not to look at her, hastened in.

A minute later Sonia, too, came in with the candle, set down the candlestick and, completely disconcerted, stood before him inexpressibly agitated and apparently frightened by his unexpected visit. The colour rushed suddenly to her pale face and tears came into her eyes . . . She felt sick and ashamed and happy, too . . . Raskolnikov turned away quickly and sat on a chair by the table. He scanned the room in a rapid glance.

It was a large but exceedingly low-pitched room, the only one let by the Kapernaumovs, to whose rooms a closed door led in the wall on the left. In the opposite side on the right-hand wall was another door, always kept locked. That led to the next flat, which formed a separate lodging. Sonia's room looked like a barn; it was a very irregular quadrangle and this gave it a grotesque appearance. A wall with three windows looking out on to the canal ran aslant so that one corner formed a very acute angle, and it was difficult to see in it without very strong light. The other corner was disproportionately obtuse. There was scarcely any furniture in the big room: in the corner on the right was a bedstead, beside it, nearest the door, a chair. A plain deal table covered by a blue cloth stood against the same wall, close to the door into the other flat. Two rush-bottom chairs stood by the table. On the opposite wall near the acute angle stood a small plain wooden chest of drawers looking, as it were, lost in a desert. That was all there was in the room. The yellow, scratched and shabby wall-paper was black in the corners. It must have been damp and full of fumes in the winter. There was every sign of poverty; even the bedstead had no curtain.

Sonia looked in silence at her visitor, who was so attentively and unceremoniously scrutinizing her room, and even began at last to tremble with terror, as though she were standing before her judge and the arbiter of her destinies.

'I am late . . . It's eleven, isn't it?' he asked, still not lifting his eyes.

'Yes,' muttered Sonia, 'oh yes, it is,' she added, hastily, as though in that lay her means of escape. 'My landlady's clock has just struck . . . I heard it myself . . .'

'I've come to you for the last time,' Raskolnikov went on gloomily, although this was the first time. 'I may perhaps not see you again . . .'

'Are you . . . going away?'

'I don't know . . . to-morrow . . .'

'Then you are not coming to Katerina Ivanovna to-morrow?' Sonia's voice shook.

'I don't know. I shall know to-morrow morning . . . Never mind that: I've come to say one word . . .'

He raised his brooding eyes to her and suddenly noticed that he was sitting down while she was all the while standing before him.

'Why are you standing? Sit down,' he said in a changed voice, gentle and friendly.

She sat down. He looked kindly and almost compassionately at her.

'How thin you are! What a hand! Quite transparent, like a dead hand.'

He took her hand. Sonia smiled faintly.

'I have always been like that,' she said.

'Even when you lived at home?'

'Yes.'

'Of course, you were,' he added abruptly, and the expression on his face and the sound of his voice changed again suddenly.

He looked round him once more.

'You rent this room from the Kapernaumovs?'

'Yes . . .'

'They live there, through that door?'

'Yes . . . They have another room like this.'

'All in one room?'

'Yes.'

'I should be afraid in your room at night,' he observed gloomily.

'They are very good people, very kind,' answered Sonia, who still seemed bewildered, 'and all the furniture, everything . . . everything is theirs. And they are very kind and the children, too, often come to see me.'

'They all stammer, don't they?'

'Yes . . . He stammers and he's lame. And his wife, too . . . It's not exactly that she stammers, but she can't speak plainly. She is a very kind woman. And he used to be a house serf. And there are seven children . . . and it's only the eldest one that stammers and the others are simply ill . . . but they don't stammer . . . But where did you hear about them?' she added with some surprise.

'Your father told me, then. He told me all about you . . . And how you went out at six o'clock and came back at nine and how Katerina Ivanovna knelt down by your bed.'

Sonia was confused.

'I fancied I saw him to-day,' she whispered hesitatingly.

'Whom?'

'Father. I was walking in the street, out there at the corner, about ten o'clock and he seemed to be walking in front. It looked just like him. I wanted to go to Katerina Ivanovna . . .'

'You were walking in the streets?'

'Yes.' Sonia whispered abruptly, again overcome with confusion and looking down.

'Katerina Ivanovna used to beat you, I dare say?'

'Oh no, what are you saying? No!' Sonia looked at him almost with dismay.

'You love her, then?'

'Love her? Of course!' said Sonia with plaintive emphasis, and she clasped her hands in distress. 'Ah, you don't . . . If you only knew! You see, she is quite like a child . . . Her mind is quite unhinged, you see . . . from sorrow. And how clever she used to be . . . how generous . . . how kind! Ah, you don't understand, you don't understand!'

Sonia said this as though in despair, wringing her hands in excitement and distress. Her pale cheeks flushed, there was a look of anguish in her eyes. It was clear that she was stirred to the very depths, that she was longing to speak, to champion, to express something. A sort of *insatiable* compassion, if one may so express it, was reflected in every feature of her face.

'Beat me! how can you? Good heavens, beat me! And if she did beat me, what then? What of it? You know nothing, nothing about it . . . She is so unhappy . . . ah, how unhappy! And ill . . . She is seeking righteousness, she is pure. She has such faith that there must be righteousness everywhere and she expects it . . . And if you were to torture her, she wouldn't do wrong. She doesn't see that it's impossible for people to be righteous and she is angry at it. Like a child, like a child. She is good!'

'And what will happen to you?'

Sonia looked at him inquiringly.

'They are left on your hands, you see. They were all on your hands before, though . . . And your father came to you to beg for drink. Well, how will it be now?'

'I don't know,' Sonia articulated mournfully.

'Will they stay here?'

'I don't know . . . They are in debt for the lodging, but the landlady, I hear, said to-day that she wanted to get rid of them, and Katerina Ivanovna says that she won't stay another minute.'

'How is it she is so bold? She relies upon you?'

'Oh, no, don't talk like that . . . We are one, we live like one.' Sonia was agitated again and even angry, as though a canary or some other little bird were to be angry. 'And what could she do? What, what could she do?' she persisted, getting hot and excited. 'And how she cried to-day! Her mind is unhinged, haven't you noticed it? At one minute she is worrying like a child that everything should be right to-morrow, the lunch and all that . . . Then she is wringing her hands, spitting blood, weeping, and all at once she will begin knocking her head against the wall, in despair. Then she will be comforted again. She builds all her hopes on you; she says that you will help her now and that she will borrow a little money somewhere and go to her native town with me and set up a boarding school for the daughters of gentlemen and take me to superintend it, and we will begin a new splendid life. And she kisses and hugs me, comforts me, and you know she has such faith, such faith in her fancies! One can't contradict her. And all the day long she has been washing, cleaning, mending. She dragged the wash-tub into the room with her feeble hands and sank on the bed, gasping for breath. We went this morning to the shops to buy shoes for Polenka and Lida, for theirs are quite worn out. Only the money we'd reckoned wasn't enough, not nearly enough. And she picked out such dear little boots, for she has taste, you don't know. And there in the shop she burst out crying before the shopmen because she hadn't enough . . . Ah, it was sad to see her . . .'

'Well, after that I can understand your living like this,' Raskolnikov said with a bitter smile.

'And aren't you sorry for them? Aren't you sorry?' Sonia flew at him again. 'Why, I know, you gave your last penny yourself, though you'd seen nothing of it, and if you'd seen everything, oh dear! And how often, how often I've brought her to tears! Only last week! Yes I! Only a week before his death, I was cruel! And how often I've done it! Ah, I've been wretched at the thought of it all day!'

Sonia wrung her hands as she spoke at the pain of remembering it.

'You were cruel?'

'Yes. I – I. I went to see them,' she went on, weeping, 'and father said, "Read me something, Sonia, my head aches, read to me, here's a book". He had a book he had got from Andrey Semyonovitch Lebeziatnikov, he lives there, he always used to get hold of such funny books. And I said, "I can't stay", as I didn't want to read, and I'd gone in chiefly to show Katerina Ivanovna some collars. Lizaveta, the pedlar, sold me some collars and cuffs cheap, pretty, new, embroidered ones. Katerina Ivanovna liked them very much; she put them on and looked at herself in the glass and was delighted with them. "Make me a present of them, Sonia," she said, "please do." "*Please do*," she said, she wanted them so much. And when could she wear them? They just reminded her of her old happy days. She looked at herself in the glass, admired herself, and she has no clothes at all, no things of her own, hasn't had all these years! And she never asks anyone for anything; she is proud, she'd sooner give away everything. And these she asked for, she liked them so much. And I was sorry to give them. "What use are they to you, Katerina Ivanovna?" I said. I spoke like that to her, I ought not to have said that! She gave me such a look. And she was so grieved, so grieved at my refusing her. And it was so sad to see . . . And she was not grieved for the collars, but for my refusing, I saw that. Ah, if only I could bring it all back, change it, take back those words! Ah, if I . . . but it's nothing to you!'

'Did you know Lizaveta, the pedlar?'

'Yes . . . Did you know her?' Sonia asked with some surprise.

'Katerina Ivanovna is in consumption, rapid consumption; she will soon die,' said Raskolnikov after a pause, without answering her question.

'Oh no, no, no!'

And Sonia unconsciously clutched both his hands, as though imploring that she should not.

'But it will be better if she does die.'

'No, not better, not at all better!' Sonia unconsciously repeated in dismay.

'And the children? What can you do except take them to live with you?'

'Oh, I don't know,' cried Sonia, almost in despair, and she put her hands to her head.

It was evident that that idea had very often occurred to her before and he had only roused it again.

'And what if, even now, while Katerina Ivanovna is alive, you get ill and are taken to the hospital, what will happen then?' he persisted pitilessly.

'How can you? That cannot be!'

And Sonia's face worked with awful terror.

'Cannot be?' Raskolnikov went on, with a harsh smile. 'You are not insured against it, are you? What will happen to them then? They will be in the street, all of them, she will cough and beg and knock her head against some wall, as she did to-day, and the children will cry . . . Then she will fall down, be taken to the police station and to the hospital, she will die, and the children . . .'

'Oh no . . . God will not let it be!' broke at last from Sonia's overburdened bosom.

She listened, looking imploringly at him, clasping her hands to dumb entreaty, as though it all depended upon him.

Raskolnikov got up and began to walk about the room. A minute passed. Sonia was standing with her hands and her head hanging in terrible dejection.

'And can't you save? Put by for a rainy day?' he asked, stopping suddenly before her.

'No,' whispered Sonia.

'Of course not. Have you tried?' he added almost ironically.

'Yes.'

'And it didn't come off! Of course not! No need to ask.'

And again he paced the room. Another minute passed.

'You don't get money every day?'

Sonia was more confused than ever and colour rushed into her face again.

'No,' she whispered with a painful effort.

'It will be the same with Polenka, no doubt,' he said suddenly.

'No, no! It can't be, no!' Sonia cried aloud in desperation, as though she had been stabbed. 'God would not allow anything so awful!'

'He lets others come to it.'

'No, no! God will protect her, God!' she repeated beside herself.

'But perhaps, there is no God at all,' Raskolnikov answered with a sort of malignance, laughed and looked at her.

Sonia's face suddenly changed; a tremor passed over it. She looked at him with unutterable reproach, tried to say something, but could not speak and broke into bitter, bitter sobs, hiding her face in her hands.

'You say Katerina Ivanovna's mind is unhinged; your own mind is unhinged,' he said after a brief silence.

Five minutes passed. He still paced up and down the room in silence, not looking at her. At last he went up to her; his eyes glittered. He put his two hands on her shoulders and looked straight into her tearful face. His eyes were hard, feverish and piercing, his lips were twitching. All at once he bent down quickly and dropping to the ground, kissed her foot. Sonia drew back from him as from a madman. And certainly he looked like a madman.

'What are you doing to me?' she muttered, turning pale, and a sudden anguish clutched at her heart.

He stood up at once.

'I did not bow down to you, I bowed down to all the suffering of humanity,' he said wildly and walked away to the window. 'Listen,' he added, turning to her a minute later. 'I said just now to an insolent man that he was not worth your little finger . . . and that I did my sister honour making her sit beside you.'

'Ach, you said that to them! And in her presence?' cried Sonia, frightened. 'Sit down with me! An honour! Why, I'm . . . dishonourable . . . Ah, why did you say that?'

'It was not because of your dishonour and your sin I said that of you, but because of your great suffering. But you are a great sinner, that's true,' he added almost solemnly, 'and your worst sin is that you have destroyed and betrayed yourself *for nothing*. Isn't that fearful? Isn't it fearful that you are living in this filth which you loathe so, and at the same time you know yourself (you've only to open your eyes) that you are not helping anyone by it, not saving anyone from anything? Tell me,' he went on almost in a frenzy, 'how this shame and degradation can exist in you side by side with other, opposite, holy feelings? It would be better, a thousand times better and wiser to leap into the water and end it all!'

'But what would become of them?' Sonia asked faintly, gazing at him with eyes of anguish, but not seeming surprised at his suggestion.

Raskolnikov looked strangely at her. He read it all in her face; so she must have had that thought already, perhaps many times, and earnestly she had thought out in her despair how to end it and so earnestly, that now she scarcely wondered at his suggestion. She had not even noticed the cruelty of his words. (The significance of his reproaches and his peculiar attitude to her shame she had, of course, not noticed either, and that, too, was clear to him.) But he saw how monstrously the thought of her disgraceful, shameful position was torturing her and had long tortured her. 'What, what,' he thought, 'could hitherto have hindered her from putting an end to it?' Only then he realized what those poor little orphan children and that pitiful half-crazy Katerina Ivanovna, knocking her head against the wall in her consumption, meant for Sonia.

But, nevertheless, it was clear to him again that with her character and the amount of education she had after all received, she could not in any case remain so. He was still confronted by the question, how could she have remained so long in that position without going out of her mind, since she could not bring herself to jump into the water? Of course he knew that Sonia's position was an exceptional case, though unhappily not unique and not infrequent, indeed; but that her very exceptionalness, her tinge of education, her previous life might, one would have thought, have killed her at the first step on that revolting path. What held her up – surely not depravity? All that infamy had obviously only touched her mechanically, not one drop of real depravity had penetrated to her heart; he saw that. He saw through her as she stood before him . . .

'There are three ways before her,' he thought, 'the canal, the madhouse, or . . . at last to sink into depravity which obscures the mind and turns the heart to stone.'

The last idea was the most revolting, but he was a sceptic, he was young, abstract, and therefore cruel, and so he could not help believing that the last end was the most likely.

'But can that be true?' he cried to himself. 'Can that creature who has still preserved the purity of her spirit be consciously drawn at last into that sink of filth and iniquity? Can the process already have begun? Can it be that she has only been able to bear it till now, because vice has begun to be less loathsome to her? No, no, that cannot be!' he cried, as Sonia had just before. 'No, what has kept her from the canal till now is the idea of sin and they, the children... And if she has not gone out of her mind... but who says she has not gone out of her mind? Is she in her senses? Can one talk, can one reason as she does? How can she sit on the edge of the abyss of loathsomeness into which she is slipping and refuse to listen when she is told of danger? Does she expect a miracle? No doubt she does. Doesn't that all mean madness?'

He stayed obstinately at that thought. He liked that explanation indeed better than any other. He began looking more intently at her.

'So you pray to God a great deal, Sonia?' he asked her. Sonia did not speak, he stood beside her waiting for an answer.

'What should I be without God?' she whispered rapidly, forcibly, glancing at him with suddenly flashing eyes, and squeezing his hand.

'Ah, so that is it!' he thought.

'And what does God do for you?' he asked, probing her further.

Sonia was silent a long while, as though she could not answer. Her weak chest kept heaving with emotion.

'Be silent! Don't ask! You don't deserve!' she cried suddenly, looking sternly and wrathfully at him.

'That's it, that's it,' he repeated to himself.

'He does everything,' she whispered quickly, looking down again.

'That's the way out! That's the explanation,' he decided, scrutinizing her with eager curiosity, with a new, strange, almost morbid feeling. He gazed at that pale, thin, irregular, angular little face, those soft blue eyes, which could flash with such fire, such stern energy, that little body still shaking with indignation and anger – and it all seemed to him more and more strange, almost impossible. 'She is a religious maniac!' he repeated to himself.

There was a book lying on the chest of drawers. He had noticed it every time he paced up and down the room. Now he took it up and looked at it. It was the New Testament in the Russian translation. It was bound in leather, old and worn.

'Where did you get that?' he called to her across the room.

She was still standing in the same place, three steps from the table.

'It was brought me,' she answered, as it were unwillingly, not looking at him.

'Who brought it?'

'Lizaveta! I asked her for it.'

'Lizaveta! strange!' he thought.

Everything about Sonia seemed to him stranger and more wonderful every moment. He carried the book to the candle and began to turn over the pages.

'Where is the story of Lazarus?' he asked suddenly.

Sonia looked obstinately at the ground and would not answer. She was standing sideways to the table.

'Where is the raising of Lazarus? Find it for me, Sonia.' She stole a glance at him.

'You are not looking in the right place . . . It's in the fourth gospel,' she whispered sternly, without looking at him.

'Find it and read it to me,' he said. He sat down with his elbow on the table, leaned his head on his hand and looked away sullenly, prepared to listen.

'In three weeks' time they'll welcome me in the madhouse! I shall be there if I am not in a worse place,' he muttered to himself.

Sonia heard Raskolnikov's request distrustfully and moved hesitating to the table. She took the book, however.

'Haven't you read it?' she asked, looking up at him across the table. Her voice became sterner and sterner.

'Long ago . . . When I was at school. Read!'

'And haven't you heard it in church?'

'I . . . haven't been. Do you often go?'

'N-no,' whispered Sonia.

Raskolnikov smiled.

'I understand . . . And you won't go to your father's funeral to-morrow?'

'Yes, I shall. I was at church last week, too . . . I had a requiem service.'

'For whom?'

'For Lizaveta. She was killed with an axe.'

His nerves were more and more strained. His head began to go round.

'Were you friends with Lizaveta?'

'Yes . . . She was good . . . she used to come . . . not often . . . she couldn't . . . We used to read together and . . . talk. She will see God.'

The last phrase sounded strange in his ears. And here was something new again; the mysterious meetings with Lizaveta and both of them – religious maniacs.

'I shall be a religious maniac myself soon! It's infectious!'

'Read!' he cried irritably and insistently.

Sonia still hesitated. Her heart was throbbing. She hardly dared to read to him. He looked almost with exasperation at the 'unhappy lunatic'.

'What for? You don't believe? . . .' she whispered softly and as it were breathlessly.

'Read! I want you to,' he persisted. 'You used to read to Lizaveta.'

Sonia opened the book and found the place. Her hands were shaking, her voice failed her. Twice she tried to begin and could not bring out the first syllable.

'Now a certain man was sick named Lazarus of Bethany . . .' she forced herself at last to read, but at the third word her voice broke like an overstrained string. There was a catch in her breath.

Raskolnikov saw in part why Sonia could not bring herself to read to him, and the more he saw this, the more roughly and irritably he insisted on her doing so. He understood only too well how painful it was for her to betray and unveil all that was her *own*. He understood that these feelings really were her *secret treasure*, which she had kept perhaps for years, perhaps from childhood, while she lived with an unhappy father and a distracted stepmother crazed by grief, in the midst of starving children and unseemly abuse and reproaches. But at the same time he knew now and knew for certain that, although it filled her with dread and suffering, yet she had a tormenting desire to read and to read to *him* that he might hear it, and to read *now* whatever might come of it! . . . He read this in her eyes, he could see it in her intense emotion. She mastered herself, controlled the spasm in her throat and went on reading the eleventh chapter of St John. She went on to the nineteenth verse:

'And many of the Jews came to Martha and Mary to comfort them concerning their brother.

Then Martha as soon as she heard that Jesus was coming went and met Him: but Mary sat still in the house.

Then said Martha unto Jesus, Lord, if Thou hadst been here, my brother had not died.

But I know that even now whatsoever Thou wilt ask of God, God will give it Thee . . .'

Then she stopped again with a shamefaced feeling that her voice would quiver and break again.

'Jesus saith unto her, thy brother shall rise again.

Martha said unto Him, I know that he shall rise again in the resurrection, at the last day.

Jesus said unto her, I am the resurrection and the life: he that believeth in Me though he were dead, yet shall he live.

And whosoever liveth and believeth in Me shall never die. Believest thou this?

She saith unto Him,'

(And drawing a painful breath, Sonia read distinctly and forcibly as though she were making a public confession of faith.)

'Yea, Lord: I believe that Thou art the Christ, the Son of God Which should come into the world.'

She stopped and looked up quickly at him, and controlling herself went on reading. Raskolnikov sat without moving, his elbows on the table and his eyes turned away. She read to the thirty-second verse.

'Then when Mary was come where Jesus was and saw Him, she fell down at His feet, saying unto Him, Lord if Thou hadst been here, my brother had not died.

When Jesus therefore saw her weeping, and the Jews also weeping which came with her, he groaned in the spirit and was troubled,

And said, Where have ye laid him? They said unto Him, Lord, come and see.

Jesus wept.

Then said the Jews, behold how He loved him!

And some of them said, could not this Man which opened the eyes of the blind, have caused that even this man should not have died?'

Raskolnikov turned and looked at her with emotion. Yes, he had known it! She was trembling in a real physical fever. He had expected it. She was getting near the story of the greatest miracle and a feeling of immense triumph came over her. Her voice rang out like a bell; triumph and joy gave it power. The lines danced before her eyes, but she knew what she was reading by heart. At the last verse 'Could not this Man which opened the eyes of the blind . . .' dropping her voice she passionately reproduced the doubt, the reproach and censure of the blind disbelieving Jews, who in another moment would fall at His feet as though struck by thunder, sobbing and believing. . . . 'And *he, he* – too, is blinded and unbelieving, he, too, will hear, he, too, will believe, yes, yes! At once, now,' was what she was dreaming, and she was quivering with happy anticipation.

'Jesus therefore again groaning in Himself cometh to the grave. It was a cave, and a stone lay upon it.

Jesus said, Take ye away the stone. Martha, the sister of him that was dead, saith unto Him, Lord, by this time he stinketh: for he hath been dead four days.'

She laid the emphasis on the word *four*.

'Jesus saith unto her, Said I not unto thee that if thou wouldest believe, thou shouldest see the glory of God?

Then they took away the stone from the place where the dead was laid. And Jesus lifted up His eyes and said, Father, I thank Thee that Thou hast heard Me.

And I know that Thou hearest Me always; but because of the people which stand by I said it, that they may believe that Thou has sent Me.

And when He thus had spoken, He cried with a loud voice, Lazarus, come forth.

And he that was dead came forth.'

(She read loudly, cold and trembling with ecstasy, as though she were seeing it before her eyes.)

'Bound hand and foot with graveclothes; and his face was bound about with a napkin. Jesus saith into them, Loose him and let him go.

Then many of the Jews which came to Mary and had seen the things which Jesus did believed on Him.'

She could read no more, closed the book and got up from her chair quickly.

'That is all about the raising of Lazarus,' she whispered severely and abruptly, and turning away she stood motionless, not daring to raise her eyes to him. She still trembled feverishly. The candle-end was flickering out in the battered candlestick, dimly lighting up in the poverty-stricken room the murderer and the harlot who had so strangely been reading together the eternal book. Five minutes or more passed.

'I came to speak of something,' Raskolnikov said aloud, frowning. He got up and went to Sonia. She lifted her eyes to him in silence. His face was particularly stern and there was a sort of savage determination in it.

'I have abandoned my family to-day,' he said, 'my mother and sister. I am not going to see them. I've broken with them completely.'

'What for?' asked Sonia amazed. Her recent meeting with his mother and sister had left a great impression which she could not analyse. She heard his news almost with horror.

'I have only you now,' he added. 'Let us go together. . . . I've come to you, we are both accursed, let us go our way together!'

His eyes glittered 'as though he were mad', Sonia thought, in her turn.

'Go where?' she asked in alarm and she involuntarily stepped back.

'How do I know? I only know it's the same road, I know that and nothing more. It's the same goal!'

She looked at him and understood nothing. She knew only that he was terribly, infinitely unhappy.

'No one of them will understand, if you tell them, but I have understood. I need you, that is why I have come to you.'

'I don't understand,' whispered Sonia.

'You'll understand later. Haven't you done the same? You, too, have transgressed . . . have had the strength to transgress. You have laid hands on yourself, you have destroyed a life . . . *your own* (it's all the same!). You might have lived in spirit and understanding, but you'll end in the Hay Market. . . . But you won't be able to stand it, and if you remain alone you'll go out of your mind like me. You are like a mad creature already. So we must go together on the same road! Let us go!'

'What for? What's all this for?' said Sonia, strangely and violently agitated by his words.

'What for? Because you can't remain like this, that's why! You must look things straight in the face at last, and not weep like a child and cry that God won't allow it. What will happen if you should really be taken to the hospital to-morrow? She is mad and in consumption, she'll soon die and the children? Do you mean to tell me Polenka won't come to grief? Haven't you seen children here at the street corners sent out by their mothers to beg? I've found out where those mothers live and in what surroundings. Children can't remain children there! At seven the child is vicious and a thief. Yet children, you know, are the image of Christ: "theirs is the kingdom of Heaven." He bade us honour and love them, they are the humanity of the future. . . .'

'What's to be done, what's to be done?' repeated Sonia, weeping hysterically and wringing her hands.

'What's to be done? Break what must be broken, once for all, that's all, and take the suffering on oneself. What, you don't understand? You'll understand later. . . . Freedom and power, and above all, power! Over all trembling creation and all the ant-heap! . . . That's the goal, remember that! That's my farewell message. Perhaps it's the last time I shall speak to you. If I don't come to-morrow, you'll hear of it all, and then remember these words. And some day later on, in years to come, you'll understand perhaps what they meant. If I come to-morrow, I'll tell you who killed Lizaveta. . . . Good-bye.'

Sonia started with terror.

'Why, do you know who killed her?' she asked, chilled with horror, looking wildly at him.

'I know and will tell . . . you, only you. I have chosen you out. I'm not coming to you to ask forgiveness, but simply to tell you. I chose you out long ago to hear this, when your father talked of you and when Lizaveta was alive, I thought of it. Good-bye, don't shake hands. To-morrow!'

He went out. Sonia gazed at him as at a madman. But she herself was like one insane and felt it. Her head was going round.

'Good heavens, how does he know who killed Lizaveta? What did those words mean? It's awful!' But at the same time *the idea* did not enter her head, not for a moment! 'Oh, he must be terribly unhappy! . . . He has abandoned his mother and sister. . . . What for? What has happened? And what had he in his mind? What did he say to her? He had kissed her foot and said . . . said (yes, he had said it clearly) that he could not live without her. . . . Oh, merciful heavens!'

Sonia spent the whole night feverish and delirious. She jumped up from time to time, wept and wrung her hands, then sank again into feverish sleep and dreamt of Polenka, Katerina Ivanovna and Lizaveta, or reading the gospel and him . . . him with pale face, with burning eyes . . . kissing her feet, weeping.

On the other side of the door on the right, which divided Sonia's room from Madame Resslich's flat, was a room which had long stood empty. A card was fixed on the gate and a notice stuck in the windows over the canal advertizing it to let. Sonia had long been accustomed to the room's being uninhabited. But all that time Mr. Svidrigaïlov had been standing, listening at the door of the empty room. When Raskolnikov went out he stood still, thought a moment, went on tiptoe to his own room which adjoined the empty one, brought a chair and noiselessly carried it to the door that led to Sonia's room. The conversation had struck him as interesting and remarkable, and he had greatly enjoyed it – so much so that he brought a chair that he might not in the future, to-morrow, for instance, have to endure the inconvenience of standing a whole hour, but might listen in comfort.

⇒ FIVE ⇐

WHEN NEXT MORNING AT ELEVEN o'clock punctually Raskolnikov went into the department of the investigation of criminal causes and sent his name in to Porfiry Petrovitch, he was surprised at being kept waiting so long: it was at least ten minutes before he was summoned. He had expected that they would pounce upon him. But he stood in the waiting-room, and people, who apparently had nothing to do with him, were continually passing to and fro before him. In the next room which looked like an office, several clerks were sitting writing and obviously they had no notion who or what Raskolnikov might be. He looked uneasily and suspiciously about him to see whether there was not some guard, some mysterious watch being kept on him to prevent his escape. But there was nothing of the sort: he saw only the faces of clerks absorbed in petty details, then other people, no one seemed to have any concern with him. He might go where he liked for them. The conviction grew stronger in him that if that enigmatic man of yesterday, that phantom sprung out of the earth, had seen everything, they would not have let him stand and wait like that. And would they have waited till he elected to appear at eleven? Either the man had not yet given information, or . . . or simply he knew nothing, had seen nothing (and how could he have seen anything?) and so all that had happened to him the day before was again a phantom exaggerated by his sick and overstrained imagination. This conjecture had begun to grow strong the day before, in the midst of all his alarm and despair. Thinking it all over now and preparing for a fresh conflict, he was suddenly aware that he was trembling – and he felt a rush of indignation at the thought that he was trembling with fear at facing that hateful Porfiry Petrovitch. What he dreaded above all was meeting that man again; he hated him with an intense, unmitigated hatred and was afraid his hatred might betray him. His indignation was such that he ceased trembling at once; he made ready to go in with a cold and arrogant bearing and vowed to himself to keep as silent as possible, to watch and listen and for once at least to control his overstrained nerves. At that moment he was summoned to Porfiry Petrovitch.

He found Porfiry Petrovitch alone in his study. His study was a room neither large nor small, furnished with a large writing-table, that stood before a sofa, upholstered in checked material, a bureau, a bookcase in the corner and several chairs – all government furniture, of polished yellow wood. In the further wall there was a closed door, beyond it there were no doubt other rooms. On Raskolnikov's entrance Porfiry Petrovitch had at once closed the door by which he had come in and they remained alone. He met his visitor with an apparently genial and good-tempered air, and it was only after a few minutes that Raskolnikov saw signs of a certain awkwardness in him, as though he had been thrown out of his reckoning or caught in something very secret.

'Ah, my dear fellow! Here you are . . . in our domain' . . . began Porfiry, holding out both hands to him. 'Come, sit down, old man . . . or perhaps you don't like to be called "my dear fellow" and "old man" – *tout court*? Please don't think it too familiar. . . . Here, on the sofa.'

Raskolnikov sat down, keeping his eyes fixed on him. 'In our domain,' the apologies for familiarity, the French phrase *tout court*, were all characteristic signs.

'He held out both hands to me, but he did not give me one – he drew it back in time,' struck him suspiciously. Both were watching each other, but when their eyes met, quick as lightning they looked away.

'I brought you this paper . . . about the watch. Here it is. Is it all right or shall I copy it again?'

'What? A paper? Yes, yes, don't be uneasy, it's all right,' Porfiry Petrovitch said as though in haste, and after he had said it he took the paper and looked at it. 'Yes, it's all right. Nothing more is needed,' he declared with the same rapidity and he laid the paper on the table.

A minute later when he was talking of something else he took it from the table and put in on his bureau.

'I believe you said yesterday you would like to question me . . . formally . . . about my acquaintance with the murdered woman?' Raskolnikov was beginning again. 'Why did I put in "I believe" ' passed through his mind in a flash. 'Why am I so uneasy at having to put in that "*I believe*"?' came in a second flash. And he suddenly felt that his uneasiness at the mere contact with Porfiry, at the first words, at the first looks, had grown in an instant to monstrous proportions, and that this was fearfully dangerous. His nerves were quivering, his emotion was increasing. 'It's bad, it's bad! I shall say too much again.'

'Yes, yes, yes! There's no hurry, there's no hurry,' muttered Porfiry Petrovitch, moving to and fro about the table without any apparent aim, as it were making dashes towards the window, the bureau and the table, at one moment avoiding Raskolnikov's suspicious glance, then again standing still and looking him straight in the face.

His fat round little figure looked very strange, like a ball rolling from one side to the other and rebounding back.

'We've plenty of time. Do you smoke? have you your own? Here, a cigarette!' he went on, offering his visitor a cigarette. 'You know I am receiving you here, but my own quarters are through there, you know, my government quarters. But I am living outside for the time, I had to have some repairs done here. It's almost finished now. . . . Government quarters, you know, are a capital thing. Eh, what do you think?'

'Yes, a capital thing,' answered Raskolnikov, looking at him almost ironically.

'A capital thing, a capital thing,' repeated Porfiry Petrovitch, as though he had just thought of something quite different. 'Yes, a capital thing,' he almost shouted at last, suddenly staring at Raskolnikov and stopped short two steps from him.

This stupid repetition was too incongruous in its ineptitude with the serious, brooding and enigmatic glance he turned upon his visitor.

But this stirred Raskolnikov's spleen more than ever and he could not resist an ironical and rather incautious challenge.

'Tell me, please,' he asked suddenly, looking almost insolently at him and taking a kind of pleasure in his own insolence. 'I believe it's a sort of

278

legal rule, a sort of legal tradition – for all investigating lawyers – to begin their attack from afar, with a trivial, or at least an irrelevant subject, so as to encourage, or rather, to divert the man they are cross-examining, to disarm his caution and then all at once to give him an unexpected knock-down blow with some fatal question. Isn't that so? It's a sacred tradition, mentioned I fancy, in all the manuals of the art?'

'Yes, yes. . . . Why, do you imagine that was why I spoke about government quarters . . . eh?'

And as he said this Porfiry Petrovitch screwed up his eyes and winked; a good-humoured, crafty look passed over his face. The wrinkles on his forehead were smoothed out, his eyes contracted, his features broadened and he suddenly went off into a a nervous prolonged laugh, shaking all over and looking Raskolnikov straight in the face. The latter forced himself to laugh, too, but when Porfiry, seeing that he was laughing, broke into such a guffaw that he turned almost crimson, Raskolnikov's repulsion overcame all precaution; he left off laughing, scowled and stared with hatred at Porfiry, keeping his eyes fixed on him while his intentionally prolonged laughter lasted. There was lack of precaution on both sides, however, for Porfiry Petrovitch seemed to be laughing in his visitor's face and to be very little disturbed at the annoyance with which the visitor received it. The latter fact was very significant in Raskolnikov's eyes: he saw that Porfiry Petrovitch had not been embarrassed just before either, but that he, Raskolnikov, had perhaps fallen into a trap; that there must be something, some motive here unknown to him; that, perhaps, everything was in readiness and in another moment would break upon him . . .

He went straight to the point at once, rose from his seat and took his cap.

'Porfiry Petrovitch,' he began resolutely, though with considerable irritation, 'yesterday you expressed a desire that I should come to you for some inquiries' (he laid special stress on the word 'inquiries'). 'I have come and if you have anything to ask me, ask it, and if not, allow me to withdraw. I have no time to spare. . . . I have to be at the funeral of that man who was run over, of whom you . . . know also,' he added, feeling angry at once at having made this addition and more irritated at his anger. 'I am sick of it all, do you hear? and have long been. It's partly what made me ill. In short,' he shouted, feeling that the phrase about his illness was still more out of place, 'in short, kindly examine me or let me go, at once. And if you must examine me, do so in the proper form! I will not allow you to do so otherwise, and so meanwhile, good-bye, as we have evidently nothing to keep us now.'

'Good heavens! What do you mean? What shall I question you about?'

cackled Porfiry Petrovitch with a change of tone, instantly leaving off laughing. 'Please don't disturb yourself,' he began fidgeting from place to place and fussily making Raskolnikov sit down. 'There's no hurry, there's no hurry, it's all nonsense. On, no, I'm very glad you've come to see me at last . . . I look upon you simply as a visitor. And as for my confounded laughter, please excuse it, Rodion Romanovitch. Rodion Romanovitch. That is your name? . . . It's my nerves, you tickled me so with your witty observation; I assure you, sometimes I shake with laughter like an india-rubber ball for half an hour at a time. . . . I'm often afraid of an attack of paralysis. Do sit down. Please do, or I shall think you are angry . . .'

Raskolnikov did not speak; he listened, watching him, still frowning angrily. He did sit down, but still held his cap.

'I must tell you one thing about myself, my dear Rodion Romanovitch,' Porfiry Petrovitch continued, moving about the room and again avoiding his visitor's eyes. 'You see, I'm a bachelor, a man of no consequence and not used to society; besides, I have nothing before me, I'm set, I'm running to seed and . . . and have you noticed, Rodion Romanovitch, that in our Petersburg circles, if two clever men meet who are not intimate, but respect each other, like you and me, it takes them half an hour before they can find a subject for conversation – they are dumb, they sit opposite each other and feel awkward? Everyone has subjects of conversation, ladies, for instance . . . people in high society always have their subjects of conversation, c'est de rigueur, but people of the middle sort like us, thinking people that is, are always tongue-tied and awkward. What is the reason for it? Whether it is the lack of public interest, or whether it is we are so honest we don't want to deceive one another, I don't know. What do you think? Do put down your cap, it looks as if you were just going, it makes me uncomfortable . . . I am so delighted . . .'

Raskolnikov put down his cap and continued listening in silence with a serious frowning face to the vague and empty chatter of Porfiry Petrovitch. 'Does he really want to distract my attention with his silly babble?'

'I can't offer you coffee here; but why not spend five minutes with a friend?' Porfiry pattered on, 'and you know all these official duties . . . please don't mind my running up and down, excuse it, my dear fellow, I am very much afraid of offending you, but exercise is absolutely indispensable for me. I'm always sitting and so glad to be moving about for five minutes . . . I suffer from my sedentary life . . . I always intend to join a gymnasium; they say that officials of all ranks, even Privy Councillors, may be seen skipping gaily there; there you have it, modern science . . . yes, yes. . . . But as for my duties here, inquiries and all such formalities . . . you mentioned inquiries yourself just now . . . I assure you these interrogations are sometimes more embarrassing for the interrogator than for the interrogated.... You made the observation yourself just now very aptly and wittily.' (Raskolnikov had made no observation of the kind.) 'One gets into a muddle! A regular muddle! One keeps harping on the same note, like a drum! There is to be a reform and we shall be called by a different name, at least, he-he-he! And as for our legal tradition, as you so wittily called it, I thoroughly agree with you. Every prisoner on trial, even the rudest peasant, knows that they begin by disarming him with irrelevant questions (as you so happily put it) and then deal him a knock-down blow, he-he-he! – your felicitous comparison, he-he! So you really imagined that I meant by "government quarters" – he-he! You are an ironical person. Come, I won't go on! Ah, by the way, yes! One word leads to another. You spoke of formality just now, apropos of the inquiry, you know. But what's the use of formality? In many cases it's nonsense. Sometimes one has a friendly chat and gets a good deal more out of it. One can always fall back on formality, allow me to assure you. And after all, what does it amount to? An examining lawyer cannot be bounded by formality at every step. The work of investigation is, so to speak, a free art in its own way, he-he-he!'

Porfiry Petrovitch took breath a moment. He had simply babbled on uttering empty phrases, letting slip a few enigmatic words and again reverting to incoherence. He was almost running about the room, moving his fat little legs quicker and quicker, looking at the ground, with his right hand behind his back, while with his left making gesticulations that were extraordinarily incongruous with his words. Raskolnikov suddenly noticed that as he ran about the room he seemed twice to stop for a moment near the door, as though he were listening.

'Is he expecting anything?'

'You are certainly quite right about it,' Porfiry began gaily, looking with extraordinary simplicity at Raskolnikov (which startled him and instantly put him on his guard); 'certainly quite right in laughing so wittily at our legal forms, he-he! Some of these elaborate psychological methods are exceedingly ridiculous and perhaps useless, if one adheres too closely to the forms. Yes ... I am talking of forms again. Well, if I recognize, or more strictly speaking, if I suspect someone or other to be a criminal in any case entrusted to me ... you're reading for the law, of course, Rodion Romanovitch?'

'Yes, I was ...'

'Well then, it is a precedent for you for the future – though don't suppose I should venture to instruct you after the articles you publish about crime! No, simply I make bold to state it by way of a fact, if I took this man or that for a criminal, why, I ask, should I worry him prematurely, even though I had evidence against him? In one case I may be bound, for instance, to arrest a man at once, but another may be in quite a different position, you know, so why shouldn't I let him walk about the town a bit? he-he-he! But I see you don't quite understand, so I'll give you a clearer example. If I put him in prison too soon, I may very likely give him, so to speak, moral support, he-he! You're laughing?'

Raskolnikov had no idea of laughing. He was sitting with compressed lips, his feverish eyes fixed on Porfiry Petrovitch's.

'Yet that is the case, with some types especially, for men are so different. You say "evidence". Well, there may be evidence. But evidence, you know, can generally be taken two ways. I am an examining lawyer and a weak man, I confess it. I should like to make a proof, so to say, mathematically clear. I should like to make a chain of evidence such as twice two are four, it ought to be a direct, irrefutable proof And if I shut him up too soon – even though I might be convinced *he* was the man, I should very likely be depriving myself of the means of getting further evidence against him. And how? By giving him, so to speak, a definite position, I shall put him out of suspense and set his mind at rest, so that he will retreat into his shell. They say that at Sevastopol, soon after Alma, the clever people were in a terrible fright that the enemy would attack openly and take Sevastopol at once. But when they saw that the enemy preferred a regular siege, they were delighted, I am told and reassured, for the thing would drag on for two months at least. You're laughing, you don't believe me again? Of course, you're right, too. You're right, you're right. These are all special cases, I admit. But you must observe this, my dear Rodion Romanovitch, the general case, the case for which all legal forms and rules are intended, for which they are calculated and laid down in books, does not exist at all, for the reason that every case, every crime, for instance, as soon as it actually occurs, at once becomes a thoroughly special case and sometimes a case unlike any that's gone before. Very comic cases of that sort sometimes occur. If I leave one man quite alone, if I don't touch him and don't worry him, but let him know or at least suspect every moment that I know all about it and am watching him day and night, and if he is in continual suspicion and terror, he'll be bound to lose his head. He'll come of himself, or maybe do something which will make it as plain as twice two are four – it's delightful. It may be so with a simple peasant, but with one of our sort, an intelligent man cultivated on a certain side, it's a dead certainty. For, my dear fellow, it's a very important matter to know on what side a man is cultivated. And then there are nerves, there are nerves, you have overlooked them! Why, they are all sick, nervous and irritable! . . . And then how they all suffer from spleen! That I assure you is a regular gold-mine for us. And it's no anxiety to me, his running about the town free! Let him, let him walk about for a bit! I know well enough that I've caught him and that he won't escape me. Where could he escape to, he-he? Abroad, perhaps? A Pole will escape abroad, but not he, especially as I am watching and have taken measures. Will he escape into the depths of the country perhaps? But you know, peasants live there, real rude Russian peasants. A modern cultivated man would prefer prison to living with such strangers as our peasants. He-he! But that's all nonsense, and on the surface. It's not merely that he has nowhere to run to, he is *psychologically* unable to escape me, he-he! What an expression! Through a law of nature he can't escape me if he had anywhere to go. Have you seen a butterfly round a candle? That's how he will keep circling and circling round me. Freedom will lose its attractions. He'll begin to brood, he'll weave a tangle round himself, he'll worry himself to death! What's more, he will provide me with a mathematical proof – if I only gave him long enough interval.... And he'll keep circling round me, getting nearer and nearer and then – flop! He'll fly straight into my mouth and I'll swallow him, and that will be very amusing, he-he-he! You don't believe me?'

Raskolnikov made no reply; he sat pale and motionless, still gazing with the same intensity into Porfiry's face.

'It's a lesson,' he thought, turning cold. 'This is beyond the cat playing with a mouse, like yesterday. He can't be showing off his power with no motive ... prompting me; he is far too clever for that ... he must have another object. What is it? It's all nonsense, my friend, you are pretending, to scare me! You've no proofs and the man I saw had no real existence. You simply want to make me lose my head, to work me up beforehand and so to crush me. But you are wrong, you won't do it! But why give me such a hint? Is he reckoning on my shattered nerves? No, my friend, you are wrong, you won't do it even though you have some trap for me ... let us see what you have in store for me.'

And he braced himself to face a terrible and unknown ordeal. At times he longed to fall on Porfiry and strangle him. This anger was what he dreaded from the beginning. He felt that his parched lips were flecked with foam, his heart was throbbing. But he was still determined not to speak till the right moment. He realized that this was the best policy in his position, because instead of saying too much he would be irritating his enemy by his silence and provoking him into speaking too freely. Anyhow, this was what he hoped for.

'No, I see you don't believe me, you think I am playing a harmless joke on you,' Porfiry began again, getting more and more lively, chuckling at every instant and again pacing round the room. 'And to be sure you're right: God has given me a figure that can awaken none but comic ideas in other people; a buffoon; but let me tell you, and I repeat it, excuse an old man, my dear Rodion Romanovitch, you are a man still young, so to say, in your first youth and so you put intellect above everything, like all young people. Playful wit and abstract arguments fascinate you and that's for all the world like the old Austrian *Hof-kriegsrat*, as far as I can judge of military matters, that is: on paper they'd beaten Napoleon and taken him prisoner, and there in their study they worked it all out in the cleverest fashion, but look you, General Mack surrendered with all his army, he-he-he! I see, I see, Rodion Romanovitch, you are laughing at a civilian like me, taking examples out of military history! But I can't help it, it's my weakness. I am fond of military science. And I'm ever so fond of reading all military histories. I've certainly missed my proper career. I ought to have been in the army, upon my word I ought. I shouldn't have been a Napoleon, but I might have been a major, he-he! Well, I will tell you the whole truth, my dear fellow, about this *special case*, I mean: actual fact and a man's temperament, my dear sir, are weighty matters and it's astonishing how they sometimes deceive the sharpest calculation! I – listen to an old man – am speaking seriously, Rodion Romanovitch' (as he said this Porfiry Petrovitch, who was scarcely five-and-thirty, actually seemed to have grown old; even his voice changed and he seemed to shrink altogether). 'Moreover, I'm a candid man . . . am I a candid man or not? What do you say? I fancy I really am: I tell you these things for nothing and don't even expect a reward for it, he-he! Well, to proceed, wit in my opinion is a splendid thing, it is, so to say, an adornment of nature and a consolation of life, and what tricks it can play! So that it sometimes is hard for a poor examining lawyer to know where he is, especially when he's liable to be carried away by his own fancy, too, for you know he is a man after all! But the poor fellow is saved by the criminal's temperament, worse luck for him! But young people carried away by their own wit don't think of that "when they overstep all obstacles", as you wittily and cleverly expressed it yesterday. He will lie – that is the man, who is a *special case*, the incognito, and he will lie well, in the cleverest fashion; you might think he would triumph and enjoy the fruits of his wit, but at the most interesting, the most flagrant moment he will faint. Of course there may be illness and a stuffy room as well, but anyway! Anyway he's given us the idea! He lied incomparably, but he didn't reckon on his temperament. That's what betrays him! Another time he will be carried away by his playful wit into making fun of the man who suspects him, he will turn pale, as it were, on purpose to mislead, but his paleness will be *too natural*, too much like the real thing, again he has given us an idea! Though his questioner may be deceived at first, he will think differently next day if he is not a fool, and, of course, it is like that at every step! He puts himself forward where he is not wanted, speaks continually when he ought to keep silent, brings in all sorts of allegorical allusions, he-he! Comes and asks, why didn't you take me long ago! he-he-he! And that can happen, you know, with the cleverest man, the psychologist, the literary man. The temperament reflects everything like a mirror! Gaze into it and admire what you see! But why are you so pale, Rodion Romanovitch? Is the room stuffy? Shall I open the window?'

'Oh, don't trouble, please,' cried Raskolnikov and he suddenly broke into a laugh. 'Please don't trouble.'

Porfiry stood facing him, paused a moment and suddenly he too laughed. Raskolnikov got up from the sofa, abruptly checked his hysterical laughter.

'Porfiry Petrovitch,' he began, speaking loudly and distinctly, though his legs trembled and he could scarcely stand. 'I see clearly at last that you actually suspect me of murdering that old woman and her sister Lizaveta. Let me tell you for my part that I am sick of this. If you find that you have a right to prosecute me legally, to arrest me, then prosecute me, arrest me. But I will not let myself be jeered at to my face and worried . . .'

His lips trembled, his eyes glowed with fury and he could not restrain his voice.

'I won't allow it!' he shouted, bringing his fist down on the table. 'Do you hear me, Porfiry Petrovitch? I won't allow it.'

'Good heavens! What does it mean?' cried Porfiry Petrovitch, apparently quite frightened. 'Rodion Romanovitch, my dear fellow, what is the matter with you?'

'I won't allow it,' Raskolnikov shouted again.

'Hush, my dear man! They'll hear and come in. Just think, what could we say to them?' Porfiry Petrovitch whispered in horror, bringing his face close to Raskolnikov's.

'I won't allow it, I won't allow it,' Raskolnikov repeated mechanically, but he too spoke in a sudden whisper.

Porfiry turned quickly and ran to open the window.

'Some fresh air! And you must have some water, my dear fellow. You're ill!' and he was running to the door to call for some when he found a decanter of water in the corner. Come, drink a little,' he whispered, rushing up to him with the decanter. 'It will be sure to do you good.'

Porfiry Petrovitch's alarm and sympathy were so natural that Raskolnikov was silent and began looking at him with wild curiosity. He did not take the water, however.

'Rodion Romanovitch, my dear fellow, you'll drive yourself out of your mind, I assure you, ach, ach! Have some water, do drink a little.'

He forced him to take the glass. Raskolnikov raised it mechanically to his lips, but set it on the table again with disgust.

'Yes, you've had a little attack! You'll bring back your illness again, my dear fellow,' Porfiry Petrovitch cackled with friendly sympathy, though he still looked rather disconcerted. 'Good heavens, you must take more care of yourself! Dmitri Prokofitch was here, came to see me yesterday – I know, I know, I've a nasty, ironical temper, but what they made of it! . . . Good heavens, he came yesterday after you'd been. We dined and he talked and talked away, and I could only throw up my hands in despair! Did he come from you? But do sit down, for mercy's sake, sit down!'

'No, not from me, but I knew he went to you and why he went,' Raskolnikov answered sharply.

'You knew?'

'I knew. What of it?'

'Why this, Rodion Romanovitch, that I know more than that about you; I know about everything. I know how you went *to take a flat* at night when it was dark and how you ran the bell and asked about the blood, so that the workmen and the porter did not know what to make of it. Yes, I understand your state of mind at that time . . . but you'll drive yourself mad like that, upon my word! You'll lose your head! You're full of generous indignation at the wrongs you've received, first from destiny, and then from the police officers, and so you rush from one thing to another to force them to speak out and make an end of it all, because you are sick of all this suspicion and foolishness. That's so, isn't it? I have guessed how you feel, haven't I? Only in that way you'll lose your head and Razumihin's too; he's too *good* a man for such a position, you must know that. You are ill and he is good and your illness is infectious for him . . . I'll tell you about it when you are more yourself. . . . But do sit down, for goodness' sake. Please rest, you look shocking, do sit down.'

Raskolnikov sat down; he no longer shivered, he was hot all over. In amazement he listened with strained attention to Porfiry Petrovitch who still seemed frightened as he looked after him with friendly solicitude. But he did not believe a word he said, though he felt a strange inclination to believe. Porfiry's unexpected words about the flat had utterly overwhelmed him. 'How can it be, he knows about the flat then,' he thought suddenly, 'and he tells it me himself!'

'Yes, in our legal practice there was a case almost exactly similar, a case of morbid psychology,' Porfiry went on quickly. 'A man confessed to murder and how he kept it up! It was a regular hallucination; he brought forward facts, he imposed upon everyone, and why? He had been partly, but only partly, unintentionally the cause of a murder and when he knew that he had given the murderers the opportunity, he sank into dejection, it got on his mind and turned his brain, he began imagining things and he persuaded himself that he was the murderer. But at last the High Court of Appeal went into it and the poor fellow was acquitted and put under proper care. Thanks to the Court of Appeal! Tut-tut-tut! Why, my dear fellow, you must drive yourself into delirium if you have the impulse to work upon your nerves, to go ringing bells at night and asking about blood! I've studied all this morbid psychology in my practice. A man is sometimes tempted to jump out of window or from a belfry. Just the same with bell-ringing. . . . It's an illness, Rodion Romanovitch! You have begun to neglect your illness. You should consult an experienced doctor, what's the good of that fat fellow? You are light-headed! You were delirious when you did all this!'

For a moment Raskolnikov felt everything going round.

'Is it possible, is it possible,' flashed through his mind, 'that he is still lying? He can't be, he can't be.' He rejected that idea, feeling to what a degree of fury it might drive him, feeling that that fury might drive him mad.

'I was not delirious. I knew what I was doing,' he cried, straining every faculty to penetrate Porfiry's game, 'I was quite myself, do you hear?'

'Yes, I hear and understand. You said yesterday you were not delirious, you were particularly emphatic about it! I understand all you can tell me! A-ach! . . . Listen, Rodion Romanovitch, my dear fellow. If you were actually a criminal, or were somehow mixed up in this damnable business, would you insist that you were not delirious but in full possession of your faculties? And so emphatically and persistently? Would it be possible? Quite impossible, to my thinking. If you had anything on your conscience, you certainly ought to insist that you were delirious. That's so, isn't it?'

There was a note of slyness in this inquiry. Raskolnikov drew back on the sofa as Porfiry bent over him and stared in silent perplexity at him.

'Another thing about Razumihin – you certainly ought to have said that he came of his own accord, to have concealed your part in it! But you don't conceal it! You lay stress on his coming at your instigation.'

Raskolnikov had not done so. A chill went down his back.

'You keep telling lies,' he said slowly and weakly, twisting his lips into a sickly smile, 'you are trying again to show that you know all my game, that you know all I shall say beforehand,' he said, conscious himself that he was not weighing his words as he ought. 'You want to frighten me . . . or you are simply laughing at me . . .'

He still stared at him as he said this and again there was a light of intense hatred in his eyes.

'You keep lying,' he cried. 'You know perfectly well that the best policy for the criminal is to tell the truth as nearly as possible . . . to conceal as little as possible. I don't believe you!'

'What a wily person you are!' Porfiry tittered, 'there's no catching you; you've a perfect monomania. So you don't believe me? But still you do believe me, you believe a quarter; I'll soon make you believe the whole, because I have a sincere liking for you and genuinely wish you good.'

Raskolnikov's lips trembled.

'Yes, I do,' went on Porfiry, touching Raskolnikov's arm genially, 'you must take care of your illness. Besides, your mother and sister are here now; you must think of them. You must soothe and comfort them and you do nothing but frighten them . . .'

'What has that to do with you? How do you know it? What concern is it of yours? You are keeping watch on me and want to let me know it?'

'Good heavens! Why, I learnt it all from you yourself! You don't notice that in your excitement you tell me and others everything. From Razumihin, too, I learnt a number of interesting details yesterday. No, you interrupted me, but I must tell you that, for all your wit, your suspiciousness makes you lose the common-sense view of things. To return to bell-ringing, for instance. I, an examining lawyer, have betrayed a precious thing like that, a real fact (for it is a fact worth having), and you see nothing in it! Why, if I had the slightest suspicion of you, should I have acted like that? No, I should first have disarmed your suspicions and not let you see I knew of that fact, should have diverted your attention and suddenly dealt you a knock-down blow (your expression) saying: "And what were you doing, sir, pray, at ten or nearly eleven at the murdered woman's flat and why did you ring the bell and why did you ask about blood? And why did you invite the porters to go with you to the police-station, to the lieutenant?" That's how I ought to have acted if I had a grain of suspicion of you. I ought to have taken your evidence in due form, searched your lodging and perhaps have arrested you, too . . . so I have no suspicion of you, since I have not done that! But you can't look at it normally and you see nothing, I say again.'

Raskolnikov started so that Porfiry Petrovitch could not fail to perceive it.

'You are lying all the while,' he cried. 'I don't know your object, but you are lying. You did not speak like that just now and I cannot be mistaken!'

'I am lying?' Porfiry repeated, apparently incensed, but preserving a good-humoured and ironical face, as though he were not in the least concerned at Raskolnikov's opinion of him. 'I am lying . . . but how did I treat you just now, I, the examining lawyer? Prompting you and giving you every means for your defence; illness, I said, delirium, injury, melancholy and the police officers and all the rest of it? Ah! He-he-he! Though, indeed, all those psychological means of defence are not very reliable and cut both ways: illness, delirium, I don't remember – that's all right, but why, my good sir, in your illness and in your delirium were you haunted by just those delusions and not by any others? There may have been others, eh? He-he-he!'

Raskolnikov looked haughtily and contemptuously at him.

'Briefly,' he said loudly and imperiously, rising to his feet and in so doing pushing Porfiry back a little, 'briefly, I want to know, do you acknowledge me perfectly free from suspicion or not? Tell me, Porfiry Petrovitch, tell me once for all and make haste!'

'What a business I'm having with you!' cried Porfiry with a perfectly good-humoured, sly and composed face. 'And why do you want to know, why do you want to know so much, since they haven't begun to worry you? Why, you are like a child asking for the matches! And why are you so uneasy? Why do you force yourself upon us, eh? He-he-he!'

'I repeat,' Raskolnikov cried furiously, 'that I can't put up with it!'

'With what? Uncertainty?' interrupted Porfiry.

'Don't jeer at me! I won't have it! I tell you I won't have it. I can't and I won't, do you hear, do you hear?' he shouted, bringing his fist down on the table again.

'Hush! Hush! They'll overhear! I warn you seriously, take care of yourself. I am not joking,' Porfiry whispered, but this time there was not the look of old womanish good nature and alarm in his face. Now he was peremptory, stern, frowning and for once laying aside all mystification.

But this was only for an instant. Raskolnikov, bewildered, suddenly fell into actual frenzy, but, strange to say, he again obeyed the command to speak quietly, though he was in a perfect paroxysm of fury.

'I will not allow myself to be tortured,' he whispered, instantly recognizing with hatred that he could not help obeying the command and driven to even greater fury by the thought. 'Arrest me, search me, but kindly act in due form and don't play with me! Don't dare!'

'Don't worry about the form,' Porfiry interrupted with the same sly smile, as it were, gloating with enjoyment over Raskolnikov. 'I invited you to see me quite in a friendly way.'

'I don't want your friendship and I spit on it! Do you hear? And here, I take my cap and go. What will you say now if you mean to arrest me?'

He took up his cap and went to the door.

'And won't you see my little surprise?' chuckled Porfiry, again taking him by the arm and stopping him at the door.

He seemed to become more playful and good-humoured, which maddened Raskolnikov.

'What surprise?' he asked, standing still and looking at Porfiry in alarm.

'My little surprise, it's sitting there behind the door, he-he-he!' (He pointed to the locked door.) 'I locked him in that he should not escape.'

'What is it? Where? What? . . .'

Raskolnikov walked to the door and would have opened it, but it was locked.

'It's locked, here is the key.'

And he brought a key out of his pocket.

'You are lying,' roared Raskolnikov without restraint, 'you lie, you damned punchinello!' and he rushed at Porfiry who retreated to the other door, not at all alarmed.

'I understand it all! You are lying and mocking so that I may betray myself to you . . .'

'Why, you could not betray yourself any further, my dear Rodion Romanovitch. You are in a passion. Don't shout, I shall call the clerks.'

'You are lying! Call the clerks! You knew I was ill and tried to work me into a frenzy to make me betray myself, that was your object! Produce your facts! I understand it all. You've no evidence, you have only wretched rubbishy suspicions like Zametov's! You knew my character, you wanted to drive me to fury and then to knock me down with priests and deputies. . . . Are you waiting for them? eh? What are you waiting for? Where are they? Produce them!'

'Why deputies, my good man? What things people will imagine! And to do so would not be acting in form as you say, you don't know the business, my dear fellow. . . . And there's no escaping form, as you see,' Porfiry muttered, listening at the door through which a noise could be heard.

'Ah, they're coming,' cried Raskolnikov. 'You've sent for them! You expected them! Well, produce them all: your deputies, your witnesses, what you like! . . . I am ready!'

But at this moment a strange incidence occurred, something so unexpected that neither Raskolnikov nor Porfiry Petrovitch could have looked for such a conclusion to their interview.

✦ SIX ✦

WHEN HE REMEMBERED THE SCENE afterwards, this is how Raskolnikov saw it.

The noise behind the door increased, and suddenly the door was opened a little.

'What is it?' cried Porfiry Petrovitch, annoyed. 'Why, I gave orders . . .'

For an instant there was no answer, but it was evident that there were several persons at the door, and that they were apparently pushing somebody back.

'What is it?' Porfiry Petrovitch repeated, uneasily.

'The prisoner Nikolay has been brought,' someone answered.

'He is not wanted! Take him away! Let him wait! What's he doing here? How irregular!' cried Porfiry, rushing to the door.

'But he . . .' began the same voice, and suddenly ceased.

Two seconds, not more, were spent in actual struggle, then someone gave a violent shove, and then a man, very pale, strode into the room.

This man's appearance was at first sight very strange. He stared straight before him, as though seeing nothing. There was a determined gleam in his eyes; at the same time there was a deathly pallor in his face, as though he were being led to the scaffold. His white lips were faintly twitching.

He was dressed like a workman and was of medium height, very young, slim, his hair cut in a round crop, with thin spare features. The man whom he had thrust back followed him into the room and succeeded in seizing him by the shoulder; he was a warder; but Nikolay pulled his arm away.

Several persons crowded inquisitively into the doorway. Some of them tried to get in. All this took place almost instantaneously.

'Go away, it's too soon! Wait till you are sent for! . . . Why have you brought him too soon?' Porfiry Petrovitch muttered, extremely annoyed, and as it were thrown out of his reckoning.

But Nikolay suddenly knelt down.

'What's the matter?' cried Porfiry surprised.

'I am guilty! Mine is the sin! I am the murderer,' Nikolay articulated suddenly, rather breathless, but speaking fairly loudly.

For ten seconds there was silence, as though all had been struck dumb; even the warder stepped back, mechanically retreated to the door, and stood immovable.

'What is it?' cried Porfiry Petrovitch, recovering from his momentary stupefaction.

'I . . . am the murderer,' repeated Nikolay, after a brief pause.

'What . . . you . . . what . . . whom did you kill?' Porfiry Petrovitch was obviously bewildered.

Nikolay again was silent for a moment.

'Alyona Ivanovna and her sister Lizaveta Ivanovna, I . . . killed . . . with an axe. Darkness came over me,' he added suddenly, and was again silent.

He still remained on his knees. Porfiry Petrovitch stood for some moments as though meditating, but suddenly roused himself and waved back the uninvited spectators. They instantly vanished and closed the door. Then he looked towards Raskolnikov, who was standing in the corner, staring wildly at Nikolay and moved towards him, but stopped short, looked from Nikolay to Raskolnikov and then again to Nikolay, and seeming unable to restrain himself darted at the latter.

'You're in too great a hurry,' he shouted at him, almost angrily. 'I didn't ask you what came over you. . . . Speak, did you kill them?'

'I am the murderer. . . . I want to give evidence,' Nikolay pronounced.

'Ach! What did you kill them with?'

'An axe. I had it ready.'

'Ach, he is in a hurry! Alone?'

Nikolay did not understand the question.

'Did you do it alone?'

'Yes, alone. And Mitka is not guilty and had no share in it.'

'Don't be in a hurry about Mitka! A-ach! How was it you ran downstairs like that at the time? The porters met you both!'

'It was to put them off the scent. . . . I ran after Mitka,' Nikolay replied hurriedly, as though he had prepared the answer.

'I knew it!' cried Porfiry, with vexation. 'It's not his own tale he is telling,' he muttered as though to himself, and suddenly his eyes rested on Raskolnikov again.

He was apparently so taken up with Nikolay that for a moment he had forgotten Raskolnikov. He was a little taken aback.

'My dear Rodion Romanovitch, excuse me!' he flew up to him, 'this won't do; I'm afraid you must go . . . it's no good your staying . . . I will . . . you see, what a surprise! . . . Good-bye!'

And taking him by the arm, he showed him to the door.

'I suppose you didn't expect it?' said Raskolnikov who, though he had not yet fully grasped the situation, had regained his courage.

'You did not expect it either, my friend. See how your hand is trembling! He-he!'

'You're trembling, too, Porfiry Petrovitch!'

'Yes, I am; I didn't expect it.'

They were already at the door; Porfiry was impatient for Raskolnikov to be gone.

'And your little surprise, aren't you going to show it to me?' Raskolnikov said, sarcastically.

'Why, his teeth are chattering as he asks, he-he! You are an ironical person! Come, till we meet!'

'I believe we can say *good-bye!*'

'That's in God's hands,' muttered Porfiry, with an unnatural smile.

As he walked through the office, Raskolnikov noticed that many people were looking at him. Among them he saw the two porters from *the* house, whom he had invited that night to the police-station. They stood there waiting. But he was no sooner on the stairs than he heard the voice of Porfiry Petrovitch behind him. Turning round, he saw the latter running after him, out of breath.

'One word, Rodion Romanovitch; as to all the rest, it's in God's hands, but as a matter of form there are some questions I shall have to ask you . . . so we shall meet again, shan't we?'

And Porfiry stood still, facing him with a smile.

'Shan't we?' he added again.

He seemed to want to say something more, but could not speak out.

'You must forgive me, Porfiry Petrovitch, for what has just passed . . . I lost my temper,' began Raskolnikov, who had so far regained his courage that he felt irresistibly inclined to display his coolness.

'Don't mention it, don't mention it,' Porfiry replied, almost gleefully. 'I myself too . . . I have a wicked temper, I admit it! But we shall meet again. If it's God's will, we may see a great deal of one another.'

'And will get to know each other through and through?' added Raskolnikov.

'Yes; know each other through and through,' assented Porfiry Petrovitch, and he screwed up his eyes, looking earnestly at Raskolnikov. 'Now you're going to a birthday party?'

'To a funeral.'

'Of course, the funeral! Take care of yourself, and get well.'

'I don't know what to wish you,' said Raskolnikov, who had begun to descend the stairs, but looked back again. 'I should like to wish you success, but your office is such a comical one.'

'Why comical?' Porfiry Petrovitch had turned to go, but he seemed to prick up his ears at this.

'Why, how you must have been torturing and harrassing that poor Nikolay psychologically, after your fashion, till he confessed! You must have been at him day and night, proving to him that he was the murderer, and now that he has confessed, you'll begin vivisecting him again. "You are lying," you'll say. "You are not the murderer! You can't be! It's not your own tale you are telling!" You must admit it's a comical business!'

'He-he-he! You noticed then that I said to Nikolay just now that it was not his own tale he was telling?'

'How could I help noticing it?'

'He-he! You are quick-witted. You notice everything! You've really a playful mind! And you always fasten on the comic side . . . he-he! They say that was the marked characteristic of Gogol, among the writers.'

'Yes, of Gogol.'

'Yes, of Gogol. . . . I shall look forward to meeting you.'

'So shall I.'

Raskolnikov walked straight home. He was so muddled and bewildered that on getting home he sat for a quarter of an hour on the sofa, trying to collect his thoughts. He did not attempt to think about Nikolay; he was stupefied; he felt that his confession was something inexplicable, amazing – something beyond his understanding. But Nikolay's confession was an actual fact. The consequences of this fact were clear to him at once, its falsehood could not fail to be discovered, and then they would be after him again. Till then, at least, he was free and must do something for himself, for the danger was imminent.

But how imminent? His position gradually became clear to him. Remembering, sketchily, the main outlines of his recent scene with Porfiry, he could not help shuddering again with horror. Of course, he did not yet know all Porfiry's aims, he could not see into all his calculations. But he had already partly shown his hand, and no one knew better than Raskolnikov how terrible Porfiry's 'lead' had been for him. A little more and he *might* have given himself away completely, circumstantially. Knowing his nervous temperament and from the first glance seeing through him, Porfiry, though playing a bold game, was bound to win. There's no denying that Raskolnikov had compromised himself seriously, but no *facts* had come to light as yet; there was nothing positive. But was he taking a true view of the position? Wasn't he mistaken? What had Porfiry been trying to get at? Had he really some surprise prepared for him? And what was it? Had he really been expecting something or not? How would they have parted if it had not been for the unexpected appearance of Nikolay?

Porfiry had shown almost all his cards – of course, he had risked something in showing them – and if he had really had anything up his sleeve (Raskolnikov reflected), he would have shown that, too. What was that 'surprise'? Was it a joke? Had it meant anything? Could it have concealed anything like a fact, a piece of positive evidence? His yesterday's visitor? What had become of him? Where was he to-day? If Porfiry really had any evidence, it must be connected with him. . . .

He sat on the sofa with his elbows on his knees and his face hidden in his hands. He was still shivering nervously. At last he got up, took his cap, thought a minute, and went to the door.

He had a sort of presentiment that for to-day, at least, he might consider himself out of danger. He had a sudden sense almost of joy; he wanted to make haste to Katerina Ivanovna's. He would be too late for the funeral, of course, but he would be in time for the memorial dinner, and there at once he would see Sonia.

He stood still, thought a moment, and a suffering smile came for a moment on to his lips.

'To-day! To-day,' he repeated to himself. 'Yes, to-day! So it must be. . . .'

But as he was about to open the door, it began opening of itself. He started and moved back. The door opened gently and slowly, and there suddenly appeared a figure – yesterday's visitor *from underground*.

The man stood in the doorway, looked at Raskolnikov without speaking, and took a step forward into the room. He was exactly the same as yesterday; the same figure, the same dress, but there was a great change in his face; he looked dejected and sighed deeply. If he had only put his hand up to his cheek and leaned his head on one side he would have looked exactly like a peasant woman.

'What do you want?' asked Raskolnikov, numb with terror.

The man was still silent, but suddenly he bowed down almost to the ground, touching it with his finger.

'What is it?' cried Raskolnikov.

'I have sinned,' the man articulated softly.

'How?'

'By evil thoughts.'

They looked at one another.

'I was vexed. When you came, perhaps in drink, and bade the porters go to the police-station and asked about the blood, I was vexed that they let you go and took you for drunken. I was so vexed that I lost my sleep. And remembering the address we came here yesterday and asked for you . . .'

'Who came?' Raskolnikov interrupted, instantly beginning to recollect.

'I did, I've wronged you.'

'Then you come from that house?'

'I was standing at the gate with them . . . don't you remember? We have carried on our trade in that house for years past. We cure and prepare hides, we take work home . . . most of all I was vexed. . . .'

And the whole scene of the day before yesterday in the gateway came clearly before Raskolnikov's mind; he recollected that there had been several people there besides the porters, women among them. He remembered one voice that suggested taking him straight to the police-station. He could not recall the face of the speaker, and even now he did not recognize it, but he remembered that he had turned round and made him some answer. . . .

So this was the solution of yesterday's horror. The most awful thought was that he had been actually almost lost, had almost done for himself on account of such a *trivial* circumstance. So this man could tell nothing except his asking about the flat and the bloodstains. So Porfiry, too, had nothing but that *delirium*, no facts but this *psychology* which *cuts both ways*, nothing positive. So if no more facts come to light (and they must not, they must not!) then . . . then what can they do to him? How can they convict him, even if they arrest him? And Porfiry then had only just heard about the flat and had not known about it before.

'Was it you who told Porfiry . . . that I'd been there?' he cried, struck by a sudden idea.

'What Porfiry?'

'The head of the detective department?'

'Yes. The porters did not go there, but I went.'

'To-day?'

'I got there two minutes before you. And I heard, I heard it all, how he worried you.'

'Where? What? When?'

'Why, in the next room. I was sitting there all the time.'

'What? Why, then you were the surprise? But how could it happen? Upon my word!'

'I saw that the porters did not want to do what I said,' began the man; 'for it's too late, said they, and maybe he'll be angry that we did not come at the time. I was vexed and I lost my sleep, and I began making inquiries. And finding out yesterday where to go, I went to-day. The first time I went he wasn't there, when I came an hour later he couldn't see me. I went the third time, and they showed me in. I informed him of everything, just as it happened, and he began skipping about the room and punching himself on the chest. "What do you scoundrels mean by it? If I'd known about it I should have arrested him!" Then he ran out, called somebody and began talking to him in the corner, then he turned to me, scolding and questioning me. He scolded me a great deal; and I told him everything, and I told him that you didn't dare to say a word in answer to me yesterday and that you didn't recognize me. And he fell to running about again and kept hitting himself on the chest, and getting angry and running about, and when you were announced he told me to go into the next room. "Sit there a bit," he said. "Don't move, whatever you may hear." And he set a chair there for me and locked me in. "Perhaps," he said, "I may call you." And when Nikolay'd been brought he let me out as soon as you were gone. "I shall send for you again and question you," he said.'

'And did he question Nikolay while you were there?'

'He got rid of me as he did of you, before he spoke to Nikolay.'

The man stood still, and again suddenly bowed down, touching the ground with his finger.

'Forgive me for my evil thoughts, and my slander.'

'May God forgive you,' answered Raskolnikov.

And as he said this, the man bowed down again, but not to the ground, turned slowly and went out of the room.

'It all cuts both ways, now it all cuts both ways,' repeated Raskolnikov, and he went out more confident than ever.

'Now we'll make a fight for it,' he said, with a malicious smile, as he went down the stairs. His malice was aimed at himself; with shame and contempt he recollected his 'cowardice'.

297

PART FIVE

❯❯ ONE ❮❮

THE MORNING THAT FOLLOWED THE fateful interview with Dounia and her mother brought sobering influences to bear on Pyotr Petrovitch. Intensely unpleasant as it was, he was forced little by little to accept as a fact beyond recall what had seemed to him only the day before fantastic and incredible. The black snake of wounded vanity had been gnawing at his heart all night. When he got out of bed, Pyotr Petrovitch immediately looked in the looking-glass. He was afraid that he had jaundice. However his health seemed unimpaired so far, and looking at his noble, clear-skinned countenance which had grown fattish of late, Pyotr Petrovitch for an instant was positively comforted in the conviction that he would find another bride and, perhaps, even a better one. But coming back to the sense of his present position, he turned aside and spat vigorously, which excited a sarcastic smile in Andrey Semyonovitch Lebeziatnikov, the young friend with whom he was staying. That smile Pyotr Petrovitch noticed, and at once set it down against his young friend's account. He had set down a good many points against him of late. His anger was redoubled when he reflected that he ought not to have told Andrey Semyonovitch about the result of yesterday's interview. That was the second mistake he had made in temper, through impulsiveness and irritability. . . . Moreover, all that morning one unpleasantness followed another. He even found a hitch awaiting him in his legal case in the senate. He was particularly irritated by the owner of the flat which had been taken in view of his approaching marriage and was being redecorated at his own expense; the owner, a rich German tradesman, would not entertain the idea of breaking the contract which had just been signed and insisted on the full forfeit money, though Pyotr Petrovitch would be giving him back the flat practically redecorated. In the same way the upholsterers refused to return a single rouble of the instalment paid for the furniture purchased but not yet removed to the flat.

'Am I to get married simply for the sake of the furniture?' Pyotr Petrovitch ground his teeth and at the same time once more he had a gleam of desperate hope. 'Can all that be really so irrevocably over? Is it no use to make another effort?' The thought of Dounia sent a voluptuous pang through his heart. He endured anguish at that moment, and if it had been possible to slay Raskolnikov instantly by wishing it, Pyotr Petrovitch would promptly have uttered the wish.

'It was my mistake, too, not to have given them money,' he thought, as he returned dejectedly to Lebeziatnikov's room, 'and why on earth was I such a Jew? It was false economy! I meant to keep them without a penny so that they should turn to me as their providence, and look at them! foo! If I'd spent some fifteen hundred roubles on them for the trousseau and presents, on knick-knacks, dressing-cases, jewellery, materials, and all that sort of trash from Knopp's and the English shop, my position would have been better and . . . stronger! They could not have refused me so easily! They are the sort of people that would feel bound to return money and presents if they broke it off; and they would find it hard to do it! And their conscience would prick them: how can we dismiss a man who has hitherto been so generous and delicate? . . . H'm! I've made a blunder.'

And grinding his teeth again, Pyotr Petrovitch called himself a fool – but not aloud, of course.

He returned home, twice as irritated and angry as before. The preparations for the funeral dinner at Katerina Ivanovna's excited his curiosity as he passed. He had heard about it the day before; he fancied, indeed, that he had been invited, but absorbed in his own cares he paid no attention. Inquiring of Madame Lippevechsel who was busy laying the table while Katerina Ivanovna was away at the cemetery, he heard that the entertainment was to be great affair, that all the lodgers had been invited, among them some who had not known the dead man, that even Andrey Semyonovitch Lebeziatnikov was invited in spite of his previous quarrel with Katerina Ivanovna, that he, Pyotr Petrovitch, was not only invited but was eagerly expected as he was the most important of the lodgers. Amalia Ivanovna herself had been invited with great ceremony in spite of the recent unpleasantness, and so she was very busy with preparations and was taking a positive pleasure in them; she was more-over dressed up to the nines, all in new black silk, and she was proud of it. All this suggested an idea to Pyotr Petrovitch and he went into his room, or rather Lebeziatnikov's, somewhat thoughtful. He had learnt that Raskolnikov was to be one of the guests.

Andrey Semyonovitch had been at home all the morning. The attitude of Pyotr Petrovitch to this gentleman was strange, though perhaps natural. Pyotr Petrovitch had despised and hated him from the day he came to stay with him and at the same time he seemed somewhat afraid of him. He had not come to stay with him on his arrival in Petersburg simply from parsimony, though that had been perhaps his chief object. He had heard of Andrey Semyonovitch, who had once been his ward, as a leading young progressive who was taking an important part in certain interesting circles, the doings of which were a legend in the provinces. It had impressed Pyotr Petrovitch. These powerful omniscient circles who despised everyone and showed everyone up had long inspired in him a peculiar but quite vague alarm. He had not, of course, been able to form even an approximate notion of what they meant. He, like everyone, had heard that there were, especially in Petersburg, progressives of some sort, nihilists and so on, and, like many people, he exaggerated and distorted the significance of those words to an absurd degree. What for many years past he had feared more than anything was *being shown up* and this was the chief ground for his continual uneasiness at the thought of transferring his business to Petersburg. He was afraid of this as little children are sometimes panic-stricken. Some years before, when he was just entering on his own career, he had come upon two cases in which rather important personages in the province, patrons of his, had been cruelly shown up. One instance had ended in great scandal for the person attacked and the other had very nearly ended in serious trouble. For this reason Pyotr Petrovitch intended to go into the subject as soon as he reached Petersburg and, if necessary, to anticipate contingencies by seeking the favour of 'our younger generation'. He relied on Andrey Semyonovitch for this and before his visit to Raskolnikov he had succeeded in picking up some current phrases. He soon discovered that Andrey Semyonovitch was a commonplace simpleton, but that by no means reassured Pyotr Petrovitch. Even if he had been certain that all the progressives were fools like him, it would not have allayed his uneasiness. All the doctrines, the ideas, the systems, with which Andrey Semyonovitch pestered him had no interest for him. He had his own object – he simply wanted to find out at once what was happening *here*. Had these people any power or not? Had he anything to fear from them? Would they expose any enterprise of his? And what precisely was now the object of their attacks? Could he somehow make up to them and get round them if they really were powerful? Was this the thing to do or not? Couldn't he gain something through them? In fact hundreds of questions presented themselves.

Andrey Semyonovitch was an anæmic, scrofulous little man, with strangely flaxen mutton-chop whiskers of which he was very proud. He was a clerk and had almost always something wrong with his eyes. He was rather soft-hearted, but self-confident and sometimes extremely conceited in speech, which had an absurd effect, incongruous with his little figure. He was one of the lodgers most respected by Amalia Ivanovna, for he did not get drunk and paid regularly for his lodging. Andrey Semyonovitch really was rather stupid; he attached himself to the cause of progress and 'our younger generation' from enthusiasm. He was one of the numerous and varied legion of dullards, of half-animate abortions, conceited, half-educated coxcombs, who attach themselves to the idea most in fashion only to vulgarize it and who caricature every cause they serve, however sincerely.

Though Lebeziatnikov was so good-natured, he, too, was beginning to dislike Pyotr Petrovitch. This happened on both sides unconsciously. However simple Andrey Semyonovitch might be, he began to see that Pyotr Petrovitch was duping him and secretly despising him, and that 'he was not the right sort of man'. He had tried expounding to him the system of Fourier and the Darwinian theory, but of late Pyotr Petrovitch began to listen too sarcastically and even to be rude. The fact was he had begun instinctively to guess that Lebeziatnikov was not merely a commonplace simpleton, but, perhaps, a liar, too, and that he had no connections of any consequence even in his own circle, but had simply picked things up third-hand; and that very likely he did not even know much about his own work of propaganda, for he was in too great a muddle. A fine person he would be to show anyone up! It must be noted, by the way, that Pyotr Petrovitch had during those ten days eagerly accepted the strangest praise from Andrey Semyonovitch; he had not protested, for instance, when Andrey Semyonovitch belauded him for being ready to contribute to the establishment of the new 'commune', or to abstain from christening his future children, or to acquiesce if Dounia were to take a lover a month after marriage, and so on. Pyotr Petrovitch so enjoyed hearing his own praises that he did not disdain even such virtues when they were attributed to him.

Pyotr Petrovitch had had occasion that morning to realize some five-per-cent bonds and now he sat down to the table and counted over bundles of notes. Andrey Semyonovitch who hardly ever had any money walked about the room pretending to himself to look at all those bank-notes with indifference and even contempt. Nothing would have convinced Pyotr Petrovitch that Andrey Semyonovitch could really look on the money unmoved, and the latter, on his side, kept thinking bitterly that Pyotr Petrovitch was capable of entertaining such an idea about him and was, perhaps, glad of the opportunity of teasing his young friend by reminding him of his inferiority and the great difference between them.

He found him incredibly inattentive and irritable, though he, Andrey Semyonovitch, began enlarging on his favourite subject, the foundation of a new special 'commune'. The brief remarks that dropped from Pyotr Petrovitch between the clicking of the beads on the reckoning frame betrayed unmistakable and discourteous irony. But the 'humane' Andrey Semyonovitch ascribed Pyotr Petrovitch's ill-humour to his recent breach with Dounia and he was burning with impatience to discourse on that theme. He had something progressive to say on the subject which might console his worthy friend and 'could not fail' to promote his development.

'There is some sort of festivity being prepared at that . . . at the widow's, isn't there?' Pyotr Petrovitch asked suddenly, interrupting Andrey Semyonovitch at the most interesting passage.

'Why, don't you know? Why, I was telling you last night what I think about all such ceremonies. And she invited you too, I heard. You were talking to her yesterday . . .'

'I should never have expected that beggarly fool would have spent on this feast all the money she got from that other fool, Raskolnikov. I was surprised just now as I came through at the preparations there, the wines! Several people are invited. It's beyond everything!' continued Pyotr Petrovitch, who seemed to have some object in pursuing the conversation. 'What? You say I am asked to? When was that? I don't remember. But I shan't go. Why should I? I only said a word to her in passing yesterday of the possibility of her obtaining a year's salary as a destitute widow of a government clerk. I suppose she has invited me on that account, hasn't she? He-he-he!'

'I don't intend to go either,' said Lebeziatnikov.

'I should think not, after giving her a thrashing! You might well hesitate, he-he!'

'Who thrashed? Whom?' cried Lebeziatnikov, flustered and blushing.

'Why, you thrashed Katerina Ivanovna a month ago. I heard so yesterday . . . so that's what your convictions amount to . . . and the same woman question, too, wasn't quite sound, he-he-he!' and Pyotr Petrovitch, as though comforted, went back to clicking his beads.

'It's all slander and nonsense!' cried Lebeziatnikov, who was always afraid of allusions to the subject. 'It was not like that at all, it was quite different. You've heard it wrong; it's a libel. I was simply defending myself. She rushed at me first with her nails, she pulled out all my whiskers. . . . It's permissible for anyone, I should hope, to defend himself and I never allow anyone to use violence to me on principle, for it's an act of despotism. What was I to do? I simply pushed her back.'

'He-he-he!' Luzhin went on laughing maliciously.

'You keep on like that because you are out of humour yourself. . . . But that's nonsense and it has nothing, nothing whatever to do with the woman question! You don't understand; I used to think, indeed, that if women are equal to men in all respects, even in strength (as is maintained now) there ought to be equality in that, too. Of course, I reflected afterwards that such a question ought not really to arise, for there ought not to be fighting and in the future society fighting is unthinkable . . . and that it would be a queer thing to seek for equality in fighting. I am not so stupid ... though, of course, there is fighting ... there won't be later, but at present there is ... confound it! How muddled one gets with you! It's not on that account that I am not going. I am not going on principle, not to take part in the revolting convention of memorial dinners, that's why! Though, of course, one might go to laugh at it. ... I am sorry there won't be any priests at it. I should certainly go if there were.'

'Then you would sit down at another man's table and insult it and those who invited you. Eh?'

'Certainly not insult, but protest. I should do it with a good object. I might indirectly assist the cause of enlightenment and propaganda. It's a duty of every man to work for enlightenment and propaganda and the more harshly, perhaps, the better. I might drop a seed, an idea. ... And something might grow up from that seed. How should I be insulting them? They might be offended at first, but afterwards they'd see I'd done them a service. You know, Terebyeva (who is in the community now) was blamed because when she left her family and ... devoted ... herself, she wrote to her father and mother that she wouldn't go on living conventionally and was entering on a free marriage and it was said that was too harsh, that she might have spared them and have written more kindly. I think that's all nonsense and there's no need of softness; on the contrary, what's wanted is protest. Varents had been married seven years, she abandoned her two children, she told her husband straight out in a letter: "I have realized that I cannot be happy with you. I can never forgive you that you have deceived me by concealing from me that there is another organization of society by means of the communities. I have only lately learned it from a great-hearted man to whom I have given myself and with whom I am establishing a community. I speak plainly because I consider it dishonest to deceive you. Do as you think best. Do not hope to get me back, you are too late. I hope you will be happy." That's how letters like that ought to be written!'

'Is that Terebyeva the one you said had made a third free marriage?'

'No, it's only the second, really! But what if it were the fourth, what if it were the fifteenth, that's all nonsense! And if ever I regretted the death of my father and mother, it is now, and I sometimes think if my parents were living what a protest I would have aimed at them! I would have done something on purpose ... I would have shown them! I would have astonished them! I am really sorry there is no one!'

'To surprise! He-he! Well, be that as you will,' Pyotr Petrovitch interrupted, 'but tell me this: do you know the dead man's daughter, the delicate-looking little thing? It's true what they say about her, isn't it?'

'What of it? I think, that is, it is my own personal conviction that this is the normal condition of women. Why not? I mean, *distinguons*. In our present society it is not altogether normal, because it is compulsory, but in the future society it will be perfectly normal, because it will be voluntary. Even as it is, she was quite right; she was suffering and that was her asset, so to speak, her capital which she had a perfect right to dispose of. Of course, in the future society there will be no need of assets, but her part will have another significance, rational and in harmony with her environment. As to Sofya Semyonovna personally, I regard her actions as a vigorous protest against the organization of society, and I respect her deeply for it; I rejoice indeed when I look at her!'

'I was told that you got her turned out of these lodgings.'

Lebeziatnikov was enraged.

'That's another slander,' he yelled. 'It was not so at all! That was all Katerina Ivanovna's invention, for she did not understand! And I never made love to Sofya Semyonovna! I was simply developing her, entirely disinterestedly, trying to rouse her to protest. . . . All I wanted was her protest and Sofya Semyonovna could not have remained here anyway!'

'Have you asked her to join your community?'

'You keep on laughing and very inappropriately, allow me to tell you. You don't understand! There is no such rôle in a community. The community is established that there should be no rôles. In a community, such a rôle is essentially transformed and what is stupid here is sensible there, what, under present conditions, is unnatural becomes perfectly natural in the community. It all depends on the environment. It's all the environment and man himself is nothing. And I am on good terms with Sofya Semyonovna to this day, which is a proof that she never regarded me as having wronged her. I am trying now to attract her to the community, but on quite, quite a different footing. What are you laughing at? We are trying to establish a community of our own, a special one, on a broader basis. We have gone further in our convictions. We reject more! And meanwhile I'm still developing Sofya Semyonovna. She has a beautiful, beautiful character!'

'And you take advantage of her fine character, eh? He-he!'

'No, no! Oh, no! On the contrary.'

'Oh, the contrary! He-he-he! A queer thing to say!'

'Believe me! Why should I disguise it? In fact, I feel it strange myself how timid, chaste and modest she is with me!'

'And you, of course, are developing her . . . he-he! trying to prove to her that all that modesty is nonsense?'

'Not at all, not at all! How coarsely, how stupidly – excuse me saying so – you misunderstand the word development! Good heavens, how . . . crude you still are! We are striving for the freedom of women and you have only one idea in your head.... Setting aside the general question of chastity and feminine modesty as useless in themselves and indeed prejudices, I fully accept her chastity with me, because that's for her to decide. Of course if she were to tell me herself that she wanted me, I should think myself very lucky, because I like the girl very much; but as it is, no one has ever treated her more courteously than I, with more respect for her dignity ... I wait in hopes, that's all!'

'You had much better make her a present of something. I bet you never thought of that.'

'You don't understand, as I've told you already! Of course, she is in such a position, but it's another question. Quite another question! You simply despise her. Seeing a fact which you mistakenly consider deserving of contempt, you refuse to take a humane view of a fellow creature. You don't know what a character she is! I am only sorry that of late she has quite given up reading and borrowing books. I used to lend them to her, I am sorry, too, that with all the energy and resolution in protesting – which she has already shown once – she has little self-reliance, little, so to say, independence, so as to break free from certain prejudices and certain foolish ideas. Yet she thoroughly understands some questions, for instance about kissing of hands, that is, that it's an insult to a woman for a man to kiss her hand, because it's a sign of inequality. We had a debate about it and I described it to her. She listened attentively to an account of the workmen's associations in France, too. Now I am explaining the question of coming into the room in the future society.'

'And what's that, pray?'

'We had a debate lately on the question: Has a member of the community the right to enter another member's room, whether man or woman, at any time ... and we decided that he has!'

'It might be at an inconvenient moment, he-he!'

Lebeziatnikov was really angry.

'You are always thinking of something unpleasant,' he cried with aversion. 'Tfoo! How vexed I am that when I was expounding our system I referred prematurely to the question of personal privacy! It's always a stumbling-block to people like you, they turn it into ridicule before they understand it. And how proud they are of it, too! Tfoo! I've often maintained that that question should not be approached by a novice till he has a firm faith in the system. And tell me, please, what do you find so shameful even in cesspools? I should be the first to be ready to clean out any cesspool you like. And it's not a question of self-sacrifice, it's simply work, honourable, useful work which is as good as any other and much better than the work of a Raphael and a Pushkin, because it is more useful.'

'And more honourable, more honourable, he-he-he!'

'What do you mean by "more honourable"? I don't understand such expressions to describe human activity. "More honourable", "nobler" – all those are old-fashioned prejudices which I reject. Everything which is *of use* to mankind is honourable. I only understand one word: *useful!* You can snigger as much as you like, but that's so!'

Pyotr Petrovitch laughed heartily. He had finished counting the money and was putting it away. But some of the notes he left on the table. The 'cesspool question' had already been a subject of dispute between them. What was absurd was that it made Lebeziatnikov really angry, while it amused Luzhin and at that moment he particularly wanted to anger his young friend.

'It's your ill-luck yesterday that makes you so ill-humoured and annoying,' blurted out Lebeziatnikov, who in spite of his 'independence' and his 'protests' did not venture to oppose Pyotr Petrovitch and still behaved to him with some of the respect habitual in earlier years.

'You'd better tell me this,' Pyotr Petrovitch interrupted with haughty displeasure, 'can you ... or rather are you really friendly enough with that young person to ask her to step in here for a minute? I think they've all come back from the cemetery ... I heard the sound of steps ... I want to see her, that young person.'

'What for?' Lebeziatnikov asked with surprise.

'Oh, I want to. I am leaving here to-day or to-morrow and therefore I wanted to speak to her about ... However, you may be present during the interview. It's better you should be, indeed. For there's no knowing what you might imagine.'

'I shan't imagine anything. I only asked and, if you've anything to say to her, nothing is easier than to call her in. I'll go directly and you may be sure I won't be in your way.'

Five minutes later Lebeziatnikov came in with Sonia. She came in very much surprised and overcome with shyness as usual. She was always shy in such circumstances and was always afraid of new people, she had been as a child and was even more so now. ... Pyotr Petrovitch met her 'politely and affably', but with a certain shade of bantering familiarity which in his opinion was suitable for a man of his respectability and weight in dealing with a creature so young and so *interesting* as she. He hastened to 'reassure' her and made her sit down facing him at the table. Sonia sat down, looked about her – at Lebeziatnikov, at the notes lying on the table and then again at Pyotr Petrovitch and her eyes remained riveted to him. Lebeziatnikov was moving to the door. Pyotr Petrovitch signed to Sonia to remain seated and stopped Lebeziatnikov.

'Is Raskolnikov in there? Has he come?' he asked him in a whisper.

'Raskolnikov? Yes. Why? Yes, he is there. I saw him just come in. . . . Why?'

'Well, I particularly beg you to remain here with us and not to leave me alone with this . . . young woman. I only want a few words with her, but God knows what they may make of it. I shouldn't like Raskolnikov to repeat anything. . . . You understand what I mean?'

'I understand!' Lebeziatnikov saw the point. 'Yes, you are right. . . . Of course, I am convinced personally that you have no reason to be uneasy, but . . . still, you are right. Certainly I'll stay. I'll stand here at the window and not be in your way . . . I think you are right. . . .'

Pyotr Petrovitch returned to the sofa, sat down opposite Sonia, looked attentively at her and assumed an extremely dignified, even severe expression, as much as to say, 'don't you make any mistake, madam'. Sonia was overwhelmed with embarrassment.

'In the first place, Sofya Semyonovna, will you make my excuses to your respected mamma. . . . That's right, isn't it? Katerina Ivanovna stands in the place of a mother to you?' Pyotr Petrovitch began with great dignity, though affably.

It was evident that his intentions were friendly.

'Quite so, yes; the place of a mother,' Sonia answered, timidly and hurriedly.

'Then will you make my apologies to her? Through inevitable circumstances I am forced to be absent and shall not be at the dinner table in spite of your mamma's kind invitation.'

'Yes . . . I'll tell her . . . at once.'

And Sonia hastily jumped up from her seat.

'Wait, that's not all,' Pyotr Petrovitch detained her, smiling at her simplicity and ignorance of good manners, 'and you know me little, my dear Sofya Semyonovna, if you suppose I would have ventured to trouble a person like you for a matter of so little consequence affecting myself only. I have another object.'

Sonia sat down hurriedly. Her eyes rested again for an instant on the grey-and-rainbow-coloured notes that remained on the table, but she quickly looked away and fixed her eyes on Pyotr Petrovitch. She felt it horribly indecorous, especially for *her*, to look at another person's money. She stared at the gold eye-glass which Pyotr Petrovitch held in his left hand and at the massive and extremely handsome ring with a yellow stone on his middle finger. But suddenly she looked away and, not knowing where to turn, ended by staring Pyotr Petrovitch again straight in the face. After a pause of still greater dignity he continued:

'I chanced yesterday in passing to exchange a couple of words with

310

Katerina Ivanovna, poor woman. That was sufficient to enable me to ascertain that she is in a position – preternatural, if one may so express it.'

'Yes . . . preternatural. . . .' Sonia hurriedly assented.

'Or it would be simpler and more comprehensible to say, ill.'

'Yes, simpler and more comprehen . . . yes, ill.'

'Quite so. So then from a feeling of humanity and so to speak compassion, I should be glad to be of service to her in any way, foreseeing her unfortunate position. I believe the whole of this poverty-stricken family depends now entirely on you?'

'Allow me to ask,' Sonia rose to her feet, 'did you say something to her yesterday of the possibility of a pension? Because she told me you had undertaken to get her one. Was that true?'

'Not in the slightest, and indeed it's an absurdity! I merely hinted at her obtaining temporary assistance as the widow of an official who had died in the service – if only she has patronage . . . but apparently your late parent had not served his full term and had not indeed been in the service at all of late. In fact, if there could be any hope, it would be very ephemeral, because there would be no claim for assistance in that case, far from it. . . . And she is dreaming of a pension already, he-he-he! . . . A go-ahead lady!'

'Yes, she is. For she is credulous and good-hearted, and she believes everything from the goodness of her heart and . . . and . . . and she is like that . . . yes. . . . You must excuse her,' said Sonia, and again she got up to go.

'But you haven't heard what I have to say.'

'No, I haven't heard,' muttered Sonia.

'Then sit down.' She was terribly confused; she sat down again a third time.

'Seeing her position with her unfortunate little ones, I should be glad, as I have said before, so far as lies in my power, to be of service, that is, so far as is in my power, not more. One might for instance get up a subscription for her, or a lottery, something of the sort, such as is always arranged in such cases by friends or even outsiders desirous of assisting people. It was of that I intended to speak to you; it might be done.'

'Yes, yes . . . God will repay you for it,' faltered Sonia gazing intently at Pyotr Petrovitch.

'It might be, but we will talk of it later. We might begin it to-day, we will talk it over this evening and lay the foundation so to speak. Come to me at seven o'clock. Mr. Lebeziatnikov, I hope, will assist us. But there is one circumstance of which I ought to warn you beforehand and for which I venture to trouble you, Sofya Semyonovna, to come here. In my opinion money cannot be, indeed it's unsafe to put it into Katerina Ivanovna's own hands. The dinner to-day is a proof of that. Though she has not, so to speak, a crust of bread for to-morrow and . . . well, boots or shoes, or anything; she has bought to-day Jamaica rum, and even, I believe, Madeira and . . . and coffee. I saw it as I passed through. To-morrow it will all fall upon you again, they won't have a crust of bread. It's absurd, really, and so, to my thinking, a subscription ought to be raised so that the unhappy widow should not know of the money, but only you, for instance. Am I right?'

'I don't know . . . this is only to-day, once in her life. . . . She was so anxious to do honour, to celebrate the memory. . . . And she is very sensible . . . but just as you think and I shall be very, very . . . they will all be . . . and God will reward . . . and the orphans. . . .'

Sonia burst into tears.

'Very well, then, keep it in mind; and now will you accept for the benefit of your relation the small sum that I am able to spare, from me personally. I am very anxious that my name should not be mentioned in connection with it. Here . . . having so to speak anxieties of my own, I cannot do more . . .'

And Pyotr Petrovitch held out to Sonia a ten-rouble note carefully unfolded. Sonia took it, flushed crimson, jumped up, muttered something and began taking leave. Pyotr Petrovitch accompanied her ceremoniously to the door. She got out of the room at last, agitated and distressed, and returned to Katerina Ivanovna, overwhelmed with confusion.

All this time, Lebeziatnikov had stood at the window or walked about the room, anxious not to interrupt the conversation; when Sonia had gone he walked up to Pyotr Petrovitch and solemnly held out his hand.

'I heard and *saw* everything,' he said, laying stress on the last verb. 'That is honourable, I mean to say, it's humane! You wanted to avoid gratitude, I saw! And although I cannot, I confess, in principle sympathize with private charity, for it not only fails to eradicate the evil but even promotes it, yet I must admit that I saw your action with pleasure – yes, yes, I like it.'

'That's all nonsense,' muttered Pyotr Petrovitch, somewhat disconcerted, looking carefully at Lebeziatnikov.

'No, it's not nonsense! A man who has suffered distress and annoyance as you did yesterday and who yet can sympathize with the misery of others, such a man . . . even though he is making a social mistake – is still deserving of respect! I did not expect it indeed of you, Pyotr Petrovitch, especially as according to your ideas . . . oh, what a drawback your ideas are to you! How distressed you are, for instance, by your ill-luck yesterday,' cried the simple-hearted Lebeziatnikov, who felt a return of affection for Pyotr Petrovitch. 'And what do you want with marriage, with *legal* marriage, my dear, noble Pyotr Petrovitch? Why do you cling to this *legality* of marriage? Well, you may beat me if you like, but I am glad, positively glad it hasn't come off, that you are free, that you are not quite lost for humanity. . . . You see, I've spoken my mind!'

'Because I don't want in your free marriage to be made a fool of and to bring up another man's children, that's why I want legal marriage,' Luzhin replied in order to make some answer.

He seemed preoccupied by something.

'Children? You referred to children,' Lebeziatnikov started off like a warhorse at the trumpet call. 'Children are a social question and a question of first importance, I agree; but the question of children has another solution. Some refuse to have children altogether, because they suggest the institution of the family. We'll speak of children later, but now as to the question of honour. I confess that's my weak point. That horrid, military, Pushkin expression is unthinkable in the dictionary of the future. What does it mean indeed? It's nonsense, there will be no deception in a free marriage! That is only the natural consequence of a legal marriage, so to say, its corrective, a protest. So that indeed it's not humiliating . . . and if I ever, to suppose an absurdity, were to be legally married, I should be positively glad of it. I should say to my wife: "My dear, hitherto I have loved you, now I respect you, for you've shown you can protest!" You laugh! That's because you are incapable of getting away from prejudices. Confound it all! I understand now where the unpleasantness is of being deceived in a legal marriage, but it's simply a despicable consequence of a despicable position in which both are humiliated. When the deception is open, as in a free marriage, then it does not exist, it's unthinkable. Your wife will only prove how she respects you by considering you incapable of opposing her happiness and avenging yourself on her for her new husband. Damn it all! I sometimes dream if I were to be married, pfoo! I mean if I were to marry, legally or not, it's just the same, I should present my wife with a lover if she had not found one for herself. "My dear," I should say, "I love you, but even more than that I desire you to respect me. See!" Am I not right?'

Pyotr Petrovitch sniggered as he listened, but without much merriment. He hardly heard it indeed. He was preoccupied with something else and even Lebeziatnikov at last noticed it. Pyotr Petrovitch seemed excited and rubbed his hands. Lebeziatnikov remembered all this and reflected upon it afterwards.

⇒ TWO ⇐

It would be difficult to explain exactly what could have originated the idea of that senseless dinner in Katerina Ivanovna's disordered brain. Nearly ten of the twenty roubles, given by Raskolnikov for Marmeladov's funeral, were wasted upon it. Possibly Katerina Ivanovna felt obliged to honour the memory of the deceased 'suitably', that all the lodgers and still more Amalia Ivanovna, might know 'that he was in no way their inferior, and perhaps very much their superior', and that no one had the right 'to turn up his nose at him'. Perhaps the chief element was that peculiar 'poor man's pride', which compels many poor people to spend their last savings on some traditional social ceremony, simply in order to do 'like other people', and not to 'be looked down upon'. It is very probable, too, that Katerina Ivanovna longed on this occasion, at the moment when she seemed to be abandoned by everyone, to show those 'wretched contemptible lodgers' that she knew 'how to do things, how to entertain' and that she had been brought up 'in a genteel, she might almost say aristocratic colonel's family' and had not been meant for sweeping floors and washing the children's rags at night. Even the poorest and most broken-spirited people are sometimes liable to these paroxysms of pride and vanity which take the form of an irresistible nervous craving. And Katerina Ivanovna was not broken-spirited; she might have been killed by circumstance, but her spirit could not have been broken, that is, she could not have been intimidated, her will could not be crushed. Moreover Sonia had said with good reason that her mind was unhinged. She could not be said to be insane, but for a year past she had been so harassed that her mind might well be overstrained. The later stages of consumption are apt, doctors tell us, to affect the intellect.

There was no great variety of wines, nor was there Madeira; but wine there was. There was vodka, rum and Lisbon wine, all of the poorest quality but in sufficient quantity. Besides the traditional rice and honey, there were three or four dishes, one of which consisted of pancakes, all prepared in Amalia Ivanovna's kitchen. Two samovars were boiling, that tea and punch might be offered after dinner. Katerina Ivanovna had herself seen to purchasing the provisions, with the help of one of the lodgers, an unfortunate little Pole who had somehow been stranded at Madame

314

Lippevechsel's. He promptly put himself at Katerina Ivanovna's disposal and had been all that morning and all the day before running about as fast as his legs could carry him, and very anxious that everyone should be aware of it. For every trifle he ran to Katerina Ivanovna, even hunting her out at the bazaar, at every instant calling her *'Pani'*. She was heartily sick of him before the end, though she had declared at first that she could not have got on without this 'serviceable and magnanimous man'. It was one of Katerina Ivanovna's characteristics to paint everyone she met in the most glowing colours. Her praises were so exaggerated as sometimes to be embarrassing; she would invent various circumstances to the credit of her new acquaintance and quite genuinely believe in their reality. Then all of a sudden she would be disillusioned and would rudely and contemptuously repulse the person she had only a few hours before been literally adoring. She was naturally of a gay, lively and peace-loving disposition, but from continual failures and misfortunes she had come to desire so *keenly* that all should live in peace and joy and should not *dare* to break the peace, that the slightest jar, the smallest disaster reduced her almost to frenzy, and she would pass in an instant from the brightest hopes and fancies to cursing her fate and raving, and knocking her head against the wall.

Amalia Ivanovna, too, suddenly acquired extraordinary importance in Katerina Ivanovna's eyes and was treated by her with extraordinary respect, probably only because Amalia Ivanovna had thrown herself heart and soul into the preparations. She had undertaken to lay the table, to provide the linen, crockery, etc., and to cook the dishes in her kitchen, and Katerina Ivanovna had left it all in her hands and gone herself to the cemetery. Everything had been well done. Even the table-cloth was nearly clean; the crockery, knives, forks and glasses were, of course, of all shapes and patterns, lent by different lodgers, but the table was properly laid at the time fixed, and Amalia Ivanovna, feeling she had done her work well, had put on a black silk dress and a cap with new mourning ribbons and met the returning party with some pride. This pride, though justifiable, displeased Katerina Ivanovna for some reason: 'as though the table could not have been laid except by Amalia Ivanovna!' She disliked the cap with new ribbons, too. 'Could she be stuck up, the stupid German, because she was mistress of the house, and had consented as a favour to help her poor lodgers! As a favour! Fancy that! Katerina Ivanovna's father who had been a colonel and almost a governor had sometimes had the table set for forty persons, and then anyone like Amalia Ivanovna, or rather Ludwigovna, would not have been allowed in the kitchen.'

Katerina Ivanovna, however, put off expressing her feelings for the time and contented herself with treating her coldly, though she decided inwardly that she would certainly have to put Amalia Ivanovna down and set her in her proper place, for goodness only knew what she was fancying herself. Katerina Ivanovna was irritated too by the fact that hardly any of the lodgers invited had come to the funeral, except the Pole who had just managed to run into the cemetery, while to the memorial dinner the poorest and the most insignificant of them had turned up, the wretched creatures, many of them not quite sober. The older and more respectable of them all, as if by common consent, stayed away. Pyotr Petrovitch Luzhin, for instance, who might be said to be the most respectable of all the lodgers, did not appear, though Katerina Ivanovna had the evening before told all the world, that is Amalia Ivanovna, Polenka, Sonia and the Pole, that he was the most generous, noble-hearted man with a large property and vast connections, who had been a friend of her first husband's, and a guest in her father's house, and that he had promised to use all his influence to secure her a considerable pension. It must be noted that when Katerina Ivanovna exalted anyone's connections and fortune, it was without any ulterior motive, quite disinterestedly, for the mere pleasure of adding to the consequence of the person praised. Probably 'taking his cue' from Luzhin, 'that contemptible wretch Lebeziatnikov had not turned up either. What did he fancy himself? He was only asked out of kindness and because he was sharing the same room with Pyotr Petrovitch and was a friend of his, so that it would have been awkward not to invite him.'

Among those who failed to appear were 'the genteel lady and her old-maidish daughter', who had only been lodgers in the house for the last fortnight, but had several times complained of the noise and uproar in Katerina Ivanovna's room, especially when Marmeladov had come back drunk. Katerina Ivanovna heard this from Amalia Ivanovna who, quarrelling with Katerina Ivanovna, and threatening to turn the whole family out of doors, had shouted at her that they 'were not worth the foot' of the honourable lodgers whom they were disturbing. Katerina Ivanovna determined now to invite this lady and her daughter, 'whose foot she was not worth', and who had turned away haughtily when she casually met them, so that they might know that 'she was more noble in her thoughts and feelings and did not harbour malice', and might see that she was not accustomed to her way of living. She had proposed to make this clear to them at dinner with allusions to her late father's governorship, and also at the same time to hint that it was exceedingly stupid of them to turn away on meeting her. The fat colonel-major (he was really a discharged officer of low rank) was also absent, but it appeared that he had been 'not himself' for the last two days. The party consisted of the Pole, a wretched-looking clerk with a spotty face and a greasy coat, who had not a word to say for himself, and smelt abominably, a deaf and almost blind old man who had once been in the post office and who had been from immemorial ages maintained by someone at Amalia Ivanovna's.

A retired clerk of the commissariat department came, too; he was drunk, had a loud and most unseemly laugh and only fancy – was without a waistcoat! One of the visitors sat straight down to the table without even greeting Katerina Ivanovna. Finally one person having no suit appeared in his dressing-gown, but this was too much, and the efforts of Amalia Ivanovna and the Pole succeeded in removing him. The Pole brought with him, however, two other Poles who did not live at Amalia Ivanovna's and whom no one had seen here before. All this irritated Katerina Ivanovna intensely. 'For whom had they made all these preparations then?' To make room for the visitors the children had not even been laid for at the table; but the two little ones were sitting on a bench in the furthest corner with their dinner laid on a box, while Polenka as a big girl had to look after them, feed them, and keep their noses wiped like well-bred children's.

Katerina Ivanovna, in fact, could hardly help meeting her guest with increased dignity and even haughtiness. She stared at some of them with special severity, and loftily invited them to take their seats. Rushing to the conclusion that Amalia Ivanovna must be responsible for those who were absent, she began treating her with extreme nonchalance, which the latter promptly observed and resented. Such a beginning was no good omen for the end. All were seated at last.

Raskolnikov came in almost at the moment of their return from the cemetery. Katerina Ivanovna was greatly delighted to see him, in the first place because he was one 'educated visitor, and, as everyone knew, was in two years to take a professorship in the university', and secondly because he immediately and respectfully apologized for having been unable to be at the funeral. She positively pounced upon him, and made him sit on her left hand (Amalia Ivanovna was on her right). In spite of her continual anxiety that the dishes should be passed round correctly, and that everyone should taste them, in spite of the agonizing cough which interrupted her every minute and seemed to have grown worse during the last few days, she hastened to pour out in a half-whisper to Raskolnikov all her suppressed feelings and her just indignation at the failure of the dinner, interspersing her remarks with lively and uncontrollable laughter at the expense of her visitors and especially of her landlady.

'It's all that cuckoo's fault! You know whom I mean? Her, her!' Katerina Ivanovna nodded towards the landlady. 'Look at her, she's making round eyes, she feels that we are talking about her and can't understand. Pfoo, the owl! Ha-ha! (Cough-cough-cough.) And what does she put on that cap for? (Cough-cough-cough.) Have you noticed that she wants everyone to consider that she is patronizing me and doing me an honour by being here? I asked her like a sensible woman to invite people, especially those who knew my late husband, and look at the set of fools she has brought! The sweeps! Look at that one with the spotty face. And those wretched Poles, ha-ha-ha! (Cough-cough-cough.) Not one of them has ever poked his nose in here, I've never set eyes on them. What have they come here for, I ask you? There they sit in a row. Hey, *pan!*' she cried suddenly to one of them. 'have you tasted the pancakes? Take some more! Have some beer! Won't you have some vodka? Look, he's jumped up and is making his bows, they must be quite starved, poor things. Never mind, let them eat! They don't make a noise, anyway, though I'm really afraid for our landlady's silver spoons . . . Amalia Ivanovna!' she addressed her suddenly, almost aloud, 'if your spoons should happen to be stolen, I won't be responsible, I warn you! Ha-ha-ha!' She laughed turning to Raskolnikov, and again nodding towards the landlady, in high glee at her sally. 'She didn't understand, she didn't understand again! Look how she sits with her mouth open! An owl, a real owl! An owl in new ribbons, ha-ha-ha!'

Here her laugh turned again to an insufferable fit of coughing that lasted five minutes. Drops of perspiration stood out on her forehead and her handkerchief was stained with blood. She showed Raskolnikov the blood in silence, and as soon as she could get her breath began whispering to him again with extreme animation and a hectic flush of her cheeks.

'Do you know, I gave her the most delicate instructions, so to speak, for inviting that lady and her daughter, you understand of whom I am speaking? It needed the utmost delicacy, the greatest nicety, but she has managed things so that that fool, that conceited baggage, that provincial nonentity, simply because she is the widow of a major, and has come to try and get a pension and to fray out her skirts in the government offices, because at fifty she paints her face (everybody knows it) . . . a creature like that did not think fit to come, and has not even answered the invitation, which the most ordinary good manners required! I can't understand why Pyotr Petrovitch has not come? But where's Sonia? Where has she gone? Ah, there she is at last! what is it, Sonia, where have you been? It's odd that even at your father's funeral you should be so unpunctual. Rodion Romanovitch, make room for her beside you. That's your place, Sonia . . . take what you like. Have some of the cold entrée with jelly, that's the best. They'll bring the pancakes directly. Have they given the children some? Polenka, have you got everything? (Cough-cough-cough.)

That's all right. Be a good girl, Lida, and, Kolya, don't fidget with your feet; sit like a little gentleman. What are you saying, Sonia?'

Sonia hastened to give her Pyotr Petrovitch's apologies, trying to speak loud enough for everyone to hear and carefully choosing the most respectful phrases which she attributed to Pyotr Petrovitch. She added that Pyotr Petrovitch had particularly told her to say that, as soon as he possibly could, he would come immediately to discuss *business* alone with her and to consider what could be done for her, etc., etc.

Sonia knew that this would comfort Katerina Ivanovna, would flatter her and gratify her pride. She sat down beside Raskolnikov; she made him a hurried bow, glancing curiously at him. But for the rest of the time she seemed to avoid looking at him or speaking to him. She seemed absent-minded, though she kept looking at Katerina Ivanovna, trying to please her. Neither she nor Katerina Ivanovna had been able to get mourning; Sonia was wearing dark brown, and Katerina Ivanovna had on her only dress, a dark-striped cotton one.

The message from Pyotr Petrovitch was very successful. Listening to Sonia with dignity, Katerina Ivanovna inquired with equal dignity how Pyotr Petrovitch was, then at once whispered almost aloud to Raskolnikov that it certainly would have been strange for a man of Pyotr Petrovitch's position and standing to find himself in such 'extraordinary company', in spite of his devotion to her family and his old friendship with her father.

'That's why I am so grateful to you, Rodion Romanovitch, that you have not disdained my hospitality, even in such surroundings,' she added almost aloud. 'But I am sure that it was only your special affection for my poor husband that has made you keep your promise.'

Then once more with pride and dignity she scanned her visitors, and suddenly inquired aloud across the table of the deaf man: 'Wouldn't he have some more meat, and had he been given some wine?' The old man made no answer and for a long while could not understand what he was asked, though his neighbours amused themselves by poking and shaking him. He simply gazed about him with his mouth open, which only increased the general mirth.

'What an imbecile? Look, look! Why was he brought? But as to Pyotr Petrovitch, I always had confidence in him,' Katerina Ivanovna continued, 'and, of course, he is not like . . .' with an extremely stern face she addressed Amalia Ivanovna so sharply and loudly that the latter was quite disconcerted, 'not like your dressed-up draggletails whom my father would not have taken as cooks into his kitchen, and my late husband would have done them honour if he had invited them in the goodness of his heart.'

'Yes, he was fond of drink, he was fond of it, he did drink!' cried the commissariat clerk, gulping down his twelfth glass of vodka.

'My late husband certainly had that weakness, and everyone knows it,' Katerina Ivanovna attacked him at once, 'but he was a kind and honourable man, who loved and respected his family. The worst of it was his good nature made him trust all sorts of disreputable people, and he drank with fellows who were not worth the sole of his shoe. Would you believe it, Rodion Romanovitch, they found a gingerbread cock in his pocket; he was dead drunk, but he did not forget the children!'

'A cock? Did you say a cock?' shouted the commissariat clerk.

Katerina Ivanovna did not vouchsafe a reply. She sighed, lost in thought.

'No doubt you think, like everyone, that I was too severe with him,' she went on, addressing Raskolnikov. 'But that's not so! He respected me, he respected me very much! He was a kind-hearted man! And how sorry I was for him sometimes! He would sit in a corner and look at me, I used to feel so sorry for him, I used to want to be kind to him and then would think to myself: "Be kind to him and he will drink again," it was only by severity that you could keep him within bounds.'

'Yes, he used to get his hair pulled pretty often,' roared the commissariat clerk again, swallowing another glass of vodka.

'Some fools would be the better for a good drubbing, as well as having their hair pulled. I am not talking of my late husband now!' Katerina Ivanovna snapped at him.

The flush on her cheeks grew more and more marked, her chest heaved. In another minute she would have been ready to make a scene. Many of the visitors were sniggering, evidently delighted. They began poking the commissariat clerk and whispering something to him. They were evidently trying to egg him on.

'Allow me to ask what you are alluding to,' began the clerk, 'that is to say, whose . . . about whom . . . did you say just now . . .? But I don't care! That's nonsense! Widow! I forgive you. . . . Pass!'

And he took another drink of vodka.

Raskolnikov sat in silence, listening with disgust. He only ate from politeness, just tasting the food that Katerina Ivanovna was continually putting on his plate, to avoid hurting her feelings. He watched Sonia intently. But Sonia became more and more anxious and distressed; she, too, foresaw that the dinner would not end peaceably, and saw with terror Katerina Ivanovna's growing irritation. She knew that she, Sonia, was the chief reason for the 'genteel' ladies' contemptuous treatment of Katerina Ivanovna's invitation. She had heard from Amalia Ivanovna that the mother was positively offended at the invitation and had asked the question: 'How could she let her daughter sit down beside *that young person?*' Sonia had a feeling that Katerina Ivanovna had already heard this and an insult to Sonia meant more to Katerina Ivanovna than an insult to herself, her children, or her father. Sonia knew that Katerina Ivanovna would not be satisfied now, 'till she had shown those draggle-tails that they were both . . .' To make matters worse someone passed Sonia, from the other end of the table, a plate with two hearts pierced with an arrow, cut out of black bread. Katerina Ivanovna flushed crimson and at once said aloud across the table that the man who sent it was 'a drunken ass'!

Amalia Ivanovna was foreseeing something amiss, and at the same time deeply wounded by Katerina Ivanovna's haughtiness, and to restore the good-humour of the company and raise herself in their esteem she began, apropos of nothing, telling a story about an acquaintance of hers 'Karl from the chemist's', who was driving one night in a cab, and that 'the cabman wanted him to kill, and Karl very much begged him not to kill, and wept and clasped hands, and frightened and from fear pierced his heart'. Though Katerina Ivanovna smiled, she observed at once that Ivanovna ought not to tell anecdotes in Russian; the latter was still more offended, and she retorted that her *Vater aus Berlin* was a very important man, and always went with his hands in pockets. Katerina Ivanovna could not restrain herself and laughed so much that Amalia Ivanovna lost patience and could scarcely control herself.

'Listen to the owl!' Katerina Ivanovna whispered at once, her good-humour almost restored, 'she meant to say he kept his hands in his pockets, but she said he put his hands in people's pockets. (Cough-cough) And have you noticed, Rodion Romanovitch, that all these Petersburg foreigners, the Germans especially, are all stupider than we? Can you fancy anyone of us telling how 'Karl from the chemist's' 'pierced his heart from fear' and that the idiot, instead of punishing the cabman, 'clasped his hands and wept, and much begged'? Ah, the fool! And you know she fancies it's very touching and does not suspect how stupid she is! To my thinking that drunken commissariat clerk is a great deal cleverer, anyway one can see that he has addled his brains with drink, but you know, these foreigners are always so well behaved and serious. . . . Look how she sits glaring! She is angry, ha-ha! (Cough-cough-cough.)'

Regaining her good-humour, Katerina Ivanovna began at once telling Raskolnikov that when she had obtained her pension, she intended to open a school for the daughters of gentlemen in her native town T—. This was the first time she had spoken to him of the project, and she launched out into the most alluring details. It suddenly appeared that Katerina Ivanovna had in her hands the very certificate of honour of which Marmeladov had spoken to Raskolnikov in the tavern, when he told him that Katerina Ivanovna, his wife, had danced the shawl dance before the governor and other great personages on leaving school. This certificate of honour was obviously intended now to prove Katerina Ivanovna's right to open a boarding-school; but she had armed herself with it chiefly with the object of overwhelming 'those two stuck-up draggletails' if they came to the dinner, and proving incontestably that Katerina Ivanovna was of the most noble, 'she might even say aristocratic family, a colonel's daughter and was far superior to certain adventuresses who have been so much to the fore of late'. The certificate of honour immediately passed into the hands of the drunken guests, and Katerina Ivanovna did not try to retain it, for it actually contained the statement *en toutes lettres*, that her father was of the rank of a major, and also a companion of an order, so that she really was almost the daughter of a colonel.

Warming up Katerina Ivanovna proceeded to enlarge on the peaceful and happy life they would lead in T—, on the gymnasium teachers whom she would engage to give lessons in her boarding-school, on a most respectable old Frenchman, one Mangot who had taught Katerina Ivanovna herself in old days and was still living in T—, and would no doubt teach in her school on moderate terms. Next she spoke of Sonia who would go with her to T— and help her in all her plans. At this someone at the further end of the table gave a sudden guffaw.

Though Katerina Ivanovna tried to appear to be disdainfully unaware of it, she raised her voice and began at once speaking with conviction of Sonia's undoubted ability to assist her, of 'her gentleness, patience, devotion, generosity and good education', tapping Sonia on the cheek and kissing her warmly twice. Sonia flushed crimson, and Katerina Ivanovna suddenly burst into tears, immediately observing that she was 'nervous and silly, that she was too much upset, that it was time to finish, and as the dinner was over, it was time to hand round the tea'.

At that moment Amalia Ivanovna, deeply aggrieved at taking no part in the conversation, and not being listened to, made one last effort, and with secret misgivings ventured on an exceedingly deep and weighty observation, that 'in the future boarding-school she would have to pay particular attention to *die Wäsche*, and that there certainly must be a good *dame* to look after the linen, and secondly that the young ladies must not novels at night read'.

Katerina Ivanovna, who certainly was upset and very tired, as well as heartily sick of the dinner, at once cut short Amalia Ivanovna, saying 'she knew nothing about it and was talking nonsense, that it was the business of the laundry maid, and not of the directress of a high-class boarding-school to look after *die Wäsche*, and as for novel-reading, that was simply rudeness, and she begged her to be silent'. Amalia Ivanovna fired up and getting angry observed that she only 'meant her good', and that 'she had meant her very good', and that 'it was long since she had paid her *gold* for the lodgings'.

Katerina Ivanovna at once 'set her down', saying that it was a lie to say she wished her good, because only yesterday when her dead husband was lying on the table, she had worried her about the lodgings. To this Amalia Ivanovna very appropriately observed that she had invited those ladies but 'those ladies had not come, because those ladies *are* ladies and cannot come to a lady who is not a lady'. Katerina Ivanovna at once pointed out to her that as she was a slut she could not judge what made one really a lady. Amalia Ivanovna at once declared that her '*Vater aus Berlin* was a very, very important man, and both hands in pockets went, and always used to say: "Poof! poof!" ' and she leapt up from the table to represent her father, sticking her hands in her pockets, puffing her cheeks, and uttering vague sounds resembling 'poof! poof!' amid loud laughter from all the lodgers, who purposely encouraged Amalia Ivanovna, hoping for a fight.

But this was too much for Katerina Ivanovna, and she at once declared, so that all could hear, that Amalia Ivanovna probably never had a father, but was simply a drunken Petersburg Finn, and had certainly once been a cook and probably something worse. Amalia Ivanovna turned as red as a lobster and squealed that perhaps Katerina Ivanovna never had a father, 'but she had a *Vater aus Berlin* and that he wore a long coat and always said poof-poof-poof!'

Katerina Ivanovna observed contemptuously that all knew what her family was and that on that very certificate of honour it was stated in print that her father was a colonel, while Amalia Ivanovna's father – if she really had one – was probably some Finnish milkman, but that probably she never had a father at all, since it was still uncertain whether her name was Amalia Ivanovna or Amalia Ludwigovna.

At this Amalia Ivanovna, lashed to fury, struck the table with her fist, and shrieked that she was Amalia Ivanovna, and not Ludwigovna, 'that her *Vater* was named Johann and that he was a burgomeister, and that Katerina Ivanovna's *Vater* was quite never a burgomeister'. Katerina Ivanovna rose from her chair, and with a stern and apparently calm voice (though she was pale and her chest was heaving) observed that 'if she dared for one moment to set her contemptible wretch of a father on a level with her papa, she, Katerina Ivanovna, would tear her cap off her head and trample it under foot'. Amalia Ivanovna ran about the room, shouting at the top of her voice that she was mistress of the house and that Katerina Ivanovna should leave the lodgings that minute; then she rushed for some reason to collect the silver spoons from the table. There was a great outcry and uproar, the children began crying. Sonia ran to restrain Katerina Ivanovna, but when Amalia Ivanovna shouted something about 'the yellow ticket', Katerina Ivanovna pushed Sonia away, and rushed at the landlady to carry out her threat.

At that minute the door opened, and Pyotr Petrovitch Luzhin appeared on the threshold. He stood scanning the party with severe and vigilant eyes. Katerina Ivanovna rushed to him.

➤ THREE ◄

'PYOTR PETROVITCH,' SHE CRIED, 'protect me . . . you at least! Make this foolish woman understand that she can't behave like this to a lady in misfortune . . . that there is a law for such things. . . . I'll go to the governor-general himself. . . . She shall answer for it. . . . Remembering my father's hospitality protect these orphans.'

'Allow me, madam. . . . Allow me.' Pyotr Petrovitch waved her off. 'Your papa as you are well aware I had not the honour of knowing' (someone laughed aloud) 'and I do not intend to take part in your everlasting squabbles with Amalia Ivanovna. . . . I have come here to speak of my own affairs . . . and I want to have a word with your step-daughter, Sofya . . . Ivanovna, I think it is? Allow me to pass.'

Pyotr Petrovitch, edging by her, went to the opposite corner where Sonia was.

Katerina Ivanovna remained standing where she was, as though thunderstruck. She could not understand how Pytor Petrovitch could deny having enjoyed her father's hospitality. Though she invented it herself, she believed in it firmly by this time. She was struck too by the businesslike, dry and even contemptuous menacing tone of Pyotr Petrovitch. All the clamour gradually died away at his entrance. Not only was this 'serious business man' strikingly incongruous with the rest of the party, but it was evident, too, that he had come upon some matter of consequence, that some exceptional cause must have brought him and that therefore something was going to happen. Raskolnikov, standing beside Sonia, moved aside to let him pass; Pyotr Petrovitch did not seem to notice him. A minute later Lebeziatnikov, too, appeared in the doorway;

he did not come in, but stood still, listening with marked interest, almost wonder, and seemed for a time perplexed.

'Excuse me for interrupting you, but it's a matter of some importance,' Pyotr Petrovitch observed, addressing the company generally. 'I am glad indeed to find other persons present. Amalia Ivanovna, I humbly beg you as mistress of the house to pay careful attention to what I have to say to Sofya Ivanovna. Sofya Ivanovna,' he went on addressing Sonia who was very much surprised and already alarmed, 'immediately after your visit I found that a hundred-rouble note was missing from my table, in the room of my friend Mr. Lebeziatnikov. If in any way whatever you know and will tell us where it is now, I assure you on my word of honour and call all present to witness that the matter shall end there. In the opposite case I shall be compelled to have recourse to very serious measures and then . . . you must blame yourself.'

Complete silence reigned in the room. Even the crying children were still. Sonia stood deadly pale, staring at Luzhin and unable to say a word. She seemed not to understand. Some seconds passed.

'Well, how is it to be then?' asked Luzhin, looking intently at her.

'I don't know. . . . I know nothing about it,' Sonia articulated faintly at last.

'No, you know nothing?' Luzhin repeated and again he paused for some seconds. 'Think a moment, mademoiselle,' he began severely, but still, as it were, admonishing her. 'Reflect, I am prepared to give you time for consideration. Kindly observe this: if I were not so entirely convinced I should not, you may be sure, with my experience venture to accuse you so directly. Seeing that for such direct accusation before witnesses, if false or even mistaken, I should myself in a certain sense be made responsible, I am aware of that. This morning I changed for my own purposes several five-per-cent securities for the sum of approximately three thousand roubles. The account is noted down in my pocket-book. On my return home I proceeded to count the money – as Mr. Lebeziatnikov will bear witness – and after counting two thousand three hundred roubles I put the rest in my pocket-book in my coat pocket. About five hundred roubles remained on the table and among them three notes of a hundred roubles each. At that moment you entered (at my invitation) – and all the time you were present you were exceedingly embarrassed; so that three times you jumped up in the middle of the conversation and tried to make off. Mr. Lebeziatnikov can bear witness to this. You yourself, mademoiselle, probably will not refuse to confirm my statement that I invited you through Mr. Lebeziatnikov, solely in order to discuss with you the hopeless and destitute position of your relative, Katerina Ivanovna (whose dinner I was unable to attend), and the advisability of getting up something of the nature of a subscription, lottery or the like, for her benefit. You thanked me and even shed tears. I describe all this as it took place, primarily to recall it to your mind and secondly to show you that not the slightest detail has escaped my recollection. Then I took a ten-rouble note from the table and handed it to you by way of first instalment of my part for the benefit of your relative. Mr. Lebeziatnikov saw all this. Then I accompanied you to the door – you being still in the same state of embarrassment – after which, being left alone with Mr. Lebeziatnikov I talked to him for ten minutes – then Mr. Lebeziatnikov went out and I returned to the table with the money lying on it, intending to count it and to put it aside, as I proposed doing before. To my surprise one hundred-rouble note had disappeared. Kindly consider the position. Mr. Lebeziatnikov I cannot suspect. I am ashamed to allude to such a supposition. I cannot have made a mistake in my reckoning, for the minute before your entrance I had finished my accounts and found the total correct. You will admit that recollecting your embarrassment, your eagerness to get away and the fact that you kept your hands for some time on the table, and taking into consideration your social position and the habits associated with it, I was, so to say, with horror and positively against my will, *compelled* to entertain a suspicion – a cruel but justifiable suspicion! I will add further and repeat that in spite of my positive conviction, I realize that I run a certain risk in making this accusation, but, as you see, I could not let it pass. I have taken action and I will tell you why: solely, madam, solely owing to your black ingratitude! Why! I invite you for the benefit of your destitute relative, I present you with my donation of ten roubles and you, on the spot, repay me for all that with such an action. It is too bad! You need a lesson. Reflect! Moreover, like a true friend I beg you – and you could have no better friend at this moment – think what you are doing, otherwise I shall be immovable! Well, what do you say?'

'I have taken nothing,' Sonia whispered in terror, 'you gave me ten roubles, here it is, take it.'

Sonia pulled her handkerchief out of her pocket, untied a corner of it, took out the ten-rouble note and gave it to Luzhin.

'And the hundred roubles you do not confess to taking?' he insisted reproachfully, not taking the note.

Sonia looked about her. All were looking at her with such awful stern ironical, hostile eyes. She looked at Raskolnikov . . . he stood against the wall, with his arms crossed, looking at her with glowing eyes.

'Good God!' broke from Sonia.

'Amalia Ivanovna, we shall have to send word to the police and therefore I humbly beg you meanwhile to send for the house porter,' Luzhin said softly and even kindly.

'*Gott der Barmherzige!* I knew she was the thief,' cried Amalia Ivanovna, throwing up her hands.

'You knew it?' Luzhin caught her up, 'then I suppose you had some reason before this for thinking so. I beg you, worthy Amalia Ivanovna, to remember your words which have been uttered before witnesses.'

There was a buzz of loud conversation on all sides. All were in movement.

'What!' cried Katerina Ivanovna, suddenly realizing the position, and she rushed to Luzhin. 'What! You accuse her of stealing? Sonia? Ah, the wretches, the wretches?'

And running to Sonia she flung her wasted arms round her and held her as in a vice.

'Sonia! how dared you take ten roubles from him? Foolish girl! Give it to me! Give me the ten roubles at once – here!'

And snatching the note from Sonia, Katerina Ivanovna crumpled it up and flung it straight into Luzhin's face. It hit him in the eye and fell to the ground. Amalia Ivanovna hastened to pick it up. Pyotr Petrovitch lost his temper.

'Hold that mad woman!' he shouted.

At that moment several other persons, besides Lebeziatnikov appeared in the doorway, among them the two ladies.

'What! Mad? Am I mad? Idiot!' shrieked Katerina Ivanovna. 'You are an idiot yourself, pettifogging lawyer, base man! Sonia, Sonia take his money! Sonia a thief! Why, she'd give away her last penny!' and Katerina Ivanovna broke into hysterical laughter. 'Did you ever see such an idiot!' she turned from side to side. 'And you too?' she suddenly saw the landlady, 'and you too, sausage-eater, you declare that she is a thief, you trashy Prussian hen's leg in a crinoline! She hasn't been out of this room: she came straight from you, you wretch, and sat down beside me, everyone saw her. She sat here, by Rodion Romanovitch. Search her! Since she's not left the room, the money would have to be on her! Search her, search her! But if you don't find it, then excuse me, my dear fellow, you'll answer for it! I'll go to our Sovereign, to our Sovereign, to our gracious Tsar himself, and throw myself at his feet, to-day, this minute! I'm alone in this world! They would let me in ! Do you think they wouldn't? You're wrong, I will get in! I will get in! You reckoned on her meekness! You relied upon that! But I am not so submissive, let me tell you! You've gone too far yourself. Search her, search her!'

And Katerina Ivanovna in a frenzy shook Luzhin and dragged him towards Sonia.

'I am ready, I'll be responsible ... but calm yourself, madam, calm yourself. I see that you are not so submissive! ... Well, well, but as to that . . .' Luzhin muttered, 'that ought to be before the police . . . though indeed there are witnesses enough as it is . . . I am ready. . . . .But in any case it's difficult for a man . . . on account of her sex. . . . But with the help of Amalia Ivanovna . . . though, of course, it's not the way to do things. . . . How is it to be done?'

'As you will! Let anyone who likes search her!' cried Katerina Ivanovna. 'Sonia, turn out your pockets! See! Look, monster, the pocket is empty, here was her handkerchief Here is the other pocket, look! D'you see, d'you see?'

And Katerina Ivanovna turned – or rather snatched – both pockets inside out. But from the right pocket a piece of paper flew out and describing a parabola in the air fell at Luzhin's feet. Everyone saw it, several cried out. Pytor Petrovitch stooped down, picked up the paper in two fingers, lifted it where all could see it and opened it. It was a hundred-rouble note folded in eight. Pyotry Petrovitch held up the note showing it to everyone.

'Thief Out of my lodging. Police, police!' yelled Amalia Ivanovna. 'They must to Siberia be sent! Away!'

Exclamations arose on all sides. Raskolnikov was silent, keeping his eyes fixed on Sonia, except for an occasional rapid glance at Luzhin. Sonia stood still, as though unconscious. She was hardly able to feel surprise. Suddenly the colour rushed to her cheeks; she uttered a cry and hid her face in her hands.

'No, it wasn't I! I didn't take it! I know nothing about it,' she cried with heartening wail, and she ran to Katerina Ivanovna, she clasped her tightly in her arms, as though she would shelter her from the world.

'Sonia! Sonia! I don't believe it! You see, I don't believe it!' she cried in the face of the obvious fact, swaying her to and fro in her arms like a baby, kissing her face continually, then snatching at her hands and kissing them, too, 'you took it! How stupid these people are! Oh dear! You are fools, fools,' she cried, addressing the whole room, 'you don't know, you don't know what a heart she has, what a girl she is! She take it, she? She'd sell her last rag, she'd go barefoot to help you if you needed it, that's what she is! She has the yellow passport because my children were starving, she sold herself for us! Ah, husband husband! Do you see? Do you see? What a memorial dinner for you! Merciful heavens! Defend her, why are you all standing still? Rodion Romanovitch, why don't you stand up for her? Do you believe it, too? You are not worth her little finger, all of you together! Good God! Defend her now, at least!'

The wail of the poor, consumptive, helpless woman seemed to produce a great effect on her audience. The agonized, wasted, consumptive face, the parched blood-stained lips, the hoarse voice, the tears unrestrained as a child's, the trustful, childish and yet despairing prayer for help was so piteous that everyone seemed to feel for her. Pyotr Petrovitch at any rate was at once moved to *compassion*.

'Madam, madam, this incident does not reflect upon you!' he cried impressively, 'no one would take upon himself to accuse you of being an instigator or even an accomplice in it, especially as you have proved her guilt by turning out her pockets showing that you had no previous idea of it. I am most ready, most ready to show compassion, if poverty, so to speak, drove Sofya Ivanovna to it, but why did you refuse to confess, mademoiselle? Were you afraid of the disgrace? The first step? You lost your head, perhaps? One can quite understand it. . . . But how could you have lowered yourself to such an action? Gentlemen,' he addressed the whole company, 'gentlemen! Compassionating and, so to say, commiserating these people, I am ready to overlook it even now in spite of the personal insult lavished upon me! And may this disgrace be a lesson to you for the future,' he said, addressing Sonia, 'and I will carry the matter no further. Enough!'

Pyotyr Petrovitch stole a glance at Raskolnikov. Their eyes met, and the fire in Raskolnikov's seemed ready to reduce him to ashes. Meanwhile Katerina Ivanovna apparently heard nothing. She was kissing and hugging Sonia like a madwoman. The children, too, were embracing Sonia on all sides, and Polenka – though she did not fully understand what was wrong – was drowned in tears and shaking with sobs, as she hid her pretty little face, swollen with weeping, on Sonia's shoulder.

'How vile!' a loud voice cried suddenly in the doorway.

Pyotr Petrovitch looked round quickly.

'What vileness!' Lebeziatnikov repeated, staring him straight in the face.

Pyotr Petrovitch gave a positive start – all noticed it and recalled it afterwards. Lebeziatnikov strode into the room.

'And you dared to call me as a witness?' he said, going up to Pyotr Petrovitch.

'What do you mean? What are you talking about?' muttered Luzhin.

'I mean that you . . . are a slanderer, that's what my words mean!' Lebeziatnikov said hotly, looking sternly at him with his short-sighted eyes.

He was extremely angry. Raskolnikov gazed intently at him, as though seizing and weighing each word. Again there was a silence. Pyotr Petrovitch indeed seemed almost dumbfounded for the first moment.

'If you mean that for me . . .' he began, stammering. 'But what's the matter with you? Are you out of your mind?'

'I'm in my mind, but you are a scoundrel! Ah, how vile! I have heard everything. I kept waiting on purpose to understand it, for I must own even now it is not quite logical. . . . What you have done it all for I can't understand.'

'Why, what have I done then? Give over talking in your nonsensical riddles! Or maybe you are drunk!'

'You may be a drunkard perhaps, vile man, but I am not! I never touch vodka, for it's against my convictions. Would you believe it, he, he himself, with his own hands gave Sofya Semyonovna that hundred-rouble note – I saw it, I was a witness, I'll take my oath! He did it, he!' repeated Lebeziatnikov, addressing all.

'Are you crazy, milksop?' squealed Luzhin. 'She is herself before you – she herself here declared just now before everyone that I gave her only ten roubles. How could I have given it to her?'

'I saw it, I saw it,' Lebeziatnikov repeated, 'and though it is against my principles, I am ready this very minute to take any oath you like before the court, for I saw how you slipped it in her pocket. Only like a fool I thought you did it out of kindness! When you were saying good-bye to her at the door, while you held her hand in one hand, with the other, the left, you slipped the note into her pocket. I saw it, I saw it!'

Luzhin turned pale.

'What lies!' he cried impudently, 'why, how could you, standing by the window, see the note? You fancied it with your short-sighed eyes. You are raving!'

'No, I didn't fancy it. And though I was standing some way off, I saw it all. And though it certainly would be hard to distinguish a note from the window – that's true – I knew for certain that it was a hundred-rouble note, because, when you were going to give Sofya Semyonovna ten roubles, you took up from the table a hundred-rouble note (I saw it because I was standing near then, and an idea struck me at once, so that I did not forget you had it in your hand). You folded it and kept it in your hand all the time. I didn't think of it again until, when you were getting up, you changed it from your right hand to your left and nearly dropped it! I noticed it because the same idea struck me again, that you meant to do her a kindness without my seeing. You can fancy how I watched you and I saw how you succeeded in slipping it into her pocket. I saw it, I saw it, I'll take my oath.'

Lebeziatnikov was almost breathless. Exclamations arose on all hands, chiefly expressive of wonder, but some were menacing in tone. They all crowded round Pyotr Petrovitch. Katerina Ivanovna flew to Lebeziatnikov.

'I was mistaken in you! Protect her! You are the only one to take her part! She is an orphan, God has sent you!'

Katerina Ivanovna, hardly knowing what she was doing, sank on her knees before him.

'A pack of nonsense!' yelled Luzhin, roused to fury, 'it's all nonsense you've been talking! "An idea struck you, you didn't think, you noticed" – what does it does amount to? So I gave it to her on the sly on purpose? What for? With what object? What have I to do with this . . .?'

'What for? That's what I can't understand, but that what I am telling you is the fact, that's certain! So far from my being mistaken, you infamous criminal man, I remember how, on account of it, a question occurred to me at once, just when I was thanking you and pressing your hand. What made you put it secretly in her pocket? Why you did it secretly, I mean? Could it be simply to conceal it from me, knowing that my convictions are opposed to yours and that I do not approve of private benevolence, which effects no radical cure. Well, I decided that you really were ashamed of giving such a large sum before me. Perhaps, too, I thought, he wants to give her a surprise, when she finds a whole hundred-rouble note in her pocket. (For I know, some benevolent people are very fond of decking out their charitable actions in that way.) Then the idea struck me, too, that you wanted to test her, to see whether, when she found it, she would come to thank you. Then, too, that you wanted to avoid thanks and that, as the saying is, your right hand should not know . . . something of that sort, in fact. I thought of so many possibilities that I put off considering it, but still thought it indelicate to show you that I knew your secret. But another idea struck me again that Sofya Semyonovna might easily lose the money before she noticed it, that was why I decided to come in here to call her out of the room and to tell her that you put a hundred roubles in her pocket. But on my way I went first to Madame Kobilatnikov's to take them the "General Treatise on the Positive Method" and especially to recommend Piderit's article (and also Wagner's); then I come on here and what a state of things I find! Now could I, could I, have all these ideas and reflections if I had not seen you put the hundred-rouble note in her pocket?'

When Lebeziatnikov finished his long-winded harangue with the logical deduction at the end, he was quite tired, and the perspiration streamed from his face. He could not, alas, even express himself correctly in Russian, though he knew no other language, so that he was quite exhausted, almost emaciated after this heroic exploit. But his speech produced a powerful effect. He had spoken with such vehemence, with such conviction that everyone obviously believed him. Pyotr Petrovitch felt that things were going badly with him.

'What it is to do with me if silly ideas did occur to you?' he shouted, 'that's no evidence. You may have dreamt it, that's all! And I tell you, you are lying, sir. You are lying and slandering from some spite against me, simply from pique, because I did not agree with your free-thinking, godless, social propositions!'

But this retort did not benefit Pyotr Petrovitch. Murmurs of disapproval were heard on all sides.

'Ah, that's your line now, is it!' cried Lebeziatnikov, 'that's nonsense! Call the police and I'll take my oath! There's only one thing I can't understand: what made him risk such a contemptible action. Oh, pitiful, despicable man!'

'I can explain why he risked such an action, and if necessary I, too, will swear to it,' Raskolnikov said at last in a firm voice, and he stepped forward.

He appeared to be firm and composed. Everyone felt clearly from the very look of him that he really knew about it and that the mystery would be solved.

'Now I can explain it all to myself,' said Raskolnikov, addressing Lebeziatnikov. 'From the very beginning of the business, I suspected that there was some scoundrelly intrigue at the bottom of it. I began to suspect it from some special circumstances known to me only, which I will explain at once to everyone: they account for everything. Your valuable evidence has finally made everything clear to me. I beg all, all to listen. This gentleman (he pointed to Luzhin) was recently engaged to be married to a young lady – my sister, Avdotya Romanovna Raskolnikov. But coming to Petersburg he quarrelled with me, the day before yesterday, at our first meeting and I drove him out of my room – I have two witnesses to prove it. He is a very spiteful man. . . . The day before yesterday I did not know that he was staying here, in your room, and that consequently on the very day we quarrelled – the day before yesterday – he saw me give Katerina Ivanovna some money for the funeral, as a friend of the late Mr. Marmeladov. He at once wrote a note to my mother and informed her that I had given away all my money, not to Katerina Ivanovna but to Sofya Semyonovna, and referred in a most contemptible way to the . . . character of Sofya Semyonovna, that is, hinted at the character of my attitude to Sofya Semyonovna. All this you understand was with the object of dividing me from my mother and sister, by insinuating that I was squandering on unworthy objects the money which they had sent me and which was all they had. Yesterday evening, before my mother and sister and in his presence, I declared that I had given the money to Katerina Ivanovna for the funeral and not to Sofya Semyonovna and that I had no acquaintance with Sofya Semyonovna and he had never seen her before, indeed. At the same time I added that he, Pyotr Petrovitch Luzhin, with all his virtues, was not worth Sofya Semyonovna's little finger, though he spoke so ill of her. To his question – would I let Sofya Semyonovna sit down beside my sister, I answered that I had already done so that day. Irritated that my mother and sister were unwilling to quarrel with me at his insinuations, he gradually began being unpardonably rude to them. A final rupture took place and he was turned out of the house. All this happened yesterday evening. Now I beg your special attention: consider: if he had now succeeded in proving that Sofya Semyonovna was a thief, he would have shown my mother and sister that he was almost right in his suspicions, that he had reason to be angry at my putting my sister on a level with Sofya Semyonovna, that, in attacking me, he was protecting and preserving the honour of my sister, his betrothed. In fact he might even, through all this, have been able to estrange me from my family, and no doubt he hoped to be restored to favour with them; to say nothing of revenging himself on me personally, for he has grounds for supposing that the honour and happiness of Sofya Semyonovna are very precious to me. That was what he was working for! That's how I understand it. That's the whole reason for it and there can be no other!'

It was like this, or somewhat like this, that Raskolnikov wound up his speech which was followed very attentively, though often interrupted by exclamations from his audience. But in spite of interruptions he spoke clearly, calmly, exactly, firmly. His decisive voice, his tone of conviction and his stern face made a great impression on everyone.

'Yes, yes, that's it,' Lebeziatnikov assented gleefully, 'that must be it, for he asked me, as soon as Sofya Semyonovna came into our room, whether you were here, whether I had seen you among Katerina Ivanovna's guests. He called me aside to the window and asked me in secret. It was essential for him that you should be here! That's it, that's it!'

Luzhin smiled contemptuously and did not speak. But he was very pale. He seemed to be deliberating on some means of escape. Perhaps he would have been glad to give up everything and get away, but at the moment this was scarcely possible. It would have implied admitting the truth of the accusations brought against him. Moreover the company, which had already been excited by drink, was now too much stirred to allow it. The commissariat clerk, though indeed he had not grasped the whole position, was shouting louder than anyone and was making some suggestions very unpleasant to Luzhin. But not all those present were drunk; lodgers came in from all the rooms. The three Poles were tremendously excited and were continually shouting at him: 'The *pan* is a *lajdak!*' and muttering threats in Polish. Sonia had been listening with strained attention, though she too seemed unable to grasp it all; she seemed as though she had just returned to consciousness. She did not take her eyes off Raskolnikov, feeling that all her safety lay in him. Katerina Ivanovna breathed hard and painfully and seemed fearfully exhausted. Amalia Ivanovna stood looking more stupid than anyone, with her mouth wide open, unable to make out what had happened. She only saw that Pyotr Petrovitch had somehow come to grief.

Raskolnikov was attempting to speak again, but they did not let him. Everyone was crowding round Luzhin with threats and shouts of abuse. But Pyotr Petrovitch was not intimidated. Seeing that his accusation of Sonia had completely failed, he had recourse to insolence:

'Allow me, gentlemen, allow me! Don't squeeze, let me pass!' he said, making his way through the crowd. 'And no threats, if you please! I assure you it will be useless, you will gain nothing by it. On the contrary, you'll have to answer, gentlemen, for violently obstructing the course of justice. The thief has been more than unmasked, and I shall prosecute. Our judges are not so blind and . . . not so drunk, and will not believe the testimony of two notorious infidels, agitators, and atheists, who accuse me from motives of personal revenge which they are foolish enough to admit. . . . Yes, allow me to pass!'

'Don't let me find a trace of you in my room! Kindly leave at once, and everything is at an end between us! When I think of the trouble I've been taking, the way I've been expounding . . . all this fortnight!'

'I told you myself to-day that I was going, when you tried to keep me; now I will simply add that you are a fool. I advise you to see a doctor for your brains and your short sight. Let me pass, gentlemen!'

He forced his way through. But the commissariat clerk was unwilling to let him off so easily: he picked up a glass from the table, brandished it in the air and flung it at Pyotr Petrovitch; but the glass flew straight at Amalia Ivanovna. She screamed, and the clerk, overbalancing, fell heavily under the table. Pyotr Petrovitch made his way to his room and half an hour later had left the house. Sonia, timid by nature, had felt before that day that she could be ill-treated more easily than anyone, and that she could be wronged with impunity. Yet till that moment she had fancied that she might escape misfortune by care, gentleness and submissiveness before everyone. Her disappointment was too great. She could, of course, bear with patience and almost without murmur anything, even this. But for the first minute she felt it too bitter. In spite of her triumph and her justification – when her first terror and stupefaction had passed and she could understand it all clearly – the feeling of her helplessness and of the wrong done to her made her heart throb with anguish and she was overcome with hysterical weeping. At last, unable to bear any more, she rushed out of the room and ran home, almost immediately after Luzhin's departure. When amidst loud laughter the glass flew at Amalia Ivanovna, it was more than the landlady could endure. With a shriek she rushed like a fury at Katerina Ivanovna, considering her to blame for everything.

'Out of my lodgings! At once! Quick march!'

And with these words she began snatching up everything she could lay her hands on that belonged to Katerina Ivanovna, and throwing it on the floor. Katerina Ivanovna, pale, almost fainting, and gasping for breath, jumped up from the bed where she had sunk in exhaustion and darted at Amalia Ivanovna. But the battle was too unequal: the landlady waved her away like a feather.

'What! As though that godless calumny was not enough – this vile creature attacks me! What! On the day of my husband's funeral I am turned out of my lodging! After eating my bread and salt she turned me out into the street, with my orphans! Where am I to go?' wailed the poor woman, sobbing and gasping. 'Good God!' she cried with flashing eyes, 'is there no justice upon earth? Whom should you protect if not us orphans? We shall see! There is law and justice on earth, there is, I will find it! Wait a bit, godless creature! Polenka, stay with the children, I'll come back. Wait for me, if you have to wait in the street. We will see whether there is justice on earth!'

And throwing over her head that green shawl which Marmeladov had mentioned to Raskolnikov, Katerina Ivanovna squeezed her way through the disorderly and drunken crowd of lodgers who still filled the room, and, wailing and tearful, she ran into the street – with a vague intention of going at once somewhere to find justice. Polenka with the two little ones in her arms crouched, terrified, on the trunk in the corner of the room, where she waited trembling for her mother to come back. Amalia Ivanovna raged about the room, shrieking, lamenting and throwing everything she came across on the floor. The lodgers talked incoherently, some commented to the best of their ability on what had happened, other quarrelled and swore at one another, while others struck up a song. . . .

'Now it's time for me to go,' thought Raskolnikov. 'Well, Sofya Semyonovna, we shall see what you'll say now!'

And he set off in the direction of Sonia's lodgings.

✎ FOUR ✎

Raskolnikov has been a vigorous and active champion of Sonia against Luzhin, although he had such a load of horror and anguish in his own heart. But having gone through so much in the morning, he found a sort of relief in a change of sensations, apart from the strong personal feeling which impelled him to defend Sonia. He was agitated too, especially at some moments, by the thought of his approaching interview with Sonia: he *had* to tell her who had killed Lizaveta. He knew the terrible suffering it would be to him and, as it were, brushed away the thought of it. So when he cried as he left Katerina Ivanovna's, 'Well, Sofya Semyonovna, we shall see what you'll say now!' he was still superficially excited, still vigorous and defiant from his triumph over Luzhin. But, strange to say, by the time he reached Sonia's lodging, he felt a sudden impotence and fear. He stood still in hesitation at the door, asking himself the strange question: 'Must he tell her who killed Lizaveta?' It was a strange question because he felt at the very time not only that he could not help telling her, but also that he could not put off the telling. He did not yet know why it must be so, he only *felt* it, and the agonizing sense of his impotence before the inevitable almost crushed him. To cut short his hesitation and suffering, he quickly opened the door and looked at Sonia from the doorway. She was sitting with her elbows on the table and her face in her hands, but seeing Raskolnikov she got up at once and came to meet him as though she were expecting him.

'What would have become of me but for you?' she said quickly, meeting him in the middle of the room.

Evidently she was in haste to say this to him. It was what she had been waiting for.

Raskolnikov went to the table and sat down on the chair from which she had only just risen. She stood facing him, two steps away, just as she had done the day before.

'Well, Sonia?' he said, and felt that his voice was trembling, 'it was all due to "your social position and the habits associated with it". Did you understand that just now?'

Her face showed her distress.

'Only don't talk to me as you did yesterday,' she interrupted him. 'Please don't begin it. There is misery enough without that.'

She made haste to smile, afraid that he might not like the reproach.

'I was silly to come away from there. What is happening there now? I wanted to go back directly, but I kept thinking that . . . you would come.'

He told her that Amalia Ivanovna was turning them out of their lodging and that Katerina Ivanovna had run off somewhere 'to seek justice'.

'My God!' cried Sonia, 'let's go at once. . . .'

And she snatched up her cape.

'It's everlastingly the same thing!' cried Raskolnikov, irritably. 'You've no thought except for them! Stay a little with me.'

'But . . . Katerina Ivanovna?'

'You won't lose Katerina Ivanovna, you may be sure, she'll come to you herself since she has run out,' he added peevishly. 'If she doesn't find you here, you'll be blamed for it. . . .'

Sonia sat down in painful suspense. Raskolnikov was silent, gazing at the floor and deliberating.

'This time Luzhin did not want to prosecute you,' he began, not looking at Sonia, 'but if he had wanted to, if it had suited his plans, he would have sent you to prison if it had not been for Lebeziatnikov and me. Ah?'

'Yes,' she assented in a faint voice. 'Yes,' she repeated, preoccupied and distressed.

'But I might easily not have been there. And it was quite an accident Lebeziatnikov's turning up.'

Sonia was silent.

'And if you'd gone to prison, what then? Do you remember what I said yesterday?'

Again she did not answer. He waited.

'I thought you would cry out again, "Don't speak of it, leave off ".' Raskolnikov gave a laugh, but rather a forced one. 'What, silence again?' he asked a minute later. 'We must talk about something, you know. It would be interesting for me to know how you would decide a certain "problem " as Lebeziatnikov would say.' (He was beginning to lose the thread.) 'No, really, I am serious. Imagine, Sonia, that you had known all Luzhin's intentions beforehand. Known, that is, for a fact, that they would be the ruin of Katerina Ivanovna and the children and yourself thrown in – since you don't count yourself for anything – Polenka too . . . for she'll go the same way. Well, if suddenly it all depended on your decision whether he or they should go on living, that is whether Luzhin should go on living and doing wicked things, or Katerina Ivanovna should die? How would you decide which of them was to die? I ask you!'

Sonia looked uneasily at him. There was something peculiar in this hesitating question, which seemed approaching something in a round-about way.

'I felt that you were going to ask some question like that,' she said, looking inquisitively at him.

'I dare say you did. But how is it to be answered?'

'Why do you ask about what could not happen?' said Sonia reluctantly.

'Then it would be better for Luzhin to go on living and doing wicked things? You haven't dared to decide even that!'

'But I can't know the Divine Providence. . . . And why do you ask what can't be answered? What's the use of such foolish questions? How could it happen that it should depend on my decision – who has made me a judge to decide who is to live and who is not to live?'

'Oh, if the Divine Providence is to be mixed up in it, there is no doing anything,' Raskolnikov grumbled morosely.

'You'd better say straight out what you want!' Sonia cried in distress. 'You are leading up to something again. . . . Can you have come simply to torture me?'

She could not control herself and began crying bitterly. He looked at her in gloomy misery. Five minutes passed.

'Of course you're right, Sonia,' he said softly at last. He was suddenly changed. His tone of assumed arrogance and helpless defiance was gone. Even his voice was suddenly weak. 'I told you yesterday that I was not coming to ask forgiveness and almost the first thing I've said is to ask forgiveness. . . . I said that about Luzhin and Providence for my own sake. I was asking forgiveness, Sonia. . . .'

He tried to smile, but there was something helpless and incomplete in his pale smile. He bowed his head and hid his face in his hands.

And suddenly a strange surprising sensation of a sort of bitter hatred for Sonia passed through his heart. As it were wondering and frightened of this sensation, he raised his head and looked intently at her; but he met her uneasy and painfully anxious eyes fixed on him; there was love in them; his hatred vanished like a phantom. It was not the real feeling; he had taken the one feeling for the other. It only meant that *that* minute had come.

He hid his face in his hands again and bowed his head. Suddenly he turned pale, got up from his chair, looked at Sonia and without uttering a word sat down mechanically on her bed.

His sensations that moment were terribly like the moment when he had stood over the old woman with the axe in his hand and felt that 'he must not lose another minute'.

'What's the matter?' asked Sonia, dreadfully frightened.

He could not utter a word. This was not at all, not at all the way he had intended to 'tell' and he did not understand what was happening to him now. She went up to him softly, sat down on the bed beside him and waited, not taking her eyes off him. Her heart throbbed and sank. It was unendurable; he turned his deadly pale face to her. His lips worked, helplessly struggling to utter something. A pang of terror passed through Sonia's heart.

'What's the matter?' she repeated, drawing a little away from him.

'Nothing, Sonia, don't be frightened. . . . It's nonsense. It really is nonsense, if you think of it,' he muttered, like a man in delirium. 'Why have I come to torture you?' he added suddenly, looking at her. 'Why, really? I keep asking myself that question, Sonia. . . .'

He had perhaps been asking himself that question a quarter of an hour before, but now he spoke helplessly, hardly knowing what he said and feeling a continual tremor all over.

'Oh, how you are suffering!' she uttered in distress, looking intently at him.

'It's all nonsense. . . . Listen, Sonia.' He suddenly smiled, a pale helpless smile for two seconds. 'You remember what I meant to tell you yesterday?'

Sonia waited uneasily.

'I said as I went away that perhaps I was saying good-bye for ever, but that if I came to-day I would tell you who . . . who killed Lizaveta.'

She began trembling all over.

'Well, here I've come to tell you.'

'Then you really meant it yesterday?' she whispered with difficulty. 'How do you know?' she asked quickly, as though suddenly regaining her reason.

Sonia's face grew paler and paler, and she breathed painfully.

'I know.'

She paused a minute.

'Have they found him?' she asked timidly.

'No.'

'Then how do you know about *it*?' she asked again, hardly audibly and again after a minute's pause.

He turned to her and looked very intently at her.

'Guess,' he said, with the same distorted helpless smile.

A shudder passed over.

'But you . . . why do you frighten me like this?' she said, smiling like a child.

'I must be a great friend of *his* . . . since I know,' Raskolnikov went on, still gazing into her face, as though he could not turn his eyes away. 'He . . . did not mean to kill that Lizaveta . . . he . . . killed her accidentally. . . . He meant to kill the old woman when she was alone and he went there . . . and then Lizaveta came in . . . he killed her too.'

Another awful moment passed. Both still gazed at one another.

'You can't guess, then?' he asked suddenly, feeling as though he were flinging himself down from a steeple.

'N-no . . .' whispered Sonia.

'Take a good look.'

As soon as he had said this again, the same familiar sensation froze his heart. He looked at her and all at once seemed to see in her face the face of Lizaveta. He remembered clearly the expression in Lizaveta's face, when he approached her with the axe and she stepped back to the wall, putting out her hand, with childish terror in her face, looking as little children do when they begin to be frightened of something, looking intently and uneasily at what frightens them, shrinking back and holding out their little hands on the point of crying. Almost the same thing happened now to Sonia. With the same helplessness and the same terror, she looked at him for a while and, suddenly putting out her left hand, pressed her fingers faintly against his breast and slowly began to get up from the bed, moving further from him and keeping her eyes fixed even more immovably on him. Her terror infected him. The same fear showed itself on his face. In the same way he stared at her and almost with the same *childish* smile.

'Have you guessed?' he whispered at last.

'Good God!' broke in an awful wail from her bosom.

She sank helplessly on the bed and with her face in the pillows, but a moment later she got up, moved quickly to him, seized both his hands and, gripping them tightly in her thin fingers, began looking into his face again with the same intent stare. In this last desperate look she tried to look into him and catch some last hope. But there was no hope; there was no doubt remaining; it was all true! Later on, indeed, when she recalled that moment, she thought it strange and wondered why she had seen at once that there was no doubt. She could not have said, for instance, that she had foreseen something of the sort – and yet now, as soon as he told her, she suddenly fancied that she had really foreseen this very thing.

'Stop, Sonia, enough! Don't torture me,' he begged her miserably.

It was not at all, not at all like this he had thought of telling her, but this is how it happened.

She jumped up, seeming not to know what she was doing, and, wringing her hands, walked into the middle of the room; but quickly went back and sat down again beside him, her shoulder almost touching his. All of a sudden she started as though she had been stabbed, uttered a cry and fell on her knees before him, she did not know why.

'What have you done – what have you done to yourself?' she said in despair, and, jumping up, she flung herself on his neck, threw her arms round him, and held him tightly.

Raskolnikov drew back and looked at her with a mournful smile.

'You are a strange girl, Sonia – you kiss me and hug me when I tell you about that. . . . You don't think what you are doing.'

'There is no one – no one in the whole world now so unhappy as you!' she cried in a frenzy, not hearing what he said, and she suddenly broke into violent hysterical weeping.

A feeling long unfamiliar to him flooded his heart and softened it at once. He did not struggle against it. Two tears started into his eyes and hung on his eyelashes.

'Then you won't leave me, Sonia?' he said, looking at her almost with hope.

'No, no, never, nowhere!' cried Sonia. 'I will follow you, I will follow you everywhere. Oh, my God! Oh, how miserable I am! . . . Why, why didn't I know you before? Why didn't you come before? Oh, dear!'

'Here I have come.'

'Yes, now! What's to be done now? . . . Together, together!' she repeated as it were unconsciously, and she hugged him again. 'I'll follow you to Siberia!'

He recoiled at this, and the same hostile, almost haughty smile came on to his lips.

'Perhaps I don't want to go to Siberia yet, Sonia,' he said.

Sonia looked at him quickly.

Again after her first passionate, agonizing sympathy for the unhappy man the terrible idea of the murder overwhelmed her. In his changed tone she seemed to hear the murderer speaking. She looked at him bewildered. She knew nothing as yet, why, how, with what object it had been. Now all these questions rushed at once into her mind. And again she could not believe it: 'He, he is a murderer! Could it be true?'

'What's the meaning of it? Where am I?' she said in complete bewilderment, as though still unable to recover herself. 'How could you, you, a man like you? . . . How could you bring yourself to it? . . . What does it mean?'

'Oh, well – to plunder. Leave off, Sonia,' he answered wearily, almost with vexation.

Sonia stood as though struck dumb, but suddenly she cried:

'You were hungry! It was . . . to help your mother? Yes?'

'No, Sonia, no,' he muttered, turning away and hanging his head. 'I was not so hungry. . . . I certainly did want to help my mother, but . . . that's not the real thing either. . . . Don't torture me, Sonia.'

Sonia clasped her hands.

'Could it, could it all be true? Good God, what a truth! Who could believe it? And how could you give away your last farthing and yet rob and murder! Ah,' she cried suddenly, 'that money you gave Katerina Ivanovna . . . that money . . . Can that money . . .'

'No, Sonia,' he broke in hurriedly, 'that money was not it. Don't worry yourself! That money my mother sent me and it came when I was ill, the day I gave it to you. . . . Razumihin saw it . . . he received it for me. . . . That money was mine – my own.'

Sonia listened to him in bewilderment and did her utmost to comprehend.

'And *that* money. . . . I don't even know really whether there was any money,' he added softly, as though reflecting. 'I took a purse off her neck, made of chamois leather . . . a purse stuffed full of something . . . but I didn't look in it; I suppose I hadn't time. . . . And the things – chains and trinkets – I buried under a stone with the purse next morning in a yard off the V – Prospect. They are all there now. . . .'

Sonia strained every nerve to listen.

'Then why . . . why, you said you did it to rob, but you took nothing?' she asked quickly, catching at a straw.

'I don't know. . . . I haven't yet decided whether to take that money or not,' he said, musing again; and, seeming to wake up with a start, he gave a brief ironical smile. 'Ach, what silly stuff I am talking, eh?'

The thought flashed through Sonia's mind, wasn't he mad? But she dismissed it at once. 'No, it was something else.' She could make nothing of it, nothing.

'Do you know, Sonia,' he said suddenly with conviction, 'let me tell you: if I'd simply killed her because I was hungry,' laying stress on every word and looking enigmatically but sincerely at her, 'I should be *happy* now. You must believe that! What would it matter to you,' he cried a moment later with a sort of despair, 'what would it matter to you if I were to confess that I did wrong? What do you gain by such a stupid triumph over me? Ah, Sonia, was it for that I've come to you to-day?'

Again Sonia tried to say something, but did not speak.

'I asked you to go with me yesterday because you are all I have left.'

'Go where?' asked Sonia, timidly.

'Not to steal and not to murder, don't be anxious,' he smiled bitterly. 'We are so different. . . . And you know, Sonia, it's only now, only this moment that I understand *where* I asked you to go with me yesterday! Yesterday when I said it I did not know where. I asked you for one thing, I came to you for one thing – not to leave me. You won't leave me, Sonia?'

She squeezed his hand.

'And why, why did I tell her? Why did I let her know?' he cried a minute later in despair, looking with infinite anguish at her. 'Here you expect an explanation from me, Sonia; you are sitting and waiting for it, I see that. But what can I tell you? You won't understand and will only suffer misery . . . on my account! Well, you are crying and embracing me again. Why do you do it? Because I couldn't bear my burden and have come to throw it on another: you suffer too, and I shall feel better! And can you love such a mean wretch?'

'But aren't you suffering, too?' cried Sonia.

Again a wave of the same feeling surged into his heart, and again for an instant softened it.

'Sonia, I have a bad heart, take note of that. It may explain a great deal. I have come because I am bad. There are men who wouldn't have come. But I am a coward and . . . a mean wretch. But . . . never mind! That's not the point. I must speak now, but I don't know how to begin.'

He paused and sank into thought.

'Ach, we are so different,' he cried again, 'we are not alike. And why, why did I come? I shall never forgive myself that.'

'No, no, it was a good thing you came,' cried Sonia. 'It's better I should know, far better!'

He looked at her with anguish.

'What if it were really that?' he said, as though reaching a conclusion. 'Yes, that's what it was! I wanted to become a Napoleon, that is why I killed her. . . . Do you understand now?'

'N-no,' Sonia whispered naïvely and timidly. 'Only speak, speak, I shall understand *in myself*' she kept begging him.

'You'll understand? Very well, we shall see!' He paused and was for some time lost in meditation.

'It was like this: I asked myself one day this question – what if Napoleon, for instance, had happened to be in my place, and if he had not had Toulon nor Egypt nor the passage of Mont Blanc to begin his career with, but instead of all those picturesque and monumental things, there had simply been some ridiculous old hag, a pawnbroker, who had to be murdered too to get money from her trunk (for his career, you understand). Well, would he have brought himself to that if there had been no other means? Wouldn't he have felt a pang at its being so far from monumental and . . . and sinful, too? Well, I must tell you that I worried myself fearfully over that "question" so that I was awfully ashamed when I guessed at last (all of a sudden, somehow) that it would not have given him the least pang, that it would not even have struck him that it was not monumental . . . that he would not have seen that there was anything in it to pause over, and that, if he had had no other way, he would have strangled her in a minute without thinking about it! Well, I too . . . left off thinking about it . . . murdered her, following her example. And that's exactly how it was! Do you think it funny? Yes, Sonia, the funniest thing of all is that perhaps that's just how it was.'

Sonia did not think it at all funny.

'You had better tell me straight out . . . without examples,' she begged, still more timidly said scarcely audibly.

He turned to her, looked sadly at her and took her hands.

'You are right again, Sonia. Of course that's all nonsense, it's almost all talk! You see, you know of course that my mother has scarcely anything, my sister happened to have a good education and was condemned to drudge as a governess. All their hopes were centred on me. I was a student, but I couldn't keep myself at the university and was forced for a time to leave it. Even if I had lingered on like that, in ten or twelve years I might (with luck) hope to be some sort of teacher or clerk with a salary of a thousand roubles' (he repeated it as though it were a lesson) 'and by that time my mother would be worn out with grief and anxiety and I could not succeed in keeping her in comfort, while my sister . . . well, my sister might well have fared worse! And it's a hard thing to pass everything by all one's life, to turn one's back upon everything, to forget one's mother and decorously accept the insults inflicted on one's sister. Why should one? When one has buried them, to burden oneself with others – wife and children – and to leave them again without a farthing? So I resolved to gain possession of the old woman's money and to use it for my first years without worrying my mother, to keep myself at the university and for a little while after leaving it – and to do this all on a broad, thorough scale, so as to build up a completely new career and enter upon a new life of independence. . . . Well . . . that's all. . . . Well, of course in killing the old woman I did wrong. . . . Well, that's enough.'

He struggled to the end of his speech in exhaustion and let his head sink.

'Oh, that's not it, that's not it,' Sonia cried in distress. 'How could one . . . no, that's not right, not right.'

'You see yourself that it's not right. But I've spoken truly, it's the truth.'

'As though that could be the truth! Good God!'

'I've only killed a louse, Sonia, a useless, loathsome, harmful creature.'

'A human being – a louse!'

'I too know it wasn't a louse,' he answered, looking strangely at her. 'But I am talking nonsense, Sonia,' he added. 'I've been talking nonsense a long time. . . . That's not it, you are right there. There were quite, quite other causes for it! I haven't talked to anyone for so long, Sonia. . . . My head aches dreadfully now.'

His eyes shone with feverish brilliance. He was almost delirious; an uneasy smile strayed on his lips. His terrible exhaustion could be seen through his excitement. Sonia saw how he was suffering. She too was growing dizzy. And he talked so strangely: it seemed somehow comprehensible, but yet . . . 'But how, how? Good God!' And she wrung her hands in despair.

'No, Sonia, that's not it,' he began again suddenly, raising his head as though a new and sudden train of thought had struck and as it were roused him – 'that's not it! Better . . . imagine – yes, it's certainly better – imagine that I am vain, envious, malicious, base, vindictive and . . . well, perhaps with a tendency to insanity. (Let's have it all out at once! They've talked of madness already, I noticed.) I told you just now I could not keep myself at the university. But do you know that perhaps I might have done? My mother would have sent me what I needed for the fees and I could have earned enough for clothes, boots and food, no doubt. Lessons had turned up at half a rouble. Razumihin works! But I turned sulky and wouldn't. (Yes, sulkiness, that's the right word for it!) I sat in my room like a spider. You've been in my den, you've seen it. . . . And do you know, Sonia, that low ceilings and tiny rooms cramp the soul and the mind? Ah, how I hated that garret! And yet I wouldn't go out of it! I wouldn't on purpose! I didn't go out for days together, and I wouldn't work, I wouldn't even eat, I just lay there doing nothing. If Natasya brought me anything, I ate it, if she didn't, I went all day without; I wouldn't ask, on purpose, from sulkiness! At night I had no light, I lay in the dark and I wouldn't earn money for candles. I ought to have studied, but I sold my books; and the dust lies an inch think on the notebooks on my table. I preferred lying still and thinking. And I kept thinking . . . And I had dreams all the time, strange dreams of all sorts, no need to describe! Only then I began to fancy that. . . . No, that's not it! Again I am telling you wrong! You see I kept asking myself then: why am I so stupid, that if others are stupid – and I know they are – yet I won't be wiser? Then I saw, Sonia, that if one waits for everyone to get wiser it will take too long. . . . Afterwards I understand that that would never come to pass, that men won't change and that nobody can alter it and that it's not worth wasting effort over it. Yes, that's so. That's the law of their nature, Sonia . . . that's so! . . . And I know now, Sonia, that whoever is strong in mind and spirit will have power over them. Anyone who is greatly daring is right in their eyes. He who despises most things will be a lawgiver among them and he who dares most of all will be most in the right! So it has been till now and so it will always be. A man must be blind not to see it!'

Though Raskolnikov looked at Sonia as he said this, he no longer cared whether she understood or not. The fever had complete hold of him; he was in a sort of gloomy ecstasy (he certainly had been too long without talking to anyone). Sonia felt that this gloomy creed had become his faith and code.

'I divined then, Sonia,' he went on eagerly, 'that powder is only vouch-safed to the man who dares to stoop and pick it up. There is only one thing, one thing needful: one has only to dare! Then for the first time in my life an idea took shape in my mind which no one had ever thought of before me, no one! I saw clear as daylight how strange it is that not a single person living in this mad world has had the daring to go straight for it all and send it flying to the devil! I . . . I wanted *to have the daring* . . . and I killed her. I only wanted to have the daring, Sonia! That was the whole cause of it!'

'Oh, hush, hush!' cried Sonia, clasping her hands. 'You turned away from God and God has smitten you, has given you over to the devil!'

'Then, Sonia, when I used to lie there in the dark and all this became clear to me, was it a temptation of the devil, eh?'

'Hush, don't laugh, blasphemer! You don't understand, you don't understand! Oh God! He won't understand!'

'Hush, Sonia! I am not laughing. I know myself that it was the devil leading me. Hush, Sonia, hush!' he repeated with gloomy insistence. 'I know it all, I have thought it all over and over and whispered it all over to myself, lying there in the dark. . . . I've argued it all over with myself, every point of it, and I know it all, all! And how sick, how sick I was then of going over it all! I kept wanting to forget it and make a new beginning, Sonia, and leave off thinking. And you don't suppose that I went into it headlong like a fool? I went into it like a wise man, and that was just my destruction. And you mustn't suppose that I didn't know, for instance, that if I began to question myself whether I had the right to gain power – I certainly hadn't the right – or that if I asked myself whether a human being is a louse it proved that it wasn't so for me, though it might be for a man who would go straight to his goal without asking questions. . . . If I worried myself in those days, wondering whether Napoleon would have done it or not, I felt clearly of course that I wasn't Napoleon. I had to endure all the agony of that battle of ideas, Sonia, and I longed to throw it off: I wanted to murder without casuistry, to murder for my own sake, for myself alone! I didn't want to lie about it even to myself. It wasn't to help my mother I did the murder – that's nonsense – I didn't do the murder to gain wealth and power and to become a benefactor of mankind. Nonsense! I simply did it; I did the murder for myself, for myself alone, and whether I became a benefactor to others, or spent my life like a spider catching men in my web and sucking the life out of men,

I couldn't have cared at that moment. . . . And it was not the money I wanted, Sonia, when I did it. It was not so much the money I wanted, but something else. . . . I know it all now. . . . Understand me! Perhaps I should never have committed a murder again. I wanted to find out something else; it was something else led me on. I wanted to find out then and quickly whether I was a louse like everybody else or a man. Whether I can step over barriers or not, whether I dare stop to pick up or not, whether I am a trembling creature or whether I have the *right* . . .'

'To kill? Have the right to kill?' Sonia clasped her hands.

'Ach, Sonia!' he cried irritably and seemed about to make some retort, but was contemptuously silent. 'Don't interrupt me, Sonia. I want to prove one thing only, that the devil led me on then and he has shown me since that I had not the right to take that path, because I am just such a louse as all the rest. He was mocking me and here I've come to you now! Welcome your guest! If I were not a louse, should I have come to you? Listen: when I went then to the old woman's I only went to *try*. . . . You may be sure of that!'

'And you murdered her!'

'But how did I murder her? Is that how men do murders? Do men go to commit a murder as I went then? I will tell you some day how I went! Did I murder the old woman? I murdered myself, not her! I crushed myself once for all, for ever. . . . But it was the devil that killed that old woman, not I. Enough, enough, Sonia, enough! Let me be!' he cried in a sudden spasm of agony, 'let me be!'

He leaned his elbows on his knees and squeezed his head in his hands as in a vice.

'What suffering!' A wail of anguish broke from Sonia.

'Well, what am I to do now?' he asked, suddenly raising his head and looking at her with a face hideously distorted by despair.

'What are you to do?' she cried, jumping up, and her eyes that had been full of tears suddenly began to shine. 'Stand up!' (She seized him by the shoulder, he got up, looking at her almost bewildered.) 'Go at once, this very minute, stand at the cross-roads, bow down, first kiss the earth which you have defiled and then bow down to all the world and say to all men aloud, "I am a murderer! " Then God will send you life again. Will you go, will you go?' she asked him, trembling all over, snatching his two hands, squeezing them tight in hers and gazing at him with eyes full of fire.

He was amazed at her sudden ecstasy.

'You mean Siberia, Sonia? I must give myself up?' he asked gloomily.

'Suffer and expiate your sin by it, that's what you must do.'

'No! I am not going to them, Sonia!'

'But how will you go on living? What will you live for?' cried Sonia, 'how is it possible now? Why, how can you talk to your mother? (Oh, what will become of them now?) But what am I saying? You have abandoned your mother and your sister already. He has abandoned them already! Oh God!' she cried, 'why, he knows it all himself. How, how can he live by himself? What will become of you now?'

'Don't be a child, Sonia,' he said softly. 'What wrong have I done them? Why should I go to them? What should I say to them? That's only a phantom. . . . They destroy men by millions themselves and look on it as a virtue. They are knaves and scoundrels, Sonia! I am not going to them. And what should I say to them – that I murdered her, but did not dare to take the money and hid it under a stone?' he added with a bitter smile. 'Why, they would laugh at me, and would call me a fool for not getting it. A coward and a fool! They wouldn't understand and they don't deserve to understand. Why should I go to them? I won't. Don't be a child, Sonia. . . .'

'It will be too much for you to bear, too much!' she repeated, holding out her hands in despairing supplication.

'Perhaps I've been unfair to myself,' he observed gloomily, pondering, 'perhaps after all I am a man and not a louse and I've been in too great a hurry to condemn myself. I'll make another fight for it.'

A haughty smile appeared on his lips.

'What a burden to bear! And your whole life, your whole life!'

'I shall get used to it,' he said grimly and thoughtfully. 'Listen,' he began a minute later, 'stop crying, it's time to talk of the facts: I've come to tell you that the police are after me, on my track. . . .'

'Ach!' Sonia cried in terror.

'Well, why do you cry out? You want me to go to Siberia and now you are frightened? But let me tell you: I shall not give myself up. I shall make a struggle for it and they won't do anything to me. They've no real evidence. Yesterday I was in great danger and believed I was lost; but to-day things are going better. All the facts they know can be explained two ways, that's to say I can turn their accusations to my credit, do you understand? And I shall, for I've learnt my lesson. But they will certainly arrest me. If it had not been for something that happened, they would have done so to-day for certain; perhaps even now they will arrest me to-day. . . . But that's no matter, Sonia: they'll let me out again . . . for there isn't any real proof against me, and there won't be, I give you my word for it. And they can't convict a man on what they have against me. Enough. . . . I only tell you that you may know. . . . I will try to manage somehow to put it to my mother and sister so that they won't be frightened. . . . My sister's future is secure, however, now, I believe . . .

and my mother's must be too. . . . Well, that's all. Be careful, though. Will you come and see me in prison when I am there?'

'Oh, I will, I will.'

They sat side by side, both mournful and dejected, as though they had been cast up by the tempest alone on some deserted shore. He looked at Sonia and felt how great was her love for him, and strange to say he felt it suddenly burdensome and painful to be so loved. Yes, it was a strange and awful sensation! On his way to see Sonia he had felt that all his hopes rested on her; he expected to be rid of at least part of his suffering, and now, when all her heart turned towards him, he suddenly felt that he was immeasurably unhappier than before.

'Sonia,' he said, 'you'd better not come and see me when I am in prison.'

Sonia did not answer, she was crying. Several minutes passed.

'Have you a cross on you?' she asked, as though suddenly thinking of it.

He did not at first understand the question.

'No, of course not? Here, take this one, of cypress wood. I have another, a copper one that belonged to Lizaveta. I changed with Lizaveta: she gave me her cross and I gave her my little ikon. I will wear Lizaveta's now and give you this. Take it . . . it's mine! It's mine, you know,' she begged him. 'We will go to suffer together, and together we will bear our cross!'

'Give it me,' said Raskolnikov.

He did not want to hurt her feelings. But immediately he drew back the hand he held out for the cross.

'Not now, Sonia. Better later,' he added to comfort her.

'Yes, yes, better,' she repeated with conviction, 'when you go to meet your suffering, then put it on. You will come to me, I'll put it on you, we will pray and go together.'

At that moment someone knocked three times at the door.

'Sofya Semyonovna, may I come in?' they heard in a very familiar and polite voice.

Sonia rushed to the door in a fright. The flaxen head of Mr. Lebeziatnikov appeared at the door.

❧ FIVE ❦

Lebeziatnikov looked perturbed.

'I've come to you, Sofya Semyonovna,' he began. 'Excuse me . . . I thought I should find you,' he said, addressing Raskolnikov suddenly, 'that is, I didn't mean anything . . . of that sort . . . but I just thought. . . . Katerina Ivanovna has gone out of her mind,' he blurted out suddenly, turning from Raskolnikov to Sonia.

Sonia screamed.

'At least it seems so. But . . . we don't know what to do, you see! She came back – she seems to have been turned out somewhere, perhaps beaten. . . . So it seems at least. . . . She had run to your father's former chief, she didn't find him at home; he was dining at some other general's. . . . Only fancy, she rushed off there, to the other general's, and, imagine, she was so persistent that she managed to get the chief to see her, had him fetched out from dinner, it seems. You can imagine what happened. She was turned out, of course; but, according to her own story, she abused him and threw something at him. One may well believe it. . . . How it is she wasn't taken up, I can't understand! Now she is telling everyone, including Amalia Ivanovna; but it's difficult to understand her, she is screaming and flinging herself about. . . . Oh yes, she shouts that since everyone has abandoned her, she will take the children and go into the street with a barrel-organ, and the children will sing and dance, and she too, and collect money, and will go every day under the general's window . . . "to let everyone see well-born children, whose father was an official, begging in the street". She keeps beating the children and they are all crying. She is teaching Lida to sing "My Village", the boy to dance, Polenka the same. She is tearing up all the clothes, and making them little caps like actors; she means to carry a tin basin and make it tinkle, instead of music. . . . She won't listen to anything. . . . Imagine the state of things! It's beyond anything!'

Lebeziatnikov would have gone on, but Sonia, who had heard him almost breathless, snatched up her cloak and hat and ran out of the room, putting on her things as she went. Raskolnikov followed her and Lebeziatnikov came after him.

'She has certainly gone mad!' he said to Raskolnikov, as they went out into the street. 'I didn't want to frighten Sofya Semyonovna, so I said "it seemed like it", but there isn't a doubt of it. They say that in consumption the tubercles sometimes occur in the brain; it's a pity I know nothing of medicine. I did try to persuade her, but she wouldn't listen.'

'Did you talk to her about the tubercles?'

'Not precisely of the tubercles. Besides, she wouldn't have understood! But what I say is, that if you convince a person logically that he has nothing to cry about, he'll stop crying. That's clear. Is it your conviction that he won't?'

'Life would be too easy if it were so,' answered Raskolnikov.

'Excuse me, excuse me; of course it would be rather difficult for Katerina Ivanovna to understand, but do you know that in Paris they have been conducting serious experiments as to the possibility of curing the insane, simply by logical argument? One professor there, a scientific man of standing, lately dead, believed in the possibility of such treatment. His idea was that there's nothing really wrong with the physical organism of the insane, and that insanity is, so to say, a logical mistake, an error of judgment, an incorrect view of things. He gradually showed the madman his error and, would you believe it, they say he was successful! But as he made use of douches too, how far success was due to that treatment remains uncertain. . . . So it seems at least.'

Raskolnikov had long ceased to listen. Reaching the house where he lived, he nodded to Lebeziatnikov and went in at the gate. Lebeziatnikov woke up with a start, looked about him and hurried on.

Raskolnikov went into his little room and stood still in the middle of it. Why had he come back here? He looked at the yellow and tattered paper, at the dust, at his sofa. . . . From the yard came a loud continuous knocking; someone seemed to be hammering. . . . He went to the window, rose on tiptoe and looked out into the yard for a long time with an air of absorbed attention. But the yard was empty and he could not see who was hammering. In the house on the left he saw some open windows; on the window-sills were pots of sickly-looking geraniums. Linen was hung out of the windows. . . . He knew it all by heart. He turned away and sat down on the sofa.

Never, never had he felt himself so fearfully alone!

Yes, he felt once more that he would perhaps come to hate Sonia, now that he had made her more miserable.

'Why had he gone to her to beg for her tears? What need had he to poison her life? Oh, the meanness of it!'

'I will remain alone,' he said resolutely, 'and she shall not come to the prison!'

Five minutes later he raised his head with a strange smile. That was a strange thought.

'Perhaps it really would be better in Siberia,' he thought suddenly.

He could not have said how long he sat there with vague thoughts surging through his mind. All at once the door opened and Dounia came in. At first she stood still and looked at him from the doorway, just as he had done at Sonia; then she came in and sat down in the same place as yesterday, on the chair facing him. He looked silently and almost vacantly at her.

'Don't be angry, brother; I've only come for one minute,' said Dounia.

Her face looked thoughtful but not stern. Her eyes were bright and soft. He saw that she too had come to him with love.

'Brother, now I know all, *all*. Dmitri Prokofitch has explained and told me everything. They are worrying and persecuting you through a stupid and contemptible suspicion. . . . Dmitri Prokofitch told me that there is no danger, and that you are wrong in looking upon it with such horror. I don't think so, and I fully understand how indignant you must be, and that that indignation may have a permanent effect on you. That's what I am afraid of. As for your cutting yourself off from us, I don't judge you, I don't venture to judge you, and forgive me for having blamed you for it. I feel that I too, if I had so great a trouble, should keep away from everyone. I shall tell mother nothing *of this*, but I shall talk about you continually and shall tell her from you that you will come very soon. Don't worry about her; *I* will set her mind at rest; but don't you try her too much – come once at least; remember that she is your mother. And now I have come simply to say' (Dounia began to get up) 'that if you should need me or should need . . . all my life or anything . . . call me, and I'll come. Good-bye!'

She turned abruptly and went towards the door.

'Dounia!' Raskolnikov stopped her and went towards her. 'That Razumihin, Dmitri Prokofitch, is a very good fellow.'

Dounia flushed slightly.

'Well?' she asked, waiting a moment.

'He is competent, hard-working, honest and capable of real love. . . . Good-bye, Dounia.'

Dounia flushed crimson, then suddenly she took alarm.

'But what does it mean, brother? Are we really parting for ever that you . . . give me such a parting message?'

'Never mind. . . . Good-bye.'

He turned away, and walked to the window. She stood a moment, looked at him uneasily, and went out troubled.

No, he was not cold to her. There was an instant (the very last one) when he had longed to take her in his arms and *say good-bye* to her, and even *to tell* her, but he had not dared even to touch her hand.

'Afterwards she may shudder when she remembers that I embraced her, and will feel that I stole her kiss.'

'And would *she* stand that test?' he went on a few minutes later to himself. 'No, she wouldn't; girls like that can't stand things! They never do.'

And he thought of Sonia.

There was a breath of fresh air from the window. The daylight was fading. He took up his cap and went out.

He could not, of course, and would not consider how ill he was. But all this continual anxiety and agony of mind could not but affect him. And if he were not lying in high fever it was perhaps just because this continual inner strain helped to keep him on his legs and in possession of his faculties. But this artificial excitement could not last long.

He wandered aimlessly. The sun was setting. A special form of misery had begun to oppress him of late. There was nothing poignant, nothing acute about it; but there was a feeling of permanence, of eternity about it; it brought a foretaste of hopeless years of this cold leaden misery, a foretaste of an eternity 'on a square yard of space'. Towards evening this sensation usually began to weigh on him more heavily.

'With this idiotic, purely physical weakness, depending on the sunset or something, one can't help doing something stupid! You'll go to Dounia, as well as to Sonia,' he muttered bitterly.

He heard his name called. He looked round. Lebeziatnikov rushed up to him.

'Only fancy, I've been to your room looking for you. Only fancy, she's carried out her plan, and taken away the children. Sofya Semyonovna and I have had a job to find them. She is rapping on a frying-pan and making the children dance. The children are crying. They keep stopping at the cross-roads and in front of shops; there's a crowd of fools running after them. Come along!'

'And Sonia?' Raskolnikov asked anxiously, hurrying after Lebeziatnikov.

'Simply frantic. That is, it's not Sofya Semyonovna's frantic, but Katerina Ivanovna, though Sofya Semyonovna's frantic too. But Katerina Ivanovna is absolutely frantic. I tell you she is quite mad. They'll be taken to the police. You can fancy what an effect that will have.... They are on the canal bank, near the bridge now, not far from Sofya Semyonovna's, quite close.'

On the canal bank near the bridge and not two houses away from the one where Sonia lodged, there was a crowd of people, consisting principally of gutter children. The hoarse broken voice of Katerina Ivanovna could be heard from the bridge, and it certainly was a strange spectacle likely to attract a street crowd. Katerina Ivanovna in her old dress with the green shawl, wearing a torn straw hat, crushed in a hideous way on one side, was really frantic. She was exhausted and breathless. Her wasted consumptive face looked more suffering than ever, and indeed out of doors in the sunshine a consumptive always looks worse than at home. But her excitement did not flag, and every moment her irritation grew more intense. She rushed at the children, shouted at them, coaxed them, told them before the crowd how to dance and what to sing, began explaining to them why it was necessary, and driven to desperation by their not understanding, beat them. . . . Then she would make a rush at the crowd; if she noticed any decently dressed person stopping to look, she immediately appealed to him to see what these children 'from a genteel, one may say aristocratic house' had been brought to. If she heard laughter or jeering in the crowd, she would rush at once at the scoffers and begin squabbling with them. Some people laughed, others shook their heads, but everyone felt curious at the sight of the 'madwoman with the frightened children. The frying-pan of which Lebeziatnikov had spoken was not there, at least Raskolnikov did not see it. But instead of rapping on the pan, Katerina Ivanovna began clapping her wasted hands, when she made Lida and Kolya dance and Polenka sing. She too joined in the singing, but broke down at the second note with a fearful cough, which made her curse in despair and even shed tears. What made her most furious was the weeping and terror of Kolya and Lida. Some effort had been made to dress the children up as street singers are dressed. The boy had on a turban made of something red and white to look like a Turk. There had been no costume for Lida; she simply had a red knitted cap, or rather a night-cap that had belonged to Marmeladov, decorated with a broken piece of white ostrich feather, which had been Katerina Ivanovna's grandmother's and had been preserved as a family possession. Polenka was in her everyday dress; she looked in timid perplexity at her mother, and kept at her side, hiding her tears. She dimly realized her mother's condition, and looked uneasily about her. She was terribly frightened of the street and the crowd. Sonia followed Katerina Ivanovna, weeping and beseeching her to return home, but Katerina Ivanovna was not to be persuaded.

'Leave off, Sonia, leave off,' she shouted, speaking fast, panting and coughing. 'You don't know what you ask; you are like a child! I've told you before that I am not coming back to that drunken German. Let everyone, let all Petersburg see the children begging in the streets, though their father was an honourable man who served all his life in truth and fidelity, and one may say died in the service.' (Katerina Ivanovna had by now invented this fantastic story and thoroughly believed it.) 'Let that wretch of a general see it! And you are silly, Sonia: what have we to eat? Tell me that. We have worried you enough, I won't go on so! Ah, Rodion Romanovitch, is that you?' she cried, seeing Raskolnikov and rushing up to him. 'Explain to this silly girl, please, that nothing better could be done! Even organ-grinders earn their living, and everyone will see at once that we are different, that we are an honourable and bereaved family reduced to beggary. And that general will lose his post, you'll see! We shall perform under his windows every day, and if the Tsar drives by, I'll fall on my knees, put the children before me, show them to him, and say, "Defend us father". He is the father of the fatherless, he is merciful, he'll protect us, you'll see, and that wretch of a general. . . . Lida, *tenez-vous droite!* Kolya, you'll dance again. Why are you whimpering? Whimpering again! What are you afraid of, stupid? Goodness, what am I to do with them, Rodion Romanovitch? If you only know how stupid they are! What's one to do with such children?'

And she, almost crying herself – which did not stop her uninterrupted, rapid flow of talk – pointed to the crying children. Raskolnikov tried to persuade her to go home, and even said, hoping to work on her vanity, that it was unseemly for her to be wandering about the streets like an organ-grinder, as she was intending to become the principal of a boarding-school.

'A boarding-school, ha-ha-ha! A castle in the air,' cried Katerina Ivanovna, her laugh ending in a cough. 'No, Rodion Romanovitch, that dream is over! All have forsaken us! . . . And that general. . . . You know, Rodion Romanovitch, I threw an inkpot at him – it happened to be standing in the waiting-room by the paper where you sign your name. I wrote my name, threw it at him and ran away. Oh, the scoundrels, the scoundrels! But enough of them, now I'll provide for the children myself, I won't bow down to anybody! She has had to bear enough for us!' she pointed to Sonia. 'Polenka, how much have you got? Show me! What, only two farthings! Oh, the mean wretches! They give us nothing, only run after us, putting their tongues out. There, what is that blockhead laughing at?' (She pointed to a man in the crowd.) 'It's all because Kolya here is so stupid; I have such a bother with him. What do you want, Polenka? Tell me in French, *parlez-moi français.* Why, I've taught you, you know some phrases. Else how are you to show that you are of good family, well brought-up children, and not at all like other organ-grinders? We aren't going to have a Punch and Judy show in the street, but to sing a genteel song. . . . Ah, yes. . . . What are we to sing? You keep putting me out, but we . . . you see, we are standing here, Rodion Romanovitch, to find something to sing and get money, something Kolya can dance to.... For, as you can fancy, our performance is all impromptu.... We must talk it over and rehearse it all thoroughly, and then we shall go to Nevsky, where there are far more people of good society, and we shall be noticed at once. Lida knows "My Village" only, nothing but "My Village", and everyone sings that. We must sing something far more genteel.... Well, have you thought of anything, Polenka? If only you'd help your mother! My memory's quite gone, or I should have thought of something. We really can't sing "An Hussar". Ah, let us sing in French, "Cinq Sous", I have taught it you, I have taught it you. And as it is in French, people will see at once that you are children of good family, and that will be much more touching.... You might sing "Malborough s'en va-t-en guerre", for that's quite a child's song and is sung as a lullaby in all the aristocratic houses.

> *Malborough s'en va-t-en guerre,*
> *Ne sait quand reviendra....'*

she began singing. 'But no, better sing "Cinq Sous". Now, Kolya, your hands on your hips, make haste, and you, Lida, keep turning the other way, and Polenka and I will sing and clap our hands!

> *Cinq sous, cinq sous*
> *Pour monter notre ménage.'*

(Cough-cough-cough!) 'Set your dress straight, Polenka, it's slipped down on your shoulders,' she observed, panting from coughing. 'Now it's particularly necessary to behave nicely and genteelly, that all may see that you are well-born children. I said at the time that the bodice should be cut longer, and made of two widths. It was your fault, Sonia, with your advice to make it shorter, and now you see the child is quite deformed by it.... Why, you're all crying again! What's the matter, stupids? Come, Kolya, begin. Make haste, make haste! Oh, what an unbearable child!

> *Cinq sous, cinq sous.*

A policeman again! What do you want?'

A policeman was indeed forcing his way through the crowd. But at that moment a gentleman in civilian uniform and an overcoat – a solid-looking official of about fifty with a decoration on his neck (which delighted Katerina Ivanovna and had its effect on the policeman) – approached and without a word handed her a green three-rouble note.

His face wore a look of genuine sympathy. Katerina Ivanovna took it and gave him a polite, even ceremonious, bow.

'I thank you, honoured sir,' she began loftily. 'The causes that have induced us (take the money, Polenka: you see there are generous and honourable people who are ready to help a poor gentlewoman in distress). You see, honoured sir, these orphans of good family – I might even say of aristocratic connections – and that wretch of a general sat eating grouse . . . and stamped at my disturbing him. "Your excellency," I said, "protect the orphans, for you knew my late husband, Semyon Zaharovitch, and on the very day of his death the basest of scoundrels slandered his only daughter. . . . That policeman again! Protect me,' she cried to the official. 'Why is that policeman edging up to me? We have only just run away from one of them. What do you want, fool?'

'It's forbidden in the streets. You mustn't make a disturbance.'

'It's you're making a disturbance. It's just the same as if I were grinding an organ. What business if it of yours?'

'You have to get a licence for an organ, and you haven't got one, and in that way you collect a crowd. Where do you lodge?'

'What, a licence?' wailed Katerina Ivanovna. 'I buried my husband to-day. What need of a licence?'

'Calm yourself, madam, calm yourself,' began the official. 'Come along; I will escort you. . . . This is no place for you in the crowd. You are ill.'

'Honoured sir, honoured sir, you don't know,' screamed Katerina Ivanovna. 'We are going to the Nevsky. . . . Sonia, Sonia! Where is she? She is crying too! What's the matter with you all? Kolya, Lida, where are you going?' she cried suddenly in alarm. 'Oh, silly children! Kolya, Lida, where are they off to? . . .'

Kolya and Lida, scared out of their wits by the crowd, and their mother's mad pranks, suddenly seized each other by the hand, and ran off at the sight of the policeman who wanted to take them away somewhere. Weeping and wailing, poor Katerina Ivanovna ran after them. She was a piteous and unseemly spectacle, as she ran, weeping and panting for breath. Sonia and Polenka rushed after her.

'Bring them back, bring them back, Sonia! Oh, stupid, ungrateful children! . . . Polenka! catch them. . . . It's for your sakes I . . .'

She stumbled as she ran and fell down.

'She's cut herself, she's bleeding! Oh dear!' cried Sonia, bending over her.

All ran up and crowded around. Raskolnikov and Lebeziatnikov were the first at her side, the official too hastened up, and behind him the policeman who muttered, 'Bother!' with a gesture of impatience, feeling that the job was going to be a troublesome one.

'Pass on! Pass on!' he said to the crowd that pressed forward.

'She's dying,' someone shouted.

'She's gone out of her mind,' said another.

'Lord have mercy upon us,' said a woman, crossing herself. 'Have they caught the little girl and the boy? They're being brought back, the elder one's got them. . . . Ah, the naughty imps!'

When they examined Katerina Ivanovna carefully, they saw that she had not cut herself against a stone, as Sonia thought, but that the blood that stained the pavement red was from her chest.

'I've seen that before,' muttered the official to Raskolnikov and Lebeziatnikov; 'that's consumption; the blood flows and chokes the patient. I saw the same thing with a relative of my own not long ago . . . nearly a pint of blood, all in a minute. . . . What's to be done though? She is dying.'

'This way, this way, to my room!' Sonia implored. 'I live here! . . . See that house, the second from here. . . . Come to me, make haste,' she turned from one to the other. 'Send for the doctor! Oh dear!'

Thanks to the official's efforts, this plan was adopted, the policeman even helping to carry Katerina Ivanovna. She was carried to Sonia's room, almost unconscious, and laid on the bed. The blood was still flowing, but she seemed to be coming to herself. Raskolnikov, Lebeziatnikov, and the official accompanied Sonia into the room and were followed by the policeman, who first drove back the crowd which followed to the very door. Polenka came in holding Kolya and Lida, who were trembling and weeping. Several persons came in too from the Kapernaumovs' room; the landlord, a lame one-eyed man of strange appearance with whiskers and hair that stood up like a brush, his wife, a woman with an everlastingly scared expression, and several open-mouthed children with wonder-struck faces. Among these, Svidrigaïlov suddenly made his appearance. Raskolnikov looked at him with surprise, not understanding where he had come from and not having noticed him in the crowd. A doctor and priest were spoken of. The official whispered to Raskolnikov that he thought it was too late now for the doctor, but he ordered him to be sent for. Kapernaumov ran himself.

Meanwhile Katerina Ivanovna had regained her breath. The bleeding ceased for a time. She looked with sick but intent and penetrating eyes at Sonia, who stood pale and trembling, wiping the sweat from her brow with a handkerchief. At last she asked to be raised. They sat her up on the bed, supporting her on both sides.

'Where are the children?' she said in a faint voice. 'You've brought them, Polenka? Oh, the sillies! Why did you run away? . . . Och!'

Once more her parched lips were covered with blood. She moved her eyes, looking about her.

'So that's how you live, Sonia! Never once have I been in your room.'

She looked at her with a face of suffering.

'We have been your ruin, Sonia. Polenka, Lida, Kolya, come here! Well, here they are, Sonia, take them all! I hand them over to you, I've had enough! The ball is over.' (Cough!) 'Lay me down, let me die in peace.'

They laid her back on the pillow.

'What, the priest? I don't want him. You haven't got a rouble to spare. I have no sins. God must forgive me without that. He knows how I have suffered. . . . And if He won't forgive me, I don't care!'

She sank more and more into uneasy delirium. At times she shuddered, turned her eyes from side to side, recognized everyone for a minute, but at once sank into delirium again. Her breathing was hoarse and difficult, there was a sort of rattle in her throat.

'I said to him, your excellency,' she ejaculated, gasping after each word. 'That Amalia Ludwigovna, ah! Lida, Kolya, hands on your hips, make haste! *Glissez, glissez! pas de basque!* Tap with your heels, be a graceful child!

Du hast Diamanten und Perlen

What next? That's the thing to sing.

Du hast die schönsten Augen,
Mädchen, was willst du mehr?

'What an idea! *Was willst du mehr?* What things the fool invents! Ah, yes!

In the heat of midday in the vale of Dagestan.

'Ah, how I loved it! I loved that song to distraction, Polenka! Your father, you know, used to sing it when we were engaged. . . . Oh, those days! Oh, that's the thing for us to sing! How does it go? I've forgotten. Remind me! how was it?'

She was violently excited and tried to sit up. At last, in a horribly hoarse, broken voice, she began, shrieking and gasping at every word, with a look of growing terror:

'In the heat of midday! . . . in the vale! . . . of Dagestan! . . . With lead in my breast! . . .

'Your excellency!' she wailed suddenly with a heart-rending scream

359

and a flood of tears, 'protect the orphans! You have been their father's guest . . . one may say aristocratic. . . .' She started, regaining consciousness, and gazed at all with a sort of terror, but at once recognized Sonia.

'Sonia, Sonia!' she articulated softly and caressingly, as though surprised to find her there. 'Sonia darling, are you here, too?'

They lifted her up again.

'Enough! It's over! Farewell, poor thing! I am done for! I am broken!' she cried with vindictive despair, and her head fell heavily back on the pillow.

She sank into unconsciousness again, but this time it did not last long. Her pale, yellow, wasted face dropped back, her mouth fell open, her leg moved convulsively, she gave a deep, deep sigh and died.

Sonia fell upon her, flung her arms about her, and remained motionless with her head pressed to the dead woman's wasted bosom. Polenka threw herself at her mother's feet, kissing them and weeping violently. Though Kolya and Lida did not understand what had happened, they had a feeling that it was something terrible; they put their heads on each other's little shoulders, stared straight at one another and both at once opened their mouths and began screaming. They were both still in their fancy dress; one in a turban, the other in the cap with the ostrich feather.

And how did 'the certificate of merit' come to be on the bed beside Katerina Ivanovna? It lay there by the pillow; Raskolniko saw it.

He walked away to the window. Lebeziatnikov skipped up to him.

'She is dead,' he said.

'Rodion Romanovitch, I must have two words with you,' said Svidrigaïlov, coming up to them.

Lebeziatnikov at once made room for him and delicately withdrew. Svidrigaïlov drew Raskolnikov further away.

'I will undertake all the arrangements, the funeral and that. You know it's a question of money and, as I told you, I have plenty to spare. I will put those two little ones and Polenka into some good orphan asylum, and I will settle fifteen hundred roubles to be paid to each on coming of age, so that Sofya Semyonovna need have no anxiety about them. And I will pull her out of the mud too, for she is a good girl, isn't she? So tell Avdotya Romanovna that that is how I am spending her ten thousand.'

'What is your motive for such benevolence?' asked Raskolnikov.

'Ah! you sceptical person!' laughed Svidrigaïlov. 'I told you I had no need of that money. Won't you admit that it's simply done from humanity? She wasn't "a louse", you know' (he pointed to the corner where the dead woman lay), 'was she, like some old pawnbroker woman? Come, you'll agree, is Luzhin to go on living, and doing wicked things or is she to die? And if I didn't help them, Polenka would go the same way.'

He said this with an air of a sort of gay winking slyness, keeping his eyes fixed on Raskolnikov, who turned white and cold, hearing his own phrases, spoken to Sonia. He quickly stepped back and looked wildly at Svidrigaïlov.

'How do you know?' he whispered, hardly able to breathe.

'Why, I lodge here at Madame Resslich's, the other side of the wall. Here is Kapernaumov, and there lives Madame Resslich, an old and devoted friend of mine. I am a neighbour.'

'You?'

'Yes,' continued Svidrigaïlov, shaking with laughter. 'I assure you on my honour, dear Rodion Romanovitch, that you have interested me enormously. I told you we should become friends, I foretold it. Well, here we have. And you will see what an accommodating person I am. You'll see that you can get on with me!'

PART SIX

✦ ONE ✦

A STRANGE PERIOD BEGAN FOR Raskolnikov: it was as though a fog had fallen upon him and wrapped him in a dreary solitude from which there was no escape. Recalling that period long after, he believed that his mind had been clouded at times, and that it had continued so, with intervals, till the final catastrophe. He was convinced that he had been mistaken about many things at that time, for instance as to the date of certain events. Anyway, when he tried later on to piece his recollections together, he learnt a great deal about himself from what other people told him. He had mixed up incidents and had explained events as due to circumstances which existed only in his imagination. At times he was a prey to agonies of morbid uneasiness, amounting sometimes to panic. But he remembered, too, moments, hours, perhaps whole days, of complete apathy, which came upon him as a reaction from his previous terror and might be compared with the abnormal insensibility, sometimes seen in the dying. He seemed to be trying in that latter stage to escape from a full and clear understanding of his position. Certain essential facts which required immediate consideration were particularly irksome to him. How glad he would have been to be free from some cares, the neglect of which would have threatened him with complete, inevitable ruin.

He was particularly worried about Svidrigaïlov, he might be said to be permanently thinking of Svidrigaïlov. From the time of Svidrigaïlov's too menacing and unmistakable words in Sonia's room at the moment of Katerina Ivanovna's death, the normal working of his mind seemed to break down. But although this new fact caused him extreme uneasiness, Raskolnikov was in no hurry for an explanation of it. At times, finding himself in a solitary and remote part of the town, in some wretched eating-house, sitting alone lost in thought, hardly knowing how he had come there, he suddenly thought of Svidrigaïlov. He recognized suddenly, clearly, and with dismay that he ought at once to come to an understanding with that man and to make what terms he could. Walking outside the city gates one day, he positively fancied that they had fixed a meeting there, that he was waiting for Svidrigaïlov. Another time he woke up before daybreak lying on the ground under some bushes and could not at first understand how he had come there.

But during the two or three days after Katerina Ivanovna's death, he had two or three times met Svidrigaïlov at Sonia's lodging, where he had gone aimlessly for a moment. They exchanged a few words and made no reference to the vital subject, as though they were tacitly agreed not to speak of it for a time.

Katerina Ivanovna's body was still lying in the coffin, Svidrigaïlov was busy making arrangements for the funeral. Sonia too was very busy. At their last meeting Svidrigaïlov informed Raskolnikov that he had made an arrangement, and a very satisfactory one, for Katerina Ivanovna's children; that he had, through certain connections, succeeded in getting hold of certain personages by whose help the three orphans could be at once placed in very suitable institutions; that the money he had settled on them had been of great assistance, as it is much easier to place orphans with some property than destitute ones. he said something too about Sonia and promised to come himself in a day or two to see Raskolnikov, mentioning that 'he would like to consult with him, that there were things they must talk over. . . .'

This conversation took place in the passage on the stairs. Svidrigaïlov looked intently at Raskolnikov and suddenly, after a brief pause, dropping his voice, asked: 'But how is it, Rodion Romanovitch; you don't seem yourself? You look and you listen, but you don't seem to understand. Cheer up! We'll talk things over; I am only sorry I've so much to do of my own business and other people's. Ah, Rodion Romanovitch,' he added suddenly, 'what all men need is fresh air, fresh air . . . more than anything!'

He moved to one side to make way for the priest and server, who were coming up the stairs. They had come for the requiem service. By Svidrigaïlov's orders it was sung twice a day punctually. Svidrigaïlov went his way. Raskolnikov stood still a moment, thought, and followed the priest into Sonia's room. He stood at the door. They began quietly, slowly and mournfully singing the service. From his childhood the thought of death and the presence of death had something oppressive and mysteriously awful; and it was long since he had heard the requiem service. And there was something else here as well, too awful and disturbing. He looked at the children: they were all kneeling by the coffin; Polenka was weeping. Behind them Sonia prayed, softly and, as it were, timidly weeping.

'These last two days she hasn't said a word to me, she hasn't glanced at me,' Raskolnikov thought suddenly. The sunlight was bright in the room; the incense rose in clouds; the priest read, 'Give rest, oh Lord. . . .'

Raskolnikov stayed all through the service. As he blessed them and took his leave, the priest looked round strangely. After the service, Raskolnikov went up to Sonia. She took both his hands and let her head sink on his shoulder. This slight friendly gesture bewildered Raskolnikov. It seemed strange to him that there was no trace of repugnance, no trace of disgust, no tremor in her hand. It was the furthest limit of self-abnegation, at least so he interpreted it.

Sonia said nothing. Raskolnikov pressed her hand and went out. He felt very miserable. If it had been possible to escape to some solitude, he would have thought himself lucky, even if he had to spend his whole life there. But although he had almost always been by himself of late, he had never been able to feel alone. Sometimes he walked out of the town on to the high road, once he had even reached a little wood, but the lonelier the place was the more he seemed to be aware of an uneasy presence near him. It did not frighten him, but greatly annoyed him, so that he made haste to return to the town, to mingle with the crowd, to enter restaurants and taverns, to walk in busy thoroughfares. There he felt easier and even more solitary. One day at dusk he sat for an hour listening to songs in a tavern and he remembered that he positively enjoyed it. But at last he had suddenly felt the same uneasiness again, as though his conscience smote him. 'Here I sit listening to singing, is that what I ought to be doing?' he thought. Yet he felt at once that that was not the only cause of his uneasiness; there was something requiring immediate decision, but it was something he could not clearly understand or put into words. It was a hopeless tangle. 'No, better the struggle again! Better Porfiry again. . . . or Svidrigaïlov. . . . Better some challenge again . . . some attack. Yes, yes!' he thought. He went out of the tavern and rushed away almost at a run. The thought of Dounia and his mother suddenly reduced him almost to a panic. That night he woke up before morning among some bushes in Krestovsky Island, trembling all over with fever; he walked home, and it was early morning when he arrived. After some hours' sleep the fever left him, but he woke up late, two o'clock in the afternoon.

He remembered that Katerina Ivanovna's funeral had been fixed for that day, and was glad that he was not present at it. Nastasya brought him some food; he ate and drank with appetite, almost with greediness. His head was fresher and he was calmer than he had been for the last three days. He even felt a passing wonder at his previous attacks of panic.

The door opened and Razumihin came in.

'Ah, he's eating and he's not ill,' said Razumihin. He took a chair and sat down at the table opposite Raskolnikov.

He was troubled and did not attempt to conceal it. He spoke with evident annoyance, but without hurry or raising his voice. He looked as though he had some special fixed determination.

'Listen,' he began resolutely. 'As far as I'm concerned, you may all go to to hell, but from what I see, it's clear to me that I can't make head or tail of it; please don't think I've come to ask you questions. I don't want to know, hang it! If you begin telling me your secrets, I dare say I shouldn't stay to listen, I should go away cursing. I have only come to find out once for all whether it's a fact that you are mad? There is a conviction in the air that you are mad or very nearly so. I admit I've been disposed to that opinion myself, judging from your stupid, repulsive and quite inexplicable actions, and from your recent behaviour to your mother and sister. Only a monster or a madman could treat them as you have; so you must be mad.'

'When did you see them last?'

'Just now. Haven't you seen them since then? What have you been doing with yourself? Tell me, please. I've been to you three times already. Your mother has been seriously ill since yesterday. She had made up her mind to come to you; Avdotya Romanovna tried to prevent her; she wouldn't hear a word. "If he is ill, if his mind is giving way, who can look after him like his mother?" she said. We all came here together, we couldn't let her come alone all the way. We kept begging her to be calm. We came in, you weren't here; she sat down, and stayed ten minutes, while we stood waiting in silence. She got up and said: "If he's gone out, that is, if he is well, and has forgotten his mother, it's humiliating, and unseemly for his mother to stand at his door begging for kindness." She returned home and took to her bed; now she is in a fever. "I see," she said, "that he has time for *his girl*." She means by *your girl* Sofya Semyonovna, your betrothed or your mistress, I don't know. I went at once to Sofya Semyonovna's, for I wanted to know what was going on. I looked round, I saw the coffin, the children crying, and Sofya Semyonovna trying them on mourning dresses. No sign of you. I apologized, came away, and reported to Avdotya Romanovna. So that's all nonsense and you haven't got a girl; the most likely thing is that you are mad. But here you sit, guzzling boiled beef as though you'd not had a bite for three days. Though, as far as that goes, madmen eat too, but though you have not said a word to me yet . . . you are not mad! That I'd swear! Above all, you are not mad! So you may go to hell, all of you, for there's some mystery, some secret about it, and I don't intend to worry my brain over your secrets. So I've simply come to swear at you,' he finished, getting up, 'to relieve my mind. And I know what to do now.'

'What do you mean to do now?'

'What business is it of yours what I mean to do?'

'You are going in for a drinking bout.'

'How . . . how did you know?'

'Why, it's pretty plain.'

Razumihin paused for a minute.

'You always have been a very rational person and you've never been mad, never,' he observed suddenly with warmth. 'You're right: I shall drink. Good-bye!'

And he moved to go out.

'I was talking with my sister – the day before yesterday, I think it was – about you, Razumihin.'

'About me! But . . . where can you have seen her the day before yesterday?' Razumihin stopped short and even turned a little pale.

One could see that his heart was throbbing slowly and violently.

'She came here by herself, sat there and talked to me.'

'She did!'

'Yes.'

'What did you say to her . . . I mean, about me?'

'I told her you were a very good, honest, and industrious man. I didn't tell her you love her, because she knows that herself.'

'She knows that herself?'

'Well, it's pretty plain. Wherever I might go, whatever happened to me, you would remain to look after them. I, so to speak, give them into your keeping, Razumihin. I say this because I know quite well how you love her, and am convinced of the purity of your heart. I know that she too may love you and perhaps does love you already. Now decide for yourself, as you know best, whether you need go in for a drinking bout or not.'

'Rodya! You see . . . well . . . Ach, damn it! But where do you mean to go? Of course, if it's all a secret, never mind. . . . But I . . . I shall find out the secret . . . and I am sure that it must be some ridiculous nonsense and that you've made it all up. Anyway you are a capital fellow, a capital fellow! . . .'

'That was just what I wanted to add, only you interrupted, that that was a very good decision of yours not to find out these secrets. Leave it to time, don't worry about it. You'll know it all in time when it must be. Yesterday a man said to me that what a man needs is fresh air, fresh air, fresh air. I mean to go to him directly to find out what he meant by that.'

Razumihin stood lost in thought and excitement, making a silent conclusion.

'He's a political conspirator! He must be. And he's on the eve of some desperate step, that's certain. It can only be that! And . . . and Dounia knows,' he thought suddenly.

'So Avdotya Romanovna comes to see you,' he said, weighing each syllable, 'and you're going to see a man who says we need more air, and so of course that letter . . . that too must have something to do with it,' he concluded to himself.

'What letter?'

'She got a letter to-day. It upset her very much – very much indeed. Too much so. I began speaking of you, she begged me not to. Then . . . then she said that perhaps we should very soon have to part . . . then she began warmly thanking me for something; then she went to her room and locked herself in.'

'She got a letter?' Raskolnikov asked thoughtfully.

'Yes, and you didn't know? hm. . . .'

They were both silent.

'Good-bye, Rodion. There was a time, brother, when I. . . . Never mind, good-bye. You see, there was a time. . . . Well, good-bye! I must be off too. I am not going to drink. There's no need now. . . . That's all stuff'

He hurried out; but when he had almost closed the door behind him, he suddenly opened it again, and said, looking away:

'Oh, by the way, do you remember that murder, you know Porfiry's, that old woman? Do you know the murderer has been found, he has confessed and given the proofs. It's one of those very workmen, the painter, only fancy! Do you remember I defended them here? Would you believe it, all that scene of fighting and laughing with his companions on the stairs while the porter and the two witnesses were going up, he got up on purpose to disarm suspicion. The cunning, the presence of mind of the young dog! One can hardly credit; but it's his own explanation, he has confessed it all. And what a fool I was about it! Well, he's simply a genius of hypocrisy and resourcefulness in disarming the suspicions of the lawyers – so there's nothing much to wonder at, I suppose! Of course people like that are always possible. And the fact that he couldn't keep up the character, but confessed, makes him easier to believe in. But what a fool I was! I was so frantic on their side!'

'Tell me, please, from whom did you hear that, and why does it interest you so?' Raskolnikov asked with unmistakable agitation.

'What next? You ask me why it interests me! . . . Well, I heard it from Porfiry, among others. . . . It was from him I heard almost all about it.'

'From Porfiry?'

'From Porfiry.'

'What . . . what did he say?' Raskolnikov asked in dismay.

'He gave me a capital explanation of it. Psychologically, after his fashion.'

'He explained it? Explained it himself?'

'Yes, yes; good-bye. I'll tell you all about it another time, but now I'm busy. There was a time when I fancied. . . . But no matter, another time! . . . What need is there for me to drink now? You have made me drunk without wine. I am drunk, Rodya! Good-bye, I'm going. I'll come again very soon.'

He went out.

'He's a political conspirator, there's not a doubt about it,' Razumihin decided, as he slowly descended the stairs. 'And he's drawn his sister in; that's quite, quite in keeping with Avdotya Romanovna's character. There are interviews between them! . . . She hinted at it too. . . . So many of her words . . . and hints . . . bear that meaning! And how else can all this tangle be explained? Hm! And I was almost thinking. . . . Good heavens, what I thought! Yes, I took leave of my senses and I wronged him! It was his doing, under the lamp in the corridor that day. Pfoo! What a crude, nasty, vile idea on my part! Nikolay is a brick, for confessing. . . . And how clear it all is now! His illness then, all his strange actions . . . before this, in the university, how morose he used to be, how gloomy. . . . But what's the meaning of that letter? There's something in that, too, perhaps. Whom was it from? I suspect . . . ! No, I must find out!'

He thought of Dounia, realizing all he had heard and his heart throbbed, and he suddenly broke into a run.

As soon as Razumihin went out, Raskolnikov got up, turned to the window, walked into one corner and then into another, as though forgetting the smallness of his room, and sat down again on the sofa. He felt, so to speak, renewed; again the struggle, so a means of escape had come.

'Yes, a means of escape had come! It had been too stifling, too cramping, the burden had been too agonizing. A lethargy had come upon him at times. From the moment of the scene with Nikolay at Porfiry's he had been suffocating, penned in without hope of escape. After Nikolay's confession, on that very day had come the scene with Sonia; his behaviour and his last words had been utterly unlike anything he could have imagined beforehand; he had grown feebler, instantly and fundamentally! And he had agreed at the time with Sonia, he had agreed in his heart he could not go on living alone with such a thing on his mind!

'And Svidrigaïlov was a riddle. . . . He worried him, that was true, but somehow not on the same point. He might still have a struggle to come with Svidrigaïlov. Svidrigaïlov, too, might be a means of escape; but Porfiry was a different matter.

'And so Porfiry himself had explained it to Razumihin, had explained it *psychologically.* He had begun bringing in his damned psychology again! Porfiry? But to think that Porfiry should for one moment believe that Nikolay was guilty, after what had passed between them before Nikolay's

371

appearance, after that tête-à-tête interview, which could have only *one* explanation? (During those days Raskolnikov had often recalled passages in that scene with Porfiry; he could not bear to let his mind rest on it.) Such words, such gestures had passed between them, they had exchanged such glances, things had been said in such a tone and had reached such a pass, that Nikolay whom Porfiry had seen through at the first word, at the first gesture, could not have shaked his conviction.'

'And to think that even Razumihin had begun to suspect! The scene in the corridor under the lamp had produced its effect then. He had rushed to Porfiry. . . . But what had induced the latter to deceive him like that? What had been his object in putting Razumihin off with Nikolay? He must have some plan; there was some design, but what was it? It was true that a long time had passed since that morning – too long a time – and no sight nor sound of Porfiry. Well, that was a bad sign. . . .'

Raskolnikov took his cap and went out of the room, still pondering. It was the first time for a long while that he had felt clear in his mind, at least. 'I must settle Svidrigaïlov,' he thought, 'and as soon as possible; he, too, seems to be waiting for me to come to him of my own accord.' And at that moment there was such a rush of hate in his weary heart that he might have killed either of those two – Porfiry or Svidrigaïlov. At least he felt that he would be capable of doing it later, if not now.

'We shall see, we shall see,' he repeated to himself.

But no sooner had he opened the door than he stumbled upon Porfiry himself in the passage. He was coming in to see him. Raskolnikov was dumbfounded for a minute, but only for one minute. Strange to say, he was not very much astonished at seeing Porfiry and scarcely afraid of him. He was simply startled, but was quickly, instantly, on his guard. 'Perhaps this will mean the end? But how could Porfiry have approached so quietly, like a cat, so that he had heard nothing? Could he have been listening at the door?'

'You didn't expect a visitor, Rodion Romanovitch,' Porfiry explained, laughing. 'I've been meaning to look in a long time; I was passing by and thought why not go in for five minutes? Are you going out? I won't keep you long. Just let me have one cigarette.'

'Sit down, Porfiry Petrovitch, sit down.' Raskolnikov gave his visitor a seat with so pleased and friendly an expression that he would have marvelled at himself if he could have seen it.

The last moment had come, the last drops had to be drained! So a man will sometimes go through half an hour of mortal terror with a brigand, yet when the knife is at this throat at last, he feels no fear.

Raskolnikov seated himself directly facing Porfiry, and looked at him without flinching. Porfiry screwed up his eyes and began lighting a cigarette.

'Speak, speak!' seemed as though it would burst from Raskolnikov's heart. 'Come, why don't you speak?'

⟫ TWO ⟪

'AH, THESE CIGARETTES!' PORFIRY Petrovitch ejaculated at last, having lighted one. 'They are pernicious, positively pernicious, and yet I can't give them up! I cough, I begin to have a tickling in my throat and a difficulty in breathing. You know I am a coward, I went lately to Dr. B — n; he always gives at least half an hour to each patient. He positively laughed looking at me; he sounded me: "Tobacco's bad for you," he said, "your lungs are affected." But how am I to give it up? What is there to take its place? I don't drink, that's the mischief, he-he-he, that I don't. Everything is relative, Rodion Romanovitch, everything is relative!'

'Why, he's playing his professional tricks again,' Raskolnikov thought with disgust. All the circumstances of their last interview suddenly came back to him, and he felt a rush of the feeling that had come upon him then.

'I came to see you the day before yesterday, in the evening; you didn't know?' Porfiry Petrovitch went on looking round the room. 'I came into this very room. I was passing by, just as I did to-day, and I thought I'd return your call. I walked in as your door was wide open, I looked round, waited and went out without leaving my name with your servant. Don't you lock your door?'

Raskolnikov's face grew more and more gloomy. Porfiry seemed to guess his state of mind.

'I've come to have it out with you, Rodion Romanovitch, my dear fellow! I owe you an explanation and must give it to you,' he continued with a slight smile, just patting Raskolnikov's knee.

But almost at the same instant a serious and careworn look came into his face; to his surprise Raskolnikov saw a touch of sadness in it. He had never seen and never suspected such an expression in his face.

'A strange scene passed between us last time we met, Rodion Romanovitch. Our first interview, too, was a strange one; but then . . . and one thing after another! This is the point: I have perhaps acted unfairly to you; I feel it. Do you remember how we parted? Your nerves were unhinged and your knees were shaking and so were mine. And, you know, our behaviour was unseemly, even ungentlemanly. And yet we are gentlemen, above all, in any case, gentlemen; that must be understood. Do you remember what we came to? . . . and it was quite indecorous.'

'What is he up to, what does he take me for?' Raskolnikov asked himself in amazement, raising his head and looking with open eyes on Porfiry.

'I've decided openness is better between us,' Porfiry Petrovitch went on, turning his head away and dropping his eyes, as though unwilling to disconcert his former victim and as though disdaining his former wiles. 'Yes, such suspicions and such scenes cannot continue for long. Nikolay put a stop to it, or I don't know what we might not have come to. That damned workman was sitting at the time in the next room – can you realize that? You know that, of course; and I am aware that he came to you afterwards. But what you supposed then was not true: I had not sent for anyone, I had made no kind of arrangements. You ask why I hadn't? What shall I say to you? it had all come upon me so suddenly. I had scarcely sent for the porters (you noticed them as you went out, I dare say). An idea flashed upon me; I was firmly convinced at the time, you see, Rodion Romanovitch. Come, I thought – even if I let one thing slip for a time, I shall get hold of something else – I shan't lose what I want, anyway. You are nervously irritable, Rodion Romanovitch, by temperament; it's out of proportion with other qualities of your heart and character, which I flatter myself I have to some extent divined. Of course I did reflect even then that it does not always happen that a man gets up and blurts out his whole story. It does happen sometimes, if you make a man lose all patience, though even then it's rare. I was capable of realizing that. If I only had a fact, I thought, the least little fact to go upon, something I could lay hold of, something tangible, not merely psychological. For if a man is guilty, you must be able to get something substantial out of him; one may reckon upon most surprising results indeed. I was reckoning on your temperament, Rodion Romanovitch, on your temperament above all things! I had great hopes of you at that time.'

'But what are you driving at now?' Raskolnikov muttered at last, asking the question without thinking.

'What is he talking about?' he wondered distractedly, 'does he really take me to be innocent?'

'What am I driving at? I've come to explain myself, I consider it my duty, so to speak. I want to make clear to you how the whole business, the whole misunderstanding arose. I've caused you a great deal of suffering, Rodion Romanovitch. I am not a monster. I understand what it must mean for a man who has been unfortunate, but who is proud, imperious and above all, impatient, to have to bear such treatment! I regard you in any case as a man of noble character, and not without elements of magnanimity, though I don't agree with all your convictions. I wanted to tell you this first, frankly and quite sincerely, for above all I don't want to deceive you. When I made your acquaintance, I felt attracted by you. Perhaps you will laugh at my saying so. You have a right to. I know you disliked me from the first and indeed you've no reason to like me. You may think what you like, but I desire now to do all I can to efface that impression and to show that I am a man of heart and conscience. I speak sincerely.'

Porfiry Petrovitch made a dignified pause. Raskolnikov felt a rush of renewed alarm. The thought that Porfiry believed him to be innocent began to make him uneasy.

'It's scarcely necessary to go over everything in detail,' Porfiry Petrovitch went on. 'Indeed, I could scarcely attempt it. To begin with, there were rumours. Through whom, how, and when those rumours came to me . . . and how they affected you, I need not go into. My suspicions were aroused by a complete accident, which might just as easily not have happened. What was it? Hm! I believe there is no need to go into that either. Those rumours and that accident led to one idea in my mind. I admit it openly – for one may as well make a clean breast of it – I was the first to pitch on you. The old woman's notes on the pledges and the rest of it – that all came to nothing. Yours was one of a hundred. I happened, too, to hear of the scene at the office, from a man who described it capitally, unconsciously reproducing the scene with great vividness. It was just one thing after another, Rodion Romanovitch, my dear fellow! How could I avoid being brought to certain ideas? From a hundred rabbits you can't make a horse, a hundred suspicions don't make a proof, as the English proverb says, but that's only from the rational point of view – you can't help being partial, for after all a lawyer is only human. I thought, too, of your article in that journal, do you remember, on your first visit we talked of it? I jeered at you at the time, but that was only to lead you on. I repeat, Rodion Romanovitch, you are ill and impatient. That you were bold, headstrong, in earnest and . . . had felt a great deal I recognized long before. I, too, have felt the same, so that your article seemed familiar to me. It was conceived on sleepless nights, with a throbbing heart, in ecstasy and suppressed enthusiasm. And that proud suppressed enthusiasm in young people is dangerous! I jeered at you then, but let me tell you that, as a literary amateur, I am awfully fond of such essays, full of the heat of youth. There is a mistiness and a chord vibrating in the mist. Your article is absurd and fantastic, but there's a transparent sincerity, a youthful incorruptible pride and the daring of despair in it. It's a gloomy article, but that's what's fine in it. I read your article and put it aside, thinking as I did so "that man won't go the common way". Well, I ask you, after that as a preliminary, how could I help being carried away by what followed? Oh dear, I am not saying anything, I am not making any statement now. I simply noted it at the time. What is there in it? I reflected. There's nothing in it, that is really nothing and perhaps absolutely nothing. And it's not at all the thing for the prosecutor to let himself be carried away by notions: here I have Nikolay on my hands with actual evidence against him – you may think what you like of it, but it's evidence. He brings in his psychology, too; one has to consider him, too, for it's a matter of life and death. Why am I explaining this to you? That you may understand, and not blame my malicious behaviour on that occasion. It was not malicious, I assure you, he-he! Do you suppose I didn't come to search your room at the time? I did, he-he! I was here when you were lying ill in bed, not officially, not in my own person, but I was here. Your room was searched to the last thread at the first suspicion; but *umsonst!* I thought to myself, now that man will come, will come of himself and quickly, too; if he's guilty, he's sure to come. Another man wouldn't, but he will. And you remember how Mr. Razumihin began discussing the subject with you? We arranged that to excite you, so we purposely spread rumours, that he might discuss the case with you, and Razumihin is not a man to restrain his indignation. Mr. Zametov was tremendously struck by your anger and your open daring. Think of blurting out in a restaurant "I killed her". It was too daring, too reckless. I thought to myself, if he is guilty he will be a formidable opponent. That was what I thought at the time. I was expecting you. But you simply bowled Zametov over and . . . well, you see, it all lies in this – that this damnable psychology can be taken two ways! Well, I kept expecting you, and so it was, you came! My heart was fairly throbbing. Ach!

'Now, why need you have come? Your laughter, too, as you came in, do you remember? I saw it all plain as daylight, but if I hadn't expected you so specially, I should not have noticed anything in your laughter. You see what influence a mood has! Mr. Razumihin then – ah, that stone, that stone under which the things were hidden! I seem to see it somewhere in a kitchen garden. It was in a kitchen garden, you told Zametov and afterwards you repeated that in my office? And when we began picking your article to pieces, how you explained it! One could take every word of yours in two senses, as though there were another meaning hidden.

'So in this way, Rodion Romanovitch, I reached the furthest limit, and knocking my head against a post, I pulled myself up, asking myself what I was about. After all, I said, you can take it all in another sense if you like, and it's more natural so, indeed. I couldn't help admitting it was more natural. I was bothered! "No, I'd better get hold of some little fact," I said. So when I heard of the bell-ringing, I held my breath and was all in a tremor. "Here is my little fact," thought I, and I didn't think it over, I simply wouldn't. I would have given a thousand roubles at that minute to have seen you with my own eyes, when you walked a hundred paces beside that workman, after he had called you murderer to your face, and you did not dare to ask him a question all the way. And then what about your trembling, what about your bell-ringing in your illness, in semi-delirium?

'And so, Rodion Romanovitch, can you wonder that I played such pranks on you? And what made you come at that very minute? Someone seemed to have sent you, by Jove! And if Nikolay had not parted us . . . and do you remember Nikolay at the time? Do you remember him clearly? It was a thunderbolt, a regular thunderbolt! And how I met him! I didn't believe in the thunderbolt not for a minute. You could see it for yourself; and how could I? Even afterwards, when you had gone and he began making very, very plausible answers on certain points, so that I was surprised at him myself, even then I didn't believe his story! You see what it is to be as firm as a rock! No, thought I, *Morgenfrüh*. What has Nikolay got to do with it!'

'Razumihin told me just now that you think Nikolay guilty and had yourself assured him of it. . . .'

His voice failed him, and he broke off. He had been listening in indescribable agitation, as this man, who had seen through and through him, went back upon himself. He was afraid of believing it and did not believe it. In those still ambiguous words he kept eagerly looking for something more definite and conclusive.

'Mr. Razumihin!' cried Porfiry Petrovitch, seeming glad of a question from Raskolnikov, who had till then been silent. 'He-he-he! But I had to put Mr. Razumihin off: two is company, three is none. Mr. Razumihin is not the right man, besides he is an outsider. He came running to me with a pale face. . . . But never mind him, why bring him in? To return to Nikolay, would you like to know what sort of a type he is, how I understand him, that is? To begin with, he is still a child and not exactly a coward, but something by way of an artist. Really, don't laugh at my describing him so. He is innocent and responsive to influence. He has a heart, and is a fantastic fellow. He sings and dances, he tells stories, they say, so that people come from other villages to hear him. He attends school too, and laughs till he cries if you hold up a finger to him; he will drink himself senseless – not as a regular vice, but at times, when people treat him, like a child. And he stole too, then, without knowing it himself, for "How can it be stealing, if one picks it up?" And do you know he is an Old Believer, or rather a dissenter? There have been Wanderers* in his family, and he was for two years in his village under the spiritual guidance of a certain elder. I learnt all this from Nikolay and from his fellow-villagers. And what's more, he wanted to run into the wilderness! He was full of fervour, prayed at nights, read the old books, the "true" ones, and read himself crazy.

'Petersburg had a great effect upon him, especially the women and the wine. He responds to everything and he forgot the elder and all that. I learnt that an artist here took a fancy to him, and used to go and see him, and now this business came upon him.

'Well, he was frightened, he tried to hang himself He ran away! How can one get over the idea the people have of Russian legal proceedings? The very word "trial" frightens some of them. Whose fault is it? We shall see what the new juries will do. God grant they do good! Well, in prison, it seems, he remembered the venerable elder; the Bible, too, made its appearance again. Do you know, Rodion Romanovitch, the force of the word "suffering" among some of these people? It's not a question of suffering for someone's benefit, but simply, "one must suffer". If they suffer at the hands of the authorities, so much the better. In my time there was a very meek and mild prisoner who spent a whole year in prison always reading his Bible on the stove at night and he read himself crazy, and so crazy, do you know, that one day, apropos of nothing, he seized a brick and flung it at the governor; though he had done him no harm. And the way he threw it too: aimed it a yard on one side on purpose, for fear of hurting him. Well, we know what happens to a prisoner who assaults an officer with a weapon. So "he took his suffering".

'So I suspect now that Nikolay wants to take his suffering or something of the sort. I know it for certain from facts, indeed. Only he doesn't know that I know. What, you don't admit that there are such fantastic people among the peasants? Lots of them. The elder now has begun influencing him, especially since he tried to hang himself. But he'll come and tell me all himself. You think he'll hold out? Wait a bit, he'll take his words back. I am waiting from hour to hour for him to come and abjure his evidence. I have come to like that Nikolay and am studying him in detail. And what do you think? He-he! He answered me very plausibly on some points, he obviously had collected some evidence and prepared himself cleverly. But on other points he is simply at sea, knows nothing and doesn't even suspect that he doesn't know!

'No, Rodion Romanovitch, Nikolay doesn't come in! This is a fantastic,

*A religious sect. – TRANSLATOR'S NOTE.

gloomy business, a modern case, an incident of to-day when the heart of man is troubled, when the phrase is quoted that blood "renews", when comfort is preached as the aim of life. Here we have bookish dreams, a heart unhinged by theories. Here we see resolution in the first stage, but resolution of a special kind: he resolved to do it like jumping over a precipice of from a bell-tower and his legs shook as he went to the crime. He forgot to shut the door after him, and murdered two people for a theory. He committed the murder and couldn't take the money, and what he did manage to snatch up he hid under a stone. It wasn't enough for him to suffer agony behind the door while they battered at the door and rang the bell, no, he had to go to the empty lodging, half delirious, to recall the bell-ringing, he wanted to feel the cold shiver over again. . . . Well, that, we grant, was through illness, but consider this: he is a murderer, but looks upon himself as an honest man, despises others, poses as injured innocence. No, that's not the work of a Nikolay, my dear Rodion Romanovitch!'

All that had been said before had sounded so like a recantation that these words were too great a shock. Raskolnikov shuddered as though he had been stabbed.

'Then . . . who then . . . is the murderer?' he asked in a breathless voice, unable to restrain himself.

Porfiry Petrovitch sank back in his chair, as though he were amazed at the question.

'Who is the murderer?' he repeated, as though unable to believe his ears. 'Why, *you*, Rodion Romanovitch! You are the murderer,' he added, almost in a whisper, in a voice of genuine conviction.

Raskolnikov leapt from the sofa, stood up for a few seconds and sat down again without uttering a word. His face twitched convulsively.

'Your lip is twitching just as it did before,' Porfiry Petrovitch observed almost sympathetically. 'You've been misunderstanding me, I think, Rodion Romanovitch,' he added after a brief pause, 'that's why you are so surprised. I came on purpose to tell you everything and deal openly with you.'

'It was not I murdered her,' Raskolnikov whispered like a frightened child caught in the act.

'No, it was you, you, Rodion Romanovitch, and no one else,' Porfiry whispered sternly, with conviction.

They were both silent and the silence lasted strangely long, about ten minutes. Raskolnikov put his elbow on the table and passed his fingers through his hair. Porfiry Petrovitch sat quietly waiting. Suddenly Raskolnikov looked scornfully at Porfiry.

'You are at your old tricks again, Porfiry Petrovitch! Your old method again. I wonder you don't get sick of it!'

'Oh, stop that, what does it matter now? It would be a different matter if there were witnesses present, but we are whispering alone. You see yourself that I have not come to chase and capture you like a hare. Whether you confess it or not is nothing to me now; for myself, I am convinced without it.'

'If so, what did you come for?' Raskolnikov asked irritably. 'I ask you the same question again: if you consider me guilty, why don't you take me to prison?'

'Oh, that's your question! I will answer you, point for point. In the first place, to arrest you so directly is not to my interest.'

'How so? If you are convinced you ought. . . .'

'Ach, what if I am convinced? That's only my dream for the time. Why should I put you in safety? You know that's it, since you ask me to do it. If I confront you with that workman for instance and you say to him, "Were you drunk or not? Who saw me with you? I simply took you to be drunk, and you were drunk, too." Well, what could I answer, especially as your story is a more likely one than his? for there's nothing but psychology to support his evidence – that's almost unseemly with his ugly mug, while you hit the mark exactly, for the rascal is an inveterate drunkard and notoriously so. And I have myself admitted candidly several times already that that psychology can be taken in two ways and that the second way is stronger and looks far more probable, and that apart from that I have as yet nothing against you. And though I shall put you in prison and indeed have come – quite contrary to etiquette – to inform you of it beforehand, yet I tell you frankly, also contrary to etiquette, that it won't be to my advantage. Well, secondly, I've come to you because . . .'

'Yes, yes, secondly?' Raskolnikov was listening breathlessly.

'Because, as I told you just now, I consider I owe you an explanation. I don't want you to look upon me as a monster, as I have a genuine liking for you, you may believe me or not. And in the third place I've come to you with a direct and open proposition – that you should surrender and confess. It will be infinitely more to your advantage and to my advantage too, for my task will be done. Well, is this open on my part or not?'

Raskolnikov thought a minute.

'Listen, Porfiry Petrovitch. You said just now you have nothing but psychology to go on, yet now you've gone on to mathematics. Well, what if you are mistaken yourself, now?'

'No, Rodion Romanovitch, I am not mistaken. I have a little fact even then, Providence sent it me.'

'What little fact?'

'I won't tell you what, Rodion Romanovitch. And in any case, I haven't the right to put it off any longer, I must arrest you. So think it over: it makes no different to me *now* and so I speak only your sake. Believe me, it will be better, Rodion Romanovitch.'

Raskolnikov smiled malignantly.

'That's not simply ridiculous, it's positively shameless. Why, even if I were guilty, which I don't admit, what reason should I have to confess, when you tell me yourself that I shall be in greater safety in prison?'

'Ah, Rodion Romanovitch, don't put too much faith in words, perhaps prison will not be altogether a restful place. That's only theory and my theory, and what authority am I for you? Perhaps, too, even now I am hiding something from you? I can't lay bare everything, he-he! And how can you ask what advantage? Don't you know how it would lessen your sentence? You would be confessing at a moment when another man has taken the crime on himself and so has muddled the whole case. Consider that! I swear before God that I will so arrange that your confession shall come as a complete surprise. We will make a clean sweep of all these psychological points, of all suspicion against you, so that your crime will appear to have been something like an aberration, for in truth it was an aberration. I am an honest man, Rodion Romanovitch, and will keep my word.'

Raskolnikov maintained a mournful silence and let his head sink dejectedly. He pondered a long while and at last smiled again, but his smile was sad and gentle.

'No!' he said, apparently abandoning all attempt to keep up appearances with Porfiry, 'it's not worth it, I don't care about lessening the sentence!'

'That's just what I was afraid of' Porfiry cried warmly and, as it seemed, involuntarily, 'that's just what I feared, that you wouldn't care about the mitigation of sentence.'

Raskolnikov looked sadly and expressively at him.

'Ah, don't disdain life!' Porfiry went on. 'You have a great deal of it still before you. How can you say you don't want a mitigation of sentence? You are an impatient fellow!'

'A great deal of what lies before me?'

'Of life. What sort of prophet are you, do you know much about it? Seek and ye shall find. This may be God's means for bringing you to Him. And it's not for ever, the bondage. . . .'

'The time will be shortened,' laughed Raskolnikov.

'Why, is it the bourgeois disgrace you are afraid of? It may be that you are afraid of it without knowing it, because you are young! But anyway *you* shouldn't be afraid of giving yourself up and confessing.'

'Ach, hang it!' Raskolnikov whispered with loathing and contempt, as though he did not want to speak aloud.

He got up again as though he meant to go away, but sat down again in evident despair.

'Hang it, if you like! You've lost faith and you think that I am grossly flattering you; but how long has your life been? How much do you understand? You made up a theory and then were ashamed that it broke down and turned out to be not at all original! It turned out something base, that's true, but you are not hopelessly base. By no means so base! At least you didn't deceive yourself for long, you went straight to the furthest point at one bound. How do I regard you ? I regard you as one of those men who would stand and smile at their torturer while he cuts their entrails out, if only they have found faith or God. Find it and you will live. You have long needed a change of air. Suffering, too, is a good thing. Suffer! Maybe Nikolay is right in wanting to suffer. I know you don't believe in it – but don't be over-wise; fling yourself straight into life, without deliberation; don't be afraid – the flood will bear you to the bank and set you safe on your feet again. What bank? How can I tell? I only believe that you have long life before you. I know that you take all my words now for a set speech prepared beforehand, but maybe you will remember them after. They may be of use some time. That's why I speak. It's as well that you only killed the old woman. If you'd invented another theory you might perhaps have done something a thousand times more hideous. You ought to thank God, perhaps. How do you know? Perhaps God is saving you for something. But keep a good heart and have less fear! Are you afraid of the great expiation before you? No, it would be shameful to be afraid of it. Since you have taken such a step, you must harden your heart. There is justice in it. You must fulfil the demands of justice. I know that you don't believe it, but indeed, life will bring you through. You will live it down in time. What you need now is fresh air, fresh air, fresh air!'

Raskolnikov positively started.

'But who are you? what prophet are you? From the height of what majestic calm do you proclaim these words of wisdom?'

'Who am I? I am a man with nothing to hope for, that's all. A man perhaps of feeling and sympathy, maybe of some knowledge too, but my day is over. But you are a different matter, there is life waiting for you. Though, who knows? maybe your life too, will pass off in smoke and come to nothing. Come, what does it matter, that you will pass into another class of men? It's not comfort you regret, with your heart! What of it that perhaps no one will see you for so long? It's not time, but yourself that will decide that. Be the sun and all will see you. The sun has before all to be the sun. Why are you smiling again? At my being such as Schiller? I bet you're imagining that I am trying to get round you by flattery. Well, perhaps I am, he-he-he! Perhaps you'd better not believe my word, perhaps you'd better never believe it altogether – I'm made that way, I confess it. But let me add, you can judge for yourself, I think, how far I am a base sort of man and how far I am honest.'

'When do you mean to arrest me?'

'Well, I can let you walk about another day or two. Think it over, my dear fellow, and pray to God. It's more in your interest, believe me.'

'And what if I run away?' asked Raskolnikov with a strange smile.

'No, you won't run away. A peasant would run away, a fashionable dissenter would run away, the flunkey of another man's thought, for you've only to show him the end of your little finger and he'll be ready to believe in anything for the rest of his life. But you've ceased to believe in your theory already, what will you run away with? And what would you do in hiding? It would be hateful and difficult for you, and what you need more than anything in life is a definite position, an atmosphere to suit you. And what sort of atmosphere would you have? If you ran away, you'd come back of yourself. *You can't get on without us.* And if I put you in prison – say you've been there a month, or two, or three – remember my word, you'll confess of yourself and perhaps to your own surprise. You won't know an hour beforehand that you are coming with a confession. I am convinced that you will decide, "to take your suffering". You don't believe my words now, but you'll come to it of yourself. For suffering, Rodion Romanovitch, is a great thing. Never mind my having grown fat, I know all the same. Don't laugh at it, there's an idea in suffering, Nikolay is right. No, you won't run away, Rodion Romanovitch.'

Raskolnikov got up and took his cap. Porfiry Petrovitch also rose.

'Are you going for a walk? The evening will be fine, if only we don't have a storm. Though it would be a good thing to freshen the air.'

He, too, took his cap.

'Porfiry Petrovitch, please don't take up the notion that I have confessed to you to-day,' Raskolnikov pronounced with sullen insistence. 'You're a strange man and I have listened to you from simple curiosity. But I have admitted nothing, remember that!'

'Oh, I know that, I'll remember. Look at him, he's trembling! Don't be uneasy, my dear fellow, have it your own way. Walk about a bit, you won't be able to walk too far. If anything happens, I have one request to make of you,' he added, dropping his voice. 'It's an awkward one, but important. If anything were to happen (though indeed I don't believe in it and think you quite incapable of it), yet in case you were taken during these forty or fifty hours with the notion of putting an end to the business in some other way, in some fantastic fashion – laying hands on yourself – (it's an absurd proposition, but you must forgive me for it), do leave a brief but precise note, only two lines, and mention the stone. It will be more generous. Come, till we meet! Good thoughts and sound decisions to you!'

Porfiry went out, stooping and avoiding looking at Raskolnikov. The latter went to the window and waited with irritable impatience till he calculated that Porfiry had reached the street and moved away. Then he too went hurriedly out of the room.

⇉ THREE ⇇

HE HURRIED TO SVIDRIGAÏLOV's. What he had to hope from that man he did not know. But that man had some hidden power over him. Having once recognized this, he could not rest, and now the time had come.

On the way, one question particularly worried him: had Svidrigaïlov been to Porfiry's?

As far as he could judge, he would swear to it, that he had not. He pondered again and again, went over Porfiry's visit; no, he hadn't been, of course he hadn't.

But if he had not been yet, would he go? Meanwhile, for the present he fancied he wouldn't. Why? He could not have explained, but if he could, he would not have wasted much thought over it at the moment. It all worried him and at the same time he could not attend to it. Strange to say, none would have believed it perhaps, but he only felt a faint vague anxiety about his immediate future. Another, much more important anxiety tormented him – it concerned himself, but in a different, more vital way. Moreover, he was conscious of immense moral fatigue, though his mind was working better that morning than it had done of late.

And was it worth while, after all that had happened, to contend with these new trivial difficulties? Was it worth while for instance to manœuvre that Svidrigaïlov should not go to Porfiry's? Was it worth while to investigate, to ascertain the facts, to waste time over anyone like Svidrigaïlov?

Oh, how sick he was of it all!

And yet he was hastening to Svidrigaïlov; could he be expecting something *new* from him, information, or means of escape? Men will catch at straws! Was it destiny or some instinct bringing them together? Perhaps it was only fatigue, despair; perhaps it was not Svidrigaïlov but some other whom he needed, and Svidrigaïlov had simply presented himself by chance. Sonia? But what should he go to Sonia for now? To beg her tears again? He was afraid of Sonia, too. Sonia stood before him as an irrevocable sentence. He must go his own way or hers. At that moment especially he did not feel equal to seeing her. No, would it not be better to try Svidrigaïlov? And he could not help inwardly owning that he had long felt that he must see him for some reason.

But what could they have in common? Their very evil-doing could not be of the same kind. The man, moreover, was very unpleasant, evidently depraved, undoubtedly cunning and deceitful, possibly malignant. Such stories were told about him. It is true he was befriending Katerina Ivanovna's children, but who could tell with what motive and what it meant? The man always had some design, some project.

There was another thought which had been continually hovering of late about Raskolnikov's mind, and causing him great uneasiness. It was so painful that he made distinct efforts to get rid of it. He sometimes thought that Svidrigaïlov was dogging his footsteps. Svidrigaïlov had found out his secret and had had designs on Dounia. What if he had them still? Wasn't it practically certain that he had? And what if, having learnt his secret and so having gained power over him, he were to use it as a weapon against Dounia?

This idea sometimes even tormented his dreams, but it had never presented itself so vividly to him as on his way to Svidrigaïlov. The very thought moved him to gloomy rage. To begin with, this would transform everything, even his own position; he would have at once to confess his secret to Dounia. Would he have to give himself up perhaps to prevent Dounia from taking some rash step? The letter? This morning Dounia had received a letter. From whom could she get letters in Petersburg? Luzhin, perhaps? It's true Razumihin was there to protect her; but Razumihin knew nothing of the position. Perhaps it was his duty to tell Razumihin? He thought of it with repugnance.

In any case he must see Svidrigaïlov as soon as possible, he decided finally. Thank God, the details of the interview were of little consequence, if only he could get at the root of the matter; but if Svidrigaïlov were capable . . . if he were intriguing against Dounia – then . . .

Raskolnikov was so exhausted by what he had passed through that month that he could only decide such questions in one way; 'then I shall kill him,' he thought in cold despair.

A sudden anguish oppressed his heart, he stood still in the middle of the street and began looking about to see where he was and which way he was going. He found himself in X. Prospect, thirty or forty paces from the Hay Market, through which he had come. The whole second storey of the house on the left was used as a tavern. All the windows were wide open; judging from the figures moving at the windows, the rooms were full to overflowing. There were sounds of singing, of clarionet and violin, and the boom of a Turkish drum. He could hear women shrieking. He was about to turn back wondering why he had come to the X. Prospect, when suddenly at one of the end windows he saw Svidrigaïlov, sitting at a tea-table right in the open window with a pipe in his mouth. Raskolnikov was dreadfully taken aback, almost terrified. Svidrigaïlov was silently watching and scrutinizing him and, what struck Raskolnikov at once, seemed to be meaning to get up and slip away unobserved. Raskolnikov at once pretended not to have seen him, but to be looking absent-mindedly away, while he watched him out of the corner of his eye. His heart was beating violently. Yes, it was evident that Svidrigaïlov did not want to be seen. He took the pipe out of his mouth and was on the point of concealing himself, but as he got up and moved back his chair, he seemed to have become suddenly aware that Raskolnikov had seen him, and was watching him. What had passed between them was much the same as what happened at their first meeting in Raskolnikov's room. A sly smile came into Svidrigaïlov's face and grew broader and broader. Each knew that he was seen and watched by the other. At last Svidrigaïlov broke into a loud laugh.

'Well, well, come in if you want me; I am here!' he shouted from the window.

Raskolnikov went up into the tavern. He found Svidrigaïlov in a tiny back room, adjoining the saloon in which merchants, clerks and numbers of people of all sorts were drinking tea at twenty little tables to the desperate bawling of a chorus of singers. The click of billiard balls could be heard in the distance. On the table before Svidrigaïlov stood an open bottle and a glass half full of champagne. In the room he found also a boy with a little hand organ, a healthy-looking red-cheeked girl of eighteen, wearing a tucked-up striped skirt, and a Tyrolese hat with ribbons. In spite of the chorus in the other room, she was singing some servants' hall song in a rather husky contralto, to the accompaniment of the organ.

'Come, that's enough,' Svidrigaïlov stopped her at Raskolnikov's entrance. The girl at once broke off and stood waiting respectfully. She had sung her gutter rhymes, too, with a serious and respectful expression in her face.

'Hey, Philip, a glass!' shouted Svidrigaïlov.

'I won't drink anything,' said Raskolnikov.

'As you like, I didn't mean it for you. Drink, Katia! I don't want anything more to-day, you can go.' He poured her out a full glass, and laid down a yellow note.

Katia drank off her glass of wine, as women do, without putting it down, in twenty gulps, took the note and kissed Svidrigaïlov's hand, which he allowed quite seriously. She went out of the room and the boy trailed after her with the organ. Both had been brought in from the street. Svidrigaïlov had not been a week in Petersburg, but everything about him was already, so to speak, on a patriarchal footing; the waiter, Philip, was by now an old friend and very obsequious.

The door leading to the saloon had a lock on it. Svidrigaïlov was at home in this room and perhaps spent whole days in it. The tavern was dirty and wretched, not even second-rate.

'I was going to see you and looking for you,' Raskolnikov began, 'but I don't know what made me turn from the Hay Market into the X. Prospect just now. I never take this turning. I turn to the right from the Hay Market. And this isn't the way to you. I simply turned and here you are. It is strange!'

'Why don't you say at once "it's a miracle"?'

'Because it may be only chance.'

'Oh, that's the way with all you folk,' laughed Svidrigaïlov. 'You won't admit it, even if you do inwardly believe it a miracle! Here you say that it may be only chance. And what cowards they all are here, about having an opinion of their own, you can't fancy, Rodion Romanovitch. I don't mean you, you have an opinion of your own and are not afraid to have it. That's how it was you attracted my curiosity.'

'Nothing else?'

'Well, that's enough, you know.' Svidrigaïlov was obviously exhilarated, but only slightly so, he had not had more than half a glass of wine.

'I fancy you came to see me before you knew that I was capable of having what you call an opinion of my own,' observed Raskolnikov.

'Oh, well, it was a different matter. Everyone has his own plans. And apropos of the miracle let me tell you that I think you have been asleep for the last two or three days. I told you of this tavern myself, there is no miracle in your coming straight here. I explained the way myself, told you where it was, and the hours you could find me here. Do you remember?'

'I don't remember,' answered Raskolnikov with surprise.

'I believe you. I told you twice. The address has been stamped mechanically on your memory. You turned this way mechanically and yet precisely according to the direction, though you are not aware of it. When I told it you then, I hardly hoped you understood me. You give yourself away too much, Rodion Romanovitch. And another thing, I'm convinced there are lots of people in Petersburg who talk to themselves as they walk. This is a town of crazy people. If only we had scientific men, doctors, lawyers and philosophers might make most valuable investigations in Petersburg each in his own line. There are few places where there are so many gloomy, strong and queer influences on the soul of man as in Petersburg. The mere influences of climate meant so much. And its the administrative centre of all Russia and its character must be reflected on the whole country. But that is neither here nor there now. The point is that I have several times watched you. You walk out of your house – holding your head high – twenty paces from home you let it sink, and fold your hands behind your back. You look and evidently see nothing before nor beside you. At last you begin moving your lips and talking to yourself, and sometimes you wave one hand and declaim, and at last stand still in the middle of the road. That's not at all the thing. Someone may be watching you besides me, and it won't do you any good. It's nothing really to do with me and I can't cure you, but, of course, you understand me.'

'Do you know that I am being followed?' asked Raskolnikov, looking inquisitively at him.

'No, I know nothing about it,' said Svidrigaïlov, seeming surprised.

'Well, then, let us leave me alone,' Raskolnikov muttered, frowning.

'Very good, let us leave you alone.'

'You had better tell me, if you come here to drink, and directed me twice to come here to you, why did you hide, and try to get away just now when I looked at the window from the street? I saw it.'

'He-he! And why was it you lay on your sofa with closed eyes and pretended to be asleep, though you were wide awake while I stood in your doorway? I saw it.'

'I may have had . . . reasons. You know that yourself.'

'And I may have had my reasons, though you don't know them.'

Raskolnikov dropped his right elbow on the table, leaned his chin in the fingers of his right hand, and stared intently at Svidrigaïlov. For a full minute he scrutinized his face, which had impressed him before. It was a strange face, like a mask; white and red, with bright red lips, with a flaxen beard, and still thick flaxen hair. His eyes were somehow too blue and their expression somehow too heavy and fixed. There was something awfully unpleasant in that handsome face, which looked so wonderfully young for his age. Svidrigaïlov was smartly dressed in light summer clothes and was particularly dainty in his linen. He wore a huge ring with a precious stone in it.

'Have I got to bother myself about you, too, now?' said Raskolnikov suddenly, coming with nervous impatience straight to the point. 'Even though perhaps you are the most dangerous man if you care to injure me, I don't want to put myself out any more. I will show you at once that I don't prize myself as you probably think I do. I've come to tell you at once that if you keep to your former intentions with regard to my sister and if you think to derive any benefit in that direction from what has been discovered of late, I will kill you before you get me locked up. You can reckon on my word. You know that I can keep it. And in the second place if you want to tell me anything – for I keep fancying all this time that you have something to tell me – make haste and tell it, for time is precious and very likely it will soon be too late.'

'Why in such haste?' asked Svidrigaïlov, looking at him curiously.

'Everyone has his plans,' Raskolnikov answered gloomily and impatiently.

'You urged me yourself to frankness just now, and at the first question you refuse to answer,' Svidrigaïlov observed with a smile. 'You keep fancying that I have aims of my own and so you look at me with suspicion. Of course it's perfectly natural in your position. But though I should like to be friends with you, I shan't trouble myself to convince you of the contrary. The game isn't worth the candle and I wasn't intending to talk to you about anything special.'

'What did you want me for, then? It was you who came hanging about me.'

'Why, simply as an interesting subject for observation. I liked the fantastic nature of your position – that's what it was! Besides, you are the brother of a person who greatly interested me, and from that person I had in the past heard a very great deal about you, from which I gathered that you had a great influence over her; isn't that enough? Ha-ha-ha! Still I must admit that your question is rather complex, and is difficult for me to answer. Here, you, for instance, have come to me not only for a definite object but for the sake of hearing something new. Isn't that so? Isn't that so?' persisted Svidrigaïlov with a sly smile. 'Well, can't you fancy than that I, too, on my way here in the train was reckoning on you, on your telling me something new, and on my making some profit out of you? You see what rich men we are!'

'What profit could you make?'

'How can I tell you? How do I know? You see in what a tavern I spend all my time and it's my enjoyment, that's to say it's no great enjoyment, but one must sit somewhere; that poor Katia now – you saw her? . . . If only I had been a glutton now, a club gourmand, but you see I can eat this.'

He pointed to a little table in the corner where the remnants of a terrible-looking beef-steak and potatoes lay on a tin dish.

'Have you dined, by the way? I've had something and want nothing more. I don't drink, for instance, at all. Except champagne I never touch anything, and not more than a glass of that all the evening, and even that is enough to make my head ache. I ordered it just now to wind myself up, for I am just going off somewhere and you see me in a peculiar state of mind. That was why I hid myself just now like a schoolboy, for I was afraid you would hinder me. But I believe,' he pulled out his watch, 'I can spend an hour with you. It's half-past four now. If only I'd been something, a landowner, a father, a cavalry officer, a photographer, a journalist . . . I am nothing, no speciality, and sometimes I am positively bored. I really thought you would tell me something new.'

'But what are you, and why have you come here?'

'What am I? You know, a gentleman, I served for two years in the cavalry, then I knocked about here in Petersburg, then I married Marfa Petrovna and lived in the country. There you have my biography!'

'You are a gambler, I believe?'

'No, a poor sort of gambler. A card-sharper – not a gambler.'

'You have been a card-sharper then?'

'Yes, I've been a card-sharper too.'

'Didn't you get thrashed sometimes?'

'It did happen. Why?'

'Why, you might have challenged them . . . altogether it must have been lively.'

'I won't contradict you, and besides I am no hand at philosophy. I confess that I hastened here for the sake of the women.'

'As soon as you buried Marfa Petrovna?'

'Quite so,' Svidrigaïlov smiled with engaging candour. 'What of it? You seem to find something wrong in my speaking like that about women?'

'You ask whether I find anything wrong in vice?'

'Vice! Oh, that's what you are after! But I'll answer you in order, first about women in general; you know I am fond of talking. Tell me, what should I restrain myself for? Why should I give up women, since I have a passion for them? It's an occupation, anyway.'

'So you hope for nothing here but vice?'

'Oh, very well, for vice then. You insist on its being vice. But anyway I like a direct question. In this vice at least there is something permanent, founded indeed upon nature and not dependent on fantasy, something

390

present in the blood like an ever-burning ember, for ever setting one on fire and, maybe, not to be quickly extinguished, even with years. You'll agree it's an occupation of a sort.'

'That's nothing to rejoice at, it's a disease and a dangerous one.'

'Oh, that's what you think, is it! I agree that it is a disease like everything that exceeds moderation. And, of course, in this one must exceed moderation. But in the first place, everybody does so in one way or another, and in the second place, of course, one ought to be moderate and prudent, however mean it may be, but what am I to do? If I hadn't this, I might have to shoot myself. I am ready to admit that a decent man ought to put up with being bored, but yet . . .'

'And could you shoot yourself?'

'Oh, come!' Svidrigaïlov parried with disgust. 'Please don't speak of it,' he added hurriedly and with none of the bragging tone he had shown in all the previous conversation. His face quite changed. 'I admit it's an unpardonable weakness, but I can't help it: I am afraid of death and I dislike its being talked of. Do you know that I am to a certain extent a mystic?'

'Ah, the apparitions of Marfa Petrovna! Do they still go on visiting you?'

'Oh, don't talk of them; there have been no more in Petersburg, confound them!' he cried with an air of irritation. 'Let's rather talk of that . . . though . . . H'm! I have not much time, and can't stay long with you, it's a pity! I should have found plenty to tell you.'

'What's your engagement, a woman?'

'Yes, a woman, a casual incident. . . . No, that's not what I want to talk of.'

'And the hideousness, the filthiness of all your surroundings, doesn't that affect you? Have you lost the strength to stop yourself?'

'And do you pretend to strength, too? He-he-he! You surprised me just now, Rodion Romanovitch, though I knew beforehand it would be so. You preach to me about vice and æsthetics! You – a Schiller, you – an idealist! Of course that's all as it should be and it would be surprising if it were not so, yet it is strange in reality. . . . Ah, what a pity I have no time, for you're a most interesting type! And by the way, are you fond of Schiller? I am awfully fond of him.'

'But what a braggart you are,' Raskolnikov said with some disgust.

'Upon my word, I am not,' answered Svidrigaïlov laughing. 'However, I won't dispute it, let me be a braggart, why not brag, if it hurts no one? I spent seven years in the country with Marfa Petrovna, so now when I come across an intelligent person like you – intelligent and highly interesting – I am simply glad to talk and, besides, I've drunk that half-glass of champagne and it's gone to my head a little. And besides, there's a certain fact that has wound me up tremendously, but about that I . . . will keep quiet. Where are you off to?' he asked in alarm.

Raskolnikov had begun getting up. He felt oppressed and stifled and, as it were, ill at ease at having come here. He felt convinced that Svidrigaïlov was the most worthless scoundrel on the face of the earth.

'A-ach! Sit down, stay a little!' Svidrigaïlov begged. 'Let them bring you some tea, anyway. Stay a little, I won't talk nonsense, about myself, I mean. I'll tell you something. If you like I'll tell you how a woman tried "to save" me, as you would call it? It will be an answer to your first question indeed, for the woman was your sister. May I tell you? It will help to spend the time.'

'Tell me, but I trust that you . . .'

'Oh, don't be uneasy. Besides, even in a worthless low fellow like me, Avdotya Romanovna can only excite the deepest respect.'

✦ FOUR ✦

'YOU KNOW PERHAPS – YES, I TOLD you myself,' began Svirdigaïlov, 'that I was in the debtors' prison here, for an immense sum, and had not any expectation of being able to pay it. There's no need to go into particulars how Marfa Petrovna bought me out; do you know to what a point of insanity a woman can sometimes love? She was an honest woman, and very sensible, although completely uneducated. Would be you believe that this honest and jealous woman, after many scenes of hysterics and reproaches, condescended to enter into a kind of contract with me which she kept throughout our married life. She was considerably older than I, and besides, she always kept a clove or something in her mouth. There was so much swinishness in my soul and honesty too, of a sort, as to tell her straight out that I couldn't be absolutely faithful to her. This confession drove her to frenzy, but yet she seems in a way to have liked my brutal frankness. She thought it showed I was unwilling to deceive her if I warned her like this beforehand and for a jealous woman, you know, that's the first consideration. After many tears an unwritten contract was drawn up between us: first, that I would never leave Marfa Petrovna and would always be her husband; secondly, that I would never absent myself without her permission; thirdly, that I would never set up a permanent mistress; fourthly, in return for this, Marfa Petrovna gave me a free hand with the maidservants, but only with her secret knowledge; fifthly, God forbid my falling in love with a woman of our class; sixthly, in case I – which God forbid – should be visited by a great serious passion I was bound to reveal it to Marfa Petrovna. On this last score, however, Marfa Petrovna was fairly at ease. She was a sensible woman and so she could not help looking upon me as a dissolute profligate incapable of real love. But a sensible woman and a jealous woman are two very different things, and that's where the trouble came in. But to judge some people impartially we must renounce certain preconceived opinions and our habitual attitude to the ordinary people about us. I have reason to have faith in your judgment rather than in anyone's. Perhaps you have already heard a great deal that was ridiculous and absurd about Marfa Petrovna. She certainly had some very ridiculous ways, but I tell you frankly that I feel really sorry for the innumerable woes of which I was the cause. Well, and that's enough, I think, by way of a decorous *oraison funèbre* for the most tender wife of a most tender husband. When we quarrelled, I usually held my tongue and did not irritate her and that gentlemanly conduct rarely failed to attain its object, it influenced her, it pleased her, indeed. There were times when she was positively proud of me. But your sister she couldn't put up with, anyway. And however she came to risk taking such a beautiful creature into her house as a governess. My explanation is that Marfa Petrovna was an ardent and impressionable woman and simply fell in love herself – literally fell in love – with your sister. Well, little wonder – look at Avdotya Romanovna! I saw the danger at the first glance and what do you think, I resolved not to look at her even. But Avdotya Romanovna herself made the first step, would you believe it? Would you believe it too that Marfa Petrovna was positively angry with me at first for my persistent silence about your sister, for my careless reception of her continual adoring praises of Avdotya Romanovna. I don't know what it was she wanted! Well, of course, Marfa Petrovna told Avdotya Romanovna every detail about me. She had the unfortunate habit of telling literally everyone all our family secrets and continually complaining of me; how could she fail to confide in such a delightful new friend? I expect they talked of nothing else but me and no doubt Avdotya Romanovna heard all those dark mysterious rumours that were current about me. . . . I don't mind betting that you too have heard something of the sort already?'

'I have. Luzhin charged you with having caused the death of a child. Is that true?'

'Don't refer to those vulgar tales, I beg,' said Svidrigaïlov with disgust and annoyance. 'If you insist on wanting to know about all that idiocy, I will tell you one day, but now . . .'

'I was told too about some footman of yours in the country whom you treated badly.'

'I beg you to drop the subject,' Svidrigaïlov interrupted again with obvious impatience.

'Was that the footman who came to you after death to fill your pipe? . . . you told me about it yourself.' Raskolnikov felt more and more irritated.

Svidrigaïlov looked at him attentively and Raskolnikov fancied he caught a flash of spiteful mockery in that look. But Svidrigaïlov restrained himself and answered very civilly:

'Yes, it was. I see that you, too, are extremely interested and shall feel it my duty to satisfy your curiosity at the first opportunity. Upon my soul! I see that I really might pass for a romantic figure with some people. Judge how grateful I must be to Marfa Petrovna for having repeated to Avdotya Romanovna such mysterious and interesting gossip about me. I dare not guess what impression it made on her, but in any case it worked in my interest. With all Avdotya Romanovna's natural aversion and in spite of my invariably gloomy and repellent aspect – she did at last feel pity for me, pity for a lost soul. And if once a girl's heart is moved to *pity*, it's more dangerous than anything. She is bound to want to "save him", to bring him to his senses, and lift him up and draw him to nobler aims, and restore him to new life and usefulness – well, we all know how far such dreams can go. I saw at once that the bird was flying into the cage of herself. And I too made ready. I think you are frowning, Rodion Romanovitch? There's no need. As you know, it all ended in smoke. (Hang it all, what a lot I am drinking!) Do you know, I always, from the very beginning, regretted that it wasn't your sister's fate to be born in the second or third century A.D., as the daughter of a reigning prince or some governor or pro-consul in Asia Minor. She would undoubtedly have been one of those who would endure martyrdom and would have smiled when they branded her bosom with hot pincers. And she would have gone to it of herself. And in the fourth or fifth century she would have walked away into the Egyptian desert and would have stayed there thirty years living on roots and ecstasies and visions. She is simply thirsting to face some torture for someone, and if she can't get her torture, she'll throw herself out of the window. I've heard something of a Mr. Razumihin – he's said to be a sensible fellow; his surname suggests it, indeed. He's probably a divinity student. Well, he'd better look after your sister! I believe I understand her, and I am proud of it. But at the beginning of an acquaintance, as you know, one is apt to be more heedless and stupid. One doesn't see clearly. Hang it all, why is she so handsome?

It's not my fault. In fact, it began on my side with a most irresistible physical desire. Avdotya Romanovna is awfully chaste, incredibly and phenomenally so. Take note, I tell you this about your sister as a fact. She is almost morbidly chaste, in spite of her broad intelligence, and it will stand in her way. There happened to be a girl in the house then, Parasha, a black-eyed wench, whom I had never seen before – she had just come from another village – very pretty, but incredibly stupid: she burst into tears, wailed so that she could be heard all over the place and caused scandal. One day after dinner Avdotya Romanovna followed me into an avenue in the garden and with flashing eyes *insisted* on my leaving poor Parasha alone. It was almost our first conversation by ourselves. I, of course, was only too pleased to obey her wishes, tried to appear disconcerted, embarrassed, in fact played my part not badly. Then came interviews, mysterious conversations, exhortations, entreaties, supplications, even tears – would you believe it, even tears? Think what the passion for propaganda will bring some girls to! I, of course, threw it all on my destiny, posed as hungering and thirsting for light, and finally resorted to the most powerful weapon in the subjection of the female heart, a weapon which never fails one. It's the well-known resource – flattery. Nothing in the world is harder than speaking the truth and nothing easier than flattery. If there's the hundredth part of a false note in speaking the truth, it leads to a discord, and that leads to trouble. But if all, to the last note, is false in flattery, it is just as agreeable, and is heard not without satisfaction. It may be a coarse satisfaction, but still a satisfaction. And however coarse the flattery, at least half will be sure to seem true. That's so for all stages of development and classes of society. A vestal virgin might be seduced by flattery. I can never remember without laughter how I once seduced a lady who was devoted to her husband, her children, and her principles. What fun it was and how little trouble! And the lady really had principles – of her own, anyway. All my tactics lay in simply being utterly annihilated and prostrate before her purity. I flattered her shamelessly, and as soon as I succeeded in getting a pressure of the hand, even a glance from her, I would reproach myself for having snatched it by force, and would declare that she had resisted, so that I could never have gained anything but for my being so unprincipled. I maintained that she was so innocent that she could not foresee my treachery, and yielded to me unconsciously, unawares, and so on. In fact, I triumphed, while my lady remained firmly convinced that she was innocent, chaste, and faithful to all her duties and obligations and had succumbed quite by accident. And how angry she was with me when I explained to her at last that it was my sincere conviction that she was just as eager as I. Poor Marfa Petrovna was awfully weak on the side of flattery, and if I had only

395

cared to, I might have had all her property settled on me during her lifetime. (I am drinking an awful lot of wine now and talking too much.) I hope you won't be angry if I mention now that I was beginning to produce the same effect on Avdotya Romanovna. But I was stupid and impatient and spoiled it all. Avdotya Romanovna had several times – and one time in particular – been greatly displeased by the expression of my eyes, would you believe it? There was sometimes a light in them which frightened her and grew stronger and stronger and more unguarded till it was hateful to her. No need to go into detail, but we parted. There I acted stupidly again. I fell to jeering in the coarsest way at all such propaganda and efforts to convert me; Parasha came on to the scene again, and not she alone; in fact there was a tremendous to-do. Ah, Rodion Romanovitch, if you could only see how your sister's eyes can flash sometimes! Never mind my being drunk at this moment and having had a whole glass of wine. I am speaking the truth. I assure you that this glance has haunted my dreams; the very rustle of her dress was more than I could stand at last. I really began to think that I might become epileptic. I could never have believed that I could be moved to such a frenzy. It was essential, indeed, to be reconciled, but by then it was impossible. And imagine what I did then! To what a pitch of stupidity a man can be brought by frenzy! Never undertake anything in a frenzy, Rodion Romanovitch. I reflected that Avdotya Romanovna was after all a beggar (ach! excuse me, that's not the word . . . but does it matter if it expresses the meaning?), that she lived by her work, that she had her mother and you to keep (ach! hang it, you are frowning again), and I resolved to offer her all my money – thirty thousand roubles I could have realized then – if she would run away with me here, to Petersburg. Of course I should have vowed eternal love, rapture, and so on. Do you know, I was so wild about her at that time that if she had told me to poison Marfa Petrovna or to cut her throat and to marry herself, it would have been done at once! But it ended in the catastrophe of which you know already. You can fancy how frantic I was when I heard that Marfa Petrovna had got hold of that scoundrelly attorney, Luzhin, and had almost made a match between them – which would really have been just the same thing as I was proposing. Wouldn't it? Wouldn't it? I notice that you've begun to be very attentive . . . you interesting young man. . . .'

Svidrigaïlov struck the table with his fist impatiently. He was flushed. Raskolnikov saw clearly that the glass or glass and a half of champagne that he had sipped almost unconsciously was affecting him – and he resolved to take advantage of the opportunity. He felt very suspicious of Svidrigaïlov.

'Well, after what you have said, I am fully convinced that you have come to Petersburg with designs on my sister,' he said directly to Svidrigaïlov in order to irritate him further.

'Oh, nonsense,' said Svidrigaïlov, seeming to rouse himself. 'Why, I told you . . . besides your sister can't endure me.'

'Yes, I am certain that she can't, but that's not the point.'

'Are you so sure that she can't?' Svidrigaïlov screwed up his eyes and smiled mockingly. 'You are right, she doesn't love me, but you can never be sure of what has passed between husband and wife or lover and mistress. There's always a little corner which remains a secret to the world and is only known to those two. Will you answer for it that Avdotya Romanovna regarded me with aversion?'

'From some words you've dropped, I notice that you still have designs – and of course evil ones – on Dounia and mean to carry them out promptly.'

'What, have I dropped words like that?' Svidrigaïlov asked in naïve dismay, taking not the slightest notice of the epithet bestowed on his designs.

'Why, you are dropping them even now. Why are you so frightened? What are you so afraid of now?'

'Me – afraid? Afraid of you? You have rather to be afraid of me, *cher ami*. But what nonsense. . . . I've drunk too much though, I see that. I was almost saying too much again. Damn the wine! Hi! there, water!'

He snatched up the champagne bottle and flung it without ceremony out of the window. Philip brought the water.

'That's all nonsense!' said Svidrigaïlov, wetting a towel and putting it to his head. 'But I can't answer you in one word and annihilate all your suspicions. Do you know that I am going to get married?'

'You told me so before.'

'Did I? I've forgotten. But I couldn't have told you so for certain, for I had not even seen my betrothed; I only meant to. But now I really have a betrothed and it's a settled thing, and if it weren't that I have business that can't be put off, I would have taken you to see them at once, for I should like to ask your advice. Ach! hang it, only ten minutes left! See, look at the watch. But I must tell you, for it's an interesting story, my marriage, in its own way. Where are you off to? Going again?'

'No, I'm not going away now.'

'Not at all? We shall see. I'll take you there, I'll show you my betrothed, only not now. For you'll soon have to be off. You have to go to the right and I to the left. Do you know that Madame Resslich, the woman I am lodging with now, eh? I know what you're thinking, that she's the woman whose girl they say drowned herself in the winter. Come, are you listening? She arranged it all for me. You're bored, she said, you want something to fill up your time. For, you know, I am a gloomy, depressed person. Do you think I'm light-hearted? No, I'm gloomy. I do no harm, but sit in a corner without speaking a word for three days at a time. And that Resslich is a sly hussy, I tell you. I know what she has got in her mind; she thinks I shall get sick of it, abandon my wife and depart, and she'll get hold of her and make a profit out of her – in our class, of course, or higher. She told me the father was a broken-down retired official, who had been sitting in a chair for the last three years with his legs paralyzed. The mamma, she said, was a sensible woman. There is a son serving in the provinces, but he doesn't help; there is a daughter, who is married, but she doesn't visit them. And they've two little nephews on their hands, as though their own children were not enough, and they've taken from school their youngest daughter, a girl who'll be sixteen in another month, so that then she can be married. She was for me. We went there. How funny it was! I present myself – a land-owner, a widower, of a well-known name, with connections, with a fortune. What if I am fifty and she is not sixteen? Who thinks of that? But it's fascinating, isn't it? It is fascinating, ha-ha! You should have seen how I talked to the papa and mamma. It was worth paying to have seen me at that moment. She comes in, curtseys, you can fancy, still in a short frock – an unopened bud! Flushing like a sunset – she had been told, no doubt. I don't know how you feel about females faces, but to my mind these sixteen years, these childish eyes, shyness and tears of bashfulness are better than beauty; and she is a perfect little picture, too. Fair hair in little curls, like a lamb's, full little rosy lips, tiny feet, a charmer! . . . Well, we made friends. I told them I was in a hurry owing to domestic circumstances, and the next day, that is the day before yesterday, we were betrothed. When I go now I take her on my knee at once and keep her there. . . . Well, she flushes like a sunset and I kiss her every minute. Her mamma of course impresses on her that this is her husband and that this must be so. It's simply delicious! The present betrothed condition is perhaps better than marriage. Here you have what is called *la nature et la vérité*, ha-ha! I've talked to her twice, she is far from a fool. Sometimes she steals a look at me that positively scorches me. Her face is like Raphael's Madonna. You know, the Sistine Madonna's face has something fantastic in it, the face of mournful religious ecstasy. Haven't you noticed it? Well, she's something in that line. The day after we'd been betrothed, I bought her presents to the value of fifteen hundred roubles – a set of diamonds and another of pearls and a silver dressing-case as large as this, with all sorts of things in it, so that even my Madonna's face glowed. I sat her on my knee yesterday, and I suppose rather too unceremoniously – she flushed crimson and the tears started, but she didn't want to show it. We were left alone, she suddenly flung herself on my neck (for the first time of her own accord), put her little arms round me, kissed me, and vowed that she would be an obedient, faithful, and good wife, would make me happy, would devote all her life, every minute of her life, would sacrifice everything, everything, and that all she asks in return is my *respect*, and that she wants "nothing, nothing more from me, no presents". You'll admit that to hear such a confession, alone, from an angel of sixteen in a muslin frock, with little curls, with a flush of maiden shyness in her cheeks and tears of enthusiasm in her eyes is rather fascinating! Isn't it fascinating? It's worth paying for, isn't it? Well . . . listen, we'll go to see my betrothed, only not just now!'

'The fact is this monstrous difference in age and development excites your sensuality! Will you really make such a marriage?'

'Why, of course. Everyone thinks of himself, and he lives most gaily who knows best how to deceive himself. Ha-ha! But why are you so keen about virtue? Have mercy on me, my good friend, I am a sinful man. Ha-ha-ha!'

'But you have provided for the children of Katerina Ivanovna. Though . . . though you had your own reasons. . . . I understand it all now.'

'I am always fond of children, very fond of them,' laughed Svidrigaïlov. 'I can tell you one curious instance of it. The first day I came here I visited various haunts, after seven years I simply rushed at them. You probably notice that I am not in a hurry to renew acquaintance with my old friends. I shall do without them as long as I can. Do you know, when I was with Marfa Petrovna in the country, I was haunted by the thought of these places where anyone who knows his way about can find a great deal. Yes, upon my soul! The peasants have vodka, the educated young people, shut out from activity, waste themselves in impossible dreams and visions and are crippled by theories; Jews have sprung up and are amassing money, and all the rest give themselves up to debauchery. From the first hour the town reeked of its familiar odours. I chanced to be in a frightful den – I like my dens dirty – it was a dance, so called, and there was a *cancan* such as I never saw in my day. Yes, there you have progress. All of a sudden I saw a little girl of thirteen, nicely dressed, dancing with a specialist in that line, with another one *vis-à-vis*. Her mother was sitting on a chair by the wall. You can't fancy what a *cancan* that was! The girl was ashamed, blushed, at last felt insulted, and began to cry. Her partner seized her and began whirling her round and performing before her; everyone laughed and – I like your public, even the *cancan* public – they laughed and shouted. "Serve her right – serve her right! Shouldn't bring children!" Well, it's not my business whether that consoling reflection was logical or not. I at once fixed on my plan, sat down by the mother, and began by saying that I too was a stranger and that people here were ill-bred and that they couldn't distinguish decent folks and treat them with respect; gave her to understand that I had plenty of money, offered to take them home in my carriage. I took them home and got to know them. They were lodging in a miserable little hole and had only just arrived from the country. She told me that she and her daughter could only regard my acquaintance as an honour. I found out that they had nothing of their own and had come to town upon some legal business. I proffered my services and money. I learnt that they had gone to the dancing saloon by mistake, believing that it was a genuine dancing class. I offered to assist in the young girl's education in French and dancing. My offer was accepted with enthusiasm as an honour – and we are still friendly. . . . If you like, we'll go and see them, only not just now.'

'Stop! Enough of your vile, nasty anecdotes, depraved, vile, sensual man!'

'Schiller, you are a regular Schiller! *O la vertue va-t-elle se nicher?* But you know I shall tell you these things on purpose, for the pleasure of hearing your outcries!'

'I dare say. I can see I am ridiculous myself,' muttered Raskolnikov angrily.

Svidrigaïlov laughed heartily; finally he called Philip, paid his bill, and began getting up.

'I say, but I am drunk, *assez causé*,' he said. 'It's been a pleasure!'

'I should rather think it must be a pleasure!' cried Raskolnikov, getting up. 'No doubt it is a pleasure for a worn-out profligate to describe such adventures with a monstrous project of the same sort in his mind – especially under such circumstances and to such a man as me. . . . It's stimulating!'

'Well, if you come to that,' Svidrigaïlov answered, scrutinizing Raskolnikov with some surprise, 'if you come to that, you are a thorough cynic yourself. You've plenty to make you so, anyway. You can understand a great deal . . . and you can do a great deal too. But enough. I sincerely regret not having had more talk with you, but I shan't lose sight of you. . . . Only wait a bit.'

Svidrigaïlov walked out of the restaurant. Raskolnikov walked out after him. Svidrigaïlov was not however very drunk, the wine had affected him for a moment, but it was passing off every minute. He was preoccupied with something of importance and was frowning. He was apparently excited and uneasy in anticipation of something. His manner to Raskolnikov had changed during the last few minutes, and he was ruder and more sneering every moment. Raskolnikov noticed all this, and he too was uneasy. He became very suspicious of Svidrigaïlov and resolved to follow him.

They came out on to the pavement.

'You go to the right, and I to the left, or if you like, the other way. Only *adieu, mon plaisir*, may we meet again.'

And he walked to the right towards the Hay Market.

⇜ FIVE ⇝

RASKOLNIKOV WALKED AFTER HIM.

'What's this?' cried Svidrigaïlov turning round. 'I thought I said . . .'

'It means that I am not going to lose sight of you now.'

'What?'

Both stood still and gazed at one another, as though measuring their strength.

'From all your half tipsy stories,' Raskolnikov observed harshly, 'I am *positive* that you have not given up your designs on my sister, but are pursuing them more actively than ever. I have learnt that my sister received a letter this morning. You have hardly been able to sit still all this time. . . . You may have unearthed a wife on the way, but that means nothing. I should like to make certain myself.'

Raskolnikov could hardly have said himself what he wanted and of what he wished to make certain.

'Upon my word! I'll call the police!'

'Call away!'

Again they stood for a minute facing each other. At last Svidrigaïlov's face changed. Having satisfied himself that Raskolnikov was not frightened at his threat, he assumed a mirthful and friendly air.

'What a fellow! I purposely refrained from referring to your affair, though I am devoured by curiosity. It's a fantastic affair. I've put it off till another time, but you're enough to rouse the dead. . . . Well, let us go, only I warn you beforehand I am only going home for a moment, to get some money; then I shall lock up the flat, take a cab and go to spend the evening at the Islands. Now, now are you going to follow me?'

'I'm coming to your lodgings, not to see you but Sofya Semyonovna, to say I'm sorry not to have been at the funeral.'

'That's as you like, but Sofya Semyonovna is not at home. She has taken the three children to an old lady of high rank, the patroness of some orphan asylums, whom I used to know years ago. I charmed the old lady by depositing a sum of money with her to provide for the three children of Katerina Ivanovna and subscribing to the institution as well. I told her too the story of Sofya Semyonovna in full detail, suppressing nothing. It produced an indescribable effect on her. That's why Sofya Semyonovna has been invited to call to-day at the X. Hotel where the lady is staying for the time.'

"No matter, I'll come all the same.'

'As you like, it's nothing to me, but I won't come with you; here we are at home. By the way, I am convinced that you regard me with suspicion just because I have shown such delicacy and have not so far troubled you with questions . . . you understand? It struck you as extraordinary; I don't mind betting it's that. Well, it teaches one to show delicacy!'

'And to listen at doors!'

'Ah, that's it, is it?' laughed Svidrigaïlov. 'Yes, I should have been surprised if you had let that pass after all that has happened. Ha-ha! Though I did understand something of the pranks you had been up to and were telling Sofya Semyonovna about, what was the meaning of it? Perhaps I am quite behind the times and can't understand. For goodness' sake, explain it, my dear boy. Expound the latest theories!'

'You couldn't have heard anything. You're making it all up!'

'But I'm not talking about that (though I did hear something). No, I'm talking of the way you keep sighing and groaning now. The Schiller in you is in revolt every moment, and now you tell me not to listen at doors. If that's how you feel, go and inform the police that you had this mischance: you made a little mistake in your theory. But if you are convinced that one mustn't listen at doors, but one may murder old women at one's pleasure, you'd better be off to America and make haste. Run, young man! There may still be time. I'm speaking sincerely. Haven't you the money? I'll give you the fare.'

'I'm not thinking of that at all,' Raskolnikov interrupted with disgust.

'I understand (but don't put yourself out, don't discuss it if you don't want to). I understand the questions you are worrying over – moral ones, aren't they? Duties of citizen and man? Lay them all aside. They are nothing to you now, ha-ha! You'll say you are still a man and a citizen. If so you ought not to have got into this coil. It's no use taking up a job you are not fit for. Well, you'd better shoot yourself, or don't you want to?'

'You seem trying to enrage me, to make me leave you.'

'What a queer fellow! But here we are. Welcome to the staircase. You see, that's the way to Sofya Semyonovna. Look, there is no one at home. Don't you believe me? Ask Kapernaumov. She leaves the key with him.

402

Here is Madame de Kapernaumov herself. Hey, what? She is rather deaf. Has she gone out? Where? Did you hear? She is not in and won't be till late in the evening probably. Well, come to my room; you wanted to come and see me, didn't you? Here we are. Madame Resslich's not at home. She is a woman who is always busy, an excellent woman, I assure you. . . . She might have been of use to you if you had been a little more sensible. Now, see! I take this five-per-cent bond out of the bureau – see what a lot I've got of them still – this one will be turned into cash to-day. I mustn't waste any more time. The bureau is locked, the flat is locked, and here we are again on the stairs. Shall we take a cab? I'm going to the Islands. Would you like a lift? I'll take this carriage. Ah, you refuse? You are tired of it? Come for a drive! I believe it will come on to rain. Never mind, we'll put down the hood. . . .'

Svidrigaïlov was already in the carriage. Raskolnikov decided that his suspicions were at least for that moment unjust. Without answering a word he turned and walked back towards the Hay Market. If he had only turned round on his way he might have seen Svidrigaïlov get out a hundred paces off, dismiss the cab and walk along the pavement. But he had turned the corner and could see nothing. Intense disgust drew him away from Svidrigaïlov.

'To think that I could for one instant have looked for help from that coarse brute, that depraved sensualist and blackguard!' he cried.

Raskolnikov's judgment was uttered too lightly and hastily: there was something about Svidrigaïlov which gave him a certain original, even a mysterious character. As concerned his sister, Raskolnikov was convinced that Svidrigaïlov would not leave her in peace. But it was too tiresome and unbearable to go on thinking and thinking about this.

When he was alone, he had not gone twenty paces before he sank, as usual, into deep thought. On the bridge he stood by the railing and began gazing at the water. And his sister was standing close by him.

He met her at the entrance to the bridge, but passed by without seeing her. Dounia had never met him like this in the street before and was struck with dismay. She stood still and did not know whether to call to him or not. Suddenly she saw Svidrigaïlov coming quickly from the direction of the Hay Market.

He seemed to be approaching cautiously. He did not go on to the bridge, but stood aside on the pavement, doing all he could to avoid Raskolnikov's seeing him. He had observed Dounia for some time and had been making signs to her. She fancied he was signalling to beg her not to speak to her brother, but to come to him.

That was what Dounia did. She stole by her brother and went up to Svidrigaïlov.

'Let us make haste away,' Svidrigaïlo whispered to her, 'I don't want Rodion Romanovitch to know of our meeting. I must tell you I've been sitting with him in the restaurant close by, where he looked me up and I had great difficulty in getting rid of him. He has somehow heard of my letter to you and suspects something. It wasn't you who told him, of course, but if not you, who then?'

'Well, we've turned the corner now,' Dounia interrupted, 'and my brother won't see us. I have to tell you that I am going no further with you. Speak to me here. You can tell it all in the street.'

'In the first place, I can't say it in the street; secondly, you must hear Sofya Semyonovna too; and, thirdly, I will show you some papers. . . . Oh well, if you won't agree to come with me, I shall refuse to give any explanation and go away at once. But I beg you not to forget that a very curious secret of your beloved brother's is entirely in my keeping.'

Dounia stood still, hesitating, and looked at Svidrigaïlov with searching eyes.

'What are you afraid of?' he observed quietly. 'The town is not the country. And even in the country you did me more harm than I did you.'

'Have you prepared Sofya Semyonovna?'

'No, I have not said a word to her and am not quite certain whether she is at home now. But most likely she is. She has buried her stepmother to-day: she is not likely to go visiting on such a day. For the time I don't want to speak to any one about it and I half regret having spoken to you. The slightest indiscretion is as bad as betrayal in a thing like this. I live there in that house, we are coming to it. That's the porter of our house – he knows me very well; you see, he's bowing; he sees I'm coming with a lady and no doubt he has noticed your face already and you will be glad of that if you are afraid of me and suspicious. Excuse my putting things so coarsely. I haven't a flat to myself; Sofya Semyonovna's room is next to mine – she lodges in the next flat. The whole floor is let out in lodgings. Why are you frightened like a child? Am I really so terrible?'

Svidrigaïlov's lips were twisted in a condescending smile; but he was in no smiling mood. His heart was throbbing and he could scarcely breathe. He spoke rather loudly to cover his growing excitement. But Dounia did not notice this peculiar excitement, she was so irritated by his remark that she was frightened of him like a child and that he was so terrible to her.

'Though I know that you are not a man of . . . honour, I am not in the least afraid of you. Lead the way,' she said with apparent composure, but her face was very pale.

Svidrigaïlov stopped at Sonia's room.

'Allow me to inquire whether she is at home. . . . She is not. How unfortunate! But I know she may come quite soon. If she's gone out, it can only be to see a lady about the orphans. Their mother is dead. . . . I've been meddling and making arrangements for them. If Sofya Semyonovna does not come back in ten minutes, I will send her to you, to-day, if you like. This is my flat. These are my two rooms. Madame Resslich, my landlady, has the next room. Now, look this way. I will show you my chief piece of evidence: this door from my bedroom leads into two perfectly empty rooms, which are to let. Here they are . . . you must look into them with some attention.'

Svidrigaïlov occupied two fairly large furnished rooms. Dounia was looking about her mistrustfully, but saw nothing special in the furniture or position of the rooms. Yet there was something to observe, for instance, that Svidrigaïlov's flat was exactly between two sets of almost uninhabited apartments. His rooms were not entered directly from the passage, but through the landlady's two almost empty rooms. Unlocking a door leading out of his bedroom, Svidrigaïlov showed Dounia the two empty rooms that were to let. Dounia stopped in the doorway, not knowing what she was called to look upon, but Svidrigaïlov hastened to explain.

'Look here, at this second large room. Notice that door, it's locked. By the door stands a chair, the only one in the two rooms. I brought it from my rooms so as to listen more conveniently. Just the other side of the door is Sofya Semyonovna's table; she sat there talking to Rodion Romanovitch. And I sat here listening on two successive evenings, for two hours each time – and of course I was able to learn something, what do you think?'

'You listened?'

'Yes, I did. Now come back to my room; we can't sit down here.'

He brought Avdotya Romanovna back into his sitting-room and offered her a chair. He sat down at the opposite side of the table, at least seven feet from her, but probably there was the same glow in his eyes which had once frightened Dounia so much. She shuddered and once more looked about her distrustfully. It was an involuntary gesture; she evidently did not wish to betray her uneasiness. But the secluded position of Svidrigaïlov's lodging had suddenly struck her. She wanted to ask whether his landlady at least were at home, but pride kept her from asking. Moreover, she had another trouble in her heart incomparably greater than fear for herself. She was in great distress.

'Here is your letter,' she said, laying it on the table. 'Can it be true what you write? You hint at a crime committed, you say, by my brother. You hint at it too clearly; you daren't deny it now. I must tell you that I'd heard of this stupid story before you wrote and don't believe a word of it. It's a disgusting and ridiculous suspicion. I know the story and why and how it was invented. You can have no proofs. You promised to prove it. Speak! But let me warn you that I don't believe you! I don't believe you!'

Dounia said this, speaking hurriedly and for an instant the colour rushed to her face.

'If you don't believe it, how could you risk coming alone to my rooms? Why have you come? Simply from curiosity?'

'Don't torment me. Speak, speak!'

'There's no denying that you are a brave girl. Upon my word, I thought you would have asked Mr. Razumihin to escort you here. But he was not with you nor anywhere near. I was on the look-out. It's spirited of you, it proves you wanted to spare Rodion Romanovitch. But everything is divine in you. . . . About your brother, what am I to say to you? You've just seen him yourself. What did you think of him?'

'Surely that's not the only thing you are building on?'

'No, not on that, but on his own words. He came here on two successive evenings to see Sofya Semyonovna. I've shown you where they sat. He made a full confession to her. He is a murderer. He killed an old woman, a pawnbroker, with whom he had pawned things himself. He killed her sister, too, a pedlar woman called Lizaveta, who happened to come in while he was murdering her sister. He killed them with an axe he brought with him. He murdered them to rob them and he did rob them. He took money and various things. . . . He told all this, word for word, to Sofya Semyonovna, the only person who knows his secret. But she has had to share by word or deed in the murder; she was as horrified at it as you are now. Don't be anxious, she won't betray him.'

'It cannot be,' muttered Dounia, with white lips. She gasped for breath. 'It cannot be. There was not the slightest cause, no sort of ground. . . . It's a lie, a lie!'

'He robbed her, that was the cause, he took money and things. It's true that by his own admission he made no use of the money or things, but hid them under a stone, where they are now. But that was because he dared not make use of them.'

'But how could he steal, rob? How could he dream of it?' cried Dounia, and she jumped up from her chair. 'Why, you know him, and you've seen him, can he be a thief?'

She seemed to be imploring Svidrigaïlov; she had entirely forgotten her fear.

'There are thousands and millions of combinations and possibilities, Avdotya Romanovna. A thief steals and knows he is a scoundrel, but I've heard of a gentleman who broke open the mail. Who knows, very likely he thought he was doing a gentlemanly thing! Of course I should not have believed it myself if I'd been told of it as you have, but I believe my own ears. He explained all the causes of it to Sofya Semyonovna too, but she did not believe her ears at first, yet she believed her own eyes at last.'

'What . . . were the causes?'

'It's a long story, Avdotya Romanovna. Here's . . . how shall I tell you? – A theory of a sort, the same one by which I for instance consider that a single misdeed is permissible if the principal aim is right, a solitary wrongdoing and hundreds of good deeds! It's galling too, of course, for a young man of gifts and overweening pride to know that if he had, for instance, a paltry three thousand, his whole career, his whole future would be differently shaped and yet not to have that three thousand. Add to that, nervous irritability from hunger, from lodging in a hole, from rags, from a vivid sense of the charm of his social position and his sister's and mother's position too. Above all, vanity, pride and vanity, though goodness knows he may have good qualities too. . . . I am not blaming him, please don't think it; besides, it's not my business. A special little theory came in too – a theory of a sort – dividing mankind, you see, into material and superior persons, that is persons to whom the law does not apply owing to their superiority, who make laws for the rest of mankind, the material, that is. It's all right as a theory, *une théorie comme une autre*. Napoleon attracted him tremendously, that is, what affected him was that a great many men of genius have not hesitated at wrongdoing, but have overstepped the law without thinking about it. He seems to have fancied that he was a genius too – that is, he was convinced of it for a time. He has suffered a great deal and is still suffering from the idea that he could make a theory, but was incapable of boldly overstepping the law, and so is not a man of genius. And that's humiliating for a young man of any pride, in our day especially. . . .'

'But remorse? You deny him any moral feeling then? Is he like that?'

'Ah, Avdotya Romanovna, everything is in a muddle now; not that it was ever in very good order. Russians in general are broad in their ideas, Avdotya Romanovna, broad like their land and exceedingly disposed to the fantastic, the chaotic. But it's a misfortune to be broad without a special genius. Do you remember what a lot of talk we had together on this subject, sitting in the evenings on the terrace after supper? Why, you used to reproach me with breadth! Who knows, perhaps we were talking at the very time when he was lying here thinking over his plan. There are no sacred traditions amongst us, especially in the educated class, Avdotya Romanovna. At the best someone will make them up somehow for himself out of books or from some old chronicle. But those are for the most part the learned and all old fogeys, so that it would be almost ill-bred in a man of society. You know my opinions in general, though. I never blame anyone. I do nothing at all, I persevere in that. But we've talked of this more than once before. I was so happy indeed as to interest you in my opinions. . . . You are very pale, Avdotya Romanovna.'

'I know his theory. I read that article of his about men to whom all is permitted. Razumihin brought it to me.'

'Mr. Razumihin? Your brother's article? In a magazine? Is there such an article? I didn't know. It must be interesting. But where are you going, Avdotya Romanovna?'

'I want to see Sofya Semyonovna,' Dounia articulated faintly. 'How do I get to her? She has come in, perhaps. I must see her at once. Perhaps she . . .'

Avdotya Romanovna could not finish. Her breath literally failed her.

'Sofya Semyonovna will not be back till night, at least I believe not. She was to have been back at once, but if not, then she will not be in till quite late.'

'Ah, then you are lying! I see . . . you were lying . . . lying all the time. . . . I don't believe you! I don't believe you!' cried Dounia, completely losing her head.

Almost fainting, she sank on to a chair which Svidrigaïlov made haste to give her.

'Avdotya Romanovna, what is it? Control yourself! Here is some water. Drink a little. . . .'

He sprinkled some water over her. Dounia shuddered and came to herself.

'It has acted violently,' Svidrigaïlov muttered to himself, frowning. 'Avdotya Romanovna, calm yourself! Believe me, he has friends. We will save him. Would you like me to take him abroad? I have money, I can get a ticket in three days. And as for the murder, he will do all sorts of good deeds yet, to atone for it. Calm yourself. He may become a great man yet. Well, how are you? How do you feel?'

'Cruel man! To be able to jeer at it! Let me go. . . .'

'Where are you going?'

'To him. Where is he? Do you know? Why is this door locked? We came in at that door and now it is locked. When did you manage to lock it?'

'We couldn't be shouting all over the flat on such a subject. I am far from jeering; it's simply that I'm sick of talking like this. But how can you go in such a state? Do you want to betray him? You will drive him to fury, and he will give himself up. Let me tell you, he is already being watched; they are already on his track. You will simply be giving him away. Wait a little: I saw him and was talking to him just now. He can still be saved. Wait a bit, sit down; let us think it over together. I asked you to come in order to discuss it alone with you and to consider it thoroughly. But do sit down!'

'How can you save him? Can he really be saved?'

Dounia sat down. Svidrigaïlov sat down beside her.

'It all depends on you, on you, on you alone,' he began with glowing eyes, almost in a whisper and hardly able to utter the words for emotion.

Dounia drew back from him in alarm. He too was trembling all over.

'You . . . one word from you, and he is saved. I . . . I'll save him. I have money and friends. I'll send him away at once. I'll get a passport, two passports, one for him and one for me. I have friends . . . capable people. . . . If you like, I'll take a passport for you . . . for your mother. . . . What do you want with Razumihin? I love you too. . . . I love you beyond everything. . . . Let me kiss the hem of your dress, let me, let me. . . . The very rustle of it is too much for me. Tell me, "Do that," and I'll do it. I'll do everything. I will do the impossible. What you believe, I will believe. I'll do anything – anything! Don't, don't look at me like that. Do you know that you are killing me? . . .'

He was almost beginning to rave. . . . Something seemed suddenly to go to his head. Dounia jumped up and rushed to the door.

'Open it! Open it!' she called, shaking the door. 'Open it! Is there no one there?'

Svidrigaïlov got up and came to himself. His still trembling lips slowly broke into an angry mocking smile.

'There is no one at home,' he said quietly and emphatically. 'The land-lady has gone out, and it's waste of time to shout like that. You are only exciting yourself uselessly.'

'Where is the key? Open the door at once, at once, base man!'

'I have lost the key and cannot find it.'

'This is an outrage,' cried Dounia, turning pale as death. She rushed to the furthest corner, where she made haste to barricade herself with a little table.

She did not scream, but she fixed her eyes on her tormentor and watched every movement he made.

Svidrigaïlov remained standing at the other end of the room, facing her. He was positively composed, at least in appearance, but his face was pale as before. The mocking smile did not leave his face.

'You spoke of outrage just now, Avdotya Romanovna. In that case you may be sure I've taken measures. Sofya Semyonovna is not at home. The Kapernaumovs are far away – there are five locked rooms between. I am at least twice as strong as you are and I have nothing to fear, besides. For you could not complain afterwards. You surely would not be willing actually to betray your brother? Besides, no one would believe you. How should a girl have come alone to visit a solitary man in his lodgings? So that even if you do sacrifice your brother, you could prove nothing. It is very difficult to prove an assault, Avdotya Romanovna.'

'Scoundrel!' whispered Dounia indignantly.

'As you like, but observe I was only speaking by way of a general proposition. It's my personal conviction that you are perfectly right – violence is hateful. I only spoke to show you that you need have no remorse even if . . . you were willing to save your brother of your own accord, as I suggest to you. You would be simply submitting to circumstances, to violence, in fact, if we must use that word. Think about it. Your brother's and your mother's fate are in your hands. I will be your slave . . . all my life. . . . I will wait here.'

Svidrigaïlov sat down on the sofa about eight steps from Dounia. She had not the slightest doubt now of his unbending determination. Besides, she knew him. Suddenly she pulled out of her pocket a revolver, cocked it and laid it in her hand on the table. Svidrigaïlov jumped up.

'Aha! So that's it, is it?' he cried, surprised but smiling maliciously. 'Well, that completely alters the aspect of affairs. You've made things wonderfully easier for me, Avdotya Romanovna. But where did you get the revolver? Was it Mr. Razumihin? Why, it's my revolver, an old friend! And how I've hunted for it! The shooting lessons I've given you in the country have not been thrown away.'

'It's not your revolver, it belonged to Marfa Petrovna, whom you killed, wretch! There was nothing of yours in her house. I took it when I began to suspect what you were capable of. If you dare to advance one step, I swear I'll kill you.' She was frantic.

'But your brother? I ask from curiosity,' said Svidrigaïlov, still standing where he was.

'Inform, if you want to! Don't stir! Don't come nearer! I'll shoot! You poisoned your wife, I know; you are a murderer yourself!' She held the revolver ready.

'Are you so positive I poisoned Marfa Petrovna?'

'You did! You hinted it yourself; you talked to me of poison. . . . I knew you went to get it . . . you had it in readiness. . . . It was your doing. . . . It must have been your doing. . . . Scoundrel!'

'Even if that were true, it would have been for your sake . . . you would have been the cause.'

'You are lying! I hated you always, always. . . .'

'Oho, Avdotya Romanovna! You seem to have forgotten how you softened to me in the heat of propaganda. I saw it in your eyes. Do you remember that moonlight night, when the nightingale was singing?'

'That's a lie,' there was a flash of fury in Dounia's eyes; 'that's a lie and a libel!'

'A lie? Well, if you like, it's a lie. I made it up. Women ought not to be reminded of such things,' he smiled. 'I know you will shoot, you pretty wild creature. Well, shoot away!'

Dounia raised the revolver, and deadly pale, gazed at him, measuring the distance and awaiting the first movement on his part. Her lower lip was white and quivering and her big black eyes flashed like fire. He had never seen her so handsome. The fire glowing in her eyes at the moment she raised the revolver seemed to kindle him and there was a pang of anguish in his heart. He took a step forward and a shot rang out. The bullet grazed his hair and flew into the wall behind. He stood still and laughed softly.

'The wasp has stung me. She aimed straight at my head. What's this? Blood?' He pulled out his handkerchief to wipe the blood, which flowed in a thin stream down his right temple. The bullet seemed to have just grazed the skin.

Dounia lowered the revolver and looked at Svidrigaïlov not so much in terror as in a sort of wild amazement. She seemed not to understand what she was doing and what was going on.

'Well, you missed! Fire again, I'll wait,' said Svidrigaïlov softly, still smiling, but gloomily. 'If you go on like that, I shall have time to seize you before you cock again.'

Dounia started, quickly cocked the pistol and again raised it.

'Let me be,' she cried in despair. 'I swear I'll shoot again. I . . . I'll kill you.'

'Well . . . at three paces you can hardly help it. But if you don't . . . then.' His eyes flashed and he took two steps forward. Dounia shot again: it missed fire.

'You haven't loaded it properly. Never mind, you have another charge there. Get it ready, I'll wait.'

He stood facing her, two paces away, waiting and gazing at her with wild determination, with feverishly passionate, stubborn, set eyes. Dounia saw that he would sooner die than let her go. 'And . . . now, of course she would kill him, at two paces!' Suddenly she flung away the revolver.

'She's dropped it!' said Svidrigaïlov with surprise, and he drew a deep breath. A weight seemed to have rolled from his heart – perhaps not only the fear of death; indeed he may scarcely have felt it at that moment. It was the deliverance from another feeling, darker and more bitter, which he could not himself have defined.

He went to Dounia and gently put his arm round her waist. She did not resist, but, trembling like a leaf, looked at him with suppliant eyes. He tried to say something, but his lips moved without being able to utter a sound.

'Let me go,' Dounia implored. Svidrigaïlov shuddered. Her voice now was quite different.

'Then you don't love me?' he asked softly. Dounia shook her head.

'And . . . and you can't? Never?' he whispered in despair.

'Never!'

There followed a moment of terrible, dumb struggle in the heart of Svidrigaïlov. He looked at her with an indescribable gaze. Suddenly he withdrew his arm, turned quickly to the window and stood facing it. Another moment passed.

'Here's the key.'

He took it out of the left pocket of his coat and laid it on the table behind him, without turning or looking at Dounia.

'Take it! Make haste!'

He looked stubbornly out of the window. Dounia went up to the table to take the key.

'Make haste! Make haste!' repeated Svidrigaïlov, still without turning or moving. But there seemed a terrible significance in the tone of that 'make haste'.

Dounia understood it, snatched up the key, flew to the door, unlocked it quickly and rushed out of the room. A minute later, beside herself, she ran out on to the canal bank in the direction of X. Bridge.

Svidrigaïlov remained three minutes standing at the window. At last he slowly turned, looked about him and passed his hand over his forehead. A strange smile contorted his face, a pitiful, sad, weak smile, a smile of despair. The blood, which was already getting dry, smeared his hand. He looked angrily at it, then wetted a towel and washed his temple. The revolver which Dounia had flung away lay near the door and suddenly caught his eye. He picked it up and examined it. It was a little pocket three-barrel revolver of old-fashioned construction. There were still two charges and one capsule left in it. It could be fired again. He thought a little, put the revolver in his pocket, took his hat and went out.

❖ SIX ❖

HE SPENT THAT EVENING TILL TEN o'clock going from one low haunt to another. Katia too turned up and sang another gutter song, how a certain 'villain and tyrant'

'began kissing Katia'

Svidrigaïlov treated Katia and the organ-grinder and some singers and the waiters and two little clerks. He was particularly drawn to these clerks by the fact that they both had crooked noses, one bent to the left and the other to the right. They took him finally to a pleasure garden, where he paid for their entrance. There was one lanky three-year-old pine-tree and three bushes in the garden, besides a 'Vauxhall', which was in reality a drinking-bar where tea too was served, and there were a few green tables and chairs standing round it. A chorus of wretched singers and a drunken but exceedingly depressed German clown from Munich with a red nose entertained the public. The clerks quarrelled with some other clerks and a fight seemed imminent. Svidrigaïlov was chosen to decide the dispute. He listened to them for a quarter of an hour, but they shouted so loudly that there was no possibility of understanding them. The only fact that seemed certain was that one of them had stolen something and had even succeeded in selling it on the spot to a Jew, but would not share the spoil with his companion. Finally it appeared that the stolen object was a teaspoon belonging to the Vauxhall. It was missed and the affair began to seem troublesome. Svidrigaïlov paid for the spoon, got up, and walked out of the garden. It was about six o'clock. He had not drunk a drop of wine all this time and had ordered tea more for the sake of appearances than anything.

It was a dark and stifling evening. Threatening storm-clouds came over the sky about ten o'clock. There was a clap of thunder, and the rain came down like a waterfall. The water fell not in drops but beat on the earth in streams. There were flashes of lightning every minute and each flash lasted while one could count five.

Drenched to the skin, he went home, locked himself in, opened the bureau, took out all his money and tore up two or three papers. Then, putting the money in his pocket, he was about to change his clothes, but, looking out of the window and listening to the thunder and the rain, he gave up the idea, took up his hat and went out of the room without locking the door. He went straight to Sonia. She was at home.

She was not alone: the four Kapernaumov children were with her. She was giving them tea. She received Svidrigaïlov in respectful silence, looking wonderingly at his soaking clothes. The children all ran away at once in indescribable terror.

Svidrigaïlov sat down at the table and asked Sonia to sit beside him. She timidly prepared to listen.

'I may be going to America, Sofya Semyonovna,' said Svidrigaïlov, 'and as I am probably seeing you for the last time, I have come to make some arrangements. Well, did you see the lady to-day? I know what she said to you, you need not tell me.' (Sonia made a movement and blushed.) 'Those people have their own way of doing things. As to your sisters and your brother, they are really provided for and the money assigned to them I've put into safe keeping and have received acknowledgments. You had better take charge of the receipts, in case anything happens. Here, take them! Well now, that's settled. Here are three 5-per-cent bonds to the value of three thousand roubles. Take those for yourself, entirely for yourself, and let that be strictly between ourselves, so that no one knows of it, whatever you hear. You will need the money, for to go on living in the old way, Sofya Semyonovna, is bad, and besides there is no need for it now.'

'I am so much indebted to you, and so are the children and my stepmother,' said Sonia hurriedly, 'and if I've said so little ... please don't consider ...'

'That's enough! that's enough!'

'But as for the money, Arkady Ivanovitch, I am very grateful to you, but I don't need it now. I can always earn my own living. Don't think me ungrateful. If you are so charitable, that money ...'

'It's for you, for you, Sofya Semyonovna, and please don't waste words over it. I haven't time for it. You will want it. Rodion Romanovitch has two alternatives: a bullet in the brain or Siberia.' (Sonia looked wildly at him, and started.) 'Don't be uneasy. I know all about it from himself and I am not a gossip; I won't tell anyone. It was good advice when you told him to give himself up and confess. It would be much better for him. Well, if it turns out to be Siberia, he will go and you will follow him. That's so, isn't it? And if so, you'll need money. You'll need it for him, do you understand? Giving it to you is the same as my giving it to him. Besides, you promised Amalia Ivanovna to pay what's owing. I heard you. How can you undertake such obligations so heedlessly, Sofya

Semyonovna? It was Katerina Ivanovna's debt and not yours, so you ought not to have taken any notice of the German woman. You can't get through the world like that. If you are ever questioned about me – tomorrow or the day after you will be asked – don't say anything about my coming to see you now and don't show the money to anyone or say a word about it. Well now, good-bye.' (He got up.) 'My greetings to Rodion Romanovitch. By the way, you'd better put the money for the present in Mr. Razumihin's keeping. You know Mr. Razumihin? Of course you do. He's not a bad fellow. Take it to him to-morrow or . . . when the time comes. And till then, hide it carefully.'

Sonia too jumped up from her chair and looked in dismay at Svidrigaïlov. She longed to speak, to ask a question, but for the first moments she did not dare and did not know how to begin.

'How can you . . . how can you be going now, in such rain?'

'Why, be starting for America, and be stopped by rain! Ha, ha! Good-bye, Sofya Semyonovna, my dear! Live and live long, you will be of use to others. By the way . . . tell Mr. Razumihin I sent my greetings to him. Tell him Arkady Ivanovitch Svidrigaïlov sends his greetings. Be sure to.'

He went out, leaving Sonia in a state of wondering anxiety and vague apprehension.

It appeared afterwards that on the same evening, at twenty past eleven, he made another very eccentric and unexpected visit. The rain still persisted. Drenched to the skin, he walked into the little flat where the parents of his betrothed lived, in Third Street in Vassilyevsky Island. He knocked some time before he was admitted, and his visit at first caused great perturbation; but Svidrigaïlov could be very fascinating when he liked, so that the first, and indeed very intelligent surmise of the sensible parents that Svidrigaïlov had probably had so much to drink that he did not know what he was doing vanished immediately. The decrepit father was wheeled in to see Svidrigaïlov by the tender and sensible mother, who as usual began the conversation with various irrelevant questions. She never asked a direct question, but began by smiling and rubbing her hands and then, if she were obliged to ascertain something – for instance, when Svidrigaïlov would like to have the wedding – she would begin by interested and almost eager questions about Paris and the court life there, and only by degrees brought the conversation round to Third Street. On other occasions this had of course been very impressive, but this time Arkady Ivanovitch seemed particularly impatient, and insisted on seeing his betrothed at once, though he had been informed, to begin with, that she had already gone to bed. The girl of course appeared.

Svidrigaïlov informed her at once that he was obliged by very important affairs to leave Petersburg for a time, and therefore brought her fifteen thousand roubles and begged her to accept them as a present from him, as he had long been intending to make her this trifling present before their wedding. The logical connection of the present with his immediate departure and the absolute necessity of visiting them for that purpose in pouring rain at midnight was not made clear. But it all went off very well; even the inevitable ejaculations of wonder and regret, the inevitable questions were extraordinarily few and restrained. On the other hand, the gratitude expressed was most glowing and was reinforced by tears from the most sensible of mothers. Svidrigaïlov got up, laughed, kissed his betrothed, patted her cheek, declared he would soon come back, and noticing in her eyes, together with childish curiosity, a sort of earnest dumb inquiry, reflected and kissed her again, though he felt sincere anger inwardly at the thought that his present would be immediately locked up in the keeping of the most sensible of mothers. He went away, leaving them all in a state of extraordinary excitement, but the tender mamma, speaking quietly in a half-whisper, settled some of the most important of their doubts, concluding that Svidrigaïlov was a great man, a man of great affairs and connections and of great wealth – there was no knowing what he had in his mind. He would start off on a journey and give away money just as the fancy took him, so that there was nothing surprising about it. Of course it was strange that he was wet through, but Englishmen, for instance, are even more eccentric, and all these people of high society didn't think of what was said of them and didn't stand on ceremony. Possibly, indeed, he came like that on purpose to show that he was not afraid of anyone. Above all, not a word should be said about it, for God knows what might come of it, and the money must be locked up, and it was most fortunate that Fedosya, the cook, had not left the kitchen. And above all not a word must be said to that old cat, Madame Resslich, and so on and so on. They sat up whispering till two o'clock, but the girl went to bed much earlier, amazed and rather sorrowful.

Svidrigaïlov meanwhile, exactly at midnight, crossed the bridge on the way back to the mainland. The rain had ceased and there was a roaring wind. He began shivering, and for one moment he gazed at the black waters of the Little Neva with a look of special interest, even inquiry. But he soon felt it very cold, standing by the water; he turned and went towards Y. Prospect. He walked along that endless street for a long time, almost half an hour, more than once stumbling in the dark on the wooden pavement, but continually looking for something on the right side of the street. He had noticed passing through this street lately that there was a hotel somewhere towards the end, built of wood, but fairly large, and its name he remembered was something like Adrianople. He was not mistaken: the hotel was so conspicuous in that God-forsaken place that he could not fail to see it even in the dark. It was a long, blackened wooden building, and in spite of the late hour there were lights in the windows and signs of life within. He went in and asked a ragged fellow who met him in the corridor for a room. The latter, scanning Svidrigaïlov, pulled himself together and led him at once to a close and tiny room in the distance, at the end of the corridor, under the stairs. There was no other, all were occupied. The ragged fellow looked inquiringly.

'Is there tea?' asked Svidrigaïlov.

'Yes, sir.'

'What else is there?'

'Veal, vodka, savouries.'

'Bring me tea and veal.'

'And you want nothing else?' he asked with apparent surprise.

'Nothing nothing.

The ragged man went away, completely disillusioned.

'It must be a nice place,' thought Svidrigaïlov. 'How was it I didn't know it? I expect I look as if I came from a café chantant and have had some adventure on the way. It would be interesting to know who stays here?'

He lighted the candle and looked at the room more carefully. It was a room so low-pitched that Svidrigaïlov could only just stand up in it; it had one window; the bed, which was very dirty, and the plain-stained chair and table almost filled it up. The walls looked as though they were made of planks, covered with shabby paper, so torn and dusty that the pattern was indistinguishable, though the general colour – yellow – could still be made out. One of the walls was cut short by the sloping ceiling, though the room was not an attic but just under the stairs.

Svidrigaïlov set down the candle, sat down on the bed and sank into thought. But a strange persistent murmur which sometimes rose to a shout in the next room attracted his attention. The murmur had not ceased from the moment he entered the room. He listened: someone was upbraiding and almost tearfully scolding, but he heard only one voice.

Svidrigaïlov got up, shaded the light with his hand and at once he saw light through a crack in the wall; he went up and peeped through. The room, which was somewhat larger than his, had two occupants. One of them, a very curly-headed man with a red inflamed face, was standing in the pose of an orator, without his coat, with his legs wide apart to preserve his balance, and smiting himself on the breast. He reproached the other with being a beggar, with having no standing whatever. He declared that he had taken the other out of the gutter and he could turn him out when he liked, and that only the finger of Providence sees it all. The object of his reproaches was sitting in a chair, and had the air of a man who wants dreadfully to sneeze, but can't. He sometimes turned sheepish and befogged eyes on the speaker, but obviously had not the slightest idea what he was talking about and scarcely heard it. A candle was burning down on the table; there were wine-glasses, a nearly empty bottle of vodka, bread and cucumber, and glasses with the dregs of stale tea. After gazing attentively at this, Svidrigaïlov turned away indifferently and sat down on the bed.

The ragged attendant, returning with the tea, could not resist asking him again whether he didn't want anything more, and again receiving a negative reply, finally withdrew. Svidrigaïlov made haste to drink a glass of tea to warm himself, but could not eat anything. He began to feel feverish. He took off his coat and, wrapping himself in the blanket, lay down on the bed. He was annoyed. 'It would have been better to be well for the occasion,' he thought with a smile. The room was close, the candle burnt dimly, the wind was roaring outside, he heard a mouse scratching in the corner and the room smelt of mice and of leather. He lay in a sort of reverie: one thought followed another. He felt a longing to fix his imagination on something. 'It must be a garden under the window,' he thought. 'There's a sound of trees. How I dislike the sound of trees on a stormy night, in the dark! They give one a horrid feeling.' He remembered how he had disliked it when he passed Petrovsky Park just now. This reminded him of the bridge over the Little Neva and he felt cold again as he had when standing there. 'I never have liked water,' he thought, 'even in a landscape,' and he suddenly smiled again at a strange idea: 'Surely now all these questions of taste and comfort ought not to matter, but I've become more particular, like an animal that picks out a special place ... for such an occasion. I ought to have gone into the Petrovsky Park! I suppose it seemed dark, cold, ha-ha! As though I were seeking pleasant sensations! ... By the way, why haven't I put out the candle?' He blew it out. 'They've gone to bed next door,' he thought, not seeing the light at the crack. 'Well, now, Marfa Petrovna, now is the time for you to turn up; it's dark, and the very time and place for you. But now you won't come!'

He suddenly recalled how, an hour before carrying out his design on Dounia, he had recommended Raskolnikov to trust her to Razumihin's keeping. 'I suppose I really did say it, as Raskolnikov guessed, to tease myself. But what a rogue that Raskolnikov is! He's gone through a good deal. He may be a successful rogue in time when he's got over his nonsense. But now he's *too* eager for life. These young men are contemptible on that point. But, hang the fellow! Let him please himself, it's nothing to do with me.'

He could not get to sleep. By degrees Dounia's image rose before him, and a shudder ran over him. 'No, I must give up all that now,' he thought, rousing himself. 'I must think of something else. It's queer and funny. I never had a great hatred for anyone, I never particularly desired to avenge myself even, and that's a bad sign, a bad sign, a bad sign. I never liked quarrelling either, and never lost my temper – that's a bad sign too. And the promises I made her just now, too! Damnation! But – who knows? – perhaps she would have made a new man of me somehow. . . .'

He ground his teeth and sank into silence again. Again Dounia's image rose before him, just as she was when, after shooting the first time, she had lowered the revolver in terror and gazed blankly at him, so that it might have seized her twice over and she would not have lifted a hand to defend herself if he had not reminded her. He recalled how at that instant he felt almost sorry for her, how he had felt a pang at his heart . . .

'Aïe! Damnation, these thoughts again! I must put it away!'

He was dozing off; the feverish shiver had ceased, when suddenly something seemed to run over his arm and leg under the bedclothes. He started. 'Ugh! hang it! I believe it's a mouse,' he thought, 'that's the veal I left on the table.' He felt fearfully disinclined to pull off the blanket, get up, get cold, but all at once something unpleasant ran over his leg again. He pulled off the blanket and lighted the candle. Shaking with feverish chill he bent down to examine the bed: there was nothing. He shook the blanket and suddenly a mouse jumped out on the sheet. He tried to catch it, but the mouse ran to and fro in zigzags without leaving the bed, slipped between his fingers, ran over his hand and suddenly darted under the pillow. He threw down the pillow, but in one instant felt something leap on his chest and dart over his body and down his back under his shirt. He trembled nervously and woke up.

The room was dark. He was lying on the bed wrapped up in the blanket as before. The wind was howling under the window. 'How disgusting,' he thought with annoyance.

He got up and sat on the edge of the bedstead with his back to the window. 'It's better not to sleep at all,' he decided. There was a cold damp draught from the window, however; without getting up he drew the blanket over him and wrapped himself in it. He was not thinking of anything and did not want to think. But one image rose after another, incoherent scraps of thought without beginning or end passed through his mind. He sank into drowsiness. Perhaps the cold, or the dampness, or the dark, or the wind that howled under the window and tossed the trees roused a sort of persistent craving for the fantastic. He kept dwelling on images of flowers, he fancied a charming flower garden, a bright, warm, almost hot day, a holiday – Trinity day. A fine, sumptuous country cottage in the English taste overgrown with fragrant flowers, with flower beds going round the house; the porch, wreathed in climbers, was surrounded with beds of roses. A light, cool staircase, carpeted with rich rugs, was decorated with rare plants in china pots. He noticed particularly in the windows nosegays of tender, white, heavily fragrant narcissus bending over their bright, green, thick long stalks. He was reluctant to move away from them, but he went up the stairs and came into a large high drawing-room and again everywhere – at the windows, the doors on to the balcony, and on the balcony itself – were flowers. The floors were strewn with freshly-cut fragrant hay, the windows were open, a fresh, cool, light air came into the room. The birds were chirruping under the window, and in the middle of the room, on a table covered with a white satin shroud, stood a coffin. The coffin was covered with white silk and edged with a thick white frill; wreaths of flowers surrounded it on all sides. Among the flowers lay a girl in a white muslin dress, with her arms crossed and pressed on her bosom, as though carved out of marble. But her loose fair hair was wet; there was a wreath of roses on her head. The stern and already rigid profile of her face looked as though chiselled of marble too, and the smile on her pale lips was full of an immense unchildish misery and sorrowful appeal. Svidrigaïlov knew that girl; there was no holy image, no burning candle beside the coffin; no sound of prayers: the girl had drowned herself. She was only fourteen, but her heart was broken. And she had destroyed herself crushed by an insult that had appalled and amazed that childish soul, had smirched that angel purity with unmerited disgrace and torn from her a last scream of despair, unheeded and brutally disregarded, on a dark night in the cold and wet while the wind howled. . . .

Svidrigaïlov came to himself, got up from the bed and went to the window. He felt for the latch and opened it. The wind lashed furiously into the little room and stung his face and his chest, only covered with his shirt, as though with frost. Under the window there must have been something like a garden, and apparently a pleasure garden. There, too, probably there were tea-tables and singing in the daytime. Now drops of rain flew in at the window from the trees and bushes; it was dark as in a cellar, so that he could only just make out some dark blurs of objects. Svidrigaïlov, bending down with elbows on the windowsill, gazed for five minutes into the darkness; the boom of a cannon, followed by a second one, resounded in the darkness of the night. 'Ah, the signal! The river is overflowing,' he thought. 'By morning it will be swirling down the street in the lower parts, flooding the basements and cellars. The cellar rats will swim out, and men will curse in the rain and wind as they drag their rubbish to their upper storeys. What time is it now?' And he had hardly thought it when, somewhere near, a clock on the wall, ticking away hurriedly, struck three.

'Aha! It will be light in an hour! Why wait? I'll go out at once straight to the park. I'll choose a great bush there drenched with rain, so that as soon as one's shoulder touches it, millions of drops drip on one's head.'

He moved away from the window, shut it, lighted the candle, put on his waistcoat, his overcoat and his hat and went out, carrying the candle, into the passage to look for the ragged attendant who would be asleep somewhere in the midst of candle-ends and all sorts of rubbish, to pay him for the room and leave the hotel. 'It's the best minute; I couldn't choose a better.'

He walked for some time through a long narrow corridor without finding anyone and was just going to call out when suddenly in a dark corner between an old cupboard and the door he caught sight of a strange object which seemed to be alive. He bent down with the candle and saw a little girl, not more than five years old, shivering and crying, with her clothes as wet as a soaking house-flannel. She did not seem afraid of Svidrigaïlov, but looked at him with blank amazement out of her big black eyes. Now and then she sobbed as children do when they have been crying a long time but are beginning to be comforted. The child's face was pale and tired, she was numb with cold. 'How can she have come here? She must have hidden here and not slept all night.' He began questioning her. The child, suddenly becoming animated, chattered away in her baby language, something about 'mammy' and that 'mammy would beat her', and about some cup that she had 'bwoken'. The child chattered on without stopping. He could only guess from what she said that she was a neglected child, whose mother, probably a drunken cook, in the service of the hotel, whipped and frightened her; that the child had broken a cup of her mother's and was so frightened that she had run away the evening before, had hidden for a long while somewhere outside in the rain, at last had made her way in here, hidden behind the cupboard and spent the night there, crying and trembling from the damp, the darkness and the fear that she would be badly beaten for it. He took her in his arms, went back to his room, sat her on the bed, and began undressing her. The torn shoes which she had on her stockingless feet were as wet as if they had been standing in a puddle all night. When he had undressed her, he put her on the bed, covered her up and wrapped her in the blanket from her head downwards. She fell asleep at once. Then he sank into dreary musing again.

'What folly to trouble myself,' he decided suddenly with an oppressive feeling of annoyance. 'What idiocy!' In vexation he took up the candle to go and look for the ragged attendant again and made haste to go away.

'Damn the child!' he thought as he opened the door, but he turned again to see whether the child was asleep. He raised the blanket carefully. The child was sleeping soundly, she had got warm under the blanket, and her pale cheeks were flushed. But strange to say that flush seemed brighter and coarser than the rosy cheeks of childhood. 'It's a flush of fever,' thought Svidrigaïlov. It was like the flush from drinking, as though she had been given a full glass to drink. Her crimson lips were hot and glowing; but what was this? He suddenly fancied that her long black eyelashes were quivering, as though the lids were opening and a sly crafty eye peeped out with an unchildlike wink, as though the little girl were not asleep, but pretending. Yes, it was so. Her lips parted in a smile. The corners of her mouth quivered, as though she were trying to control them. But now she quite gave up all effort, now it was a grin, a broad grin; there was something shameless, provocative in that quite unchildish face; it was depravity, it was the face of a harlot, the shameless face of a French harlot. Now both eyes opened wide; they turned a glowing, shameless glance upon him; they laughed, invited him.... There was something infinitely hideous and shocking in that laugh, in those eyes, in such nastiness in the face of a child. 'What, at five years old?' Svidrigaïlov muttered in genuine horror. 'What does it mean?' And now she turned to him, her little face all aglow, holding out her arms.... 'Accursed child!' Svidrigaïlov cried, raising his hand to strike her, but at that moment he woke up.

He was in the same bed, still wrapped in the blanket. The candle had not been lighted, and daylight was streaming in at the windows.

'I've had nightmares all night!' He got up angrily, feeling utterly shattered; his bones ached. There was a thick mist outside and he could see nothing. It was nearly five. He had overslept himself! He got up, put on his still damp jacket and overcoat. Feeling the revolver in his pocket, he took it out and then he sat down, took a notebook out of his pocket and in the most conspicuous place on the title-page wrote a few lines in large letters. Reading them over, he sank into thought with his elbows on the table. The revolver and the notebook lay beside him. Some flies woke up and settled on the untouched veal, which was still on the table. He stared at them and at last with his free right hand began trying to catch one. He tried till he was tired, but could not catch it. At last, realizing that he was engaged in this interesting pursuit, he started, got up and walked resolutely out of the room. A minute later he was in the street.

A thick milky mist hung over the town. Svidrigaïlov walked along the slippery dirty wooden pavement towards the Little Neva. He was picturing the waters of the Little Neva swollen in the night, Petrovsky Island, the wet paths, the wet grass, the wet trees and bushes and at last the bush. . . . He began ill-humouredly staring at the houses, trying to think of something else. There was not a cabman or a passer-by in the street. The bright yellow, wooden, little houses looked dirty and dejected with their closed shutters. The cold and damp penetrated his whole body and he began to shiver. From time to time he came across shop signs and read each carefully. At last he reached the end of the wooden pavement and came to a big stone house. A dirty shivering dog crossed his path with its tail between its legs. A man in a greatcoat lay face downwards, dead drunk, across the pavement. He looked at him and went on. A high tower stood up on the left. 'Bah!' he thought, 'here is a place. Why should it be Petrovsky? It will be in the presence of an official witness, anyway. . . .'

He almost smiled at this thought and turned into the street where there was the big house with the tower. At the great closed gates of the house, a little man stood with his shoulder leaning against them, wrapped in a grey soldier's coat, with a copper Achilles helmet on his head. He cast a drowsy and indifferent glance at Svidrigaïlov. His face wore that perpetual look of peevish dejection which is so sourly printed on all faces of Jewish race without exception. They both, Svidrigaïlov and Achilles, stared at each other for a few minutes without speaking. At last it struck Achilles as irregular for a man not drunk to be standing three steps from him, staring and not saying a word.

'What do you want here?' he said, without moving or changing his position.

'Nothing, brother, good morning,' answered Svidrigaïlov.

'This isn't the place.'

'I am going to foreign parts, brother.'

'To foreign parts?'

'To America.'

'America?'

Svidrigaïlov took out the revolver and cocked it. Achilles raised his eyebrows.

'I say, this is not the place for such jokes!'

'Why shouldn't it be the place?'

'Because it isn't.'

'Well, brother, I don't mind that. It's a good place. When you are asked, you just say he was going, he said, to America.'

He put the revolver to his right temple.

'You can't do it here, it's not the place,' cried Achilles, rousing himself, his eyes growing bigger and bigger.

Svidrigaïlov pulled the trigger.

✦ SEVEN ✦

THE SAME DAY, ABOUT SEVEN o'clock in the evening, Raskolnikov was on his way to his mother's and sister's lodging – the lodging in Bakaleyev's house which Razumihin had found for them. The stairs went up from the street. Raskolnikov walked with lagging steps, as though still hesitating whether to go or not. But nothing would have turned him back: his decision was taken.

'Besides, it doesn't matter, they still know nothing,' he thought, 'and they are used to thinking of me as eccentric.'

He was appallingly dressed: his clothes torn and dirty, soaked with a night's rain. His face was almost distorted from fatigue, exposure, the inward conflict that had lasted for twenty-four hours. He had spent all the previous night alone, God knows where. But, anyway, he had reached a decision.

He knocked at the door, which was opened by his mother. Dounia was not at home. Even the servant happened to be out. At first Pulcheria Alexandrovna was speechless with joy and surprise; then she took him by the hand and drew him into the room.

'Here you are!' she began, faltering with joy. 'Don't be angry with me, Rodya, for welcoming you so foolishly with tears: I am laughing, not crying. Did you think I was crying? No, I am delighted, but I've got into such a stupid habit of shedding tears. I've been like that ever since your father's death. I cry for anything. Sit down, dear boy, you must be tired; I see you are. Ah, how muddy you are.'

'I was in the rain yesterday, mother. . . .' Raskolnikov began.

'No, no,' Pulcheria Alexandrovna hurriedly interrupted, 'you thought I was going to cross-question you in the womanish way I used to; don't be anxious, I understand, I understand it all: now I've learned the ways here and truly I see for myself that they are better. I've made up my mind once for all: how could I understand your plans and expect you to give an account of them? God knows what concerns and plans you may have, or what ideas you are hatching; so it's not for me to keep nudging your elbow, asking you what you are thinking about? But, my goodness! why am I running to and fro as though I were crazy . . .? I am reading your article in the magazine for the third time, Rodya. Dmitri Prokofitch brought it to me. Directly I saw it I cried out to myself: "There, foolish one, " I thought, "that's what he is busy about; that's the solution of the mystery! Learned people are always like that. He may have some new ideas in his head just now; he is thinking them over and I worry him and upset him. " I read it, my dear, and of course there was a great deal I did not understand; but that's only natural – how should I?'

'Show me, mother.'

Raskolnikov took the magazine and glanced at his article. Incongruous as it was with his mood and his circumstances, he felt that strange and bitter sweet sensation that every author experiences the first time he sees himself in print; besides, he was only twenty-three. It lasted only a moment. After reading a few lines he frowned and his heart throbbed with anguish. He recalled all the inward conflict of the preceding months. He flung the article on the table with disgust and anger.

'But however foolish I may be, Rodya, I can see for myself that you will very soon be one of the leading – if not the leading man – in the world of Russian thought. And they dared to think you were mad! You don't know, but they really thought that. Ah, the despicable creatures, how could they understand genius? And Dounia, Dounia was all but believing it – what do you say to that? Your father sent twice to magazines – the first time poems (I've got the manuscript and will show you) and the second time a whole novel (I begged him to let me copy it out) and how we prayed that they should be taken – they weren't! I was breaking my heart, Rodya, six or seven days ago over your food and your clothes and the way you are living. But now I see again how foolish I was, for you can attain any position you like by your intellect and talent. No doubt you don't care about that for the present and you are occupied with much more important matters. . . .'

'Dounia's not at home, mother?'

'No, Rodya. I often don't see her; she leaves me alone. Dmitri Proko-fitch comes to see me, it's so good of him, and he always talks about you. He loves and respects you, my dear. I don't say that Dounia is very wanting in consideration. I am not complaining. She has her ways and I have mine; she seems to have got some secrets of late and I never have any secrets from you two. Of course, I am sure that Dounia has far too much sense, and besides she loves you and me . . . but I don't know what it will all lead to. You've made me so happy by coming now, Rodya, but she has missed you by going out; when she comes in I'll tell her: "Your brother came in while you were out. Where have you been all this time? " You mustn't spoil me, Rodya, you know; come when you can, but if you can't, it doesn't matter, I can wait. I shall know, anyway, that you are fond of me, that will be enough for me. I shall read what you write, I shall hear about you from everyone, and sometimes you'll come yourself to see me. What could be better? Here you've come now to comfort your mother, I see that.'

Here Pulcheria Alexandrovna began to cry.

'Here I am again! Don't mind my foolishness. My goodness, why am I sitting here?' she cried, jumping up. 'There is coffee and I don't offer you any. Ah, that's the selfishness of old age. I'll get it at once!'

'Mother, don't trouble, I am going at once. I haven't come for that. Please listen to me.'

Pulcheria Alexandrovna went up to him timidly.

'Mother, whatever happens, whatever you hear about me, whatever you are told about me, will you always love me as you do now?' he asked suddenly from the fullness of his heart, as though not thinking of his words and not weighing them.

'Rodya, Rodya, what is the matter? How can you ask me such a question? Why, who will tell me anything about you? Besides, I shouldn't believe anyone, I should refuse to listen.'

'I've come to assure you that I've always loved you and I am glad that we are alone, even glad Dounia is out,' he went on with the same impulse. 'I have come to tell you that though you will be unhappy, you must believe that your son loves you now more than himself, and that all you thought about me, that I was cruel and didn't care about you, was all a mistake. I shall never cease to love you. . . . Well, that's enough: I thought I must do this and begin with this. . . .'

Pulcheria Alexandrovna embraced him in silence, pressing him to her bosom and weeping gently.

'I don't know what is wrong with you, Rodya,' she said at last. 'I've been thinking all this time that we were simply boring you and now I see that there is a great sorrow in store for you, and that's why you are miserable. I've foreseen it a long time, Rodya. Forgive me for speaking about it. I keep thinking about it and lie awake at nights. Your sister lay talking in her sleep all last night, talking of nothing but you. I caught something, but I couldn't make it out. I felt all the morning as though I were going to be hanged, waiting for something, expecting something, and now it has come? Rodya, Rodya, where are you going? You are going away somewhere?'

'Yes.'

'That's what I thought! I can come with you, you know, if you need me. And Dounia, too; she loves you, she loves you dearly – and Sofya Semyonovna may come with us if you like. You see, I am glad to look upon her as a daughter even. . . . Dmitri Prokofitch will help us to go together. But . . . where . . . are you going?'

'Good-bye, mother.'

'What, to-day?' she cried, as though losing him for ever.

'I can't stay, I must go now. . . .'

'And can't I come with you?'

'No, but kneel down and pray to God for me. Your prayer perhaps will reach Him.'

'Let me bless you and sign you with the cross. That's right, that's right. Oh God, what are we doing?'

Yes, he was glad, he was very glad that there was no one there, that he was alone with his mother. For the first time after all those awful months his heart was softened. He fell down before her, he kissed her feet and both wept, embracing. And she was not surprised and did not question him this time. For some days she had realized that something awful was happening to her son and that now some terrible minute had come for him.

'Rodya, my darling, my first born,' she said sobbing, 'now you are just as when you were little. You would run like this to me and hug me and kiss me. When your father was living and we were poor, you comforted us simply by being with us and when I buried your father, how often we wept together at his grave and embraced, as now. And if I've been crying lately, it's that my mother's heart had a foreboding of trouble. The first time I saw you, that evening, you remember, as soon as we arrived here, I guessed simply from your eyes. My heart sank at once, and to-day when I opened the door and looked at you, I thought the fatal hour had come. Rodya, Rodya, you are not going away to-day?'

'No!'

'You'll come again?'

'Yes . . . I'll come.'

'Rodya, don't be angry, I don't dare to question you. I know I mustn't. Only say two words to me – is it far where you are going?'

'Very far.'

'What is awaiting you there? Some post or career for you?'

'What God sends . . . only pray for me.' Raskolnikov went to the door, but she clutched him and gazed despairingly into his eyes. Her face worked with terror.

'Enough, mother,' said Raskolnikov, deeply regretting that he had come.

'Not for ever, it's not yet for ever? You'll come, you'll come to-morrow?'

'I will, I will, good-bye.' He tore himself away at last.

It was a warm, fresh, bright evening; it had cleared up in the morning. Raskolnikov went to his lodgings; he made haste. He wanted to finish all before sunset. He did not want to meet anyone till then. Going up the stairs he noticed that Nastasya rushed from the samovar to watch him intently. 'Can anyone have come to see me?' he wondered. He had a disgusted vision of Porfiry. But opening his door he saw Dounia. She was sitting alone, plunged in deep thought, and looked as though she had been waiting a long time. He stopped short in the doorway. She rose from the sofa in dismay and stood up facing him. Her eyes, fixed upon him, betrayed horror and infinite grief. And from those eyes alone he saw at once that she knew.

'Am I to come in or go away?' he asked uncertainly.

'I've been all day with Sofya Semyonovna. We were both waiting for you. We thought that you would be sure to come there.'

Raskolnikov went into the room and sank exhausted on a chair.

'I feel weak, Dounia, I am very tired; and I should have liked at this moment to be able to control myself.'

He glanced at her mistrustfully.

'Where were you all night?'

'I don't remember clearly. You see, sister, I wanted to make up my mind once for all, and several times I walked by the Neva, I remember that I wanted to end it all there, but . . . I couldn't make up my mind,' he whispered, looking at her mistrustfully again.

'Thank God! That was just what we were afraid of, Sofya Semyonovna and I. Then you still have faith in life? Thank God, thank God!'

Raskolnikov smiled bitterly.

'I haven't faith, but I have just been weeping in mother's arms; I haven't faith, but I have just asked her to pray for me. I don't know how it is, Dounia, I don't understand it.'

'Have you been at mother's? Have you told her?' cried Dounia, horror-stricken. 'Surely you haven't done that?'

'No, I didn't tell her . . . in words; but she understood a great deal. She heard you talking in your sleep. I am sure she half understands it already. Perhaps I did wrong in going to see her. I don't know why I did go. I am a contemptible person, Dounia.'

'A contemptible person, but ready to face suffering! You are, aren't you?'

'Yes, I am going. At once. Yes, to escape the disgrace I thought of drowning myself, Dounia, but as I looked into the water, I thought that if I had considered myself strong till now I'd better not be afraid of disgrace,' he said, hurrying on. 'It's pride, Dounia.'

'Pride, Rodya.'

There was a gleam of fire in his lustreless eyes; he seemed to be glad to think that he was still proud.

'You don't think, sister, that I was simply afraid of the water?' he asked, looking into her face with a sinister smile.

'Oh, Rodya, hush!' cried Dounia bitterly. Silence lasted for two minutes. He sat with his eyes fixed on the floor; Dounia stood at the other end of the table and looked at him with anguish. Suddenly he got up.

'It's late, it's time to go! I am going at once to give myself up. But I don't know why I am going to give myself up.'

Big tears fell down her cheeks.

'You are crying, sister, but can you hold out your hand to me?'

'You doubted it?'

She threw her arms round him.

'Aren't you half expiating your crime by facing the suffering?' she cried, holding him close and kissing him.

'Crime? What crime?' he cried in sudden fury. 'That I killed a vile noxious insect, an old pawnbroker woman, of use to no one! . . . Killing her was atonement for forty sins. She was sucking the life out of poor people. Was that a crime? I am not thinking of it and I am not thinking of expiating it, and why are you all rubbing it in on all sides? "A crime! a crime!" Only now I see clearly the imbecility of my cowardice, now that I have decided to face this superfluous disgrace. It's simply because I am contemptible and have nothing in me that I have decided to, perhaps too for my advantage, as that . . . Porfiry . . . suggested!'

'Brother, brother, what are you saying? Why, you have shed blood?' cried Dounia in despair.

'Which all men shed,' he put in almost frantically, 'which flows and had always flowed in streams, which is spilt like champagne, and for which men are crowned in the Capitol and are called afterwards benefactors of mankind. Look into it more carefully and understand it! I too wanted to do good to men and would have done hundreds, thousands of good deeds to make up for that one piece of stupidity, not stupidity even, simply clumsiness, for the idea was by no means so stupid as it seems now that it has failed. . . . (Everything seems stupid when it fails.) By that stupidity I only wanted to put myself into an independent position, to take the first step, to obtain means, and then everything would have been smoothed over by benefits immeasurable in comparison. . . . But I . . . I couldn't carry out even the first step, because I am contemptible, that's what's the matter! And yet I won't look at it as you do. If I had succeeded I should have been crowned with glory, but now I'm trapped.'

'But that's not so, not so! Brother, what are you saying?'

'Ah, it's not picturesque, not æsthetically attractive! I fail to understand why bombarding people by regular siege is more honourable. The fear of appearances is the first symptom of impotence. I've never, never recognized this more clearly than now, and I am further than ever from seeing that what I did was a crime. I've never, never been stronger and more convinced than now.'

The colour had rushed into his pale exhausted face, but as he uttered his last explanation, he happened to meet Dounia's eyes and he saw such anguish in them that he could not help being checked. He felt that he had, anyway, made these two poor women miserable, that he was, anyway, the cause. . . .

'Dounia darling, if I am guilty forgive me (though I cannot be forgiven if I am guilty). Good-bye! We won't dispute. It's time, high time to go. Don't follow me, I beseech you, I have somewhere else to go. . . . But you go at once and sit with mother. I entreat you to! It's my last request of you. Don't leave her at all; I left her in a state of anxiety, that she is not fit to bear; she will die or go out of her mind. Be with her! Razumihin will be with you. I've been talking to him. . . . Don't cry about me: I'll try to be honest and manly all my life, even if I am a murderer. Perhaps I shall some day make a name. I won't disgrace you, you will see; I'll still show. . . . Now good-bye for the present,' he concluded hurriedly, noticing again a strange expression in Dounia's eyes at his last words and promises. 'Why are you crying? Don't cry, don't cry: we are not parting for ever! Ah yes! Wait a minute, I'd forgotten!'

He went to the table, took up a thick dusty book, opened it and took from between the pages a little water-colour portrait on ivory. It was the portrait of his landlady's daughter, who had died of fever, that strange girl who had wanted to be a nun. For a minute he gazed at the delicate expressive face of his betrothed, kissed the portrait and gave it to Dounia.

'I used to talk a great deal about it to her, only to her,' he said thoughtfully. 'To her heart I confided much of what has since been so hideously realized. Don't be uneasy,' he turned to Dounia, 'she was as much opposed to it as you, and I am glad that she is gone. The great point is that everything now is going to be different, is going to be broken in two,' he cried, suddenly returning to his dejection. 'Everything, everything, and am I prepared for it? Do I want it myself? They say it is necessary for me to suffer! What's the object of these senseless sufferings? Shall I know any better what they are for, when I am crushed by hardships and idiocy, and weak as an old man after twenty years' penal servitude? And what shall I have to live for then? Why am I consenting to that life now? Oh, I knew I was contemptible when I stood looking at the Neva at daybreak to-day!'

At last they both went out. It was hard for Dounia, but she loved him. She walked away, but after going fifty paces she turned round to look at him again. He was still in sight. At the corner he too turned and for the last time their eyes met; but noticing that she was looking at him, he motioned her away with impatience and even vexation, and turned the corner abruptly.

'I am wicked, I see that,' he thought to himself, feeling ashamed a moment later of his angry gesture to Dounia. 'But why are they so fond of me if I don't deserve it? Oh, if only I were alone and no one loved me and I too had never loved anyone! *Nothing of all this would have happened.* But I wonder shall I in those fifteen or twenty years grow so meek that I shall humble myself before people and whimper at every word that I am a criminal? Yes, that's it, that's it, that's what they are sending me there for, that's what they want. Look at them running to and fro about the streets, every one of them a scoundrel and a criminal at heart and, worse still, an idiot. But try to get me off and they'd be wild with righteous indignation. Oh, how I hate them all!'

He fell to musing by what process it could come to pass, that he could be humbled before all of them, indiscriminately – humbled by conviction. And yet why not? It must be so. Would not twenty years of continual bondage crush him utterly? Water wears out a stone. And why, why should he live after that? Why should he go now when he knew that it would be so? It was the hundredth time perhaps that he had asked himself that question since the previous evening, but still he went.

➤ EIGHT ◆

WHEN HE WENT INTO SONIA'S ROOM, it was already getting dark. All day Sonia had been waiting for him in terrible anxiety. Dounia had been waiting with her. She had come to her that morning, remembering Svidrigaïlov's words that Sonia knew. We will not describe the conversation and tears of the two girls, and how friendly they became. Dounia gained one comfort at least from that interview, that her brother would not be alone. He had gone to her, Sonia, first with his confession; he had gone to her for human fellowship when he needed it; she would go with him wherever fate might send him. Dounia did not ask, but she knew it was so. She looked at Sonia almost with reverence and at first almost embarrassed her by it. Sonia was almost on the point of tears. She felt herself, on the contrary, hardly worthy to look at Dounia. Dounia's gracious image when she had bowed to her so attentively and respectfully at their first meeting in Raskolnikov's room had remained in her mind as one of the fairest visions of her life.

Dounia at last became impatient and, leaving Sonia, went to her brother's room to await him there; she kept thinking that he would come there first. When she had gone, Sonia began to be tortured by the dread of his committing suicide, and Dounia too feared it. But they had spent the day trying to persuade each other that that could not be, and both were less anxious while they were together. As soon as they parted, each thought of nothing else. Sonia remembered how Svidrigaïlov had said to her the day before that Raskolnikov had two alternatives – Siberia or . . . Besides she knew his vanity, his pride and his lack of faith.

'Is it possible that he has nothing but cowardice and fear of death to make him live?' she thought at last in despair.

Meanwhile the sun was setting. Sonia was standing in dejection, looking intently out of the window, but from it she could see nothing but the unwhitewashed blank wall of the next house. At last when she began to feel sure of his death – he walked into the room.

She gave a cry of joy, but looking carefully into his face she turned pale.

'Yes,' said Raskolnikov, smiling. 'I have come for your cross, Sonia. It was you told me to go to the cross-roads; why is it you are frightened now it's come to that?'

Sonia gazed at him astonished. His tone seemed strange to her; a cold shiver ran over her, but in a moment she guessed that the tone and the words were a mask. He spoke to her looking away, as though to avoid meeting her eyes.

'You see, Sonia, I've decided that it will be better so. There is one fact. . . . But it's a long story and there's no need to discuss it. But do you know what angers me? It annoys me that all those stupid brutish faces will be gaping at me directly, pestering me with their stupid questions, which I shall have to answer – they'll point their fingers at me. . . . Tfoo! You know I am not going to Porfiry, I am sick of him, I'd rather go to my friend, the Explosive Lieutenant; how I shall surprise him, what a sensation I shall make! But I must be cooler; I've become too irritable of late. You know I was nearly shaking my fist at my sister just now, because she turned to take a last look at me. It's a brutal state to be in! Ah! what am I coming to? Well, where are the crosses?'

He seemed hardly to know what he was doing. He could not stay still or concentrate his attention on anything; his ideas seemed to gallop after one another, he talked incoherently, his hands trembling slightly.

Without a word Sonia took out of the drawer two crosses, one of cypress wood and one of copper. She made the sign of the cross over herself and over him, and put the wooden cross on his neck.

'It's the symbol of my taking up the cross,' he laughed. 'As though I had not suffered much till now! The wooden cross, that is the peasant one; the copper one, that is Lizaveta's – you will wear yourself, show me! So she had it on . . . at that moment? I remember two things like these too, a silver one and a little ikon. I threw them back on the old woman's neck. Those would be appropriate now, really, those are what I ought to put on now. . . . But I am talking nonsense and forgetting what matters; I'm somehow forgetful. . . . You see I have come to warn you, Sonia, so that you might know . . . that's all – that's all I came for. But I thought I had more to say. You wanted me to go yourself. Well, now I am going to prison and you'll have your wish. Well, what are you crying for? You too? Don't. Leave off! Oh, how I hate it all!'

But his feeling was stirred; his heart ached, as he looked at her. 'Why is she grieving too?' he thought to himself. 'What am I to her? Why does she weep? Why is she looking after me, like my mother or Dounia? She'll be my nurse.'

'Cross yourself, say at least one prayer,' Sonia begged in a timid broken voice.

'Oh certainly, as much as you like! And sincerely, Sonia, sincerely. . . .'

But he wanted to say something quite different.

He crossed himself several times. Sonia took up her shawl and put it over her head. It was the green *drap de dames* shawl of which Marmeladov had spoken, 'the family shawl'. Raskolnikov thought of that looking at it, but he did not ask. He began to feel himself that he was certainly forgetting things and was disgustingly agitated. He was frightened at this. He was suddenly struck too by the thought that Sonia meant to go with him.

'What are you doing? Where are you going? Stay here, stay! I'll go alone,' he cried in cowardly vexation, and almost resentful, he moved towards the door. 'What's the use of going in procession?' he muttered going out.

Sonia remained standing in the middle of the room. He had not even said good-bye to her; he had forgotten her. A poignant and rebellious doubt surged in his heart.

'Was it right, was it right, all this?' he thought again as he went down the stairs. 'Couldn't he stop and retract it all . . . and not go?'

But still he went. He felt suddenly once for all that he mustn't ask himself questions. As he turned into the street he remembered that he had not said good-bye to Sonia, that he had left her in the middle of the room in her green shawl, not daring to stir after he had shouted at her, and he stopped short for a moment. At the same instant, another thought dawned upon him, as though it had been lying in wait to strike him then.

'Why, with what object did I go to her just now? I told her – on business; on what business? I had no sort of business! To tell her I was *going*; but where was the need? Do I love her? No, no, I drove her away just now like a dog. Did I want her crosses? Oh, how low I've sunk! No, I wanted her tears, I wanted to see her terror, to see how her heart ached! I had to have something to cling to, something to delay me, some friendly face to see! And I dared to believe in myself, to dream of what I would do! I am a beggarly contemptible wretch, contemptible!'

He walked along the canal bank, and he had not much further to go. But on reaching the bridge he stopped and turning out of his way along it went to the Hay Market.

He looked eagerly to right and left, gazed intently at every object and could not fix his attention on anything; everything slipped away. 'In another week, another month I shall be driven in a prison van over this bridge, how shall I look at the canal then? I should like to remember this!' slipped into his mind. 'Look at this sign! How shall I read those letters then? It's written here "Campany ", that's a thing to remember, that letter *a*, and to look at it again in a month – how shall I look at it then? What shall I be feeling and thinking then? . . . How trivial it all must be, what I am fretting about now! Of course it must all be interesting . . . in its way . . . (Ha-ha-ha! What am I thinking about?) I am becoming a baby, I am showing off to myself; why am I ashamed? Foo! how people shove! that fat man – a German he must be – who pushed against me, does he know whom he pushed? There's a peasant woman with a baby, begging. It's curious that she thinks me happier than she is. I might give her something, for the incongruity of it. Here's a five-copeck piece left in my pocket, where did I get it? Here, here . . . take it, my good woman!'

'God bless you,' the beggar chanted in a lachrymose voice.

He went into the Hay Market. It was distasteful, very distasteful to be in a crowd, but he walked just where he saw most people. He would have given anything in the world to be alone; but he knew himself that he would not have remained alone for a moment. There was a man drunk and disorderly in the crowd; he kept trying to dance and falling down. There was a ring round him. Raskolnikov squeezed his way through the crowd, stared for some minutes at the drunken man and suddenly gave a short jerky laugh. A minute later he had forgotten him and did not see him, though he still stared. He moved away at last, not remembering where he was; but when he got into the middle of the square an emotion suddenly came over him, overwhelming him body and mind.

He suddenly recalled Sonia's words, 'Go to the cross-roads, bow down to the people, kiss the earth, for you have sinned against it too, and say aloud to the whole world, "I am a murderer ".' He trembled, remembering that. And the hopeless misery and anxiety of all that time, especially of the last hours, had weighed so heavily upon him that he positively clutched at the chance of this new unmixed, complete sensation. It came over him like a fit; it was like a single spark kindled in his soul and spreading fire through him. Everything in him softened at once and the tears started into his eyes. He fell to the earth on the spot. . . .

He knelt down in the middle of the square, bowed down to the earth, and kissed that filthy earth with bliss and rapture. He got up and bowed down a second time.

'He's boozed,' a youth near him observed.

There was a roar of laughter.

'He's going to Jerusalem, brothers, and saying good-bye to his children and his country. He's bowing down to all the world and kissing the great city of St. Petersburg and its pavement,' added a workman who was a little drunk.

'Quite a young man, too!' observed a third.

'And a gentleman,' someone observed soberly.

'There's no knowing who's a gentleman and who isn't nowadays.'

These exclamations and remarks checked Raskolnikov, and the words, 'I am a murderer', which were perhaps on the point of dropping from his lips, died away. He bore these remarks quietly, however, and, without looking round, he turned down a street leading to the police office. He had a glimpse of something on the way which did not surprise him; he had felt that it must be so. The second time he bowed down in the Hay Market he saw, standing fifty paces from him on the left, Sonia. She was hiding from him behind one of the wooden shanties in the market-place. She had followed him then on his painful way! Raskolnikov at that moment felt and knew once for all that Sonia was with him for ever and would follow him to the ends of the earth, wherever fate might take him. It wrung his heart . . . but he was just reaching the fatal place.

He went into the yard fairly resolutely. He had to mount to the third storey. 'I shall be some time going up,' he thought. He felt as though the fateful moment was still far off, as though he had plenty of time left for consideration.

Again the same rubbish, the same eggshells lying about on the spiral stairs, again the open doors of the flats, again the same kitchens and the same fumes and stench coming from them. Raskolnikov had not been here since that day. His legs were numb and gave way under him, but still they moved forward. He stopped for a moment to take breath, to collect himself, so as to enter *like a man*. 'But why? what for?' he wondered, reflecting. 'If I must drink the cup what difference does it make? The more revolting the better.' He imagined for an instant the figure of the 'explosive lieutenant', Ilya Petrovitch. Was he actually going to him? Couldn't he go to someone else? To Nikodim Fomitch? Couldn't he turn back and go straight to Nikodim Fomitch's lodgings? At least then it would be done privately. . . . No, no! To the 'explosive lieutenant'! If he must drink it, drink it off at once.

Turning cold and hardly conscious, he opened the door of the office. There were very few people in it this time – only a house porter and a peasant. The doorkeeper did not even peep out from behind his screen. Raskolnikov walked into the next room. 'Perhaps I still need not speak,' passed through his mind. Some sort of clerk not wearing a uniform was settling himself at a bureau to write. In a corner another clerk was seating himself. Zametov was not there, nor, of course, Nikodim Fomitch.

'No one in?' Raskolnikov asked, addressing the person at the bureau.

'Whom do you want?'

'A-ah! Not a sound was heard, not a sight was seen, but I scent the Russian . . . how does it go on in the fairy tale? . . . I've forgotten! "At your service! " ' a familiar voice cried suddenly.

Raskolnikov shuddered. The Explosive Lieutenant stood before him. He had just come in from the third room. 'It is the hand of fate,' thought Raskolnikov. 'Why is he here?'

'You've come to see us? What about?' cried Ilya Petrovitch. He was obviously in an exceedingly good humour and perhaps a trifle exhilarated. 'If it's on business you are rather early.* It's only a chance that I am here . . . however, I'll do what I can. I must admit, I . . . what is it, what is it? Excuse me. . . .'

'Raskolnikov.'

'Of course, Raskolnikov. You didn't imagine I'd forgotten? Don't think I am like that . . . Rodion Ro – Ro – Rodionovitch, that's it, isn't it?'

'Rodion Romanovitch.'

'Yes, yes, of course, Rodion Romanovitch! I was just getting at it. I made many inquiries about you. I assure you I've been genuinely grieved since that . . . since I behaved like that . . . it was explained to me afterwards that you were a literary man . . . and a learned one too . . . and so to say the first steps. . . . Mercy on us! What literary or scientific man does not begin by some originality of conduct! My wife and I have the greatest respect for literature, in my wife it's a genuine passion! Literature and art! If only a man is a gentleman, all the rest can be gained by talents, learning, good sense, genius. As for a hat – well, what does a hat matter?

*Dostoevsky appears to have forgotten that it is after sunset, and that the last time Raskolnikov visited the police office at two in the afternoon he was reproached for coming too late.–TRANSLATOR.

I can buy a hat as easily as I can a bun; but what's under the hat, what the hat covers, I can't buy that! I was even meaning to come and apologize to you, but thought maybe you'd. . . . But I am forgetting to ask you, is there anything you want really? I hear your family have come?'

'Yes, my mother and sister.'

'I've even had the honour and happiness of meeting your sister – a highly cultivated and charming person. I confess I was sorry I got so hot with you. There it is! But as for my looking suspiciously at your fainting fit – that affair has been cleared up splendidly! Bigotry and fanaticism! I understand your indignation. Perhaps you are changing your lodging or account of your family's arriving?'

'No, I only looked in . . . I came to ask . . . I thought that I should find Zametov here.'

'Oh, yes! Of course, you've made friends, I heard. Well, no, Zametov is not here. Yes, we've lost Zametov. He's not been here since yesterday . . . he quarrelled with everyone on leaving . . . in the rudest way. He is a feather-headed youngster, that's all; one might have expected something from him, but there, you know what they are, our brilliant young men. He wanted to go in for some examination, but it's only to talk and boast about it, it will go no further than that. Of course it's a very different matter with you or Mr. Razumihin there, your friend. Your career is an intellectual one and you won't be deterred by failure. For you, one may say, all the attractions of life *nihil est* – you are an ascetic, a monk, a hermit! . . . A book, a pen behind your ear, a learned research – that's where your spirit soars! I am the same way myself. . . . Have you read Livingstone's Travels?'

'No.'

'Oh, I have. There are a great many Nihilists about nowadays, you know, and indeed it is not to be wondered at. What sort of days are they? I ask you. But we thought . . . you are not a Nihilist of course? Answer me openly, openly!'

'N-no. . . .'

'Believe me, you can speak openly to me as you would to yourself! Official duty is one thing but . . . you are thinking I meant to say *friendship* is quite another? No, you're wrong! It's not friendship, but the feeling of a man and a citizen, the feeling of humanity and of love for the Almighty. I may be an official, but I am always bound to feel myself a man and a citizen. . . . You were asking about Zametov. Zametov will make a scandal in the French style in a house of bad reputation, over a glass of champagne . . . that's all your Zametov is good for! While I'm perhaps, so to speak, burning with devotion and lofty feelings, and besides I have rank, consequence, a post! I am married and have children, I fulfil the duties of a man and a citizen, but who is he, may I ask? I appeal to you as a man ennobled by education . . . Then these midwives, too, have become extraordinarily numerous.'

Raskolnikov raised his eyebrows inquiringly. The words of Ilya Petrovitch, who had obviously been dining, were for the most part a stream of empty sounds for him. But some of them he understood. He looked at him inquiringly, not knowing how it would end.

'I mean those crop-headed wenches,' the talkative Ilya Petrovitch continued. 'Midwives is my name for them. I think it a very satisfactory one, ha-ha! They go to the Academy, study anatomy. If I fall ill, am I to send for a young lady to treat me? What do you say? Ha-ha!' Ilya Petrovitch laughed, quite pleased with his own wit. 'It's an immoderate zeal for education, but once you're educated, that's enough. Why abuse it? Why insult honourable people, as that scoundrel Zametov does? Why did he insult me, I ask you? Look at these suicides, too, how common they are, you can't fancy! People spend their last halfpenny and kill themselves, boys and girls and old people. Only this morning we heard about a gentleman who had just come to town. Nil Pavlitch, I say, what was the name of that gentleman who shot himself?'

'Svidrigaïlov,' someone answered from the other room with drowsy listlessness.

Raskolnikov started.

'Svidrigaïlov! Svidrigaïlov has shot himself' he cried.

'What, do you know Svidrigaïlov?'

'Yes . . . I knew him. . . . . He hadn't been here long.'

'Yes, that's so. He had lost his wife, was a man of reckless habits and all of a sudden shot himself, and in such a shocking way. . . . He left in his notebook a few words: that he dies in full possession of his faculties and that no one is to blame for his death. He had money, they say. How did you come to know him?'

'I . . . was acquainted . . . my sister was governess in his family.'

'Bah-bab-bah! Then no doubt you can tell us something about him. You had no suspicion?'

'I saw him yesterday . . . he . . . was drinking wine; I knew nothing.'

Raskolnikov felt as though something had fallen on him and was stifling him.

'You've turned pale again. It's so stuffy here. . . .'

'Yes, I must go,' muttered Raskolnikov. 'Excuse my troubling you. . . .'

'Oh, not at all, as often as you like. It's a pleasure to see you and I am glad to say so.'

Ilya Petrovitch held out his hand.

'I only wanted . . . I came to see Zametov.'

'I understand, I understand, and it's a pleasure to see you.'

'I . . . am very glad . . . good-bye,' Raskolnikov smiled.

He went out; he reeled, he was overtaken with giddiness and did not know what he was doing. He began going down the stairs, supporting himself with his right hand against the wall. He fancied that a porter pushed past him on his way upstairs to the police office, that a dog in the lower storey kept up a shrill barking and that a woman flung a rolling-pin at it and shouted. He went down and out into the yard. There, not far from the entrance, stood Sonia, pale and horror-stricken. She looked wildly at him. He stood still before her. There was a look of poignant agony, of despair, in her face. She clasped her hands. His lips worked in an ugly, meaningless smile. He stood still a minute, grinned and went back to the police office.

Ilya Petrovitch had sat down and was rummaging among some papers. Before him stood the same peasant who had pushed by on the stairs.

'Hulloa! Back again! have you left something behind? What's the matter?'

Raskolnikov, with white lips and staring eyes, came slowly nearer. He walked right to the table, leaned his hand on it, tried to say something, but could not; only incoherent sounds were audible.

'You are feeling ill, a chair! Here, sit down! Some water!'

Raskolnikov dropped on to a chair, but he kept his eyes fixed on the face of Ilya Petrovitch, which expressed unpleasant surprise. Both looked at one another for a minute and waited. Water was brought.

'It was I . . .' began Raskolnikov.

'Drink some water.'

Raskolnikov refused the water with his hand, and softly and brokenly, but distinctly said:

'*It was I killed the old pawnbroker woman and her sister Lizaveta with an axe and robbed them.*'

Ilya Petrovitch opened his mouth. People ran up on all sides.

Raskolnikov repeated his statement.

✺ EPILOGUE ✺

➤ ONE ➤

SIBERIA. ON THE BANKS OF A broad solitary river stands a town, one of the administrative centres of Russia; in the town there is a fortress, in the fortress there is a prison. In the prison the second-class convict Rodion Raskolnikov has been confined for nine months. Almost a year and a half has passed since his crime.

There had been little difficulty about his trial. The criminal adhered exactly, firmly, and clearly to his statement. He did not confuse nor misrepresent the facts, nor soften them in his own interest, nor omit the smallest detail. He explained every incident of the murder, the secret of *the pledge* (the piece of wood with a strip of metal) which was found in the murdered woman's hand. He described minutely how he had taken her keys, what they were like, as well as the chest and its contents; he explained the mystery of Lizaveta's murder; described how Koch and after him, the student knocked, and repeated all they had said to one another; how he afterwards had run downstairs and heard Nikolay and Dmitri shouting; how he had hidden in the empty flat and afterwards gone home. He ended by indicating the stone in the yard off the Voznesensky Prospect under which the purse and the trinkets were found. The whole thing, in fact, was perfectly clear. The lawyers and the judges were very much struck, among other things, by the fact that he had hidden the trinkets and the purse under a stone, without making use of them, and that, what was more, he did not now remember what the trinkets were like, or even how many there were. The fact that he had never opened the purse and did not even know how much was in it seemed incredible. There turned out to be in the purse three hundred and seventeen roubles and sixty copecks. From being so long under the stone, some of the most valuable notes lying uppermost had suffered from the damp. They were a long while trying to discover why the accused man should tell a lie about this, when about everything else he had made a truthful and straightforward confession. Finally some of the lawyers more versed in psychology admitted that it was possible he had really not looked into the purse, and so didn't know what was in it when he hid it under the stone. But they immediately drew the deduction that the crime could only have been committed through temporary mental derangement, through homicidal mania, without object or the pursuit of gain. This fell in with the most recent fashionable theory of temporary insanity, so often applied in our days in criminal cases. Moreover Raskolnikov's hypochondriacal condition was proved by many witnesses, by Dr. Zossimov, his former fellow students, his landlady and her servant. All this pointed strongly to the conclusion that Raskolnikov was not quite like an ordinary murderer and robber, but that there was another element in the case.

To the intense annoyance of those who maintained this opinion, the criminal scarcely attempted to defend himself. To the decisive question as to what motive impelled him to the murder and the robbery, he answered very clearly with the coarsest frankness that the cause was his miserable position, his poverty and helplessness, and his desire to provide for his first steps in life by the help of the three thousand roubles he had reckoned on finding. He had been led to the murder through his shallow and cowardly nature, exasperated moreover by privation and failure. To the question what led him to confess, he answered that it was his heartfelt repentance. All this was almost coarse. . . .

The sentence however was more merciful than could have been expected, perhaps partly because the criminal had not tried to justify himself, but had rather shown a desire to exaggerate his guilt. All the strange and peculiar circumstances of the crime were taken into consideration. There could be no doubt of the abnormal and poverty-stricken condition of the criminal at the time. The fact that he had made no use of what he had stolen was put down partly to the effect of remorse, partly to his abnormal mental condition at the time of the crime. Incidentally the murder of Lizaveta served indeed to confirm the last hypothesis: a man commits two murders and forgets that the door is open! Finally, the confession, at the very moment when the case was hopelessly muddled by the false evidence given by Nikolay through melancholy and fanaticism, and when, moreover, there were no proofs against the real criminal, no suspicions even (Porfiry Petrovitch fully kept his word) – all this did much to soften the sentence. Other circumstances, too, in the prisoner's favour came out quite unexpectedly. Razumihin somehow discovered and proved that while Raskolnikov was at the university he had helped a poor consumptive fellow student and had spent his last penny on supporting him for six months, and when this student died, leaving a decrepit old father whom he had maintained almost from his thirteenth year, Raskolnikov had got the old man into a hospital and paid for his funeral when he died. Raskolnikov's landlady bore witness, too, that when they had lived in another house at Five Corners, Raskolnikov had rescued two little children from a house on fire and was burnt in doing so. This was investigated and fairly well confirmed by many witnesses. These facts made an impression in his favour.

And in the end the criminal was, in consideration of extenuating circumstances, condemned to penal servitude in the second class for a term of eight years only.

At the beginning of the trial Raskolnikov's mother fell ill. Dounia and Razumihin found it possible to get her out of Petersburg during the trial. Razumihin chose a town on the railway not far from Petersburg, so as to be able to follow every step of the trial and at the same time to see Avdotya Romanovna as often as possible. Pulcheria Alexandrovna's illness was a strange nervous one and was accompanied by a partial derangement of her intellect.

When Dounia returned from her last interview with her brother, she had found her mother already ill, in feverish delirium. That evening Razumihin and she agreed what answers they must make to her mother's questions about Raskolnikov and made up a complete story for her mother's benefit of his having to go away to a distant part of Russia on a business commission, which would bring him in the end money and reputation.

But they were struck by the fact that Pulcheria Alexandrovna never asked them anything on the subject, neither then nor thereafter. On the contrary, she had her own version of her son's sudden departure; she told them with tears how he had come to say good-bye to her, hinting that she alone knew many mysterious and important facts, and that Rodya had many very powerful enemies, so that it was necessary for him to be in hiding. As for his future career, she had no doubt that it would be brilliant when certain sinister influences could be removed. She assured Razumihin that her son would be one day a great statesman, that his article and brilliant literary talent proved it. This article she was continually reading, she even read it aloud, almost took it to bed with her, but scarcely asked where Rodya was, though the subject was obviously avoided by the others, which might have been enough to awaken her suspicions.

They began to be frightened at last at Pulcheria Alexandrovna's strange silence on certain subjects. She did not, for instance, complain of getting no letters from him, though in previous years she had only lived on the hope of letters from her beloved Rodya. This was the cause of great uneasiness to Dounia; the idea occurred to her that her mother suspected that there was something terrible in her son's fate and was afraid to ask, for fear of hearing something still more awful. In any case, Dounia saw clearly that her mother was not in full possession of her faculties.

It happened once or twice, however, that Pulcheria Alexandrovna gave such a turn to the conversation that it was impossible to answer her without mentioning where Rodya was, and on receiving unsatisfactory and suspicious answers she became at once gloomy and silent, and this mood lasted for a long time. Dounia saw at last that it was hard to deceive her and came to the conclusion that it was better to be absolutely silent on certain points; but it became more and more evident that the poor mother suspected something terrible. Dounia remembered her brother's telling her that her mother had overheard her talking in her sleep on the night after her interview with Svidrigaïlov and before the fatal day of the confession: had not she made out something from that? Sometimes days and even weeks of gloomy silence and tears would be succeeded by a period of hysterical animation, and the invalid would begin to talk almost incessantly of her son, of her hopes of his future. . . . Her fancies were sometimes very strange. They humoured her, pretended to agree with her (she saw perhaps that they were pretending), but she still went on talking.

Five months after Raskolnikov's confession, he was sentenced. Razumihin and Sonia saw him in prison as often as it was possible. At last the moment of separation came. Dounia swore to her brother that the separation should not be for ever, Razumihin did the same. Razumihin, in his youthful ardour, had firmly resolved to lay the foundations at least of a secure livelihood during the next three or four years, and saving up a certain sum, to emigrate to Siberia, a country rich in every natural resource and in need of workers, active men and capital. There they would settle in the town where Rodya was and all together would begin a new life. They all wept at parting.

Raskolnikov had been very dreamy for a few days before. He asked a great deal about his mother and was constantly anxious about her. He worried so much about her that it alarmed Dounia. When he heard about his mother's illness he became very gloomy. With Sonia he was particularly reserved all the time. With the help of the money left to her by Svidrigaïlov, Sonia had long ago made her preparations to follow the party of convicts in which he was despatched to Siberia. Not a word passed between Raskolnikov and her on the subject, but both knew it would be so. At the final leave-taking he smiled strangely at his sister's and Razumihin's fervent anticipations of their happy future together when he should come out of prison. He predicted that their mother's illness would soon have a fatal ending. Sonia and he at last set off.

Two months later Dounia was married to Razumihin. It was a quiet and sorrowful wedding; Porfiry Petrovitch and Zossimov were invited however. During all this period Razumihin wore an air of resolute determination. Dounia put implicit faith in his carrying out his plans and indeed she could not but believe in him. He displayed a rare strength of will. Among other things he began attending university lectures again in order to take his degree. They were continually making plans for the future; both counted on settling in Siberia within five years at least. Till then they rested their hopes on Sonia.

Pulcheria Alexandrovna was delighted to give her blessing to Dounia's marriage with Razumihin; but after the marriage she became even more melancholy and anxious. To give her pleasure Razumihin told her how Raskolnikov had looked after the poor student and his decrepit father and how a year ago he had been burnt and injured in rescuing two little children from a fire. These two pieces of news excited Pulcheria Alexandrovna's disordered imagination almost to ecstasy. She was continually talking about them, even entering into conversation with strangers in the street, though Dounia always accompanied her. In public conveyances and shops, wherever she could capture a listener, she would begin to discourse about her son, his article, how he had helped the student, how he had burnt at the fire, and so on! Dounia did not know how to restrain her. Apart from the danger of her morbid excitement, there was the risk of someone's recalling Raskolnikov's name and speaking of the recent trial. Pulcheria Alexandrovna found out the address of the mother of the two children her son had saved and insisted on going to see her.

At last her restlessness reached an extreme point. She would sometimes begin to cry suddenly and was often ill and feverishly delirious. One morning she declared that by reckoning Rodya ought soon to be home, that she remembered when he said good-bye to her he said that they must expect him back in nine months. She began to prepare for his coming, began to do up her room for him, to clean the furniture, to wash and put up new hangings and so on. Dounia was anxious, but said nothing and helped her to arrange the room. After a fatiguing day spent in continual fancies, in joyful day-dreams and tears, Pulcheria Alexandrovna was taken ill in the night and by morning she was feverish and delirious. It was brain fever. She died within a fortnight. In her delirium she dropped words which showed that she knew a great deal more about her son's terrible fate than they had supposed.

For a long time Raskolnikov did not know of his mother's death, though a regular correspondence had been maintained from the time he reached Siberia. It was carried on by means of Sonia, who wrote every month to the Razumihins and received an answer with unfailing regularity. At first they found Sonia's letters dry and unsatisfactory, but later on they came to the conclusion that the letters could not be better, for from these letters they received a complete picture of their unfortunate brother's life. Sonia's letters were full of the most matter-of-fact detail, the simplest and clearest description of all Raskolnikov's surroundings as a convict. There was no word of her own hopes, no conjecture as to the future, no description of her feelings. Instead of any attempt to interpret his state of mind and inner life, she gave the simple facts – that is, his own words, an exact account of his health, what he asked for at their interviews, what commission he gave her and so on. All these facts she gave with extraordinary minuteness. The picture of their unhappy brother stood out at last with great clearness and precision. There could be no mistake, because nothing was given but facts.

But Dounia and her husband could get little comfort out of the news, especially at first. Sonia wrote that he was constantly sullen and not ready to talk, that he scarcely seemed interested in the news she gave him from their letters, that he sometimes asked after his mother and that when, seeing that he had guessed the truth, she told him at last of her death, she was surprised to find that he did not seem greatly affected by it, not externally at any rate. She told them that, although he seemed so wrapped up in himself and, as it were, shut himself off from everyone – he took a very direct and simple view of his new life; that he understood his position, expected nothing better for the time, had no ill-founded hopes (as is so common in his position) and scarcely seemed surprised at anything in his surroundings, so unlike anything he had known before. She wrote that his health was satisfactory; he did his work without shirking or seeking to do more; he was almost indifferent about food, but except on Sundays and holidays the food was so bad that at last he had been glad to accept some money from her, Sonia, to have his own tea every day. He begged her not to trouble about anything else, declaring that all this fuss about him only annoyed him. Sonia wrote further that in prison he shared the same room with the rest, that she had not seen the inside of their barracks, but concluded that they were crowded, miserable and unhealthy; that he slept on a plank bed with a rug under him and was unwilling to make any other arrangement. But that he lived so poorly and roughly, not from any plan or design, but simply from inattention and indifference.

Sonia wrote simply that he had at first shown no interest in her visits, had almost been vexed with her indeed for coming, unwilling to talk and rude to her. But that in the end these visits had become a habit and almost a necessity for him, so that he was positively distressed when she was ill for some days and could not visit him. She used to see him on holidays at the prison gates or in the guard-room, to which he was brought for a few minutes to see her. On working days she would go to see him at work either at the workshops or at the brick kilns, or at the sheds on the banks of the Irtish.

About herself, Sonia wrote that she had succeeded in making some acquaintances in the town, that she did sewing, and, as there was scarcely a dressmaker in the town, she was looked upon as an indispensable person in many houses. But she did not mention that the authorities were, through her, interested in Raskolnikov; that his task was lightened and so on.

At last the news came (Dounia had indeed noticed signs of alarm and uneasiness in the preceding letters) that he held aloof from everyone, that his fellow prisoners did not like him, that he kept silent for days at a time and was becoming very pale. In the last letter Sonia wrote that he had been taken very seriously ill and was in the convict ward of the hospital.

✦ TWO ✦

HE WAS ILL A LONG TIME. But it was not the horrors of prison life, not the hard labour, the bad food, the shaven head, or the patched clothes that crushed him. What did he care for all those trials and hardships! He was even glad of the hard work. Physically exhausted, he could at least reckon on a few hours of quiet sleep. And what was the food to him – the thin cabbage soup with beetles floating in it? In the past as a student he had often not had even that. His clothes were warm and suited to his manner of life. He did not even feel the fetters. Was he ashamed of his shaven head and parti-coloured coat? Before whom? Before Sonia? Sonia was afraid of him, how could he be ashamed before her? And yet he was ashamed even before Sonia, whom he tortured because of it with his contemptuous rough manner. But it was not his shaven head and his fetters he was ashamed of: his pride had been stung to the quick. It was wounded pride that made him ill. Oh, how happy he would have been if he could have blamed himself! He could have borne anything then, even shame and disgrace. But he judged himself severely, and his exasperated conscience found no particularly terrible fault in his past, except a simple *blunder* which might happen to anyone. He was ashamed just because he, Raskolnikov, had so hopelessly, stupidly come to grief through some decree of blind fate, and must humble himself and submit to 'the idiocy' of a sentence, if he were anyhow to be at peace.

Vague and objectless anxiety in the present, and in the future a continual sacrifice leading to nothing – that was all that lay before him. And what comfort was it to him that at the end of eight years he would only be thirty-two and able to begin a new life! What had he to live for? What had he to look forward to? Why should he strive? To live in order to exist? Why, he had been ready a thousand times before to give up existence for the sake of an idea, for a hope, even for a fancy. Mere existence had always been too little for him; he had always wanted more. Perhaps it was just because of the strength of his desires that he had thought himself a man to whom more was permissible than to others.

And if only fate would have sent him repentance – burning repentance that would have torn his heart and robbed him of sleep, that repentance, the awful agony of which brings visions of hanging or drowning! Oh, he would have been glad of it! Tears and agonies would at least have been life. But he did not repent of his crime.

At least he might have found relief in raging at his stupidity, as he had raged at the grotesque blunders that had brought him to prison. But now in prison, *in freedom*, he thought over and criticized all his actions again and by no means found them so blundering and so grotesque as they had seemed at the fatal time.

'In what way,' he asked himself, 'was my theory stupider than others that have swarmed and clashed from the beginning of the world? One has only to look at the thing quite independently, broadly, and uninfluenced by commonplace ideas, and my idea will by no means seem so . . . strange. Oh, sceptics and halfpenny philosophers, why do you halt halfway?'

'Why does my action strike them as so horrible?' he said to himself. 'Is it because it was a crime? What is meant by crime? My conscience is at rest. Of course it was a legal crime, of course the letter of the law was broken and blood was shed. Well, punish me for the letter of the law . . . and that's enough. Of course, in that case many of the benefactors of mankind who snatched power for themselves instead of inheriting it ought to have been punished at their first steps. But those men succeeded and so *they were right*, and I didn't, and so I had no right to have taken that step.'

It was only in that that he recognized his criminality, only in the fact that he had been unsuccessful and had confessed it.

He suffered too from the question: why had he not killed himself? Why had he stood looking at the river and preferred to confess? Was the desire to live so strong and was it so hard to overcome it? Had not Svidrigaïlov overcome it, although he was afraid of death?

In misery he asked himself this question, and could not understand that, at the very time he had been standing looking into the river, he had perhaps been dimly conscious of the fundamental falsity in himself and his convictions. He didn't understand that that consciousness might be the promise of a future crisis, of a new view of life and of his future resurrection.

He preferred to attribute it to the dead weight of instinct which he could not step over, again through weakness and meanness. He looked at his fellow prisoners and was amazed to see how they all loved life and prized it. It seemed to him that they loved and valued life more in prison than in freedom. What terrible agonies and privations some of them, the tramps for instance, had endured! Could they care so much for a ray of sunshine, for the primeval forest, the cold spring hidden away in some unseen spot, which the tramp had marked three years before, and longed to see again, as he might to see his sweetheart, dreaming of the green grass round it and the bird singing in the bush? As he went on he saw still more inexplicable examples.

In prison, of course, there was a great deal he did not see and did not want to see; he lived as it were with downcast eyes. It was loathsome and unbearable for him to look. But in the end there was much that surprised him and he began, as it were involuntarily, to notice much that he had not suspected before. What surprised him most of all was the terrible impossible gulf that lay between him and all the rest. They seemed to be a different species, and he looked at them and they at him with distrust and hostility. He felt and knew the reasons of his isolation, but he would never have admitted till then that those reasons were so deep and strong. There were some Polish exiles, political prisoners, among them. They simply looked down upon all the rest as ignorant churls; but Raskolnikov could not look upon them like that. He saw that these ignorant men were in many respects far wiser than the Poles. There were some Russians who were just as contemptuous, a former officer and two seminarists. Raskolnikov saw their mistake as clearly. He was disliked and avoided by everyone; they even began to hate him at last – why he could not tell. Men who had been far more guilty despised and laughed at his crime.

'You're a gentleman,' they used to say. 'You shouldn't hack about with an axe; that's not a gentleman's work.'

The second week in Lent, his turn came to take the sacrament with his gang. He went to church and prayed with the others. A quarrel broke out one day, he did not know how. All fell on him at once in a fury.

'You're an infidel! You don't believe in God,' they shouted. 'You ought to be killed.'

He had never talked to them about God nor his belief, but they wanted to kill him as an infidel. He said nothing. One of the prisoners rushed at him in perfect frenzy. Raskolnikov awaited him calmly and silently; his eyebrows did not quiver, his face did not flinch. The guard succeeded in intervening between him and his assailant, or there would have been bloodshed.

There was another question he could not decide: why were they all so fond of Sonia? She did not try to win their favour; she rarely met them, sometimes only she came to see him at work for a moment. And yet everybody knew her, they knew that she had come out to follow *him*, knew how and where she lived. She never gave them money, did them no particular services. Only once at Christmas she sent them all presents of pies and rolls. But by degrees closer relations sprang up between them and Sonia. She would write and post letters for them to their relations. Relations of the prisoners who visited the town, at their instructions, left with Sonia presents and money for them. Their wives and sweethearts knew her and used to visit her. And when she visited Raskolnikov at work, or met a party of the prisoners on the road, they all took off their hats to her. 'Little mother Sofya Semyonovna, you are our dear, good little mother,' coarse branded criminals said to that frail little creature. She would smile and bow to them and everyone was delighted when she smiled. They even admired her gait and turned round to watch her walking; they admired her too for being so little, and, in fact, did not know what to admire her most for. They even came to her for help in their illnesses.

He was in the hospital from the middle of Lent till after Easter. When he was better, he remembered the dreams he had had while he was feverish and delirious. He dreamt that the whole world was condemned to a terrible new strange plague that had come to Europe from the depths of Asia. All were to be destroyed except a very few chosen. Some new sorts of microbes were attacking the bodies of men, but these microbes were endowed with intelligence and will. Men attacked by them became at once mad and furious. But never had men considered themselves so intellectual and so completely in possession of the truth as these sufferers, never had they considered their decisions, their scientific conclusions, their moral convictions so infallible. Whole villages, whole towns and peoples went mad from the infection. All were excited and did not understand one another. Each thought that he alone had the truth and was wretched looking at the others, beat himself on the breast, wept, and wrung his hands. They did not know how to judge and could not agree what to consider evil and what good; they did not know whom to blame, whom to justify. Men killed each other in a sort of senseless spite. They gathered together in armies against one another, but even on the march the armies would begin attacking each other, the ranks would be broken and the soldiers would fall on each other, stabbing and cutting, biting and devouring each other. The alarm bell was ringing all day long in the towns; men rushed together, but why they were summoned and who was summoning them no one knew. The most ordinary trades were abandoned, because everyone proposed his own ideas, his own improvements, and they could not agree. The land too was abandoned. Men met in groups, agreed on something, swore to keep together, but at once began on something quite different from what they had proposed. They accused one another, fought and killed each other. There were conflagrations and famine. All men and all things were involved in destruction. The plague spread and moved further and further. Only a few men could be saved in the whole world. They were a pure chosen people, destined to found a new race and a new life, to renew and purify the earth, but no one had seen these men, no one had heard their words and their voices.

Raskolnikov was worried that this senseless dream haunted his memory so miserably, the impression of this feverish delirium persisted so long. The second week after Easter had come. There were warm bright spring days; in the prison ward the grating windows under which the sentinel paced were opened. Sonia had only been able to visit him twice during his illness; each time she had to obtain permission, and it was difficult. But she often used to come to the hospital yard, especially in the evening, sometimes only to stand a minute and look up at the windows of the ward.

One evening, when he was almost well again, Raskolnikov fell asleep. On waking up he chanced to go to the window, and at once saw Sonia in the distance at the hospital gate. She seemed to be waiting for someone. Something stabbed him to the heart at that minute. He shuddered and moved away from the window. Next day Sonia did not come, nor the day after; he noticed that he was expecting her uneasily. At last he was discharged. On reaching the prison he learnt from the convicts that Sofya Semyonovna was lying ill at home and was unable to go out.

He was very uneasy and sent to inquire after her; he soon learnt that her illness was not dangerous. Hearing that he was anxious about her, Sonia sent him a pencilled note, telling him that she was much better, that she had a slight cold and that she would soon, very soon come and see him at his work. His heart throbbed painfully as he read it.

Again it was a warm bright day. Early in the morning, at six o'clock he went off to work on the river bank, where they used to pound alabaster and where there was a kiln for baking it in a shed. There were only three of them sent. One of the convicts went with the guard to the fortress to fetch a tool; the other began getting the wood ready and laying it in the kiln. Raskolnikov came out of the shed on to the river bank, sat down on a heap of logs by the shed and began gazing at the wide deserted river. From the high bank a broad landscape opened before him, the sound of singing floated faintly audible from the other bank. In the vast steppe, bathed in sunshine, he could just see, like black specks, the nomads' tent. There there was freedom, there other men were living, utterly unlike those here; there time itself seemed to stand still, as though the age of Abraham and his flocks had not passed. Raskolnikov sat gazing, his thoughts passed into day-dreams, into contemplation; he thought of nothing, but a vague restlessness excited and troubled him. Suddenly he found Sonia beside him; she had come up noiselessly and sat down at his side. It was still quite early; the morning chill was still keen. She wore her poor old burnous and the green shawl; her face still showed signs of illness, it was thinner and paler. She gave him a joyful smile of welcome, but held out her hand with her usual timidity. She was always timid of holding out her hand to him and sometimes did not offer it at all, as though afraid he would repel it. He always took her hand as though with repugnance, always seemed vexed to meet her and was sometimes obstinately silent throughout her visit. Sometimes she trembled before him and went away deeply grieved. But now their hands did not part. He stole a rapid glance at her and dropped his eyes on the ground without speaking. They were alone, no one had seen them. The guard had turned away for the time.

How it happened he did not know. But all at once something seemed to seize him and fling him at her feet. He wept and threw his arms round her knees. For the first instant she was terribly frightened and she turned pale. She jumped up and looked at him trembling. But at the same moment she understood, and a light of infinite happiness came into her eyes. She knew and had no doubt that he loved her beyond everything and that at last the moment had come. . . .

They wanted to speak, but could not; tears stood in their eyes. They were both pale and thin; but those sick pale faces were bright with the dawn of a new future, of a full resurrection into a new life. They were renewed by love; the heart of each held infinite sources of life for the heart of the other.

They resolved to wait and be patient. They had another seven years to wait, and what terrible suffering and what infinite happiness before then! But he had risen again and he knew it and felt in it all his being, while she – she only lived in his life.

On the evening of the same day, when the barracks were locked, Raskolnikov lay on his plank bed and thought of her. He had even fancied that day that all the convicts who had been his enemies looked at him differently; he had even entered into talk with them and they answered him in a friendly way. He remembered that now, and thought it was bound to be so. Wasn't everything now bound to be changed?

He thought of her. He remembered how continually he had tormented her and wounded her heart. He remembered her pale and thin little face. But these recollections scarcely troubled him now; he knew with what infinite love he would now repay all her sufferings. And what were all, *all* the agonies of the past! Everything, even his crime, his sentence and imprisonment, seemed to him now in the first rush of feeling an external, strange fact with which he had no concern. But he could not think for long together of anything that evening, and he could not have analyzed anything consciously; he was simply feeling. Life had stepped into the place of theory and something quite different would work itself out in his mind.

Under his pillow lay the New Testament. He took it up mechanically. The book belonged to Sonia; it was the one from which she had read the raising of Lazarus to him. At first he was afraid that she would worry him about religion, would talk about the gospel and pester him with books. But to his great surprise she had not once approached the subject and had not even offered him the Testament. He had asked her for it himself not long before his illness and she brought him the book without a word. Till now he had not opened it.

He did not open it now, but one thought passed through his mind: 'Can her convictions not be mine now? Her feelings, her aspirations at least. . . .'

She too had been greatly agitated that day, and at night she was taken ill again. But she was so happy – and so unexpectedly happy – that she was almost frightened of her happiness. Seven years, *only* seven years! At the beginning of their happiness at some moments they were both ready to look on those seven years as though they were seven days. He did not know that the new life would not be given him for nothing, that he would have to pay dearly for it, that it would cost him great striving, great suffering.

But that is the beginning of a new story – the story of the gradual renewal of a man, the story of his gradual regeneration, of his passing from one world into another, of his initiation into a new unknown life. That might be the subject of a new story, but our present story is ended.

THE GAMBLER

✦ ONE ✦

AT LENGTH I RETURNED FROM TWO weeks' leave of absence to find that my patrons had arrived three days ago in Roulettenberg. I received from them a welcome quite different to that which I had expected. The General eyed me coldly, greeted me in rather haughty fashion, and dismissed me to pay my respects to his sister. It was clear that from *somewhere* money had been acquired. I thought I could even detect a certain shamefacedness in the General's glance. Maria Philipovna, too, seemed distraught, and conversed with me with an air of detachment. Nevertheless, she took the money which I handed to her, counted it, and listened to what I had to tell. To luncheon there were expected that day a Monsieur Mezentsov, a French lady, and an Englishman; for, whenever money was in hand, a banquet in Muscovite style was always given. Polina Alexandrovna, on seeing me, inquired why I had been so long away. Then, without waiting for an answer, she departed. Evidently this was not mere accident, and I felt that I must throw some light upon matters. It was high time that I did so.

I was assigned a small room on the fourth floor of the hotel (for you must know that I belonged to the General's suite). So far as I could see, the party had already gained some notoriety in the place, which had come to look upon the General as a Russian nobleman of great wealth. Indeed, even before luncheon he charged me, among other things, to get two thousand-franc notes changed for him at the hotel counter, which put us in a position to be thought millionaires – at all events for a week! Later I was about to take Mischa and Nadia for a walk when a summons reached me from the staircase that I must attend the General. He began by deigning to inquire of me where I was going to take the children; and as he did so I could see that he failed to look me in the eyes. He *wanted* to do so, but each time was met by me with such a fixed, disrespectful stare that he desisted in confusion. In pompous language, however, which jumbled one sentence into another, and at length grew disconnected, he gave me to understand that I was to lead the children altogether away from the Casino, and out into the park. Finally his anger exploded, and he added sharply:

459

'I suppose you would like to take them to the Casino to play roulette? Well, excuse my speaking so plainly, but I know how addicted you are to gambling. Though I am not your mentor, nor wish to be, at least I have a right to require that you shall not actually *compromise* me.'

'I have no money for gambling,' I quietly replied.

'But you will soon be in receipt of some,' retorted the General, reddening a little as he dived into his writing desk and applied himself to a memorandum book. From it he saw that he had 120 roubles of mine in his keeping.

'Let us calculate,' he went on. 'We must translate these roubles into thalers. Here – take 100 thalers, as a round sum. The rest will be safe in my hands.'

In silence I took the money.

'You must not be offended at what I say,' he continued. 'You are too touchy about these things. What I have said I have said merely as a warning. To do so is no more than my right.'

When returning home with the children before luncheon, I met a cavalcade of our party riding to view some ruins. Two splendid carriages, magnificently horsed, with Mlle Blanche, Maria Philipovna, and Polina Alexandrovna in one of them, and the Frenchman, the Englishman, and the General in attendance on horseback! The passers-by stopped to stare at them, for the effect was splendid – the General could not have improved upon it. I calculated that, with the 4000 francs which I had brought with me, added to what my patrons seemed already to have acquired, the party must be in possession of at least 7000 or 8000 francs – though that would be none too much for Mlle Blanche, who, with her mother and the Frenchman, was also lodging in our hotel. The latter gentleman was called by the lacqueys 'Monsieur le Comte,' and Mlle Blanche's mother was dubbed 'Madame la Comtesse.' Perhaps in very truth they *were* 'Comte et Comtesse.'

I knew that 'Monsieur le Comte' would take no notice of me when we met at dinner, as also that the General would not dream of introducing us, nor of recommending me to the 'Comte.' However, the latter had lived awhile in Russia, and knew that the person referred to as 'uchitel' is never looked upon as a bird of fine feather. Of course, strictly speaking, he *knew* me; but I was an uninvited guest at the luncheon – the General had forgotten to arrange otherwise, or I should have been dispatched to dine at the table d'hôte. Nevertheless I presented myself in such guise that the General looked at me with a touch of approval; and though the good Maria Philipovna was for showing me my place, the fact of my having previously met the Englishman, Mr Astley, saved me, and thenceforward I figured as one of the company.

This strange Englishman I had met first in Prussia, where we had happened to sit *vis-à-vis* in a railway train in which I was travelling to overtake our party; while, later, I had run across him in France, and again in Switzerland – twice within the space of two weeks! To think, therefore, that I should suddenly encounter him again here, in Roulettenberg! Never in my life had I known a more retiring man, for he was shy to the pitch of imbecility, yet well aware of the fact (for he was no fool). At the same time, he was a gentle, amiable sort of an individual, and, even on our first encounter in Prussia I had contrived to draw him out, and he had told me that he had just been to the North Cape, and was now anxious to visit the fair at Nizhni Novgorod. How he had come to make the General's acquaintance I do not know, but, apparently, he was much struck with Polina. Also, he was delighted that I should sit next to him at table, for he appeared to look upon me as his bosom friend.

During the meal the Frenchman was in great feather: he was discursive and pompous to every one. In Moscow too, I remembered, he had blown a great many bubbles. Interminably he discoursed on finance and Russian politics, and though, at times, the General made feints to contradict him, he did so humbly, and as though wishing not wholly to lose sight of his own dignity.

For myself, I was in a curious frame of mind. Even before luncheon was half finished I had asked myself the old, eternal question: '*Why* do I continue to dance attendance upon the General, instead of having left him and his family long ago?' Every now and then I would glance at Polina Alexandrovna, but she paid me no attention; until eventually I became so irritated that I decided to play the boor.

First of all I suddenly, and for no reason whatever, plunged loudly and gratuitously into the general conversation. Above everything I wanted to pick a quarrel with the Frenchman; and with that end in view I turned to the General, and exclaimed in an overbearing sort of way – indeed, I think that I actually interrupted him – that that summer it had been almost impossible for a Russian to dine anywhere at tables d'hôte. The General bent upon me a glance of astonishment.

'If one is a man of self-respect,' I went on, 'one risks abuse by so doing, and is forced to put up with insults of every kind. Both at Paris and on the Rhine – yes, and even in Switzerland – there are so many Poles, with their sympathizers, the French, at these tables d'hôte that one cannot get a word in edgeways if one happens only to be a Russian.'

This I said in French. The General eyed me doubtfully, for he did not know whether to be angry or merely to feel surprised that I should so far forget myself.

'Of course, one always learns *something everywhere*,' said the Frenchman in a careless, contemptuous sort of tone.

'In Paris, too, I had a dispute with a Pole,' I continued, 'and then with a French officer who supported him. After that a section of the Frenchmen present took my part. They did so as soon as I told them the story of how once I threatened to spit into Monsignor's coffee.'

'To spit into it?' the General inquired with grave disapproval in his tone, and a stare of astonishment, while the Frenchman looked at me unbelievingly.

'Just so,' I replied. 'You must know that, on one occasion, when, for two days, I had felt certain that at any moment I might have to depart for Rome on business, I repaired to the Embassy of the Holy See in Paris, to have my passport visaed. There I encountered a sacristan of about fifty, and a man dry and cold of mien. After listening politely, but with great reserve, to my account of myself, this sacristan asked me to wait a little. I was in a great hurry to depart, but of course I sat down, pulled out a copy of *L'Opinion Nationale*, and fell to reading an extraordinary piece of invective against Russia which it happened to contain. As I was thus engaged I heard some one enter an adjoining room and ask for Monsignor; after which I saw the sacristan make a low bow to the visitor, and then another bow as the visitor took his leave. I ventured to remind the good man of my own business also; whereupon, with an expression of, if anything, increased dryness, he again asked me to wait. Soon a third visitor arrived who, like myself, had come on business (he was an Austrian of some sort); and as soon as ever he had stated his errand he was conducted upstairs! This made me very angry. I rose, approached the sacristan, and told him that, since Monsignor was receiving callers, his lordship might just as well finish off *my* affair as well. Upon this the sacristan shrunk back in astonishment. It simply passed his understanding that any insignificant Russian should dare to compare himself with other visitors of Monsignor's! In a tone of the utmost effrontery, as though he were delighted to have a chance of insulting me, he looked me up and down, and then said: 'Do you suppose that Monsignor is going to put aside his coffee for *you*?' But I only cried the louder: 'Let me tell you that I am going to *spit* into that coffee! Yes, and if you do not get me my passport visaed this very minute, I shall take it to Monsignor myself.'

'What? While he is engaged with a Cardinal?' screeched the sacristan, again shrinking back in horror. Then, rushing to the door, he spread out his arms as though he would rather die than let me enter.

Thereupon I declared that I was a heretic and a barbarian – 'Je suis hérétique et barbare,' I said – and that these archbishops and cardinals and monsignors, and the rest of them, meant nothing at all to me. In a word, I showed him that I was not going to give way. He looked at me with an air of infinite resentment. Then he snatched up my passport, and departed with it upstairs. A minute later the passport had been visaed! Here it is now, if you care to see it,' – and I pulled out the document, and exhibited the Roman visa.

'But — ' the General began.

'What really saved you was the fact that you proclaimed yourself a heretic and a barbarian,' remarked the Frenchman with a smile. 'Cela n'était pas si bête.'

'But is *that* how Russian subjects ought to be treated? Why, when they settle here they dare not utter even a word – they are ready even to deny the fact that they are Russians! At all events, at my hotel in Paris I received far more attention from the company after I had told them about the fracas with the sacristan. A fat Polish nobleman, who had been the most offensive of all who were present at the table d'hôte, at once went upstairs, while some of the Frenchmen were simply disgusted when I told them that two years ago I had encountered a man at whom, in 1812, a French 'hero' fired for the mere fun of discharging his musket. That man was then a boy of ten, and his family are still residing in Moscow.'

'Impossible!' the Frenchman spluttered. '*No* French soldier would fire at a child!'

'Nevertheless the incident was as I say,' I replied. 'A very respected ex-captain told me the story, and I myself could see the scar left on his cheek.'

'The Frenchman then began chattering volubly, and the General supported him; but I recommended the former to read, for example, extracts from the memoirs of General Perovski, who, in 1812, was a prisoner in the hands of the French. Finally Maria Philipovna said something to interrupt the conversation. The General was furious with me for having started the altercation with the Frenchman. On the other hand, Mr Astley seemed to take great pleasure in my brush with Monsieur, and, rising from the table, proposed that we should go and have a drink together. The same afternoon, at four o'clock, I went to have my customary talk with Polina Alexandrovna; and the talk soon extended to a stroll. We entered the Park, and approached the Casino, where Polina seated herself upon a bench near the fountain, and sent Nadia away to a little distance to play with some other children. Mischa also I dispatched to play by the fountain, and in this fashion we – that is to say, Polina and myself – contrived to find ourselves alone.

Of course, we began by talking on business matters. Polina seemed furious when I handed her only 700 gülden, for she had thought to receive from Paris, as the proceeds of the pledging of her diamonds, at least 2000 gülden, or even more.

'Come what may, I *must* have money,' she said. 'And get it somehow I will – otherwise I shall be ruined.'

I asked her what had happened during my absence.

'Nothing; except that two pieces of news have reached us from St Petersburg. In the first place, my grandmother is very ill, and unlikely to last another couple of days. We had this from Timothy Petrovitch himself, and he is a reliable person. Every moment we are expecting to receive news of the end.'

'All of you are on the tiptoe of expectation?' I queried.

'Of course – all of us, and every minute of the day. For a year-and-a-half now we have been looking for this.'

'Looking for it?'

'Yes, looking for it. I am not her blood relation, you know – I am merely the General's step-daughter. Yet I am certain that the old lady has remembered me in her will.'

'Yes, I believe that you *will* come in for a good deal,' I said with some assurance.

'Yes, for she is fond of me. But how come you to think so?'

I answered this question with another one. 'That Marquis of yours,' I said, ' – is *he* also familiar with your family secrets?'

'And why are you yourself so interested in them?' was her retort as she eyed me with dry grimness.

'Never mind. If I am not mistaken, the General has succeeded in borrowing money of the Marquis.'

'It may be so.'

'Is it likely that the Marquis would have lent the money if he had not known something or other about your grandmother? Did you notice, too, that three times during luncheon, when speaking of her, he called her "La Baboulenka"?* What loving, friendly behaviour, to be sure!'

'Yes, that is true. As soon as ever he learnt that I was likely to inherit something from her he began to pay me his addresses. I thought you ought to know that.'

'Then he has only just begun his courting? Why, I thought he had been doing so a long while!'

'You *know* he has not,' retorted Polina angrily. 'But where on earth did you pick up this Englishman?' She said this after a pause.

'I *knew* you would ask about him!' Whereupon I told her of my previous encounters with Astley while travelling.

---

*Dear little Grandmother.

'He is very shy,' I said, 'and susceptible. Also, he is in love with you.'

'Yes, he *is* in love with me,' she replied.

'And he is ten times richer than the Frenchman. In fact, what does the Frenchman possess? To me it seems at least doubtful that he possesses anything at all.'

'Oh, no, there is no doubt about it. He does possess some château or other. Last night the General told me that for certain. *Now* are you satisfied?'

'Nevertheless, in your place I should marry the Englishman.'

'And why?' asked Polina.

'Because, though the Frenchman is the handsomer of the two, he is also the baser; whereas the Englishman is not only a man of honour, but ten times the wealthier of the pair.'

'Yes? But then the Frenchman is a marquis, and the cleverer of the two,' remarked Polina imperturbably.

'Is that so?' I repeated.

'Yes; absolutely.'

Polina was not at all pleased at my questions; I could see that she was doing her best to irritate me with the brusquerie of her answers. But I took no notice of this.

'It amuses me to see you grow angry,' she continued. 'However, inasmuch as I allow you to indulge in these questions and conjectures, you ought to pay me something for the privilege.'

'I consider that I have a perfect right to put these questions to you,' was my calm retort; 'for the reason that I am ready to pay for them, and also care little what becomes of me.'

Polina giggled.

'Last time you told me – when on the Schlangenberg – that at a word from me you would be ready to jump down a thousand feet into the abyss. Some day I may remind you of that saying, in order to see if you will be as good as your word. Yes, you may depend upon it that I shall do so. I hate you because I have allowed you to go to such lengths, and I also hate you – and still more – because you are so necessary to me. For the time being I want you, so I must keep you.'

Then she made a movement to rise. Her tone had sounded very angry. Indeed, of late her talks with me had invariably ended on a note of temper and irritation – yes, of real temper.

'May I ask you who is this Mlle Blanche?' I inquired (since I did not wish Polina to depart without an explanation).

'You *know* who she is – just Mlle Blanche. Nothing further has transpired. Probably she will soon be Madame General – that is to say, if the rumours that Grandmamma is nearing her end should prove true. Mlle

Blanche, with her mother and her cousin, the Marquis, know very well that, as things now stand, we are ruined.'

'And is the General at last in love?'

'That has nothing to do with it. Listen to me. Take these 700 florins, and go and play roulette with them. Win as much for me as you can, for I am badly in need of money.'

So saying, she called Nadia back to her side, and entered the Casino, where she joined the rest of our party. For myself, I took, in musing astonishment, the first path to the left. Something had seemed to strike my brain when she told me to go and play roulette. Strangely enough, that something had also seemed to make me hesitate, and to set me analysing my feelings with regard to her. In fact, during the two weeks of my absence I had felt far more at my ease than I did now, on the day of my return; although, while travelling, I had moped like an imbecile, rushed about like a man in a fever, and actually beheld her in my dreams. Indeed, on one occasion (this happened in Switzerland, when I was asleep in the train) I had spoken aloud to her, and set all my fellow-travellers laughing. Again, therefore, I put to myself the question: 'Do I, or do I not, love her?' and again I could return myself no answer – or, rather, for the hundredth time I told myself that I detested her. Yes, I detested her; there were moments (more especially at the close of our talks together) when I would gladly have given half my life to have strangled her! I swear that, had there, at such moments, been a sharp knife ready to my hand, I would have seized that knife with pleasure, and plunged it into her breast. Yet I also swear that if, on the Schlangen-berg, she had *really* said to me, 'Leap into that abyss,' I should have leapt into it, and with equal pleasure. Yes, this I knew well. One way or the other, the thing must soon be ended. She, too, knew it in some curious way; the thought that I was fully conscious of her inaccessibility, and of the impossibility of my ever realizing my dreams, afforded her, I am certain, the keenest possible pleasure. Otherwise, is it likely that she, the cautious and clever woman that she was, would have indulged in this familiarity and openness with me? Hitherto (I concluded) she had looked upon me in the same light that the old Empress did upon her servant – the Empress who hesitated not to unrobe herself before her slave, since she did not account a slave a man. Yes, often Polina must have taken me for something less than a man!'

Still, she had charged me with a commission – to win what I could at roulette. Yet all the time I could not help wondering *why* it was so necessary for her to win something, and what new schemes could have sprung to birth in her ever-fertile brain. A host of new and unknown factors seemed to have arisen during the last two weeks. Well, it behoved me to divine them, and to probe them, and that as soon as possible. Yet not now: at the present moment I must repair to the roulette-table.

⋙ TWO ⋘

I CONFESS I DID NOT LIKE IT. ALTHOUGH I had made up my mind to play, I felt averse to doing so on behalf of some one else. In fact, it almost upset my balance, and I entered the gaming-rooms with an angry feeling at my heart. At first glance the scene irritated me. Never at any time have I been able to bear the flunkeyishness which one meets in the Press of the world at large, but more especially in that of Russia, where, almost every evening, journalists write on two subjects in particular – namely, on the splendour and luxury of the casinos to be found in the Rhenish towns, and on the heaps of gold which are daily to be seen lying on their tables. Those journalists are not paid for doing so: they write thus merely out of a spirit of disinterested complaisance. For there is nothing splendid about the establishments in question; and not only are there no heaps of gold to be seen lying on their tables, but also there is very little money to be seen at all. Of course, during the season, *some* madman or another may make his appearance – generally an Englishman, or an Asiatic, or a Turk – and (as had happened during the summer of which I write) win or lose a great deal; but, as regards the rest of the crowd, it plays only for petty gülden, and seldom does much wealth figure on the board. When, on the present occasion, I entered the gaming-rooms (for the first time in my life), it was several moments before I could even make up my mind to play. For one thing, the crowd oppressed me. Had I been playing for myself, I think I should have left at once, and never have embarked upon gambling at all, for I could feel my heart beginning to beat, and my heart was anything but cold-blooded. Also, I knew, I had long ago made up my mind, that never should I depart from Roulettenberg until some radical, some final, change had taken place in my fortunes. Thus it must and would be. However ridiculous it may seem to you that I was expecting to win at roulette, I look upon the generally accepted opinion concerning the folly and the grossness of hoping to win at gambling as a thing even *more* absurd. For why is gambling a whit worse than any other method of acquiring money? How, for instance, is it worse than trade? True, out of a hundred persons, only one can win; yet what business is that of yours or of mine?

At all events, I confined myself at first simply to looking on, and decided to attempt nothing serious. Indeed, I felt that, if I began to do anything at all, I should do it in an absent-minded, haphazard sort of way – of that I felt certain. Also, it behoved me to learn the game itself; since, despite a thousand descriptions of roulette which I had read with ceaseless avidity, I knew nothing of its rules, and had never even seen it played.

In the first place, everything about it seemed to me so foul – so morally mean and foul. Yet I am not speaking of the hungry, restless folk who, by scores – nay, even by hundreds – could be seen crowded around the gaming-tables. For in a desire to win quickly and to win much I can see nothing sordid; I have always applauded the opinion of a certain dead and gone, but cocksure, moralist who replied to the excuse that 'one may always gamble moderately' by saying that to do so makes things worse, since, in that case, the profits too will always be moderate. Insignificant profits and sumptuous profits do not stand on the same footing. No, it is all a matter of proportion. What may seem a small sum to a Rothschild may seem a large sum to me, and it is not the fault of stakes or of winnings that everywhere men can be found winning, can be found depriving their fellows of something, just as they do at roulette. As to the question whether stakes and winnings are, in themselves, immoral is another question altogether, and I wish to express no opinion upon it. Yet the very fact that I was full of a strong desire to win caused this gambling for gain, in spite of its attendant squalor, to contain, if you will, something intimate, something sympathetic, to my eyes: for it is always pleasant to see men dispensing with ceremony, and acting naturally, and in an unbuttoned mood. . . . Yet why should I so deceive myself? I could see that the whole thing was a vain and unreasoning pursuit; and what, at the first glance, seemed to me the ugliest feature in this mob of roulette players was their respect for their occupation – the seriousness, and even the humility with which they stood around the gaming-tables.

Moreover, I had always drawn sharp distinctions between a game which is *de mauvais genre* and a game which is permissible to a decent man. In fact, there are two sorts of gaming – namely, the game of the gentleman and the game of the plebs – the game for gain, and the game of the herd. Herein, as said, I draw sharp distinctions. Yet how essentially base are the distinctions! For instance, a gentleman may stake, say, five or ten louis d'or – seldom more, unless he is a very rich man, when he may stake, say, a thousand francs; but he must do this simply for the love of the game itself – simply for sport, simply in order to observe the process of winning or of losing, and, above all things, as a man who remains quite uninterested in the possibility of his issuing a winner. If he wins, he will be at liberty, perhaps, to give vent to a laugh, or to pass a remark on the circumstance to a bystander, or to stake again, or to double his stake; but even this he must do solely out of curiosity, and for the pleasure of watching the play of chances and of calculations, and not because of any vulgar desire to win. In a word, he must look upon the gaming-table, upon roulette, and upon trente et quarante, as mere relaxations which have been arranged solely for his amusement. Of the existence of the lures and gains upon which the bank is founded and maintained he must profess to have not an inkling. Best of all, he ought to imagine his fellow-gamblers and the rest of the mob which stands trembling over a coin to be equally rich and gentlemanly with himself, and playing solely for recreation and pleasure. This complete ignorance of the realities, this innocent view of mankind, is what, in my opinion, constitutes the truly aristocratic.

For instance, I have seen even fond mothers so far indulge their guile-less, elegant daughters – misses of fifteen or sixteen – as to give them a few gold coins and teach them how to play; and though the young ladies may have won or have lost, they have invariably laughed, and departed as though they were well pleased. In the same way, I saw our General once approach the table in a stolid, important manner. A lacquey darted to offer him a chair, but the General did not even notice him. Slowly he took out his money bags, and slowly extracted 300 francs in gold, which he staked on the black, and won. Yet he did not take up his winnings – he left them there on the table. Again the black turned up, and again he did not gather in what he had won; and when, in the third round, the *red* turned up he lost, at a stroke, 1200 francs. Yet even then he rose with a smile, and thus preserved his reputation; yet I knew that his money bags must be chafing his heart, as well as that, had the stake been twice or thrice as much again, he would still have restrained himself from venting his disappointment. On the other hand, I saw a Frenchman first win, and then lose, 30,000 francs – cheerfully, and without a murmur. Yes; even if a gentleman should lose his whole substance, he must never give way to annoyance. Money must be so subservient to gentility as never to be worth a thought. Of course, the *supremely* aristocratic thing is to be entirely oblivious of the mire of rabble, with its setting; but sometimes a reverse course may be aristocratic – to remark, to scan, and even to gape at, the mob (for preference, through a lorgnette), even as though one were taking the crowd and its squalor for a sort of rare show which had been organized specially for a gentleman's diversion. Though one may be squeezed by the crowd, one must look as though one were fully assured of being the observer – of having neither part nor lot with the observed. At the same time, to stare fixedly about one is unbecoming; for that, again, is ungentlemanly, seeing that no spectacle is worth an open stare – there are no spectacles in the world which merit from a gentleman too pronounced an inspection. However, to me personally the scene *did* seem to be worth undisguised contemplation – more especially in view of the fact that I had come there not only to look at, but also to number myself sincerely and wholeheartedly with, the mob. As for my secret moral views, I had no room for them amongst my actual, practical opinions. Let that stand as written: I am writing only to relieve my conscience. Yet let me say also this: that from the first I have been consistent in having an intense aversion to any trial of my acts and thoughts by a moral standard. Another standard altogether has directed my life. . . .

As a matter of fact, the mob was playing in exceedingly foul fashion. Indeed, I have an idea that sheer robbery was going on around that gaming-table. The croupiers who sat at the two ends of it had not only to watch the stakes, but also to calculate the game – an immense amount of work for two men! As for the crowd itself – well, it consisted mostly of Frenchmen. Yet I was not then taking notes merely in order to be able to give you a description of roulette, but in order to get my bearings as to my behaviour when I myself should begin to play. For example, I noticed that nothing was more common than for another's hand to stretch out and grab one's winnings whenever one had won. Then there would arise a dispute, and frequently an uproar; and it would be a case of 'I beg of you to prove, and to produce witnesses to the fact, that the stake is yours.'

At first the proceedings were pure Greek to me. I could only divine and distinguish that stakes were hazarded on numbers, on 'odd' or 'even,' and on colours. Polina's money I decided to risk, that evening, only to the amount of 100 gülden. The thought that I was not going to play for myself quite unnerved me. It was an unpleasant sensation, and I tried hard to banish it. I had a feeling that, once I had begun to play for Polina, I should wreck my own fortunes. Also, I wonder if any one has *ever* approached a gaming-table without falling an immediate prey to superstition? I began by pulling out fifty gülden, and staking them on 'even.' The wheel spun and stopped at 13. I had lost! With a feeling like a sick qualm, as though I would like to make my way out of the crowd and go home, I staked another fifty gülden – this time on the red. The red turned up. Next time I staked the 100 gülden just where they lay – and again the red turned up. Again I staked the whole sum, and again the red turned up. Clutching my 400 gülden, I placed 200 of them on twelve figures, to see what would come of it. The result was that the croupier paid me out three times my total stake! Thus from 100 gülden my store had grown to 800! Upon that such a curious, such an inexplicable, unwonted feeling overcame me that I decided to depart. Always the thought kept recurring to me that if I had been playing for myself alone I should never have had such luck. Once more I staked the whole 800 gülden on the 'even.' The wheel stopped at 4. I was paid out another 800 gülden, and, snatching up my pile of 1600, departed in search of Polina Alexandrovna.

I found the whole party walking in the park, and was able to get an interview with her only after supper. This time the Frenchman was absent from the meal, and the General seemed to be in a more expansive vein. Among other things he thought it necessary to remind me that he would be sorry to see me playing at the gaming-tables. In his opinion, such conduct would greatly compromise him – especially if I were to lose much. 'And even if you were to *win* much I should be compromised,' he added in a meaning sort of way. 'Of course I have no *right* to order your actions, but you yourself will agree that — ' As usual, he did not finish his sentence. I answered drily that I had very little money in my possession, and that, consequently, I was hardly in a position to indulge in any conspicuous play, even if I did gamble. At last, when ascending to my own room, I succeeded in handing Polina her winnings, and told her that, next time, I should not play for her.

'Why not?' she asked excitedly.

'Because I wish to play *for myself*,' I replied with a feigned glance of astonishment. 'That is my sole reason.'

'Then are you so certain that your roulette-playing will get us out of our difficulties?' she inquired with a quizzical smile.

I said very seriously, 'Yes;' and then added: 'Possibly my certainty about winning may seem to you ridiculous; yet pray leave me in peace.'

None the less she insisted that I ought to go halves with her in the day's winnings, and offered me 800 gülden on condition that henceforth I gambled only on those terms; but I refused to do so, once and for all – stating, as my reason, that I found myself unable to play on behalf of any one else, 'I am not unwilling so to do,' I added, 'but in all probability I should lose.'

'Well, absurd though it be, I place great hopes on your playing of roulette,' she remarked musingly: 'Wherefore you ought to play as my partner and on equal shares; wherefore, of course, you will do as I wish.'

Then she left me without listening to any further protests on my part.

✴ THREE ✴

ON THE MORROW SHE SAID not a word to me about gambling. In fact, she purposely avoided me, although her old manner to me had not changed: the same serene coolness was hers on meeting me – a coolness that was mingled even with a spice of contempt and dislike. In short, she was at no pains to conceal her aversion to me. That I could see plainly. Also, she did not trouble to conceal from me the fact that I was necessary to her, and that she was keeping me for some end which she had in view. Consequently there became established between us relations which, to a large extent, were incomprehensible to me, considering her general pride and aloofness. For example, although she knew that I was madly in love with her, she allowed me to speak to her of my passion (though she could not well have showed her contempt for me more than by permitting me, unhindered and unrebuked, to mention to her my love).

'You see,' her attitude expressed, 'how little I regard your feelings, as well as how little I care for what you say to me, or for what you feel for me.' Likewise, though she spoke as before concerning her affairs, it was never with complete frankness. In her contempt for me there were refinements. Although she knew well that I was aware of a certain circumstance in her life – of something which might one day cause her trouble, she would speak to me about her affairs (whenever she had need of me for a given end) as though I were a slave or a passing acquaintance – yet tell them me only in so far as one would need to know them if one were going to be made temporary use of. Had I not known the whole chain of events, or had she not seen how much I was pained and disturbed by her teasing insistency, she would never have thought it worth while to soothe me with this frankness – even though, since she not infrequently used me to execute commissions that were not only troublesome, but risky, she ought, in my opinion, to have been frank in *any* case. But, forsooth, it was not worth her while to trouble about *my* feelings – about the fact that *I* was uneasy, and, perhaps, thrice as put about by her cares and misfortunes as she was herself!

For three weeks I had known of her intention to take to roulette. She had even warned me that she would like me to play on her behalf, since it was unbecoming for her to play in person; and from the tone of her words I had gathered that there was something on her mind besides a mere desire to win money. As if money could matter to *her!* No, she had some end in view, and there were circumstances at which I could guess, but which I did not know for certain. True, the slavery and abasement in which she held me might have given me (such things often do so) the power to question her with abrupt directness (seeing that, inasmuch as I figured in her eyes as a mere slave and nonentity, she could not very well have taken offence at any rude curiosity); but the fact was that, though she let me question her, she never returned me a single answer, and at times did not so much as notice me. That is how matters stood.

Next day there was a good deal of talk about a telegram which, four days ago, had been sent to St. Petersburg, but to which there had come no answer. The General was visibly disturbed and moody, for the matter concerned his mother. The Frenchman, too, was excited, and after dinner the whole party talked long and seriously together – the Frenchman's tone being extraordinarily presumptuous and off-hand to everybody. It almost reminded one of the proverb, 'Invite a man to your table, and soon he will place his feet upon it.' Even to Polina he was brusque almost to the point of rudeness. Yet still he seemed glad to join us in our walks in the Casino, or in our rides and drives about the town. I had long been aware of certain circumstances which bound the General to him; I had long been aware that in Russia they had hatched some scheme together – although I did not know whether the plot had come to anything, or whether it was still only in the stage of being talked of. Likewise I was aware, in part, of a family secret – namely, that, last year, the Frenchman had bailed the General out of debt, and given him 30,000 roubles wherewith to pay his Treasury dues on retiring from the service. And now, of course, the General was in a vice – although the chief part in the affair was being played by Mlle. Blanche. Yes, of this last I had no doubt.

But *who* was this Mlle. Blanche? It was said of her that she was a Frenchwoman of good birth who, living with her mother, possessed a colossal fortune. It was also said that she was some relation to the Marquis, but only a distant one – a cousin, or cousin-german, or something of the sort. Likewise I knew that, up to the time of my journey to Paris, she and the Frenchman had been more ceremonious towards our party – they had stood on a much more precise and delicate footing with them; but that now their acquaintanceship – their friendship, their intimacy – had taken on a much more off-hand and rough-and-ready air. Perhaps they thought that our means were too modest for them, and therefore unworthy of politeness or reticence. Also, for the last three days I had noticed certain looks which Astley had kept throwing at Mlle. Blanche and her mother; and it had occurred to me that he must have had some previous acquaintance with the pair. I had even surmised that the Frenchman too must have met Mr. Astley before. Astley was a man so shy, reserved, and taciturn in his manner that one might have looked for anything from him. At all events the Frenchman accorded him only the slightest of greetings, and scarcely even looked at him. Certainly he did not seem to be afraid of him; which was intelligible enough. But why did Mlle. Blanche also never look at the Englishman? – particularly since, *á propos* of something or another, the Marquis had declared the Englishman to be immensely and indubitably rich? Was not that a sufficient reason to make Mlle. Blanche look at the Englishman? Anyway the General seemed extremely uneasy; and one could well understand what a telegram to announce the death of his mother would mean for him!

Although I thought it probable that Polina was avoiding me for a definite reason, I adopted a cold and indifferent air; for I felt pretty certain that it would not be long before she of herself approached me. For two days, therefore, I devoted my attention to Mlle. Blanche. The poor General was in despair! To fall in love at fifty-five, and with such vehemence, is indeed a misfortune! And add to that his widowerhood, his children, his ruined property, his debts, and the woman with whom he had fallen in love! Though Mlle. Blanche was extremely good-looking, I may or may not be understood when I say that she had one of those faces which one is afraid of. At all events, I myself have always feared such women. Apparently about twenty-five years of age, she was tall and broad-shouldered, with shoulders that sloped; yet though her neck and bosom were ample in their proportions, her skin was dull yellow in colour, while her hair (which was extremely abundant – sufficient to make two coiffures) was as black as Indian ink. Add to that a pair of black eyes with yellowish whites, a proud glance, gleaming teeth, and lips which were perennially pomaded and redolent of musk. As for her dress, it was invariably rich, effective, and chic, yet in good taste. Lastly, her feet and hands were astonishing, and her voice a deep contralto. Sometimes, when she laughed, she displayed her teeth, but at ordinary times her air was taciturn and haughty – especially in the presence of Polina and Maria Philipovna. Yet she seemed to me almost destitute of education, and even of wits, though cunning and suspicious. This, apparently, was not because her life had been lacking in incident. Perhaps, if all were known, the Marquis was not her kinsman at all, nor her mother her mother; but there was evidence that in Berlin, where we had first come across the pair, they had possessed acquaintances of good standing. As for the Marquis himself, I doubt to this day if he *was* a marquis – although about the fact that he had formerly belonged to high society (for instance, in Moscow and Germany) there could be no doubt whatever. What he had formerly been in France I had not a notion. All I knew was that he was said to possess a château. During the last two weeks I had looked for much to transpire, but am still ignorant whether at that time anything decisive ever passed between Mademoiselle and the General. Everything seemed to depend upon our means – upon whether the General would be able to flourish sufficient money in her face. If ever the news should arrive that the grandmother was not dead, Mlle. Blanche, I felt sure, would disappear in a twinkling. Indeed, it surprised and amused me to observe what a passion for intrigue I was developing. But how I loathed it all! With what pleasure would I have given everybody and everything the go-by! Only – I could not leave Polina. How, then, could I show contempt for those who surrounded her? Espionage is a base thing, but – what have I to do with that?

Mr. Astley, too, I found a curious person. I was only sure that he had fallen in love with Polina. A remarkable and diverting circumstance is the amount which may lie in the mien of a shy and painfully modest man who has been touched with the divine passion – especially when he would rather sink into the earth than betray himself by a single word or look. Though Mr. Astley frequently met us when we were out walking, he would merely take off his hat and pass us by, though I knew he was dying to join us. Even when invited to do so, he would refuse. Again, in places of amusement – in the Casino, at concerts, or near the fountain – he was never far from the spot where we were sitting. In fact, *wherever* we were – in the Park, in the forest, or on the Schlangenberg – one needed but to raise one's eyes and glance around to catch sight of at least a *portion* of Mr. Astley's frame sticking out – whether on an adjacent path or behind a bush. Yet never did he lose any chance of speaking to myself; and one morning when we had met, and exchanged a couple of words, he burst out in his usual abrupt way, without saying 'Good-morning.'

'That Mlle. Blanche,' he said. 'Well, I have seen a good many women like her.'

After that he was silent as he looked me meaningly in the face. What he meant I did not know, but to my glance of inquiry he returned only a dry nod, and a reiterated 'It is so.' Presently, however, he resumed:

'Does Mlle. Polina like flowers?'

'I really cannot say,' was my reply.

'What? You cannot say?' he cried in great astonishment.

'No; I have never noticed whether she does so or not,' I repeated with a smile.

'Hm! Then I have an idea in my mind,' he concluded. Lastly, with a nod, he walked away with a pleased expression on his face. The conversation had been carried on in execrable French.

✦ FOUR ✦

To-DAY HAS BEEN A DAY OF folly, stupidity, and ineptness. The time is now eleven o'clock in the evening, and I am sitting in my room and thinking. It all began, this morning, with my being forced to go and play roulette for Polina Alexandrovna. When she handed me over her store of six hundred gülden I exacted two conditions – namely, that I should *not* go halves with her in her winnings, if any (that is to say, I should not take anything for myself), and that she should explain to me, that same evening, why it was so necessary for her to win, and how much was the sum which she needed. For I could not suppose that she was doing all this merely for the sake of money. Yet clearly she *did* need some money, and that as soon as possible, and for a special purpose. Well, she promised to explain matters, and I departed. There was a tremendous crowd in the gaming-rooms. What an arrogant, greedy crowd it was! I pressed forward towards the middle of the room until I had secured a seat at a croupier's elbow. Then I began to play in timid fashion; venturing only twenty or thirty gülden at a time. Meanwhile I observed and took notes. It seemed to me that calculation was superfluous, and by no means possessed of the importance which certain other players attached to it, even though they sat with ruled papers in their hands, whereon they set down the coups, calculated the chances, reckoned, staked, and – lost exactly as we more simple mortals did who played without any reckoning at all. However, I deduced from the scene one conclusion which seemed to me reliable – namely, that in the flow of fortuitous chances there is, if not a system, at all events a sort of order. This, of course, is a very strange thing. For instance, after a dozen middle figures there would always occur a dozen or so outer ones. Suppose the ball stopped twice at a dozen outer figures; it would then pass to a dozen of the first ones, and then, again, to a dozen of the middle ciphers, and fall upon them three or four times, and then revert to a dozen outers; whence, after another couple of rounds, the ball would again pass to the first figures, strike upon them once, and then return thrice to the middle series – continuing thus for an hour and a half, or two hours. One, three, two: one, three, two. It was all very curious. Again, for the whole of a day or a morning the red would alternate with the black, but almost without any order, and from moment

476

to moment, so that scarcely two consecutive rounds would end upon either the one or the other. Yet, next day, or, perhaps, the next evening, the red alone would turn up, and attain a run of over two score, and continue so for quite a length of time – say, for a whole day. Of these circumstances the majority were pointed out to me by Mr. Astley, who stood by the gaming-table the whole morning, yet never once staked in person. For myself, I lost all that I had on me, and with great speed. To begin with, I staked two hundred gülden on 'even,' and won. Then I staked the same amount again, and won: and so on some two or three times. At one moment I must have had in my hands – gathered there within a space of five minutes – about 4000 gülden. That, of course, was the proper moment for me to have departed, but there arose in me a strange sensation as of a challenge to Fate – as of a wish to deal her a blow on the cheek, and to put out my tongue at her. Accordingly I set down the largest stake allowed by the rules – namely, 4000 gülden – and lost. Fired by this mishap, I pulled out all the money left to me, staked it all on the same venture, and – again lost! Then I rose from the table, feeling as though I were stupefied. What had happened to me I did not know, but before luncheon I told Polina of my losses; until which time I walked about the Park.

At luncheon I was as excited as I had been at the meal three days ago. Mlle. Blanche and the Frenchman were lunching with us, and it appeared that the former had been to the Casino that morning, and had seen my exploits there. So now she showed me more attention when talking to me; while, for his part, the Frenchman approached me, and asked outright if it had been my own money that I had lost. He appeared to be suspicious as to something being on foot between Polina and myself, but I merely fired up, and replied that the money had been all my own.

At this the General seemed extremely surprised, and asked me whence I had procured it; whereupon I replied that, though I had begun only with 100 gülden, six or seven rounds had increased my capital to 5000 or 6000 gülden, and that subsequently I had lost the whole in two rounds.

All this, of course, was plausible enough. During my recital I glanced at Polina, but nothing was to be discerned on her face. However, she had allowed me to fire up without correcting me, and from that I concluded that it was my *cue* to fire up, and to conceal the fact that I had been playing on her behalf. 'At all events,' I thought to myself, 'she, in her turn, has promised to give me an explanation to-night, and to reveal to me something or another.'

Although the General appeared to be taking stock of me, he said nothing. Yet I could see uneasiness and annoyance in his face. Perhaps his straitened circumstances made it hard for him to have to hear of piles of gold passing through the hands of an irresponsible fool like myself within the space of a quarter of an hour. Now, I have an idea that, last night, he and the Frenchman had a sharp encounter with one another. At all events they closeted themselves together, and then had a long and vehement discussion; after which the Frenchman departed in what appeared to be a passion, but returned, early this morning, to renew the combat. On hearing of my losses, however, he only remarked with a sharp, and even a malicious, air that a man ought to go more carefully. Next, for some reason or another, he added that, though a great many Russians go in for gambling, they are no good at the game.

'I think that roulette was devised specially for Russians,' I retorted; and when the Frenchman smiled contemptuously at my reply I further remarked that I was sure I was right; also that, speaking of Russians in the capacity of gamblers, I had far more blame for them than praise – of that he could be quite sure.

'Upon what do you base your opinion?' he inquired.

'Upon the fact that to the virtues and merits of the civilized Westerner there has become historically added – though this is not his chief point – a capacity for acquiring capital; whereas not only is the Russian incapable of acquiring capital, but also he exhausts it wantonly and of sheer folly. None the less we Russians often need money; wherefore we are glad of, and greatly devoted to, a method of acquisition like roulette – whereby, in a couple of hours, one may grow rich without doing any work. This method, I repeat, has a great attraction for us, but since we play in wanton fashion, and without taking any trouble, we almost invariably lose.'

'To a certain extent that is true,' assented the Frenchman with a self-satisfied air.

'Oh no, it is not true,' put in the General sternly. 'And you,' he added to me, 'you ought to be ashamed of yourself for traducing your own country!'

'I beg pardon,' I said. 'Yet it would be difficult to say which is the worst of the two – Russian ineptitude or the German method of growing rich through honest toil.'

'What an extraordinary idea,' cried the General.

'And what a *Russian* idea!' added the Frenchman.

I smiled, for I was rather glad to have a quarrel with them.

'I would rather live a wandering life in tents,' I cried, 'than bow the knee to a German idol!'

'To *what* idol?' exclaimed the General, now seriously angry.

'To the German method of heaping up riches. I have not been here very long, but I can tell you that what I have seen and verified makes my Tartar blood boil. Good Lord! I wish for no virtues of that kind. Yesterday

I went for a walk of about ten versts; and everywhere I found that things were even as we read of them in good German picture-books – that every house has its "Vater," who is horribly beneficent and extraordinarily honourable. So honourable is he that it is dreadful to have anything to do with him; and I cannot bear people of that sort. Each such "Vater" has his family, and in the evenings they read improving books aloud. Over their roof-trees there murmur elms and chestnuts; the sun has sunk to his rest; a stork is roosting on the gable; and all is beautifully poetic and touching. Do not be angry, General. Let me tell you something that is even more touching than that. I can remember how, of an evening, my own father, now dead, used to sit under the lime trees in his little garden, and to read books aloud to myself and my mother. Yes, I know how things ought to be done. Yet every German family is bound to slavery and to submission to its "Vater." They work like oxen, and amass wealth like Jews. Suppose the "Vater" has put by a certain number of gülden which he hands over to his eldest son, in order that the said son may acquire a trade or a small plot of land. Well, one result is to deprive the daughter of a dowry, and so leave her among the unwedded. For the same reason, the parents will have to sell the younger son into bondage or the ranks of the army, in order that he may earn more towards the family capital. Yes, such things *are* done, for I have been making inquiries on the subject. It is all done out of sheer rectitude – out of a rectitude which is magnified to the point of the younger son believing that he has been *rightly* sold, and that it is simply idyllic for the victim to rejoice when he is made over into pledge. What more have I to tell? Well, this – that matters bear just as hardly upon the eldest son. Perhaps he has his Gretchen to whom his heart is bound; but he cannot marry her, for the reason that he has not yet amassed sufficient gülden. So the pair wait on in a mood of sincere and virtuous expectation, and smilingly deposit themselves in pawn the while. Gretchen's cheeks grow sunken, and she begins to wither; until at last, after some twenty years, their substance has multiplied, and sufficient gülden have been honourably and virtuously accumulated. Then the "Vater" blesses his forty-year-old heir and the thirty-five-year-old Gretchen with the sunken bosom and the scarlet nose; after which he bursts into tears, reads the pair a lesson on morality, and dies. In turn the eldest son becomes a virtuous "Vater," and the old story begins again. In fifty or sixty years' time the grandson of the original "Vater" will have amassed a considerable sum; and that sum he will hand over to his son, and the latter to *his* son, and so on for several generations; until at length there will issue a Baron Rothschild, or a "Hoppe and Company," or the devil knows what! Is it not a beautiful spectacle – the spectacle of a century or two of inherited labour, patience,

479

intellect, rectitude, character, perseverance, and calculation, with a stork sitting on the roof above it all? What is more, they think there can never be anything better than this; wherefore from *their* point of view they begin to judge the rest of the world, and to censure all who are at fault – that is to say, who are not exactly like themselves. Yes, there you have it in a nutshell. For my own part, I would rather grow fat after the Russian manner, or squander my whole substance at roulette. I have no wish to be "Hoppe and Company" at the end of five generations. I want the money for *myself*, for in no way do I look upon my personality as necessary to, or meet to be given over to, capital. I may be wrong, but there you have it. Those are *my* views.'

'How far you may be right in what you have said I do not know,' remarked the General moodily; 'but I *do* know that you are becoming an insufferable *farçeur* whenever you are given the least chance.'

As usual, he left his sentence unfinished. Indeed, whenever he embarked upon anything that in the least exceeded the limits of daily small-talk, he left unfinished what he was saying. The Frenchman had listened to me contemptuously, with a slight protruding of his eyes; but he could not have understood very much of my harangue. As for Polina, she had looked on with serene indifference. She seemed to have heard neither my voice nor any other during the progress of the meal.

➤ FIVE ➤

YES, SHE HAD BEEN EXTRAORDINARILY meditative. Yet, on leaving the table, she immediately ordered me to accompany her for a walk. We took the children with us, and set out for the fountain in the Park.

I was in such an irritated frame of mind that in rude and abrupt fashion I blurted out a question as to 'why our Marquis de Griers had ceased to accompany her for strolls, or to speak to her for days together.'

'Because he is a brute,' she replied in rather a curious way. It was the first time that I had heard her speak so of De Griers: consequently I was momentarily awed into silence by this expression of resentment.

'Have you noticed, too, that to-day he is by no means on good terms with the General?' I went on.

'Yes; and I suppose you want to know why,' she replied with dry captiousness. 'You are aware, are you not, that the General is mortgaged to the Marquis, with all his property? Consequently, if the General's mother does not die, the Frenchman will become the absolute possessor of everything which he now holds only in pledge.'

'Then it is really the case that everything is mortgaged? I have heard rumours to that effect, but was unaware how far they might be true.'

'Yes, they *are* true. What then?'

'Why, it will be a case of "Farewell, Mlle. Blanche," ' I remarked; 'for in such an event she would never become Madame General. Do you know, I believe the old man is so much in love with her that he will shoot himself if she should throw him over. At his age it is a dangerous thing to fall in love.'

'Yes, something, I believe, *will* happen to him,' assented Polina thoughtfully.

'And what a fine thing it all is!' I continued. 'Could anything be more abominable than the way in which she has agreed to marry for money alone? Not one of the decencies has been observed; the whole affair has taken place without the least ceremony. And as for the grandmother, what could be more comical, yet more dastardly, than the sending of telegram after telegram to know if she is dead? What do *you* think of it, Polina Alexandrovna?'

'Yes, it is very horrible,' she interrupted with a shudder. 'Consequently I am the more surprised that *you* should be so cheerful. What are *you* so pleased about? About the fact that you have gone and lost my money?'

'What? The money that you gave me to lose? I told you I should never win for other people – least of all for you. I obeyed you simply because you ordered me to; but you must not blame me for the result. I warned you that no good would ever come of it. You seem much depressed at having lost your money. Why do you need it so greatly?'

'Why do *you* ask me these questions?'

'Because you promised to explain matters to me. Listen. I am certain that, as soon as ever I begin to play for myself (and I still have 120 gülden left), I shall win. You can then take off me what you require.'

She made a contemptuous grimace.

'You must not be angry with me,' I continued, 'for making such a proposal. I am so conscious of being only a nonentity in your eyes that you need not mind accepting money from me. A gift from me could not possibly offend you. Moreover, it was I who lost your gülden.'

She glanced at me, but, seeing that I was in an irritable, sarcastic mood, changed the subject.

'My affairs cannot possibly interest you,' she said. 'Still, if you *do* wish to know, I am in debt. I borrowed some money, and must pay it back again. I have a curious, a senseless idea that I am bound to win at the gaming-tables. Why I think so I cannot tell, but I do think so, and with some assurance. Perhaps it is because of that assurance that I now find myself without any other resource.'

'Or perhaps it is because it is so *necessary* for you to win. It is like a drowning man catching at a straw. You yourself will agree that, unless he were drowning he would not mistake a straw for the trunk of a tree.'

Polina looked surprised.

'What?' she said. 'Do not you also hope something from it? Did you not tell me again and again, two weeks ago, that you were certain of winning at roulette if you played here? And did you not ask me not to consider you a fool for doing so? Were you joking? You cannot have been, for I remember that you spoke with a gravity which forbade the idea of your jesting.'

'True,' I replied gloomily. 'I always felt certain that I should win. Indeed, what you say makes me ask myself – Why have my absurd, senseless losses of to-day raised a doubt in my mind? Yet I am *still* positive that, so soon as ever I begin to play for myself, I shall infallibly win.'

'And why are you so certain?'

'To tell the truth, I do not know. I only know that I *must* win – that it is the one resource I have left. Yes, why do I feel so assured on the point?'

'Perhaps because one cannot help winning if one is fanatically certain of doing so.'

'Yet I dare wager that you do not think me capable of serious feeling in the matter?'

'I do not care whether you are so or not,' answered Polina with calm indifference. 'Well, since you ask me, I *do* doubt your ability to take anything seriously. You are capable of worrying, but not deeply. You are too ill-regulated and unsettled a person for that. But why do you want money? Not a single one of the reasons which you have given can be looked upon as serious.'

'By the way,' I interrupted, 'you say you want to pay off a debt. It must be a large one. Is it to the Frenchman?'

'What do you mean by asking all these questions? You are very clever to-day. Surely you are not drunk?'

'You know that you and I stand on no ceremony, and that sometimes I put to you very plain questions. I repeat that I am your slave – and slaves cannot be shamed or offended.'

'You talk like a child. It is always possible to comport oneself with dignity. If one has a quarrel it ought to elevate rather than to degrade one.'

'A maxim straight from the copybook! Suppose I *cannot* comport myself with dignity. By that I mean that, though I am a man of self-respect, I am unable to carry off a situation properly. Do you know the reason? It is because we Russians are too richly and multifariously gifted to be able at once to find the proper mode of expression. It is all a question of mode. Most of us are so bounteously endowed with intellect as to require also a spice of genius to choose the right form of behaviour. And genius is lacking in us for the reason that so little genius at all exists. It belongs only to the French – though a few other Europeans have elaborated their forms so well as to be able to figure with extreme dignity, and yet be wholly undignified persons. That is why, with us, the mode is so all-important. The Frenchman may receive an insult – a real, a venomous insult: yet he will not so much as frown. But a tweaking of the nose he cannot bear, for the reason that such an act is an infringement of the accepted, of the time-hallowed, order of decorum. That is why our good ladies are so fond of Frenchmen – the Frenchman's manners, they say, are perfect! But in my opinion there is no such thing as a Frenchman's manners. The Frenchman is only a bird – the *coq gaulois*. At the same time, as I am not a woman, I do not properly understand the question. Cocks may be excellent birds. If I am wrong you must stop me. You ought to stop and correct me more often when I am speaking to you, for I am too apt to say everything that is in my head. You see, I have lost my manners. I agree that I have none, nor yet any dignity. I will tell you why. I set no store upon such things. Everything in me has undergone a check. You know the reason. I have not a single human thought in my head. For a long while I have been ignorant of what is going on in the world – here or in Russia. I have been to Dresden, yet am completely in the dark as to what Dresden is like. You know the cause of my obsession. I have no hope now, and am a mere cipher in your eyes; wherefore I tell you outright that wherever I go I see only you – all the rest is a matter of indifference. Why or how I have come to love you I do not know. It may be that you are not altogether fair to look upon. Do you know, I am ignorant even as to what your face is like. In all probability, too, your heart is not comely, and it is possible that your mind is wholly ignoble.'

'And because you do not believe in my nobility of soul you think to purchase me with money?' she said.

'*When* have I thought to do so?' was my reply.

'You are losing the thread of the argument. If you do not wish to purchase me, at all events you wish to purchase my respect.'

'Not at all. I have told you that I find it difficult to explain myself. You are hard upon me. Do not be angry at my chattering. You know why you ought not to be angry with me – that I am simply an imbecile. However, I do not mind if you *are* angry. Sitting in my room, I need but to think of you, to imagine to myself the rustle of your dress, and at once I fall almost to biting my hands. Why should you be angry with me? Because I call myself your slave? Revel, I pray you, in my slavery – revel in it. Do you know that sometimes I could kill you? – not because I do not love, or am jealous of, you, but because I feel as though I could simply devour you. You are laughing!'

'No, I am not,' she retorted. 'But I order you, nevertheless, to be silent.'

She stopped, well nigh breathless with anger. God knows, she may not have been a beautiful woman, yet I loved to see her come to a halt like this, and was therefore the more fond of arousing her temper. Perhaps she divined this, and for that very reason gave way to rage. I said as much to her.

'What rubbish!' she cried with a shudder.

'I do not care,' I continued. 'Also, do you know that it is not safe for us to take walks together? Often I have a feeling that I should like to strike you, to disfigure you, to strangle you. Are you certain that it will never come to that? You are driving me to frenzy. Am I afraid of a scandal, or of your anger? Why should I fear your anger? I love without hope, and know that hereafter I shall love you a thousand times more. If ever I should kill you I should have to kill myself too. But I shall put off doing so as long as possible, for I wish to continue enjoying the unbearable pain which your coldness gives me. Do you know a very strange thing? It is that, with every day, my love for you increases – though that would seem to be almost an impossibility. Why should I not become a fatalist? Remember how, on the third day that we ascended the Schlangenberg, I was moved to whisper in your ear: "Say but the word, and I will leap into the abyss." Had you said it, I should have leapt. Do you not believe me?'

'What stupid rubbish!' she cried.

'I care not whether it be wise or stupid,' I cried in return. 'I only know that in your presence I must speak, speak, speak. Therefore I am speaking. I lose all conceit when I am with you, and everything ceases to matter.'

'Why should I have wanted you to leap from the Schlangenberg?' she said drily, and (I think) with wilful offensiveness. '*That* would have been of no use to me.'

'Splendid!' I shouted. 'I know well that you must have used the words "of no use" in order to crush me. I can see through you. "Of no use," did you say? Why, to give pleasure is *always* of use; and as for barbarous, unlimited power – even if it be only over a fly – why, it is a kind of luxury. Man is a despot by nature, and loves to torture. You, in particular, love to do so.'

I remember that at this moment she looked at me in a peculiar way.

The fact is that my face must have been expressing all the maze of senseless, gross sensations which were seething within me. To this day I can
remember, word for word, the conversation as I have written it down.
My eyes were suffused with blood, and the foam had caked itself on my
lips. Also, on my honour I swear that, had she bidden me cast myself
from the summit of the Schlangenberg, I should have done it. Yes, had
she bidden me in jest, or only in contempt and with a spit in my face, I
should have cast myself down.

'Oh no! Why so? I believe you,' she said, but in such a manner – in the
manner of which, at times, she was a mistress – and with such a note of
disdain and viperish arrogance in her tone, that God knows I could have
killed her.

Yes, at that moment she stood in peril. I had not lied to her about that.

'Surely you are not a coward?' suddenly she asked me.

'I don't know,' I replied. 'Perhaps I am, but I do not know. I have long
given up thinking about such things.'

'If I said to you, "Kill that man," would you kill him?'

'Whom?'

'Whomsoever I wish?'

'The Frenchman?'

'Do not ask me questions; return me answers. I repeat, whomsoever I
wish? I desire to see if you were speaking seriously just now.'

She awaited my reply with such gravity and impatience that I found
the situation unpleasant.

'Do *you*, rather, tell me,' I said, 'what is going on here. Why do you
seem half-afraid of me? I can see for myself what is wrong. You are the
step-daughter of a ruined and insensate man who is smitten with love for
this devil of a Blanche. And there is this Frenchman, too, with his mysterious influence over you. Yet you actually ask me such a question! If you
do not tell me how things stand I shall have to put in my oar and do
something. Are you ashamed to be frank with me? Are you shy of me?'

'I am not going to talk to you on that subject. I have asked you a
question, and am waiting for an answer.'

'Well, then – I will kill whomsoever you wish,' I said. 'But are you *really*
going to bid me do such deeds?'

'Why should you think that I am going to let you off? I shall bid you
do it, or else renounce me. Could you ever do the latter? No, you know
that you couldn't. You would first kill whom I had bidden you, and then
kill *me* for having dared to send you away.'

Something seemed to strike upon my brain as I heard these words. Of
course, at the time I took them half in jest and half as a challenge: yet
she had spoken them with great seriousness. I felt thunderstruck that she

should so express herself, that she should assert such a right over me, that she should assume such authority and say outright: 'Either you kill whom I bid you, or I will have nothing more to do with you.' Indeed, in what she had said there was something so cynical and unveiled as to pass all bounds. For how could she ever regard me as the same after the killing was done? This was more than slavery and abasement; it was sufficient to bring a man back to his right senses. Yet, despite the outrageous improbability of our conversation, my heart shook within me.

Suddenly she burst out laughing. We were seated on a bench near the spot where the children were playing – just opposite the point in the alleyway before the Casino where the carriages drew up in order to set down their occupants.

'Do you see that fat Baroness?' she cried. 'It is the Baroness Burmergelm. She arrived three days ago. Just look at her husband – that tall, wizened Prussian there, with the stick in his hand. Do you remember how he stared at us the other day? Well, go to the Baroness, take off your hat to her, and say something in French.'

'Why?'

'Because you have sworn that you would leap from the Schlangenberg for my sake, and that you would kill any one whom I might bid you kill. Well, instead of such murders and tragedies, I wish only for a good laugh. Go without answering me, and let me see the Baron give you a sound thrashing with his stick.'

'Then you throw me out a challenge? – you think that I will not do it?'

'Yes, I do challenge you. Go, for such is my will.'

'Then I *will* go, however mad be your fancy. Only, look here: shall you not be doing the General a great disservice, as well as, through him, a great disservice to yourself? It is not about myself I am worrying; it is about you and the General. Why, for a mere fancy, should I go and insult a woman?'

'Ah! Then I can see that you are only a trifler,' she said contemptuously. 'Your eyes are swimming with blood – but only because you have drunk a little too much at luncheon. Do I not know that what I have asked you to do is foolish and wrong, and that the General will be angry about it? But I want to have a good laugh, all the same. I want that, and nothing else. Why should you insult a woman, indeed? Well, you will be given a sound thrashing for so doing.'

I turned away, and went silently to do her bidding. Of course the thing was folly, but I could not get out of it. I remember that, as I approached the Baroness, I felt as excited as a schoolboy. I was in a frenzy, as though I were drunk.

⇒ SIX ⇐

TWO DAYS HAVE PASSED SINCE THAT day of lunacy. What a noise and a fuss and a chattering and an uproar there was! And what a welter of unseemliness and disorder and stupidity and bad manners! And *I* the cause of it all! Yet part of the scene was also ridiculous – at all events to myself it was so. I am not quite sure what was the matter with me – whether I was merely stupefied or whether I purposely broke loose and ran amok. At times my mind seems all confused; while at other times I seem almost to be back in my childhood, at the school desk, and to have done the deed simply out of mischief.

It all came of Polina – yes, of Polina. But for her, there might never have been a fracas. Or perhaps I did the deed in a fit of despair (though it may be foolish of me to think so)? What there is so attractive about her I cannot think. Yet there *is* something attractive about her – something passing fair, it would seem. Others besides myself she has driven to distraction. She is tall and straight, and very slim. Her body looks as though it could be tied into a knot, or bent double, like a cord. The imprint of her foot is long and narrow. It is a maddening imprint – yes, simply a maddening one! And her hair has a reddish tint about it, and her eyes are like cat's eyes – though able also to glance with proud, disdainful mien. On the evening of my first arrival, four months ago, I remember that she was sitting and holding an animated conversation with De Griers in the salon. And the way in which she looked at him was such that later, when I retired to my own room upstairs, I kept fancying that she had smitten him in the face – that she had smitten him right on the cheek, so peculiar had been her look as she stood confronting him. Ever since that evening I have loved her.

But to my tale.

I stepped from the path into the carriage-way, and took my stand in the middle of it. There I awaited the Baron and the Baroness. When they were but a few paces distant from me I took off my hat, and bowed.

I remember that the Baroness was clad in a voluminous silk dress, pale grey in colour, and adorned with flounces and a crinoline and train. Also, she was short and inordinately stout, while her gross, flabby chin completely concealed her neck. Her face was purple, and the little eyes in

487

it had an impudent, malicious expression. Yet she walked as though she were conferring a favour upon everybody by so doing. As for the Baron, he was tall, wizened, bony-faced after the German fashion, spectacled, and, apparently, about forty-five years of age. Also, he had legs which seemed to begin almost at his chest – or, rather, at his chin! Yet, for all his air of peacock-like conceit, his clothes sagged a little, and his face wore a sheepish air which might have passed for profundity.

These details I noted within a space of a few seconds.

At first my bow and the fact that I had my hat in my hand barely caught their attention. The Baron only scowled a little, and the Baroness swept straight on.

'Madame la Baronne,' said I, loudly and distinctly – embroidering each word, as it were – 'j'ai l'honneur d'être votre esclave.'

Then I bowed again, put on my hat, and walked past the Baron with a rude smile on my face.

Polina had ordered me merely to take off my hat: the bow and the general effrontery were of my own invention. God knows what instigated me to perpetrate the outrage! In my frenzy I felt as though I were walking on air.

'Hein!' ejaculated – or, rather, growled – the Baron as he turned towards me in angry surprise.

I too turned round, and stood waiting in pseudo-courteous expectation. Yet still I wore on my face an impudent smile as I gazed at him. He seemed to hesitate, and his brows contracted to their utmost limits. Every moment his visage was growing darker. The Baroness also turned in my direction, and gazed at me in wrathful perplexity, while some of the passers-by also began to stare at us, and others of them halted outright.

'Hein!' the Baron vociferated again, with a redoubled growl and a note of growing wrath in his voice.

'Ja wohl!' I replied, still looking him in the eyes.

'Sind Sie rasend?' he exclaimed, brandishing his stick, and, apparently, beginning to feel nervous. Perhaps it was my costume which intimidated him, for I was well and fashionably dressed, after the manner of a man who belongs to indisputably good society.

'Ja wo-o-ohl!' cried I again with all my might – with a long-drawn rolling of the 'ohl' sound after the fashion of the Berliners (who constantly use the phrase 'Ja wohl!' in conversation, and more or less prolong the syllable 'ohl!' according as they desire to express different shades of meaning or of mood).

At this the Baron and the Baroness faced sharply about, and almost fled in their alarm. Some of the bystanders gave vent to excited exclamations, and others remained staring at me in astonishment. But I do not remember the details very well.

Wheeling quietly about, I returned in the direction of Polina Alexandrovna. But when I had got within a hundred paces of her seat I saw her rise, and set out with the children towards the hotel.

At the portico I caught her up.

'I have perpetrated the – the piece of idiocy,' I said as I came level with her.

'Have you? Then you can take the consequences,' she replied without so much as looking at me. Then she moved towards the staircase.

I spent the rest of the evening walking in the park. Thence I passed into the forest, and walked on until I found myself in a neighbouring principality. At a wayside restaurant I partook of an omelette and some wine, and was charged for the idyllic repast a thaler and a half.

Not until eleven o'clock did I return home – to find a summons awaiting me from the General.

Our party occupied two suites in the hotel; each of which contained two rooms. The first (the larger suite) comprised a salon and a smoking-room, with, adjoining the latter, the General's study. It was here that he was awaiting me as he stood posed in a majestic attitude beside his writing-table. Lolling on a divan close by was De Griers.

'My good sir,' the General began, 'may I ask you what this is that you have gone and done?'

'I should be glad,' I replied, 'if we could come straight to the point. Probably you are referring to my encounter of to-day with a German?'

'With a German? Why, the German was the Baron Burmergelm – a most important personage! I hear that you have been rude both to him and to the Baroness?'

'No, I have not.'

'But I understand that you simply terrified them, my good sir?' shouted the General.

'Not in the least,' I replied. 'You must know that when I was in Berlin I frequently used to hear the Berliners repeat, and repellently prolong, a certain phrase – namely, "Ja wohl!"; and, happening to meet this couple in the carriage-drive, I found, for some reason or another, that this phrase suddenly recurred to my memory, and exercised a rousing effect upon my spirits. Moreover, on the three previous occasions that I have met the Baroness she has walked towards me as though I were a worm which could easily be crushed with the foot. Not unnaturally, I too possess a measure of self-respect; wherefore on *this* occasion I took off my hat, and said politely (yes, I assure you it was said politely): "Madame, j'ai l'honneur d'être votre esclave." Then the Baron turned round, and said "Hein!";

whereupon I felt moved to ejaculate in answer "Ja wohl!" Twice I shouted it at him – the first time in an ordinary tone, and the second time with the greatest prolonging of the words of which I was capable. That is all.'

I must confess that this puerile explanation gave me great pleasure. I felt a strong desire to overlay the incident with an even added measure of grossness; so, the further I proceeded, the more did the gusto of my proceeding increase.

'You are only making fun of me!' vociferated the General as, turning to the Frenchman, he declared that my bringing about of the incident had been gratuitous. De Griers smiled contemptuously, and shrugged his shoulders.

'Do not think *that*,' I put in. 'It was not so at all. I grant you that my behaviour was bad – I fully confess that it was so, and make no secret of the fact. I would even go so far as to grant you that my behaviour might well be called stupid and indecent tomfoolery; but *more* that that it was not. Also, let me tell you that I am very sorry for my conduct. Yet there is one circumstance which, in my eyes, almost absolves me from regret in the matter. Of late – that is to say, for the last two or three weeks – I have been feeling not at all well. That is to say, I have been in a sick, nervous, irritable, fanciful condition, so that I have periodically lost control over myself. For instance, on more than one occasion I have tried to pick a quarrel even with Monsieur le Marquise here; and under the circumstances he had no choice but to answer me. In short, I have recently been showing signs of ill-health. Whether the Baroness Burmergelm will take this circumstance into consideration when I come to beg her pardon (for I *do* intend to make her amends) I do not know, but I doubt if she will, and the less so since, so far as I know, the circumstance is one which, of late, has begun to be abused in the legal world, in that advocates in criminal cases have taken to justifying their clients on the ground that, at the moment of the crime, they (the clients) were unconscious of what they were doing – that, in short, they were out of health. "My client committed the murder – that is true; but he has no recollection of having committed it." And doctors actually support these advocates by affirming that there really *is* such a malady – that there really *can* arise temporary delusions which make a man remember nothing of a given deed, or only a half or a quarter of it! But the Baron and Baroness are members of an older generation, as well as Prussian Jünkers and landowners. To them such a process in the medico-judicial world will be unknown, and therefore they are the more unlikely to accept any such explanation. What is *your* opinion about it, General?'

'Enough sir!' he thundered with barely restrained fury. 'Enough, I say! Once and for all I must endeavour to rid myself of you and your impertinence. To justify yourself in the eyes of the Baron and Baroness will be impossible. Any intercourse with you, even though it be confined to a begging of their pardons, they would look upon as a degradation. I may tell you that, on learning that you formed part of my household, the Baron approached me in the Casino, and demanded of me additional satisfaction. Do you understand, then, what it is that you have entailed upon me – upon *me*, my good sir? You have entailed upon me the fact of my being forced to sue humbly to the Baron, and to give him my word of honour that this very day you shall cease to belong to my establishment!'

'Excuse me, General,' I interrupted, 'but did he make an express point of it that I should "cease to belong to your establishment," as you call it?'

'No; I of my own initiative thought that I ought to afford him that satisfaction: and with it he was satisfied. So we must part, good sir. It is my duty to hand over to you forty gülden, three florins, as per the accompanying statement. Here is the money, and here the account, which you are at liberty to verify. Farewell. From henceforth we are strangers. From you I have never had anything but trouble and unpleasantness. I am about to call the landlord, and explain to him that from to-morrow onwards I shall no longer be responsible for your hotel expenses. Also I have the honour to remain your obedient servant.'

I took the money and the account (which was indited in pencil), and, bowing low to the General, said to him very gravely:

'The matter cannot end here. I regret very much that you should have been put to unpleasantness at the Baron's hands; but the fault (pardon me) is your own. How came you to answer for me to the Baron? And what did you mean by saying that I formed part of your household? I am merely your family tutor – not a son of yours, nor yet your ward, nor a person of any kind for whose acts you need be responsible. I am a judicially competent person, a man of twenty-five years of age, a university graduate, a gentleman, and, until I met yourself, a complete stranger to you. Only my boundless respect for your merits restrains me from demanding satisfaction at your hands, as well as a further explanation as to the reasons which have led you to take it upon yourself to answer for my conduct.'

So struck was he with my words that, spreading out his hands, he turned to the Frenchman, and interpreted to him that I had challenged himself (the General) to a duel. The Frenchman laughed aloud.

'Nor do I intend to let the Baron off,' I continued calmly, but with not a little discomfiture at De Griers' merriment. 'And since you, General, have to-day been so good as to listen to the Baron's complaints, and to enter into his concerns – since you have made yourself a participator in the affair – I have the honour to inform you that, to-morrow morning at the latest, I shall, in my own name, demand of the said Baron a formal explanation as to the reasons which have led him to disregard the fact that the matter lies between him and myself alone, and to put a slight upon me by referring it to another person, as though I were unworthy to answer for my own conduct.'

Then there happened what I had foreseen. The General, on hearing of this further intended outrage, showed the white feather.

'What?' he cried. 'Do you intend to go on with this damned nonsense? Do you not realize the harm that it is doing me? I beg of you not to laugh at me, sir – not to laugh at me, for we have police authorities here who, out of respect for my rank, and for that of the Baron – In short, sir, I swear to you that I will have you arrested, and marched out of the place, to prevent any further brawling on your part. Do you understand what I say?' He was almost breathless with anger, as well as in a terrible fright.

'General,' I replied with that calmness which he never could abide, 'one cannot arrest a man for brawling until he has brawled. I have not so much as begun my explanations to the Baron, and you are altogether ignorant as to the form and time which my intended procedure is likely to assume. I wish but to disabuse the Baron of what is, to me, a shameful supposition – namely, that I am under the guardianship of a person who is qualified to exercise control over my freewill. It is vain for you to disturb and alarm yourself.'

'For God's sake, Alexis Ivanovitch, do put an end to this senseless scheme of yours!' he muttered, but with a sudden change from a truculent tone to one of entreaty as he caught me by the hand. 'Do you know what is likely to come of it? Merely further unpleasantness. You will agree with me, I am sure, that at present I ought to move with especial care – yes, with very especial care. You cannot be fully aware of how I am situated. When we leave this place I shall be ready to receive you back into my household; but for the time being I – Well, I cannot tell you all my reasons.' With that he wound up in a despairing voice: 'O Alexis Ivanovitch, Alexis Ivanovitch!'

I moved towards the door – begging him to be calm, and promising that everything should be done decently and in order; whereafter I departed.

Russians, when abroad, are over-apt to play the poltroon, and to watch all their words, and to wonder what people are thinking of their conduct, or whether such and such a thing is *comme il faut*. In short, they are over-apt to cosset themselves, and to lay claim to great importance. Always they prefer the form of behaviour which has once and for all become accepted and established. This they will follow slavishly – whether in hotels, on promenades, at meetings, or when on a journey. But the General had avowed to me that, over and above such considerations as these, there were circumstances which compelled him to 'move with especial care at present': and the fact had actually made him poor-spirited and a coward – had made him altogether change his tone towards me. This fact I took into my calculations, and duly noted it, for, of course, he *might* apply to the authorities to-morrow, and it behoved me to go carefully.

Yet it was not the General but Polina that I wanted to anger. She had treated me with such cruelty, and had got me into such a hole, that I felt a longing to force her to beseech me to stop. Of course, my tomfoolery might compromise her; yet certain other feelings and desires had begun to form themselves in my brain. If I was never to rank in her eyes as anything but a nonentity, it would not greatly matter if I figured as a draggle-tailed cockerel, and the Baron were to give me a good thrashing; but the fact was that I desired to have the laugh of them all, and to come out myself unscathed. Let people see what they *would* see. Let Polina, for once, have a good fright, and be forced to whistle me to heel again. But, however much she might whistle, she should see that I was at least no draggle-tailed cockerel!

I have just received a surprising piece of news. I have just met our chambermaid on the stairs, and been informed by her that Maria Philipovna departed to-day, by the night train, to stay with a cousin at Carlsbad. What can that mean? The maid declares that Madame packed her trunks early in the day. Yet how is it that no one else seems to have been aware of the circumstance? Or is it that *I* have been the only person to be unaware of it? Also, the maid has just told me that, three days ago, Maria Philipovna had some high words with the General. I understand, then! Probably the words were concerning Mlle. Blanche. Certainly something decisive is approaching.

✦ SEVEN ✦

IN THE MORNING I SENT FOR THE maitre d'hôtel, and explained to him that, in future, my bill was to be rendered to me personally. As a matter of fact, my expenses had never been so large as to alarm me, nor to lead me to quit the hotel; while, moreover, I still had 160 gülden left to me, and – in them – yes, in them, perhaps, riches awaited me. It was a curious fact, that, though I had not yet won anything at play, I nevertheless acted, thought, and felt as though I were sure, before long, to become wealthy, since I could not imagine myself otherwise.

Next I bethought me, despite the earliness of the hour, of going to see Mr. Astley, who was staying at the Hôtel de l'Angleterre (a hostelry at no great distance from our own). But suddenly De Griers entered my room. This had never before happened, for of late that gentleman and I had stood on the most strained and distant of terms – he attempting no concealment of his contempt for me (he even made an express point of showing it), and I having no reason to desire his company. In short, I detested him. Consequently his entry at the present moment the more astounded me. At once I divined that something out of the way was on the carpet.

He entered with marked affability, and began by complimenting me on my room. Then, perceiving that I had my hat in my hands, he inquired whither I was going so early; and no sooner did he hear that I was bound for Mr. Astley's than he stopped, looked grave, and seemed plunged in thought.

He was a true Frenchman in so far as that, though he could be lively and engaging when it suited him, he became insufferably dull and wearisome as soon as ever the need for being lively and engaging had passed. Seldom is a Frenchman *naturally* civil: he is civil only as though to order and of set purpose. Also, if he thinks it incumbent upon him to be fanciful, original, and out of the way, his fancy always assumes a foolish, unnatural vein, for the reason that it is compounded of trite, hackneyed forms. In short, the natural Frenchman is a conglomeration of commonplace, petty, everyday positiveness, so that he is the most tedious person in the world. Indeed, I believe that none but greenhorns and excessively Russian people feel an attraction towards the French; for, to any man of sensibility, such a compendium of outworn forms – a compendium which is built up of drawing-room manners, expansiveness, and gaiety – becomes at once over noticeable and unbearable.

'I have come to see you on business,' De Griers began in a very offhand, yet polite, tone; 'nor will I seek to conceal from you the fact that I have come in the capacity of an emissary, of an intermediary, from the General. Having small knowledge of the Russian tongue, I lost most of what was said last night; but the General has now explained matters, and I must confess that — '

'See here, Monsieur de Griers,' I interrupted. 'I understand that you have undertaken to act in this affair as an intermediary. Of course I am only "un utchitel," a tutor, and have never claimed to be an intimate of this household, nor to stand on at all familiar terms with it. Consequently I do not know the whole of its circumstances. Yet pray explain to me this: have you yourself become one of its members, seeing that you are beginning to take such a part in everything, and are now present as an intermediary?'

The Frenchman seemed not over-pleased at my question. It was one which was too outspoken for his taste – and he had no mind to be frank with me.

'I am connected with the General,' he said drily, 'partly through business affairs, and partly through special circumstances. My principal has sent me merely to ask you to forego your intentions of last evening. What you contemplate is, I have no doubt, very clever; yet he has charged me to represent to you that you have not the slightest chance of succeeding in your end, since not only will the Baron refuse to receive you, but also he (the Baron) has at his disposal every possible means for obviating further unpleasantness from you. Surely you can see that yourself? What, then, would be the good of going on with it all? On the other hand, the General promises that at the first favourable opportunity he will receive you back into his household, and, in the meantime, will credit you with your salary – with "vos appointements." Surely that will suit you, will it not?'

Very quietly I replied that he (the Frenchman) was labouring under a delusion; that perhaps, after all, I should *not* be expelled from the Baron's presence, but, on the contrary, be listened to; finally, that I should be glad if Monsieur de Griers would confess that he was now visiting me merely in order to see how far I intended to go in the affair.

'Good heavens!' cried de Griers. 'Seeing that the General takes such an interest in the matter, is there anything very unnatural in his desiring also to know your plans?'

Again I began my explanations, but the Frenchman only fidgeted and rolled his head about as he listened with an expression of manifest and unconcealed irony on his face. In short, he adopted a supercilious attitude. For my own part, I endeavoured to pretend that I took the affair very seriously. I declared that, since the Baron had gone and complained of me to the General, as though I were a mere servant of the General's, he had, in the first place, lost me my post, and, in the second place, treated me like a person to whom, as to one not qualified to answer for himself, it was not even worth while to speak. Naturally, I said, I felt insulted at this. Yet, comprehending, as I did, differences of years, of social status, and so forth (here I could scarcely help smiling), I was not anxious to bring about further scenes by going personally to demand or to request satisfaction of the Baron. All that I felt was that I had a right to go in person and beg the Baron's and the Baroness's pardon – the more so since, of late, I had been feeling unwell and unstrung, and had been in a fanciful condition. And so forth, and so forth. Yet (I continued) the Baron's offensive behaviour to me of yesterday (that is to say, the fact of his referring the matter to the General) as well as his insistence that the General should deprive me of my post, had placed me in such a position that I could not well express my regret to him (the Baron) and to his good lady, for the reason that in all probability both he and the Baroness, with the world at large, would imagine that I was doing so merely because I hoped, by my action, to recover my post. Hence I found myself forced to request the Baron to express to me *his own* regrets, as well as to express them in the most unqualified manner – to say, in fact, that he had never had any wish to insult me. After the Baron had done *that*, I should, for my part, at once feel free to express to him, whole-heartedly and without reserve, my own regrets. 'In short,' I declared in conclusion, 'my one desire is that the Baron may make it possible for me to adopt the latter course.'

'Oh fie! What refinements and subtleties!' exclaimed De Griers. 'Besides, what have you to express regret for? Confess. Monsieur, Monsieur – pardon me, but I have forgotten your name – confess, I say, that all this is merely a plan to annoy the General? Or perhaps you have some other and special end in view? Eh?'

'In return you must pardon *me*, mon cher Marquis, and tell me what *you* have to do with it.'

'The General — '

'But what of the General? Last night he said that, for some reason or another, it behoved him to "move with especial care at present;" wherefore he was feeling nervous. But I did not understand the reference.'

'Yes, there *do* exist special reasons for his doing so,' assented De Griers in a conciliatory tone, yet with rising anger. 'You are acquainted with Mlle de Cominges, are you not?'

'Mlle Blanche, you mean?'

'Yes, Mlle Blanche de Cominges. Doubtless you know also that the General is in love with this young lady, and may even be about to marry her before he leaves here? Imagine, therefore, what any scene or scandal would entail upon him!'

'I cannot see that the marriage scheme need be affected by scenes or scandals.'

'Mais le Baron est si irascible – un caractère prussien, vous savez! Enfin il fera une querelle d'Allemand.'

'I do not care,' I replied, 'seeing that I no longer belong to his household' (of set purpose I was trying to talk as senselessly as possible). 'But is it quite settled that Mlle is to marry the General? What are they waiting for? Why should they conceal such a matter – at all events from ourselves, the General's own party?'

'I cannot tell you. The marriage is not yet a settled affair, for they are awaiting news from Russia. The General has business transactions to arrange.'

'Ah! Connected, doubtless, with madame his mother?'

De Griers shot at me a glance of hatred.

'To cut things short,' he interrupted, 'I have complete confidence in your native politeness, as well as in your tact and good sense. I feel sure that you will do what I suggest, even if it is only for the sake of this family which has received you as a kinsman into its bosom and has always loved and respected you.'

'Be so good as to observe,' I remarked, 'that the same family has just *expelled* me from its bosom. All that you are saying you are saying but for show; but when people have just said to you, "Of course we do not wish to turn you out, yet, for the sake of appearances, you must *permit* yourself to be turned out," nothing can matter very much.'

'Very well, then,' he said, in a sterner and more arrogant tone. 'Seeing that my solicitations have had no effect upon you, it is my duty to mention that other measures will be taken. There exist here police, you must remember, and this very day they shall send you packing. Que diable! To think of a blanc bec like yourself challenging a person like the Baron to a duel! Do you suppose that you will be *allowed* to do such things? Just try doing them, and see if any one will be afraid of you! The reason why I have asked you to desist is that I can see that your conduct is causing the General annoyance. Do you believe that the Baron could not tell his lacquey simply to put you out of doors?'

'Nevertheless I should not *go* out of doors,' I retorted with absolute calm. 'You are labouring under a delusion, Monsieur de Griers. The thing will be done in far better trim than you imagine. I was just about to start for Mr Astley's, to ask him to be my intermediary – in other words, my second. He has a strong liking for me, and I do not think that he will refuse. He will go and see the Baron on my behalf, and the Baron will certainly not decline to receive him. Although I am only a tutor – a kind of subaltern, Mr Astley is known to all men as the nephew of a real English lord, the Lord Piebroch, as well as a lord in his own right. Yes, you may be pretty sure that the Baron will be civil to Mr Astley, and listen to him. Or, should he decline to do so, Mr Astley will take the refusal as a personal affront to himself (for you know how persistent the English are?) and thereupon introduce to the Baron a friend of his own (and he has many friends in a good position). That being so, picture to yourself the issue of the affair – an affair which will not quite end as you think it will.'

This caused the Frenchman to bethink him of playing the coward. 'Really things may be as this fellow says,' he evidently thought. 'Really he *might* be able to engineer another scene.'

'Once more I beg of you to let the matter drop,' he continued in a tone that was now entirely conciliatory. 'One would think that it actually *pleased* you to have scenes! Indeed, it is a brawl rather than genuine satisfaction that you are seeking. I have said that the affair may prove to be diverting, and even clever, and that possibly you may attain something by it; yet none the less I tell you' (he said this only because he saw me rise and reach for my hat) 'that I have come hither also to hand you these few words from a certain person. Read them, please, for I must take her back an answer.'

So saying, he took from his pocket a small, compact, wafer-sealed note, and handed it to me. In Polina's handwriting I read:

'I hear that you are thinking of going on with this affair. You have lost your temper now, and are beginning to play the fool! Certain circumstances, however, I may explain to you later. Pray cease from your folly, and put a check upon yourself. For folly it all is. I have need of you, and, moreover, you have promised to obey me. Remember the Schlangenberg. I ask you to be obedient. If necessary, I shall even *bid* you be obedient. – Your own

POLINA.

'P.S. – If so be that you still bear a grudge against me for what happened last night, pray forgive me.'

Everything, to my eyes, seemed to change as I read these words. My lips grew pale, and I began to tremble. Meanwhile the cursed Frenchman was eyeing me discreetly and askance, as though he wished to avoid witnessing my confusion. It would have been better if he had laughed outright.

'Very well,' I said, 'you can tell Mlle. not to disturb herself. But,' I added sharply, 'I would ask you why you have been so long in handing me this note? Instead of chattering about trifles, you ought to have delivered me the missive at once – if you have really come commissioned as you say.'

'Well, pardon some natural haste on my part, for the situation is so strange. I wished first to gain some personal knowledge of your intentions; and, moreover, I did not know the contents of the note, and thought that it could be given you at any time.'

'I understand,' I replied. 'So you were ordered to hand me the note only in the last resort, and if you could not otherwise appease me? Is it not so? Speak out, Monsieur de Griers.'

'Perhaps,' said he, assuming a look of great forbearance, but gazing at me in a meaning way.

I reached for my hat; whereupon he nodded, and went out. Yet on his lips I fancied that I could see a mocking smile. How could it have been otherwise?

'You and I are to have a reckoning later, Master Frenchman,' I muttered as I descended the stairs. 'Yes, we will measure our strength together.' Yet my thoughts were all in confusion, for again something seemed to have struck me dizzy. Presently the air revived me a little, and, a couple of minutes later, my brain had sufficiently cleared to enable two ideas in particular to stand out in it. Firstly, I asked myself, which of the absurd, boyish, and extravagant threats which I had uttered at random last night had made everybody so alarmed? Secondly, what was the influence which this Frenchman appeared to exercise over Polina? He had but to give the word, and at once she did as he desired – at once she wrote me a note to beg of me to forbear! Of course, the relations between the pair had, from the first, been a riddle to me – they had been so ever since I had first made their acquaintance, but of late I had remarked in her a strong aversion for – even a contempt for – him, while, for his part, he had scarcely even looked at her, but had behaved towards her always in the most churlish fashion. Yes, I had noted that. Also, Polina herself had mentioned to me her dislike for him, and delivered herself of some remarkable confessions on the subject. Hence he must have got her into his power somehow – somehow he must be holding her as in a vice.

✦ EIGHT ✦

ALL AT ONCE, ON THE PROMENADE, as it was called – that is to say, in the Chestnut Avenue – I came face to face with my Englishman.

'I was just coming to see you,' he said; 'and you appear to be out on a similar errand. So you have parted with your employers?'

'How do you know that?' I asked in astonishment. 'Is *every one* aware of the fact?'

'By no means. Not every one would consider such a fact to be of moment. Indeed, I have never heard any one speak of it.'

'Then how come you to know it?'

'Because I have had occasion to do so. Whither are you bound? I like you, and was therefore coming to pay you a visit.'

'What a splendid fellow you are, Mr. Astley!' I cried, though still wondering how he had come by his knowledge. 'And since I have not yet had my coffee, and you have, in all probability, scarcely tasted yours, let us adjourn to the Casino Café, where we can sit and smoke and have a talk.'

The café in question was only a hundred paces away; so when coffee had been brought we seated ourselves, and I lit a cigarette. Astley was no smoker, but, taking a seat by my side, he prepared himself to listen.

'I do not intend to go away,' was my first remark. 'I intend, on the contrary, to remain here.'

'That I never doubted,' he answered good-humouredly.

It is a curious fact that, on my way to see him, I had never even thought of telling him of my love for Polina. In fact, I had purposely meant to avoid any mention of the subject. Nor, during our stay in the place, had I ever made aught but the scantiest reference to it. You see, not only was Astley a man of great reserve, but also from the first I had perceived that Polina had made a great impression upon him, although he never spoke of her. But now, strangely enough, he had no sooner seated himself and bent his steely gaze upon me, than, for some reason or another, I felt moved to tell him everything – to speak to him of my love in all its phases. For an hour and a half did I discourse on the subject, and found it a pleasure to do so, even though this was the first occasion on which I had referred to the matter. Indeed, when, at certain moments, I perceived that my more ardent passages confused him, I purposely increased my ardour of narration. Yet one thing I regret: and that is that I made references to the Frenchman which were a little over-personal.

Mr. Astley sat without moving as he listened to me. Not a word nor a sound of any kind did he utter as he stared into my eyes. Suddenly, however, on my mentioning the Frenchman, he interrupted me, and inquired sternly whether I did right to speak of an extraneous matter (he had always been a strange man in his mode of propounding questions).

'No, I fear not,' I replied.

'And concerning this Marquis and Mlle. Polina you know nothing beyond surmise?'

Again I was surprised that such a categorical question should come from such a reserved individual.

'No, I know nothing *for certain* about them,' was my reply. 'No – nothing.'

'Then you have done very wrong to speak of them to me, or even to imagine things about them.'

'Quite so, quite so,' I interrupted in some astonishment. 'I admit that. Yet that is not the question.' Whereupon I related to him in detail the incident of two days ago. I spoke of Polina's outburst, of my encounter with the Baron, of my dismissal, of the General's extraordinary pusilla-nimity, and of the call which De Griers had that morning paid me. In conclusion, I showed Astley the note which I had lately received.

'What do you make of it?' I asked. 'When I met you I was just coming to ask you your opinion. For myself, I could have killed this Frenchman, and am not sure that I shall not do so even yet.'

'I feel the same about it,' said Mr. Astley. 'As for Mlle. Polina – well, you yourself know that, if necessity drives, one enters into relation with people whom one simply detests. Even between this couple there may be something which, though unknown to you, depends upon extraneous circumstances. For my own part, I think that you may reassure yourself – or at all events partially. And as for Mlle. Polina's proceedings of two days ago, they were, of course, strange; not because she can have meant to get rid of you, or to earn for you a thrashing from the Baron's cudgel (which, for some curious reason, he did not use, although he had it ready in his hands), but because such proceedings on the part of such – well, of such a refined lady as Mlle. Polina are, to say the least of it, unbecoming. But she cannot have guessed that you would carry out her absurd wish to the letter?'

'Do you know what?' suddenly I cried as I fixed Mr. Astley with my gaze. 'I believe that you have already heard the story from some one – very possibly from Mlle. Polina herself?'

In return he gave me an astonished stare.

'Your eyes look very fiery,' he said with a return of his former calm, 'and in them I can read suspicion. Now, you have no right whatever to be suspicious. It is not a right which I can for a moment recognize, and I absolutely refuse to answer your questions.'

'Enough! You need say no more,' I cried with a strange emotion at my heart, yet not altogether understanding what had aroused that emotion in my breast. Indeed, when, where, and how could Polina have chosen Astley to be one of her confidants? Of late I had come rather to overlook him in this connection, even though Polina had always been a riddle to me – so much so that now, when I had just permitted myself to tell my friend of my infatuation in all its aspects, I had found myself struck, during the very telling, with the fact that in my relations with her I

501

could specify nothing that was explicit, nothing that was positive. On the contrary, my relations had been purely fantastic, strange, and unreal; they had been unlike anything else that I could think of.

'Very well, very well,' I replied with a warmth equal to Astley's own. 'Then I stand confounded, and have no further opinions to offer. But you are a good fellow, and I am glad to know what you think about it all, even though I do not need your advice.'

Then, after a pause, I resumed:

'For instance, what reason should you assign for the General taking fright in this way? Why should my stupid clowning have led the world to elevate it into a serious incident? Even De Griers has found it necessary to put in his oar (and he only interferes on the most important occasions), and to visit me, and to address to me the most earnest supplications. Yes, *he*, De Griers, has actually been playing the suppliant to *me!* And, mark you, although he came to me as early as nine o'clock, he had ready-prepared in his hand Mlle. Polina's note. When, I would ask, was that note written? Mlle. Polina must have been aroused from sleep for the express purpose of writing it. At all events the circumstance shows that she is an absolute slave to the Frenchman, since she actually begs my pardon in the note – actually begs my pardon! Yet what is her personal concern in the matter? Why is she interested in it at all? Why, too, is the whole party so afraid of this precious Baron? And what sort of a business do you call it for the General to be going to marry Mlle. Blanche de Cominges? He told me last night that, because of the circumstance, he must "move with especial care at present." What is your opinion of it all? Your look convinces me that you know more about it than I do.'

Mr. Astley smiled and nodded.

'Yes, I think I *do* know more about it than you do,' he assented. 'The affair centres around this Mlle. Blanche. Of that I feel certain.'

'And what of Mlle. Blanche?' I cried impatiently (for in me there had dawned a sudden hope that this would enable me to discover something about Polina).

'Well, my belief is that at the present moment Mlle. Blanche has, in very truth, a special reason for wishing to avoid any trouble with the Baron and the Baroness. It might lead not only to some unpleasantness, but even to a scandal.'

'Oh, oh!'

'Also I may tell you that Mlle. Blanche has been in Roulettenberg before, for she was staying here three seasons ago. I myself was in the place at the time, and in those days Mlle. Blanche was not known as Mlle. de Cominges, nor was her mother, the Widow de Cominges, even in existence. In any case no one ever mentioned the latter. De Griers, too, had not materialized, and I am convinced that not only do the parties stand in no relation to one another, but also they have not long enjoyed one another's acquaintance. Likewise the *Marquisate* de Griers is of recent creation. Of that I have reason to be sure, owing to a certain circumstance. Even the name De Griers itself may be taken to be a new invention, seeing that I have a friend who once met the said "Marquis" under a different name altogether.'

'Yet he possesses a good circle of friends?'

'Possibly. Mlle. Blanche also may possess that. Yet it is not three years since she received from the local police, at the instance of the Baroness, an invitation to leave the town. And she left it.'

'But why?'

'Well, I must tell you that she first appeared here in company with an Italian – a prince of some sort, a man who bore an historic name (Barberini or something of the kind). The fellow was simply a mass of rings and diamonds – real diamonds, too – and the couple used to drive out in a marvellous carriage. At first Mlle. Blanche played trente et quarante with fair success, but, later, her luck took a marked change for the worse. I distinctly remember that in a single evening she lost an enormous sum. But worse was to ensue, for one fine morning her prince disappeared – horses, carriage, and all. Also, the hotel bill which he left unpaid was enormous. Upon this Mlle. Zelma (the name which she assumed after figuring as Madame Barberini) was in despair. She shrieked and howled all over the hotel, and even tore her clothes in her frenzy. In the hotel there was staying also a Polish count (you must know that *all* travelling Poles are counts!), and the spectacle of Mlle. Zelma tearing her clothes and, catlike, scratching her face with her beautiful, scented nails produced upon him a strong impression. So the pair had a talk together, and by luncheon time she was consoled. Indeed, that evening the couple entered the Casino arm in arm – Mlle. Zelma laughing loudly, according to her custom, and showing even more expansiveness in her manners than she had before shown. For instance, she thrust her way into the file of women roulette-players in the exact fashion of those ladies who, to clear a space for themselves at the tables, push their fellow-players roughly aside. Doubtless you have noticed them?'

'Yes, certainly.'

'Well, they are not worth noticing. To the annoyance of the decent public they are allowed to remain here – at all events such of them as daily change 4000 franc notes at the tables (though, as soon as ever these women cease to do so, they receive an invitation to depart). However, Mlle. Zelma continued to change notes of this kind, but her play grew more and more unsuccessful, despite the fact that such ladies' luck is frequently good, for they have a surprising amount of cash at their disposal. Suddenly the Count too disappeared, even as the Prince had done, and that same evening Mlle Zelma was forced to appear in the Casino alone. On this occasion no one offered her a greeting. Two days later she had come to the end of her resources; whereupon, after staking and losing her last louis d'or, she chanced to look around her, and saw standing by her side the Baron Burmergelm, who had been eyeing her with fixed disapproval. To his distaste, however, Mlle paid no attention, but, turning to him with her well-known smile, requested him to stake, on her behalf, ten louis on the red. Later that evening a complaint from the Baroness led the authorities to request Mlle not to re-enter the Casino. If you feel in any way surprised that I should know these petty and unedifying details, the reason is that I had them from a relative of mine who, later that evening, drove Mlle Zelma in his carriage from Roulettenberg to Spa. Now, mark you, Mlle wants to become Madame General, in order that, in future, she may be spared the receipt of such invitations from Casino authorities as she received three years ago. At present she is not playing; but that is only because, according to the signs, she is lending money to other players. Yes, that is a much more paying game. I even suspect that the unfortunate General is himself in her debt, as well as, perhaps, also De Griers. Or it may be that the latter has entered into a partnership with her. Consequently you yourself will see that, until the marriage shall have been consummated, Mlle would scarcely like to have the attention of the Baron and the Baroness drawn to herself. In short, to any one in her position, a scandal would be most detrimental. You form a member of the ménage of these people; wherefore any act of yours might cause such a scandal – and the more so since daily she appears in public arm in arm with the General or with Mlle Polina. *Now* do you understand?'

'No, I do not!' I shouted as I banged my fist down upon the table – banged it with such violence that a frightened waiter came running towards us. 'Tell me, Mr Astley, why, if you knew this history all along, and, consequently, always knew who this Mlle Blanche is, you never warned either myself or the General, nor, most of all, Mlle Polina (who is accustomed to appear in the Casino – in public everywhere – with Mlle Blanche)? How could you do it?'

'It would have done no good to warn you,' he replied quietly, 'for the reason that you could have effected nothing. Against what was I to warn you? As likely as not, the General knows more about Mlle Blanche even than I do; yet the unhappy man still walks about with her and Mlle Polina. Only yesterday I saw this Frenchwoman riding, splendidly mounted, with De Griers, while the General was careering in their wake on a roan horse. He had said, that morning, that his legs were hurting him, yet his riding-seat was easy enough. As he passed I looked at him, and the thought occurred to me that he was a man lost for ever. However, it is no affair of mine, for I have only recently had the happiness to make Mlle Polina's acquaintance. Also' – he added this as an afterthought – 'I have already told you that I do not recognize your right to ask me certain questions, however sincere be my liking for you.'

'Enough,' I said rising. 'To me it is as clear as day that Mlle Polina knows all about this Mlle Blanche, but cannot bring herself to part with her Frenchman; wherefore she consents also to be seen in public with Mlle Blanche. You may be sure that nothing else would ever have induced her either to walk about with this Frenchwoman or to send me a note not to touch the Baron. Yes, it is *there* that the influence lies before which everything in the world must bow! Yet she herself it was who launched me at the Baron! The devil take it, but I was left no choice in the matter.'

'You forget, in the first place, that this Mlle de Cominges is the General's inamorata, and, in the second place, that Mlle Polina, the General's step-daughter, has a younger brother and sister who, though they are the General's own children, are completely neglected by this madman, and robbed as well.'

'Yes, yes; that is so. For me to go and desert the children now would mean their total abandonment; whereas, if I remain, I should be able to defend their interests, and, perhaps, to save a moiety of their property. Yes, yes; that is quite true. And yet, and yet – Oh, I can well understand why they are all so interested in the General's mother!'

'In whom?' asked Mr Astley.

'In the old woman of Moscow who declines to die, yet concerning whom they are for ever expecting telegrams to notify the fact of her death.'

'Ah, then of course their interests centre around her. It is a question of succession. Let that but be settled, and the General will marry, Mlle Polina will be set free, and De Griers — '

'Yes, and De Griers?'

'Will be repaid his money, which is what he is now waiting for.'

'What? You think that he is waiting for *that*?'

'I know of nothing else,' asserted Mr Astley doggedly.

'But, I do, I do!' I shouted in my fury. 'He is waiting also for the old woman's will, for the reason that it awards Mlle Polina a dowry. As soon as ever the money is received, she will throw herself upon the Frenchman's neck. All women are like that. Even the proudest of them become abject slaves where marriage is concerned. What Polina is good for is to fall head over ears in love. That is *my* opinion. Look at her – especially when she is sitting alone, and plunged in thought. All this was pre-ordained and foretold, and is accursed. Polina could perpetrate any mad act. She – she – But who called me by name?' I broke off. 'Who is shouting for me? I heard some one calling in Russian, "Alexis Ivanovitch!" It was a woman's voice. Listen!'

At the moment we were approaching my hotel. We had left the café long ago, without even noticing that we had done so.

'Yes, I *did* hear a woman's voice calling, but whose I do not know. The some one was calling you in Russian. Ah! *Now* I can see whence the cries come. They come from that lady there – the one who is sitting on the settee, the one who has just been escorted to the verandah by a crowd of lacqueys. Behind her see that pile of luggage! She must have arrived by train.'

'But why should she be calling *me*? Hear her calling again! See! She is beckoning to us!'

'Yes, so she is,' assented Mr Astley.

'Alexis Ivanovitch, Alexis Ivanovitch! Good heavens, what a stupid fellow!' came in a despairing wail from the verandah.

We had almost reached the portico, and I was just setting foot upon the space before it, when my hands fell to my sides in limp astonishment, and my feet glued themselves to the pavement!

✦ NINE ✦

FOR ON THE TOPMOST TIER OF THE hotel verandah, after being carried up the steps in an armchair amid a bevy of footmen, maid-servants, and other menials of the hotel, headed by the landlord (that functionary had actually run out to meet a visitor who arrived with so much stir and din, attended by her own retinue, and accompanied by so great a pile of trunks and port-manteaux) – on the topmost tier of the verandah, I say, there was sitting – *the Grandmother*! Yes, it was *she* – rich, and imposing, and seventy-five years of age – Antonida Vassilievna Tarassevitcha, land-owner and *grande dame* of Moscow – the 'La Baboulenka' who had caused so many telegrams to be sent off and received – who had been dying, yet not dying – who had, in her own person, descended upon as even as snow might fall from the clouds! Though unable to walk, she had arrived borne aloft in an armchair (her mode of conveyance for the last five years), yet as brisk, aggressive, self-satisfied, bolt-upright, loudly imperious, and generally abusive as ever. In fact, she looked exactly as she had done on the only two occasions when I had seen her since my appointment to the General's household. Naturally enough, I stood petrified with astonishment. She had sighted me a hundred paces off Even while she was being carried along in her chair she had recognized me, and called me by name and surname (which as usual, after hearing once, she had remembered ever afterwards).

'And this is the woman whom they had thought to see in her grave after making her will!' I thought to myself. 'Yet she will outlive us, and every one else in the hotel. Good Lord! what is going to become of us now? What on earth is to happen to the General? She will turn the place upside down!'

'My good sir,' the old woman continued in a stentorian voice, 'what are you standing *there* for, with your eyes almost falling out of your head? Cannot you come and say how-do-you-do? Are you too proud to shake hands? Or do you not recognize me? Here, Potapitch!' she cried to an old servant who, dressed in a frock coat and white waistcoat, had a bald, red head (he was the chamberlain who always accompanied her on her journeys). 'Just think! Alexis Ivanovitch does not recognize me! They have buried me for good and all! Yes, and after sending hosts of telegrams to know if I were dead or not! Yes, yes, I have heard the whole story. I am very much alive, though, as you may see.'

'Pardon me, Antonida Vassilievna, 'I replied good humouredly as I recovered my presence of mind. '*I* have no reason to wish you ill. I am merely rather astonished to see you. Why should I not be so, seeing how unexpected — '

'*Why* should you be astonished? I just got into my chair, and came. Things are quiet enough in the train, for there is no one there to chatter. Have you been out for a walk?'

'Yes. I have just been to the Casino.'

'Oh? Well, it is quite nice here,' she went on as she looked about her. 'The place seems comfortable, and all the trees are out. I like it very well. Are your people at home? Is the General, for instance, indoors?'

'Yes; and probably all of them.'

'Do they observe the convenances, and keep up appearances? Such things always give one tone. I have heard that they are keeping a carriage, even as Russian gentlefolks ought to do. When abroad, our Russian people always cut a dash. Is Prascovia here too?'

'Yes. Polina Alexandrovna is here.'

'And the Frenchwoman? However, I will go and look for them myself. Tell me the nearest way to their rooms. Do *you* like being here?'

'Yes, I thank you, Antonida Vassilievna.'

'And you, Potapitch, go you and tell that fool of a landlord to reserve me a suitable suite of rooms. They must be handsomely decorated, and not too high up. Have my luggage taken up to them. But what are you tumbling over yourselves for? Why are you all tearing about? What scullions these fellows are! – Who is that with you?' she added to myself.

'A Mr. Astley,' I replied.

'And who is Mr. Astley?'

'A fellow-traveller, and my very good friend, as well as an acquaintance of the General's.'

'Oh, an Englishman? Then that is why he stared at me without even opening his lips. However, I like Englishmen. Now, take me upstairs, direct to their rooms. Where are they lodging?'

Madame was lifted up in her chair by the lacqueys, and I preceded her up the grand staircase. Our progress was exceedingly effective, for every one whom we met stopped to stare at the cortège. It happened that the hotel had the reputation of being the best, the most expensive, and the most aristocratic in all the spa, and at every turn on the staircase or in the corridors we encountered fine ladies and important-looking Englishmen – more than one of whom hastened downstairs to inquire of the awestruck landlord who the newcomer was. To all such questions he returned the same answer – namely, that the old lady was an influential foreigner, a Russian, a Countess, and a *grande dame*, and that she had taken the suite which, during the previous week, had been tenanted by the Grande Duchesse de N. Meanwhile the cause of the sensation – the Grandmother – was being borne aloft in her armchair. Every person whom she met she scanned with an inquisitive eye, after first of all interrogating me about him or her at the top of her voice. She was stout of figure, and, though she could not leave her chair, one felt, the moment that one first looked at her, that she was also tall of stature. Yet her back was as straight as a board, and never did she lean back in her seat. Also, her large grey head, with its keen, rugged features, remained always erect as she glanced about her in an imperious, challenging sort of way, with looks and gestures that clearly were unstudied. Though she had reached her seventy-sixth year, her face was still fresh, and her teeth had not decayed. Lastly, she was dressed, in a black silk gown and white mobcap.

'She interests me tremendously,' whispered Mr. Astley as, still smoking, he walked by my side. Meanwhile I was reflecting that probably the old lady knew all about the telegrams, and even about De Griers, though little or nothing about Mlle. Blanche. I said as much to Mr. Astley.

But what a frail creature is man! No sooner was my first surprise abated than I found myself rejoicing in the shock which we were about to administer to the General. So much did the thought inspire me that I marched ahead in the gayest of fashions.

Our party was lodging on the third floor. Without knocking at the door, or in any way announcing our presence, I threw open the portals, and the Grandmother was borne through them in triumph. As though of set purpose, the whole party chanced at that moment to be assembled in the General's study. The time was eleven o'clock, and it seemed that an outing of some sort (at which a portion of the party were to drive in carriages, and others to ride on horseback, accompanied by one or two extraneous acquaintances) was being planned. The General was present, and also Polina, the children, the latter's nurses, De Griers, Mlle. Blanche (attired in a riding-habit), her mother, the young Prince, and a learned German whom I beheld for the first time. Into the midst of this assembly the lacqueys conveyed Madame in her chair, and set her down within three paces of the General! Good heavens! Never shall I forget the spectacle which ensued! Just before our entry the General had been holding forth to the company, with De Griers in support of him. I may also mention that, for the last two or three days, Mlle. Blanche and De Griers had been making a great deal of the young Prince, under the very nose of the poor General. In short, the company, though decorous and conventional, was in a gay, familiar mood. But no sooner did the Grandmother appear than the General stopped dead in the middle of a word, and, with jaw dropping, stared hard at the old lady – his eyes almost starting out of his head, and his expression as spellbound as though he had just seen a basilisk. In return the Grandmother stared at him silently and without moving – though with a look of mingled challenge, triumph, and ridicule in her eyes. For ten seconds did the pair remain thus eyeing one another, amid the profound silence of the company; and even De Griers sat petrified – an extraordinary look of uneasiness dawning on his face. As for Mlle. Blanche, she too stared wildly at the Grandmother, with eyebrows raised and her lips parted; while the Prince and the German savant contemplated the tableau in profound amazement. Only Polina looked anything but perplexed or surprised. Presently, however, she too turned as white as a sheet, and then reddened to her temples. Truly the Grandmother's arrival seemed to be a catastrophe for everybody! For my own part, I stood looking from the Grandmother to the company, and back again, while Mr. Astley, as usual, remained in the background, and gazed calmly and decorously at the scene.

'Well, here I am – and instead of a telegram, too!' the Grandmother at last ejaculated, to dissipate the silence. 'What? You were not expecting me?'

'Antonida Vassilievna! O my dearest mother! But how on earth did you, did you – ?' The mutterings of the unhappy General died away.

I verily believe that if the Grandmother had held her tongue a few seconds longer she would have had a stroke.

'How on earth did I *what*?' she exclaimed. 'Why, I just got into the train and came here. What else is the railway meant for? But you thought that I had turned up my toes and left my property to the lot of you. Oh, I know *all* about the telegrams which you have been dispatching. They must have cost you a pretty sum, I should think, for telegrams are not sent from abroad for nothing. Well, I picked up my heels, and came here. Who is the Frenchman? Monsieur de Griers, I suppose?'

'Oui, madame,' assented De Griers. 'Et, croyez, je suis si enchanté! Votre santé – c'est un miracle de vous voir ici. Une surprise charmante!'

'Just so. "Charmante" I happen to know you as a mountebank, and therefore trust you no more than *this*.' She indicated her little finger. 'And who is *that*?' she went on, turning towards Mlle. Blanche. Evidently the Frenchwoman looked so becoming in her riding-habit, with her whip in her hand, that she had made an impression upon the old lady. 'Who is that woman there?'

'Mlle. de Cominges,' I said. 'And this is her mother, Madame de Cominges. They also are staying in the hotel'.

'Is the daughter married?' asked the old lady, without the least semblance of ceremony.

'No,' I replied as respectfully as possible, but under my breath.

'Is she good company?'

I failed to understand the question.

'I mean, is she or is she not a bore? Can she speak Russian? When this De Griers was in Moscow he soon learnt to make himself understood.'

I explained to the old lady that Mlle. Blanche had never visited Russia.

'Bonjour, then,' said Madame, with sudden brusquerie.

'Bonjour, madame,' replied Mlle. Blanche with an elegant, ceremonious bow as, under cover of an unwonted modesty, she endeavoured to express, both in face and figure, her extreme surprise at such strange behaviour on the part of the Grandmother.

'How the woman sticks out her eyes at me! How she mows and minces!' was the Grandmother's comment. Then she turned suddenly to the General, and continued: 'I have taken up my abode here, so am going to be your next-door neighbour. Are you glad to hear that, or are you not?'

'My dear mother, believe me when I say that I am sincerely delighted,' returned the General, who had now, to a certain extent, recovered his senses; and inasmuch as, when occasion arose, he could speak with fluency, gravity, and a certain effect, he set himself to be expansive in his remarks, and went on: 'We have been so dismayed and upset by the news of your indisposition! We have received such hopeless telegrams about you! Then suddenly — '

'Fibs, fibs!' interrupted the Grandmother.

'How on earth, too, did you come to decide upon the journey?' continued the General, with raised voice as he hurried to overlook the old lady's last remark. 'Surely, at your age, and in your present state of health, the thing is so unexpected that our surprise is at least intelligible. However, I am glad to see you (as indeed, are we all' – he said this with a dignified, yet conciliatory, smile), 'and will use my best endeavours to render your stay here as pleasant as possible.'

'Enough! All this is empty chatter. You are talking the usual nonsense. I shall know quite well how to spend my time. How did I come to undertake the journey, you ask? Well, is there anything so very surprising about it? It was done quite simply. What is every one going into ecstasies about? – How do you do, Prascovia? What are *you* doing here?'

'And how are *you*, Grandmother?' replied Polina, as she approached the old lady. 'Were you long on the journey?'

'The most sensible question that I have yet been asked! Well, you shall hear for yourself how it all happened. I lay and lay, and was doctored and doctored; until at last I drove the physicians from me, and called in an apothecary from Nicolai who had cured an old woman of a malady similar to my own – cured her merely with a little hayseed. Well, he did me a great deal of good, for on the third day I broke into a sweat, and was able to leave my bed. Then my German doctors held another consultation, put on their spectacles, and told me that if I would go abroad, and take a course of the waters, the indisposition would finally pass away. "Why should it not?" I thought to myself. So I had things got ready, and on the following day – a Friday – set out for here. I occupied a special compartment in the train, and wherever I had to change I found at the station bearers who were ready to carry me for a few coppers. You have nice quarters here,' she went on as she glanced around the room. 'But where on earth did you get the money for them, my good sir? I thought that everything of yours had been mortgaged? This Frenchman alone must be your creditor for a good deal. Oh, I know all about it, all about it.'

'I – I am surprised at you, my dearest mother,' said the General in some confusion. 'I – I am greatly surprised. But I do not need any extraneous control of my finances. Moreover, my expenses do not exceed my income, and we — '

'They do not exceed it? Fie! Why, you are robbing your children of their last kopeck – you, their guardian!'

'After this,' said the General, completely taken aback, ' – after what you have just said, I do not know whether — '

'You do not know *what*? By heavens, are you *never* going to drop that roulette of yours? Are you going to whistle all your property away?'

This made such an impression upon the General that he almost choked with fury.

'Roulette, indeed? *I* play roulette? Really, in view of my position — Recollect what you are saying, my dearest mother. You must still be unwell.'

'Rubbish, rubbish!' she retorted. 'The truth is that you *cannot* be got away from that roulette. You are simply telling lies. This very day I mean to go and see for myself what roulette is like. Prascovia, tell me what there is to be seen here; and do you, Alexis Ivanovitch, show me everything; and do you, Potapitch, make me a list of excursions. What *is* there to be seen?' again she inquired of Polina.

'There is a ruined castle, and the Schlangenberg.'

'The Schlangenberg? What is it? A forest?'

'No, a mountain on the summit of which there is a place fenced off. From it you can get a most beautiful view.'

'Could a chair be carried up that mountain of yours?'

'Doubtless we could find bearers for the purpose.' I interposed.

At this moment Theodosia, the nursemaid, approached the old lady with the General's children.

'No, I *don't* want to see them,' said the Grandmother. 'I hate kissing children, for their noses are always wet. How are you getting on, Theodosia?'

'I am very well, thank you, Madame,' replied the nursemaid. 'And how is your ladyship? We have been feeling so anxious about you!'

'Yes, I know, you simple soul. – But who are those other guests?' the old lady continued, turning again to Polina. 'For instance, who is that old rascal in the spectacles?'

'Prince Nilski, Grandmamma,' whispered Polina.

'Oh, a Russian? Why, I had no idea that he could understand me! Surely he did not hear what I said? As for Mr. Astley, I have seen him already, and I see that he is here again. How do you do?' she added to the gentleman in question.

Mr. Astley bowed in silence.

'Have you *nothing* to say to me?' the old lady went on. 'Say something, for goodness' sake! Translate to him, Polina.'

'Polina did so.

'I have only to say,' replied Mr. Astley gravely, but also with alacrity, 'that I am indeed glad to see you in such good health.' This was interpreted to the Grandmother, and she seemed much gratified.

'How well English people know how to answer one!' she remarked. 'That is why I like them so much better than French. Come here,' she added to Mr. Astley. 'I will try not to bore you too much. Polina, translate to him that I am staying in rooms on a lower floor. Yes, on a lower floor,' she repeated to Astley, pointing downwards with her finger.

Astley looked pleased at receiving the invitation.

Next the old lady scanned Polina from head to foot with minute attention.

'I could almost have liked you, Prascovia,' suddenly she remarked, 'for you are a nice girl – the best of the lot. You have some character about you. I too have character. Turn round. Surely that is not false hair that you are wearing?'

'No, Grandmamma. It is my own.'

'Well, well. I do not like the stupid fashions of to-day. You are very good looking. I should have fallen in love with you if I had been a man. Why do you not get married? It is time now that I was going. I want to walk, yet I always have to ride. Are you still in a bad temper?' she added to the General.

'No, indeed,' rejoined the now mollified General. 'I quite understand that at your time of life — '

'Cette vieille est tombée en enfance,' De Griers whispered to me.

'But I want to look round a little,' the old lady added to the General. 'Will you lend me Alexis Ivanovitch for the purpose?'

'As much as you like. But I myself – yes, and Polina and Monsieur de Griers too – we all of us hope to have the pleasure of escorting you.'

'Mais, madame, cela sera un plaisir,' De Griers commented with a bewitching smile.

' "Plaisir" indeed! Why, I look upon you as a perfect fool, monsieur.' Then she remarked to the General: 'I am not going to let *you* have any of my money. I must be off to my rooms now, to see what they are like. Afterwards we will look round a little. Lift me up.'

Again the Grandmother was borne aloft, and carried down the staircase amid a perfect bevy of followers – the General walking as though he had been hit over the head with a cudgel, and De Griers seeming to be plunged in thought. Endeavouring to be left behind, Mlle. Blanche next thought better of it, and followed the rest, with, in her wake, the Prince. Only the German savant and Madame de Cominges did not leave the General's apartments.

✦ TEN ✦

AT SPAS – AND, PROBABLY, ALL over Europe – 'hotel landlords and managers are guided in their allotment of rooms to visitors, not so much by the wishes and requirements of those visitors, as by their personal estimate of the same. It may also be said that these landlords and managers seldom make a mistake. To the Grandmother, however, our landlord, for some reason or another, allotted such a sumptuous suite that he fairly overreached himself; for he assigned her a suite consisting of four magnificently appointed rooms, with bathroom, servants' quarters, a separate room for her maid, and so on. In fact, during the previous week the suite had been occupied by no less a personage than a Grand Duchess: which circumstance was duly explained to the new occupant, as an excuse for raising the price of these apartments. The Grandmother had herself carried – or, rather, wheeled – through each room in turn, in order that she might subject the whole to a close and attentive scrutiny, while the landlord – an elderly, bald-headed man – walked respectfully by her side.

What every one took the Grandmother to be I do not know, but it appeared, at least, that she was accounted a person not only of great importance, but also, and still more, of great wealth; and without delay they entered her in the hotel register as 'Madame la générale, princesse de Tarassevitcheva,' although she had never been a princess in her life. Her retinue, her reserved compartment in the train, her pile of unnecessary trunks, portmanteaux, and strong-boxes, all helped to increase her prestige; while her wheeled chair, her sharp tone and voice, her eccentric questions (put with an air of the most overbearing and unbridled imperiousness), her whole figure – upright, rugged, and commanding as it was – completed the general awe in which she was held. As she inspected her new abode she ordered her chair to be stopped at intervals in order that, with finger extended towards some article of furniture, she might ply the respectfully smiling, yet secretly apprehensive, landlord with unexpected questions. She addressed them to him in French, although her pronunciation of the language was so bad that sometimes I had to translate them. For the most part, the landlord's answers were unsatisfactory, and failed to please her; nor were the questions themselves of a practical nature, but related, generally, to God knows what.

For instance, on one occasion she halted before a picture which, a poor copy of a well-known original, had a mythological subject.

'Of whom is this a portrait?' she inquired.

The landlord explained that it was probably that of a countess.

'But how know you that?' the old lady retorted. 'You live here, yet you cannot say for certain! And why is the picture there at all? And why do its eyes look so crooked?'

To all these questions the landlord could return no satisfactory reply, despite his floundering endeavours.

'The blockhead!' exclaimed the Grandmother in Russian.

Then she proceeded on her way – only to repeat the same story in front of a Saxon statuette which she had sighted from afar, and had commanded, for some reason or another, to be brought to her. Finally she inquired of the landlord what was the value of the carpet in her bedroom, as well as where the said carpet had been manufactured; but the landlord could do no more than promise to make inquiries.

'What donkeys these people are!' she commented. Next, she turned her attention to the bed.

'What a huge counterpane!' she exclaimed. 'Turn it back, please.' The lacqueys did so.

'Further yet, further yet,' the old lady cried. 'Turn it *right* back. Also, take off those pillows and bolsters, and lift up the feather bed.'

The bed was opened for her inspection.

'Mercifully it contains no bugs,' she remarked. 'Pull off the whole thing, and then put on my own pillows and sheets. The place is too luxurious for an old woman like myself. It is too large for any one person. Alexis Ivanovitch, come and see me whenever you are not teaching your pupils.'

'After to-morrow I shall no longer be in the General's service,' I replied, 'but merely living in the hotel on my own account.'

'Why so?'

'Because, the other day, there arrived from Berlin a German and his wife – persons of some importance; and it chanced that, when taking a walk, I spoke to them in German without having properly compassed the Berlin accent.'

'Indeed?'

'Yes: and this action on my part the Baron held to be an insult, and complained about it to the General, who yesterday dismissed me from his employ.'

'But I suppose you must have threatened that precious Baron, or something of the kind? However, even if you did so, it was a matter of no moment.'

'No, I did not. The Baron was the aggressor by raising his stick at me.'

515

Upon that the Grandmother turned sharply to the General.

'What? You permitted yourself to treat your tutor thus, you nincompop, and to dismiss him from his post? You are a blockhead – an utter blockhead! I can see that clearly.'

'Do not alarm yourself, my dear mother,' the General replied with a lofty air – an air in which there was also a tinge of familiarity. 'I am quite capable of managing my own affairs. Moreover, Alexis Ivanovitch has not given you a true account of the matter.'

'What did you do next?' The old lady inquired of me.

'I wanted to challenge the Baron to a duel,' I replied as modestly as possible; 'but the General protested against my doing so.'

'And *why* did you so protest?' she inquired of the General. Then she turned to the landlord, and questioned him as to whether *he* would not have fought a duel, if challenged. 'For,' she added, 'I can see no difference between you and the Baron; nor can I bear that German visage of yours.' Upon this the landlord bowed and departed, though he could not have understood the Grandmother's compliment.

'Pardon me, Madame,' the General continued with a sneer; 'but are duels really feasible?'

'Why not? All men are crowing cocks, and that is why they quarrel. *You*, though, I perceive, are a blockhead – a man who does not even know how to carry his breeding. Lift me up. Potapitch, see to it that you always have *two* bearers ready. Go and arrange for their hire. But we shall not require more than two, for I shall need only to be carried upstairs. On the level or in the street I can be *wheeled* along. Go and tell them that, and pay them in advance, so that they may show me some respect. You too, Potapitch, are always to come with me, and *you*, Alexis Ivanovitch, are to point out to me this Baron as we go along, in order that I may get a squint at the precious "Von." And where is that roulette played?'

I explained to her that the game was carried on in the salons of the Casino; whereupon there ensued a string of questions as to whether there were many such salons, whether many people played in them, whether those people played a whole day at a time, and whether the game was managed according to fixed rules. At length I thought it best to say that the most advisable course would be for her to go and see it for herself, since a mere description of it would be a difficult matter.

'Then take me straight there,' she said; 'and do you walk on in front of me, Alexis Ivanovitch.'

'What, mother? Before you have so much as rested from your journey?' the General inquired with some solicitude. Also, for some reason which I could not divine, he seemed to be growing nervous; and, indeed, the whole party was evincing signs of confusion, and exchanging glances with one another. Probably they were thinking that it would be a ticklish – even an embarrassing – business to accompany the Grandmother to the Casino, where, very likely, she would perpetrate further eccentricities, and in public too! Yet on their own initiative they had offered to escort her!

'Why should I rest?' she retorted. 'I am not tired, for I have been sitting still these past five days. Let us see what your medicinal springs and waters are like, and where they are situated. What, too, about that, that – what did you call it, Prascovia? – oh, about that mountain top?'

'Yes, we are going to see it, Grandmamma.'

'Very well. Is there anything else for me to see here?'

'Yes; quite a number of things,' Polina forced herself to say.

'Martha, *you* must come with me as well,' went on the old lady to her maid.

'No, no, mother!' ejaculated the General. 'Really she cannot come. They would not admit even Potapitch to the Casino.'

'Rubbish! Because she is my servant, is that a reason for turning her out? Why, she is only a human being like the rest of us; and as she has been travelling for a week she might like to look about her. With whom else could she go out but myself? She would never dare to show her nose in the street alone.'

'But, mother — '

'Are you ashamed to be seen with me? Stop at home, then, and you will be asked no questions. A pretty General *you* are, to be sure! I am a general's widow myself. But, after all, why should I drag the whole party with me? I will go and see the sights with only Alexis Ivanovitch as my escort.'

De Griers strongly insisted that *every one* ought to accompany her. Indeed, he launched out into a perfect shower of charming phrases concerning the pleasure of acting as her cicerone, and so forth. Every one was touched with his words.

'Mais elle est tombée en enfance,' he added aside to the General. 'Seule, elle fera des bêtises.' More than this I could not overhear, but he seemed to have got some plan in his mind, or even to be feeling a slight return of his hopes.

The distance to the Casino was about half a verst, and our route led us through the Chestnut Avenue until we reached the square directly fronting the building. The General, I could see, was a trifle reassured by the fact that, though our progress was distinctly eccentric in its nature, it was, at least, correct and orderly. As a matter of fact, the spectacle of a person who is unable to walk is not anything to excite surprise at a spa. Yet it was clear that the General had a great fear of the Casino itself: for why should a person who had lost the use of her limbs – more especially an old woman – be going to rooms which were set apart only for roulette? On either side of the wheeled chair walked Polina and Mlle. Blanche – the latter smiling, modestly jesting, and, in short, making herself so agreeable to the Grandmother that in the end the old lady relented towards her. On the other side of the chair Polina had to answer an endless flow of petty questions – such as 'Who was it passed just now?' 'Who is that coming along?' 'Is the town a large one?' 'Are the public gardens extensive?' 'What sort of trees are those?' 'What is the name of those hills?' 'Do I see eagles flying yonder?' 'What is that absurd-looking building?' and so forth. Meanwhile Astley whispered to me, as he walked by my side, that he looked for much to happen that morning. Behind the old lady's chair marched Potapitch and Martha – Potapitch in his frockcoat and white waistcoat, with a cloak over all, and the forty-year-old and rosy, but slightly grey-headed, Martha in a mobcap, cotton dress, and squeaking shoes. Frequently the old lady would twist herself round to converse with these servants. As for De Griers, he spoke as though he had made up his mind to do something (though it is also possible that he spoke in this manner merely in order to hearten the General, with whom he appeared to have held a conference). But, alas, the Grandmother had uttered the fatal words, 'I am not going to give you any of my money;' and though De Griers might regard these words lightly, the General knew his mother better. Also, I noticed that De Griers and Mlle. Blanche were still exchanging looks; while of the Prince and the German savant I lost sight at the end of the Avenue, where they had turned back and left us.

Into the Casino we marched in triumph. At once, both in the person of the commissionaire and in the persons of the footmen, there sprang to life the same reverence as had arisen in the lacqueys of the hotel. Yet it was not without some curiosity that they eyed us. Without loss of time the Grandmother gave orders that she should be wheeled through every room in the establishment; of which apartments she praised a few, while to others she remained indifferent. Concerning everything, however, she asked questions. Finally we reached the gaming-salons, where a lacquey who was acting as guard over the doors flung them open as though he were a man possessed.

The Grandmother's entry into the roulette-salon produced a profound impression upon the public. Around the tables, and at the further end of the room, where the trente-et-quarante table was set out, there may have been gathered from 150 to 200 gamblers, ranged in several rows. Those who had succeeded in pushing their way to the tables were standing with their feet firmly planted, in order to avoid having to give up their places until they should have finished their game (since merely to stand looking

on – thus occupying a gambler's place for nothing – was not permitted).
True, chairs were provided around the tables, but few players made use
of them – more especially if there was a large attendance of the general
public; since to stand allowed of a closer approach, and therefore of
greater facilities for calculation and staking. Behind the foremost row
were herded a second and a third row of people awaiting their turn; but
sometimes their impatience led these people to stretch a hand through
the first row, in order to deposit their stakes. Even third-row individuals
would dart forward to stake; whence seldom did more than five or ten
minutes pass without a scene over disputed money arising at one or
another end of the table. On the other hand, the police of the Casino were
an able body of men; and though to escape the crush was an impossibility,
however much one might wish it, the eight croupiers apportioned to each
table kept an eye upon the stakes, performed the necessary reckoning,
and decided disputes as they arose. In the last resort they always called
in the Casino police, and the disputes would immediately come to an
end. Policemen were stationed about the Casino in ordinary costume,
and mingled with the spectators so as to make it impossible to recognize
them. In particular they kept a look-out for pickpockets and swindlers,
who simply swarmed in the roulette salons, and reaped a rich harvest.
Indeed, in every direction money was being filched from pockets or
purses – though, of course, if the attempt miscarried, a great uproar
ensued. One had only to approach a roulette table, and begin to play, and
then openly grab some one else's winnings, for a din to be raised, and the
thief to start vociferating that the stake was *his*; and if the coup had been
carried out with sufficient skill, and the witnesses wavered at all in their
testimony, the thief would as likely as not succeed in getting away with
the money, provided that the sum was not a large one – not large enough
to have attracted the attention of the croupiers or some fellow-player.
Moreover, if it were a stake of insignificant size, its true owner would
sometimes decline to continue the dispute, rather than become involved
in a scandal. Conversely, if the thief was detected he was ignominiously
expelled from the building.

Upon all this the Grandmother gazed with open-eyed curiosity; and,
on some thieves happening to be turned out of the place, she was
delighted. Trente-et-quarante interested her but little; she preferred roulette, with its ever-revolving wheel. At length she expressed a wish to
view the game closer; whereupon in some mysterious manner the lacqueys and other officious agents (especially one or two ruined Poles of
the kind who keep offering their services to successful gamblers and
foreigners in general) at once found and cleared a space for the old lady
among the crush, at the very centre of one of the tables, and next to the

chief croupier; after which they wheeled her chair thither. Upon this a number of visitors who were not playing, but only looking on (particularly some Englishmen with their families), pressed closer forward towards the table, in order to watch the old lady from among the ranks of the gamblers. Many a lorgnette I saw turned in her direction, and the croupiers' hopes rose high that such an eccentric player was about to provide them with something out of the common. An old lady of seventy-five years who, though unable to walk, desired to play was not an everyday phenomenon. I too pressed forward towards the table, and ranged myself by the Grandmother's side; while Martha and Potapitch remained somewhere in the background among the crowd, and the General, Polina, and De Griers, with Mlle. Blanche, also remained hidden among the spectators.

At first the old lady did no more than watch the gamblers, and ply me, in a half-whisper, with sharp-spoken questions as to who was so-and-so. Especially did her favour light upon a very young man who was plunging heavily, and had won (so it was whispered) as much as 40,000 francs, which were lying before him on the table in a heap of gold and banknotes. His eyes kept flashing, and his hands shaking; yet all the while he staked without any sort of calculation – just what came to his hand, as he kept winning and winning, and raking and raking in his gains. Around him lacqueys fussed – placing chairs just behind where he was standing, and clearing the spectators from his vicinity, so that he should have more room, and not be crowded – the whole done, of course, in expectation of a generous largesse. From time to time other gamblers would hand him part of their winnings – being glad to let him stake for them as much as his hand could grasp; while beside him stood a Pole in a state of violent, but respectful, agitation, who, also in expectation of a generous largesse, kept whispering to him at intervals (probably telling him what to stake, and advising and directing his play). Yet never once did the player throw him a glance as he staked and staked, and raked in his winnings. Evidently the player in question was dead to all besides.

For a few minutes the Grandmother watched him.

'Go and tell him,' suddenly she exclaimed with a nudge at my elbow, ' – go and tell him to stop, and to take his money with him, and go home. Presently he will be losing – yes, losing everything that he has now won.' She seemed almost breathless with excitement. 'Where is Potapitch?' she continued. 'Send Potapitch to speak to him. No; *you* must tell him, *you* must tell him,' – here she nudged me again – 'for I have not the least notion where Potapitch is. Sortez, sortez,' she shouted to the young man, until I leant over in her direction and whispered in her ear that no shouting was allowed, nor even loud speaking, since to do so disturbed the calculations of the players, and might lead to our being ejected.

'How provoking?' she retorted. 'Then the young man is done for! I suppose he *wishes* to be ruined. Yet I could not bear to see him have to return it all. What a fool the fellow is!' – and the old lady turned sharply away.

On the left, among the players at the other half of the table, a young lady was playing, with, beside her, a dwarf. Who the dwarf may have been – whether a relative or a person whom she took with her to act as a foil – I do not know; but I had noticed her there on previous occasions, since, every day, she entered the Casino at once o'clock precisely, and departed at two – thus playing for exactly one hour. Being well-known to the attendants, she always had a seat provided for her; and, taking some gold and a few thousand-franc notes out of her pocket – would begin quietly, coldly, and after much calculation, to stake, and mark down the figures in pencil on a paper, as though striving to work out a system according to which, at given moments, the odds might group themselves. Always she staked large coins, and either lost or won one, two, or three thousand francs a day, but not more; after which she would depart. The Grandmother took a long look at her.

'*That* woman is not losing,' she said. 'To whom does she belong? Do you know her? Who is she?'

'She is, I believe, a Frenchwoman,' I replied.

'Ah! A bird of passage, evidently. Besides, I can see that she has her shoes polished. Now, explain to me the meaning of each round in the game, and the way in which one ought to stake.'

Upon this I set myself to explain the meaning of all the combinations – of 'rouge et noir,' of 'pair et impair,' of 'manque et passe,' with, lastly, the different values in the system of numbers. The Grandmother listened attentively, took notes, put questions in various forms, and laid the whole thing to heart. Indeed, since an example of each system of stakes kept constantly occurring, a great deal of information could be assimilated with ease and celerity. The Grandmother was vastly pleased.

'But what is zero?' she inquired. 'Just now I heard the flaxen-haired croupier call out "zero!" And why does he keep raking in all the money that is on the table? To think that he should grab the whole pile for himself! What does zero mean?'

'Zero is what the bank takes for itself. If the wheel stops at that figure, everything lying on the table becomes the absolute property of the bank. Also, whenever the wheel has begun to turn, the bank ceases to pay out anything.'

'Then I should receive nothing if I were staking?'

'No; unless by any chance you had *purposely* staked on zero; in which case you would receive thirty-five times the value of your stake.'

'Why thirty-five times, when zero so often turns up? And if so, why do not more of these fools stake upon it?'

'Because the number of chances against its occurrence is thirty-six.'

'Rubbish! Potapitch, Potapitch! Come here, and I will give you some money.' The old lady took out of her pocket a tightly-clasped purse, and extracted from its depths a ten-gülden piece. 'Go at once, and stake that upon zero.'

'But, Madame, zero has only this moment turned up,' I remonstrated; 'wherefore it may not do so again for ever so long. Wait a little, and you may then have a better chance.'

'Rubbish! Stake, please.'

'Pardon me, but zero might not turn up again until, say, to-night, even though you had staked thousands upon it. If often happens so.'

'Rubbish, rubbish! Who fears the wolf should never enter the forest. What? We have lost? Then stake again.'

A second ten-gülden piece did we lose, and then I put down a third. The Grandmother could scarcely remain seated in her chair, so intent was she upon the little ball as it leapt through the notches of the ever-revolving wheel. However, the third ten-gülden piece followed the first two. Upon this the Grandmother went perfectly crazy. She could no longer sit still, and actually struck the table with her fist when the croupier cried out, 'Trente-six,' instead of the desiderated zero.

'To listen to him!' fumed the old lady. 'When will that accursed zero ever turn up? I cannot breathe until I see it. I believe that infernal croupier is *purposely* keeping it from turning up. Alexis Ivanovitch, stake *two* golden pieces this time. The moment we cease to strike, that cursed zero will come turning up, and we shall get nothing.'

'My good Madame — '

'Stake, stake! It is not *your* money.'

Accordingly I staked two ten-gülden pieces. The ball went hopping round the wheel until it began to settle through the notches. Meanwhile the Grandmother sat as though petrified, with my hand convulsively clutched in hers.

'Zero!' called the croupier.

'There! You see, you see!' cried the old lady, as she turned and faced me, wreathed in smiles. 'I told you so! It was the Lord God himself who suggested to me to stake those two coins. Now, how much ought I to receive? Why do they not pay it out to me? Potapitch! Martha! Where are they? What has become of our party? Potapitch, Potapitch!'

'Presently, Madame,' I whispered. 'Potapitch is outside, and they would decline to admit him to these rooms. See! You are being paid out your money. Pray take it.' The croupiers were making up a heavy packet of coins, sealed in blue paper, and containing fifty ten-gülden pieces, together with an unsealed packet containing another twenty. I handed the whole to the old lady in a money-shovel.

'Faites le jeu, messieurs! Faites le jeu, messieurs! Rien ne va plus,' proclaimed the croupier as once more he invited the company to stake, and prepared to turn the wheel.

'We shall be too late! He is going to spin again! Stake, stake!' The Grandmother was in a perfect fever. 'Do not hang back! Be quick!' She seemed almost beside herself, and nudged me as hard as she could.

'Upon what shall I stake, Madame?'

'Upon zero, upon zero! Again upon zero! Stake as much as ever you can. How much have we got? Seventy ten-gülden pieces? We shall not miss them, so stake twenty pieces at a time.'

'Think a moment, Madame. Sometimes zero does not turn up for two hundred rounds in succession. I assure you that you may lose all your capital.'

'You are wrong – utterly wrong. Stake, I tell you! What a chattering tongue you have! I know perfectly well what I am doing.' The old lady was shaking with excitement.

'But the rules do not allow of more than 120 gülden being staked upon zero at a time.'

'How "do not allow"? Surely you are wrong? Monsieur, monsieur — ' here she nudged the croupier who was sitting on her left, and preparing to spin – 'combien zero? Douze? Douze?'

I hastened to translate.

'Oui, Madame,' was the croupier's polite reply. 'No single stake must exceed four thousand florins. That is the regulation.'

'Then there is nothing else for it. We must risk 120 gülden.'

'Le jeu est fait!' the croupier called. The wheel revolved, and stopped at thirty. We had lost!

'Again, again, again! Stake again!' shouted the old lady. Without attempting to oppose her further, but merely shrugging my shoulders, I placed twelve more ten-gülden pieces upon the table. The wheel whirled around and around, with the Grandmother simply quaking as she watched its revolutions.

'Does she again think that zero is going to be the winning coup?' thought I as I stared at her in astonishment. Yet an absolute assurance of winning was shining on her face; she looked perfectly convinced that zero was about to be called again. At length the ball dropped off into one of the notches.

'Zero!' cried the croupier.

'Ah!!!' screamed the old lady as she turned to me in a whirl of triumph.

I myself was at heart a gambler. At that moment I became acutely conscious both of that fact and of the fact that my hands and knees were shaking, and that the blood was beating in my brain. Of course this was a rare occasion – an occasion on which zero had turned up no less than three times within a dozen rounds; yet in such an event there was nothing so very surprising, seeing that, only three days ago, I myself had been a witness to zero turning up *three times in succession*, so that one of the players who was recording the coups on paper was moved to remark that for several days past zero had never turned up at all!

With the Grandmother, as with any one who has won a very large sum, the management settled up with great attention and respect, since she was fortunate to have to receive no less than 4200 gülden. Of these gülden the odd 200 were paid her in gold, and the remainder in bank notes.

This time the old lady did not call for Potapitch; for that she was too preoccupied. Though not outwardly shaken by the event (indeed, she seemed perfectly calm) she was trembling inwardly from head to foot. At length, completely absorbed in the game, she burst out:

'Alexis Ivanovitch, did not the croupier just say that 4000 florins were the most that could be staked at any one time? Well, take these 4000, and stake them upon the red.'

To oppose her was useless. Once more the wheel revolved.

'Rouge!' proclaimed the croupier.

Again 4000 florins – in all 8000!

'Give me them,' commanded the Grandmother, 'and stake the other 4000 upon the red again.'

I did so.

'Rouge!' proclaimed the croupier.

'Twelve thousand!' cried the old lady. 'Hand me the whole lot. Put the gold into this purse here, and count the bank notes. Enough! Let us go home. Wheel my chair away.'

⇥ ELEVEN ⇤

THE CHAIR, WITH THE OLD LADY beaming in it, was wheeled away towards the doors at the further end of the salon, while our party hastened to crowd around her, and to offer her their congratulations. In fact, eccentric as was her conduct, it was also overshadowed by her triumph; with the result that the General no longer feared to be publicly compromised by being seen with such a strange woman, but, smiling in a condescending, cheerfully familiar way, as though he were soothing a child, he offered his greetings to the old lady. At the same time, both he and the rest of the spectators were visibly impressed. Everywhere people kept pointing to the Grandmother, and talking about her. Many people even walked beside her chair, in order to view her the better, while, at a little distance, Astley was carrying on a conversation on the subject with two English acquaintances of his. De Griers was simply overflowing with smiles and compliments, and a number of fine ladies were staring at the Grandmother as though she had been something curious.

'Quelle victoire!' exclaimed De Griers.

'Mais, Madame, c'était du feu!' added Mlle. Blanche with an elusive smile.

'Yes, I have won twelve thousand florins,' replied the old lady. 'And then there is all this gold. With it the total ought to come to nearly thirteen thousand. How much is that in Russian money? Six thousand roubles, I think?'

However, I calculated that the sum would exceed seven thousand roubles – or, at the present rate of exchange, even eight thousand.

'Eight thousand roubles! What a splendid thing! And to think of you simpletons sitting there and doing nothing! Potapitch! Martha! See what I have won!'

'How *did* you do it, Madame?' Martha exclaimed ecstatically. 'Eight thousand roubles!'

'And I am going to give you fifty gülden apiece. There they are.'

Potapitch and Martha rushed towards her to kiss her hand.

'And to each bearer also I will give a ten-gülden piece. Let them have it out of the gold, Alexis Ivanovitch. But why is this footman bowing to me, and that other man as well? Are they congratulating me? Well, let them have ten gülden apiece.'

'Madame la princesse – Un pauvre expatrié – Malheur continuel – Les princes russes sont si généreux!' said a man who for some time past had been hanging around the old lady's chair – a personage who, dressed in a shabby frockcoat, and coloured waistcoat, kept taking off his cap, and smiling pathetically.

'Give him ten gülden,' said the Grandmother. 'No, give him twenty. Now, enough of that, or I shall never get done with you all. Take a moment's rest, and then carry me away. Prascovia, I mean to buy a new dress for you to-morrow. Yes, and for you too, Mlle. Blanche. Please translate, Prascovia.'

'Merci, Madame,' replied Mlle. Blanche gratefully as she twisted her face into the mocking smile which usually she kept only for the benefit of De Griers and the General. The latter looked confused, and seemed greatly relieved when we reached the Avenue.

'How surprised Theodosia too will be!' went on the Grandmother (thinking of the General's nursemaid). 'She, like yourselves, shall have the price of a new gown. Here, Alexis Ivanovitch! Give that beggar something' (a crooked-backed ragamuffin had approached to stare at us).

'But perhaps he is *not* a beggar – only a rascal,' I replied.

'Never mind, never mind. Give him a gülden.'

I approached the beggar in question, and handed him the coin. Looking at me in great astonishment, he silently accepted the gülden, while from his person there proceeded a strong smell of liquor.

'Have you never tried your luck, Alexis Ivanovitch?'

'No, Madame.'

'Yet just now I could see that you were burning to do so?'

'I *do* mean to try my luck presently.'

'Then stake everything upon zero. You have seen how it ought to be done? How much capital do you possess?'

'Two hundred gülden, Madame.'

'Not very much. See here; I will lend you five hundred if you wish. Take this purse of mine.' With that she added sharply to the General: 'But *you* need not expect to receive any.'

This seemed to upset him, but he said nothing, and De Griers contented himself by scowling.

'Que diable!' he whispered to the General. 'C'est une terrible vieille.'

'Look! Another beggar, another beggar!' exclaimed the Grandmother. 'Alexis Ivanovitch, go and give him a gülden.'

As she spoke I saw approaching us a greyheaded old man with a wooden leg – a man who was dressed in a blue frockcoat and carrying a staff. He looked like an old soldier. As soon as I tendered him the coin he fell back a step or two, and eyed me threateningly.

'Was ist der Teufel!' he cried, and appended thereto a round dozen of oaths.

'The man is a perfect fool!' exclaimed the Grandmother, waving her hand. 'Move on now, for I am simply famished. When we have lunched we will return to that place.'

'What?' cried I. 'You are going to play *again*?'

'What else do you suppose?' she retorted. 'Are you going only to sit here, and grow sour, and let me look at you?'

'Madame,' said De Griers confidentially, 'les chances peuvent tourner. Une seule mauvaise chance, et vous perdrez tout – surtout avec votre jeu. C'était terrible!'

'Oui; vous perdrez absolument,' put in Mlle. Blanche.

'What has that got to do with *you*?' retorted the old lady. 'It is not *your* money that I am going to lose; it is my own. And where is that Mr. Astley of yours?' she added to myself.

'He stayed behind in the Casino.'

'What a pity! He is such a nice sort of man!'

Arriving home, and meeting the landlord on the staircase, the Grandmother called him to her side, and boasted to him of her winnings – thereafter doing the same to Theodosia, and conferring upon her thirty gülden; after which she bid her serve luncheon. The meal over, Theodosia and Martha broke into a joint flood of ecstasy.

'I was watching you all the time, Madame,' quavered Martha, 'and I asked Potapitch what mistress was trying to do. And, my word! the heaps and *heaps* of money that were lying upon the table! Never in my life have I seen so much money. And there were gentlefolk around it, and other gentlefolk sitting down. So I asked Potapitch where all these gentry had come from; for, thought I, maybe the Holy Mother of God will help our mistress among them. Yes, I prayed for you, Madame, and my heart died within me, so that I kept trembling and trembling. The Lord be with her, I thought to myself; and in answer to my prayer He has now sent you what He has done! Even yet I tremble – I tremble to think of it all.'

'Alexis Ivanovitch,' said the old lady, 'after luncheon, – that is to say, about four o'clock – get ready to go out with me again. But in the meanwhile, good-bye. Do not forget to call a doctor, for I must take the waters. Now go and get rested a little.'

I left the Grandmother's presence in a state of bewilderment. Vainly I endeavoured to imagine what would become of our party, or what turn the affair would next take. I could perceive that none of the party had yet recovered their presence of mind – least of all the General. The factor of the Grandmother's appearance in place of the hourly expected telegram to announce her death (with, of course, resultant legacies) had so upset the whole scheme of intentions and projects that it was with a decided feeling of apprehension and growing paralysis that the conspirators viewed any future performances of the old lady at roulette. Yet this second factor was not quite so important as the first, since, though the Grandmother had twice declared that she did not intend to give the General any money, that declaration was not a complete ground for the abandonment of hope. Certainly De Griers, who, with the General, was up to the neck in the affair, had not wholly lost courage; and I felt sure that Mlle. Blanche also – Mlle. Blanche who was not only as deeply involved as the other two, but also expectant of becoming Madame General and an important legatee – would not lightly surrender the position, but would use her every resource of coquetry upon the old lady, in order to afford a contrast to the impetuous Polina, who was difficult to understand, and lacked the art of pleasing. Yet now, when the Grandmother had just performed an astonishing feat at roulette; now, when the old lady's personality had been so clearly and typically revealed as that of a rugged arrogant woman who was 'tombée en enfance'; now, when everything appeared to be lost, – why, now the Grandmother was as merry as a child which plays with thistle-down. 'Good Lord!' I thought with, may God forgive me, a most malicious smile, 'every ten-gülden piece which the Grandmother staked must have raised a blister on the General's heart, and maddened De Griers, and driven Mlle. de Cominges almost to frenzy with the sight of this spoon dangling before her lips.' Another factor is the circumstance that even when, overjoyed at winning, the Grandmother was distributing alms right and left, and taking every one to be a beggar, she again snapped out to the General that he was not going to be allowed any of her money: which meant that the old lady had quite made up her mind on the point, and was sure of it. Yes, danger loomed ahead.

All these thoughts passed through my mind during the few moments that, having left the old lady's rooms, I was ascending to my own room on the top storey. What most struck me was the fact that, though I had divined the chief, the stoutest, threads which united the various actors in the drama, I had, until now, been ignorant of the methods and secrets of the game. For Polina had never been completely open with me. Although, on occasions, it had happened that involuntarily, as it were, she had revealed to me something of her heart, I had noticed that in most cases – in fact, nearly always – she had either laughed away these revelations, or grown confused, or purposely imparted to them a false guise. Yes, she must have concealed a great deal from me. But I had a presentiment that now the end of this strained and mysterious situation was approaching. Another stroke, and all would be finished and exposed. Of my own fortunes, interested though I was in the affair, I took no account. I was in the strange position of possessing but two hundred gülden, of being at a loose end, of lacking both a post, the means of subsistence, a shred of hope, and any plans for the future, yet of caring nothing for these things. Had not my mind been so full of Polina, I should have given myself up to the comical piquancy of the impending dénouement, and laughed my fill at it. But the thought of Polina was torture to me. That her fate was settled I already had an inkling; yet *that* was not the thought which was giving me so much uneasiness. What I really wished for was to penetrate her secrets. I wanted her to come to me and say, 'I love you;' and if she would not so come, or if to hope that she would ever do so was an unthinkable absurdity – why, then there was nothing else for me to want. Even now I do not know what I am wanting. I feel like a man who has lost his way. I yearn but to be in her presence, and within the circle of her light and splendour – to be there now, and for ever, and for the whole of my life. More I do not know. How can I ever bring myself to leave her?

On reaching the third story of the hotel I experienced a shock. I was just passing the General's suite when something caused me to look round. Out of a door about twenty paces away there was coming Polina! She hesitated for a moment on seeing me, and then beckoned me to her.

'Polina Alexandrovna!'

'Hush! No so loud.'

'Something startled me just now,' I whispered, 'and I looked round, and saw you. Some electrical influence seems to emanate from your form.'

'Take this letter,' she went on with a frown (probably she had not even heard my words, she was so preoccupied), 'and hand it personally to Mr. Astley. Go as quickly as ever you can, please. No answer will be required. He himself — ' She did not finish her sentence.

'To Mr. Astley?' I asked, in some astonishment.

But she had vanished again.

Aha! So the two were carrying on a correspondence! However, I set off to search for Astley – first at his hotel, and then at the Casino, where I went the round of the salons in vain. At length, vexed, and almost in despair, I was on my way home when I ran across him among a troop of English ladies and gentlemen who had been out for a ride. Beckoning to him to stop, I handed him the letter. We had barely time even to look at one another, but I suspect that it was of set purpose that he restarted his horse so quickly.

Was jealousy, then, gnawing at me? At all events, I felt exceedingly depressed, despite the fact that I had no desire to ascertain what the correspondence was about. To think that *he* should be her confidant! 'My friend, mine own familiar friend!' passed through my mind. Yet *was* there any love in the matter? 'Of course not,' reason whispered to me. But reason goes for little on such occasions. I felt that the matter must be cleared up, for it was becoming unpleasantly complex.

I had scarcely set foot in the hotel when the commissionaire and the landlord (the latter issuing from his room for the purpose) alike informed me that I was being searched for high and low – that three separate messages to ascertain my whereabouts had come down from the General. When I entered his study I was feeling anything but kindly disposed. I found there the General himself, De Griers, and Mlle. Blanche, but not Mlle.'s mother, who was a person whom her reputed daughter used only for show purposes, since in all matters of business the daughter fended for herself, and it is unlikely that the mother knew anything about them.

Some very heated discussion was in progress, and meanwhile the door of the study was open – an unprecedented circumstance. As I approached the portals I could hear loud voices raised, for mingled with the pert, venomous accents of De Griers were Mlle. Blanche's excited, impudently abusive tongue and the General's plaintive wail as, apparently, he sought to justify himself in something. But on my appearance every one stopped speaking, and tried to put a better face upon matters. De Griers smoothed his hair, and twisted his angry face into a smile – into the mean, studiedly polite French smile which I so detested; while the downcast, perplexed General assumed an air of dignity – though only in a mechanical way. On the other hand, Mlle. Blanche did not trouble to conceal the wrath that was sparkling in her countenance, but bent her gaze upon me with an air of impatient expectancy. I may remark that hitherto she had treated me with absolute superciliousness, and, so far from answering my salutations, had always ignored them.

'Alexis Ivanovitch,' began the General in a tone of affectionate upbraiding, 'may I say to you that I find it strange, exceedingly strange, that — In short, your conduct towards myself and my family — In a word, your – er – extremely — '

'Eh! Ce n'est pas ça,' interrupted De Griers in a tone of impatience and contempt (evidently he was the ruling spirit of the conclave). 'Mon cher monsieur, notre général se trompe. What he means to say is that he warns you – he begs of you most earnestly – not to ruin him. I use the expression because — '

'Why? Why?' I interjected.

'Because you have taken upon yourself to act as guide to this, to this –

how shall I express it? – to this old lady, à cette pauvre terrible vieille. But she will only gamble away all that she has – gamble it away like thistle-down. You yourself have seen her play. Once she has acquired the taste for gambling, she will never leave the roulette-table, but, of sheer perversity and temper, will stake her all, and lose it. In cases such as hers a gambler can never be torn away from the game; and then – and then — '

'And then,' asseverated the General, 'you will have ruined my whole family. I and my family are her heirs, for she has no nearer relatives than ourselves. I tell you frankly that my affairs are in great – very great disorder; how much they are so you yourself are partially aware. If she should lose a large sum, or, may be, her whole fortune, what will become of us – of my children' (here the General exchanged a glance with De Griers) 'or of me?' (here he looked at Mlle. Blanche, who turned her head contemptuously away). 'Alexis Ivanovitch, I beg of you to save us.'

'Tell me, General, how am I to do so? On what footing do I stand here?'

'Refuse to take her about. Simply leave her alone.'

'But she would soon find some one else to take my place?'

'Ce n'est pas ça, ce n'est pas ça,' again interrupted De Griers. 'Que diable! Do not leave her alone so much as advise her, persuade her, draw her away. In any case do not let her gamble; find her some counter-attraction.'

'And how am I to do that? If only you would undertake the task, Monsieur de Griers!' I said this last as innocently as possible, but at once saw a rapid glance of excited interrogation pass from Mlle. Blanche to De Griers, while in the face of the latter also there gleamed something which he could not repress.

'Well, at the present moment she would refuse to accept my services,' said he with a gesture. 'But if, later — '

Here he gave Mlle. Blanche another glance which was full of meaning; whereupon she advanced towards me with a bewitching smile, and seized and pressed my hands. Devil take it, but how that devilish visage of hers could change! At the present moment it was a visage full of supplication, and as gentle in its expression as that of a smiling, roguish infant. Stealthily she drew me apart from the rest, as though the more completely to separate me from them; and though no harm came of her doing so – for it was merely a stupid manœuvre, and no more – I found the situation very unpleasant.

The General hastened to lend her his support.

'Alexis Ivanovitch,' he began, 'pray pardon me for having said what I did just now – for having said more than I meant to do. I beg and beseech you, I kiss the hem of your garment, as our Russian saying has it, for you, and only you, can save us. I and Mlle. de Cominges, we all of us beg of you — But you understand, do you not? Surely you understand?' and with his eyes he indicated Mlle. Blanche. Truly he was cutting a pitiful figure!

At this moment three low, respectful knocks sounded at the door; which, on being opened, revealed a chambermaid, with Potapitch behind her – come from the Grandmother to request that I should attend her in her rooms. 'She is in a bad humour,' added Potapitch.

The time was half-past three.

'My mistress was unable to sleep,' explained Potapitch; 'so, after tossing about for a while, she suddenly rose, called for her chair, and sent me to look for you. She is now in the verandah.'

'Quelle mégère!' exclaimed De Griers.

True enough, I found Madame in the hotel verandah – much put about at my delay, for she had been unable to contain herself until four o'clock.

'Lift me up,' she cried to the bearers, and once more we set out for the roulette-salons.

❧ TWELVE ❧

THE GRANDMOTHER WAS IN AN impatient, irritable frame of mind. Without doubt the roulette had turned her head, for she appeared to be indifferent to everything else, and, in general, seemed much distraught. For instance, she asked me no questions about objects *en route*, except that, when a sumptuous barouche passed us and raised a cloud of dust, she lifted her hand for a moment, and inquired, 'What was that?' Yet even then she did not appear to hear my reply, although at times her abstraction was interrupted by sallies and fits of sharp, impatient fidgeting. Again, when I pointed out to her the Baron and Baroness Burmergelm walking to the Casino, she merely looked at them in an absent-minded sort of way, and said with complete indifference, 'Ah!' Then, turning sharply to Potapitch and Martha, who were walking behind us, she rapped out:

'Why have *you* attached yourselves to the party? We are not going to take *you* with us every time. Go home at once.' Then, when the servants had pulled hasty bows and departed, she added to me: '*You* are all the escort I need.'

At the Casino the Grandmother seemed to be expected, for no time was lost in procuring her her former place beside the croupier. It is my opinion that though croupiers seem such ordinary, humdrum officials – men who care nothing whether the bank wins or loses – they are, in reality, anything but indifferent to the bank's losing, and are given instructions to attract players, and to keep a watch over the bank's interests; as also that for such services these officials are awarded prizes and premiums. At all events, the croupiers of Roulettenberg seemed to look upon the Grandmother as their lawful prey: whereafter there befell what our party had foretold.

It happened thus.

As soon as ever we arrived the Grandmother ordered me to stake twelve ten-gülden pieces in succession upon zero. Once, twice, and thrice I did so, yet zero never turned up.

'Stake again,' said the old lady with an impatient nudge of my elbow, and I obeyed.

'How many times have we lost?' she inquired – actually grinding her teeth in her excitement.

'We have lost 144 ten-gülden pieces,' I replied. 'I tell you, Madame, that zero may not turn up until nightfall.'

'Never mind,' she interrupted. 'Keep on staking upon zero, and also stake a thousand gülden upon rouge. Here is a bank-note with which to do so.

The red turned up, but zero missed again, and we only got our thousand gülden back.

'But you see, you see!' whispered the old lady. 'We have now recovered almost all that we staked. Try zero again. Let us do so another ten times, and then leave off.'

By the fifth round, however, the Grandmother was weary of the scheme.

'To the devil with that zero!' she exclaimed. 'Stake four thousand gülden upon the red.'

'But, Madame, that will be so much to venture!' I remonstrated. 'Suppose the red should *not* turn up?' The Grandmother almost struck me in her excitement. Her agitation was rapidly making her quarrelsome. Consequently, there was nothing for it but to stake the whole four thousand gülden as she had directed.

The wheel revolved while the Grandmother sat as bolt upright, and with as proud and quiet a mien, as though she had not the least doubt of winning.

'Zero!' cried the croupier.

At first the old lady failed to understand the situation; but as soon as she saw the croupier raking in her four thousand gülden, together with everything else that happened to be lying on the table, and recognized that the zero which had been so long turning up, and on which we had lost nearly two hundred ten-gülden pieces, had at length, as though of set purpose, made a sudden reappearance – why, the poor old lady fell to cursing it, and to throwing herself about, and wailing and gesticulating at the company at large. Indeed, some people in our vicinity actually burst out laughing.

'To think that that accursed zero should have turned up *now!*' she sobbed. 'The accursed, accursed thing! And it is all *your* fault,' she added, rounding upon me in a frenzy. 'It was *you* who persuaded me to cease staking upon it.'

'But, Madame, I only explained the game to you. How am *I* to answer for every mischance which may occur in it?'

'You and your mischances!' she whispered threateningly. 'Go! Away at once!'

'Farewell, then, Madame.' And I turned to depart.

'No; stay,' she put in hastily. 'Where are you going to? Why should you leave me? You fool! No, no; stay here. It is *I* who was the fool. Tell me what I ought to do.'

'I cannot take it upon myself to advise you, for you will only blame me if I do so. Play at your own discretion. Say exactly what you wish staked, and I will stake it.'

'Very well. Stake another four thousand gülden upon the red. Take this banknote to do it with. I have still got twenty thousand roubles in actual cash.'

'But,' I whispered, 'such a quantity of money — '

'Never mind. I cannot rest until I have won back my losses. Stake!'

I staked, and we lost.

'Stake again, stake again – eight thousand at a stroke!'

'I cannot, Madame. The largest stake allowed is four thousand gülden.'

'Well, then; stake four thousand.'

This time we won, and the Grandmother recovered herself a little.

'You see, you see!' she exclaimed as she nudged me. 'Stake another four thousand.'

I did so, and lost. Again, and yet again, we lost.

'Madame, your twelve thousand gülden are now gone,' at length I reported.

'I see they are,' she replied with, as it were, the calmness of despair. 'I see they are,' she muttered again as she gazed straight in front of her, like a person lost in thought. 'Ah well, I do not mean to rest until I have staked another four thousand.'

'But you have no money with which to do it, Madame. In this satchel I can see only a few five per cent. bonds and some transfers – no actual cash.'

'And in the purse?'

'A mere trifle.'

'But there is a money-changer's office here, is there not? They told me I should be able to get any sort of paper security changed?'

'Quite so; to any amount you please. But you will lose on the transaction what would frighten even a Jew.'

'Rubbish! I am *determined* to retrieve my losses. Take me away, and call those fools of bearers.'

'I wheeled the chair out of the throng, and, the bearers making their appearance, we left the Casino.

'Hurry, hurry!' commanded the Grandmother. 'Show me the nearest way to the money-changer's. Is it far?'

'A couple of steps, Madame.'

At the turning from the square into the Avenue we came face to face with the whole of our party – the General, De Griers, Mlle. Blanche, and her mother. Only Polina and Mr. Astley were absent.

'Well, well, well!' exclaimed the Grandmother. 'But we have no time to stop. What do you want? I can't talk to you here.'

I dropped behind a little, and immediately was pounced upon by De Griers.

'She has lost this morning's winnings,' I whispered, 'and also twelve thousand gülden of her original money. At the present moment we are going to get some bonds changed.'

De Griers stamped his foot with vexation, and hastened to communicate the tidings to the General. Meanwhile we continued to wheel the old lady along.

'Stop her, stop her,' whispered the General in consternation.

'You had better try and stop her yourself,' I returned – also in a whisper.

'My good mother,' he said as he approached her, ' – my good mother, pray let, let – ' (his voice was beginning to tremble and sink) ' –let us hire a carriage, and go for a drive. Near here there is an enchanting view to be obtained. We – we – we were just coming to invite you to go and see it.'

'Begone with you and your views!' said the Grandmother angrily as she waved him away.

'And there are trees there, and we could have tea under them,' continued the General – now in utter despair.

'Nous boirons du lait, sur l'herbe fraiche,' added De Griers with the snarl almost of a wild beast.

'Du lait, de l'herbe fraiche' – the idyll, the ideal of the Parisian bourgeois – his whole outlook upon 'la nature et la verité'!

'Have done with you and your milk!' cried the old lady. 'Go and stuff *yourself* as much as you like, but *my* stomach simply recoils from the idea. What are you stopping for? I have nothing to say to you.'

'Here we are, Madame,' I announced. 'Here is the money-changer's office.'

I entered to get the securities changed, while the Grandmother remained outside in the porch, and the rest waited at a little distance, in doubt as to their best course of action. At length the old lady turned such an angry stare upon them that they departed along the road towards the Casino.

The process of changing involved complicated calculations which soon necessitated my return to the Grandmother for instructions.

'The thieves!' she exclaimed as she clapped her hands together. 'Never mind, though. Get the documents cashed.- No; send the banker out to me,' she added as an afterthought.

'Would one of the clerks do, Madame?'

'Yes, one of the clerks. The thieves!'

The clerk consented to come out when he perceived that he was being asked for by an old lady who was too infirm to walk; after which the Grandmother began to upbraid him at length, and with great vehemence, for his alleged usuriousness, and to bargain with him in a mixture of Russian, French, and German – I acting as interpreter. Meanwhile the grave-faced official eyed us both, and silently nodded his head. At the Grandmother, in particular, he gazed with a curiosity which almost bordered upon rudeness. At length, too, he smiled.

'Pray recollect yourself' cried the old lady. 'And may my money choke you! Alexis Ivanovitch, tell him that we can easily repair to some one else.'

'The clerk says that others will give you even less than he.'

Of what the ultimate calculations consisted I do not exactly remember, but at all events they were alarming. Receiving twelve thousand florins in gold, I took also the statement of accounts, and carried it out to the Grandmother.

'Well, well,' she said, 'I am no accountant. Let us hurry away, hurry away.' And she waved the paper aside.

'Neither upon that accursed zero, however, nor upon that equally accursed red do I mean to stake a cent,' I muttered to myself as I entered the Casino.

This time I did all I could to persuade the old lady to stake as little as possible – saying that a turn would come in the chances when she would be at liberty to stake more. But she was so impatient that, though at first she agreed to do as I suggested, nothing could stop her when once she had begun. By way of prelude she won stakes of a hundred and two hundred gülden.

'There you are!' she said as she nudged me. 'See what we have won! Surely it would be worth our while to stake four thousand instead of a hundred, for we might win another four thousand, and then —! Oh, it was *your* fault before – all your fault.'

I felt greatly put out as I watched her play, but I decided to hold my tongue, and to give her no more advice.

Suddenly De Griers appeared on the scene. It seemed that all this while he and his companions had been standing beside us – though I noticed that Mlle. Blanche had withdrawn a little from the rest, and was engaged in flirting with the Prince. Clearly the General was greatly put out at this. Indeed, he was in a perfect agony of vexation. But Mlle. was careful never to look his way, though he did his best to attract her notice. Poor General! By turns his face blanched and reddened, and he was trembling to such an extent that he could scarcely follow the old lady's play. At length Mlle. and the Prince took their departure, and the General followed them.

'Madame, Madame,' sounded the honeyed accents of De Griers as he leant over to whisper in the Grandmother's ear. 'That stake will never win. No, no, it is impossible,' he added in Russian with a writhe. 'No, no!'

'But why not?' asked the Grandmother, turning round. 'Show me what I ought to do.'

Instantly De Griers burst into a babble of French as he advised, jumped about, declared that such and such chances ought to be waited for, and started to make calculations of figures. All this he addressed to me in my capacity as translator – tapping the table the while with his finger, and pointing hither and thither. At length he seized a pencil, and began to reckon sums on paper until he had exhausted the Grandmother's patience.

'Away with you!' she interrupted. 'You talk sheer nonsense, for, though you keep on saying "Madame, Madame," you haven't the least notion what ought to be done. Away with you, I say!'

'Mais, Madame,' cooed De Griers – and straightway started afresh with his fussy instructions.

'Stake just *once* as he advises,' the Grandmother said to me, 'and then we shall see what we *shall* see. Of course, his stake *might* win.'

As a matter of fact, De Grier's one object was to distract the old lady from staking large sums; wherefore he now suggested to her that she should stake upon certain numbers, singly and in groups. Consequently, in accordance with his instructions I staked a ten-gülden piece upon several odd numbers in the first twenty, and five ten-gülden pieces upon certain groups of numbers – groups of from twelve to eighteen, and from eighteen to twenty-four. The total staked amounted to 160 gülden.

The wheel revolved. 'Zero!' cried the croupier.

We had lost it all!

'The fool!' cried the old lady as she turned upon De Griers. 'You infernal Frenchman, to think that *you* should advise! Away with you! Though you fuss and fuss, you don't even know what you're talking about.'

Deeply offended, De Griers shrugged his shoulders, favoured the Grandmother with a look of contempt, and departed. For some time past he had been feeling ashamed of being seen in such company, and this had proved the last straw.

An hour later we had lost everything in hand.

'Home!' cried the Grandmother.

Not until we had turned into the Avenue did she utter a word; but from that point onwards, until we arrived at the hotel, she kept venting exclamations of 'What a fool I am! What a silly fool I am, to be sure!'

Arrived at the hotel, she called for tea, and then gave orders for her luggage to be packed.

'We are off again,' she announced.

'But whither, Madame?' inquired Martha.

'What business is that of *yours*? Let the cricket stick to its hearth.* Potapitch, have everything packed, for we are returning to Moscow at once. I have fooled away fifteen thousand roubles.'

'Fifteen thousand roubles, good mistress? My God!' and Potapitch spat upon his hands – probably to show that he was ready to serve her in any way he could.

'Now then, you fool! At once you begin with your weeping and wailing! Be quiet, and pack. Also, run downstairs, and get my hotel bill.'

'The next train leaves at 9.30, Madame,' I interposed, with a view to checking her agitation.

'And what is the time now?'

'Half-past eight.'

'How vexing! But never mind. Alexis Ivanovitch, I have not a kopeck left; I have but these two bank notes. Please run to the office and get them changed. Otherwise I shall have nothing to travel with.'

Departing on her errand, I returned half an hour later to find the whole party gathered in her rooms. It appeared that the news of her impending departure for Moscow had thrown the conspirators into consternation even greater than her losses had done. For, said they, even if her departure should save her fortune, what will become of the General later? And who

* The Russian form of 'Mind your own business.'

is to repay De Griers? Clearly Mlle. Blanche would never consent to wait until the Grandmother was dead, but would at once elope with the Prince or some one else. So they had all gathered together – endeavouring to calm and dissuade the Grandmother. Only Polina was absent. For her part the Grandmother had nothing for the party but abuse.

'Away with you, you rascals!' she was shouting. 'What have my affairs to do with you? Why, in particular, do *you*' – here she indicated De Griers – 'come sneaking here with your goat's beard? And what do *you*' – here she turned to Mlle. Blanche – 'want of me? What are *you* finicking for?'

'Diantre!' muttered Mlle. under her breath, but her eyes were flashing. Then all at once she burst into a laugh, and left the room – crying to the General as she did so: 'Elle vivra cent ans!'

'So you have been counting upon my death have you?' fumed the old lady. 'Away with you! Clear them out of the room, Alexis Ivanovitch. What business is it of *theirs*? It is not *their* money that I have been squandering, but my own.'

The General shrugged his shoulders, bowed, and withdrew, with De Griers behind him.

'Call Prascovia,' commanded the Grandmother, and in five minutes Martha reappeared with Polina, who had been sitting with the children in her own room (having purposely determined not to leave it that day). Her face looked grave and careworn.

'Prascovia,' began the Grandmother, 'is what I have just heard through a side wind true – namely, that this fool of a stepfather of yours is going to marry that silly whirligig of a Frenchwoman – that actress, or something worse? Tell me, is it true?'

'I do not know *for certain*, Grandmamma,' replied Polina; 'but from Mlle. Blanche's account (for she does not appear to think it necessary to conceal anything) I conclude that — '

'You need not say any more,' interrupted the Grandmother energetically. 'I understand the situation. I always thought we should get something like this from him, for I always looked upon him as a futile, frivolous fellow who gave himself unconscionable airs on the fact of his being a general (though he only became one because he retired as a colonel). Yes, I know *all* about the sending of the telegrams to inquire whether "the old woman is likely to turn up her toes soon." Ah, they were looking for the legacies! Without money that wretched woman (what is her name? – Oh, De Cominges) would never dream of accepting the General and his false teeth – no, not even for him to be her lacquey – since she herself, they say, possesses a pile of money, and lends it on interest, and makes a good thing out of it. However, it is not *you*, Prascovia, that I am blaming: it was not *you* who sent those telegrams. Nor, for that matter, do I wish to recall old scores. True, I know that you are a vixen by nature – that you are a wasp which will sting one if one touches it; yet my heart is sore for you, for I loved your mother, Katerina. Now, will you leave everything here, and come away with me? Otherwise I do not know what is to become of you, and it is not right that you should continue living with these people. Nay,' she interposed, the moment that Polina attempted to speak, 'I have not yet finished. I ask of you nothing in return. My house in Moscow is, as you know, large enough for a palace, and you could occupy a whole floor of it if you liked, and keep away from me for weeks together. Will you come with me, or will you not?'

'First of all, let me ask of *you*,' replied Polina, 'whether you are intending to depart at once?'

'What? You suppose me to be jesting? I have said that I am going, and I *am* going. To-day I have squandered fifteen thousand roubles at that accursed roulette of yours, and though, five years ago, I promised the people of a certain suburb of Moscow to build them a stone church in place of a wooden one, I have been fooling away my money here! However, I am going back now to build my church.'

'But what about the waters, Grandmamma? Surely you came here to take the waters?'

'You and your waters! Do not anger me, Prascovia. Surely you are trying to? Say, then: will you, or will you not, come with me?'

'Grandmamma,' Polina replied with deep feeling, 'I am very, very grateful to you for the shelter which you have so kindly offered me. Also, to a certain extent you have guessed my position aright, and I am beholden to you to such an extent that it may be that I *will* come and live with you, and that very soon; yet there are important reasons why – why I cannot make up my mind just yet. If you would let me have, say, a couple of weeks to decide in —?'

'You mean that you are *not* coming?'

'I mean only that I cannot come just yet. At all events, I could not well leave my little brother and sister here, since – since – if I were to leave them, they would be abandoned altogether. But if, Grandmamma, you would take the little ones *and* myself, then, of course, I could come with you, and would do all I could to serve you' (this she said with great earnestness). 'Only, without the little ones I *cannot* come.'

'Do not make a fuss' (as a matter of fact, Polina never at any time either fussed or wept). 'The Great Foster-Father* can find for all his chicks a place. You are not coming without the children? But see here, Prascovia.

* Translated literally – The Great Poulterer.

I wish you well, and nothing but well: yet I have divined the reason why you will not come. Yes, I know all, Prascovia. That Frenchman will never bring you good of any sort.'

Polina coloured hotly, and even I started. 'For,' thought I to myself, 'every one seems to know about that affair. Or perhaps I am the only one who does *not* know about it?

'Now, now! Do not frown,' continued the Grandmother. 'But I do not intend to slur things over. You will take care that no harm befalls you, will you not? For you are a girl of sense, and I am sorry for you – I regard you in a different light to the rest of them. And now, please, leave me. Good-bye.'

'But let me stay with you a little longer,' said Polina.

'No,' replied the other; 'you need not. Do not bother me, for you and all of them have tired me out.'

Yet when Polina tried to kiss the Grandmother's hand, the old lady withdrew it, and herself kissed the girl on the cheek. As she passed me, Polina gave me a momentary glance, and then as swiftly averted her eyes.

'And good-bye to you, also, Alexis Ivanovitch. The train starts in an hour's time, and I think that you must be weary of me. Take these five hundred gülden for yourself.

'I thank you humbly, Madame, but I am ashamed to — '

'Come, come!' cried the Grandmother so energetically, and with such an air of menace, that I did not dare refuse the money further.

'If, when in Moscow, you have no place where you can lay your head,' she added, 'come and see me, and I will give you a recommendation. Now, Potapitch, get things ready.'

I ascended to my room, and lay down upon the bed. A whole hour I must have lain thus, with my head resting upon my hand. So the crisis had come! I needed time for its consideration. To-morrow I would have a talk with Polina. Ah! The Frenchman! So it *was* true? But how could it be so? Polina and De Griers! What a combination!

No, it was too improbable. Suddenly I leapt up with the idea of seeking Astley and forcing him to speak. There could be no doubt that he knew more than I did. Astley? Well, he was another problem for me to solve.

Suddenly there came a knock at the door, and I opened it to find Potapitch awaiting me.

'Sir,' he said, 'my mistress is asking for you.'

'Indeed? But she is just departing, is she not? The train leaves in ten minutes' time.'

'She is uneasy, sir; she cannot rest. Come quickly, sir; do not delay.'

I ran downstairs at once. The Grandmother was just being carried out of her rooms into the corridor. In her hands she held a roll of bank-notes.

'Alexis Ivanovitch,' she cried, 'walk on ahead, and we will set out again.'

'But whither, Madame?'

'I cannot rest until I have retrieved my losses. March on ahead, and ask me no questions. Play continues until midnight, does it not?'

For a moment I stood stupefied – stood deep in thought; but it was not long before I had made up my mind.

'With your leave, Madame,' I said, 'I will not go with you.'

'And why not? What do you mean? Is *every one* here a stupid-good-for-nothing?'

'Pardon me, but I have nothing to reproach myself with. I merely will not go. I merely intend neither to witness nor to join in your play. I also beg to return you your five hundred gülden. Farewell.'

Laying the money upon a little table which the Grandmother's chair happened to be passing, I bowed and withdrew.

'What folly!' the Grandmother shouted after me. 'Very well, then. Do not come, and I will find my way alone. Potapitch, *you* must come with me. Lift up the chair, and carry me along.'

I failed to find Mr. Astley, and returned home. It was now growing late – it was past midnight, but I subsequently learnt from Potapitch how the Grandmother's day had ended. She had lost all the money which, earlier in the day, I had got for her paper securities – a sum amounting to about ten thousand roubles. This she did under the direction of the Pole whom, that afternoon, she had dowered with two ten-gülden pieces. But before his arrival on the scene she had commanded Potapitch to stake for her; until at length she had told him also to go about his business. Upon that the Pole had leapt into the breach. Not only did it happen that he knew the Russian language, but also he could speak a mixture of three different dialects, so that the pair were able to understand one another. Yet the old lady never ceased to abuse him, despite his deferential manner, and to compare him unfavourably with myself (so, at all events, Potapitch declared). 'You,' the old chamberlain said to me, 'treated her as a gentleman should, but he – he robbed her right and left, as I could see with my own eyes. Twice she caught him at it, and rated him soundly. On one occasion she even pulled his hair, so that the bystanders burst out laughing. Yet she lost everything, sir – that is to say, she lost all that you had changed for her. Then we brought her home, and, after asking for some water and saying her prayers, she went to bed. So worn out was she that she fell asleep at once. May God send her dreams of angels! And *this* is all that foreign travel has done for us! Oh, my own Moscow! For what have we not at home there, in Moscow? Such a garden and flowers as you could never see here, and fresh air and apple-trees coming into blossom, and a beautiful view to look upon. Ah, but what must she do but go travelling abroad? Alack, alack!'

➤ THIRTEEN ◄

ALMOST A MONTH HAS PASSED since I last touched these notes – notes which I began under the influence of impressions at once poignant and disordered. The crisis which I then felt to be approaching has now arrived, but in a form a hundred times more extensive and unexpected than I had looked for. To me it all seems strange, uncouth, and tragic. Certain occurrences have befallen me which border upon the marvellous. At all events, that is how I view them. I view them so in one regard at least. I refer to the whirlpool of events in which, at the time, I was revolving. But the most curious feature of all is my relation to those events, for hitherto I had never clearly understood myself. Yet now the actual crisis has passed away like a dream. Even my passion for Polina is dead. *Was* it ever so strong and genuine as I thought? If so, what has become of it now? At times I fancy that I must be mad; that somewhere I am sitting in a madhouse; that these events have merely *seemed* to happen; that still they merely *seem* to be happening.

I have been arranging and re-perusing my notes (perhaps for the purpose of convincing myself that I am not in a madhouse). At present I am lonely and alone. Autumn is coming – already it is mellowing the leaves; and as I sit brooding in this melancholy little town (and how melancholy the little towns of Germany can be!), I find myself taking no thought for the future, but living under the influence of passing moods, and of my recollections of the tempest which recently drew me into its vortex, and then cast me out again. At times I seem still to be caught within that vortex. At times the tempest seems once more to be gathering, and, as it passes overhead, to be wrapping me in its folds, until I have lost my sense of order and reality, and continue whirling and whirling and whirling around.

Yet it may be that I shall be able to stop myself from revolving if once I can succeed in rendering myself an exact account of what has happened within the month just past. Somehow I feel drawn towards the pen; on many and many an evening I have had nothing else in the world to do. But, curiously enough, of late I have taken to amusing myself with the works of M. Paul de Kock, which I read in German translations obtained from a wretched local library. These works I cannot abide, yet I read them, and find myself marvelling that I should be doing so. Somehow I seem to be afraid of any *serious* book – afraid of permitting any *serious* preoccupation to break the spell of the passing moment. So dear to me is the formless dream of which I have spoken, so dear to me are the impressions which it has left behind, that I fear to touch the vision with anything new, lest it should dissolve in smoke. But *is* it so dear to me? Yes, it *is* dear to me, and will ever be fresh in my recollections – even forty years hence. . . .

So let me write of it, but only partially, and in a more abridged form than my full impressions might warrant.

First of all, let me conclude the history of the Grandmother. Next day she lost every gülden that she possessed. Things were bound to happen so, for persons of her type who have once entered upon that road descend it with ever-increasing rapidity, even as a sledge descends a toboggan-slide. All day until eight o'clock that evening did she play; and though I personally did not witness her exploits, I learnt of them later through report.

All that day Potapitch remained in attendance upon her; but the Poles who directed her play she changed more than once. As a beginning she dismissed her Pole of the previous day – the Pole whose hair she had pulled – and took to herself another one; but the latter proved worse even than the former, and incurred dismissal in favour of the first Pole, who, during the time of his unemployment, had nevertheless hovered around the Grandmother's chair, and from time to time obtruded his head over her shoulder. At length the old lady became desperate, for the second Pole, when dismissed, imitated his predecessor by declining to go away; with the result that one Pole remained standing on the right of the victim, and the other on her left; from which vantage points the pair quarrelled, abused each other concerning the stakes and rounds, and exchanged the epithet 'laidak'* and other Polish terms of endearment. Finally they effected a mutual reconciliation, and, tossing the money about anyhow, played simply at random. Once more quarrelling, each of them staked money on his own side of the Grandmother's chair (for instance, the one Pole staked upon the red, and the other one upon the black), until they had so confused and browbeaten the old lady that, nearly weeping, she was forced to appeal to the head croupier for protection, and to have

* Rascal.

the two Poles expelled. No time was lost in this being done, despite the rascals' cries and protestations that the old lady was in their debt, that she had cheated them, and that her general behaviour had been mean and dishonourable. The same evening the unfortunate Potapitch related the story to me with tears – complaining that the two men had filled their pockets with money (he himself had seen them do it) which had been shamelessly pilfered from his mistress. For instance one Pole demanded of the Grandmother fifty gülden for his trouble, and then staked the money by the side of her stake. She happened to win; whereupon he cried out that the winning stake was his, and hers the loser. As soon as the two Poles had been expelled, Potapitch left the room, and reported to the authorities that the men's pockets were full of gold; and, on the Grandmother also requesting the head croupier to look into the affair, the police made their appearance, and, despite the protests of the Poles (who, indeed, had been caught redhanded), their pockets were turned inside out, and the contents handed over to the Grandmother. In fact, in view of the circumstances that she lost all day, the croupiers and other authorities of the Casino showed her every attention; and on her fame spreading through the town, visitors of every nationality – even the most knowing of them, the most distinguished – crowded to get a glimpse of 'la vieille comtesse russe, tombée en enfance,' who had lost 'so many millions.'

Yet with the money which the authorities restored to her from the pockets of the Poles the Grandmother effected very, very little, for there soon arrived to take his countrymen's place a third Pole – a man who could speak Russian fluently, was dressed like a gentleman (albeit in lacqueyish fashion), and sported a huge moustache. Though polite enough to the old lady, he took a high hand with the bystanders. In short, he offered himself less as a servant than as an *entertainer*. After each round he would turn to the old lady, and swear terrible oaths to the effect that he was a 'Polish gentleman of honour' who would scorn to take a kopeck of her money; and though he repeated these oaths so often that at length she grew alarmed, he had her play in hand, and began to win on her behalf; wherefore she felt that she could not well get rid of him. An hour later the two Poles who, earlier in the day, had been expelled from the Casino made a reappearance behind the old lady's chair, and renewed their offers of service – even if it were only to be sent on messages; but from Potapitch I subsequently had it that between these rascals and the said 'gentleman of honour' there passed a wink, as well as that the latter put something into their hands. Next, since the Grandmother had not yet lunched – she had scarcely for a moment left her chair – one of the two Poles ran to the restaurant of the Casino, and brought her thence a cup of soup, and afterwards some tea. In fact, *both* the Poles hastened to perform this office. Finally, towards the close of the day, when it was clear that the Grandmother was about to play her last bank-note, there could be seen standing behind her chair no fewer than six natives of Poland – persons who, as yet, had been neither audible nor visible; and as soon as ever the old lady played the note in question, they took no further notice of her, but pushed their way past her chair to the table, seized the money, and staked it – shouting and disputing the while, and arguing with the 'gentleman of honour' (who also had forgotten the Grandmother's existence), as though he were their equal. Even when the Grandmother had lost her all, and was returning (about eight o'clock) to the hotel, some three or four Poles could not bring themselves to leave her, but went on running beside her chair and volubly protesting that the Grandmother had cheated them, and that she ought to be made to surrender what was not her own. Thus the party arrived at the hotel; whence, presently, the gang of rascals was ejected neck and crop.

According to Potapitch's calculations, the Grandmother lost, that day, a total of ninety thousand roubles, in addition to the money which she had lost the day before. Every paper security which she had brought with her – five per cent. bonds, internal loan scrip, and what not – she had changed into cash. Also, I could not but marvel at the way in which, for seven or eight hours at a stretch, she sat in that chair of hers, almost never leaving the table. Again, Potapitch told me that there were three occasions on which she really began to win; but that, led on by false hopes, she was unable to tear herself away at the right moment. Every gambler knows how a person may sit a day and a night at cards without ever casting a glance to right or to left.

Meanwhile, that day, some other very important events were passing in our hotel. As early as eleven o'clock – that is to say, before the Grandmother had quitted her rooms – the General and De Griers decided upon their last stroke. In other words, on learning that the old lady had changed her mind about departing, and was bent on setting out for the Casino again, the whole of our gang (Polina only excepted) proceeded *en masse* to her rooms, for the purpose of finally and frankly treating with her. But the General, quaking and greatly apprehensive as to his possible future, overdid things. After half an hour's prayers and entreaties, coupled with a full confession of his debts, and even of his passion for Mlle. Blanche (yes, he had quite lost his head), he suddenly adopted a tone of menace, and started to rage at the old lady – exclaiming that she was sullying the family honour, that she was making a public scandal of herself, and that she was smirching the fair name of Russia. The upshot was that the Grandmother turned him out of the room with her stick (it was a real stick, too!). Later in the morning he held several consultations with De Griers – the question which occupied him being: Is it in any way possible to make use of the police – to tell them that 'this respected, but unfortunate, old lady has gone out of her mind, and is squandering her last kopeck,' or something of the kind? In short, is it in any way possible to engineer a species of supervision over, or of restraint upon, the old lady? De Griers, however, shrugged his shoulders at this, and laughed in the General's face, while the old warrior went on chattering volubly, and running up and down his study. Finally De Griers waved his hand, and disappeared from view; and by evening it became known that he had left the hotel, after holding a very secret and important conference with Mlle. Blanche. As for the latter, from early morning she had taken decisive measures, by completely excluding the General from her presence, and bestowing upon him not a glance. Indeed, even when the General pursued her to the Casino, and met her walking arm in arm with the Prince, he (the General) received from her and her mother not the slightest recognition. Nor did the Prince himself bow. The rest of the day Mlle. spent in probing the Prince, and trying to make him declare himself; but in this she made a woeful mistake. The little incident occurred in the evening. Suddenly Mlle. Blanche realized that the Prince had not even a copper to his name, but, on the contrary, was minded to borrow of her money wherewith to play at roulette. In high displeasure she drove him from her presence, and shut herself up in her room.

The same morning I went to see – or, rather, to look for – Mr. Astley, but was unsuccessful in my quest. Neither in his rooms nor in the Casino nor in the Park was he to be found; nor did he, that day, lunch at his hotel as usual. However, at about five o'clock I caught sight of him walking from the railway station to the Hotel d'Angleterre. He seemed to be in a great hurry and much preoccupied, though in his face I could discern no actual traces of worry or perturbation. He held out to me a friendly hand, with his usual ejaculation of 'Ah!' but did not check his stride. I turned and walked beside him, but found, somehow, that his answers forbade any putting of definite questions. Moreover, I felt reluctant to speak to him of Polina; nor, for his part, did he ask me any questions concerning her, although, on my telling him of the Grandmother's exploits, he listened attentively and gravely, and then shrugged his shoulders.

'She is gambling away everything that she has,' I remarked.

'Indeed? She arrived at the Casino even before I had taken my departure by train, so I knew she had been playing. If I should have time I will go to the Casino to-night, and take a look at her. The thing interests me.'

'Where have you been to-day?' I asked – surprised at myself for having, as yet, omitted to put to him that question.

'To Frankfurt.'

'On business?'

'On business.'

What more was there to be asked after that? I accompanied him until, as we drew level with the Hotel des Quatre Saisons, he suddenly nodded to me and disappeared. For myself, I returned home, and came to the conclusion that, even had I met him at *two* o'clock in the afternoon, I should have learnt no more from him than I had done at five o'clock, for the reason that I had no definite question to ask. It was bound to have been so. For me to formulate the query which I really wished to put was a simple impossibility.

Polina spent the whole of that day either in walking about the park with the nurse and children or in sitting in her own room. For a long while past she had avoided the General and had scarcely had a word to say to him (scarcely a word, I mean, on any *serious* topic). Yes, that I had noticed. Still, even though I was aware of the position in which the General was placed, it had never occurred to me that he would have any reason to avoid *her*, or to trouble her with family explanations. Indeed, when I was returning to the hotel after my conversation with Astley, and chanced to meet Polina and the children, I could see that her face was as calm as though the family disturbances had never touched her. To my salute she responded with a slight bow, and I retired to my room in a very bad humour.

Of course, since the affair with the Burmergelms I had exchanged not a word with Polina, nor had with her any kind of intercourse. Yet I had been at my wits' end, for, as time went on, there was arising in me an ever-seething dissatisfaction. Even if she did not love me she ought not to have trampled upon my feelings, nor to have accepted my confessions with such contempt, seeing that she must have been aware that I loved her (of her own accord she had allowed me to tell her as much). Of course the situation between us had arisen in a curious manner. About two months ago I had noticed that she had a desire to make me her friend, her confidant – that she was making trial of me for the purpose; but for some reason or another the desired result had never come about, and we had fallen into the present strange relations, which had led me to address her as I had done. At the same time, if my love was distasteful to her, why had she not *forbidden* me to speak of it to her?

But she had not so forbidden me. On the contrary, there had been occasions when she had even *invited* me to speak. Of course, this might have been done out of sheer wantonness, for I well knew – I had remarked it only too often! – that, after listening to what I had to say, and angering me almost beyond endurance, she loved suddenly to torture me with some fresh outburst of contempt and aloofness. Yet she must have known that I could not live without her. Three days had elapsed since the affair with the Baron, and I could bear the severance no longer. When, that afternoon, I met her near the Casino, my heart almost made me faint, it beat so violently. She too could not live without me, for had she not said that she had *need* of me? Or had that too been spoken in jest?

That she had a secret of some kind there could be no doubt. What she had said to the Grandmother had stabbed me to the heart. On a thousand occasions I had challenged her to be open with me, nor could she have been ignorant that I was ready to give my very life for her. Yet always she had kept me at a distance with that contemptuous air of hers; or else she had demanded of me, in lieu of the life which I offered to lay at her feet, such escapades as I had perpetrated with the Baron. Ah, was it not torture to me, all this? For could it be that her whole world was bound up with the Frenchman? What, too, about Mr. Astley? The affair was inexplicable throughout. My God, what distress it caused me!

Arrived home, I, in a fit of frenzy, indited the following:

'Polina Alexandrovna, I can see that there is approaching us an exposure which will involve you too. For the last time I ask of you – have you, or have you not, any need of my life? If you have, then make such dispositions as you wish, and I shall always be discoverable in my room if required. If you have need of my life, write or send for me.'

I sealed the letter, and dispatched it by the hand of a corridor lacquey, with orders to hand it to the addressee in person. Though I expected no answer, scarcely three minutes had elapsed before the lacquey returned with 'the compliments of a certain person.'

Next, about seven o'clock, I was sent for by the General. I found him in his study, apparently preparing to go out again, for his hat and stick were lying on the sofa. When I entered he was standing in the middle of the room – his feet wide apart, and his head bent down. Also, he appeared to be talking to himself. But as soon as ever he saw me at the door he came towards me in such a curious manner that involuntarily I retreated a step, and was for leaving the room; whereupon he seized me by both hands, and, drawing me towards the sofa, and seating himself thereon, he forced me to sit down on a chair opposite him. Then, without letting go of my hands, he exclaimed with quivering lips and a sparkle of tears on his eyelashes:

'Oh, Alexis Ivanovitch! Save me, save me! have some mercy upon me!'

For a long time I could not make out what he meant, although he kept talking and talking, and constantly repeating to himself, 'Have mercy, mercy!' At length, however, I divined that he was expecting me to give him something in the nature of advice – or, rather, that, deserted by every one, and overwhelmed with grief and apprehension, he had bethought himself of my existence, and sent for me to relieve his feelings by talking and talking and talking.

In fact, he was in such a confused and despondent state of mind that, clasping his hands together, he actually went down upon his knees and begged me to go to Mlle. Blanche, and beseech and advise her to return to him, and to accept him in marriage.'

'But, General,' I exclaimed, 'possibly Mlle. Blanche has scarcely even remarked my existence? What could I do with her?'

It was in vain that I protested, for he could understand nothing that was said to him. Next he started talking about the Grandmother, but always in a disconnected sort of fashion – his one thought being to send for the police.

'In Russia,' said he, suddenly boiling over with indignation, 'or in any well-ordered State where there exists a government, old women like my mother are placed under proper guardianship. Yes, my good sir,' he went on, relapsing into a scolding tone as he leapt to his feet and started to pace the room, 'do you not know this' (he seemed to be addressing some imaginary auditor in the corner) ' – do you not know this, that in Russia old women like her are subjected to restraint, the devil take them?' Again he threw himself down upon the sofa.

A minute later, though sobbing and almost breathless, he managed to gasp out that Mlle. Blanche had refused to marry him, for the reason that the Grandmother had turned up in place of a telegram, and it was therefore clear that he had no inheritance to look for. Evidently he supposed that I had hitherto been in entire ignorance of all this. Again, when I referred to De Griers, the General made a gesture of despair. 'He has gone away,' he said, 'and everything which I possess is mortgaged to him. I stand stripped to my skin. Even of the money which you brought me from Paris I know not if seven hundred francs be left. Of course that sum will do to go on with, but, as regards the future, I know nothing, I know nothing.'

'Then how will you pay your hotel bill?' I cried in consternation. 'And what shall you do afterwards?'

He looked at me vaguely, but it was clear that he had not understood – perhaps had not even heard – my questions. Then I tried to get him to speak of Polina and the children, but he only returned brief answers of 'Yes, yes,' and again started to maunder about the Prince, and the likelihood of the latter marrying Mlle. Blanche. 'What on earth am I to do?' he concluded. 'What on earth am I to do? Is not this ingratitude? Is it not sheer ingratitude?' And he burst into tears.

Nothing could be done with such a man. Yet to leave him alone was dangerous, for something might happen to him. I withdrew from his rooms for a little while, but warned the nursemaid to keep an eye upon him, as well as exchanged a word with the corridor lacquey (a very talkative fellow), who likewise promised to remain on the look-out.

Hardly had I left the General when Potapitch approached me with a summons from the Grandmother. It was now eight o'clock, and she had returned from the Casino after finally losing all that she possessed. I found her sitting in her chair – much distressed and evidently fatigued. Presently Martha brought her up a cup of tea, and forced her to drink it; yet even then I could detect in the old lady's tone and manner a great change.

'Good evening, Alexis Ivanovitch,' she said slowly, with her head drooping. 'Pardon me for disturbing you again. Yes, you must pardon an old, old woman like myself, for I have left behind me all that I possess – nearly a hundred thousand roubles! You did quite right in declining to come with me this evening. Now I am without money – without a single groat. But I must not delay a moment; I must leave by the 9.30 train. I have sent for that English friend of yours, and am going to beg of him three thousand francs for a week. Please try and persuade him to think nothing of it, nor yet to refuse me, for I am still a rich woman who possesses three villages and a couple of mansions. Yes, the money shall be found, for I have not yet squandered *everything*. I tell you this in order that he may have no doubts about — Ah, but here he is! Clearly he is a good fellow.'

True enough, Astley had come hot-foot on receiving the Grandmother's appeal. Scarcely stopping even to reflect, and with scarcely a word, he counted out the three thousand francs under a note of hand which she duly signed. Then, his business done, he bowed, and lost no time in taking his departure.

'You too leave me, Alexis Ivanovitch,' said the Grandmother. 'All my bones are aching, and I still have an hour in which to rest. Do not be hard upon me, old fool that I am. Never again shall I blame young people for being frivolous. I should think it wrong even to blame that unhappy General of yours. Nevertheless I do not mean to let him have any of my money (which is all that he desires), for the reason that I look upon him as a perfect blockhead, and consider myself, simpleton though I be, at least wiser than *he* is. How surely does God visit old age, and punish it for its presumption! Well, goodbye. Martha, come and lift me up.'

However, I had a mind to see the old lady off; and, moreover, I was in an expectant frame of mind – somehow I kept thinking that *something* was going to happen; wherefore I could not rest quietly in my room, but stepped out into the corridor, and then into the Chestnut Avenue for a few minutes' stroll. My letter to Polina had been clear and firm, and the present crisis, I felt sure, would prove final. I had heard of De Griers' departure, and, however much Polina might reject me as a *friend*, she might not reject me altogether as a *servant*. She would need me to fetch and carry for her, and I was ready to do so. How could it have been otherwise?

Towards the hour of the train's departure I hastened to the station, and put the Grandmother into her compartment – she and her party occupying a reserved family saloon.

'Thanks for your disinterested assistance,' she said at parting. 'Oh, and please remind Prascovia of what I said to her last night. I expect soon to see her.'

Then I returned home. As I was passing the door of the General's suite, I met the nursemaid, and inquired after her master. 'There is nothing new to report, sir,' she replied quietly. Nevertheless I decided to enter, and was just doing so when I halted thunderstruck on the threshold. For before me I beheld the General and Mlle. Blanche – laughing gaily at one another! while beside them, on the sofa, there was seated her mother. Clearly the General was almost out of his mind with joy, for he was talking all sorts of nonsense, and bubbling over with a long-drawn, nervous laugh – a laugh which twisted his face into innumerable wrinkles, and caused his eyes almost to disappear. Afterwards I learnt from Mlle. Blanche herself that, after dismissing the Prince and hearing of the General's tears, she bethought her of going to comfort the old man, and had just arrived for the purpose when I entered. Fortunately the poor General did not know that his fate had been decided – that Mlle. had long ago packed her trunks in readiness for the first morning train to Paris!

Hesitating a moment on the threshold I changed my mind as to entering, and departed unnoticed. Ascending to my own room, and opening the door, I perceived in the semi-darkness a figure seated on a chair in the corner by the window. The figure did not rise when I entered, so I approached it swiftly, peered at it closely, and felt my heart almost stop beating. The figure was Polina!

❖ FOURTEEN ❖

THE SHOCK MADE ME UTTER an exclamation.

'What is the matter? What is the matter?' she asked in a strange voice. She was looking pale, and her eyes were dim.

'What is the matter?' I re-echoed. 'Why the fact that you are *here!*'

'If I am here, I have come with all that I have to bring,' she said. 'Such has always been my way, as you shall presently see. Please light a candle.'

I did so; whereupon she rose, approached the table, and laid upon it an open letter.

'Read it,' she added.

'It is De Griers' handwriting!' I cried as I seized the document. My hands were so tremulous that the lines on the pages danced before my eyes. Although, at this distance of time, I have forgotten the exact phraseology of the missive, I append, if not the precise words, at all events the general sense.

'Mademoiselle,' the document ran, 'certain untoward circumstances compel me to depart in haste. Of course, you have of yourself remarked that hitherto I have always refrained from having any final explanation with you, for the reason that I could not well state the whole circumstances; and now to my difficulties the advent of the aged Grandmother, coupled with her subsequent proceedings, has put the final touch. Also, the involved state of my affairs forbids me to write with any finality concerning those hopes of ultimate bliss upon which, for a long while past, I have permitted myself to feed. I regret the past, but at the same time hope that in my conduct you have never been able to detect anything that was unworthy of a gentleman and a man of honour. Having lost, however, almost the whole of my money in debts incurred by your stepfather, I find myself driven to the necessity of saving the remainder; wherefore I have instructed certain friends of mine in St. Petersburg to arrange for the sale of all the property which has been mortgaged to myself. At the same time, knowing that, in addition, your frivolous stepfather has squandered money which is exclusively yours, I have decided to absolve him from a certain moiety of the mortgages on his property, in order that you may be in a position to recover of him what you have lost, by suing him in legal fashion. I trust, therefore, that, as matters now stand, this action of mine may bring you some advantage. I trust also that this same action leaves me in the position of having fulfilled every obligation which is incumbent upon a man of honour and refinement. Rest assured that your memory will for ever remain graven in my heart.'

'All this is clear enough,' I commented. 'Surely you did not expect aught else from him?' Somehow I was feeling annoyed.

'I expected nothing at all from him,' she replied – quietly enough, to all outward seeming, yet with a note of irritation in her tone. 'Long ago I made up my mind on the subject, for I could read his thoughts, and knew what he was thinking. He thought that possibly I should sue him – that one day I might become a nuisance.' Here Polina halted for a moment, and stood biting her lips. 'So of set purpose I redoubled my contemptuous treatment of him, and waited to see what he would do. If a telegram to say that we had become legatees had arrived from St. Petersburg, I should have flung at him a quittance for my foolish stepfather's debts, and then dismissed him. For a long time I have hated him. Even in earlier days he was not a man; and now! — Oh, how gladly I could throw those fifty thousand roubles in his face, and spit in it, and then rub the spittle in!'

'But the document returning the fifty-thousand-rouble mortgage – has the General got it? If so, possess yourself of it, and send it to De Griers.'

'No, no; the General has not got it.'

'Just as I expected! Well, what is the General going to do?' Then an idea suddenly occurred to me. 'What about the Grandmother?' I asked.

Polina looked at me with impatience and bewilderment.

'What makes you speak of *her*?' was her irritable inquiry. 'I cannot go and live with her. Nor,' she added hotly, 'will I go down upon my knees to *any one*.'

'Why should you?' I cried. 'Yet to think that you should have loved De Griers! The villain, the villain! But I will kill him in a duel. Where is he now?'

'In Frankfort, where he will be staying for the next three days.'

'Well, bid me do so, and I will go to him by the first train to-morrow,' I exclaimed with enthusiasm.

She smiled.

'If you were to do that,' she said, 'he would merely tell you to be so good as first to return him the fifty thousand francs. What, then, would be the use of having a quarrel with him? You talk sheer nonsense.'

I ground my teeth.

'The question,' I went on, 'is how to raise the fifty thousand francs. We cannot expect to find them lying about on the floor. Listen. What of Mr.

Astley?' Even as I spoke a new and strange idea formed itself in my brain.

Her eyes flashed fire.

'What? *You yourself* wish me to leave you for him?' she cried with a scornful look and a proud smile. Never before had she addressed me thus.

Then her head must have turned dizzy with emotion, for suddenly she seated herself upon the sofa, as though she were powerless any longer to stand.

A flash of lightning seemed to strike me as I stood there. I could scarcely believe my eyes or my ears. She *did* love me, then! It *was* to me, and not to Mr. Astley, that she had turned! Although she, an unprotected girl, had come to me in my room – in an hotel room – and had probably compromised herself thereby, I had not understood!

Then a second mad idea flashed into my brain.

'Polina,' I said, 'give me but an hour. Wait here just one hour until I return. Yes, you *must* do so. Do you not see what I mean? Just stay here for that time.'

And I rushed from the room without so much as answering her look of inquiry. She called something after me, but I did not return.

Sometimes it happens that the most insane thought, the most impossible conception, will become so fixed in one's head that at length one believes the thought or the conception to be reality. Moreover, if with the thought or the conception there is combined a strong, a passionate, desire, one will come to look upon the said thought or conception as something fated, inevitable, and foreordained – something bound to happen. Whether by this there is connoted something in the nature of a combination of presentiments, or a great effort of will, or a self-annulment of one's true expectations, and so on, I do not know; but at all events that night saw happen to me (a night which I shall never forget) something in the nature of the miraculous. Although the occurrence can easily be explained by arithmetic, I still believe it to have been a miracle. Yet why did this conviction take such a hold upon me at the time, and remain with me ever since? Previously I had thought of the idea, not as an occurrence which was ever likely to come about, but as something which *never* could come about.

The time was a quarter past eleven o'clock when I entered the Casino in such a state of hope (though, at the same time, of agitation) as I had never before experienced. In the gaming-rooms there were still a large number of people, but not half as many as had been present in the morning.

At eleven o'clock there usually remained behind only the real, the desperate gamblers – persons for whom, at spas, there existed nothing beyond roulette, and who went thither for that alone. These gamesters took little note of what was going on around them, and were interested in none of the appurtenances of the season, but played from morning till night, and would have been ready to play through the night until dawn had that been possible. As it was, they used to disperse unwillingly when, at midnight, roulette came to an end. Likewise, as soon as ever roulette was drawing to a close and the head croupier had called 'Les trois derniers coups,' most of them were ready to stake on the last three rounds all that they had in their pockets – and, for the most part, lost it. For my own part I proceeded towards the table at which the Grandmother had lately sat; and since the crowd around it was not very large, I soon obtained standing room among the ring of gamblers, while directly in front of me, on the green cloth, I saw marked the word 'Passe.'

'Passe' was a row of numbers from 19 to 36 inclusive; while a row of numbers from 1 to 18 inclusive was known as 'Manque.' But what had that to do with me? I had not noticed – I had not so much as heard – the numbers upon which the previous coup had fallen, and so took no bearings when I began to play, as, in my place, any *systematic* gambler would have done. No, I merely extended my stock of twenty ten-gülden pieces, and threw them down upon the space 'Passe' which happened to be confronting me.

'Vingt-deux!' called the croupier.

I had won! I staked upon the same again – both my original stake and my winnings.

'Trente-et-un!' called the croupier.

Again I had won, and was now in possession of eighty ten-gülden pieces. Next I moved the whole eighty on to twelve middle numbers (a stake which, if successful, would bring me in a triple profit, but also involved a risk of two chances to one). The wheel revolved, and stopped at twenty-four. Upon this I was paid out notes and gold until I had by my side a total sum of two thousand gülden.

It was as in a fever that I moved the pile, *en bloc*, on to the red. Then suddenly I came to myself (though that was the only time during the evening's play when fear cast its cold spell over me, and showed itself in a trembling of the hands and knees). For with horror I had realized that I *must* win, and that upon that stake there depended all my life.

'Rouge!' called the croupier. I drew a long breath, and hot shivers went coursing over my body. I was paid out my winnings in bank-notes – amounting, of course, to a total of four thousand florins, eight hundred gülden (I could still calculate the amounts).

After that, I remember, I again staked two thousand florins upon twelve middle numbers, and lost. Again I staked the whole of my gold, with eight hundred gülden in notes, and lost. Then madness seemed to come upon me, and seizing my last two thousand florins, I staked them upon twelve of the first numbers – wholly by chance, and at random, and without any sort of reckoning. Upon my doing so there followed a moment of suspense only comparable to that which Madame Blanchard must have experienced when, in Paris, she was descending earthwards from a balloon.

'Quatre!' called the croupier.

Once more, with the addition of my original stake I was in possession of six thousand florins! Once more I looked around me like a conqueror – once more I feared nothing as I threw down four thousand of these florins upon the black. The croupiers glanced around them, and exchanged a few words; the bystanders murmured expectantly.

The black turned up. After that I do not exactly remember either my calculations or the order of my stakings. I only remember that, as in a dream, I won in one round sixteen thousand florins; that in the three following rounds I lost twelve thousand; that I moved the remainder (four thousand) on to 'Passe' (though quite unconscious of what I was doing – I was merely waiting, as it were, mechanically, and without reflection, for something), and won; and that, finally, four times in succession I lost. Yes, I can remember raking in money by thousands – but most frequently on the twelve middle numbers, to which I constantly adhered, and which kept appearing in a sort of regular order – first, three or four times running, and then, after an interval of a couple of rounds, in another break of three or four appearances. Sometimes, this astonishing regularity manifested itself in patches; a thing to upset all the calculations of note-taking gamblers who play with a pencil and a memorandum-book in their hands. Fortune perpetrates some terrible jests at roulette!

Since my entry not more than half an hour could have elapsed. Suddenly a croupier informed me that I had won thirty thousand florins, as well as that, since the latter was the limit for which, at any one time, the bank could make itself responsible, roulette at that table must close for the night. Accordingly I caught up my pile of gold, stuffed it into my pocket, and, grasping my sheaf of bank-notes, moved to the table in an adjoining salon, where a second game of roulette was in progress. The crowd followed me in a body, and cleared a place for me at the table; after which I proceeded to stake as before – that is to say, at random and without calculating. What saved me from ruin I do not know.

Of course there were times when fragmentary reckonings *did* come flashing into my brain. For instance, there were times when I attached myself for a while to certain figures and coups – though always leaving them again before long, without knowing what I was doing. In fact, I cannot have been in possession of all my faculties, for I can remember the croupiers correcting my play more than once, owing to my having made mistakes of the gravest order. My brows were damp with sweat, and my hands were shaking. Also, Poles came around me to proffer their services, but I heeded none of them. Nor did my luck fail me now. Suddenly there arose around me a loud din of talking and laughter. 'Bravo, bravo!' was the general shout, and some people even clapped their hands. I had raked in thirty thousand florins, and again the bank had had to close for the night!

'Go away now, go away now,' a voice whispered to me on my right. The person who had spoken to me was a certain Jew of Frankfurt – a man who had been standing beside me the whole while, and occasionally helping me in my play.

'Yes, for God's sake go,' whispered a second voice in my left ear. Glancing around, I perceived that the second voice had come from a modestly, plainly dressed lady of rather less than thirty – a woman whose face, though pale and sickly-looking, bore also very evident traces of former beauty. At the moment I was stuffing the crumpled bank-notes into my pockets, and collecting all the gold that was left on the table. Seizing up my last note for five hundred gülden, I contrived to insinuate it, unperceived, into the hand of the pale lady. An overpowering impulse had made me do so, and I remember how her thin little fingers pressed mine in token of her lively gratitude. The whole affair was the work of a moment.

Then, collecting my belongings, I crossed to where trente et quarante was being played – a game which could boast of a more aristocratic public, and was played with cards instead of with a wheel. At this diversion the bank made itself responsible for a hundred thousand thalers as the limit, but the highest stake allowable was, as in roulette, four thousand florins. Although I knew nothing of the game – although I scarcely knew the stakes, except those on black and red – I joined the ring of players, while the rest of the crowd massed itself around me. At this distance of time I cannot remember whether I ever gave a thought to Polina; I seemed only to be conscious of a vague pleasure in seizing and raking in the bank-notes which kept massing themselves in a pile before me.

But, as ever, fortune seemed to be at my back. As though of set purpose, there came to my aid a circumstance which not infrequently repeats itself in gaming. The circumstance is that not infrequently luck attaches itself to, say, the red, and does not leave it for a space of, say, ten, or even fifteen, rounds in succession. Three days ago I had heard that, during the previous week, there had been a run of twenty-two coups on the red – an occurrence never before known at roulette, so that men spoke of it with astonishment. Naturally enough, many deserted the red after a dozen rounds, and practically no one could now be found to stake upon it. Yet upon the black also – the antithesis of the red – no experienced gambler would stake anything, for the reason that every practised player knows the meaning of 'capricious fortune.' That is to say, after the sixteenth (or so) success of the red, one would think that the seventeenth coup would inevitably fall upon the black; wherefore novices would be apt to back the latter in the seventeenth round, and even to double or treble their stakes upon it – only, in the end, to lose.

Yet some whim or other led me, on remarking that the red had come up consecutively for seven times, to attach myself to that colour. Probably this was mostly due to self-conceit, for I wanted to astonish the bystanders with the riskiness of my play. Also, I remember that – oh, strange sensation! – I suddenly, and without any challenge from my own presumption, became obsessed with a *desire* to take risks. If the spirit has passed through a great many sensations, possibly it can no longer be sated with them, but grows more excited, and demands more sensations, and stronger and stronger ones, until at length it falls exhausted. Certainly, if the rules of the game had permitted even of my staking fifty thousand florins at a time, I should have staked them. All of a sudden I heard exclamations arising that the whole thing was a marvel, since the red was turning up for the fourteenth time!

'Monsieur a gagné cent mille florins,' a voice exclaimed beside me.

I awoke to my senses. What? I had won a hundred thousand florins? If so, what more did I need to win? I grasped the bank-notes, stuffed them into my pockets, raked in the gold without counting it, and started to leave the Casino. As I passed through the salons people smiled to see my bulging pockets and unsteady gait, for the weight which I was carrying must have amounted to half a pood! Several hands I saw stretched out in my direction, and as I passed I filled them with all the money that I could grasp in my own. At length two Jews stopped me near the exit.

'You are a bold young fellow,' one said; 'but mind you depart early to-morrow – as early as you can, for if you do not you will lose everything that you have won.'

But I did not heed them. The Avenue was so dark that it was barely possible to distinguish one's hand before one's face, while the distance to the hotel was half a verst or so; but I feared neither pickpockets nor highwaymen. Indeed, never since my boyhood have I done that. Also, I cannot remember what I thought about on the way. I only felt a sort of fearful pleasure – the pleasure of success, of conquest, of power (how can

I best express it?). Likewise, before me there flitted the image of Polina; and I kept remembering, and reminding myself, that it was to *her* I was going, that it was in *her* presence I should soon be standing, that it was *she* to whom I should soon be able to relate and show everything. Scarcely once did I recall what she had lately said to me, or the reason why I had left her, or all those varied sensations which I had been experiencing a bare hour and a half ago. No, those sensations seemed to be things of the past, to be things which had righted themselves and grown old, to be things concerning which we needed to trouble ourselves no longer, since, for us, life was about to begin anew. Yet I had just reached the end of the Avenue when there *did* come upon me a fear of being robbed or murdered. With each step the fear increased until, in my terror, I almost started to run. Suddenly, as I issued from the Avenue, there burst upon me the lights of the hotel, sparkling with a myriad lamps! Yes, thanks be to God, I had reached home!

Running up to my room, I flung open the door of it. Polina was still on the sofa, with a lighted candle in front of her, and her hands clasped. As I entered she stared at me in astonishment (for, at the moment, I must have presented a strange spectacle). All I did, however, was to halt before her, and fling upon the table my burden of wealth.

⇉ FIFTEEN ⇇

I REMEMBER, TOO, HOW, WITHOUT moving from her place, or changing her attitude, she gazed into my face.

'I have won two hundred thousand francs!' cried I as I pulled out my last sheaf of bank-notes. The pile of paper currency occupied the whole table. I could not withdraw my eyes from it. Consequently, for a moment or two Polina escaped my mind. Then I set myself to arrange the pile in order, and to sort the notes, and to mass the gold in a separate heap. That done, I left everything where it lay, and proceeded to pace the room with rapid strides as I lost myself in thought. Then I darted to the table once more, and began to recount the money; until all of a sudden, as though I had remembered something, I rushed to the door, and closed and double-locked it. Finally I came to a meditative halt before my little trunk.

'Shall I put the money there until to-morrow?' I asked, turning sharply round to Polina as the recollection of her returned to me.

She was still in her old place – still making not a sound. Yet her eyes had followed every one of my movements. Somehow in her face there was a strange expression – an expression which I did not like. I think that I shall not be wrong if I say that it indicated sheer hatred.

Impulsively I approached her.

'Polina,' I said, 'here are twenty-five thousand florins – fifty thousand francs, or more. Take them, and to-morrow throw them in De Griers' face.'

She returned no answer.

'Or, if you should prefer,' I continued, 'let me take them to him myself to-morrow – yes, early to-morrow morning. Shall I?'

Then all at once she burst out laughing, and laughed for a long while. With astonishment and a feeling of offence I gazed at her. Her laughter was too like the derisive merriment which she had so often indulged in of late – merriment which had broken forth always at the time of my most passionate explanations. At length she ceased, and frowned at me from under her eyebrows.

'I am *not* going to take your money,' she said contemptuously.

'Why not?' I cried. 'Why not, Polina?'

'Because I am not in the habit of receiving money for nothing.'

'But I am offering it to you as a *friend*. In the same way I would offer you my very life.'

Upon this she threw me a long, questioning glance, as though she were seeking to probe me to the depths.

'You are giving too much for me,' she remarked with a smile. 'The beloved of De Griers is not worth fifty thousand francs.'

'Oh Polina, how can you speak so?' I exclaimed reproachfully. 'Am *I* De Griers?'

'You?' she cried with her eyes suddenly flashing. 'Why, I *hate* you! Yes, yes, I *hate* you! I love you no more than I do De Griers.'

Then she buried her face in her hands, and relapsed into hysterics. I darted to her side. Somehow I had an intuition of something having happened to her which had nothing to do with myself. She was like a person temporarily insane.

'Buy me, would you, would you? Would you buy me for fifty thousand francs as De Griers did?' she gasped between her convulsive sobs.

I clasped her in my arms, kissed her hands and feet, and fell upon my knees before her.

Presently the hysterical fit passed away, and, laying her hands upon my shoulders, she gazed for a while into my face, as though trying to read it. Something I said to her, but it was clear that she did not hear it. Her face looked so dark and despondent that I began to fear for her

reason. At length she drew me towards herself – a trustful smile playing over her features; and then, as suddenly, she pushed me away again as she eyed me dimly.

Finally she threw herself upon me in an embrace.

'You love me?' she said. '*Do* you? – you who were willing even to quarrel with the Baron at my bidding?'

Then she laughed – laughed as though something dear, but laughable, had recurred to her memory. Yes, she laughed and wept at the same time. What was I to do? I was like a man in a fever. I remember that she began to say something to me – though *what* I do not know, since she spoke with a feverish lisp, as though she were trying to tell me something very quickly. At intervals, too, she would break off into the smile which I was beginning to dread. 'No, no!' she kept repeating. '*You* are my dear one; *you* are the man I trust.' Again she laid her hands upon my shoulders, and again she gazed at me as she reiterated: 'You love me, you love me? Will you *always* love me?' I could not take my eyes off her. Never before had I seen her in this mood of humility and affection. True, the mood was the outcome of hysteria; but – ! All of a sudden she noticed my ardent gaze, and smiled slightly. The next moment, for no apparent reason, she began to talk of Astley.

She continued talking and talking about him, but I could not make out all she said – more particularly when she was endeavouring to tell me of something or other which had happened recently. On the whole, she appeared to be laughing at Astley, for she kept repeating that he was waiting for her, and did I know whether, even at that moment, he was not standing beneath the window? 'Yes, yes, he is there,' she said. 'Open the window, and see if he is not.' She pushed me in that direction; yet no sooner did I make a movement to obey her behest than she burst into laughter, and I remained beside her, and she embraced me.

'Shall we go away to-morrow?' presently she asked, as though some disturbing thought had recurred to her recollection. 'How would it be if we were to try and overtake Grandmamma? I think we should do so at Berlin. And what think you she would have to say to us when we caught her up, and her eyes first lit upon us? What, too, about Mr. Astley? *He* would not leap from the Schlangenberg for my sake! No! Of that I am *very* sure!' – and she laughed. 'Do you know where he is going next year? He says he intends to go to the North Pole for scientific investigations, and has invited me to go with him! Ha, ha, ha! He also says that we Russians know nothing, can do nothing, without European help. But he is a good fellow all the same. For instance, he does not blame the General in the matter, but declares that Mlle. Blanche – that love — But no; I do not know, I do not know.' She stopped suddenly, as though she had said her say, and were feeling bewildered. 'What poor creatures these people are. How sorry I am for them, and for Grandmamma! But when are you going to kill De Griers? Surely you do not intend actually to murder him? You fool! Do you suppose that I should *allow* you to fight De Griers? Nor shall you kill the Baron.' Here she burst out laughing. 'How absurd you looked when you were talking to the Burmergelms! I was watching you all the time – watching you from where I was sitting. And how unwilling you were to go when I sent you! Oh, how I laughed and laughed!'

Then she kissed and embraced me again; again she pressed her face to mine with tender passion. Yet I neither saw nor heard her, for my head was in a whirl . . .

It must have been about seven o'clock in the morning when I awoke. Daylight had come, and Polina was sitting by my side – a strange expression on her face, as though she had seen a vision and were unable to collect her thoughts. She too had just awoken, and was now staring at the money on the table. My head ached; it felt heavy. I attempted to take Polina's hand, but she pushed me from her, and leapt from the sofa. The dawn was full of mist, for rain had fallen, yet she moved to the window, opened it, and, leaning her elbows upon the window-sill, thrust out her head and shoulders to take the air. In this position did she remain for several minutes, without ever looking round at me, or listening to what I was saying. Into my head there came the uneasy thought: What is to happen now? How is it all to end? Suddenly Polina rose from the window, approached the table, and, looking at me with an expression of infinite aversion, said with lips which quivered with anger:

'Well? Are you going to hand me over my fifty thousand francs?'

'Polina, you say that *again, again*?' I exclaimed.

'You have changed your mind, then? Ha, ha, ha! You are sorry you ever promised them?'

On the table where, the previous night, I had counted the money there still was lying the packet of twenty-five thousand florins. I handed it to her.

'The francs are mine, then, are they? They are mine?' she inquired viciously as she balanced the money in her hands.

'Yes; they have *always* been yours,' I said.

'Then *take* your fifty thousand francs!' and she hurled them full in my face. The packet burst as she did so, and the floor became strewed with bank-notes. The instant that the deed was done she rushed from the room.

At that moment she cannot have been in her right mind: yet what was the cause of her temporary aberration I cannot say. For a month past she had been unwell. Yet what had brought about this *present* condition of mind – above all things, this outburst? Had it come of wounded pride? Had it come of despair over her decision to come to me? Had it come of the fact that, presuming too much on my good fortune, I had seemed to be intending to desert her (even as De Griers had done) when once I had given her the fifty thousand francs? But, on my honour, I had never cherished any such intention. What was at fault, I think, was her own pride, which kept urging her not to trust me, but, rather, to insult me – even though she had not realized the fact. In her eyes I corresponded to De Griers, and therefore had been condemned for a fault not wholly my own. Her mood, of late, had been a sort of delirium, a sort of lightheaded-ness – that I knew full well; yet never had I sufficiently taken it into consideration. Perhaps she would not pardon me now? Ah, but this was *the present*. What about the future? Her delirium and sickness were not likely to make her forget what she had done in bringing me De Griers' letter. No, she must have known what she was doing when she brought it.

Somehow I contrived to stuff the pile of notes and gold under the bed, to cover them over, and then to leave the room some ten minutes after Polina. I felt sure that she had returned to her own room; wherefore I intended quietly to follow her, and to ask the nursemaid who opened the door how her mistress was. Judge, therefore, of my surprise when, meet-ing the domestic on the stairs, she informed me that Polina had not yet returned, and that she (the domestic) was at that moment on her way to my room in quest of her!

'Mlle. left me but ten minutes ago,' I said. 'What can have become of her?'

The nursemaid looked at me reproachfully.

Already sundry rumours were flying about the hotel. Both in the office of the commissionaire and in that of the landlord it was whispered that, at seven o'clock that morning, the Fraülein had left the hotel, and set off, despite the rain, in the direction of the Hôtel d'Angleterre. From words and hints let fall I could see that the fact of Polina having spent the night in my room was now public property. Also, sundry rumours were circulating concerning the General's family affairs. It was known that last night he had gone out of his mind, and paraded the hotel in tears; also, that the old lady who had arrived was his mother, and that she had come from Russia on purpose to forbid her son's marriage with Mlle. de Cominges, as well as to cut him out of her will if he should disobey her; also that, because he had disobeyed her, she had squandered all her money at roulette, in order to have nothing more to leave to him. 'Oh, these Russians!' exclaimed the landlord, with an angry toss of the head; while the bystanders laughed and the clerk betook himself to his accounts. Also, every one had learnt about my winnings; Karl, the corridor lacquey, was the first to congratulate me. But with these folk I had nothing to do. My business was to set off at full speed to the Hôtel d'Angleterre.

As yet it was early for Mr. Astley to receive visitors; but as soon as he learnt that it was *I* who had arrived, he came out into the corridor to meet me, and stood looking at me in silence with his steel-grey eyes as he waited to hear what I had to say. I inquired after Polina.

'She is ill,' he replied, still looking at me with his direct, unwavering glance.

'And she is in your rooms?'

'Yes, she is in my rooms.'

'Then you are minded to keep her there?'

'Yes, I am minded to keep her there.'

'But, Mr. Astley, that will raise a scandal. It ought not to be allowed. Besides, she is very ill. Perhaps you had not remarked that?'

'Yes, I have. It was *I* who told *you* about it. Had she not been ill, she would not have gone and spent the night with you.'

'Then you know all about it?'

'Yes; for last night she was to have accompanied me to the house of a relative of mine. Unfortunately, being ill, she made a mistake, and went to your rooms instead.'

'Indeed? Then I wish you joy, Mr. Astley. Apropos, you have reminded me of something. Were you beneath my window last night? Every moment Mlle. Polina kept telling me to open the window and see if you were there; after which she always smiled.'

'Indeed? No, I was *not* there; but I *was* waiting in the corridor, and walking about the hotel.'

'She ought to see a doctor, you know, Mr. Astley.'

'Yes, she ought. I have sent for one, and, if she dies, I shall hold you responsible.'

This surprised me.

'Pardon me,' I replied, 'but what do you mean?'

'Never mind. Tell me if it is true that, last night, you won two hundred thousand thalers?'

'No; I won a hundred thousand florins.'

'Good heavens! Then I suppose you will be off to Paris this morning?'

'Why?'

'Because all Russians who have grown rich go to Paris,' explained Astley, as though he had read the fact in a book.

'But what could I do in Paris in summer time? – I *love* her, Mr. Astley! Surely you know that?'

'Indeed? I am sure that you do *not*. Moreover, if you were to stay here, you would lose everything that you possess, and have nothing left with which to pay your expenses in Paris. Well, good-bye now. I feel sure that to-day will see you gone from here.'

'Good-bye. But I am *not* going to Paris. Likewise – pardon me – what is to become of this family? I mean that the affair of the General and Mlle. Polina will soon be all over the town.'

'I daresay; yet I hardly suppose that that will break the General's heart. Moreover, Mlle. Polina has a perfect right to live where she chooses. In short, we may say that, as a family, this family has ceased to exist.'

I departed, and found myself smiling at the Englishman's strange assurance that I should soon be leaving for Paris, 'I suppose he means to shoot me in a duel, should Polina die. Yes, that is what he intends to do.' Now, although I was honestly sorry for Polina, it is a fact that, from the moment when, the previous night, I had approached the gaming-table, and begun to rake in the packets of bank-notes, my love for her had entered upon a new plane. Yes, I can say that now; although, at the time, I was barely conscious of it. Was I, then, at heart a gambler? Did I, after all, love Polina not so *very* much? No, no! As God is my witness, I loved her! Even when I was returning home from Mr. Astley's my suffering was genuine, and my self-reproach sincere. But presently I was to go through an exceedingly strange and ugly experience.

I was proceeding to the General's rooms when I heard a door near to me open, and a voice call me by name. It was Mlle.'s mother, the Widow de Cominges, who was inviting me, in her daughter's name, to enter.

I did so; whereupon I heard a laugh and a little cry proceed from the bedroom (the pair occupied a suite of two apartments), where Mlle. Blanche was just arising.

'Ah, c'est lui! Viens, donc, bête! Is it true that you have won a mountain of gold and silver? J'aimerais mieux l'or.'

'Yes,' I replied with a smile.

'How much?'

'A hundred thousand florins.'

'Bibi, comme tu es bête! Come in here, for I can't hear you where you are now. Nous ferons bombance, n'est-ce pas?'

Entering her room, I found her lolling under a pink satin coverlet, and revealing a pair of swarthy, wonderfully healthy shoulders – shoulders such as one sees in dreams – shoulders covered over with a white cambric nightgown which, trimmed with lace, stood out, in striking relief, against the darkness of her skin.

'Mon fils, as-tu du cœur?' she cried when she saw me, and then giggled. Her laugh had always been a very cheerful one, and at times it even sounded sincere.

'Tout autre — ' I began, paraphrasing Corneille.

'See here,' she prattled on. 'Please search for my stockings and help me to dress. Aussi, si tu n'es pas trop bête, je te prends à Paris. I am just off, let me tell you.'

'This moment?'

'In half an hour.'

True enough, everything stood ready-packed – trunks, portmanteaux, and all. Coffee had long been served.

'Eh bien, tu verras Paris. Dis donc, qu'est-ce que c'est qu'un "utchitel"? Tu étais bien bête quand tu étais "utchitel." Where are my stockings? Please help me to dress.'

And she lifted up a really ravishing foot – small, swarthy, and not misshappen like the majority of feet which look dainty only in bottines. I laughed, and started to draw on to the foot a silk stocking, while Mlle. Blanche sat on the edge of the bed, and chattered.

'Eh bien, que feras-tu si je te prends avec moi? First of all I must have fifty thousand francs, and you shall give them to me at Frankfurt. Then we will go on to Paris, where we will live together, et je te ferai voir des étoiles en plein jour. Yes, you shall see such women as your eyes have never lit upon.'

'Stop a moment. If I were to give you those fifty thousand francs, what should I have left for myself?'

'Another hundred thousand francs, please to remember. Besides, I could live with you in your rooms for a month, or even for two, or even for longer. But it would not take us more than two months to get through fifty thousand francs; for, look you, je suis bonne enfante, et tu verras des étoiles, you may be sure.'

'What? You mean to say that we should spend the whole in two months?'

'Certainly. Does that surprise you very much? Ah, vil esclave! Why, one month of that life would be better than all your previous existence. One month – et après, le déluge! Mais tu ne peux comprendre. Va! Away, away! You are not worth it. – Ah, que fais-tu?'

For, while drawing on the other stocking, I had felt constrained to kiss her. Immediately she shrunk back, kicked me in the face with her toes, and turned me neck and crop out of the room.

'Eh, bien, mon "utchitel",' she called after me, 'je t'attends, si tu veux. I start in a quarter of an hour's time.'

I returned to my own room with my head in a whirl. It was not *my* fault that Polina had thrown a packet in my face, and preferred Mr. Astley to myself. A few bank-notes were still fluttering about the floor, and I picked them up. At that moment the door opened, and the landlord appeared – a person who, until now, had never bestowed upon me so much as a glance. He had come to know if I would prefer to move to a lower floor – to a suite which had just been tenanted by Count V.

For a moment I reflected.

'No!' I shouted. 'My account, please, for in ten minutes I shall be gone.'

'To Paris, to Paris!' I added to myself. 'Every man of birth must make her acquaintance.'

Within a quarter of an hour all three of us were seated in a family compartment – Mlle. Blanche, the Widow de Cominges, and myself. Mlle. kept laughing hysterically as she looked at me, and Madame re-echoed her; but I did not feel so cheerful. My life had broken in two, and yesterday had infected me with a habit of staking my all upon a card. Although it might be that I had failed to win my stake, that I had lost my senses, that I desired nothing better, I felt that the scene was to be changed only *for a time*. 'Within a month from now,' I kept thinking to myself. 'I shall be back again in Roulettenberg; and *then* I mean to have it out with you, Mr. Astley!' Yes, as now I look back at things, I remember that I felt greatly depressed, despite the absurd gigglings of the egregious Blanche.

'What is the matter with you? How dull you are!' she cried at length as she interrupted her laughter to take me seriously to task.

'Come, come! We are going to spend your two hundred thousand francs for you, et tu seras heureux comme un petit roi. I myself will tie your tie for you, and introduce you to Hortense. And when we have spent your money you shall return here, and break the bank again. What did those two Jews tell you? – that the thing most needed is daring, and that you possess it. Consequently this is not the first time that you will be hurrying to Paris with money in your pocket. Quant à moi, je veux cinquante mille francs de rente, et alors — '

'But what about the General?' I interrupted.

'The General? You know well enough that at about this hour every day he goes to buy me a bouquet. On this occasion I took care to tell him that he must hunt for the choicest of flowers; and when he returns home the poor fellow will find the bird flown? Possibly he may take wing in pursuit – ha, ha, ha! And if so, I shall not be sorry, for he could be useful to me in Paris, and Mr. Astley will pay his debts here.'

In this manner did I depart for the Gay City.

✦ SIXTEEN ✦

OF PARIS WHAT AM I TO SAY? The whole proceeding was a delirium, a madness. I spent a little over three weeks there, and, during that time, saw my hundred thousand francs come to an end. I speak only of the *one* hundred thousand francs, for the other hundred thousand I gave to Mlle. Blanche in pure cash. That is to say, I handed her fifty thousand francs at Frankfurt, and, three days later (in Paris), advanced her another fifty thousand on note of hand. Nevertheless a week had not elapsed before she came to me for more money. 'Et les cent mille francs qui nous restent,' she added, 'tu les mangeras avec moi, mon utchitel.' Yes, she always called me her 'utchitel.' A person more economical, grasping, and mean than Mlle. Blanche one could not imagine. But this was only as regards *her own* money. *My* hundred thousand francs (as she explained to me later) she needed to set up her establishment in Paris, 'so that once and for all I may be on a decent footing, and proof against any stones which may be thrown at me – at all events for a long time to come.' Nevertheless I saw nothing of those hundred thousand francs, for my own purse (which she inspected daily) never managed to amass in it more than a hundred francs at a time; and generally the sum did not reach even that figure.

'What do *you* want with money?' she would say to me with air of absolute simplicity; and I never disputed the point. Nevertheless, though she fitted out her flat very badly with the money, the fact did not prevent her from saying when, later, she was showing me over the rooms of her new abode: 'See what care and taste can do with the most wretched of means!' However, her 'wretchedness' had cost fifty thousand francs, while with the remaining fifty thousand she purchased a carriage and horses. Also, we gave a couple of balls – evening parties attended by Hortense and Lisette and Cléopatre, who were women remarkable both for the number of their liaisons and (though only in some cases) for their good looks. At these reunions I had to play the part of host – to meet and entertain fat mercantile parvenus who were impossible by reason of their rudeness and braggadocio, colonels of various kinds, hungry authors, and journalistic hacks: all of whom disported themselves in fashionable tailcoats and pale yellow gloves, and displayed such an aggregate of conceit and gasconade as would be unthinkable even in St. Petersburg – which is saying a great deal! They used to try to make fun of me, but I would console myself by drinking champagne, and then lolling in a retiring-room. Nevertheless I found it deadly work. 'C'est un utchitel,' Blanche would say of me, 'qui a gagné deux cent mille francs, and but for me, would have had not a notion how to spend them. Presently he will have to return to his tutoring. Does any one know of a vacant post? You know, one *must* do something for him.' I had the more frequent recourse to champagne in that I constantly felt depressed and bored, owing to the fact that I was living in the most bourgeois commercial milieu imaginable – a milieu wherein every sou was counted and grudged. Indeed, two weeks had not elapsed before I perceived that Blanche had no real affection for me, even though she dressed me in elegant clothes, and herself tied my tie each day. In short, she utterly despised me. But that caused me no concern. Blasé and inert, I spent my evenings generally at the Château des Fleurs, where I would get fuddled and then dance the cancan (which, in that establishment, was a very indecent performance) with éclat. At length the time came when Blanche had drained my purse dry. She had conceived an idea that, during the term of our residence together, it would be well if I were always to walk behind her with a paper and pencil, in order to jot down exactly what she spent, and what she had saved – what she was paying out, and what she was laying by. Well, of course I could not fail to be aware that this would entail a battle over every ten francs; so, although for every possible objection that I might make she had prepared a suitable answer, she soon saw that I made no objections, and therefore had to start disputes herself. That is to say, she would burst out into tirades which were met only with silence as I lolled on a sofa and stared fixedly at the ceiling. This greatly surprised her. At first she imagined that it was due merely to the fact that I was a fool, 'un utchitel'; wherefore she would break off her harangue in the belief that, being too stupid to understand, I was a hopeless case. Then she would leave the room, but return, ten minutes later, to resume the contest. This continued throughout her squandering of my money – a squandering altogether out of proportion to our means. An example is the way in which she changed her first pair of horses for a pair which cost sixteen thousand francs.

'Bibi,' she said on the latter occasion as she approached me, 'surely you are not angry?'

'No-o-o: I am merely tired,' was my reply as I pushed her from me. This seemed to her so curious that straightway she seated herself by my side.

'You see,' she went on, 'I decided to spend so much upon these horses only because I can easily sell them again. They would go at any time for *twenty* thousand francs.'

'Yes, yes. They are splendid horses, and you have got a splendid turn-out. I am quite content. Let me hear no more of the matter.'

'Then you are not angry?'

'No. Why should I be? You are wise to provide yourself with what you need, for it will all come in handy in the future. Yes, I quite see the necessity of your establishing yourself on a good basis, for without it you will never earn your million. My hundred thousand francs I look upon merely as a beginning – as a mere drop in the bucket.'

Blanche, who had by no means expected such declarations from me, but, rather, an uproar and protests, was rather taken aback.

'Well, well, what a man you are!' she exclaimed. 'Mais tu as l'esprit pour comprendre. Sais-tu, mon garçon, although you are a tutor, you ought to have been born a prince. Are you not sorry that your money should be going so quickly?'

'No. The quicker it goes the better.'

'Mais – sais-tu – mais dis donc, are you *really* rich? Mais sais-tu, you have too much contempt for money. Qu'est-ce que tu feras après, dis donc?'

'Après, I shall go to Homburg, and win another hundred thousand francs.'

'Oui, oui, c'est ça, c'est magnifique! Ah, I *know* you will win them, and bring them to me when you have done so. Dis donc – you will end by making me love you. Since you are what you are, I mean to love you all the time, and never to be unfaithful to you. You see, I have not loved you before parce que je croyais que tu n'es qu'un utchitel (quelque chose comme un lacquais, n'est-ce pas?) Yet all the time I have been true to you, parce que je suis bonne fille.'

'You lie!' I interrupted. 'Did I not see you, the other day, with Albert – with that black-jowled officer?'

'Oh, oh! Mais tu es —'

'Yes, you are lying right enough. But what makes you suppose that I should be angry? Rubbish! Il faut que jeunesse se passe. Even if that officer were here *now*, I should refrain from putting him out of the room if I thought you really cared for him. Only, mind you, do not give him any of my money. You hear?'

'You say, do you, that you would not be angry? Mais tu es un vrai philosophe, sais-tu? Oui, un vrai philosophe! Eh bien, je t'aimerai, je t'aimerai. Tu verras – tu seras content.'

True enough, from that time onward she seemed to attach herself only to me, and in this manner we spent our last ten days together. The promised 'étoiles' I did not see, but in other respects she, to a certain extent, kept her word. Moreover, she introduced me to Hortense, who was a remarkable woman in her way, and known among us as Thérèse Philosophe.

But I need not enlarge further, for to do so would require a story to itself, and entail a colouring which I am loth to impart to the present narrative. The point is that with all my faculties I desired the episode to come to an end as speedily as possible. Unfortunately, our hundred thousand francs lasted us, as I have said, for very nearly a month – which greatly surprised me. At all events Blanche bought herself articles to the tune of eighty thousand francs, and the rest sufficed just to meet our expenses of living. Towards the close of the affair Blanche grew almost frank with me (at least, she scarcely lied to me at all) – declaring, amongst other things, that none of the debts which she had been obliged to incur were going to fall upon my head. 'I have purposely refrained from making you responsible for my bills or borrowings,' she said, 'for the reason that I am sorry for you. Any other woman in my place would have done so, and have let you go to prison. See, then, how much I love you, and how goodhearted I am! Think, too, what this accursed marriage with the General is going to cost me!'

True enough, the marriage took place. It did so at the close of her and my month together, and I am bound to suppose that it was upon the ceremony that the last remnants of my money were spent. With it the episode – that is to say, my sojourn with the Frenchwoman – came to an end, and I formally retired from the scene.

It happened thus. A week after we had taken up our abode in Paris there arrived thither the General. He came straight to see us, and thenceforward lived with us practically as our guest, though he had a flat of his own as well. Blanche met him with merry badinage and laughter, and even threw her arms around him. In fact, she managed it so that he had to follow everywhere in her train – whether when promenading on the Boulevards, or when driving, or when going to the theatre, or when paying calls; and this use which she made of him quite satisfied the General. Still of imposing appearance and presence, as well as of fair height, he had a dyed moustache and whiskers (he had formerly been in the cuirassiers), and a handsome, though a somewhat wrinkled, face. Also, his manners were excellent, and he could carry a frockcoat well – the more so since, in Paris, he took to wearing his orders. To promenade the Boulevards with such a man was not only a thing possible, but also, so to speak, a thing advisable; and with this programme the good, but foolish, General had not a fault to find. The truth is that he had never counted upon this programme when he came to Paris to seek us out. On that occasion he had made his appearance nearly shaking with terror, for he had supposed that Blanche would at once raise an outcry, and have him put from the door; wherefore he was the more enraptured at the turn that things had taken, and spent the month in a state of senseless ecstasy. Already I had learnt that, after our unexpected departure from Roulettenberg, he had had a sort of a fit – that he had fallen into a swoon, and spent a week in a species of garrulous delirium. Doctors had been summoned to him, but he had broken away from them, and suddenly taken train to Paris. Of course Blanche's reception of him had acted as the best of all possible cures, but for long enough he carried the marks of his affliction, despite his present condition of rapture and delight. To think clearly, or even to engage in any serious conversation, had now become impossible for him; he could only ejaculate after each word 'Hm!' and then nod his head in confirmation. Sometimes, also, he would laugh, but only in a nervous, hysterical sort of a fashion; while at other times he would sit for hours looking as black as night, with his heavy eyebrows knitted. Of much that went on he remained wholly oblivious, for he grew extremely absent-minded, and took to talking to himself. Only Blanche could awake him to any semblance of life. His fits of depression and moodiness in corners always meant either that he had not seen her for some while, or that she had gone out without taking him with her, or that she had omitted to caress him before departing. When in this condition he would refuse to say what he wanted; nor had he the least idea that he was thus sulking and moping. Next, after remaining in this condition for an hour or two (this I remarked on two occasions when Blanche had gone out for the day – probably to see Albert), he would begin to look about him, and to grow uneasy, and to hurry about with an air as though he had suddenly remembered something, and must try and find it; after which, not perceiving the object of his search, nor succeeding in recalling what that object had been, he would as suddenly relapse into oblivion, and continue so until the reappearance of Blanche – merry, wanton, half-dressed, and laughing her strident laugh as she approached to pet him, and even to kiss him (though the latter reward he seldom received). Once he was so overjoyed at her doing so that he burst into tears. Even I myself was surprised.

From the first moment of his arrival in Paris Blanche set herself to plead with me on his behalf; and at such times she even rose to heights of eloquence – saying that it was for *me* she had abandoned him, though she had almost become his betrothed and promised to become so; that it was for *her* sake he had deserted his family; that, having been in his service, I ought to remember the fact, and to feel ashamed. To all this I would say nothing, however much she chattered on; until at length

I would burst out laughing, and the incident would come to an end (at first, as I have said, she had thought me a fool, but since she had come to deem me a man of sense and sensibility). In short, I had the happiness of calling her better nature into play; for though, at first, I had not deemed her so, she was, in reality, a kind-hearted woman – after her own fashion. 'You are good and clever,' she said to me towards the finish, 'and my one regret is that you are also so wrong-headed. You will *never* be a rich man!' 'Un vrai Russe – un Kalmuk' she usually called me.

Several times she sent me to give the General an airing in the streets, even as she might have done with a lacquey and her spaniel; but I preferred to take him to the theatre, to the Bal Mabille, and to restaurants. For this purpose she usually allowed me some money, though the General had a little of his own, and enjoyed taking out his purse before strangers. Once I had to use actual force to prevent him from buying a phaeton at a price of seven hundred francs, after a vehicle had caught his fancy in the Palais Royal as seeming to be a desirable present for Blanche. What could *she* have done with a seven-hundred-franc phaeton? – and the General possessed in the world but a thousand francs! The origin even of those francs I could never determine, but imagined them to have emanated from Mr. Astley – the more so since the latter had paid the family's hotel bill. As for what view the General took of myself, I think that he never divined the footing on which I stood with Blanche. True, he had heard, in a dim sort of way, that I had won a good deal of money; but more probably he supposed me to be acting as secretary – or even as a kind of servant – to his inamorata. At all events he continued to address me in his old haughty style, as my superior. At times he even took it upon himself to scold me. One morning, in particular, he started to sneer at me over our matutinal coffee. Though not a man prone to take offence, he suddenly, and for some reason of which to this day I am ignorant, fell out with me. Of course even he himself did not know the reason. To put things shortly, he began a speech which had neither beginning nor ending, and cried out, à bâtons rompus, that I was a boy whom he would soon put to rights – and so forth, and so forth. Yet no one could understand what he was saying, and at length Blanche exploded in a burst of laughter. Finally something appeased him, and he was taken out for his walk. More than once, however, I noticed that his depression was growing upon him; that he seemed to be feeling the want of somebody or something; that, despite Blanche's presence, he was missing some person in particular. Twice, on these occasions, did he plunge into a conversation with me, though he could not make himself intelligible, and only went on rambling about the service, his late wife, his home, and his property. Every now and then, also, some particular word would please him;

whereupon he would repeat it a hundred times in the day – even though the word happened to express neither his thoughts nor his feelings. Again, I would try to get him to talk about his children, but always he cut me short in his old snappish way, and passed to another subject. 'Yes, yes – my children,' was all that I could extract from him.' Only once did he disclose his real feelings. That was when we were taking him to the theatre, and suddenly he exclaimed: 'My unfortunate children! Yes, sir, they *are* unfortunate children.' Once, too, when I chanced to mention Polina, he grew quite bitter against her. 'She is an ungrateful woman!' he exclaimed. 'She is a bad and ungrateful woman! She has broken up a family. If there were laws here, I would have her impaled. Yes, I would.' As for De Griers, the General would not have his name mentioned. 'He has ruined me,' he would say. 'He has robbed me, and cut my throat. For two years he was a perfect nightmare to me. For months at a time he never left me in my dreams. Do not speak of him again.'

It was now clear to me that Blanche and he were on the point of coming to terms: yet, true to my usual custom, I said nothing. At length Blanche took the initiative in explaining matters. She did so a week before we parted.

'Il a de la chance,' she prattled; 'for the Grandmother is now *really* ill, and therefore bound to die. Mr. Astley has just sent a telegram to say so, and you will agree with me that the General is likely to be her heir. Even if he should not be so, he will not come amiss, since, in the first place, he has his pension, and, in the second place, he will be content to live in a back room; whereas *I* shall be Madame General, and get into a good circle of society' (she was always thinking of this) 'and become a Russian châtelaine. Yes, I shall have a mansion of my own, and peasants, and a million of money at my back.'

'But, suppose he should prove jealous? He might demand all sorts of things, you know. Do you follow me?'

'Oh, dear no! How ridiculous that would be of him! Besides, I have taken measures to prevent it. You need not be alarmed. That is to say, I have induced him to sign notes of hand in Albert's name. Consequently, at any time I could get him punished. Isn't he ridiculous?'

'Very well, then. Marry him.'

And, in truth, she did so – though the marriage was a family one only, and involved no pomp or ceremony. In fact, she invited to the nuptials none but Albert and a few other friends. Hortense, Cléopatre, and the rest she kept firmly at a distance. As for the bridegroom, he took a great interest in his new position. Blanche herself tied his tie, and Blanche herself pomaded him: with the result that, in his frockcoat and white waistcoat, he looked quite comme il faut.

'Il est, pourtant, *très* comme il faut,' Blanche remarked when she issued from his room, as though the idea that he was '*très* comme il faut' had impressed even her. For myself, I had so little knowledge of the minor details of the affair, and took part in it so much as a supine spectator, that I have forgotten most of what passed on this occasion. I only remember that Blanche and the Widow figured at it, not as 'de Cominges,' but as 'du Placet.' Why they had hitherto been 'de Cominges' I do not know: I only know that this entirely satisfied the General – that he liked the name 'du Placet' even better than he had liked the name 'de Cominges.' On the morning of the wedding he paced the salon in his gala attire, and kept repeating to himself with an air of great gravity and importance: 'Mlle. Blanche du Placet! Mlle. Blanche du Placet, du Placet!' He beamed with satisfaction as he did so. Both in the church and at the wedding breakfast he remained, not only pleased and contented, but even proud. She too underwent a change, for now she assumed an air of added dignity.

'I must behave altogether differently,' she confided to me with a serious air. 'Yet, mark you, there is a tiresome circumstance of which I had never before thought – which is, how best to pronounce my new family name. Zagorianski, Zagozianski, Madame la Générale de Sago, Madame la Générale de Fourteen Consonants – oh, these infernal Russian names! The *last* of them would be the best to use, don't you think?'

At length the time had come for us to part, and Blanche, the egregious Blanche, shed real tears as she took her leave of me. 'Tu étais bon enfant,' she said with a sob. 'Je te croyais bête, et tu en avais l'air, but it suited you.' Then, having given me a final handshake, she exclaimed, 'Attends!'; whereafter, running into her boudoir, she brought me thence two thousand-franc notes. I could scarcely believe my eyes! 'They may come in handy for you,' she explained; 'for, though you are a very learned tutor, you are a very stupid man. More than two thousand francs, however, I am not going to give you, for the reason that, if I did so, you would gamble them all away. Now good-bye. Nous serons toujours bons amis, and if you win again, do not fail to come to me, et tu seras heureux.'

I myself had still five hundred francs left, as well as a watch worth a thousand francs, a few diamond studs, and so on. Consequently, I could subsist for quite a length of time without particularly bestirring myself. Purposely I have taken up my abode where I am now – partly to pull myself together, and partly to wait for Mr. Astley, who, I have learnt, will soon be here for a day or so on business. Yes, I know that, and then – and then I shall go to Homburg. But to Roulettenberg I shall not go until next year, for they say it is bad to try one's luck twice in succession at a table. Moreover, Homburg is where the *best* play is carried on.

⋙ SEVENTEEN ⋘

IT IS A YEAR AND EIGHT MONTHS since I last looked at these notes of mine. I do so now only because, being overwhelmed with depression, I wish to distract my mind by reading them through at random. I left them off at the point where I was just going to Homburg. My God, with what a light heart (comparatively speaking) did I write the concluding lines! – though, it may be, not so much with a light heart as with a measure of self-confidence and unquenchable hope. At that time had I any doubts of myself? Yet behold me now. Scarcely a year and a half have passed, yet I am in a worse position than the meanest beggar. But what *is* a beggar? A fig for beggary! I have ruined myself – that is all. Nor is there anything with which I can compare myself; there is no moral which it would be of any use for you to read to me. At the present moment nothing could well be more incongruous than a moral. Oh, you self-satisfied persons who, in your unctuous pride, are for ever ready to mouth your maxims – if only you knew how fully I myself comprehend the sordidness of my present state, you would not trouble to wag your tongues at me! What could you say to me that I do not already know? Well, wherein lies my difficulty? It lies in the fact that by a single turn of a roulette wheel everything, for me, has become changed. Yet, had things befallen otherwise, these moralists would have been among the first (yes, I feel persuaded of it) to approach me with friendly jests and congratulations. Yes, they would never have turned from me as they are doing now! A fig for all of them! What am I? I am zero – nothing. What shall I be to-morrow? I may be risen from the dead, and have begun life anew. For still I may discover the man in myself, if only my manhood has not become utterly shattered.

I went, I say, to Homburg, but afterwards went also to Roulettenberg, as well as to Spa and Baden; in which latter place, for a time, I acted as valet to a certain rascal of a Privy Councillor, by name Heintze, who until lately was also my master here. Yes, for five months I lived my life with lacqueys! That was just after I had come out of Roulettenberg prison, where I had lain for a small debt which I owed. Out of that prison I was bailed by – by whom? By Mr. Astley? By Polina? I do not know. At all events the debt was paid to the tune of two hundred thalers, and I sallied forth a free man. But what was I to do with myself? In my dilemma I had recourse to this Heintze, who was a young scapegrace, and the sort of man who could speak and write three languages. At first I acted as his secretary, at a salary of thirty gülden a month, but afterwards I became his lacquey, for the reason that he could not afford to keep a secretary – only an unpaid servant. I had nothing else to turn to, so I remained with him, and allowed myself to become his flunkey. But by stinting myself in meat and drink I saved, during my five months of service, some seventy gülden; and one evening, when we were at Baden, I told him that I wished to resign my post, and then hastened to betake myself to roulette. Oh, how my heart beat as I did so! No, it was not the money that I valued: what I wanted was to make all this mob of Heintzes, hotel proprietors, and fine ladies of Baden talk about me, recount my story, wonder at me, extol my doings, and worship my winnings. True, these were childish fancies and aspirations, but who knows but that I might meet Polina, and be able to tell her everything, and see her look of surprise at the fact that I had overcome so many adverse strokes of fortune. No, I had no desire for money for its own sake, for I was perfectly well aware that I should only squander it upon some new Blanche, and spend another three weeks in Paris after buying a pair of horses which had cost sixteen thousand francs. No, I never believed myself to be a hoarder; in fact, I knew only too well that I was a spendthrift. And already, with a sort of fear, a sort of sinking, in my heart, I could hear the cries of the croupiers – 'Trente et un, rouge, impair et passe,' 'Quarte, noir, pair et manque'! How greedily I gazed upon the gaming-table, with its scattered louis d'or, ten-gülden pieces, and thalers; upon the streams of gold as they issued from the croupier's hands, and piled themselves up into heaps of gold scintillating as fire; upon the ell-long rolls of silver lying around the croupier. Even at a distance of two rooms I could hear the chink of that money – so much so that I nearly fell into convulsions.

Ah, the evening when I took those seventy gülden to the gaming table was a memorable one for me. I began by staking ten gülden upon passe. For passe I had always had a sort of predilection, yet I lost my stake upon it. This left me with sixty gülden in silver. After a moment's thought I selected zero – beginning by staking five gülden at a time. Twice I lost, but the third round suddenly brought up the desired coup. I could almost have died with joy as I received my one hundred and seventy-five gülden. Indeed, I have been less pleased when, in former times, I have won a hundred thousand gülden. Losing no time, I staked another hundred gülden upon the red, and won; two hundred upon the red, and won; four hundred upon the black, and won; eight hundred upon manque, and won. Thus, with the addition of the remainder of my original capital, I found myself possessed, within five minutes, of seventeen hundred gülden! Ah, at such moments one forgets both oneself and one's former failures! This I had gained by risking my very life. I had dared so to risk, and, behold, again I was a member of mankind!

I went and hired a room, I shut myself up in it, and sat counting my money until three o'clock in the morning. To think that when I awoke on the morrow, I was no lacquey! I decided to leave at once for Homburg. There I should neither have to serve as a footman nor to lie in prison. Half an hour before starting I went and ventured a couple of stakes – no more; with the result that, in all, I lost fifteen hundred florins. Nevertheless I proceeded to Homburg, and have now been there for a month.

Of course I am living in constant trepidation – playing for the smallest of stakes, and always looking out for something – calculating, standing whole days by the gaming-tables to watch the play – even seeing that play in my dreams – yet seeming, the while, to be in some way stiffening, to be growing caked, as I were, in mire. But I must conclude my notes, which I finish under the impression of a recent encounter with Mr. Astley. I had not seen him since we parted at Roulettenberg, and now we met quite by accident. At the time I was walking in the public gardens, and meditating upon the fact that not only had I still some fifty gülden in my possession, but also I had fully paid up my hotel bill three days ago. Consequently I was in a position to try my luck again at roulette; and if I won anything I should be able to continue my play, whereas, if I lost what I now possessed, I should once more have to accept a lacquey's place, provided that, in the alternative, I failed to discover a Russian family which stood in need of a tutor. Plunged in these reflections, I started on my daily walk through the Park and forest towards a neighbouring principality. Sometimes, on such occasions, I spent four hours on the way, and would return to Homburg tired and hungry; but on this particular occasion I had scarcely left the gardens for the Park when I caught sight of Astley, seated on a bench. As soon as he perceived me, he called me by name, and I went and sat down beside him; but on noticing that he seemed a little stiff in his manner, I hastened to moderate the expression of joy which the sight of him had called forth.

'*You* here?' he said. 'Well, I had an idea that I should meet you. Do not trouble to tell me anything, for I know all – yes, all. In fact, your whole life during the past twenty months lies within my knowledge.'

'How closely you watch the doings of your old friends!' I replied. 'That does you infinite credit. But stop a moment. You have reminded me of something. Was it you who bailed me out of Roulettenberg prison when I was lying there for a debt of two hundred gülden? *Some one* did so.'

'Oh dear no! – though I knew all the time that you were lying there.'

'Perhaps you could tell me who *did* bail me out?'

'No; I am afraid I could not.'

'What a strange thing! For I know no Russians at all here, so it cannot have been a Russian who befriended me. In Russia we Orthodox folk *do* go bail for one another, but in this case I thought it must have been done by some English stranger who was not conversant with the ways of the country.'

Mr. Astley seemed to listen to me with a sort of surprise. Evidently he had expected to see me looking more crushed and broken than I was.

'Well,' he said – not very pleasantly, 'I am none the less glad to find that you retain your old independence of spirit, as well as your buoyancy.'

'Which means that you are vexed at not having found me more abased and humiliated than I am?' I retorted with a smile.

Astley was not quick to understand this, but presently did so and laughed.

'Your remarks please me as they always did,' he continued. 'In those words I see the clever, triumphant, and, above all things, cynical friend of former days. Only Russians have the faculty of combining within themselves so many opposite qualities. Yes, most men love to see their best friend in abasement; for generally it is on such abasement that friendship is founded. All thinking persons know that ancient truth. Yet, on the present occasion, I assure you, I am sincerely glad to see that you are *not* cast down. Tell me, are you never going to give up gambling?'

'Damn the gambling! Yes, I should certainly have given it up, were it not that — '

'That you are losing? I thought so. You need not tell me any more. I know how things stand, for you have said that last in despair, and therefore truthfully. Have you no other employment than gambling?'

'No; none whatever.'

Astley gave me a searching glance. At that time it was ages since I had last looked at a paper or turned the pages of a book.

'You are growing blasé,' he said. 'You have not only renounced life, with its interests and social ties – the duties of a citizen and a man; you have not only renounced the friends whom I know you to have had, and every aim in life but that of winning money; but you have also renounced your memory. Though I can remember you in the strong, ardent period of your life, I feel persuaded that you have now forgotten every better feeling of that period – that your present dreams and aspirations of subsistence do not rise above pair, impair, rouge, noir, the twelve middle numbers, and so forth.'

'Enough, Mr. Astley!' I cried with some irritation – almost in anger. 'Kindly do not recall to me any more recollections, for I can remember things for myself. Only for a time have I put them out of my head. Only until I shall have rehabilitated myself am I keeping my memory dulled. When that hour shall come you will see me arise from the dead.'

'Then you will have to be here another ten years,' he replied. 'Should I then be alive, I will remind you – here, on this very bench – of what I have just said. In fact, I will bet you a wager that I shall do so.'

'Say no more,' I interrupted impatiently. 'And to show you that I have not wholly forgotten the past, may I enquire where Mlle. Polina is? If it was not you who bailed me out of prison, it must have been she. Yet never have I heard a word concerning her.'

'No, I do not think it was she. At the present moment she is in Switzerland, and you will do me a favour by ceasing to ask me these questions about her.' Astley said this with a firm, and even an angry, air.

'Which means that she has dealt you a serious wound?' I burst out with an involuntary sneer.

'Mlle. Polina,' he continued, 'is the best of all possible living beings; but I repeat that I shall thank you to cease questioning me about her. You never really knew her, and her name on your lips is an offence to my moral feeling.'

'Indeed? On what subject, then, have I a better right to speak to you than on this? With it are bound up all your recollections and mine. However, do not be alarmed: I have no wish to probe too far into your private, your secret affairs. My interest in Mlle. Polina does not extend beyond her outward circumstances and surroundings. About them you could tell me in two words.'

'Well, on condition that the matter shall end there, I will tell you that for a long time Mlle. Polina was ill, and still is so. My mother and sister entertained her for a while at their home in the north of England, and thereafter Mlle. Polina's grandmother (you remember the mad old woman?) died, and left Mlle. Polina a personal legacy of seven thousand pounds sterling. That was about six months ago, and now Mlle. is travelling with my sister's family – my sister having since married. Mlle.'s little brother and sister also benefited by the Grandmother's will, and are now being educated in London. As for the General, he died in Paris last month, of a stroke. Mlle. Blanche did well by him, for she succeeded in having transferred to herself all that he received from the Grandmother. That, I think, concludes all that I have to tell.'

'And De Griers? Is he too travelling in Switzerland?'

'No; nor do I know where he is. Also I warn you once more that you had better avoid such hints and ignoble suppositions; otherwise you will assuredly have to reckon with me.'

'What? In spite of our old friendship?'

'Yes, in spite of our old friendship.'

'Then I beg your pardon a thousand times, Mr. Astley. I meant nothing offensive to Mlle. Polina, for I have nothing of which to accuse her. Moreover, the question of there being anything between this Frenchman and this Russian lady is not one which you and I need discuss, nor even attempt to understand.'

'If,' replied Astley, 'you do not care to hear their names coupled together, may I ask you what you mean by the expressions "this Frenchman," "this Russian lady," and "there being anything between them?" Why do you call them so particularly a "Frenchman" and a "Russian lady"?'

'Ah, I see you are interested, Mr. Astley. But it is a long, long story, and calls for a lengthy preface. At the same time, the question is an important one, however ridiculous it may seem at the first glance. A Frenchman, Mr. Astley, is merely a fine figure of a man. With this you, as a Britisher, may not agree. With it I also, as a Russian, may not agree – out of envy. Yet possibly our good ladies are of another opinion. For instance, one may look upon Racine as a broken-down, hobbledehoy, perfumed individual – one may even be unable to read him; and I too may think him the same, as well as, in some respects, a subject for ridicule. Yet about him, Mr. Astley, there is a certain charm, and above all things, he is a great poet – though one might like to deny it. Yes, the Frenchman, the Parisian, as a national figure, was in process of developing into a figure of elegance before we Russians had even ceased to be bears. The Revolution bequeathed to the French nobility its heritage, and now every whipper-snapper of a Parisian may possess manners, methods of expression, and even thoughts that are above reproach in form, while all the time he himself may share in that form neither in initiative nor in intellect nor in soul – his manners, and the rest, having come to him through inheritance. Yes, taken by himself, the Frenchman is frequently a fool of fools and a villain of villains. Per contra, there is no one in the world more worthy of confidence and respect than this young Russian lady. De Griers might so mask his face and play a part as easily to overcome her heart, for he had an imposing figure, Mr. Astley, and this young lady might easily take that figure for his real self – for the natural form of his heart and soul instead of the mere cloak with which heredity has dowered him. And even though it may offend you, I feel bound to say that the majority also of English people are uncouth and unrefined, whereas we Russian folk can recognize beauty wherever we see it, and are always eager to cultivate the same. But to distinguish beauty of soul and personal originality there is needed far more independence and freedom than is possessed by our women, especially by our younger ladies. At all events they need more *experience*. For instance, this Mlle. Polina – pardon me, but the name has passed my lips, and I cannot well recall it – is taking a very long time to make up her mind to prefer you to Monsieur de Griers. She may respect you, she may become your friend, she may open out her heart to you; yet over that heart there will be reigning that loathsome villain, that mean and petty usurer, De Griers. This will be due to obstinacy and self-love – to the fact that De Griers once appeared to her in the transfigured guise of a marquis, of a disenchanted and ruined liberal who was doing his best to help her family and the frivolous old General; and although these transactions of his have since been exposed, you will find that the exposure has made no impression upon her mind. Only give her the De Griers of former days, and she will ask of you no more. The more she may detest the present De Griers, the more will she lament the De Griers of the past – even though the latter never existed but in her own imagination. You are a sugar refiner, Mr. Astley, are you not?'

'Yes, I belong to the well-known firm of Lovell and Co.'

'Then see here. On the one hand, you are a sugar refiner, while, on the other hand, you are an Apollo Belvedere. But the two characters do not mix with one another. I, again, am not even a sugar refiner; I am a mere roulette gambler who has also served as a lacquey. Of this fact Mlle. Polina is probably well aware, since she appears to have an excellent force of police at her disposal.'

'You are saying this because you are feeling bitter,' said Astley with cold indifference. 'Yet there is not the least originality in your words.'

'I agree. But therein lies the horror of it all – that, however mean and farcical my accusations may be, they are none the less *true*. But I am only wasting words.'

'Yes, you are, for you are only talking nonsense!' exclaimed my companion – his voice now trembling and his eyes flashing fire. 'Are you aware,' he continued, 'that, wretched, ignoble, petty, unfortunate man though you are, it was at *her* request I came to Homburg, in order to see you, and to have a long, serious talk with you, and to report to her your feelings and thoughts and hopes – yes, and your recollections of her, too?'

'Indeed? Is that really so?' I cried – the tears beginning to well from my eyes. Never before had this happened.

'Yes, poor unfortunate,' continued Astley. 'She *did* love you: and I may tell you this now for the reason that now you are utterly lost. Even if I were also to tell you that she still loves you, you would none the less have to remain where you are. Yes, you have ruined yourself beyond redemption. Once upon a time you had a certain amount of talent, and you were of a lively disposition, and your good looks were not to be despised. You might even have been useful to your country, which needs men like you. Yet you remained here, and your life is now over. I am not blaming you for this: in my view all Russians resemble you, or are inclined to do so. If it is not roulette, then it is something else. The exceptions are very rare. Nor are you the first to learn what a taskmaster is yours. For roulette is not exclusively a Russian game. Hitherto you have honourably preferred to serve as a lacquey rather than to act as a thief; but what the future may have in store for you I tremble to think. Now good-bye. You are in want of money, I suppose? Then take these ten louis d'or. More I shall not give you, for you would only gamble it away. Take care of these coins, and farewell. Once more, *take care* of them.'

'No, Mr. Astley. After all that has been said I — '

'*Take care* of them!' repeated my friend. 'I am certain you are still a gentleman, and therefore I give you the money as one gentleman may give money to another. Also, if I could be certain that you would leave both Homburg and the gaming-tables, and return to your own country, I would give you a thousand pounds down to start life afresh; but I give you ten louis d'or instead of a thousand pounds for the reason that at the present time a thousand pounds and ten louis d'or will be all the same to you – you will lose the one as readily as you will the other. Take the money, therefore, and good-bye.'

'Yes, I *will* take it if at the same time you will embrace me.'

'With pleasure.'

So we parted – on terms of sincere affection.

But he was wrong. If *I* was hard and undiscerning as regards Polina and De Griers, *he* was hard and undiscerning as regards Russian people generally. Of myself I say nothing. Yet – yet words are only words. I need to *act*. Above all things I need to think of Switzerland. To-morrow, to-morrow – Ah, but if only I could set things right to-morrow, and be born again, and rise again from the dead! But no – I cannot. Yet I must show her what I can do. Even if she should do no more than learn that I can still play the man, it would be worth it. To-day it is too late, but *to-morrow.* Yet I have a presentiment that things can never be otherwise. I have got fifteen louis d'or in my possession, although I began with fifteen gülden. If I were to play carefully at the start — But no, no! Surely I am not such a fool as that? Yet *why* should I not rise from the dead? I should require at first but to go cautiously and patiently and the rest would follow. I should require but to put a check upon my nature for one hour, and my fortunes would be changed entirely. Yes, my nature is my weak point. I have only to remember what happened to me some months ago at Roulettenberg, before my final ruin. What a notable instance that was of my capacity for resolution! On the occasion in question I had lost every-thing – everything; yet, just as I was leaving the Casino, I heard another gülden give a rattle in my pocket! 'Perhaps I shall need it for a meal,' I thought to myself; but a hundred paces further on, I changed my mind, and returned. That gülden I staked upon manque – and there *is* something in the feeling that, though one is alone, and in a foreign land, and far from one's own home and friends, and ignorant of whence one's next meal is to come, one is nevertheless staking one's very last coin! Well, I won the stake, and in twenty minutes had left the Casino with a hundred and seventy gülden in my pocket! That is a fact, and it shows what a last remaining gülden can do. . . . But what if my heart had failed me, or I had shrunk from making up my mind? . . .

No; to-morrow all shall be ended!

LETTERS FROM THE
UNDERWORLD

➤ PREFACE BY THE AUTHOR ◀

IT need hardly be said that both the writer of these 'Letters' and the 'Letters' themselves are creatures of the imagination. Nevertheless, in view of the circumstances under which, in general, our community has become formed, such men as the writer in question not only may, but are bound to, exist. I have tried, therefore, to set before the public, in more striking guise than usual, a character which is peculiar to the present age – a representative type of the generation which has not yet passed away. In the 'Letter' headed 'The Underworld' this individual presents himself and his views of life, and purports to explain the causes which have created his personality – a personality due to the *milieu* which all of us share in Russia; while in the second of the two 'Letters' he describes certain incidents which are supposed actually to have occurred during his life.

FYODOR DOSTOYEVSKY

1846

PART ONE

The Underworld

✦ ONE ✦

I AM ILL; I AM FULL OF SPLEEN AND repellent. I conceive there to be something wrong with my liver, for I cannot even think for the aching of my head. Yet what my complaint is I do not know. Medicine I cannot, I never could, take, although for medicine and doctors I have much reverence. Also, I am extremely superstitious: which, it may be, is why I cherish such a respect for the medical profession. I am well-educated, and therefore might have risen superior to such fancies, yet of them I am full to the core.

Also, I have no real desire to be cured of my ill-humour. I suppose you cannot understand this? No, I thought not; but *I* can understand it, although it would puzzle me to tell you exactly whom I am vexed with. I only know that I do not choose to offend the doctors by telling them that I am unable to accept their treatment. Also, I know – better than any one else can do – that I alone am my worst enemy, and that I am my own worst enemy far more than I am any one else's. However, if I am not to be cured, so much the worse for me and my evil passions. If my liver is out of order, so much the worse for my liver.

I have been living like this for a long while now – for fully twenty years. I am forty years old, and, in my day, have been a civil servant. But I am a civil servant no longer. Moreover, I was a bad civil servant at that. I used to offend every one, and to take pleasure in doing so. Yet never once did I accept a bribe, though it would have been easy enough for me to have feathered my nest in that way. This may seem to you a poor sort of a witticism, yet I will not erase it. I had written it down in the belief that it would wear rather a clever air when indited, yet I will not – no, not even now, when I see that I was but playing the buffoon – alter the *mot* by a single iota.

Whenever people approached my office table to ask for information, or what not, I used to grind my teeth at them, and invariably to feel pleased when I had offended their dignity. I seldom failed in my aim. Men, for the most part, are timid creatures – and we all of us know the sort of men favour-seekers are. Of such dolts there was one in particular – an officer – whom I could not bear, for he refused to defer to me at all, and always kicked up a most disgusting clatter with his sword. For a year and a half we joined battle over that sword; but it was I who won the victory, I who caused him to cease clattering his precious weapon. All this happened during my early manhood.

Do you wish to know wherein the sting of my evil temper has always lain? It has always lain (and therein also has always lain its peculiar offensiveness) in the fact that, even at moments of my bitterest spleen, I have been forced to acknowledge with shame that not only am I not at all bad-tempered, but also I have never received any real cause of offence – that I have been but roaring to frighten away sparrows, and amusing myself with doing so. Foam though I might at the mouth, I needed but to be given a doll to play with, or a cup of sweet tea to drink, and at once I sank to quiescence. Yes, I have always grown calm for the moment – even though, later, I have gnashed my teeth at myself, and suffered from months of insomnia. Such has invariably been my way.

For a long time past I have been belying my own personality by calling myself an irascible fellow. It has been pure rancour that has made me tell that lie against myself. As a matter of fact, I only played, so to speak, with my office callers, and with that officer, while all the while it was impossible for me to lose my temper. Every day I keep discovering in myself elements of the most opposite order conceivable, and can feel them swarming within me, and am aware that, to the very end of my life, they will continue so to swarm. Yet, often as they have striven to manifest themselves outwardly, I have never allowed them to do so. Of set purpose I always prevent that from happening, even though they torture me shamefully with their presence, and sometimes throw me into convulsions of *ennui* – ah, of how much *ennui* indeed! . . . Would not all this lead you, gentlemen, to suppose that I am expressing a sort of regret – that I am asking, as it were, your pardon? I am sure that you think so? Well, I can only say that I do not care a rap for your opinion.

No, I am not really bad-tempered. Rather, the fact is that I have never succeeded in being anything at all – whether kind-hearted or cruel, a villain or a saint, a hero or an insect. I just crouch here in this den of mine, and worry myself with the irritating, the useless, reflection that, after all, a man of parts cannot become anything; for only a fool does that. Yes (I say to myself), a man of the nineteenth century is morally bound, above all things, to be a colourless being, since a man of character, a man of action, is a being who is essentially limited. Such is the conviction which forty years have forced upon me. Forty years have been the span of my life, and forty years are a lifetime – they are the most extreme limit of old age. To live longer than that seems indecent, base, immoral. Who would want to live longer than that? Answer me – sincerely, and from your heart. Well, I will tell you who want to live longer. Only fools and rogues. This I say to all old men in the world – to respected old men, to silver-haired old men, to old men of repute. Yes, I say it to the whole universe. And I have the right to say it, for I myself am going to live to be sixty, or seventy, or even eighty! . . . Wait a minute. Give me a moment to recover my breath. . . .

Probably you think that I am trying to make fun of you? If so, you are wrong. I am not such a merry fellow as you suppose, or as you *may* suppose. At the same time, if, in irritation at my fooling (and I suspect that you *are* so irritated), you were to ask me exactly what sort of man I am, I should reply that I am a college graduate who, for my living (and for that purpose alone), served the State for a season, but who last year, on the death of a distant relative who left me six thousand roubles, retired from the service, and settled down in this den which you see. I used to live in it before, but since then I have taken up my abode in it for good. It is a mean, shabby room on the outskirts of the city, while for servant I have an old country-woman whose deafness makes her crusty, and whose person smells to heaven. They tell me that the climate of St. Petersburg is doing me harm, and that, in view of my insignificant means, it is sheer extravagance for me to go on living in the capital. Well, I know all that. Yes, I know it better than all the wisest and most experienced counsellors and tossers of heads in the world could possibly do. Yet I remain in St. Petersburg, nor do I intend to leave it. No, I intend to remain where I am . . . Ah! As though it matters one way or the other whether I stay here or take my departure!

By the way, what is it that all respectable men talk about most readily? Answer – about themselves. So I too will talk about myself.

➔ TWO ◆

I WISH TO TELL YOU, GENTLEMEN (no matter whether you care to hear it or not), why I have never even been able to become an insect. I solemnly declare to you that I have often *wished* to become an insect, but could never attain my desire. I swear to you, gentlemen, that to be overcharged with sensibility is an actual malady – a real, a grievous malady. For humanity's daily needs mere ordinary human sensibility ought to suffice, or about one-half or one-quarter of the sensibility which falls to the lot of the average educated man of our miserable nineteenth century, if he has the additional misfortune to reside in St. Petersburg (the most abstract, the most deviously-minded, city on this terrestrial sphere of ours, where towns, in their psychology, may be complex or non-complex). At all events such sensibility as falls to the lot of (for instance) the generality of so-called independent persons and men of action ought to suffice. I dare wager, now, that you think that I am writing this with my tongue in my cheek, and solely to make fun of men of action; that you think that it is sheer bad taste that is making me rattle my sword in the way that that officer used to do? Yet, to tell the truth, gentlemen, who would be vain of one's weaknesses while at the same time one is using them as a means for poking fun at others?

Yet why should I *not* do this? All men do it. All men are proud of their weaknesses, and I, perhaps, more so than my fellows. Let us not quarrel about it. It may be that I have used an awkward expression. Yet I am persuaded that not only is excess of sensibility, but also sensibility of any kind whatsoever, a malady. Of that I have not the smallest doubt in the world. For the moment, however, let us drop the point. Tell me this: how is it that always, and of set purpose, as it were, and at the very moment – yes, at the very moment – when I have appeared to be most in a position to appreciate the finer shades of 'the great and the beautiful' (to use the term once current amongst us), I have not only invariably failed to recognize as unseemly, but also have never failed to commit, actions which – well, in a word, actions which all men commit, but which I have always perpetrated just when I was most acutely sensible that I ought not to do them? The more I have recognized what is good and what constitutes 'the great and the beautiful,' the deeper I have plunged into the mire, and the more I have been ready to smear myself over with the sticky stuff. But the most curious point of all this – that the mood which I have described never seemed to be a mere fortuitous happening with me, but my permanent, my normal, condition, and therefore neither a weakness nor a vice. Consequently I have gradually come to lose all desire to combat this failing of mine. Indeed, things have reached the point that I almost believe (I might almost say, I *wholly* believe) that it is my normal condition. At first, however – *i.e.* at the actual beginning of things – I suffered terrible pangs in the struggle against my weakness, for I never could bring myself to believe that other men were not in the same position as I. Yet I kept the fact a secret close-locked in my breast, for I was ashamed of it then, and am ashamed of it now – yes, ashamed of the fact that I used to experience a sort of mysterious, abnormal, base gratification in recalling to my memory (say) some filthy nocturnal revel in St. Petersburg, and in recognizing that once again I had acted foully, but that what had been done could never be undone. Inwardly and secretly I often licked my lips at the thought of these revels, and chewed the cud of my recollections until their bitterness turned to a sort of base, accursed sweetness, and then to an actual, an assured, sensation of delight. Yes, I say of delight, of delight. I insist upon that. I often told myself that I would greatly like to know whether the same delight fell to the lot of other men. First of all, however, let me explain to you wherein that delight lay. It lay in a clear consciousness of my degradation – in a feeling that I had reached the last wall, and that the whole thing was base, and could never be otherwise, and that no escape therefrom was to be looked for, and that it was not possible for me to become a different man, and that, even if I still retained sufficient faith and energy to become a different man, I should not wish to become so, but that I would rather do nothing at all in the matter, since to undergo such a change might not be worth my while. And the chief thing about it was that one felt that the process was ruled by the normal, the fundamental, laws of acute sensibility, added to the inertia which arises from the working of those laws; wherefore one was never likely to alter, nor yet to lift a finger to effect an alteration. Hence may be deduced the fact that over-sensibility causes a villain to hug his villainy to himself if he really *perceives* that he is a villain. . . . However, enough of this. Have you understood all that I have said? Can you explain to me what that delight of mine consisted of? No; so I will explain it myself. I will pursue the matter to the end, seeing that I have taken up my pen to write.

I am extremely self-conscious. Also, no hunch-back, no dwarf, could be more prone to resentment and to offence than I. I have been through moments when, had I happened to receive a blow in the face, I should have been glad! Yes, I say it in all seriousness, that I should have derived the greatest possible gratification from a blow – the gratification of being able to feel desperate (since it is in desperation that one finds one's most glorious moments, especially when one has recognized that one cannot possibly draw back from the position taken up). Yes, a blow, and nothing but a blow, can wholly erase the consciousness of the grease in which one has been rubbed. Yet, averse though I am to scenes, it has always befallen me that *I* have been the offending party; as well as that (a still more shameful thing) I have been at fault without actually having transgressed – I have been, as it were, guilty through the mere working of the laws of nature. In the first place, I have often been at fault in that I have thought myself cleverer than any one else with whom I have come in contact. Such has always been my way. Sometimes, though – would you believe it? – I have felt sorry for this. At all events I know that, all my life long, I have preferred to look people under the eyes rather than in them. And in the second place, I have often been at fault in that, if there lies within me any nobility of soul, such ability has never been able to do anything for me beyond torment me with a consciousness of the utter uselessness of possessing it. I have never been able to *do* anything with that nobility, for the reason that, however much an offender might strike me in obedience to the laws of nature, it is not feasible to forgive laws of nature, nor yet to overlook them, while, despite the existence of those laws, an insult still remains an insult. Hence, were I able to divest myself of all magnanimity, and to take revenge upon each and every person who offended me, I should never really be able to revenge myself upon such persons, for the reason that, in all probability, I should never be able finally to make up my mind to any given course of action, even if I had the power to carry it out. Why should I be so unable to make up my mind? On that subject I have a word or two to say.

⇥ THREE ⇤

PEOPLE WHO ARE ABLE TO WREAK vengeance upon an assailant, and, in general, to stand up for themselves – how do they do it? It can only be supposed that, momentarily, their whole being is possessed by a desire for revenge, and that no other element is, for the time being, within them. A man of that sort goes as straight to his goal as a mad bull charges with lowered crest; and nothing but a stone wall will stop him. (*A propos*, such persons – that is to say, independent persons and men of action – make no bones about *yielding* to the wall. For them a wall is not an excuse for turning aside [as it is for us, the men of thought, and therefore the men who do nothing]; it is not a pretext for swerving from the path [a pretext in which, as a rule, no one – not even oneself – believes, but for which one is nevertheless thankful]. No, they just come to a halt before it. For them a wall connotes something calming, something morally decisive, final, and even mystical. . . . But about the wall later). I do not consider an independent man of that type to be the real, the normal, man as his fond mother, Nature, who has borne him upon earth, would have him be. Yet I envy such a man with all the power of my spleen. True, he is gross – but then the normal man may *have* to be gross. How, indeed, do you know that his grossness is not one of his very best points? Anyway I daily grow more and more confirmed in my suspicion that if he were to take the antithesis of the normal man – that is to say, the man of acute sensibility, the man who hails, not from Nature's womb, but from a chemical retort (this approaches a little nearly to mysticism – a thing which I also suspect) – the man born of the retort would sometimes feel so conscious that he was outclassed by his antithesis, the man of action, that he would come to look upon himself, despite his acute sensibility, as a mouse rather than as a human being. A very sensitive mouse, it is true (he would say to himself), yet none the less a mouse; whereas the other is a man, and therefore, *etcetera, etcetera*. Above all things, it would be he – he, the man of sensibility – who, of his own volition, would dub himself a mouse. He would ask no one else's opinion on the matter. This is an important point. Next let us observe the mouse in action. Suppose, for example, that it receives an insult (and it nearly always *is* so receiving an insult), and that it wishes to revenge itself. Perhaps it will be capable of harbouring malice in its breast to an even greater extent than *l'homme de la nature et de la vérité*. Yes, a mean, debased little yearning to repay the offender in his own coin might wax in that mouse's bosom in an even meaner way than it would do in that of *l'homme de la nature et de la vérité*, since the innate grossness of the latter would cause him to look upon revenge as bare justice, whereas the mouse, with its hypersensibility, might very possibly deny the existence of such justice. Lastly we come to the act itself – to the actual deed of revenge. By this time the unfortunate mouse will have augmented the original insult by surrounding itself, through doubts and questionings, with such a number of other insults – it will have added to the main question such a string of questions which are still undecided – that involuntarily it will have collected about itself a fatal quagmire, a stinking morass, of misunderstandings, emotions, and, lastly, spittle discharged at it by the independent persons, judges, and dictators who are solemnly standing around it in a ring, and saluting the little animal with full-throated laughter. Naturally nothing will be left for the mouse to do but to make a disdainful gesture with its little paw, indulge in a smile of deprecatory contempt wherein even the smiler itself will have no belief, and retire shamefacedly into its hole. There, in its dirty, stinking underworld, our poor insulted, brow-beaten mouse will soon have immersed itself in a state of cold, malignant, perpetual rancour. For forty long years (so it may very well be) it will continue to recall to its mind the most minute, the most shameful, details of the insult which it has sustained, and to add to them, as it does so, other details more shameful still, and to taunt and worry itself with its own fancies. Of those fancies it will be ashamed, yet it will nevertheless remember them all, exaggerate them all, and even imagine to itself things which have never happened, on the mere pretext that one day it may obtain its revenge, and that therefore it must, in the meanwhile, forget nothing. Or perhaps it *will* actually embark upon a scheme of revenge; but if it does so the thing will be done only by fits and starts, and from behind a stone, and incognito, and in a manner which makes it clear that the mouse distrusts alike its right to wreak vengeance and the ultimate success of its scheme, since it knows in advance that its poor attempts at retribution will bring upon its own head a hundred times more suffering than will fall to the lot of the person against whom the vengeance is aimed, but upon whom not so much as a scratch will be inflicted. Yes, upon its very deathbed the mouse will again recall the whole story, with compound interest added.

Now, it is just in this same cold, loathsome semi-mania, this same half-belief in oneself, this same conscious burying of oneself in the under-world for forty years, this same voluntarily imagined, yet privately dis-trusted, powerlessness to escape from one's position, this same poison of unsatisfied wishes that for ever penetrates inwards, this same fever of vacillation, of resolutions adopted for all eternity, and of regrets that come upon one in a moment, that there lies the essence of the strange delight of which I have spoken. So subtle is this delight, so elusive to the senses, that merely limited persons, or persons who merely possess a strong nervous system, cannot grasp a single one of its features. 'Perhaps, too,' you may add with a simper, 'persons who have never received a blow in the face cannot understand it?' – thereby implying that, at some date or another during my life, *I* have received such a blow, and therefore am speaking as an expert. Yes, I dare wager that that is what you are thinking. Do not disturb yourselves, gentlemen. Never once have I received a blow in the face – though I do not care a pin what *your* imaginings on the subject may be. My only regret is that I have dealt so few blows in my life. . . . But enough of this. Suppose we say no more concerning this theme which you seem to find so extraordinarily interest-ing? Let me quietly continue what I was saying about strong-nerved individuals who do not understand the higher refinements of the pleasure which I have described.

Good people who, under other circumstances, bellow as loudly as bulls (of course, we must suppose that the performance does them infinite credit) at once become mute in the face of the Impossible. By the Imposs-ible I mean the stone wall of which I have spoken. What stone wall, do you say? Why, the stone wall constituted of the laws of nature, of the deductions of learning, and of the science of mathematics. When, for instance, people of this kind seek to prove to you that you are descended from an ape, it is of no use for you to frown; you must just accept what they say. When, again, they seek to prove to you that a single drop of your fat is of more essential value to you than the bodies of a hundred thousand men who resemble yourself, and that by this deduction there become finally resolved the so-called virtues and duties and other inventions of unreason and prejudice, you must just accept what they tell you, and make up your mind to do nothing at all, since the formula that twice two make four is mathematics. To that find an objection if you can!

'Pardon us,' so these people bawl, 'but you simply *cannot* refute what we tell you. Twice two make four; Nature does not ask *your* leave for that; she has nothing to do with *your* wishes on the subject, no matter whether you approve of her laws or not. You must just take her as she is, and, with her, her results. A wall still remains a wall.' – and so forth, and so forth. . . . Good Lord! What have *I* to do with the laws of Nature, or with arithmetic, when all the time those laws and the formula that twice two make four do not meet with my acceptance? Of course, I am not going to beat my head against a wall if I have not the requisite strength to do so; yet I am not going to *accept* that wall merely because I have run up against it, and have no means to knock it down.

Does a wall, forsooth, constitute a full-stop, a signal for a cessation of the struggle, for the mere reason that it and the formula that twice two make four are one? Oh, blindness of blindnesses! What, rather, we should all do is to comprehend everything, to envisage everything – to comprehend and to envisage every impossibility and every stone wall; to accept no single impossibility, no single stone wall, if we do not feel inclined to accept it; to attain (in spite of the most inevitable combinations and the most refutative conclusions of logic) to the eternal truth that one may be at fault even in regard to a stone wall, no matter how much one may *seem* not to be at fault; lastly, on recognizing that fact, to subside silently, and with lips compressed to resignation, and with a bitter-sweet feeling in one's heart, into a state of inertia, there to dream that one need not *really* be angry with any one, since one's reasons for being so never existed, and never will exist, and have become changed, and shuffled, and substituted for one another, and half obliterated (though how, or by whom, one cannot think, except that those unknown factors and changes cause one's head to ache more and more as the mysteries in the question remain unsolved).

➣ FOUR ➤

'Ha, ha, ha! then we presume that you would find pleasure even in toothache?' you say to me with a grin?

'Well, why not?' answer I. 'Even toothache may afford one gratification. I myself have had it for a month, so I know what it means. When one has toothache one does not, of course, sit glowering in silence; one groans aloud. But those groans are not candid ones – they are uttered with suppressed venom; and in such a venomous state as that anything may turn to a jest. In reality those groans express the sufferer's *delight*. If he found no pleasure in them, he would not groan.'

Yes, you have suggested an excellent theme to me, gentlemen, and I will hasten to exploit it. Those groans express, firstly, the degrading futility of one's complaint, a legalized tyranny of nature which one despises, but from which one, unlike nature, is bound to suffer. They also express a sense of the fact that at the moment one has no other foe than the pain; a sense of the fact that one is utterly at the mercy of one's teeth; a sense of the fact that Providence is in a position either to will that your teeth shall cease on the instant to ache or to will that they shall go on aching another three months; and, lastly, a sense of the fact that if you do not agree with, but, on the contrary, protest against, the situation, your only resource, your only comfort, will be either to cut your throat or to go on beating the walls of your room ever harder and harder with your fists, since there is nothing else for you to do. Now, all these dire self-insultings, self-mockings, at length lead to a pleasure which often attains to supreme heights of voluptuousness. Let me beg of you, gentlemen, to seize the first opportunity of listening to the groans of a cultured man of the nineteenth century who is suffering from toothache. But this you should do only on the second or the third day of his malady, when he is beginning to groan in an altogether different manner from what he has done on the first day (when he will groan simply from the pain); when he is beginning to groan, not as a rude peasant, but as a man who has felt the touch of European progress and civilization; when he is beginning to groan as a man who has 'divorced himself from the soil and from vulgar principles' (to use the phrase now current). Well, by that time his groans will have become malicious and meanly irascible; and though he may

602

continue them whole nights and days at a stretch, he will be aware all the time that he is doing himself no good by his utterances, but merely uselessly angering and annoying himself and others. Better than any one else will he be aware that his family, as also the public before whom he is cutting such a figure, have for a long while been listening to him with disgust; that they think him an utter rascal, and have it in mind that he might just as well have groaned in a simpler manner (that is to say, without any turns or roulades), since his present style of groaning is due simply to temper, and is leading him to play the fool out of sheer viciousness. Now, all this self-expression, all these insults to others, connote a certain voluptuous delight. 'I am disturbing you,' you can say to your friends, 'and driving you to distraction, and preventing every one in the house from sleeping. Very well. Pray do not sleep, but join me in my constant recognition of the fact that I have got the toothache. I am no longer the hero whom I have hitherto seemed, but only a public nuisance. Very well; be it so. I am very glad that you have found me out. Do you dislike having to listen to my villainous groans? Then go on disliking it, and I will execute a few more of these infernal roulades.' Do you understand it *now*, gentlemen? No, I wager that you do not. It is clear that I must develop and expound my theme much further if you are ever to comprehend all the ins and outs of the pleasure which I mean. You laugh, do you? Then I am delighted. If my jests are in bad taste, and rude, and obscure, and halting, that arises from the fact that I have no self-respect. Indeed, what man of sensibility could possess self-respect?

✦ FIVE ✦

HOW COULD ANY MAN RESPECT himself who wilfully takes pleasure in a consciousness of his self-abasement? I do not say this out of any feeling of puling regret, for never at any time have I found it possible to say, 'Father, forgive me, and I will sin no more.' This is not so much because I have actually felt myself *incapable* of uttering the words as because they have always come too easily to my lips. And whenever I have said them, what has happened next? Why, that, as though bound to fall, I have plunged straight into sin, when all the time I have been innocent both in thought and intent. A worse thing could not be. Next I have felt softened in heart, and shed tears, and reproved myself, and seen things as they were, and felt unclean of soul. Yet for this I cannot very well blame the laws of Nature, since to offend against them has been the chief, the constant, occupation of my life. It is a degrading fact to have to recall, but the fact remains. Then, a moment or two later, I have always angrily reminded myself that my whole conduct had been false – horribly, gratuitously false (by 'it,' of course, I mean all my regrets, my softenings of heart, my vows of regeneration). So I would ask you, gentlemen – what caused me to rack and torture myself in this way? Well, the answer is that I always found it irksome merely to sit with folded hands. That is why I have given myself up to so much wrongdoing. Mark what I say, gentlemen, for what I say is true, and will give you the key to the whole business. Of set purpose I used to devise opportunities for ordering my existence in such a way as to – well, as at least to see a certain amount of life. For instance, I have often been *careful* to take offence at something – not for any good reason, but merely because I wanted to. Gentlemen, you yourselves know that if one takes causeless offence – the sort of offence which one brings upon oneself – one ends by being really, and in very truth, offended. I have been at pains, all my life, to play tricks of this sort; with the result that I have come to be destitute of any sort of self-control. Also, I have twice tried to fall in love; but I can assure you, gentlemen, that I suffered greatly in the doing so! One's heart may not *seem* to be suffering as the smiles pass over one's face, yet one *is* in pain all the while, and that in a very real, a very demonstrable, fashion, since at such times one is jealous, and above oneself. The sole cause of it all, gentlemen, is *ennui;* yes, the sole cause of it all is *ennui.* The fact is that one comes to feel crushed with the tedium, the conscious folding of the hands in contemplation, which is the direct, the inevitable, the automatic outcome of sensibility. Of this I have spoken above. . . . I repeat, therefore, I earnestly repeat, that all men of independence and action – men who are men of action because they are *prone* to action – are both gross and limited in their purview. How is this to be explained? Thus. Such men are led by their limitations to mistake approximate and secondary causes for primary, and so to persuade themselves, more easily and more readily than other men do, that they have an assured basis for their action, and therefore may cease to trouble themselves further. That is the truth, and the whole truth, of the matter. To embark upon action one must first of all feel perfectly sure of oneself, so that no doubts as to the wisdom of that action may remain. But how does a man like myself bring himself to the requisite state of assurance? Whence do I derive my primary causes? Whence my bases? Well, first of all I begin thinking things over; which has the effect of leading each original cause thought of to attract to itself some cause a good deal more primary, more original, still. And it is in this that there lies the essence of self-realization and thought (though perhaps it is also the law of Nature). What is the result? Always one and the same thing. You will remember that, just now, I spoke of revenge (though perhaps you did not altogether follow me?). I said that a man may wreak vengeance because he believes it to be justice; wherefore he has found his original cause for action in justice, and may feel sure of himself, and proceed to wreak his vengeance quietly, and with success, since he is persuaded that what he is doing is altogether right and honourable. But, for my part, I never can perceive either justice or virtue in such a course: wherefore, if I embark upon a scheme of revenge, I do so, rather, out of malice. Of course, malice *may* succeed in overcoming one's doubts – it *may* serve (and with perfect success, too) as a first cause for action (though it is nothing of the sort); but what am I to do if even malice be wanting in me (which is the point whence I originally started)? Under the accursed laws of sensibility, malice becomes subject to a process of chemical disintegration, since it always happens that if a given object of action be volatile, the reasons for such action easily turn to gas, and responsibility disappears, and the offence ceases to have been an offence at all – it becomes merely a delusion wherein (as in toothache) no one is guilty, and wherefrom there is no other way of escape than from toothache – namely, by beating one's head against the wall. Perhaps, in despair of finding a first cause for action, one shrugs one's shoulders? Well, my advice is blindly and unthinkingly to leave first causes alone, and to give oneself up to one's impulses, and, for once in a while, to let volition lie altogether in abeyance. That is to say, either hate or love, but in any case do anything rather than sit with folded hands. If you do this I wager that by the day after to-morrow (at the very latest) you will have come to despise yourself for having ever got into a fluster at all; with the result that once again you will relapse calmly into inertia and the blowing of soap-bubbles. Ah, gentlemen, at least I can look upon myself as a wise man in that I have never succeeded in beginning or ending *anything*. Grant that I am a foolish, useless, troublesome chatterer, as we all are – yes, grant that: yet may not the one true function of every man of sensibility be to act as a chatterer – to act, that is to say, as a dissipator of airy trifles into space?

⇻ SIX ⇺

I<small>F ONLY I HAD NEVER DONE</small> anything but out of sheer laziness! How I should have respected myself! Yes, I should have respected myself for the reason that I *was* capable of being lazy – that in me there *was* at least one positive quality of which I could rest assured. If you were to ask me, 'Who are you?' I should be thankful to be able to say, 'A lazy man.' Yes, I place it beyond doubt that I should like it to be said of myself that I am a sluggard. 'A lazy man' – in that there is connoted a whole calling, a whole destiny, a whole career! Do not laugh at me. What I say is true. Once upon a time I used to belong to a leading club, and to cultivate the art of self-respect; and among my club acquaintances there was a man whose lifelong boast it was that he was an infallible judge of 'Chateau Lafitte.' Upon this accomplishment he looked as a positive merit, and was never in doubt about it; with the result that he died, if not with a quiet conscience, at all events respectably. And he was right in his way of life. I, too, used to wish to have a similar career. I, too, longed to become a sluggard and a glutton – though not *merely* a sluggard and a glutton, but a sluggard and a glutton who could sympathize with 'the great and the beautiful.' Does that meet with your approval? It is a long time now since I had such fancies; yet all through my forty years of subterranean life that craze for 'the great and the beautiful' has remained as an obsession. Once upon a time things were different. Once upon a time I longed for a congenial sphere of activity in which I should be able ceaselessly to drink to the health of 'the great and the beautiful.' Yes, I used to seek every possible opportunity of dropping a tear into my cup before emptying a bumper to the health of 'the great and the beautiful.' I used to refer everything in the world to that standard, and, even in regard to the most damnable and indisputable rubbish, would first of all consult 'the great and the beautiful,' and be as ready with my tears as a wet sponge. For instance, an artist would paint some picture or another, and I would hasten to drink to the health of the artist who had painted that picture, since I loved only 'the great and the beautiful.' Or an author would write some book or another, and again I would hasten to drink to the health of the author who had written that book, since I loved only 'the great and the beautiful.'

Also, I was firmly persuaded that I ought to be looked up to for this; so that at any time I was ready to put a man through his paces who refused to show me that respect. To live in peace, and to die with *éclat* – yes, that constituted my whole aim and object in life. I even dreamed of growing a fat stomach, developing a triple chin, and fashioning for myself a purple nose, in the hope that every one who met me would exclaim as he gazed upon my figure, 'See, there goes something *substantial*, something *positive!*' Well, they might have said that as much as they liked; for, in this negative age, gentlemen, it is always pleasant to hear of anything positive.

❧ SEVEN ❧

BUT THESE ARE MERE GOLDEN dreams. Who was it first said, first propounded the theory, that man does evil only because he is blind to his own interests, but that if he were enlightened, if his eyes were opened to his real, his normal interests, he would at once cease to do evil, and become virtuous and noble for the reason that, being now enlightened and brought to understand what is best for him, he would discern his true advantage only in what is good (since it is a known thing that no man of set purpose acts against his own interests), and therefore would of necessity also *do* what is good? Oh, the simplicity of the youth who said this! Oh, the utter artlessness of the prattler! To begin with, since when, during these thousands of years, has man ever acted solely in accordance with his own interests? What about the millions of facts which go to show that only too often man knowingly (that is to say, with a full comprehension of what is his true advantage) puts that advantage aside in favour of some other plan, and betakes himself to a road, to risks, to the unknown, to which no agent nor agency has compelled him, as though, unwilling to follow the appointed path, he preferred to essay a difficult and awkward road along which he must feel his way in darkness? Would it not almost seem as though the directness, the voluntariness, of such a course had for him a greater attraction than any advantage? Advantage, indeed? What, after all, *is* advantage? Would *you*, gentlemen, undertake exactly to define wherein human advantage consists? What if human advantage not only *may*, but *does*, consist of the fact that, on certain occasions, man may desire, not what is good for him, but what is bad?

And if this be so, if this really be so, the rule falls to the ground at once. What is your opinion about it? Can it be so? I see you smiling. Well, smile away, gentlemen, but also answer me this: Can human interests *ever* be properly reckoned up? May there not always remain interests which never have been, never can be, included in any classification? You, gentlemen, take your lists of human interests from averages furnished by statistics and economic formulæ. Your lists of interests include only prosperity, riches, freedom, tranquillity, and so forth, and any one who openly and knowingly disagreed with those lists would, in your opinion (as in mine also, for that matter), be either an obscurantist or a madman. Would he not? But the most surprising point is this – that statists, savants, and lovers of the human race never fail, in their summing up of human interests, to overlook *one interest in particular*. This interest is never taken into account in the shape in which it ought to be taken; and this fact vitiates all their calculations. Yet, were they to add this interest to their summaries, no great harm would be done. The mischief lies in the fact that this particular interest declines to fall under any particular heading, or to enter into any particular schedule. For instance, I might have a friend – as also might you yourselves, gentlemen (for who has not?) – who, when about to embark upon a given piece of work, might tell one, clearly and grandiloquently, that he intends to proceed strictly on lines of truth and reason. He might even go so far as to speak with emotion and enthusiasm of the nature of true, normal human interests, and with a smile to inveigh against short-sighted dolts who do not understand either their own interests or the proper meaning of virtue. Yet within only a quarter of an hour, and without any sudden, unforeseen event having arisen – merely in accordance with something which is stronger than all his other interests put together – this same man may cut straight across what he himself has said – that is to say, cut straight across both the dictates of reason and his own true interests and everything else! Yet this friend of mine is but one of a type; wherefore the fault cannot be laid at his door alone. May there not, therefore, exist something which to most men is even dearer than their true interests? Or, not to infringe the logical sequence, may there not exist some supreme interest of interests (the additional interest of which I am speaking) which is greater and more absorbing than any other interest, and for which man, if the need should arise, is ready to contravene every law, and to lose sight alike of common sense, honour, prosperity, and ease – in a word, of all the things which are fair and expedient – if haply he can gain for himself that primal, that supreme, advantage which he conceives to be the dearest thing on earth?

'Ah well, there are interests and interests,' you might interrupt me at this point. Pardon me, gentlemen, but I ought to make it clear that, not to juggle with words, this interest of which I am speaking is a notable one, and escapes all classification, and shatters every system which has ever been established by lovers of the human race for that race's improvement. In short, let it be understood that it is an interest which introduces general confusion into everything. Before naming to you that interest I should like to damn myself for ever in your eyes by telling you bluntly that all those fine systems of, and schemes for, demonstrating to mankind its true, its normal, interests, and for explaining to it that, so long as it strives to attain its true interests, it will ever grow better and more noble, are so much dialectic. Yes, I say so much dialectic. To maintain theories of renovating the human race through systems of classification of true interests is, in my opinion, about the same thing as – well, about the same thing as to maintain that man grows milder with civilization, and, consequently, less bloodthirsty, less addicted to fighting. Logically, per-haps, that *does* happen; yet he is so prone to systems and to abstract deductions that he is for ever ready to mutilate the truth, to be blind to what he sees, and deaf to what he hears, so long only as he can succeed in vindicating his logic. Of this let me give an example which will be clear to all. Look around you at the world. Everywhere you will see blood flowing in streams, and as merrily as champagne. Look at our nineteenth century; look at Napoleon – the great Napoleon and the modern one; look at North America, with its everlasting 'Union'; look at the present caricature of Schleswig-Holstein. What has civilization done to instil greater mildness into our bosoms? Civilization develops in man nothing but an added capacity for receiving impressions. That is all. And the growth of that capacity further augments man's tendency to seek pleasure in blood-letting. Nothing else has civilization conferred upon him. You may have noticed that the most enthusiastic blood-letters have almost invariably been the most civilized of men – men whose shoes even Attila* and Stenka Razin** would have been unworthy to unloose; and if such men as the former have not bulked in the public eye quite so largely as have Attila and Stenka Razin, it is only because the former have been too numerous, too transitory. At all events civilization has rendered man, if not more bloodthirsty, at least a worse (in the sense of a meaner) thirster after blood than before. Once upon a time he considered blood-letting to be just retribution, and could therefore, with a quiet conscience, extermi-nate any one whom he wanted to; but now we account blood-letting a crime – and indulge in that crime even more than in former days. Which, then, is the worst of the two? Well, judge for yourselves. It is said that

---

* Chieftain of the Huns who conquered Rome.

** Leader of a Cossack rebellion during the reign of Catherine the Great.

Cleopatra (if I may take an instance from Roman history) loved to thrust golden pins into the breasts of her slaves, and took pleasure in the cries and contortions of her victims. Possibly you may say that all this happened in a comparatively barbarous age – that even at the present day the times are barbarous – that golden pins are still being thrust into people's breasts – that though man, in many things, has learnt to see clearer now than he used to do in *more* barbarous ages, he has not yet learnt to act wholly as reason and science would have him do. Yet all the while, I know, you are persuaded in your own minds that man is bound to improve as soon as ever he has dropped some old, bad customs of his, and allowed science and healthy thought alone to nourish, to act as the normal directors of, human nature. Yes, I know that you are persuaded that eventually man will cease to err *of set purpose*, or to let his will clash with his normal interests. On the contrary (say you), science will in time show man (though, in our opinion, it is superfluous to do so) that he does not possess *any* will or initiative of his own, and never has done, but that he is as the keyboard of a piano, or as the handle of a hurdy-gurdy. Above all, science will show him that in the world there exist certain laws of nature which cause everything to be done, not of man's volition, but of nature's, and in accordance with her laws. Consequently, say you, those laws will only need to be *explained* to man, and at once he will become divested of all responsibility, and find life a much easier thing to deal with. All human acts will then be mathematically computed according to nature's laws, and entered in tables of logarithms which extend to about the 108,000th degree, and can be combined into a calendar. Better still, there will be published certain carefully revised editions of this calendar (after the manner of modern encyclopædias) in which everything will be enumerated and set down so exactly that henceforth the world will cease to know wrong-doing, or any occasion for the same.

Then (I am supposing *you* still to be speaking) there will arise new economic relations – relations all ready for use, and calculated with mathematical precision, so that in a flash all possible questions will come to an end, for the reason that to all possible questions there will have been compiled a store of all possible answers. Then there will arise the Golden Palace of the legends. Then – well, *then*, in a word, there will dawn the millennium! . . . Of course, though (it is *I* who am now speaking), you cannot very well guarantee that things will not have come to be excessively dull, seeing that there will be nothing left for us to do when everything has been computed beforehand and tabulated? By this I do not mean to say that things will not also be excessively *regular*. I only mean to say, is there anything which dullness will not lead men to devise? For instance, out of sheer *ennui*, golden pins may again be inserted into victims' breasts. That is all. It is shameful to have to think that into everything which is goodly man loves to thrust golden pins! Yes, he is a gross animal, phenomenally gross. Rather, he is not so much gross as ungrateful to a degree which nothing else in the world can equal. For instance, I should not be surprised if, amid all this order and regularity of the future, there should suddenly arise, from some quarter or another, some gentleman of lowborn – or, rather, of retrograde and cynical – demeanour who, setting his arms akimbo, should say to you all: 'How now, gentlemen? Would it not be a good thing if, with one consent, we were to kick all this solemn wisdom to the winds, and to send those logarithms to the devil, and to begin to live our lives again according to our own stupid whims?' Yet this would be as nothing; the really shameful part of the business would be that this gentleman would find a goodly number of adherents. Such is always man's way. And he might act thus for the shallowest of reasons; for a reason which is not worth mentioning; for the reason that, always, and everywhere, and no matter what his station, man loves to act as he *likes*, and not necessarily as reason and self-interest would have him do. Yes, he will even act straight against his own interests. Indeed, he is sometimes *bound* to do so. Such, at least, is my notion of the matter. His own will, free and unfettered; his own untutored whims; his own fancies, sometimes amounting almost to a madness – here we have that superadded interest of interests which enters into no classification, which for ever consigns systems and theories to the devil. Whence do savants have it that man needs a normal, a virtuous, will? What, in particular, has made these pundits imagine that what man most needs is a will which is acutely alive to man's interests? Why, what man most needs is an *independent* will – no matter what the cost of such independence of volition, nor what it may lead to. Yet the devil only knows what man's will —

✤ EIGHT ✤

'HA, HA, HA!' I CAN IMAGINE you interrupting me with a chuckle. 'Whether you choose to think so or not, there is no such thing in the world as human will. Science has so far dissected man as to make it absolutely clear that his volition and so-called freewill are but — '

Wait a moment, gentlemen. I was just going to say the same thing myself, though I confess that I was feeling a little nervous about it. I was just going to observe that the devil only knows what man's will depends upon, when suddenly (the Lord be thanked!) I recalled that precious science of yours, and broke off short. However, you have now said it for me. As a matter of fact, if ever there shall be discovered a formula which shall exactly express our wills and whims; if ever there shall be discovered a formula which shall make it absolutely clear what those wills depend upon, and what laws they are governed by, and what means of diffusion they possess, and what tendencies they follow under given circumstances; if ever there shall be discovered a formula which shall be mathematical in its precision, well, gentlemen, whenever such a formula shall be found, man will have ceased to have a will of his own – he will have ceased even to exist. Who would care to exercise his willpower according to a table of logarithms? In such a case man would become, not a human being at all, but an organ-handle, or something of the kind. What but the handle of a hurdy-gurdy *could* a human being represent who was devoid either of desires or volition? Is it not so? Reckoning all the possibilities, could things ever come to be thus?

'Hm,' you might conceivably reply, 'our wills mostly err through adopting false views of our interests. Sometimes we will what is sheer rubbish, for the reason that in such rubbish we foolish fellows perceive the easiest way to the attainment of some presupposed advantage. But if all were to be tabulated and set forth on paper (which it would be quite an easy thing to do, seeing that to assume that man is incapable of learning a few laws of nature is senseless and absurd), there would, of course, be an end to our so-called power of volition. If, on the other hand, our volition were always to march with our reason, we should invariably exercise that reason in preference to our freewill, since such exercise of one's reasoning powers would prevent us from ever again desiderating foolish things, or wilfully cutting across our own judgment by desiderating for ourselves what would be harmful.' Well, *if* all desires and resolutions (of course, it is *I* who am now supposed to be speaking) can be exactly computed, for the reason that they are revealed to us beforehand by the laws of our so-called freewill, I do not really see that I am jesting when I say that something after the manner of tables *might* be compiled, and that we should be forced to exercise our volition only according to what might be found in them. Yet were those tables to tell me, to reckon for me, that, should I (say) point with my finger to an object, I should be doing so simply because it would have been impossible for me to do otherwise, or even to point to the object in question with any other finger than the one I used – well, in that case what element of freedom would remain to me, even though I were an educated man, and had gone through a course of science? In short, if things were so arranged, I might be able to forecast my life for (say) the next thirty years, and there would be nothing left for me to do, and I should not so much as require an intelligence. All that I should need to do would be to keep on reminding myself that never, and under no circumstances, will nature ask me what I *desire* to do, but must be taken just as she is rather than as what we would have liked her to be. Therefore, if our tendency is towards tablets and calendars – yes, or even towards retorts – we shall just have to accept them. Nature is always herself, and therefore requires her retorts to be taken with her.

For me, however, all such matters are bagatelles. Pardon my philosophizing like this, gentlemen, but it is the fruit of forty years in the underworld, and you must not mind my building castles in the air. See here: reason is an excellent thing – I do not deny that for a moment; but reason is reason, and no more, and satisfies only the reasoning faculty in man, whereas volition is a manifestation of all life (that is to say, of human life as a whole, with reason and every other sort of appendage included). It is true that, in this particular manifestation of it, human life is all too frequently a sorry failure; yet it nevertheless *is* life, and not the mere working out of a square root. For my own part, I naturally wish to satisfy *all* my faculties, and not my reasoning faculty alone (that is to say, a mere twentieth portion of my capacity for living). For what does reason know? Reason only knows that man possesses a certain capability of apprehension. Anything else, believe me, it does *not* know. This may be poor comfort, yet why should it not be said? On the other hand, human nature acts as a whole, and with all that is contained in it; so that, whether conscious or unconscious, sane or mad, it is always human nature. Now, I suspect, gentlemen, that you regard me with pity, for you keep telling me that man can never be really enlightened or developed – he can never be what the *future* human being will be – through the fact that he knowingly desiderates for himself what is harmful to his best interests. This is mathematical deduction, you say. I do not dispute it. It *is* mathematical deduction. Yet *I* tell *you* (and for about the hundredth time) that there is one occasion, and one occasion only, when man can wilfully, consciously desiderate for himself what is foolish and harmful. This is the occasion when he yearns *to have the right* to desiderate for himself what is foolish and harmful, and to be bound by no obligation whatsoever to desiderate anything that is sensible. It is his crowning folly; it is wherein we see his ineradicable waywardness. Yet such folly may also be the best thing in the world for him, even though it work him harm, and contradict our soundest conclusions on the subject of interests. This is because it is possible for his folly to preserve to him, under all circumstances, the chief, the most valuable, of all his possessions – namely, his personality, his individuality. Yes, it is not I alone who maintain that this is the most priceless asset whereof man can boast. Of course, he *may* make his volition march with his reason, and the more so if the former does not abuse the latter, but uses it with moderation. Such a proceeding is expedient, and may, at times, even be praiseworthy; but only too often do we see volition clashing with reason, and – and — Yet, do you know, gentlemen, *this too*, at times, may be both expedient and praiseworthy. For suppose man *not* to be innately foolish (in reality this could never be said of him, except in so far as that it might be urged that, if he be foolish, who in the world is wise?); yet, though he may not be foolish, he is at least monstrously ungrateful, phenomenally ungrateful. In fact, I believe that the best possible definition of man would be 'A creature which walks on two legs and is devoid of gratitude.' And this is not all – this is not his principal failing. No; his greatest failing is his constant immorality, which began with the Flood, and has lasted up to the present Schleswig-Holstein period of human history. Consequently, immorality being his leading weakness, so also is unreason, for it is an axiom that unreason arises from immorality. Try if it does not. Glance at the history of mankind, and tell me what you see there. Immensity? Well, what availed even the Colossus of Rhodes? Not for nothing did some people maintain that it was the work of human hands, while others asserted that it had been fashioned by nature herself. Variety? Well, in all ages and in all nations, what has been the use of discriminating between certain uniforms worn by military men and civilians, so long as there were no non-uniformed people, nor yet any men of learning? Uniformity? Well, in history men fight and fight, and are fighting now, and have always fought, and fought again. I should imagine that *here* you see an *excess* of uniformity! Everything, therefore, which could possibly enter into the most disordered of imaginations might well be said of the history of the world. Yet there is one thing which could *not* be said of it – and that is, that it affords much of a spectacle of reason. If one were to state the contrary one would choke at the very first word. In particular, we are continually confronted, in history, with the diverting circumstance that there continually figure in its pages large numbers of moral, sensible men and scholars and lovers of the human race who make it their prime object in life to behave as morally and as sensibly as possible – to, as it were, enlighten their neighbours by proving to them the possibility of leading, in this world, both a moral and a sensible existence. Yet what is the good of all this? We know that, sooner or later, many of these philanthropists undergo a change, and display phases of a most unseemly order. Consequently, I would ask you – what are we to expect from man, seeing that he is a creature endowed with such strange qualities? You may heap upon him every earthly blessing, you may submerge him in well-being until the bubbles shoot to the surface of his prosperity as though it were a pond, you may give him such economic success that nothing will be left for him to do but to sleep and to eat dainties and to prate about the continuity of the world's history; yes, you may do all this, but none the less, out of sheer ingratitude, sheer devilment, he will end by playing you some dirty trick. He will imperil his comfort, and purposely desiderate for himself deleterious rubbish, some improvident trash, for the sole purpose that he may alloy all the solemn good sense which has been lavished upon him with a portion of the futile, fantastical element which forms part of his very composition. Yes, it is these same fantastical dreams, this same debased stupidity, that he most wishes to retain in order to feel assured of the one thing with which he cannot dispense – namely, of the knowledge that men are still men, and not keyboards of pianos over which the hands of Nature may play at their own sweet will, and continue so to play until they threaten to deprive him of all volition, save by rote and according to calendars. Moreover, even if man *were* the keyboard of a piano, and could be convinced that the laws of nature and of mathematics had made him so, he would still decline to change. On the contrary, he would once more, out of sheer ingratitude, attempt the perpetration of something which would enable him to insist upon himself; and if he could not effect this, he would then proceed to introduce chaos and disruption into everything, and to devise enormities of all kinds, for the sole purpose, as before, of asserting his personality. He would need but to launch a single curse upon the world, and the mere fact that man alone is able to utter curses (the one privilege by which he is differentiated from the other animals) would, through the very act of commination, effect his purpose for him – namely, the purpose of convincing himself that he really *is* a man, and not the keyboard of a piano. But if you were to tell me that all this could be set down in tables – I mean the chaos, and the confusion, and the curses, and all the rest of it – so that the possibility of computing everything might remain, and reason continue to rule the roost – well, in that case, I believe, man would *purposely* become a lunatic, in order to become devoid of reason, and therefore able to insist upon himself. I believe this, and I am ready to vouch for this, simply for the reason that every human act arises out of the circumstance that man is for ever striving to prove to his own satisfaction that he is a man and not an organ-handle. And, however devious his methods, he *has* succeeded in proving it; however troglodyte-like his mode of working may have been, he *has* succeeded in proving it. So in future, perhaps, you will refrain from asserting that this particular interest of his is nugatory, or that his volition depends upon anything at all?

Also, you often tell me (or, rather you tell me whenever you deign to favour me with a single word) that no one can deprive me of my freewill, and that I ought so to arrange matters that my freewill shall, of its own volition, coincide with my normal interest, and with the laws of nature, and with arithmetic.

Ah, gentlemen! How much freewill should I have left to me when we had come to tables and arithmetic – when only the rule that twice two make four had come to hold the board? However much twice two might make four, my will would, to the end, remain my will.

➤ NINE ❖

GENTLEMEN, I NEED HARDLY SAY that, so far, I have been jesting. Yet, poor as my jests may have been, not everything which I have said has been uttered in mockery: for some of my jests have been spoken through clenched teeth. Certain questions are disturbing my soul, and I beg of you to solve them. For instance, you say that you desire man to unlearn certain of his old customs, and to regulate his will according to the dictates of science and of sane thought. But how know you that man not only *can*, but *must*, change? What leads you to suppose that the human will stands in need of being regulated? In short, how come you to feel certain that such regulation of man's will would bring him any advantage, or that if he refrained from flying in the face of his real, his normal interests (as guaranteed by the deductions of reason and of arithmetic) such a course would *really* be good for him, or require to be made the law for all humanity? So far all this is only a proposition put forward by yourselves – a mere law (we must suppose) that has been made by logicians rather than by humanity as a whole. Perhaps you think me mad, gentlemen? Well, if so, I plead guilty; I quite agree with you. Man is essentially a constructive animal – an animal for ever destined to strive towards a goal, and to apply himself to the pursuit of engineering, in the shape of ceaseless attempts to build a road which shall lead him to an unknown destination. But that is just why man so often *turns aside* from the road. He turns aside for the reason that he is *constrained* to attempt the journey; he turns aside because, being at once foolish and an independent agent, he sometimes takes it into his head that, though the road in question may eventually bring him to a destination of some sort, that destination always lies ahead of him. Consequently, as an irresponsible child, he is led at times to disregard his trade as an engineer, and to give himself up to that fatal indolence which, as we know, is the mother of all vices. Man loves to construct and to lay out roads – of that there can be no question; but why does he also love so passionately to bring about general ruin and chaos? Answer me that. First of all, however, I myself have a word or two to say about it. May not his passion for bringing about general disorder (a passion which, we must admit, allows of no dispute) arise from the fact that he has an instinctive dread of *completely* attaining his end, and so of finishing his building operations? May it not be the truth that only from a distance, and not from close at hand, does he love the edifice which he is erecting? That is to say, may it not be that he loves to create it, but not to *live* in it – only to hand it over, when completed, to *les animaux domestiques*, in the shape of ants, sheep, and so forth?

Ants are creatures of quite a different taste. They are constantly constructing marvellous edifices, but ones that shall be for ever indestructible. From the antheap all respectable ants take their origin, and in it (probably) they meet their end. This does credit alike to their continuity and to their perseverance. On the other hand, man is a frivolous, a specious creature, and, like a chess-player, cares more for the process of attaining his goal than for the goal itself. Besides, who knows (for it never does to be too sure) that the aim which man strives for upon earth may not be contained in this ceaseless continuation of the process of attainment (that is to say, in the process which is comprised in the living of life) rather than in the aim itself, which, of course, is contained in the formula that twice two make four? Yet, gentlemen, this formula is not life at all; it is only the beginning of death! At all events men have always been afraid to think that twice two make four, and I am afraid of it too. Can it be, therefore, that, though man is for ever working to attain this formula, and though, in his search for it, he sails all the seas and sacrifices his whole life to the acquisition of his end, he fears *really* to succeed in the quest, for the reason that, if he were suddenly to come upon the formula, he would feel that he had nothing left to look for? Workmen, on completing their weekly tasks, receive their wages, and betake themselves to the tavern to make merry. Such is their weekly diversion. But whither can man in the mass betake himself? It is plain that he feels ill at ease when the end of his labour has really been reached. That is to say, he loves to attain, but not *completely* to attain; which, of course, is an exceedingly ridiculous *trait* in his character, and would appear to contain a paradox. In any case the formula that twice two make four is the factor which, of all others, he cannot stomach; nor do *I* look upon it in any other light than as an abomination, since it is a formula which wears an impertinent air as, meeting you on the road, it sets its arms akimbo, and spits straight in your face. True, I agree that, in its way, it is well enough; yet I also beg leave to say (if I must apportion praise all round) that the formula 'Twice two make five' is not without its attractions.

Why, then, are you so absolutely, so portentously, certain that one thing, and one thing only, is normal and positive – in a word, good – for mankind? Does reason never err in estimating what is advantageous? May it not be that man occasionally loves something besides prosperity? May it not be that he also loves *adversity*? And may not adversity be as good for him as is happiness? Certainly there are times when man *does* love adversity, and love it passionately; so do not resort to history for your justification, but, rather, put the question to *yourselves*, if you are men, and have had any experience of life. For my part, I look upon undivided love of prosperity as something almost indecent; for to cause an occasional catastrophe, come weal come woe, seems to me a very pleasant thing to do. Yet I am not altogether for adversity, any more than I am altogether for prosperity; what I most stand for is my personal freewill, and for what it can do for me when I feel in the right mood to use it. I know that adversity is not thought acceptable in vaudeville plays, and that in the Palace of Crystal* it would be a thing quite unthinkable, for the reason that, since adversity connotes a denial and a doubt, no edifice of the kind could exist wherein a doubt was harboured. Nevertheless, I feel certain that man never wholly rejects adversity (in the sense of chaos and disruption of his schemes); for adversity is the mainspring of self-realization. When beginning these letters I said that, in my opinion, self-realization is, for a man, a supreme misfortune; yet I am sure that he loves it dearly, and that he would not exchange it for any other sort of delight. For example, adversity is immeasurably superior to the formula that twice two make four; for if the latter were ever to be found, what would there remain for us to do or to realize? All that there would remain for us to do would be to muzzle our five senses, and to relapse into a state of perpetual contemplation. The same result (namely, that there might remain nothing for us to do) might arise from self-realization; yet in that case one could at least give oneself an occasional castigation, and revivify oneself. This might be a retrograde course to take, yet at least it would be better than nothing.

* A Russian expression for the millennium.

TEN

You believe, do you not, in a palace of crystal which shall be for ever unbreakable – in an edifice, that is to say, at which no one shall be able to put out his tongue, or in any other way to mock? Now, for the very reason that it must be made of crystal, and for ever unbreakable, and one whereat no one shall put out his tongue, I should fight shy of such a building. For do you not see that if the edifice were not a palace, but a hencoop, and rain were to begin falling, I might take refuge in that hencoop, yet should hardly be likely, out of mere gratitude for its shelter, to mistake it for the residence of a king? At this you may laugh, or you may even go so far as to say that, in such a matter, a hencoop would do as well as the most stately fane. If so, I should retort, 'Yes – provided that one's sole object in life is to avoid getting wet.'

But how if I were to take it into my head that one need not live for that purpose alone, and that if one *must* live, it were best done in a palace? I am supposing such to be my will, my desire. In that case you could not rid me of my desire by any method save that of abrogating my will-power. And even supposing such abrogation to be possible for you to accomplish, and that you had some counter attraction to offer me, and that you could provide me with a new ideal, I might *still* decline to mistake a hencoop for a palace. And even if a palace of crystal were only a thing of dreams and, by the laws of nature, a sheer impossibility, and even if only my individual folly, added to certain old-established, irrational customs of my generation, had made me imagine it, what, even then, should I care if it *were* an impossibility? Would it not be all one to me whether it existed or not – or, rather, whether it existed or not so long as my desire for its existence ceased? . . . Again I see you smiling. Well, smile away. I take your smiles for what they are worth, for at least I am not in the habit of saying that I am surfeited when I am hungry, or that I do not know that my hopes are based upon something better than a mere compromise, an ever-recurring nought, which the laws of nature may (and, indeed, *do*) allow to exist. The crown of my desires is not a block of flats, with its tenements let as offices to dentists, or as homes to poor lodgers on thousand-year leases; but if you were to annul my volition, to erase my ideals, and to show me something *better*, I might then come to fall in with your views. To this you might reply that to convince me would not be worth your while; whereupon I might make a similar retort: after which we might solemnly discuss the matter a little further, until finally you decided that I was not deserving of your attention. I should not greatly care. For me there will always remain the underworld.

Meanwhile, I go on living, and exercising my volition: and may my hand wither ere ever I use it to add so much as a brick to any block of tenements! Never mind that only a short while ago I rejected the idea of a crystal edifice, for the sole reason that I should not be able to put out my tongue at it. What I then said I did not say because I am fond of putting out my tongue at things, but because, of all buildings, an edifice whereat no one can mock is the only one that has not yet come into existence. On the contrary, of sheer gratitude I would cut out my tongue if matters could be so arranged that I should never at any time feel a desire to protrude that member. What care I that an edifice of such a kind is impossible, and that I must rest content with my present lodgings? Why should such desires occur to me at all? Merely in order that, eventually, I may come to the conclusion that my whole organization is a fraud? Is that the object of it all? I do not believe it.

Yet of one thing I am certain – namely, that a denizen of the underworld ought always to ride himself upon the bit; for although for forty years he may sit silently in his den, let him once issue into the light of day, and straightway he will take the bit in his teeth, and continue talking, and talking, and talking. . . .

⇒ ELEVEN ⇐

SO AT LENGTH, GENTLEMEN, we have reached the conclusion that the best thing for us to do is to do nothing at all, but to sink into a state of contemplative inertia. For that purpose all hail the underworld! True, I said above that I profoundly envy the normal man; yet, under the conditions in which I see him placed, I have no wish to be he. That is to say, though I envy him, I find the underworld better, since at least one can — Yet I am lying. I am lying because, even as I know that two and two make four, so do I know that it is not the underworld which is so much better, but something else, something else – something for which I am hungry, but which I shall never find. Ah no! To the devil with the underworld!

At least, though, I should find things better if I could bring myself to believe a single word of all that I have written. I swear to you, gentlemen, that not a single syllable of what I have been jotting down enjoys my confidence. That is to say, I *believe* it all, but at the same time I suspect – somehow I feel – that, throughout, I have been lying like a bootmaker.

'Why, then, have you written it?' you might ask me; to which I should reply –

'Supposing I were to submerge *you* somewhere for forty years, and that you had no occupation to beguile the time, and that, during the whole of those forty years, you were forced to keep peering out of the underworld, what would become of *you* under such circumstances? Can a man spend forty years alone, yet do nothing at all?'

'But it is no shame, no degradation, to you,' you might retort, with a toss of the head. 'It is only natural for you to hunger for life, but the mischief is that you seek to decide the *questions* of life by a mass of logical tangles. How daring, how insolent, are your sallies, though all the while you are shaking with fear! You talk arrant nonsense, yet you are delighted with it. You give vent to impertinences, yet you are afraid of them, and hasten to beg our pardon. You assure us that you care for nothing, yet in the same breath you come cringing to us for our opinion. You declare that you speak through clenched teeth, yet the next moment you attempt witticisms in order to make us laugh. In short, though well aware that your witticisms are not witty, you appear to rest perfectly satisfied with them, so long only as they are orthographically correct. Possibly, in your time, you have had to suffer, but at least you do not show any respect for your suffering. A grain or two of truth may lie in you, yet not an atom of reticence, since your petty vanity leads you to make a show of everything – to befoul it, and to air it in the market place. You try to speak concisely, yet your nervousness leads you to spin a perfect web of words, for the reason that you have not a particle of self-confidence, but only a sort of pusillanimous knavery. You keep praising self-knowledge, yet at the same time you continue to vacillate, for the reason that, though your mind be working, your heart is befogged with corruption. Without a pure heart there can be no full, no true, realization of self. And what an impudent way you have with it all! What strings of questions you ask, and what fearful grimaces you make! Yet all of what you say is lies, lies from beginning to end.'

This speech I have, of course, invented for you out of my own head – another trick which the underworld has taught me. You must remember that for forty years I, in my cranny here, have been listening to the kind of stuff which you usually utter. Yes, I have been listening to it, and thinking it over, until it is no great marvel that I have learnt it all by heart, and can set it down in more or less literary form.

But are you actually so credulous as to suppose that I intend to have it all printed, and to give it to you to read? True, I myself am rather puzzled to know why I keep on calling you 'gentlemen,' and addressing you as though you were destined to be my readers. Confessions such as mine should never be printed, nor handed to others for perusal. At all events *I* have not sufficient self-confidence for that course, nor do I think it necessary. My reason for writing must be that the idea of it has entered my head and stuck there. That is how it must be.

Every man's reminiscences include things which he reveals, not to all men and sundry, but to his friends alone. Again, every man's reminiscences include things which he does not reveal even to his friends, but to himself alone, and then only under a close seal of secrecy. Lastly, every man's reminiscences include things which he hesitates to reveal even to himself. Of this latter category there soon becomes accumulated in the mind of every decent man a large store. The more decent he be, the larger will his store of such recollections become. Recently I decided to recall to my memory certain of my old experiences, but until now have always deferred doing so, through a feeling of uneasiness even at the idea. Now, however, that I am minded, not only to recall things, but to write them down, I wish, in particular, to try whether one can *ever* be really open with oneself – *ever* be really fearless of any item of truth. *En passant*, Heine has said that a true autobiography is practically impossible, since every man lies to himself. In his (Heine's) opinion, even Rousseau, in his *Confessions*, lied – partly out of set purpose, and partly out of vanity. And I believe that Heine is right. I myself know how vanity may lead a man to impute whole crimes to himself; of the working of such vanity I have a good idea. But Heine was speaking of men who write their confessions *for the public eye*, whereas I wish to write but for myself alone. Let me therefore state, once and for all, that, though I may seem to be writing for the eye of a reader, I do so out of mere show, and for the reason that I find that that kind of writing comes easier. It is all mere form – all a mere empty form, for I shall never have a reader. This I have explained before.

Moreover, I do not wish to be restricted in the scope of my writing. Consequently I intend to observe therein no order or system. What I remember, that I shall write down.

Upon this you might catch me up, and say: 'If you do not count upon being read, why is it that you make these compacts with yourself, and set them down on paper? – the compacts, we mean, that you will observe no order or system in your writing, and that you will write down just what you remember, and so forth? To whom are you speaking? In whose eyes are you seeking to excuse yourself?'

I should merely reply: 'Wait and see.'

For it may be that there is a whole psychology of reasons for what I do. Possibly I am simply a coward. Or possibly it is that I have purposely imagined to myself a public in order to cut the better figure when I *really* come to write for the public. In short, there may exist a thousand reasons for my action.

Again, for precisely what reason, for precisely what purpose, do I desire to write? If not for the benefit of the public, why cannot I remember things without committing them to paper?

Certainly I *could* adopt that course; but on paper my reminiscences are more likely to come out regularly and in order. Besides, in doing so there will be something inspiring, and I shall be able to keep a better rein over myself, and to add a word or two here and there. Again, it is possible that I shall gain from the mere labour of writing a certain *relief*, for one oppressive reminiscence in particular in weighing heavily upon my mind – a reminiscence which recently came back to me, and remains in my thoughts like a musical *motif* which refuses to be banished. I must banish it somehow! A hundred others like it there are, yet at times this one in particular persists in standing out from the rest, and troubling me. Somehow I feel confident that, once it were written down, it would vanish for ever. Why should I not try the experiment?

Lastly, I wish to write because I am *ennuyé*, and have nothing in the world to do; whereas writing is at least work of a kind. They say that labour renders man good-hearted and honourable; wherefore I wish to avail myself even of *that* chance.

To-day half-melted, yellow, dirty snow is falling. It was falling yesterday, and it does so nearly every day. I believe that it is that same half-melted snow which has once more recalled to me the episode of which I cannot rid my thoughts; so here goes for my confession *ápropos* of the fall of sleet.

PART TWO

Apropos of the Falling Sleet

When from th' abyss, the darkness,
　A word of earnest prayer
Plucked your soul for an instant –
　For an instant dulled its care;
Wringing your hands, black curses
　You heaped upon your sin
As memory, that dread rider,
　Spurred with the rowels in.
Then did you, weeping, tell me
　The secrets of the past.
Till, torn, at bay, shame-stricken,
　Your soul stood bare at last.

　　　　From a poem by NEKRASSOV

✦ ONE ✦

I WAS THEN THIRTY YEARS old, and, so far, had lived a dull, ill-regulated existence that was wellnigh as solitary as that of a savage. I had no friends or intimates, and was gradually coming to confine myself more and more to my lodgings. In the same way, when working in my office, I never even looked at those around me, for I knew that my colleagues not only regarded me as an eccentric, but also felt for me a distinct distaste. Often I would ask myself why I, of all men, should excite such aversion. For instance, one of my comrades had a repellent, pox-riddled face that was almost ruffianly in its expression; it was a face of the kind (so it always seemed to me) with which no man would care to face the world; while another of my office-associates was so dirty in his person that he smelt aloud. Yet neither of these two gentlemen seemed in the least put about by this. They seemed to care not a pin about their faces, their clothes, or anything else. Neither the one nor the other of them seemed to think that he was detested; or, if he thought so, at least he did not care, so long as his superiors approved of his work. On the other hand, I was led by my boundless vanity and pretentiousness to look upon myself with a dissatisfaction that, at times, amounted almost to loathing. Consequently I attributed to every one the view of my personality which I myself took. For instance, I detested my face because I thought it had a knavish expression. I even suspected it of looking a little vicious. The result was that, while working in our office, I used to make constant and desperate attempts to look as 'pure' as possible, in order to escape any imputation of viciousness, while I would also endeavour to make my face express the utmost possible refinement. 'Even if I *have* an ugly face,' I used to say, 'at least I will force it to look distinguished, speaking, and, above all things, clever.' Yet I knew, I knew only too painfully well, that my face would never come to express any one of those things. Worse still, I would take it into my head that my countenance looked positively stupid, and feel overwhelmed with despair. Indeed, I would not have minded its vicious expression if only I could have ensured its also being thought extremely clever.

Of course I hated and despised my colleagues. Yet somehow, also, I was afraid of them, and at times felt them to be my superiors. Yes, though I despised them, there were times when I rated them above myself. In fact, a man of the nineteenth century who is at all educated and refined cannot be vain without alternating between boundless self-assertion and envious self-depreciation. Contemptuous or respectful, I lowered my eyes before persons with whom I was brought in contact; and though sometimes I would try to outstare them, I always proved the first to avert my gaze. Also, I was desperately afraid of appearing ridiculous, and paid slavish heed to routine, and to everything that partook of an external nature. Yes, I took great care to walk always in the general rut, and dreaded lest I should discover in myself anything that savoured of eccentricity. But how was I to keep this up? I was a man of advanced tendencies, as befits a gentleman of the nineteenth century, whereas my comrades were men of dull habit, and as like one another as a flock of sheep. Probably I was the only man in our office who thought himself a poltroon and a slave because he was also a gentleman. Moreover, not only did I *think* myself a poltroon and a slave, but I was so in very truth. I say this without the least tinge of shame. Every educated man of the nineteenth century is, and must always be, a poltroon and a slave; it is his normal condition. Of that I, in those days, felt perfectly certain. Modern man is fashioned and constructed to that end and no other. Nor is it *now* only, and owing to fortuitous circumstances, that an educated man is bound to be both a coward and a bondsman; but for all time, and generally. Such is the law of nature for every educated man on this earth. If there should be anything upon which a man of refinement has cause to congratulate himself, he will derive no comfort or solace therefrom, since in all other matters he will still have to truckle to his neighbours. It is the inevitable, the eternal, result of his being what he is. Only the asinine family and its derivatives practise self-congratulation; and that only to a limited extent. But *them* we need not heed, since they signify precisely nothing.

One circumstance in particular used to torment me – namely, the circumstance that no one else was like me, and that I was like no one else. 'I am a person to myself, whereas they are *everybody*,' was my usual thought whenever I engaged in meditations on the subject. From this you will see that I was also extremely young.

In some ways, too, I was inconsistent, for though at times I would find my office work perfectly abhorrent – so much so that I often returned home from it ill – at other times I would fall into an unexpected vein of scepticism and indifference (this often occurred), and laugh at my own impatience and distaste, and blame myself for what I called my 'romanticism.' At such times I would talk with any one, and not only argue with him, but also consort with him on terms of friendship. Yes, my dislike of my fellow men sometimes disappeared entirely. Possibly I never really possessed that dislike, but derived it from books. Even to this day I cannot quite decide the point. However, no sooner had I broken the ice than I used to visit these friends of mine, to play cards with them, to drink vodka, and to talk 'shop.' . . . Here let me make a slight digression.

Generally speaking, we Russians have never gone in for that stupid transcendental romanticizing of German and, still more, French origin in which nothing is ever done by anybody, though the ground be shaking beneath one's feet and all France be going to pieces at the barricades, so long only as decorum forbids one to change, and one can go on singing transcendental songs in what I might call the grave of one's existence, for the reason that one is a fool. In the Russian land there *are* no fools. That is a fact, and one that distinguishes us from all the other Germanic countries. Consequently, Russia contains no transcendental natures in the pure meaning of the term. Yet many of our publicists and critics have been in the habit of imagining that our romanticists are similar to those of France and Germany! On the contrary, the qualities of our romanticists are directly opposed to the transcendental-European standard, and not a single stanza in the European style finds acceptance here. (You must not mind my using the term 'romanticism.' I do so only because it is an old and a respected one, and has seen much service, and is familiar to everybody.) The nature of *our* romanticists is to comprehend everything, to see everything, and frequently to see everything incomparably more clearly than do more practical intellects; not to accord offhand acceptance to anyone or anything, but nevertheless to be squeamish of nothing; to skate around everything, to yield politic way in everything; never to lose sight of the useful and the practical (as represented by such things as lodgings at the State's expense, pensions, and medals); to keep that end in view through all the enthusiasms and depressions of lyrical poetry; to cherish always within themselves 'the great and the beautiful'; and to devote their own personalities, like so many precious jewels, to the furtherance – no matter in what trifles – of 'the great and the beautiful.' Yes, our romanticist is a man of wide sympathies, and the chief rogue whom we possess – that I can assure you from personal experience. Or at all events he is so if he is a wise man. But what am I saying? The romanticist is *in any case* a wise man. Rather, I mean that, though we used to have some mad romanticists among us, we need not take *them* into account, since, when just in the flower of their vigour, they became converted into Germans, and, the better to safeguard their treasures, went and settled in Weimar or Schwartzwald or some other German town. For my part, I used to have a sincere contempt for my official work, over and above the necessity which compelled me to sit on a stool and receive money for that work – an obligation, mark you, which I did *not* so greatly regret. On the other hand, if the ordinary foreign romantic were to lose his senses (though this does not very often happen) he would not feel in the least distressed at the prospect of having to be taken to the madhouse as 'the King of Spain' or some such personage (that is to say, if he had gone *sufficiently* out of his mind); whereas with us only frail and aged romantics lose their reason. Moreover, the number of romantic writers could never be computed; which fact has led to their being divided into hosts and hosts of grades. Also, their many-sidedness is astonishing. For instance, what a faculty they possess for combining within themselves the most opposite of qualities! I used to derive great amusement from the fact – from the fact, that is to say, that among us there are numbers of 'broad-minded' writers who never lose their ideals, and who, though unwilling to stir a finger on behalf of those ideals, or to cease to be anything but declared robbers and brigands, continue, to the point of weeping, to cherish their original aspirations, while at the same time showing extraordinary singleness of heart. Yes, it is only in Russia that the most abandoned of rascals can be wholly, even splendidly, honourable men, while also continuing to be rascals. Therefore I repeat that the ranks of our romantics have given rise to bands of such absolute scoundrels (I use the term 'scoundrels' with particular pleasure) – to bands of men who display such a sense of the realities, such a knowledge of the practical – that a bewildered Government and public can but stand and gape at them!

Yes, their many-sidedness is astonishing, and God only knows whither at the present day it is being bent and developed, or what it promises for the future. Yet, after all, it does not make bad material. I do not say this out of patriotism, nor in a sour or sneering way, though I have an idea that once more you will believe me to be poking fun at you. Well, I greatly value and appreciate your opinion, and would ask you to pardon me if I have offended.

With my comrades I, of course, maintained no intimacy, and soon grew tired of them. Indeed, my then youthful inexperience led me not to curse them, but simply to drop them. At home I read a great deal, in a vain endeavour to drown in a flood of external impressions what was seething within me. The way to attain this lay, so far as I could see, only in reading. Books helped me, for by turns they soothed, stimulated, and pained my intellect. Yet at times I grew terribly weary of it all, and felt that, come what might, I must embark upon some kind of activity. Hence I would suddenly plunge into the lowest depths of foul, dark – well, not so much debauchery, as lewdness, for at that time my passions were keen, and derived all the greater heat from the aching, perpetual discontent with the world of which I was full: and to these bouts there would succeed intervals of hysteria which threw me into convulsions of weeping. I had no resource beyond reading. That is to say, there was nothing in my daily life which attracted me, or which I could respect. Above all things, constant depression seethed within me – a depression which, causing me to thirst for something different, for some sharp contrast, plunged me into vice. This I am not saying merely out of self-justification — But again I have lied. I *am* saying it merely in order to justify myself. I make this confession for my own eyes alone, since I do not wish *you*, gentlemen, to think me a liar.

Stealthily, and by night, I used to indulge in solitary rounds of dissipation, but always with a timid, blackguardly, shamefaced sort of feeling which never deserted me even in my moments of greatest abasement (though at such times, true, it caused me to curse myself). It was the fruit of my long carrying of the underworld within me. Always, too, I had a great dread of being seen, or met, or recognized by any one; wherefore I would frequently change the venue of my dark proceedings.

One night, when passing a tavern, I saw, through some lighted panes, a party of gentlemen playing at billiards. Presently they fell to fighting one another with their cues, and one of their number was thrown out of the window by his companions. At any other time I should have felt only disgusted at this, but on the present occasion I conceived a sort of envy of the expelled individual – so great an envy that I entered the tavern, and approached the billiard-room. 'Come,' I thought to myself, 'let me but pick a quarrel, and they will expel me too.' I was not drunk; I was merely ready for anything – to such a pitch can hysteria and depression eat into a man's soul. Yet nothing happened. Seeing that I could not, if necessary, spring from the window, I was on the point of departing without joining in the brawl when I was brought up short by an officer. At the moment, all unwittingly, I was blocking the door of the room, and he was trying to pass out of it. Taking me by the shoulder, and saying not a word of warning or explanation, he pushed me aside, and pursued his way as though he had not noticed me. Under ordinary circumstances I should have apologized to him, but, as it was, I felt that I could not do so, seeing that he had not only thrust me out of his path, but also departed without deigning me a single glance.

The devil only knows what, at that moment, I would have given to pick a real, a regular, a more decent, a more (if I might use the term) literary, quarrel! I had been treated like a fly! Whereas the officer had been a man of six feet, I was only a thin, mean little fellow; yet the quarrel had lain entirely in my hands, and, had I protested, I too could have been thrown out of the window. But I had wasted time in a mass of thinking and proposing, and so had incurred the shame of seeing myself snubbed!

So angry and disturbed was I that when I left the tavern I went straight home, and next day continued my course of dissipation – but in an even more timid, cowed, and lugubrious manner than usual. Indeed, I did so with, as it were, tears in my eyes. Yet I *did* continue it. Do not think that I was *afraid* of that officer. I have never yet been a coward at heart, however much I have been so in action. No, you need not smile; I have an explanation for this, even as I have, you may rest assured, an explanation for everything else.

Oh, if that officer could have been one of those who will fight duels! But no, he was essentially one of those gentlemen (now, alas! a vanished race) who prefer to take action with billiard cues, or, like Gogol's Colonel Pirogov, in obedience only to orders. Such men do *not* fight duels; a duel even with a fellow fire-eater they consider inexpedient, since they look upon the duel as a senseless, free-thinking institution which savours of Frenchism. Consequently they remain ever ready to insult others – especially if they (the aggressors) can boast of six feet of stature!

No, it was not out of cowardice that I held my hand, but through boundless vanity. I feared neither six feet of stature nor the fact that I might be beaten and thrown out of the window. *Physical* courage has never been wanting in me: what I then lacked was *moral* courage. I was afraid lest every one present, from the head marker to the lowest official, with his blotched and pimpled face and greasy collar, would fail to understand me, and laugh when I protested and addressed them in really literary language. For of the point of honour – not of honour pure and simple, mind you, but of the *point* of honour – it has never been the custom to speak in any but the most refined and literary diction. No ordinary words have I ever heard spoken concerning that same point of honour. Therefore I felt certain (it was due to the practical sense in me, as distinguished from the romantic) that every one present would burst their sides with laughter, while the officer would not merely – that is to say, inoffensively – thrash me, but also trip me in the back with his knee, lead me a dance around the billiard-table, and, finally, have sufficient pity upon me to expel me through the window. But of course I could not let this wretched episode end where it was. Frequently in after days I met the officer in the street, and took the most careful note of him. I do not know whether he recognized *me*, but I think that he did not. None the less I always regarded him with hatred and envy. Thus things continued for several years, my grudge against him growing ever deeper and stronger as the years passed on.

Early in the proceedings I tried to make some cautious inquiries about the man, but found the task very difficult, for the reason that I knew no one. At last one day some one spoke to him in the street (I was then following him as closely as though I were tied to his person), and I learnt his name. Another time I followed him home to his flat, and for the sum of one *grivennik** ascertained from the porter what number the officer lived at, on which floor, and whether alone or with some one else – in short, all that *could* be ascertained from a porter. Another morning, though it was my first essay in literature, I took it into my head to indite this officer a letter, in the form of a caricature embodying a story. With great zest I wrote it, and, making it fairly scurrilous, at first appended to my enemy a name which he was bound to recognize at first sight; but later I decided to change it for another one, and then sent the whole to *Tales of the Fatherland*. But, to my grief, it never got into print. Sometimes my wrath almost stifled me; so much so that at length I decided to challenge the foe to a duel. To this end I composed a beautiful, a most attractive letter, wherein I adjured him to expiate his fault, and hinted that, in case of refusal, I should call him out to fight me. Yet the missive was couched in such terms as would lead the officer, if he were at all capable of comprehending 'the great and the beautiful,' to at once seek me out, fall upon my neck, and proffer me his friendship. 'And how splendid that would be!' I said to myself. 'We will have such a time of it together – yes, such a time of it! He shall hold over me the ægis of his professional position, and I shall give him the benefit of my refinement – er – and – and of my ideas. Much, much will come of it!' You must remember that it was now two years since he had offered me the insult, and my challenge was simply a gross anachronism, without mentioning the added *gaucherie* of my letter, which at once disclosed and concealed that anachronism. However, thank God! (even to this day I can never bless the Almighty without tears), I failed to send the letter. Indeed, whenever I think what *might* have happened, had I sent it, I turn cold. In the end it befell that I wreaked vengeance in the most simple, the most genial, of fashions, for a brilliant idea suddenly occurred to me. You must know that, at four o'clock on the afternoon of festival days, I would go for a walk along the sunny side of the Nevski Prospect; or, rather, I would not so much go for a walk as go to indulge in a series of annoyances, humiliations, and outpourings of spleen – things which seemed to me an absolute necessity. Like a lamprey, I would, in uncouth fashion, go wriggling my way through the throng, and give room, now to a general, now to an officer of the Horse or of the Foot Guards, now to a civilian, and so on. Yet all the while there would be spasms of pain at my heart, and

* Ten kopecks, or 2¹/₂*d*.

shivers running down my back, at the mere thought of the wretched appearance that my costume and figure must be presenting. To me it was sheer misery and degradation – sheer, ceaseless, unbearable misery and degradation – to have to think, always and *apropos* of everything, that, in the eyes of this shining world, I was no more than an unclean and useless fly. True, the fly was one that was much cleverer, better educated, and better born than those who were jostling him, yet none the less it was a fly that had to give way to every one, to be looked down upon by every one, to be scorned by every one. *Why* I should voluntarily have incurred the misery which I used to suffer on the Nevski Prospect I do not know. I only know that I found myself drawn thither on every possible occasion.

It was at that period that I began to experience the species of delight to which I have referred in Part I; and after the incident with the officer I began more than ever to be attracted to the Nevski Prospect, for it was there that I most often encountered and found myself obsessed by him. He, like myself, walked there mostly on festival days; he, too, stepped aside to make room for generals and big-wigs; he, too, wormed his way along like a lamprey, while common folk like myself he merely jostled, or else walked straight into, as though the space in front of him were perfectly clear. Never did I see him make way for such people, and as I gazed at him I used to feel perfectly drunk with rancour – though I gave him room with the rest whenever I met him. How it hurt me to think that even in the streets I was powerless to get on even terms with him. 'Why the devil *do* you step aside?' I would ask myself in a sort of idiotic, hysterical way when I awoke, say, at three in the morning. 'Why is it always *you*, not *he*? Is there no law for such a man – no precept? Supposing that we were to meet on equal terms, in the usual way that gentlemen meet one another, what would happen? Well, he would yield me half the path, and I the same to him, and we should pass one another with mutual respect.' Yet never did this befall. Always I turned aside for him, whereas *he* – he never even seemed to notice that I had done so. It was then that there first occurred to me the brilliant idea of which I have spoken. 'What,' was my thought, 'if I were to meet him and *not* leave the path – to *purposely* not leave it, even though my not doing so should entail a collision?' This daring notion gradually obsessed me until I could not rest. Ceaselessly, deeply I pondered over it, while of set intent I patrolled the Prospect more frequently than ever, so as to realize the more clearly what I ought to do when actually I *did* come to make the attempt. All the while I was in transports, for more and more it was dawning upon me that my scheme was not only feasible, but a very good one. 'Of course, I shall not actually *push* him,' I would add to myself, anticipatorily considerate in my joy, 'I will simply omit to turn aside, so that without

coming into violent contact with him, I may rub shoulders with him so far as the conventions ordain. Exactly as he jostles *me* so will I jostle *him*.'
At length my mind was made up, though the preparatory process had taken a long time. In the first place, I felt that at the moment of execution I should need to be looking my best, and therefore must take some thought for my raiment, seeing that, if a public scene should ensue (the public itself, of course, did not matter, but promenading there would also be the Countess A. and the Prince B. and the whole of the literary world), I should require to be at least *decently* dressed. To be so would inspire respect, and at once place myself and my antagonist on an equal footing in the eyes of society. Accordingly I drew some salary in advance, and bought, at Tchurkin's, a pair of black gloves and a smart hat. Somehow black gloves seemed to look more respectable, more *bon ton*, than the yellow ones which I first tried on. 'Coloured gloves are too loud, and make a man look too conspicuous,' said I to myself as I rejected the yellow articles referred to. As for a shirt, I had long had one ready – one that was not only in pretty good repair, but also was fitted with white bone studs. The only thing that gave me pause was my overcoat. In itself it was not a bad one, for it was at least warm; but it had a wadded lining and a raccoon collar, and both of those things were the height of flunkeyism. Consequently it would be necessary to change the collar for a beaver one, such as all the officers wore. For this purpose I made the round of the shops, and at length lit upon a piece of beaver of cheap German extraction. Though German beaver soon comes to wear shabby and present a miserable appearance, it easily passes muster at first, if properly furbished up. Consequently a piece of it would do well enough for this occasion only. On asking the price, however, I found that it was too dear; so, after further grave consideration, I decided to sell my raccoon collar, and to borrow the deficit from the head of my department, Anton Antonitch Sietochkin. The latter, though an easy-going man, was of serious and opinionated bent and anything but a money-lender; where-fore, despite the fact that on my entry to the service I had been highly recommended to his favour by the gentleman who had procured me my nomination, I dreaded the prospect of begging a loan of him. Somehow it seemed such a monstrous, such a shameful, thing to do that for three whole nights I never slept, little though my fevered condition had for some while past inclined me to slumber. By turns my heart would sink to nothing and turn to throbbing and throbbing and throbbing. At the first blush Anton Antonitch seemed surprised at my request; then he frowned, considered the matter again, and, finally, handed me the cash in exchange for a note of hand which empowered him to recoup himself, in two weeks' time, out of my salary. Thus I had everything prepared. The

beautiful beaver had now dethroned the miserable raccoon, and I could set myself to the work in hand. No rash decision must be come to, I felt; the affair was one which called for gradual and guarded management. Yet it must be confessed that, though I made many attempts to carry out my enterprise, I soon found myself beginning to despair of ever coming into actual contact with the enemy.

For instance, on one occasion I was not ready; on a second occasion I had not properly thought the matter out. More than once the officer and myself were on the point of colliding when – again I stepped aside, and he passed me by without looking at me. Sometimes I even went so far as to mutter fervent prayers as I approached him – prayers that God might steel me to the effort. At length I had really made up my mind to jostle him when, at the very last moment, when only a couple of paces from him, my breath failed, and I tripped and fell under his feet. Nonchalantly he stepped over me, and I rolled away out of the throng like a ball. That night fever again seized me, and I became delirious. However, the affair ended in the best way possible, for it struck me, the next afternoon, that I might as well desist from my abortive enterprise, and accordingly I made my way to the Nevski Prospect for the last time, to see whether I really could effect my purpose. Suddenly, when my foe was within three paces of me, I came to a sudden decision, put on a ferocious scowl, and – and came into a violent collision with his shoulder! Not an inch did I budge, but continued my way with unshaken stride. Again he did not look at me, again he did not appear even to have noticed me; yet I felt certain that he was shamming. Yes, to this day I am sure of it. In any case it was I who had gained the most from the encounter. Though he might remain the stronger of the two, that did not matter. What really mattered was that I had attained my end, I had upheld my dignity, I had not yielded to him an inch, and I had publicly placed myself on an equality with him in the eyes of society. I returned home revenged, revenged! I felt transported with delight, and trolled an Italian aria as I proceeded. I need not tell you how I spent the next three days. Those of you who have read my *Underworld* will be able to guess it for themselves. Later, the officer was transferred to another station, and it is fourteen years since I last saw him. What has become of my idol? Whom is he now bullying?

❧ TWO ❧

AFTER THIS MY PHASE OF dissipation came to an end, and I found the time hang heavy on my hands. Occasionally repentance would seize me, but I always drove it forth again, for I was too weary to do aught but fall in with – rather, put up with – whatsoever chanced to happen. Yet all the while there was a way of escape which reconciled me to everything – namely, the way of escape contained in my visionary cult of 'the great and the beautiful.' I did nothing but dream and dream of it; for three whole months on end I, crouching in my den, did nothing else. You may be sure that at this period there was nothing in common between myself and the individual who, in chickenish perturbation of heart, had sewed a piece of German beaver on to the collar of his overcoat. No; of a sudden I had become a hero. Even my six-foot colonel I would not have deigned to admit to my rooms. As a matter of fact, I had forgotten all about him. What my dreams were, and how I was able to rest satisfied with them, it is difficult, at this distance of time, to conjecture, but at all events they *did* give me pleasure. Moreover, they always came to me with greater strength and sweetness after a bout of dissipation; they came in company with tears and regrets, transports and curses. Indeed, such moments of rapture, of happiness, had I that, thank God, it never entered into my head to deride them. Ah, how full they were of faith and hope and love for my fellowmen! That is to say, I had a sort of blind belief that one day some miracle, some external circumstance, would suddenly cause the present to break and become widened, and that suddenly there would dawn before me a horizon of congenial, productive, fair, and, above all things, *instant* activity (though in what manner *instant* I did not know), and that at last I should issue into God's world, mounted on a white horse, and crowned with laurels. Any secondary rôle I found myself unable to envisage, and that is why I thought so much about the subject. Whether a hero, or whether a groveller in dung, for me there could be no medium. Hence my undoing; since, when grovelling in dung, I always comforted myself with the reflection that at other times I was a hero, and that the hero overlaid the dung-groveller; for, thought I, though a man is usually ashamed when he bathes in mire, a hero stands on too lofty a plane ever to be wholly immersed in the stuff; wherefore he may grovel as he pleases. It is curious that my aspirations towards 'the great and the beautiful' should always have come to me precisely in moments of dissipation – on the very day that a bout of debauchery had occurred. Yes, they always came to me in isolated bursts, as though to remind me of their existence, but without repairing the dissipation by this manifestation of themselves. On the contrary, they seemed, through the mere force of contrast, to revivify my debauched instincts – to arrive, as it were, in time to make a sauce for those instincts. Of that sauce the ingredients were remorse and a sense of contradiction, added to torturing self-analysis; all of which pains and torments communicated to my degradation a sort of piquancy, and even a meaning. In short, my aspirations towards 'the great and the beautiful' fulfilled all the functions of a relish. Yet behind this there was something else; for how, otherwise, could I have reconciled myself to debauchery that was worthy only of an underclerk, or have covered myself to such an extent with mire? What was there in it all to attract me, or to lead me to cheat the night in brothels? Ah, I had a good excuse for everything. . . .

How much love – my God! how much love – I used to expend in those dreams, in those yearnings for 'the great and the beautiful'! – yes, even though my affection was of a fantastical order which could not possibly have been applied to a human being, but the abundance of which was such that I never felt any need so to apply it, seeing that, throughout, it was love of a superfluous, luxurious kind. Fortunately, it usually ended by turning to an indolent, sensuous cult of art, in the shape of beautiful forms of life which I borrowed readymade from poets and romanticists, and then adapted to every possible use and requirement of my own. In those visions I would rise superior to all mankind; all men were in the dust before me, and forced to recognize my perfection as I extended to them my pardon. Rapturously I would imagine myself to be a famous poet or courtier, or the fortunate possessor of untold millions which I was devoting to the benefit of the human race, while confessing to the latter my sins – though not sins in the actual sense of the word, but, rather, acts which partook of 'the great and the beautiful' (something after the Manfredian style). Yes, I would picture the whole world weeping and embracing me (it was bound to do so if it were not wholly gross), and myself walking abroad, barefooted and hungry, to preach my new ideas, and to deal out to reaction its Austerlitz. Then a grand march would sound, and a general amnesty would be issued; after which the Pope would consent to leave Rome for Brazil, and a ball to which all Italy would be invited would be held at the Villa Borghese (the said Villa Borghese being situated, for that occasion only, on Lake Como, which, also for that occasion only, would have been transferred to the neighbourhood of Rome). Then, again, the scene would become shadowy — But does not every one know the kind of thing? Not long ago you said that it is wrong for a man to expose his all in the market-place – to expose such tears and raptures as those to which I have confessed. But why? Do you really think that I am ashamed of them, or that any of them were a whit worse than is anything in your own lives? Moreover, not *all* my ideas were badly conceived; not *all* of them centred around Lake Como. However, you may be right; they *may* have been low and degraded. The lowest thing of all is that I should have sought to justify my conduct in your eyes. A lower thing still is the fact that I have said so. . . . However, enough of this, or I shall never have finished with it. Always one thing lower than the last will keep occurring to me.

Yet I had not spent more than three months upon these ecstasies of mine when I began to feel a renewed inclination for intercourse with my fellowmen, although, for me, the social round meant only an occasional visit to the house of my official superior, Anton Antonitch Sietochkin. Indeed, he was the one friend whom ever I have permanently retained; and to this day I marvel at the circumstance. Even him, however, I never visited except when one of my curious moods had come over me, and my dreams had reached a pitch of delight which impelled me forthwith to embrace humanity at large (which I could not well do without having at hand at least one concrete, one existing, human being). Also, since my calls upon Anton Antonitch had always to be paid on a Tuesday (such being his reception day), I had to make my yearnings towards humanity also fall upon the second day in the week. His abode consisted of four rooms on the fourth floor of a block in Five Corners Street – rooms poorly furnished, and charged with the most penurious, the most jaundiced, air conceivable. With him lived two daughters and an aunt; the last-named of whom always poured out tea. At that time the daughters were thirteen and fourteen respectively, and had flaxen hair; while their habit of whispering and giggling together used greatly to embarrass me. As for the master of the house himself, he usually passed the time on a horsehair sofa near his study table, while beside him would sit a grey-haired guest who was one of the officials of our (or, possibly some other?) office. In all, I never encountered more than two or three guests at these gatherings, and their conversation invariably turned upon the Stock Exchange, the last debate in the Senate, salaries, routine business, the Minister of our Department, and the best means of winning the Minister's favour. For some four hours or so I would sit stupidly beside these people, and listen to them without either a smile or a chance of joining in the conversation. Very dull I found it; but since, at times, I became so stricken with shyness that I would actually break out into a sweat, the whole thing did me good, since on the way home I would find no difficulty whatever in temporarily ridding myself of any desire to fall upon the neck of humanity.

Also, I had an acquaintance named Simonov, an old schoolfellow of mine. At that time many of my old schoolfellows were residing in St. Petersburg, but in most cases I had dropped them, and ceased even to salute them in the street. Moreover, I had gone so far as to procure my transfer to another department, for the sole purpose of severing all ties with my hateful boyhood. Yes, a curse upon the school at which I studied, and upon its horrible years of servitude! In short, from the moment when I regained my liberty I broke with the majority of my old comrades, save two or three. Of these, Simonov was one, since his retiringness and docility had saved us from any serious difference at school, and I could discern in him a certain amount of independence and uprightness of character. Nor did I look upon him as wholly a limited man; wherefore I spent many a friendly hour with him, and it was only comparatively recently that these reunions had ceased to be, and a mist had descended over their brightness. The truth was that suddenly he seemed to have grown weary of exchanging confidences, and to have taken fright lest we should again slip into the old footing. Yet, despite the fact that I gathered that I was no longer a *persona grata* with him, I still continued to pay him occasional visits.

So, one Thursday evening, when I felt unable any longer to bear my loneliness, and knew that on Thursdays Anton Antonitch's door would be closed to me, I bethought me of Simonov. As I mounted the stairs to the fourth floor where he lived I remember I felt more than ever assured that he had grown tired of me, and that I had come in vain; but considerations of this sort invariably ended by drawing me on the more to fill ambiguous positions, and I therefore entered his apartments. It was now almost a year since I had last seen him.

➤ THREE ◄

WITH HIM I FOUND TWO OTHER old schoolfellows of mine who were discussing what appeared to be a very important subject. On my entry neither of them paid me the least attention: which seemed to me an odd thing, seeing that I had not seen either of them for the space of a year.

Evidently they looked upon me as some kind of ordinary fly. Even at school, much as, in those days, they had disliked me, they had not treated me so. I, for my part, felt sure that their contempt was due to my unsuccessful career in the service, my social descent, my shabby clothes, and such other things as, in their eyes, would constitute signs of my incompetence and low standing. Yet I had not expected quite such a lack of ceremony as this. For his part, Simonov seemed surprised to see me enter – though it had always been his way to appear so (a circumstance which had never failed to annoy me). Consequently I seated myself in rather a dejected mood, and set myself to listen to the conversation.

A grave, and even heated, discussion was in progress concerning a farewell dinner which these three gentlemen wished to offer, the next evening, to a friend of theirs named Zvierkov, an officer in the army, who was about to leave for a distant post. He too had been a companion of mine at school, but during our latter days he had led me to conceive an intense dislike for him. Even when we were juniors I had envied him because he was a gay, good-looking young fellow whom every one liked. Yet he had never done his lessons aught but badly, and the more so as time went on. Indeed, that he passed his examinations at all was due to the fact that he had some influence behind him, for during his last year at school he had inherited a legacy of two hundred souls;* and since nearly all of us, his schoolfellows, were poor, he had taken to assuming rather grand airs over us. Yet, though in the highest degree vicious, he was also good-natured, even when swaggering his worst; with the result that, despite our purely external, fantastic, stilted forms of honour and *esprit de corps*, we all of us, except a few, grovelled before him, and the more so in proportion as he played the lord. Nor was it altogether out of self-interest that he was fawned upon; it was equally because he was so favoured of nature. Moreover, it was, with us, an accepted axiom that he was a specialist in good manners and deportment. But the latter assumption simply maddened me. I could not bear either the grating, boastful intonation of his voice, or his admiration of his own stupid witticisms, or the sight of his vapid, handsome face (gladly though I would have given in exchange my own supposedly 'clever' one), or his free and easy assumption of the manners of an officer of forty years' standing, or his talk about his intended conquest of the fair sex (which, since he had decided to leave it unentered upon until he had assumed an officer's epaulets, he was the more eager to initiate), or his everlasting prattle about his future prowess in duels. Once, when, during a play hour, he was holding forth to his comrades about the property which was one day

* That is to say, land sufficient to employ two hundred serfs.

to be his, and sporting at the prospect of it like a young puppy in the sun, and stating that he meant to take stock of every serf girl on the estate (he asserted that this would be no more than his *droit de seigneur*), and that if the peasants dared to utter a protest he would flog them all, greybeards included, and impose double tithes upon their holdings; when, as I say, he was declaiming all this, I suddenly dropped my customary rôle of silent auditor, and joined issue with him. Some of our fellows clapped their hands at this; which made me fasted upon my antagonist the more, since my prime motive was not so much pity for the serf girls and their fathers as rage at the thought that a louse of a fellow should ever have his utterances applauded. True, on this occasion I won the day, but Zvierkov, though foolish, was also proud and good-tempered, and contrived to laugh off the affair in such a manner that I was partly cheated of the fruits of victory, and forced to see the laugh remain on the other side. Several times afterwards he managed to turn the tables upon me in the same way, but this he did without malice, and merely in jest, or in passing, or with a smile, though I felt too angry and contemptuous to respond. Nay, when our school days were over, he even made overtures of friendship which I did not altogether resist, since they rather attracted me; but soon we drifted apart again. Next, I heard of some doings of his in barracks, and of the dissipated life that he was leading there; subsequently of the fact that he was getting on in the service. Yet whenever he passed me in the street he used to give me the cut direct; wherefore I suspected that he was afraid of compromising himself by being seen in converse with such an insignificant individual as myself. Also, on one occasion I saw him in a third-tier box at the theatre – already adorned with shoulder-knots, and engaged in bowing and scraping to the daughters of an old general. During the last three years, however, he had become much thinner in the face, though he was still handsome and engaging; his body had grown bloated, and it was clear that by the time he had reached the age of thirty he would have come to be a mass of wrinkles. Such was the Zvierkov to whom the farewell dinner was to be given by my fellow guests at Simonov's. For the last three years these gentlemen had been his constant companions; although, as I could easily discern, they in no way considered themselves his equals.

Of Simonov's two guests one was Ferfitchkin – a Russo-German of dwarfish stature and ape-like face, who, in his stupidity, laughed at everybody, and had, from our earliest school days, been my bitterest foe. Yet, though a vicious, conceited *farceur*, he aspired to the nicest sense of honour – he a man who, all the while was essentially a coward! Lastly, he was one of those panderers of Zvierkov's who openly flattered him, and secretly borrowed of him money. The other of the two guests was a military nonentity named Trudoliubov – a man of tall stature and frigid mien, but possessed of a certain notion of honour, even though he worshipped success in every form, and could talk only 'shop.' In addition, he could trace a certain relationship to Zvierkov; which fact, I am ashamed to state, conferred upon him a certain standing in our circle. Me, however, he seemed to rate very low for he treated me, if not with actual rudeness, at all events with the barest toleration.

'Seven roubles apiece,' said Trudoliubov. 'In all, that will make twenty-one roubles, and provide us with a very good dinner indeed. Of course *Zvierkov* need not pay his share.'

'Of course not, seeing that he is the guest,' agreed Simonov.

'But do you suppose,' put in Ferfitchkin, with all the insolence of a valet who is flaunting his master's, the general's, medals, 'do you suppose that he will *permit* us to pay his share? In all probability he will accept the invitation rather than hurt our feelings; yet he will be sure also to contribute at least half-a-dozen of champagne.'

'Then how are we to apportion the other half-dozen among ourselves?' asked Trudoliubov – his attention now riveted upon the wine question.

'I propose that the three of us (each of us contributing seven roubles) meet Zvierkov at the Hôtel de Paris at five o'clock to-morrow evening,' said Simonov, who appeared to be the prime organizer of the feast.

'What? Only twenty-one roubles?' I put in, in as excited a tone as though I were offended. 'Then accept me also as a guest, and we shall raise the total to twenty-eight roubles.'

The truth was that there had suddenly come to me an idea that to cut in unexpectedly in this fashion was a clever thing to do, and would be sure to win the respect of all present.

'So *you* wish to take part in it?' exclaimed Simonov, though without looking at me. He always avoided my gaze, because he knew me by heart, and I felt furious that he should do so.

'Why not?' I spluttered. 'I also am a comrade of Zvierkov's, and might well have taken offence at being passed over like this.'

'We did not know where to find you,' said Ferfitchkin brusquely.

'Besides, Zvierkov and yourself are not exactly *friends*,' added Trudoliubov, with a frown.

Nevertheless, I stuck to my idea, and retorted with a stutter –

'I – I do not consider that any one has the right to judge between Zvierkov and myself. It is precisely because we *have* been on bad terms that I now wish to meet him again.'

'Oh, who could understand *your* fine ideas?' said Trudoliubov, with a sneer.

'Well, well,' decided Simonov, 'you *shall* form one of the party. To-morrow, then, if you please, at the Hôtel de Paris at five. And mind you come.'

'And mind you bring the money, too,' added Ferfitchkin gruffly, with a wink at Simonov. Further than this he did not venture, for even Simonov looked confused at what he (Ferfitchkin) had just said.

'All right,' said Trudoliubov, rising. 'If he wants to come, *let* him come.'

'But the affair is a private party, not an official reception,' persisted Ferfitchkin as he too rose and reached for his hat. In leaving the room he omitted to accord me any salute whatever, and Trudoliubov gave me only a very faint one as he averted his eyes. Simonov, too, seemed annoyed when he found himself left *tête-à-tête* with me, and kept throwing stealthy glances in my direction.

'Hm! Yes, to-morrow,' he stammered. 'Er – by the way, would you mind handing me your contribution *now,* so as to make quite sure of it?'

For the moment I felt beside myself with rage; but the next minute I remembered that for a long while past I had been owing him fifteen roubles, which, though never paid, I had not wholly forgotten.

'Surely,' I replied, 'you yourself see that I could not be expected to know what was in the wind when I came? Of course I regret my negligence.'

'Very well, very well. You can pay me to-morrow, after dinner. I merely wanted to know; that is all. Pray do not – '

Without finishing his sentence he began to pace the room with an air of ever-growing annoyance, and a constant clicking of his heels.

'No,' he went on. 'That is to say, yes. . . . However, I must be off now. I am not going far.' This last he said almost apologetically.

'Why did you not tell me before?' I cried, as I seized my hat.

'Oh, it is not very far – merely a couple of steps,' he repeated, as he escorted me to the door with a preoccupied air which did not sit well upon him. 'To-morrow, at five,' he cried for the last time, as I was descending the staircase – doubtless signifying that he was only too glad to see me go. I felt furious.

'May the devil take the lot of them!' I thought, as I wended my way home. 'Why on earth have I gone and mixed myself up in the affair? Why, indeed? And to entertain an idiotic pig like Zvierkov, too! Good Lord! Of course, I *need* not go. But how am I to get out of the engagement? To-morrow I shall send Simonov word that – '

What really maddened me was the knowledge that I *should* go to the dinner. The more tactless, the more out of place it seemed to me to go, the more was I bent upon going. Yet one difficulty confronted me: I had no money. True, I had nine roubles in my possession, but, to-morrow, seven of these would need to be paid over to my servant, Apollon, who received from me, as wages, board and lodging and the monthly sum specified. Not to pay his wages punctually was, for me, a thing impossible, owing to his character. But of this brute, of this plague of my life, more anon.

All the time I knew that I should *not* pay those wages, but, on the contrary, go to the dinner.

I had terrible dreams that night – a not very remarkable thing, seeing that I had spent the evening in company with memories of my servitude at school – memories which I could not banish. To that school I had been sent by some distant relatives in whose care I had been, and of whom I had long since lost sight. They had sent me to that school an orphan whom they had cowed with scoldings until I had become a prematurely silent, introspective, curiously observant boy; and there I had been saluted by my comrades with nothing but cruel, pitiless jeers, owing to the fact that I was not like any of them. Those jeers I could not stand; I could not get on good terms with my companions in the easy way which *they* could with one another, but conceived an instant grudge against them, and shut myself up in a world of nervous, sensitive, boundless pride. My comrades' roughness was a sheer torture to me, for they never grew tired of making cynical jests on the subject of my face and ungainly figure. Yet how stupid their own faces were! Indeed, our school fostered a sort of facial expression that was unique for its innate, ever-growing dullness. However good-looking a boy might be when he first came to us, a few years would succeed in making him look simply repulsive. Even at sixteen I found myself astonished at the pettiness of my companions' thought, and at the inanity of their pursuits, games and subjects of conversation. They did not understand even the most ordinary things of life, while things that were at all striking or inspiring aroused in them no interest whatever. Consequently I had no choice but to regard my fellow students with disdain. Yet it was not mere wounded vanity that impelled me to do so, so for the love of God do not pounce upon me with the sickeningly hackneyed phrase that 'you were then only a boy of dreams, whereas *they* knew what life meant.' I tell you that these boys knew simply *nothing*, whether of life or of anything else: and this incensed me all the more against them. On the other hand, the plainest, the most evident, actuality was viewed by them in fantastically stupid fashion, for they were already accustomed to worship only success. Everything which, though of good report, was also lowly and unassuming they flouted with insults and cruelty. Rank they mistook for brains, and even at the age of sixteen they could speak familiarly of places of bad resort. Of course, much of this *may* have arisen from the crass, debased conditions which surrounded their early boyhood and adolescence; yet, even so, it must be said that, taken as a whole, they were almost monstrously vicious. True, that viciousness may, in its turn, have been largely cynical and external, for at times a certain youthful freshness glimmered amid the vice; yet even that freshness was devoid of all attractiveness, and showed itself mostly in a sort of premature pruriency. In short, I had the greatest horror of them all, even though I myself may have been the worst of the lot; and this detestation they repaid – and very openly, too – in kind. However, I did not want their liking. On the contrary, my one desire was to see them humbled to the dust. As a means of escaping their ridicule I set myself earnestly to pursue my studies, and soon had risen almost to the top of the school. This *did* make a certain impression upon them, for it gradually dawned upon them that I could read books which they could not even decipher, and that I understood things (beyond the school curriculum) which they had never so much as heard of. Of this they took their usual derisive, barbaric view, but, morally, it gave me the whip hand over them – and the more so since the circumstance led the tutors themselves to pay me some respect. Thus the sneers died away, but there still remained a feeling of hostility which caused cold, constrained relations to subsist between my schoolfellows and myself. Indeed, the situation was too irksome to be borne, and as the years passed on I developed a yearning for *real* comrades, *real* friends. But, try though I might to form some extraneous intimacies, the latter always seemed unnatural, and soon came to an end of their own volition. True, I had *one* school friend for a while, but at heart I was tyrant enough to try to exercise an excessive sway over him as, in an endeavour to inspire him with dislike for our environment, I demanded of him a final, an unconditional divorcement from everything. The result was that I only frightened him with my passionate friendship, and reduced him to tears and sullenness. By nature he was unspoilt and of a yielding disposition; yet no sooner had he surrendered to me his all than I disliked him as much as I did his companions, and drove him from me as though he had been congenial to me only so long as I could hector him and keep him in subjection. Yet it was not *all* my companions that I could bully in this way, for my friend was unlike the rest of the gang, and constituted a bright exception. On leaving school, my first act was to refuse the post to which I had been nominated; my object being to sever all ties with the past, and to bury it wholly in the dust. . . . And God only knows what, later, drew me towards the man Simonov of whom I have just spoken!

Early next morning I sprang out of bed in as agitated a state as though something important were soon about to happen. Somehow I had an idea that some radical change in my life was approaching, inevitably approaching. All my life it has been my way, on the least external occurrence, to feel that some fundamental break in my existence is at hand. However, I went to my office as usual, and slipped away home again two hours before the usual time, to prepare myself for the dinner. 'Above all things,' I thought to myself, 'I must not be the first arrival, or I shall be thought over-eager about the thing.' Important points like this seemed to multiply by thousands, and worried me until I almost fainted. Next with my own hands I cleaned my shoes, for Apollon would never have done them twice in the same day; he would have thought such a proceeding quite irregular. That done, I swept the hall clear of the litter which I had made, in order that he should not afterwards see the remains and despise me for what I had done. Then I looked through my wardrobe in detail, and found that it was old and worn and creased. Yes, I had grown very slovenly in my dress. True, my uniform* looked decent, but one cannot very well go out to dinner in a uniform. Worst of all, my trousers had a large yellow stain on one of their knees, and I felt that that stain alone would deprive me of nine-tenths of my dignity, well though I knew it was beneath me to feel like that. 'Come, come,' I thought to myself with a sinking of the spirits, 'enough of what I may or may not think. I have now to deal with *reality*.' Yet, though well aware that I was exaggerating everything to a perfectly monstrous degree, the thought of what lay before me shook my soul as with ague. Distractedly I pictured myself the cold, superior manner in which 'that rascal' Zvierkov would greet me; the dull, invincible contempt with which 'that blockhead' Trudoliubov would eye me; the rude, insulting giggles which 'that skunkish' Ferfitch-kin would vent at my expense (if by so doing he could curry favour with Zvierkov); the manner in which Simonov would size me up, and despise me for my wretched vanity and want of spirit; and, lastly, the degree to which the affair, from start to finish, would be sordid and shameful rather than 'refined.' Of course, it would be best for me not to go, but this was impossible, since no sooner do I take a thing into my head than it drags my head along with it. That is to say, it is always *after* the event that I reproach myself. 'But why,' was my reflection, 'should I be afraid of, play the coward before, reality?' Yet, passionately desirous though I was of showing all this riff-raff that I was not the coward whom I imagined myself to be, it was in a perfect storm of pusillanimous agitation that I fancied myself getting the better of the company – first snubbing them, then attracting them, then forcing them to like me for 'the elevation of my thoughts and my undoubted wit.' Zvierkov I should first of all displace from his perch, and then force to sit in shame and silence while I simply *crushed* him. Lastly, if you please, I should have pity upon him,

* In Russia even officials of the civil service wear uniform.

and drink his health, and address him in the second person singular.* None the less, the cruellest and most shameful thought of all was the knowledge – yes, the certain knowledge – that none of these things would *really* happen; that, as a matter of fact, I had no desire to crush, or to get the better of, or to attract my fellow guests, and that for such a result (were it even attainable) I should be the last man in the world to care. Oh, how I prayed God that the evening might pass as quickly as possible! Finally it was in inexpressible anguish that I went to the window, opened the sliding pane, and looked out into the dim swirl of wet, falling snow. . . .

At length my shabby wall clock whirred, and struck the hour of five. Instantly I seized my hat, and, trying not to catch Apollon's eye (ever since the morning he had been awaiting receipt of his wages, yet had been fool enough never to speak of them), I darted past him through the door, and, in a cab which I had ordered beforehand, drove in state (and in return for my last half-rouble) to the Hôtel de Paris.

➤ FOUR ◄

As LONG AGO AS THE PREVIOUS night I had known that I *should* be the first to arrive. Yet that did not greatly matter. What really mattered was that I had great difficulty in finding our room. Nor, as yet, was the table even laid! What could this mean? After many inquiries of the servants, I learnt that dinner had been ordered for six o'clock, not for five; and this the attendants in the buffet confirmed. It was bad enough even to have to ask them! As yet the clock showed twenty-five minutes to six. If the change of hour was in any way due to my fellow guests they ought to have let me know by post rather than have lowered me in my own eyes and in those of the servants. However, I sat down, and a waiter began to lay the table – greatly embarrassing me by his presence as he did so. Towards six o'clock candles were brought in, to aid the lamps, though the waiter evidently had not thought it worth while to bring them in when I first arrived. In a neighbouring room there were dining two sombre-looking customers who appeared, from their mien, to be out of temper and disin-

* In Russia, as in France, the second person singular denotes familiarity, intimacy, or condescension.

clined to talk; while in a room further on a considerable noise, and even some shouting, was in progress – the chattering of a whole party of people being audible, with stray little exclamations in French. Evidently the company included ladies. In short, I found the time of waiting excessively tedious – so much so that when (exactly at six o'clock) my fellow guests arrived *en masse*, I felt momentarily so delighted (as if they were my deliverers) that I almost forgot my rôle of an offended personage.

Zvierkov entered at the head of the band, as their manifest leader. At the moment he and his companions were laughing loudly, but when he became aware of my presence he straightened his face, came forward slowly, and with a sort of coquettish wriggling of the waist, gave me his hand with a faintly benevolent, yet faintly reserved, air in his manner, as though, even in the act, he desired to guard himself against something. On the other hand, I had expected him to break into his old thin, high-pitched laughter, and, at the first word, to lapse into his old way of cracking sorry jests and witticisms. Indeed, ever since the previous evening, I had been looking for this to happen. Consequently I was the more dumbfounded by his condescending and superior *bonhomie*. Could it be that he conceived himself immeasurably above my level in all the relations of life? If so, and if his design was only to insult me by his patronage, it did not greatly matter, since I could get even with him somehow; but what if, without actually intending to offend, he really cherished in his sheep's brain the idea that he was the better man of the two, and therefore in a position to treat me with condescension? The very supposition made me gasp!

'I have learnt with pleasure of your wish to join us,' he began, with a drawl and a lisp and an even greater mouthing of his words than in the old days. 'Somehow we never seem to meet one another now, for you keep so much to yourself. Yet you need not do so, for we are not nearly such queer creatures as you think. At all events I am very glad to renew your acquaintance now,' and he turned away with a slighting air to lay his hat upon the window-sill.

'Have you been waiting long?' Trudoliubov asked me.

'Yes,' I replied in a voice which presaged a coming explosion. 'I arrived exactly at five o'clock, as warned to do yesterday.'

'Then did no one let him know that the hour had been changed?' cried Trudoliubov, turning to Simonov.

'No; I forgot to do so,' answered the latter in an unrepentant tone, as, without a word of apology to myself, he departed to order dinner to be brought in.

'So you have been here an hour, my poor fellow!' cried Zvierkov with a laugh (naturally it would seem to him a laughing matter). In imitation of his patron, Ferfitchkin also burst into a shrill, mean chuckle like the barking of a small dog, for he too evidently thought my position an extremely ridiculous and absurd one.

'There is nothing to laugh at,' I exclaimed to Ferfitchkin, growing more and more exasperated. 'It was somebody else's fault, not mine. No one ever warned me. It was, it was – well, it was simply rude.'

'Not only rude, but something else,' remarked Trudoliubov, naïvely taking my part. 'You put things too mildly. It was simply an insult – though, of course, not an intentional one. How Simonov could have done it I — Ahem!'

'If *I* had been played such a trick,' said Ferfitchkin, 'I should have — '

'Yes, you would have ordered up something to go on with, or simply told them to lay dinner,' concluded Zvierkov for him.

'Certainly I *could* have so acted without any one's permission,' I rapped out. 'If I waited, it was only because — '

'Well, well; let us take our seats, gentlemen,' said Simonov, at that moment re-entering. 'Everything is ready, and I will answer for it that the champagne is well iced. You see,' he added to myself, 'I did not know your address, nor where to find you.' Again he avoided my eye, for he evidently bore me a grudge of some sort. After my experiences of last night I was determined to find out what it was.

Every one – myself included – seated himself at the table, which was a circular one. On my left I had Trudoliubov, and, on my right, Simonov; while Zvierkov confronted me, with, between him and Trudoliubov, Ferfitchkin.

'Tell me, are you in a government department?' Zvierkov said to me. Clearly, seeing that I was ill at ease, he had decided to interest himself in my affairs, and really thought that he ought to be kind to me – to, in a way, 'hearten' me.

'Does he want me to throw a bottle at his head?' thought I to myself. Somehow, the strangeness of the situation had made me unnaturally prone to take offence. But aloud I said drily, with my eyes on my plate –

'I am in the Ministry of — .'

'And do you like it? Also, tell me – what led you to resign your former post?'

'What led me to resign my former post?' I re-echoed, involuntarily assuming a drawl thrice as pronounced as Zvierkov's own. 'I resigned it simply because I wanted to.'

Ferfitchkin giggled, and Simonov looked at me with an ironical air. As for Trudoliubov, his fork remained poised in the air, so petrified was he with astonishment.

Zvierkov winced, yet he did not mean to show it.

'And what is your present income?' he continued.

'My present income?'

'Well, your *salary*?'

'Am I, then, to be put through a regular examination?' I retorted. However, I told him the amount of my salary, and grew very red in the face while doing so.

'Not much indeed!' he observed pompously.

'No, one couldn't afford good restaurants every night on *that*,' added Ferfitchkin mischievously.

'In my opinion it is sheer poverty,' was Trudoliubov's comment.

'And how thin you have grown! You have changed a good deal since I last saw you,' continued Zvierkov, with a glance of impertinent commiseration at my person and clothes.

'Come,' said Ferfitchkin, with a snigger, 'we have put our good friend sufficiently out of countenance.'

'Sir,' I retorted, 'it is not in your power to put me out of countenance. Do you hear? I am dining in this restaurant at my own expense, at my own expense, and not at that of some one else, Monsieur Ferfitchkin.'

'What?' cried Ferfitchkin, turning as red as a boiled lobster, and looking at me with fury. '*Which* of us is dining at the expense of some one else?'

'Never mind,' I replied, feeling that I was in for it. 'We should do well to talk on some more intellectual topic.'

'Yes; to give you an opportunity of airing your wonderful gifts, eh?'

'No, not at all. That would be out of place here.'

'More so than in your *leper*-tment?'*

'Enough, gentlemen, enough!' cried Zvierkov imperiously.

'What folly this is!' murmured Simonov.

'Yes – and utter stupidity!' assented Trudoliubov. 'We have met here to spend a few friendly hours together, and to wish our friend *bon voyage*; yet *you*' – this was addressed to me exclusively 'must start quarrelling! Since you invited yourself to the dinner, pray do not disturb the general harmony at it.'

'That will do, that will do,' said Zvierkov again. 'Let us drop the subject, gentlemen. Allow me to tell you how, three days ago, I came very near to getting married.' And he embarked upon a story which bore no relation at all to marriage, but only to the amorous exploits of some old generals, colonels, and court chamberlains, with the narrator himself as the leading spirit. A general chorus of laughter followed, and Ferfitchkin fairly shrieked. No one noticed me any longer, and I sat crushed and humiliated.

---

* A play upon the Russian word *departament*.

'My God! Look at the company that I am keeping!' thought I to myself. 'Yet what a fool I must look to them all! And I used to forgive Ferfitchkin so many things! Do these blockheads really imagine that they are doing me an honour by giving me a place at their table? Cannot they understand that it is *I* who am doing *them* an honour? I have grown thin, have I? I wear shabby clothes? Oh, the cursed clowns! Long ago Zvierkov must have noticed the yellow stain on my knee. What then? I have a great mind to rise – yes, this very minute – from the table, and to take my hat, and simply go without another word. Yes, go out of sheer contempt. To-morrow, perhaps, there will be a duel? Oh, the blackguards! But I do not think that they would miss my seven roubles very much. Perhaps they intend to — Oh, the devil take them all! I don't care a hang for the seven roubles. I'll go this very instant.'

However, I stayed, and kept drinking glass after glass, both of claret and sherry. Lack of usedness to wine soon began to turn my head, and my anger increased with my fuddlement. Suddenly I felt as though I should like to insult everyone in the rudest possible fashion, and then go. I had an idea that I should like to seize a favourable moment to show myself in my true colours. 'Let them say what they like!' I thought to myself. 'Even if I *am* ridiculous, I have some brains in my head, and – and – in short, they can go to the devil!'

From time to time I glared at the company, but every one seemed to have forgotten my existence, and to be merged in a din of shouting and merriment. Zvierkov was holding forth, and I set myself to listen. His story related to a fine lady whom he had induced to confess to a passion for himself (of course the fellow was lying throughout), as well as to an intimate friend of his – a certain Prince Kolia, of the Hussars, the alleged owner of three thousand souls* – who had rendered him valuable assistance in the affair.

I broke into the conversation. 'This Prince Kolia,' I said, 'this owner of three thousand souls, how comes it about that *he* is not here to entertain you to-night?'

For a moment or two no one spoke; but presently Trudoliubov threw a contemptuous nod in my direction, and even went so far as to remark that for some time past I had been drunk. Zvierkov, for his part, sat gazing at me like a cow, until I was forced to lower my eyes, while Simonov seized the opportunity to pour out fresh bumpers of champagne. As soon as he had done so, Trudoliubov raized his glass, and every one except myself did the same.

'Your very good health, and a pleasant journey to you!' he cried to

---

* *i.e.* three thousand serfs.

Zvierkov. 'Let us drink to the years which are gone, and to the years which are coming! Hurrah!'

The whole company honoured the toast, and then rushed to embrace Zvierkov. I alone did not stir, and my glass remained untouched upon the table before me.

'And are not *you* going to drink it?' rapped out Trudoliubov impatiently, as he turned to me with a threatening air.

'Yes, but first of all I wish to make a speech of my own, Monsieur Trudoliubov. When I have done *that* I will drink the toast.'

'Oh, the abominable cad!' muttered Simonov.

I straightened myself with the aid of the table, and feverishly clutched at my glass. I felt as though I were preparing to say something very important, yet had not a notion what it was going to be.

'Silence!' cried Ferfitchkin. 'We are about to hear something worth hearing!'

Zvierkov sat waiting gravely. He had an inkling of what was coming.

'Monsieur le Lieutenant Zvierkov,' I began, 'please to know that I detest phrases, phrasers, and fools with waists. That is my first point. Follows my second.'

There was a general stir of astonishment.

'My second point is that I detest blackguards and blackguardism, but more especially the former. My third point is that I love truth and frankness, and honesty.' I was speaking almost mechanically, and beginning to shiver with apprehension at my own words. 'Yes, and I love high thinking, Monsieur Zvierkov, and I love genuine good-fellowship and equality and — No. Ahem! — I love – I love – However, Monsieur Zvierkov, I drink to your good health. May you conquer the whole Caucasus, and slay your country's enemies, and – and – here is your very good health, Monsieur Zvierkov.'

He rose, bowed, and said, 'Thank you.' Plainly he was very much put about, for he had turned quite pale.

'The devil take it!' exclaimed Trudoliubov, striking his fist upon the table.

'That sort of thing ought to have been answered with a blow on the mouth,' squeaked Ferfitchkin.

'Let us throw him out,' muttered Simonov.

'Not a word, gentlemen! Do not lose your tempers!' cried Zvierkov, endeavouring to appease the general indignation. 'I thank you, but *I* shall know what value to set upon his words.'

'Monsieur Ferfitchkin,' I shouted at the top of my voice, 'to-morrow you shall make good to me what you have just said.'

'A duel?' he replied. 'Then I accept.' Yet so absurd did I look as I

challenged him, and so ill did it consort with my figure, that every one –
Ferfitchkin included – burst our laughing.

'Oh, leave him alone,' said Trudoliubov disgustedly. 'He is drunk.'

'I shall never forgive myself for having included him in the party,'
added Simonov.

'Now is the time for me to throw bottles at them,' thought I to myself.
I seized up one, and – calmly poured myself out another glassful.

'I had better stay on to the end,' I reflected. 'I dare say you fellows
would be thankful to see me go, but I don't intend to do so. I intend,
rather, to sit on here and drink, as a sign that I think you of no importance
whatever. I intend to sit on here and drink because the place is a tavern,
and I have duly paid my entrance money. I intend to sit on here and
drink because I look upon you all as so many unsubstantial dummies. I
intend to sit on here and drink because – yes, and to sing too if I want to,
and because I have the right to sing, and because – ahem!'

As a matter of fact, I did *not* sing that night, but exerted all my faculties
to avoid meeting my companions' eyes, the while I struck attitudes
expressive of independence, and impatiently waited for some one to be
the first to address me. But, alas! no one was so. How I wished, how I
wished that at that moment I could have made my peace with my companions! The clock struck eight, and then nine. Presently the revellers
moved from the table to a divan, where Zvierkov stretched his full length,
and rested one foot upon a what-not. Also, more wine was handed round
– he producing three bottles of his own, but omitting to include me in the
invitation. Round him sat his admirers, who seemed to listen to him with
such absolute veneration that it was clear they really liked him. 'But why,
but why?' thought I to myself. From time to time, in their drunken rapture, they actually embraced him as they talked of the Caucasus, of the
nature of true passion, of lucrative service posts, of the astounding
income of the hussar officer Podcharzhevski (whom none of them personally knew), of the marvellous beauty and grace of the Princess D – (whom
none of them had even seen), and of the immortality of Shakespeare.

I smiled contemptuously, and, placing myself in front of the divan,
started to pace the length of the room – from the table to the stove, and
back again. My one desire was to show my companions that I could get
on without them; wherefore I purposely clicked my heels together, and
stamped a good deal with my soles. Yet it was all to no purpose, for the
party paid me no attention whatever. Thus, from eight o'clock to eleven,
I tramped to and fro before the company, always keeping to the same
beat (namely, from the table to the stove, and back again). 'Here I walk,'
was what my attitude expressed, 'and no one can prevent me from doing
so.' Several times, when he entered the room, the waiter stopped to stare

at me, while the frequent turning and turning made me giddy, and every moment I thought that I should have a fit, seeing that three times, during those three hours, I burst into a sweat, and then grew dry again. Also, every now and then there pierced my heart, with deep and venomous pain, the thought that ten, twelve, or, maybe, forty, years might pass, yet I should still remember, with horror and humiliation, the most ridiculous, the most degraded, the most disgusting evening of my life. More unconscionable, more gratuitous, my degradation could not have been, and I fully understood that as I paced up and down between the table and the stove. 'Oh, if you only knew what thoughts and feelings I am capable of, and what a man of refinement you have in me!' was my incessant reflection as I purposely turned towards the divan where my enemies were seated. But my enemies comported themselves as though I were not so much as present. Once, and only once, did they pay me the slightest attention – namely, when Zvierkov was speaking of Shakespeare, and I gave a contemptuous laugh. So scurrilous, so mean was my snigger that, as with one consent, they stopped speaking, and for two or three minutes gazed at me gravely, and in silence the while I continued pacing the room, and making as though I had not noticed them. Yet nothing came of it. None of them spoke, and the next moment I was again forgotten. At length eleven o'clock struck.

'Gentlemen,' cried Zvierkov as he rose from the divan, 'let us now go to the place of which you know.'

'Of course, of course!' came the general exclamation.

Upon this I moved sharply towards Zvierkov. I felt so tortured and shattered in mind that I could almost have cut my throat, and put an end to things then and there. A sort of fever had got hold of me, and my sweat-soaked hair was clinging to my forehead and temples.

'Zvierkov,' I said harshly, but firmly. 'I beg your pardon. Ferfitchkin. I beg yours also, as I do that of every one present; for I have done a wrong to each one of you.'

'Aha!' So a duel is not in your line, after all?' hissed Ferfitchkin venomously.

This cut me to the heart.

'Do not think that I fear a duel, Ferfitchkin,' I retorted. 'I shall be ready to fight you to-morrow, but only after a reconciliation. Upon the latter I insist, and it is not for you to refuse it me. Yet, to show that there is no duel of which I am afraid, I propose that you shall fire first, and that I shall fire in the air.'

'He is only playing the fool,' remarked Simonov.

'Or clean gone out of his mind,' added Trudoliubov.

'Please let me pass,' said Zvierkov contemptuously. 'Why do you block my way like this? What is it you want?'

Every one was red in the face, with glittering eyes, for much wine had been drunk.

'I only seek your friendship, Zvierkov,' I replied. 'I have offended you, but — '

'Offended *me? You* offended *me?* Please to understand, my good sir, that never, and under no circumstances whatsoever, could you offend *me.*'

'Besides, we have had enough of you,' growled Trudoliubov. 'Come on, you fellows. Let us be off.'

'Olympia for me, gentlemen!' cried Zvierkov. 'That was a bargain.'

'Yes; we don't dispute it,' came the laughing response.

I remained alone in my shame as the party left the room. Trudoliubov drawled out some idiotic song or another as they went. Only Simonov lingered a moment to tip the waiters. Suddenly I approached him.

'Simonov,' I said in a tone of absolute despair, 'please to lend me six roubles.'

Extreme astonishment dawned in his stupid eyes (for he too was drunk).

'Do you also wish to go *there* with us?' he inquired.

'Yes.'

'Then I have no money to lend you,' he retorted with a contemptuous smile as he moved towards the door.

I seized him by the greatcoat, for a sort of nightmare was upon me.

'Simonov,' I remonstrated, 'I have just seen that you *have* some money. Why do you refuse me? Am I such a rascal? Besides, mind how you refuse me, for you cannot know the real reason why I make the request. Everything depends upon this – my future, my plans, my — '

Taking some money from his pocket, he almost threw it at me.

'Here you are, then!' he said in a hard voice, 'if you care to be such a cur.' Then he left the room at a run, to rejoin his companions.

For a moment or two I remained where I was – alone with the litter, the leavings, the dregs of liqueur, the spilt wine, the odds and ends of cigarettes; alone with the fumes and the fever in my head, and the aching depression in my heart; alone with the waiter, who, having seen and heard all, was now staring at me with intense curiosity.

'Yes; *I* will go there too!' I cried. 'Either they shall kneel to me, and clasp me by the feet, and beseech my friendship, or – or I will hit Zvierkov full in the face!'

⟫ FIVE ⟪

'So, at length, *this* is contact with reality!' I muttered as I tore down the staircase. 'Surely to learn *this* it was not necessary that the Pope should leave Rome and go to Brazil, or that a ball should be given on Lake Como?'

'You cur!' I went on, in objurgation of Zvierkov. 'What if you should get the laugh of me even now?'

'No matter if he does,' I cried the next moment, in answer to myself. 'By now you have lost everything.'

The scent of my quarry had now had time to grow cool, yet I knew where to find the man for whom I was seeking.

At the door of the hotel there was lounging a solitary night cabman, with his greatcoat dusted over with the moist – almost warm – snow which was still falling and making everything look dim and oppressive; while his shaggy little piebald pony also had a powdering of snow upon its back, and from time to time, I remember, kept coughing. Leaping into the rough bark sledge, I was in the act of bending my legs to sit down when the recollection of Simonov's recent loan of six roubles threw me into such a state of mind that I rolled backwards on to the seat like a sack.

'Yes, it will take a great deal to set all this right,' I exclaimed as I did so. 'Yet I *will* set things right, or perish in the attempt. Forward!'

Off we started – I with a veritable whirlwind circling in my brain.

'Yet is is unlikely that they will go upon their knees to win *my* friendship,' I reflected. 'It is all a mirage – a horrible, disgusting, romantic, fantastic mirage, like the ball on Lake Como. Consequently I shall have no choice but to strike Zvierkov in the face. I shall simply *have* to. *That* at least is decided upon. Get on with you, cabman!'

The cabman gave his reins a jerk.

'I shall deal Zvierkov the blow as soon as ever I enter the room. But ought I first to say a few words, by way of preface? No, I shall just enter and hit him. They will all be in the salon together, with Zvierkov seated by Olympia's side, on the divan. That cursed Olympia! Once she refused me, and laughed in my face. I will pull out her hair by the roots, and Zvierkov's ears as well! Or, rather, I will take him by one of those ears, and drag him about the room! Perhaps his companions will hurl themselves upon me, and beat me. At the very least they will throw me out of doors. What then? At all events I shall have dealt him the blow; I shall have taken the initiative, and branded him, and placed it beyond his power to efface my blow with one of his own – only with a duel. Yes, he will simply *have* to fight me. But suppose they should beat me first? Well, let them, the brutes! Trudoliubov would do the most in that way, for he is very strong, whereas Ferfitchkin would probably steal up from behind, and hang on to my hair. However, be it so, be it so! I am going there for that very purpose. Yes, at last their sheep's brains shall be forced to taste the tragic note in this. And when they are dragging me to the door I shall cry to them that the whole gang is not worth my little finger. . . . Drive on, drive on!' I shouted to the cabman, who started, and then flourished his whip, for my shout had been a wild one.

'Yes, at dawn we shall fight,' I went on. 'That is decided. Likewise, my work in the office is ended. I remember Ferfitchkin making a joke about a department and a *leper*-tment. . . . But where am I to get pistols? Pshaw! I shall draw an advance of salary and purchase some. And powder and ball? Oh, *they* are the business of the seconds. But how is everything to be arranged by dawn to-morrow? And where am I to get seconds? I have not so much as a friend in the world. Pshaw! Why, the first person whom I meet in the street will be glad to act as my second, just as he would do if he were asked to come and save a drowning man. Extraordinary circumstances must be specially allowed for. Even if I were to ask the head of my department to second me to-morrow, he would consent out of very chivalry, and keep my secret as well. Anton Antonitch is – '

At that moment I suddenly realized, with absolute and increasing clearness, the idiotic folly of my plans. Yes, I saw the reverse side of the medal. But – !

'Drive on, cabman! Drive on, you brute! Drive on, I tell you!'

'Aye, aye, sir!' responded the son of the soil.

Next, a cold fit seized me.

'Would it not be better,' I thought, 'would it not be better if I were to go straight home now? Oh, my God! Why on earth did I ever invite myself to that dinner? It is impossible for me to go home after that three hours' walk between the table and the stove. They – yes, they and no one else – must reckon with me for that walk. They alone can purge me of my dishonour. Drive on, cabman!

'But what if they should give me into custody? No, they would never dare to do such a thing, for they would be afraid of the scandal. Again, what if Zvierkov should contemptuously refuse to fight a duel? It is quite probable that he would do so. Well, in that case I should show him that – But no; I should wait for him at his door to-morrow, and, just when he was coming out, and about to get into the cab, I should seize him, and tear the greatcoat off his back, and fasten my teeth into his hand, and bite him. "See, every one!" I should cry. "See to what lengths a desperate man may be driven!" Yes, even though he were striking me over the head, and the rest of the gang were clinging to me from behind, I should still continue to cry to the public: "Look! Here is a young man going out to conquer the Caucasus! Look at the mark of my spittle on his face!"'

After this (so it seemed to me) all would be over, and my Department would, as it were, disappear from the face of the earth. I should be arrested, tried, dismissed the service, thrown into gaol, and, finally, sent to a penal settlement in Siberia. No matter! Five years later, when released from prison, I should set out – poor, and clad only in a shirt – to look for Zvierkov. Probably I should find him in some provincial capital – a married man, happy, and with a young daughter just beginning to grow up; and I should say to him: 'Look, villain, upon my hollow cheeks and ragged clothes! Everything have I now lost – my career, my happiness, my art, my learning, the woman whom I love, and all because of you! Here are pistols. I had come hither to fight a duel with you, but – but now I pardon you.' Then I should fire in the air, and be seen and heard of no more.

I could almost have wept at the pathos of my own imaginings. Yet all the while I knew that every one of them came out of *Sylvia*, or Lermontov's *Masquerade*, or some such piece. Suddenly I began to feel ashamed of myself – so ashamed that I stopped the cab, got out of it, and stood in the snow, in the middle of the street, with the driver looking on in openmouthed amazement.

'What am I to do?' was my reflection. 'It is clear that to go on is folly, while to stop at the present stage is impossible, now that I have got so far. Good Lord! I only wish that I could put an end to the matter! Yet how am I to do that after all the insults I have received?'

'No!' finally I shouted, as I sprang into the cab again. 'It is foreordained! It is fate! Drive on, cabman!' – and, beside myself, I struck him a blow on the back of his neck.

'What are you hitting *me* for?' cried the little peasant; but nevertheless the blow had the effect of causing him to whip his steed until it began to kick. Wet snow was still falling in large flakes, but I took no heed of the elements as I sat there with my coat unbuttoned. Everything was now forgotten save that I had finally decided upon dealing the blow. With horror, too, I realized that, come what might, the blow must be dealt, and that no power on earth could save me. In the streets the solitary lamps glimmered dimly through the mist, like torches at a funeral, while snow was drifting under my greatcoat, jacket and scarf, and melting there. Yet I scorned to wrap myself up, for I felt that all was lost.

At length we arrived at our destination. Leaping from the cab, I ascended the steps at a single stride, and banged with feet and fists upon the door. It opened as quickly as though I had been expected. As a matter of fact, Simonov had warned the people of the house that another member of the party might soon be following, and in houses of that kind it is best always to give warnings, and to take precautions. The house was one of those *magasins de modes* which used to be so numerous, but have now been closed by the police. During the daytime it was a dressmaker's establishment, but at night only those who had the *entrée* could resort thither for entertainment.

Passing rapidly through the show-room (which was unlighted), I reached a *salon* to which I was not altogether a stranger, and where a solitary wax candle was burning.

'Where are they?' I found myself asking of some one; but it turned out that they had that moment departed.

Presently I perceived that the proprietress herself – a woman with a foolish, smiling face, whom I knew a little – was standing before me. Then a door opened, and another person entered. Without paying any attention to either of them, I started pacing the room, and muttering to myself as I did so. I felt as though I had been saved from death. Certainly and beyond all doubt I should have dealt the intended blow, but my antagonist, by leaving the place, had altered the whole situation. I kept throwing vague glances around the room, for I could not properly rally my thoughts. Then, in mechanical sort of fashion, I looked at the woman who had just entered, and saw before me a pale, fresh young face which, though a trifle sallow, had straight black eyebrows and a serious, an astonished sort of an expression. It was a face which pleased me at once, for I should have detested it if it had been a smiling one. As I looked at her with increased attention I could discern in that serious countenance – a countenance that was grave almost to the point of singularity – a species of good-humoured *naïveté*. Assuredly she was not the sort of woman to attract those sots, and probably had passed unnoticed by them. True, she could not be called exactly pretty, but her figure was tall, strong, and well-made, and she was dressed in quite simple fashion.

Then an evil impulse stirred within me, and I approached her. At that moment I caught sight of myself in a mirror, and could see that my face was pale and agitated, my expression sullen, repellent, and vicious, and my hair dishevelled.

'So much the better!' I thought. 'I would rather seem to her disgusting than attractive. It is just what I want.'

⇶ SIX ⇷

SOMEWHERE BEHIND THE PARTITION-WALL, and with a strangled sound as though it were being violently squeezed, a clock emitted a prolonged whirring. Then, after continuing to do so for an almost unnaturally long time, it gave forth a thin, a mean, and, as it were, an unexpected stroke with its gong, as though some one had suddenly sprung at and hit it. The gong struck twice. Hitherto I had been dozing rather than sleeping – lying in a sort of half-comatose condition.

The room – a low, narrow, confined apartment in which there was a huge wardrobe, and which was littered over with cards, rags, and every sort of odds and ends of clothing – was almost dark, since a candle which had been burning on a table at the further end of the apartment had gone out, save for an occasional flicker. In a few moments the darkness would be complete.

Soon I recovered my faculties. At once, without the least effort, everything came back to my memory, as though it had been watching its opportunity to revive. Yet all through my slumber I had seemed to be conscious of some point which had never quite sunk into oblivion, and around which all the fantasies of my sleep had laboured in anguish. Another curious circumstance was that all the events of the previous day now seemed, at the moment of my awaking, to have happened a long while ago, and as though I had lived through them at some far distant period.

My head was filled with fumes, for something seemed to have come over me – to be catching at, exciting, disturbing me, until my old bilious depression began again to seethe within my breast and to search vainly for an outlet. Suddenly, by my side, I perceived a pair of widely-opened eyes regarding me with intent curiosity. Their gaze was so cold, so detached, so sullen, that they seemed hardly to belong to a human being. Indeed, I found their inspection irksome to bear.

But presently a morose idea sprang to birth in my brain, and diffused itself over my body with a sort of unclean sensation which resembled what one experiences when for the first time one penetrates to the musty, fusty underworld. Somehow, too, I thought it unnatural that those eyes should have chosen such a moment to scrutinize me. Also, I remembered

661

that never once throughout the two hours since I had entered the room had I spoken to this creature beside me so much as a word. I had not thought it necessary to do so. Indeed, it had been a sort of pleasure to me to preserve the silence unbroken. Now, however, there suddenly rose to my mind an image as uncouth and repellent as a spider – an image of the debased passion which, destitute of love, begins, grossly and shamelessly, where true love ought to receive its final crown. For a long time we lay thus – looking intently at one another. Yet at last, since she neither lowered her eyes nor once changed her expression, I could stand it no longer.

'What is your name?' I asked brusquely, and the sooner to put an end to the situation.

'Lisa,' she replied in a half-whisper, and with a sort of reluctance. Then she turned her eyes away.

I remained silent for a moment.

'It is bad weather – snowy and horrible,' I went on, though more to myself than to her, as I clasped my hands indolently behind my head, and lay staring up at the ceiling.

She said nothing. The whole thing was becoming unpleasant.

'Do you belong to St. Petersburg?' I continued, almost angrily, with a slight turn of my head in her direction.

'No.'

'To where, then?'

'To Riga,' she replied, with a very bad grace.

'You are a German, then?'

'No; a Russian.'

'And have you been here long?'

'Where?'

'In this house?'

'Two weeks.'

Her replies grew shorter and shorter. Soon the candle finally expired, and I could no longer see her face.

'Have you a father and a mother?'

'Yes – no – yes.'

'Where are they?'

'There – in Riga.'

'*Who* are they?'

'Somebody.'

'How "somebody"? What sort of people are they? What is their profession?'

'They are *miestchané*.'*

* Persons of the commercial class.

'And have you always lived with them?'

'Yes.'

'How old are you?'

'Twenty.'

'Why did you leave your parents?'

'Because – ' Her 'because' evidently signified: 'Leave me alone, for I am tired.' A silence ensued.

God knows why I did not seize the opportunity to get up and go, for I was growing more and more disgusted and depressed. In spite of my efforts to banish them, pictures of the happenings of the previous day would keep wandering through my brain. Suddenly I recalled an incident which I had witnessed in the street when leaving the office early in the afternoon.

'Yesterday,' I said loudly, and as though I had not wished to begin the conversation again, 'I saw some men carrying a coffin. They very nearly let it fall.'

'A coffin?'

'Yes; in Sennaia Street. It had just been brought out of a cellar.'

'Out of a cellar?'

'Well, out of a basement – you know the sort of place – the basement of a brothel. There was mud everywhere and filth. The place simply stank. It was horrible.'

Another pause ensued.

'Bad weather for a funeral,' I went on, in order at any cost to break the silence.

'That would make no difference,' she remarked after a further pause.

'Oh, but it would,' I replied, with a yawn.

'How so?' she inquired – again after a pause.

'Because it *would*. In the first place, it would wet the gravediggers' jackets and make them swear, and, in the second place, it would fill the grave with water.'

'Why with water?' she asked, with a touch of curiosity, and in a sharper, rougher tone than she had hitherto employed. For some reason or another this irritated me.

'Because at any depth below six *vershoks* there is *always* water. In Volkhovo cemetery it is impossible to dig a grave dry.'

'Why so?'

'Why so? Because it is a damp spot – marshy all over. They just tip the dead into the water. I have seen it done myself – yes, several times.'

(As a matter of fact, I had never once seen it done, for I had never been in Volkhovo at all – I was relying upon mere hearsay.)

'Does not that make you afraid to die?' I went on.

'*Why* should I be going to die?' she exclaimed, as though defending herself against some imputation.

'Well, you will have to die *some* day, and precisely as that woman of Sennaia Street died. She, like yourself, was a young girl once, but now she lies dead of consumption.'

'A woman should go and die in a hospital.'

('Evidently she knows all about it,' I thought to myself; 'for she said, "a woman," not "a young girl." ')

'When that woman died she was deeply in debt to her mistress,'* I resumed aloud (for I was growing more and more cantankerous). 'Yet up to the very end she was forced to serve her old woman, despite the consumption. I heard some cabmen – probably they were old friends of hers – telling some soldiers about it. Lord, how they laughed! They were just about to repair to a neighbouring tavern to celebrate the funeral.' By this time I was inventing right and left.

There fell a silence – a profound silence. Not a sound came from the woman.

'Then it is better to go and die in a hospital?' at length I asked.

'It is much the same thing, is it not?' she asked irritably. Then she added: 'But *why* should I be going to die?'

'Not now; but, later on, will you not have to?'

'Perhaps – later on.'

'But look here. As yet you are young and fresh and comely; consequently you can still name your price; but remember that after another year of this life your good looks will have faded.'

'After *one* year only?'

'Well, after a year your value will at least have lessened.' Somehow I felt inclined to be captious. 'When that has come about you will be forced to leave this house, and to enter an inferior one, and then a third, and then a fourth, and so on, always descending lower and lower and lower, until, after some seven years of it, you will find yourself landed in a Sennaia Street cellar. That will be glorious, will it not? On the other hand, it is probable that some day you will catch a disease – pneumonia, or a chill, or something of the sort; and the kind of life that you are leading makes such an illness progress very rapidly. It will cling fast to you and refuse to be shaken off until you die.'

'Ah, well – then I must die, that is all.' She spoke as though she were exasperated, and at the same time made a quick movement of impatience.

'But do you not at all regret it?'

'Regret what?'

* The proprietress of the brothel of which the woman was an inmate.

'Your life?'

There came no answer.

'Have you ever had a sweetheart?' I resumed.

'What is that to you?'

'Oh, I do not wish to press you. Quite so; what is it to me? But why should you be so angry about it? However, probably you have your troubles like every one else, and they are no business of mine. Only, I am sorry for — '

'Sorry for what?'

'For you.'

'You need not be,' was her almost inaudible rejoinder, as again she made a movement of impatience.

This angered me the more. What? I had spoken to her kindly, and she —!

'Do you ever think?' I persisted. 'Do you suppose, for instance, that you are treading the right road?'

'No, I *never* think.'

'Ah, well, that is just where the evil lies. Open your eyes while there is yet time. There *is* yet time. As yet you are young and good-looking, and might fall in love, and marry, and – '

'But not all married people are happy, are they?' she interrupted in her old rough, rapid way.

'No, not all; but at least their life is better than yours. Indeed, in comparison with your life there could not be a better one. And if one loves, one can live even without happiness; and should sorrow come, such life is still good – it is still good to be alive and to live. But *here*, what is there but foulness? Pah!'

I turned away in disgust, for I could not reason with her coldly. Besides, I was beginning to feel the force of what I was saying, and to grow warm over it. Also, I was thirsting to expound certain ideas which I had long ago conceived in my solitary den. Something in me had suddenly caught fire; there had suddenly dawned before my vision a definite aim.

'Never mind the fact that I too am here,' I said, 'for I cannot be taken as an example, even though I may be worse than you. As a matter of fact, when I came to this house to-night I was drunk' (it will be seen that I was in a very great hurry to justify myself), 'and in that respect a man is no example for a woman. You and I are different persons, for, however much I may bedaub and befoul myself, I am no slave. I come, I go, and it is as though I had not come. I can shake it off, and become, as it were, a new man. But you – you have been a slave from the beginning. Yes, a slave. For have you not surrendered your all, and even your freewill? Consequently, later on, when you may wish to break your chain, you will never be able to do so. It will fasten itself closer and closer upon you. And a right cursed chain it is, too! I know its nature only too well. But since, I suppose, you will not be able to understand me if I put it in any other way, I will ask you – Are you not in debt to your landlady? Ah! *Now* you see how it is, *now* you see your chain. Nor will you ever escape from it, for that is how it is done. The fact that your soul must go to the devil matters nothing to your employer. I, on the other hand, am an unfortunate who plunge into the mire simply out of despondency. Some men drink out of despondency, but I – well, I come *here*. Yet what good does it do? Here have we been lying together without a single friendly word to say to one another all the time. You have merely looked at me like a wild beast, and I at you. Is it *thus* that one should love? Is it *thus* that a man should mate with a woman? No, it is foulness, foulness, from start to finish.'

'*Yes!*' came a hasty confirmation of all that I had said. Indeed, I was astounded at the precipitancy with which she accorded her assent. Surely it meant that similar ideas had been wandering in *her* brain also while she had been looking at me? Surely, then, she was capable at least of *some* thought?

'Devil take it all, but this is curious, for it comes so pat,' I thought to myself, as I almost rubbed my hands with joy. 'Why should I not probe a little further into this youthful soul?' By this time I was getting more and more excited with the game.

She turned towards me, and (so far as I could judge in the darkness) raised herself upon her elbow. How I regretted that at that moment I could not watch her eyes! Yet I could hear her deep breathing.

'Why did you ever come to this house?' I resumed, with something of an authoritative air.

'For a certain reason.'

'Would it not have been much better for you to have gone on living with your father? There you would have been at least safe and well. There you would have been, as it were, in the nest.'

'But what if things were *worse* there than here?'

'It still remains for me to find the right note,' thought I in passing; 'for evidently she does not appreciate sentimentality.'

Yet this was only a momentary thought. I swear that she really interested me. Also, I was feeling weak and unstrung, and knavery goes all too easily with such a mood.

'Who can say?' I hastened to answer aloud. 'Such things often happen. Indeed, I feel sure that some one has ill-treated you, and that you have been sinned against rather than sinning. Of your history I know nothing, yet, I *do* know that a girl of your type does not lightly enter a place like this.'

'What sort of a girl am I, then?' she whispered almost inaudibly: yet I heard it.

'The devil take it all!' I reflected. 'Here have I been actually flattering her! This is horrible. Yet it is possible that good may come of it.'

'Look here, Lisa,' I went on; 'let me speak of myself a little. Had I, since childhood, had parents to live with, I should never have become what I am to-day. This often occurs to my mind, for, however miserable life at home may be, there one has at least one's father and mother, not enemies or strangers. Yes, and even though those parents show one love but once a year, still one knows that one is at home. On the other hand, I had to grow up an orphan: whence it has come about that I am what you see me now – a man of no feeling.'

Again I stopped and waited. 'Perhaps she does not understand me!' I thought. 'Perhaps all this moralizing seems to her ridiculous!'

'If I were a father,' I continued, 'and had a daughter, I should love her even more than I did my sons.' I confess to blushing as I said this.

'And why?' she inquired (she *had* heard, after all!).

'Because – well, I hardly know, Lisa. I know a father – a stern, grave man – who adores his daughter, and often kisses her hands and feet, and never grows tired of looking at her. For a whole evening he will sit and follow her with his eyes as she dances. In short, he is absolutely mad about her, and I can understand his being so. When night time comes she may be weary, and goes to rest. Then the father rises, and folds her in his arms as she lies asleep, and makes the sign of the cross over her. He wears but a threadbare coat, for he is a miser; yet for her no gift is too costly – for her he will spend his last coin, and feel happy if, in return for the gift, he receive but a smile. A father is always fonder of a daughter than a mother is. Yes, young girls are indeed fortunate to be living at home with their parents. For myself, I think that I should never have allowed any daughter of mine to marry.'

'Why not?' she asked, with a faint laugh.

'Because, by heavens, I should have been jealous. What? She to kiss another man – to love a stranger more than she did her own father? It hurts me even to think of it! Certainly, many follies are committed, and all men come to their senses at last; but I believe that to the very day of my death I should have hated giving my daughter away. On the other hand, I would have put every suitor in the world through his paces to ensure that she should fall to the man she loved. Unfortunately, the man whom the daughter loves is generally the man who cuts the worst figure in the father's eyes. 'Tis always so, and causes much trouble in families.'

'Some parents prefer to *sell* their daughters rather than give them honestly away,' she broke in quickly.

'Ah, ha!' I thought. 'So *this* is how the wind lies!' Aloud I said, with some heat: 'Lisa, that happens only in families which are unfortunate enough to be destitute either of love or of God. Where there is no love there can be no wisdom. True, I know that such families exist, but it was not of them that I was speaking. To judge by your words, I think that you yourself cannot come of a very loving family – that you have been made to suffer. On the other hand, conduct of that kind sometimes arises from poverty.'

'Are things any better in gentle families? There are plenty of poor people who live honourably.'

'Yes – perhaps. But, Lisa, man loves to count his misfortunes, and to forget his blessings. If he were a little juster he would admit that every one has an equal share of both – that, so long as all goes well in a family, God distributes His benefits to each member alike. The father will be jovial, affectionate, and faithful – a man who makes every one around him happy. Even in times of trouble everything, through him, will come to seem cheerful. For where, in marriage, does one not find trouble? If ever you should marry, you too will know trouble. But how happy is the honeymoon of a girl who has wedded the man she loves! Everywhere and always she will be happy. Even the most trivial disputes will be hushed during those few blessed weeks. At the same time, there are women who, the more they love, the more they desire to quarrel. I assure you that it is so. Once I knew a woman of that type. "I love you," they say, "and it is *because* I love you that I wish to torment you. Do you not see how it is?" I wonder if you know what torture a man may be put to on this plea? Yes, there *are* such women. They think to themselves: "How I mean to love him afterwards! I will caress him for ever if only I may tease him a little now." Yet even *they* tend to happiness in the home – to the making of everything cheerful and comfortable and peaceable and in order. Then other women there are who are jealous. I myself used to know such a one. If her husband went out she could never rest quietly at home, but must go out (even in the middle of the night!) to see if he were not "*there*" – that is to say, in a certain house, or with a certain woman. Yet she knew better than any one else that it was all a mistake on her part. Yes, she suffered from it more than any one else could do. And that was her punishment. Yet such women love, and are all for love. How pleasant, too, are reconciliations after a quarrel! The wife of her own accord acknowledges her fault to her husband, and he and she pardon one another with equal delight. Both are so happy! 'Tis like a reproduction of their first meeting, a second nuptial, a rebirth of love. Nor has any one in the world a right to know what passes between husband and wife if they really love one another. However much they may quarrel, the wife's mother should never be called in to act as arbitrator. That she should so much as suspect the *existence* of a quarrel is wrong, for husband and wife are their own best judges. Love is a secret of two, and should live hidden from all eyes, whosoever they be. It is better so, it is more religious, and it tends to develop self-respect. Now, from self-respect there spring many things, and if love has come at the right time – if it is for love that a man and a woman have married each other – why should that love ever pass? Cannot it be fostered? If so, why not? Very seldom is such a thing impossible. Why should love ever pass if the husband be kind and honourable? Of course, the fervid passion of the first few weeks cannot last eternally; but to that love there sometimes succeeds another and a better love. When that has come about, husband and wife are twin souls who have everything in common. Not a secret is there between them, and if children should result of the union, even the most difficult moments in life will have a sweetness of their own. It is sufficient to love steadfastly, and work becomes a pleasure. A married couple will then be happy indeed, and tell themselves that one day their children will repay them with love for all the present pain, and that therefore it is for themselves that they (the parents) are working. In time, too, the children will begin to grow up, and you will feel that you must set them an example, and be their support, and that when you are dead they will, for all their lives, preserve in their hearts your precepts and your thoughts as they have received them from you. In short, you will feel that your children will ever cleave faithfully to your remembrance. But what an onerous duty does that impose upon you! Therefore, for the better ordering of your conduct, is it not better to be united in as close a bond as possible? It is said that child-bearing is a painful thing. Who said that? On the contrary, it is the happiness of heaven. Do you love little children, Lisa? For myself, I adore them. Think if you had a little child to dangle at your breast! What husband would harbour even a single bitter thought against his wife if he could watch her nursing her firstborn – a little, rosy, chubby thing that stretches itself, and rubs itself, with its tiny feet and hands all swelling with milk, and its nails clean and so small, so small, that it is laughable to see them, and its little eyes so full of intelligence that one could not say *what* they do not see? Yes, look at a baby sucking – how he shakes and plays with the breast! Presently the father draws near, and at once the baby drops the teat, and turns over upon his back, and, gazing at his parent, falls to laughing as though he would never stop. Then he takes up the teat again, and sometimes falls to biting it if he has got sufficient teeth to do so, while at the same time he looks at his mother, as much as to say, "See how I have sucked my fill of you." Yes; is it not perfect happiness when all three are united in one – husband, wife and child? What would one not give to attain such moments as they enjoy? No, Lisa; first one must learn the lesson of life before proceeding to lay the blame upon fate.'

('By such pictures as these I shall certainly catch you,' was my secret thought the while. Yet what I had said I had spoken in all sincerity.)

Suddenly I turned very red in the face, for it had suddenly occurred to me, 'What if I were to find that all this time she has been bursting with laughter at me?' The idea simply enraged me. Towards the end of my speech, I had grown really heated; and to find that my conceit was in danger of being wounded! The silence continued until I had a great mind to nudge her with my elbow.

'What made you say it all?' she began, and then stopped.

Even that was sufficient for me. In a flash I understood the situation, for quite a new note could be heard quavering in her voice. No longer was there in it the old rude, brutal, obstinate intonation, but, rather, an intonation eloquent of gentleness and timidity – a timidity so great that even I felt touched, as well as (it must be confessed) a little guilty towards her.

'What do you mean?' I asked with intense curiosity.

'Well, you — '

'I what?'

'Well, one would almost think that you were speaking from a book,' she said. In her tone I could detect the mocking note.

The speech irritated me – it irritated me greatly. Nor could I understand what point lay in that mockery, seeing that such an artifice is usually the last defence of a heart which is not only diffident of itself, but, as yet, free from vice; of a heart which is holding out to the last against rudely insistent efforts to penetrate its recesses; of a heart which is seeking to conceal its true feelings. As a matter of fact, it was from those stray silences, during the period when she was making feeble attempts to rail and failing to accomplish it, that I ought to have derived enlightenment, but *that* I was not clever enough to see; and, moreover, I was blinded by my ill-humour.

'Wait a little,' I thought to myself.

✦ SEVEN ✦

'REALLY, LISA,' I SAID ALOUD, 'had vice been foreign to me, I *might* have been speaking like a book; but, you see, it is *not* foreign to me. Consequently everything that I have said to you has come from my heart. Is it, then, possible that you are not conscious of the vileness of your present life? Truly, if you are not, then great must be the force of habit, and the devil only knows whither it can lead a human being! Do you in all seriousness think that you will never grow old – that you will always be comely, and allowed to stay here? I am not speaking of your infamy in general, but of the following consideration. As yet you are young and attractive and pretty, as well as not altogether devoid of feeling. Are you, then, aware that, no sooner had I recovered my senses to-night, than I felt disgusted at finding myself here by your side? To have the hardihood to enter such a den as this one needs to be drunk. But if you had been of a different kind, if you had been leading an honest life, I might have courted and fallen in love with you. Then your every look, your every word, would have been delightful to me. I should have watched at your door, and knelt to you when you came out, and it would have been my highest boast to proclaim that I regarded you as my sweetheart. Never should I have harboured – never *could* I have harboured – a single impure thought concerning you. But *here* I know that I have but to whistle for you, and that you will come, since I need not consult *your* pleasure, but, rather, *you* must consult *mine*. The lowest peasant who sells his labour is none the less not a slave, for the reason that he knows that one day his labour will have an end. But when, for you, will that end come? Think, then: what it is that you have surrendered? What is it that you have delivered over into bondage? Why, your very soul – the soul of which you had no right to dispose, but which you have none the less enslaved to your body! You suffer your love to be profaned by drunkards when all the while love is the whole world, love is the most precious of jewels, love is the cherished treasure of virgins, love is what men will give their souls, their very lives, for! But what is *your* love worth? You have sold it beyond redemption, for who would seek to attain love where everything may be attained without love's presence at all? What worse offence could a woman commit? Do you understand me? True, I have heard that you wretched women are given a certain amount of amusement, and, at times, are allowed to have particular lovers of your own. Yet that is a mockery, a mere make-believe. You take what is given you, and get laughed at for your pains. For what sort of a man would such a lover make? Would he be even capable of love? Never! How could a man love you when all the while he knows that at any moment you may be summoned to attend someone else? No, the whole thing, for him, would be a piece of indecency, and no more. And could such a man have any respect for you? Could there be anything in common between you and him? No, he would only laugh at you and plunder you. Such would be *his* way of loving. You might consider yourself fortunate if some day he did not kill you. Could you ever be sure that he would not do so? Why, at the merest hint that he should marry you he would laugh in your face, even if he did not also spit in it, and then put you to death. And all the while, save that you had grown used to him, you might not care for him the amount of a couple of cracked kopecks! To think of it! Then why have you buried your life here? Is it because you are given coffee and fed well? But for what purpose are you fed? Food of that kind would choke any honest woman, since beneath such generosity she would always discern the hidden motive. Besides, you are in debt to your landlady, and will always be so – to the very end, to the very moment when your customers have ceased to care about you. And that moment will soon come! Do not trust too much to your youth, since in this place one year counts as three, and you will soon find yourself outside, though not before there have been many intrigues against you, and disputes and revilings, even as though you had not already handed over your health and youth to your landlady, even as though you had not already lost your soul for nothing, even as though your taskmistress had not already despoiled and beggared you and stolen your goods! No, do not trust to her always to keep you. And, to please her, your companions will never be backward in attacking you, for they are slaves like yourself, and have long since lost sight of conscience and pity. In your life the prize goes to her who is the most unclean, the most vile, the most abominable. In your life, too, they know how to inflict such injuries as are undreamt of elsewhere. All that you possess, all that you hold most dear – your health, your looks, your youth, your last remaining shred of hope – will soon be lost. At twenty-two you will be aged thirty-five; and if by that time you have not also become diseased you may think yourself lucky, and render thanks to God. Perhaps you suppose that at least you do not *work* here, that you are always "making holiday"? Wretched woman! I tell you that in all the world there is no more horrible trade than yours – in all the world there exists no form of forced labour which is even *comparable* to your existence.

Ought not that one thought – let alone any others – to make your heart weep? And when you come to be turned out of this house not a word, not a syllable, will there be that you can say for yourself. For ever you will have to go your way an outcast. Yes, you will have to enter another brothel, and then a third one, and others, until at last you find yourself landed in Sennaia Street. There you will often be beaten, for the place has its own endearments, and its *habitués* are apt to confound caresses with blows. Its horrors pass belief! Pay but a single visit there, and when you have seen it for yourself you will believe the evidence of your eyes. One New Year's Eve, when I was walking through that quarter, I saw a woman outside a door. Her companions had turned her out of the house because they could not bear to hear her weeping. Despite the fearful cold, they had closed the door upon her! There she sat at nine o'clock at night – drunken, dishevelled, half-naked, and almost dead with the beating which she had received. Terrible was the contrast between her painted cheeks and blackened eyes; her nose and gums were running with blood from a blow which had been given her by a cabman. In her hands she was holding a piece of salt fish, and as she sat there on the pavement, and wept bitter tears of pain, and lamented her lot, she kept striking this piece of fish against the doorsteps of the house, while a group of cabmen and soldiers on the kerb were engaged in egging her on. Surely *you* do not wish to become like that? Personally I do not think that you ever will; but how can any of us tell? Perhaps, some eight or ten years ago, even that woman with the fish came to this house as fresh as a cherub, and innocent, and pure, and ignorant of evil, and ready to blush at the least word. Perhaps she too was once proud, like yourself, and sensitive, like yourself, and different to all her companions, and full of the idea that nothing but happiness awaited her and the man who said he loved her, and whom she loved. Yet see the end to which she has now come! Ah, can it be that, when, drunken and dishevelled, she was striking that fish against the dirty doorsteps, she was recalling to her memory her unsullied past, and her father's house, and her school days, and the road where the young man used to wait for her to swear that he would love her always and devote his whole future to her, and the moment when they decided that their affection would be eternal, and that they must marry as soon as ever they came of age? Lisa, it would be a sheer blessing for you if you were to die to-morrow, in some cellar, some hidden corner, like the consumptive woman who died the other day in Sennaia Street. You say you will go to the hospital, do you? But they would not receive you there, because of your debt to your landlady. Consumption is not a rapid sickness, like a fever, which to the last moment leaves the patient some hope of recovery. No, a consumptive woman goes on deceiving herself, and believing herself still strong and well, while all the time she is playing into her landlady's hands. Slowly and surely you will be dying, and seeing yourself dying, and gradually being cast aside; until, at last, what will there be left for you to say? True, you will have sold your soul; but you will still be owing your landlady money. Consequently you will be left alone, utterly alone, for what else could they do with you? Perhaps they will reproach you for not earning your keep, as well as for being so long a-dying! And should you be thirsty, they will give you water, and, with it, insults, and the words: "When are you going to get out of this, you slut? You keep us awake at night with your groans, and the customers do not like it." I myself have heard things like that said to a woman. And at length, when death has nearly come to you, you will be thrown into a corner of some stinking cellar, to lie helpless in the darkness and the wet. What will you have to think of during the long, long, endless nights? ... And when death has come, some strange, some grudging hand will shroud you; and around your corpse there will be heard, not prayers, but vile oaths. No one will be there to bless you, no one to bewail you. You will be placed upon a bier similar to that which they allotted to the consumptive woman of Sennaia Street, and when that has been done the bearers will repair to a tavern and talk of you, while your body will be left to lie in the mud and the filth and the half-melted snow. And what of your funeral rites? "Lower away at that end, Vaniukha.* Even here she keeps up her heels in the air, just as she used to do when she was plying her trade. Yes, that is the sort she was." "Don't bear too heavily upon that rope there. Let it down a bit. Yes, that's the way." "No, no; you will upset her if you do that. After all, she was a human being like ourselves." "Well, so much the worse for her! On we go." Nor will they quarrel long over you. As quickly as it can be done they will throw over you a few shovelfuls of wet blue clay, and then betake themselves once more to the tavern. Such is the future before you. Other women are accompanied to the graveyard by children, fathers, or husbands; but for *you* not a tear will be shed, not a sigh will be heaved, not a regret will be uttered. Nor will any one come to pray over your grave, but your name will vanish as utterly as though you had never existed, as though you had never been born. "Dust to dust!" And at night, when the dead raise the lids of their coffins, you will cry aloud: "Suffer me to go and live a little longer in the world, good people. I lived, but I never knew life, for my life served but as a cloth for others to wipe their lust upon. All my existence was drunken away in the mire of Sennaia Street. Suffer me to go and live a little longer in the world, good people." '

* A diminutive of Ivan.

Here my own pathos began to get the better of me, and I felt such a choking sensation in the throat that I was forced to stop. Presently a nervous feeling also came upon me, and with beating heart I raised myself to listen. I had good reason to do so.

For a long while past I had been suspecting that my words would probably end by overwhelming Lisa's soul, and breaking her heart; and the more assured that that would be so I had become, the more I desired to attain my end as quickly and as thoroughly as possible. It was a game which greatly attracted me. Yet it was not *all* a game.

Though I knew that, throughout, I had spoken in a sententious, stilted, bookish manner, and could not have spoken otherwise, the fact in no way disturbed me, since I was well aware, and had a sure presentiment, that she would end by understanding me, as well as that my very bookishness would help me to further my plans. Yet even in the moment of success I recoiled and stood aghast at what I had done! For never, never in my life have I witnessed such despair as now came upon her! She lay there with her head buried in the pillow, her face pressed into its folds, and her frame shaken from head to foot with convulsive tremors. And just at the moment when her sobs seemed to be passing altogether beyond control, she broke forth into shrill cries and moans as she glued herself still closer to the pillow, in the hope that she might prevent any other inmate of the house – indeed, any living soul in the world – from hearing her agony. Tearing the sheet with her teeth, she bit her hands until (as I afterwards saw for myself) the blood came, while she twined her hands convulsively through her disordered hair. Lastly she lay motionless, almost without breathing, and with her teeth tightly clenched together. At first I tried to speak to her, to calm her agitation, but I had not the requisite courage. Shaking from head to foot, I groped my way from the bed, with the intention of dressing myself and departing; but the room was so dark that despite my efforts, my movements were greatly retarded. At length I found a box of matches and a new and unburnt candle. As soon as the flame had lit up the room Lisa raised her form with a sharp contortion, seated herself – a sorry figure – upon the edge of the bed, and looked at me with a gaze which had in it almost the smile of a mad woman. Seating myself by her side, I took her hand. Instantly she appeared to recall all that had passed during the preceding hour, and, leaning in my direction, as though to embrace me, seemed suddenly to change her mind, and ended by gently kissing my head.

'Lisa, my dear one,' I began, 'I did not mean it. Pray pardon me.'

Upon that she clasped my hands with such force that in an instant I understood that I had said the wrong thing. So for a moment I held my tongue. Then I went on –

'Here is my address, Lisa. Come and see me.'

'Yes, I will come,' she murmured, though a little irresolutely, and with her head drooping.

'Now I must go. Good-bye until we meet again.'

I rose, and she did the same. Suddenly I saw her start and blush. Then she seized a shawl which was lying on a chair, threw it over her shoulders, and muffled herself up to the chin. After that she threw me a half-whimsical glance – a sort of sickly smile. It hurt me so much that I made all the more haste to depart. I had a longing to be gone.

'Wait a moment,' came her unexpected request when we had reached the entrance-hall, and were standing by the door while I put on my overcoat. Setting down the candle, she ran back into the house.

'She must have remembered something which she had wished to show me,' thought I. 'When she left me her face was red, her eyes were shining, and her smile had quite a different air to what it had before. What can it all mean?' I waited. Presently she returned with a sort of petitioning or deprecatory look in her face. Nor was it the same face as a few hours ago, for it no longer had in it the mournful, suspicious, obstinate eyes which I had seen before. On the contrary, those eyes were now gentle, beseeching, full of confidence and tenderness, yet timid. It was the face of a child who is gazing at some one whom it loves, and from whom it is hoping to receive a gift. They were clear and grey; they were beautiful, animated eyes which could with equal intensity express either love or hate.

Without any explanation, but as though I had been some sort of a superior being who could divine everything, she tendered me a paper. As she did so her face looked brilliantly radiant – naïvely, almost childishly, triumphant. I unfolded the paper. It was a letter from a medical student (or something of the kind) which, though florid in tone and highly coloured, expressed in an entirely respectful manner a declaration of love. I have forgotten its exact terms, but can remember that, despite its flowery diction, it contained between its lines a certain amount of genuine feeling of the sort which cannot be feigned. When I had finished reading it I chanced to encounter Lisa's gaze. It was eager, full of curiosity, and as impatient as that of a child. Next, since I was slow to make a remark of any kind, she told me rapidly, and in a few words (as well as with a kind of joyous pride), that, some few days ago, she had been to a ball at 'a good house' where there lived people 'who knew nothing of what I am now – no, nothing at all,' since she was then quite new to the brothel, and had once, only once, *etcetera, etcetera*, and had now no intention of remaining there, but was resolved to leave as soon as ever she could get clear of the place. Well, at this ball she had met the medical student, and they had danced and talked together the whole evening, and the student had known and played with her as a little girl at Riga, and had also known her parents. Of *this*, however, he had known nothing, nothing whatever – he had never even suspected it. And, the day after the ball (that is to say, three days ago), he had sent her this letter by the hand of a friend who had gone with her to the dance; and – and – well, that was all. She lowered her eyes in confusion.

Poor girl! So she had been keeping this letter as a precious thing, and had yearned to show me her poor little treasure because she would not have me depart without knowing that even *she* could win honest, sincere affection, and be addressed with respect. Doubtless the letter was destined to lead to no result, but only to grow old and faded in a casket; yet sure am I that she would have treasured it to the end, as at once her visible trophy and her visible excuse. And now, in this moment of pride and desire for extenuation, she had thought of bringing me this poor little missive, that she might naïvely parade her triumph before me, and rehabilitate herself in my eyes, and (perhaps) even earn my congratulations! . . . However, I said nothing; I only pressed her hand and departed. Somehow I was in a great hurry to depart.

Large flakes of snow were falling, but I walked the whole way home. Tired, overdone, astonished though I was, there was yet dawning in me a consciousness of the truth. And a sorry truth it was!

✦ EIGHT ✦

At FIRST I COULD NOT BRING myself to accept that truth; but, next morning, on awaking from a heavy sleep of several hours, I at once recalled all the events of the night, and felt astounded at the sentimentality which I had displayed towards Lisa. 'What was the use of that horror and that pity?' I said to myself. 'Am I getting as nerve-diseased as an old woman? Pah! And why did I give her my address? What if she should avail herself of it? Well, *let* her come. It will not matter.' Evidently the point – the chief, the most important point of all – was to hasten to retrieve my reputation in the eyes of Zvierkov and Simonov. Consequently for that morning, at all events, Lisa escaped my anxious mind altogether.

First of all it behoved me to repay Simonov my debt of last night; and to effect this I decided upon desperate means – namely, to borrow fifteen roubles from Anton Antonitch. As it befell, the latter was in an exceedingly good temper that morning, and acceded to my request at the first asking. This so delighted me that, in signing the promissory note, I told him negligently, but with some archness of bearing, that, the previous evening, I had 'dined with friends at the Hôtel de Paris.' 'The occasion,' I went on, 'was a farewell dinner to a comrade – I might even say, to a friend of my boyhood – who had gone the pace right royally. Of good family and unexceptionable standing, he has also had a distinguished career, is clever and good-natured, and can boast of very great success among the fair sex. We drank champagne by the dozen,' – and so on, and so on. Rubbish though it all was, it nevertheless came quite easily, disconnectedly, and unbidden to my lips.

On reaching home I at once wrote to Simonov; and to this day I am lost in admiration when I recall the truly gentlemanly, the perfectly frank and good-humoured, tone of my letter. Easily and with grace – above all things, with no superfluous expenditure of words – I begged pardon for all that had happened, and justified myself – 'if I may be permitted to do so' – by the fact that, from the moment when, between five and six o'clock (that is to say, previous to my companions' arrival), I had imbibed a first liqueur at the Hôtel de Paris, sheer unusedness to wine had turned my head. Of Simonov I begged pardon by name, and then asked him to make my excuses to the rest of my fellow diners, but more especially to Zvier-kov, when I declared that I 'remembered only as in a dream,' but whom I must undoubtedly have offended. To this I added that assuredly I would have called upon each of my fellow diners in turn had not my head – still more, my conscience – been too sore to permit of my doing so. Upon this facile, this, as it were, careless (yet entirely becoming), touch which had suddenly manifested itself in my pen I particularly plumed myself, since, better than anything else, it would give my friends to understand that I took an absolutely independent view of 'my unseemly behaviour of last night,' and that I did not look upon myself as the crushed individual whom 'you, my good sirs, may suppose me to be,' but as a gentleman who knows how to respect himself. 'Let me not be blamed for my youthful indiscretions,' I wrote in conclusion.

'What marquis-like playfulness!' I commented admiringly, as I read the document through. 'What a refined, what a well-mannered person it makes me appear to be! Others, in my place, would have been at a loss to extricate themselves from the difficulty, whereas *I* have wormed my way out, and can go to dinner again, simply through the fact that I am a refined, educated man of the nineteenth century. To think that all this should have arisen out of last night's wine! Hm! But no; it was not due to the wine, for, as a matter of fact, between five and six o'clock I never touched a single drop of vodka, and have therefore told Simonov a lie.

Yes, I have lied to him most unconscionably; and to do so was wrong. No matter; the main thing is that I *have* got out of it safely.

With this letter I enclosed six roubles, and, having sealed the lot, requested Apollon to take it to Simonov's; whereupon, Apollon having learnt that the package contained some money, the rascal became more respectful, and consented to perform the errand. Towards evening I went for a walk, for the previous night's festivities had left me very bilious, and my head was swimming badly. The further the evening advanced, and the darker the shadows grew, the more did my reflections become varied and involved. In the recesses of my heart and conscience there seemed to be lurking something which would not die – a sort of mysterious feeling which hurt me even as a burn might have done. Generally, on such occasions, I directed my steps towards the most crowded spots and most populous thoroughfares – especially at dusk, at the hour when the throng of hurrying workmen and artisans (their faces worn almost to brutality) becomes denser, and the daily toil has reached an end. It was precisely the humble pursuits of these humble breadwinners – the blatant prose of life – that interested me most. Yet, that evening, the jostling of the pavements only served to exasperate me, and to prevent me from properly connecting my thoughts. Within me there was arising a carking uneasiness which would not be quieted. At length so unstrung was I that I betook myself homewards. Something like a crime seemed to be weighing upon my conscience.

Also, the thought that one day Lisa might call upon me kept torturing my soul. It was strange that, of all my recollections of the previous night, the memory of her should disturb me with a kind of a special, separate force. Everthing else had by this time escaped my mind, since everything else had been put right by my letter to Simonov. Only as regards the point of which I have spoken did I still remain uneasy. It was as though only Lisa had the power to make me suffer. 'What if she *should* come?' was my constant thought. 'Well, it will not greatly matter. *Let* her come. Hm! Yet I cannot bear to think that she should see the way in which I live. Last night I must have seemed to her a perfect hero; whereas now – ! Also, I cannot bear to think that I am so out-at-elbows. My rooms speak of nothing but poverty. Look at the suit in which I had to go out to dinner last night! Look at that deal sofa shedding its straw, and at the dressing-gown which barely covers me! What a set of rags! And to think that she should see all this, and see Apollon too! And the brute will be sure to insult her, and to pick a quarrel with her, if only he can do me a rudeness. And I, as usual, shall play the cad, and fall to prancing before her, and wrapping myself in the folds of my dressing-gown, and grinning, and telling endless lies. Oh, the foulness of it all! Yet even that would not be the worst thing that I should do, for in me there is something fouler, baser, more serious yet. Yes, in me there is something baser – something which will once more make don the mask of falsehood and dishonour.'

The thought of this fired my anger the more. 'But why dishonour?' I cried. 'What is there so dishonourable in it? What I said last night I really meant, for I genuinely felt it. What I did was to try and arouse her to better instincts. The fact that she wept was all to the good, and may prove the saving of her.'

Yet somehow I could not reassure myself. Continually during that evening – even after nine o'clock, when (so my calculations told me) there was no chance of her coming that night – I could see her present before me, and always in the same attitude. For, of all the incidents of the previous night, one in particular was for ever graven on my memory. It was the moment when the light of the match had revealed to me her pale, wrung face and martyred expression. What a strangely pitiful, futile smile there had been playing on her lips! Nor did I know that, even so long as fifteen years after the event, she would still be present to my mental eye, with that strangely pitiful, futile smile of hers.

But next morning I felt disposed to look upon the whole affair as nonsense and a mere lapse of the nervous system – above all, as an 'exaggeration.' Of this latter weakness in me I had always recognized the existence, and was afraid of its effects. 'I invariably magnify things; wherefore I invariably come to grief,' what what I kept saying from hour to hour.

At length I summed up my reflections in the thought that possibly she *might* come. Yet still the uncertainty annoyed me.

'Yes, she *will* come,' I burst out as I paced the room. 'If not to-day, at all events to-morrow. Oh, the cursed romanticism of these "pure hearts"! Oh, the damnableness, the folly, the obtuseness, of pruriently sentimental souls like hers! Yet how is it that I do not understand her? How is it, indeed?'

I stopped in strange perplexity.

'To think,' I resumed, 'that a few words, a mere fragment of an idyll (and a bookish, artificial, invented idyll at that) should bring about such a revolution in the life of a human being! It only shows of what a virgin, an untouched soil, is capable.'

At times I even thought of going to see *her*, and telling her all, and asking her not to come; but at these times such wrath again seized upon me that I verily believe that, had she at that moment been within my reach, I should have fallen tooth and nail upon her. Yes, I should have insulted her, spat upon her, chased her out of the house, and beaten her black and blue!

However, another day passed, and then another one, and then a third; yet no Lisa came, and I began to feel a little easier. Especially after nine o'clock did I feel cheerful as I went out for my walk. In fact, I came to take a brighter view of things altogether, and would say to myself: 'I will save Lisa by having her to visit me, and talking to her. Yes, I will develop and shape her mind. I know that she loves me, and loves me passionately, yet I mean to pretend that I am unaware of it (though *why* I should so pretend I do not know, unless it be because she is comely). Then one day, with an air at once confused and beautiful, she will throw herself into my arms, in a transport of tears and tremors, and tell me that I have been her deliverer, and that she loves me more than all the world beside. Then I shall feign surprise, and say: 'Lisa, is it possible that you suppose that I have never divined your love? Why, I saw it, and understood it, long ago, but dared not, of my own initiative, lay seige to your heart, since I had an influence over you, and feared lest, should you ever become aware of it, you would think it incumbent upon you to respond to my passion, and to force a similar passion in yourself; which would never have been in accordance with my wish, since such a course would have been sheer despotism and indelicacy on my part.' At this point I shall plunge into a sea of Western-European, George-Sandian subtleties, and then continue: "But now you are *mine*, Lisa. Now you are my own creation, a thing pure and beautiful, and my fairest of wives. So –

> ' "Into my house, with daring step and free,
> Enter thou and reign.""*

'From that point onwards we shall tread the road of life together, and travel abroad,' etcetera, etcetera, etcetera.

But in the end I used to feel ashamed of myself, and to put out my tongue at my own folly.

'Perhaps,' also I thought at times, 'they will not let this tiresome woman leave the house. I believe such women are *not* allowed to go out very much – least of all in the evenings' (for some reason I always thought that she would come at night, and precisely at seven o'clock). 'But,' I suddenly remembered, 'she told me that, as yet, she was not completely a slave – that she still stood upon a special footing. That means – hm! well, what the devil *does* it mean? Nevertheless, she will come some day; infallibly she will come.'

Really I must think myself fortunate in that, throughout that time, Apollon's rudeness did much to distract me. He simply exhausted my

* From a poem by Nekrassov.

patience. He was my prime cross, my constant plague, in life. For years we had been wrangling with one another, night and morning, until I had come positively to hate him. My God, how I hated him! Never before nor since have I so hated a human being! An elderly man of imposing aspect, he not only acted as my servant, but also did a little tailoring in his spare moments. Why he had such a contempt for me I do not know. For he *did* despise me, and that to an unreasonable extent. Yet, though he looked down upon me from heights of unspeakable superiority, he treated every one in the same way. Merely to see his tow-coloured head, his excessively sleek hair, the tuft which he grew on the top of his forehead (and which he periodically greased with olive oil), his huge mouth, and his V-shaped lips, made one feel that one was in the presence of a being who was supremely sure of himself. Besides, he was an intolerable precisian – the most precise person on earth, and could boast of a conceit which would have presumed to patronize Alexander of Macedon himself. Also, for every button on his coat, and for every nail on his fingers, he cherished an affection which positively amounted to adoration. Myself, however, he treated with a high hand. He always spoke to me very shortly, and, when looking at me, did so with invincible self-sufficiency, supreme hauteur, and a sort of rallying mockery which drove me nearly to distraction. Yet, though he made such a favour of his services, those services amounted to very little, for he appeared to think himself under no particular obligation to work. In short, there can be no doubt that he thought me an absolute idiot; and if for a single moment he endured my presence, it was only because he took pleasure in drawing, at my hands, the seven roubles per month which I awarded him for his idling. Much, much may be forgiven me on his account. Sometimes, owing to our mutual enmity, the very sound of his footsteps would make me feel as though an attack of nerves were imminent. But the feature in him which disgusted me most of all was a sort of whistling noise which he always made when speaking. Surely he must have had a tongue too long for his mouth (or some such deformity) to make him suck his lips and whistle as he spoke? Yet of this circumstance he actually seemed proud – probably because he believed that it gave him a distinguished air! Usually he spoke low, and very slowly, with one hand clasped behind his back, and his eyes cast down. Above all things he infuriated me when he was reading his nightly Psalms (between my room and his there was only a thin partition-wall), and we had many a battle over those devotions. Yet with him they were a sheer passion. Every day he would fall to conning them over in a voice that was as level and devoid of intonation as the voice of a man keeping vigil over a corpse. Curiously enough, the last-mentioned pursuit is the very trade that he has now come to, for at the present time he is a professional reciter of Psalms over the dead, while the rest of his time he divides between the professions of rat-catcher and bottle-washer. However, I was powerless to dismiss him; he was, as it were, chemically soldered to my existence. Besides, nothing in the world would ever have induced him to give me notice; while, for my part, I could not have endured life in a furnished tenement. My present tenement was an isolated one, and therefore my sheath, my box into which I could withdraw from all humanity; and for some infernal reason or another Apollon always seemed to form part of it. Consequently for seven whole years I found myself unable to make up my mind to dismiss him.

As for my retaining his wages for a day or two, I had always found the scheme impossible, for the reason that whenever I had attempted to do so he had told me tales which had made me wonder where best I could flee to hide my head. On the present occasion, however, I was so exasperated with the world that I resolved (never mind why) to punish Apollon by making him wait as much as a fortnight for his emoluments. For the last two years I had been vowing to do this thing, even if it were only to show him that he could not take a high hand with me, and that I was his master; but on the present occasion I decided to say nothing to him about it, and so force him to take the initiative in referring to his wages. As soon as he should do so (I decided) I would go to my cash-box, show him the seven roubles in order to let him see for himself that they had duly been set apart for him, and say that I did not choose, *I did not choose*, to hand them to him now. Yes, I would say quite simply that *I did not choose* to do so, since I had a mind to be master, although for a long time past he had been rude and overbearing in his manner. On the other hand, if he chose to come and ask me for them respectfully, I would (perhaps) pardon him: or perhaps three weeks, or, possibly, a whole month.

Yet, for all my resolution, he proved the victor, for I failed to maintain the struggle longer than four days. He began in the manner which he always adopted on such occasions, and, since I had been making the same sort of attempt for three years, I knew exactly what to expect. Yes, I knew all his villainous tactics by heart. He would begin by staring me in the face with long-drawn-out severity; more especially if he met me in the street, or if he were leaving the flat at the same moment as myself. If I bore the ordeal well, or if I seemed to be paying him no attention, he would embark upon other, though always silent, persecutions. Unsummoned, he would suddenly enter the room on noiseless tiptoe, at a moment when I was either reading or quietly walking up and down. Halting on the threshold, he would then lay one hand behind his back, advance one foot a step, and train upon me a look less of severity than of absolute, whole-souled contempt. If I asked him sharply what he wanted he would return me no answer, but continue to stare me in the eyes. Lastly, with a very special, a very meaning sucking of the lips, he would turn on his heel, and slowly – very slowly – retire to his den. Two hours later he would return. This time, unable any longer to contain myself, I would not ask him what he wanted, but raise my head with a sharp, imperious movement, and fix him with my gaze. In this manner we would remain staring at one another for two or three minutes; after which, with great dignity, he would once more turn on his heel (even as he had done the first time), and take his departure for another couple of hours.

In case even *that* did not suffice to bring me to terms, and I still had the hardihood to continue rebellious, he would begin sighing as he looked at me – sighing long and deeply, as though by his sighs he wished to make clear to me the measure of my moral abasement. It need hardly be said that this last stratagem had always worsted me. I might be beside myself, I might even foam at the mouth with rage, but in the end I had always had to take the road which he desired me to take.

On the present occasion, however, he had no sooner reached the stage of 'stern looks' than I issued from my fastness and attacked him (I was sufficiently irritated, you may be sure, for the deed).

'Stop!' I cried. 'Remain where you are!'

With slow, silent and dignified bearing he continued to leave the room, with his hand still clasped behind his back.

'Return!' I cried after him. 'Return at once!'

My voice must have reached an almost supernatural intensity, for he *did* return, and stood gazing at me in some astonishment. Not a word did he speak, however, and that angered me the more.

'How dare you enter my room without being sent for?' I shouted. 'And how *dare* you look at me like that? Answer!'

For fully half a minute he continued calmly to look at me. Then again he turned to depart.

'Stop!' I yelled as I made for him at a run. 'Do not move an inch! Stop where you are, and answer my questions! For what did you come here?'

'To see if you had any orders for me,' he replied with gentle deliberation after a moment's silence; the interval having been employed in sucking his lips and poising his head, first upon one shoulder, and then upon the other. His voice, his attitude, his whole self exuded a lethargy which drove me to distraction.

'It is *not* so, you ruffian!' I cried in a voice which trembled with rage. 'I never sent for you at all. *I* can tell you why you have come here. You have seen that I have not paid you your wages; yet your vanity will not allow you actually to ask for them. *That* is what you have come here for, with those damned looks of yours. Yes, you have come here just to punish and to torture me, without having the sense, you brute, to understand what a damnable, damnable, damnable thing you are doing!'

Again he was on the point of turning on his heel when I caught him by the arm.

'Listen!' I cried. 'Here is your money. Do you see it? It is *there!*' (I drew the sum from a drawer). 'Yes, the seven roubles are *there!* But you are not going to have them until you choose, humbly and respectfully, to beg my pardon.'

'That is impossible,' he replied, with almost a superhuman amount of assurance.

'Very well!' I shouted. 'Then I swear to you that you shall *never* have your wages at all!'

'There is nothing that I need beg your pardon for,' he went on, as though he had not heard me. 'On the other hand, you have called me a rascal, and I intend to go and see the superintendent about it.'

'Go, then!' I yelled. 'Go at once! Yes, this very minute, this very second! 'Go, you rascal, you rascal, you rascal!'

Scarcely looking at me, he moved towards the door; whence, paying me no further attention, nor once glancing in my direction, he re-entered his own room.

'But for Lisa, all this would never have happened,' I reflected. I felt so agitated that my heart had well-nigh stopped beating as for a moment or two I preserved my solemn, dignified attitude. Then I pursued Apollon to his room.

'Appollon,' I said in a voice the low, restrained tone of which was really due to the fact that I was half-stifled with rage, 'go at once for the superintendent of the buildings.'

Apollon had just seated himself at his table, after donning his spectacles, and begun to sew; but, on hearing my command, he burst into a loud snigger.

'Yes, go this instant!' I repeated. 'Go this instant, I tell you! If you do not go, more will happen than you have bargained for.'

'You yourself are not feeling very comfortable about it, I think,' he observed. As he spoke he did not even raise his head, but sucked his lips in, and slowly threaded his needle. 'Is it usual for a man to go for a policeman to effect his own arrest? And as for frightening me, you might as well save yourself the trouble, for you will never succeed in doing *that.*'

'Nevertheless, I tell you to go!' Barking out the words like a dog, I had just seized Apollon by the collar when – the door opened, and slowly and softly a figure appeared, came towards us, and stood gazing in astonishment at the spectacle. I felt so overcome with shame that, diving hastily into my room, I seized hold of my hair with both hands, staggered back against the wall, and remained crouching there.

A couple of minutes later I heard Apollon's slow footsteps approaching.

'Some one to see you,' he said, with a look of amazing severity. Then he stood aside for Lisa to pass. When she had done so, he made no attempt to depart, but stood there with his mocking smile.

'Go, go!' was my frantic command.

At that moment the clock, emitting a laboured whirring and creaking, struck seven.

➤ NINE ◆

'Into my house, with daring step and free,
Enter thou and reign.'

I FOUND MYSELF STANDING thunderstruck – standing shamed to the core. Yet I have an idea that I smiled, and tried to dispose my dilapidated dressing-gown to the best advantage – even as, in previous moments of doubting, I had imagined that I *should* do. She too seemed greatly confused – a thing for which I had been in no way prepared; yet it was my embarrassment which eventually rose superior to the occasion.

'Pray sit down,' I said in mechanical fashion as, placing a chair for her near the table, I withdrew to the sofa. She seated herself obediently, and gazed at me in evident expectation that I should continue. I strove to keep myself in hand, but must confess that this artless attention on her part nearly drove me mad, for I conceived that she must be merely *pretending* to have noticed nothing, merely *pretending* to be looking upon everything as the normal state of things; whereas all the time she — ! Inwardly I swore that I would make her pay for this.

'You have surprised me under odd circumstances, Lisa,' I began, though somehow conscious that that was just what I ought *not* to have said. 'No, no,' I went on (for I saw her face suddenly colour), 'I am not speaking of my *furniture*. I am not in the least ashamed of my poverty, but, on the contrary, am proud of it. I may be poor, but at least I am honourable. One *may* be poor and honourable, you know' (here I stammered a little). 'By the way, will you have some tea?'

'No, thank you,' she began, 'but — '

'Wait a moment,' I interrupted. Rising swiftly, I ran to Apollon's room, where, in default of any other resort, I was only too thankful to take refuge.

'Apollon,' I stuttered, with feverish eagerness, as I threw him the seven roubles which I had been holding in my hand the while, 'here are your wages – do you see? Yes, I will give them you *now*, but, in return, I beg of you to run to a shop, and get me some tea and a dozen lumps of sugar. If you refuse to do this, you will render me a dishonoured man, for you do not know who this lady is. Yes, that will be all. Er – perhaps you are thinking things about her? That is only because you do not know who she is.'

Apollon, who had now resumed his work and spectacles, squinted at the money without even laying aside his needle. Then, according me neither word nor glance, he continued to wrestle with his thread, which somehow seemed to be finding it difficult to pass through the eye of the needle. For fully three minutes, with my hands crossed *à la* Napoleon, I stood waiting. My temples were damp with sweat, and I could feel that I was turning pale all over. But at last, thank God, he had some compassion upon me. Relinquishing his thread, he slowly rose, pushed his chair back in the same manner, took off his spectacles with equal deliberation, counted his money at a similar pace, and, after asking me over his shoulder how much tea he was to purchase, departed as lethargically as he had executed his previous movements. On the way to rejoin Lisa I could not help debating whether my best plan were not to flee away, no matter whither, in my dressing-gown, just as I was.

In the end I reseated myself. As I did so she looked at me anxiously, and for a few moments silence reigned.

'I will *kill* him!' suddenly I exclaimed as I struck the table with my fist – struck it so violently that the ink fairly spurted out of the inkstand.

'What do you mean?' she asked, trembling all over.

'I will *kill* him, I will *kill* him!' I repeated, barking out the words like a dog and (keenly though I felt the absurdity of my behaviour) continuing to thump the table with my fist.

'Oh, Lisa, you cannot think what a torment the man is!' I went on. 'You must know that he is my rascal of a servant. Just now he has gone out to get some tea and sugar. Oh, Lisa!' – and I burst into tears.

Here was a situation! How ashamed I felt of my weakness! Yet, do what I would, I could not master myself.

Lisa was terrified.

'What *is* the matter?' she exclaimed, as she came fluttering towards me.

'Some water! Give me some water!' I stuttered in a strangled voice (though, as a matter of fact, I knew that I had no real reason for my stuttering). 'The water is over there.' *Per se* the situation was real enough, but at the same time it may be said that at that moment I was only playing a comedy, to keep up appearances.

In great agitation she fetched what I had asked for, and presently Apollon entered with the tea. It seemed to me that anything so *bizarre* and prosaic as tea was a terribly unsuitable commodity after all that had just happened. So I turned a little red in the face. Lisa looked at Apollon with a timid air, but he went out without giving us even a glance.

'How you must despise me, Lisa!' I said as I stared at her with an almost agonized anxiety to know what she was thinking. However, she was too confused to reply. Angry with myself though I was, I laid the bulk of the blame upon *her.* A horrible sort of resentment against her was rising in my heart, and I felt that I could even have killed her. To revenge myself I registered an inward vow that never again on this earth would I address to her a single word.

'*She* is the cause of everything,' I reflected.

The silence continued for something like five minutes, while the tea remained untouched upon the table. Such was my perversity that I purposely refrained from drinking any, that I might make her feel the more uncomfortable (since it would not have been proper for her to take the initiative). But from time to time she kept throwing covert glances at me, with astonishment and distress in her looks. I remained obstinately silent. It was *I* now that was undergoing martyrdom, for, although I recognized the abominable baseness of my folly and rancour, I could not, for the world, help myself.

'I – I wish to leave that place for good,' she began – probably her object having been, by some means, no matter what, to break the intolerable silence. Poor woman! She had begun, as I had, precisely as she ought *not* to have begun. To think of mentioning *that*, at such a moment, and to such a man! For a few seconds my heart contracted with pity for her clumsiness and futile frankness; but to this feeling there succeeded, almost instantly, a renewed access of spleen. Indeed, the slight instinct towards compassion which I had experienced only served to redouble my fury. 'Let everything go to the devil!' I said to myself; and again there followed a five minutes of silence.

Presently she rose; saying in a tone which was scarcely articulate –

'Am I in any way inconveniencing you?'

In her tone there were both weariness and offended dignity; whereat my anger burst all bounds, and I too rose – trembling and well-nigh suffocated with rage.

'Why did you come here?' I shouted. 'Tell me, if you please!'

The logical order of my words I did not heed, for I felt as though I must say *all* that I had to say at once, in a volley, and without caring in the least at what point I began.

'Why did you come here?' I repeated. 'Tell me, tell me! Ah, *I* will tell you, my good woman – *I* will tell you why you came here. You came here because, the other night, I said to you a few words of compassion which touched your heart, and made you long for more. Let me inform you, then, that I was only making fun of you that night, and that I am making fun of you *now*. Yes, I have only been amusing myself a little. At dinner I had been insulted by some friends of mine, and had gone to your house to challenge one of them, an officer, whom I thought to find at your house before me. But I happened just to miss him, and felt that I must revenge myself upon some one, and get my own back. *You* chanced to be at hand, and so I vented all my rage and venom upon *you*. I had been humiliated, so I humiliated *you*. I had been rinsed out like a rag, so I exerted my strength upon *you*. There you have the whole truth of the matter. Yet you – you actually thought that I had gone there to save you! Is it not so? Is not that what you are thinking?'

I guessed that, though some of the details of my harangue might escape her, she would nevertheless catch the main gist of it. Nor was I wrong. She turned as white as a sheet, and tried to speak, as, with lips twisting painfully, she fell backwards across her chair like a woman who has been felled with a hatchet. All the while that I continued declaiming she listened to me with her mouth open, her eyes distended, and her whole form trembling with horror. The utter cynicism of my words seemed simply to stupefy her senses.

'To save you, indeed!' I went on as I leapt from my chair and began pacing the room. '*Why* should I save you, seeing that, for all I know, I am even worse than yourself? Why did you not give me a slap in the face while I was doing all that moralizing, and say, "Why have you come here, then? To read me a lesson?" . . . No, power, power over some one, is what I want. I wanted to play the game of forcing your tears, your humiliation, your hysterics. *That* was my object the other night. Yet I felt loathsome even to myself, for I knew that I was both a villain and a coward, and God knows why I gave *you* – yes, gave *you*, you wretched woman – my address. As soon as I reached home I fell to cursing you, for all I was worth, because I *had* given you the address. I hated you because I had lied to you; I hated you also because I had only juggled with words, and dreamed dreams, while all the while I wanted – well, what do you think? – to see you go hang! What I wish for is rest and quietness, and, to gain it, I would sell the whole world for a song. Indeed, if I were given the choice between the world coming to an end and my retaining my liberty to drink tea, I tell you that the universe might go to the devil so long only as I could go on drinking tea. Did you guess this the other night, or did you not? Of course I know that I am a brute, a villain, an egotist, a poltroon – so much so that for three whole days I have been trembling with fear lest you should come. And do you know what most disquieted me during those three days? It was the thought that I had seemed to you a hero, whereas at any moment you might come here and surprise me, looking dirty and out-at-elbows, in this old, torn dressing-gown! A little while ago I said that I am not ashamed of my poverty; yet I tell you that I *am* ashamed of it – more ashamed, more afraid, of it than of anything else in the world, even of being accounted a thief, since I am so full of vanity that every moment I feel as though my skin were being stripped from me, and I were being exposed to the outer air. Surely, too, you have divined that I shall never be able to pardon you for having surprised me in this dressing-gown at a moment when, like a savage dog, I was flinging myself upon Apollon? To think that the saviour, the former hero, should be brawling with his servant like a scabby vagabond, and so give you the laugh over him! Nor shall I ever be able to pardon you for the tears which, like an old woman who has been put out of countenance, I was shedding just now in your presence, despite my best efforts to restrain them. Nor shall I ever be able to pardon you the reason why I am confessing this to you. For it is you, and you alone, who must answer for it all, since it is you who have chanced to cross my path – the path of the foulest, the most blackguardly, the most ridiculous, the most trivial, the most obtuse, the most ill-grained worm upon earth. Other worms may be no better than I am, yet at least, for some God-only-known reason, they seem never to look foolish as I do, who all my life shall have to be slapped on the cheek by lice, since that is my *métier*. But what does it matter to me whether you understand this or not? And what does it matter to me whether you meet your ruin in that house or not? And cannot you understand that, having told you all this, I shall for ever hate you for having heard it? Man but once in his life makes such confessions as mine, and then only when he is in a fit of hysteria. And, after it all, how is it that you are still here to flout and torture me, instead of taking your departure?'

At this point a strange thing happened.

I have such an inveterate habit of thinking and meditating in purely bookish fashion – of regarding persons as I may have previously pictured them in fancy, that at first I did not grasp the inwardness of this strange occurrence. Yet the poor outraged, insulted Lisa had gauged the position of affairs with far greater accuracy than I had done. In spite of all that had passed, she had divined what at once becomes clear to every woman who truly loves a man. She had divined that the wretch who had spoken to her in such terms was himself desperately unhappy.

Instantly the look of fear and resentment in her face gave place to a sort of mournful sympathy; and when I called myself a scoundrel and a blackguard, as also when my tears began to flow (for I wept a good deal during the course of my harangue), I saw her features contract as she rose and tried to interrupt me. Even when I had finished she did not seem frightened at my violence, nor appear to hear my reproaches to her for lingering; on the contrary her face expressed nothing but the fact that she was aware how greatly I must be suffering to make me speak thus. Besides, the poor woman was feeling so crushed and cowed, and thought herself so immeasurably inferior to me, that it never occurred to her to grow angry or to take offence. With a sort of impulse at once shy and irresistible she advanced towards me. Then, not daring to approach any nearer, she held out to me her arms. For a moment my heart contracted, and as she saw my face change she threw herself upon me, clasped me round the neck, and burst into tears. I too could no longer restrain myself, and fell to sobbing as never in my life had I sobbed before.

'I cannot be – I have not a chance to be – a good man,' I murmured brokenly as, sinking upon the sofa, I sobbed for a quarter of an hour in a perfectly hysterical way. She clasped me to herself, and, folding me in her arms, seemed to forget the whole world as she did so.

But in time (and therein lay the mockery of it all) the fit passed (I wish but to reveal the sordid truth, and nothing else) as, with my form prone upon the sofa, and my face buried in its shabby leather cushions, I began, little by little, yet involuntarily and irresistibly, to feel that it would be an effort to raise my head and look Lisa in the eyes. Of what, then, was I ashamed? I do not know. I only know that I *was* ashamed. Also, my clouded brain had taken unto itself an idea that our respective rôles had now changed; that she was now the heroine, and I the wounded, humiliated creature whom, four nights ago, *she* had appeared to be. All this passed through my mind as I lay there on the sofa.

My God! Is is possible that I *really* hated Lisa? I do not know. Even to this day I have no clear idea of how things were. I only know that never at any time in my life have I found it possible to live without playing the tyrant over some one, and – But reasoning is a useless pursuit; so why reason?

After a while I so far got the better of myself as to venture to raise my head. Yet I wonder whether it was precisely because I felt ashamed to look Lisa in the face that there suddenly revived in me a sense of domination, of possession. All unexpectedly my eyes began to blaze with passion as I clasped her hands in mine.

Yet how (so it seemed to me) I hated her! And how strangely that very hatred drew me to her arms! The one feeling spurred the other, until both of them came to resemble a desire for revenge. At first she appeared overcome with surprise – a surprise which amounted almost to terror; but that lasted only for a moment. Almost before I was aware of it she had strained me to herself in a passionate embrace.

✦ TEN ✦

A QUARTER OF AN HOUR LATER I was pacing the room with feverish strides. At intervals I would approach the screen, and, through a crack in it, take a peep at Lisa. Seated on the floor, with her head against the bed, she seemed to be weeping. Yet she had not gone away, and that irritated me. By this time she knew all. She knew that I had outraged her to the core, and that (how am I to express it?) my short-lived passion had sprung only from a desire for vengeance, from a yearning to subject her to a new indignity; that to my formless enmity there had succeeded a *personal* hatred which was founded upon jealousy. However, I do not say that all this was manifest to her. I only know that henceforth she was bound to look upon me as a man utterly vile and, above all things, incapable of loving her.

Yes, I am aware that I shall be told that to have acted with such blackguardism and cruelty was an impossibility. Perhaps you will even add that not to have loved such a woman as Lisa – at all events, not to have appreciated her love – was also an impossibility. But wherein does the impossibility lie? In the first place, I could not love her for the reason that, to me, love always connotes tyrannization and moral ascendancy. And other love has never come within my purview, and I have even gone so far as to arrive at the firm conclusion that, properly speaking, love lies in the peculiar right of tyrannization which the fact of being loved confers. Even in my most secret soul I have never been able to think of love as aught but a struggle which begins with hatred and ends with moral subjection. And, in the second place, I did not know what to do with the woman after I had subjected her. Again, therefore, I ask – wherein does the impossibility lie? Was I not depraved beyond belief? Had I not so fallen out of touch with everyday life as to think of taunting Lisa with having come to hear 'further words of compassion' when all the time she had come to me for *love* (for it is in love alone that woman can find salvation and refuge from shipwreck; it is in love, and love alone, that she can attain regeneration)? So once again I ask – was it hatred, and *nothing but hatred*, that I felt for Lisa during the time that I was pacing the room, and stopping, at intervals, to peep at her through the screen? I do not think so. Rather it was that I could not bear to feel that she was there, for I wanted her to go, and was longing for peace and solitude. I had lost the sociable habit, and she disturbed me to such an extent that she hindered my very breathing.

A few moments passed, but still she did not stir from her profound stupor. At last I was callous enough to tap the screen, to recall her to herself; whereupon she gave a violent start, rose in haste, and resumed her hat, shawl and furs, as though her one desire were to get away from me, no matter whither. Two minutes later she issued slowly from behind the screen, and stood looking at me with sombre gaze. In return I smiled a smile which I forced for the occasion. Yet the moment that her eyes met mine I found myself forced to avert my gaze.

'Good-bye,' she said as she moved towards the door.

I ran to her, took and opened her hand, put something into it, and closed the fingers again. Next, turning my back upon her, I retired precipitately into a corner, where at least I could not see her. . . .

I was going to have lied to you, my readers – to have pretended to you that it was without thinking, and purely through absence of mind and stupidity, that I put that something into her hand. Yet I will not lie. No; I will tell you frankly that it was out of sheer malice that I opened her hand and put the money into it. The idea had occurred to me while I was pacing up and down the room and Lisa was seated on the floor behind the screen. At the same time I can honestly say that the factor which caused me to perpetrate that gratuitous insult was malice of the brain rather than depravity of the heart. True, the act *was* an insult, but only a calculated, bookish, unreal one; and the moment that it had been perpetrated I retired, as I have said, into a corner – thence almost as instantly to dart back again in a storm of shame and despair. But Lisa had gone. I opened the door, and shouted down the staircase (nervously, and in an undertone): 'Lisa, Lisa!'

No answer came, though I thought I could hear her footsteps on the bottom flight of stairs.

'Lisa!' I cried once more – this time a little louder.

Still no answer came, except that the glass entrance-door of the building opened with a creak, and then shut to with a bang. The sound reached me even where I stood at the head of the staircase.

She had gone!

I returned thoughtfully to my room. My heart was heavy within me, and for a moment or two I remained standing before the table at which Lisa, on her arrival, had seated herself. I gazed with unseeing eyes. But suddenly I started. Lying right in front of me I had just discerned the crumpled bank-note for five roubles which I had a moment or two ago put into her hand! It was the same note, and no other, for it had been the only one that I had possessed. She had taken advantage of the moment when my back was turned to throw it upon the table!

Well, I might have foreseen that. Yet *could* I have foreseen it? No; I was too much of an egotist to have done that; I had too great a contempt for the world to have thought *her*, of all persons, capable of such an act.

The sight was unendurable to me. With all speed I dressed myself (taking for the purpose the first garments which came to hand) and darted off in pursuit. As yet she could not have covered more than two hundred paces.

The air was so still that snow was falling almost perpendicularly, and forming a thick coverlet upon the pavements of the deserted streets. Not a sound was there to be heard, nor a soul to be seen. The street lamps seemed to be burning with a curious sort of dimness. Running a couple of hundred paces to the nearest corner, I stopped.

Where could she have got to? And why was I running after her at all?

Ah, why indeed? To go upon my knees to her, to weep out tears of repentance, to kiss her feet, to ask of her pardon? Yes, all these things I, at that instant, longed to do. My breast seemed to be bursting with a longing to do them. Never to the end of my days shall I be able to remember that moment without a spasm of emotion.

'Yet what good would it do us?' I went on. 'Should I not, to-morrow, be hating her for the very reason that to-night I had kissed her feet? And should I ever be able to make her happy? Have I not to-night proved to myself – for about the hundredth time – what I am worth? Should I not be a constant torture to her?'

For a long while I remained standing in the snow – standing in the dark, shadowy street – plunged in meditation.

'Surely things are best as they are?' I continued as I regained my room and set myself to drown with fancies the terrible aching of my heart. 'Surely it is best that to the end she should carry the remembrance of her humbling? Of her humbling? May it not, rather, prove a cleansing – a painful, yet an intimate, reminder to her of her human dignity? To-morrow I should only have soiled her soul and wounded her heart;

whereas the insult will *never* fade from her recollection. Yes, despite the filth and the horrors of the end which is awaiting her, the offence will never cease to raise and purify her – through hatred of the offender. Hm! And through pardon too? . . . *Will* she be happier so?'

In philosophic style I next proceeded to put to myself the following question – to be studied at leisure: Which of the two is better – moderate happiness or splendid suffering? . . . Which of them *is* the better?

To the solution of that problem I devoted the remainder of that agonizing night. I felt half-dead for the pain in my heart. Never before nor since have I suffered, have I repented, as I did then.

Yet I still believe that, at the very moment when I left my rooms to go in pursuit of her, I was aware that I should return after going two hundred paces!

Never since that night have I seen her, nor have I heard of her.

To this I may add that, though for a time I derived considerable pleasure from my formula concerning the respective uses of insult and hatred, the agitation which I had suffered brought me near to being seriously ill.

Even now, after all these years, I find these bitter memories to recall; and though I can recollect many another bitter memory, had I not better, at this point, bring these 'Letters' to an end? For it seems to me that I have made a mistake in writing them at all. At all events I know that, from start to finish, I have felt ashamed while writing the story which I have just related. Truly its inditing has been, for me, not so much literature as a well-merited punishment? Nor can it interest any one that I should spin long tales as to how I have wasted my life in moral corruption – wasted it in solitude and poverty and detachment from reality – wasted it in vain-glorious searchings of heart in the underworld. A romance requires a hero, and in me fate seems to have combined only the materials for a *non*-hero. Consequently the whole thing is bound to produce an unpleasant impression, since all of us stand divorced from reality – all of us halt in greater or less degree. So unfamiliar with life have we become that at times we feel for reality a positive loathing, and cannot bear to have it brought to our notice. Indeed, so far have we advanced as to look upon real life almost as a burden, a term of servitude, and to agree that the better course is to live strictly in the bookish manner. But why do we also, at times, grow restless, captious and querulous? Even you do not know the reason. Yet if our querulous petitions were to be granted we should find ourselves in a far worse plight. For suppose we were given complete independence, and freedom to bestow our love where we willed, and a wider sphere of activity, and increased exemption from tutelage. Why, I assure you that we should very soon be asking to be taken in hand again! I know that you will be angry with me for saying this, and raise an uproar, and stamp your feet. 'Speak for yourself and your own miseries in the underworld,' you will cry; 'but do not dare to use the expression "*all* of us." ' Well, gentlemen, heaven forbid that I should justify myself by seeking to include all my fellowmen with myself; yet, so far as I am concerned, I have but carried to a finish, in my life, what you have never even dared to carry half-way, although you have constantly mistaken your cowardice for prudence, you have constantly cheated yourself with comforting reflections. The truth is that I have been more *alive* than you. That is all. But look a little closer. We do not even know where present-day reality is to be found, nor what it is called. Whenever we are left to our own devices, and deprived of our bookish rules, we at once grow confused, and lose our way – we know not what to do, nor what to observe, nor what to love, nor what to hate, not what to respect, nor what to despise. We grow weary of being human beings at all – of possessing real, individual flesh and blood. We are *ashamed* of being human – we account it beneath our dignity. Rather, we aim at becoming personalities of a general, a fictitious type. Yes, all of us are still-born creatures, not children sprung of living fathers; and that fact is coming more and more to please us. Soon we shall have invented a way of being born of nothing but ideas! But enough of this: I intend to bring these 'Letters from the Underworld' to a close.

It may be added that the 'Letters' of this dealer in paradoxes did *not* end here, since the writer could not forbear continuing them; but I who have been responsible for their transcription choose no longer to perform the task.